Archie's

BiG BOOk

VOLUME 2: FANTASY

Publisher / Co-CEO: Jon Goldwater

Co-CEO: Nancy Silberkleit

Co-President / Editor-In-Chief: Victor Gorelick

Co-President: Mike Pellerito

Co-President: Alex Segura

Chief Creative Officer: Roberto Aguirre-Sacasa

Chief Operating Officer: William Mooar

Chief Financial Officer: Robert Wintle

Director of Book Sales & Operations: Jonathan Betancourt

Production Manager: Stephen Oswald

Lead Designer: Kari McLachlan

Associate Editor: Carlos Antunes

Editorial Assistant / Proofreader: Jamie Lee Rotante

Published by Archie Comic Publications, Inc. 629 Fifth Avenue, Suite 100, Pelham, NY 10803-1242

ISBN: 978-1-68255-907-9

WRITTEN BY

Angelo DeCesare, Tom DeFalco, Tania Del Rio, Steven Duvall
George Gladir, Dan Parent and Alex Segura

ART BY

Bob Bolling, Dan DeCarlo, Mike DeCarlo, Bill Galvan, Stan Goldberg,
Barry Grossman, Pat Kennedy, Tim Kennedy, Rich Koslowski,
Gisele Lagace, Rudy Lapick, Laura Martin, Al Milgrom, Jack Morelli,
Dan Parent, Rosario "Tito" Peña, Fernando Ruiz, Bob Smith,
Glenn Whitmore, John Workman, Bill Yoshida and Digikore Studios

COVER ART BY Dan Parent, Fernando Ruiz and Walter Simonson

Archie's® BIG

TABLE OF CONTENTS

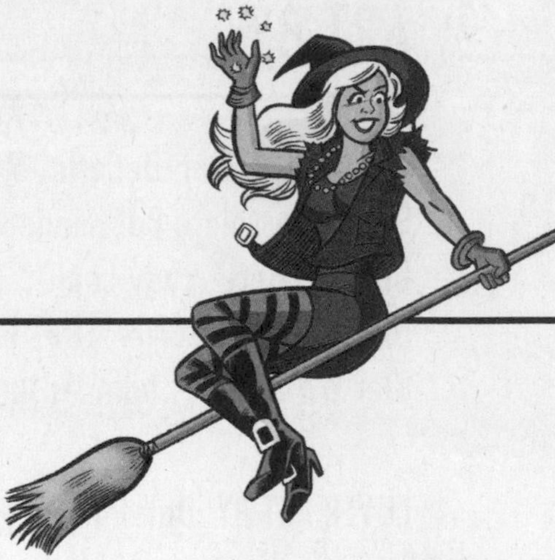

CHAPTER ONE

CHAPTER TWO

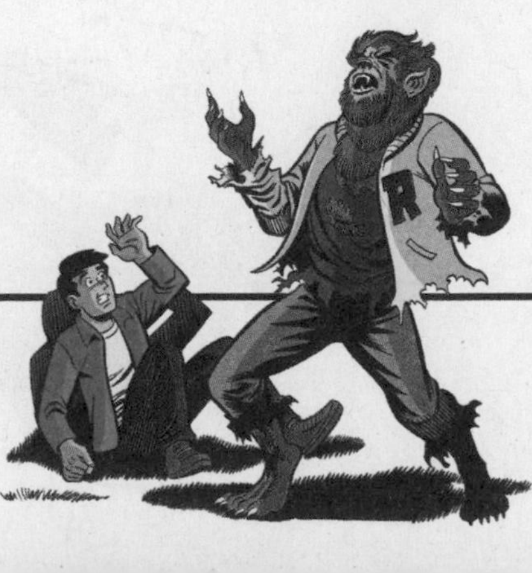

CHAPTER THREE

CHAPTER FOUR

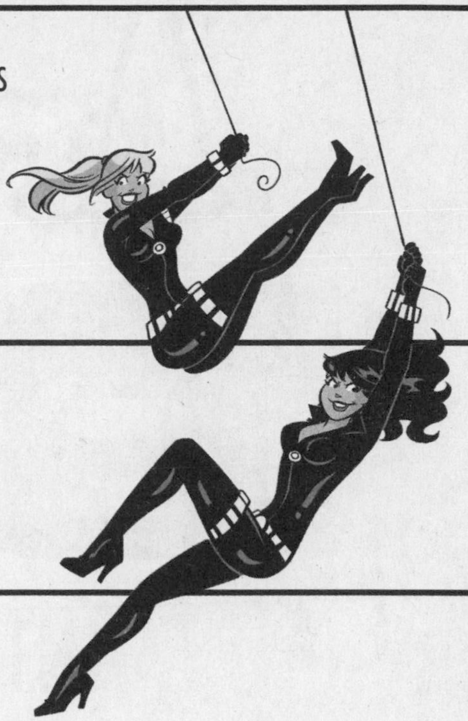

CHAPTER FIVE

CHAPTER SIX

CHAPTER SEVEN

CHAPTER EIGHT

CHAPTER NINE

CHAPTER TEN

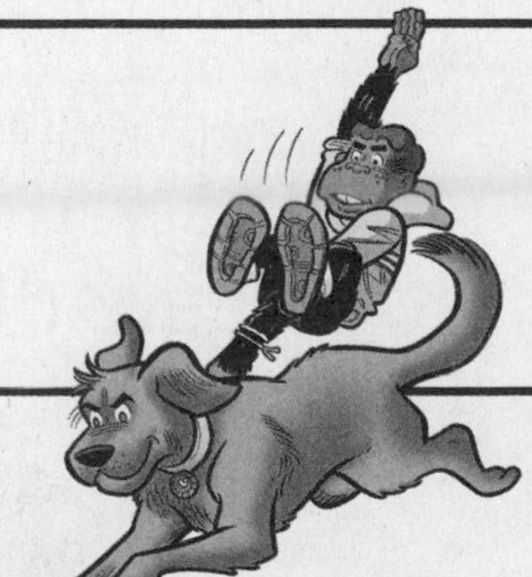

Archie's BiG

INTRODUCTION

Archie Andrews and his group of friends are just a bunch of ordinary kids who live in the small town of Riverdale, USA. They get into teenage shenanigans, high school hilarity, dating mix-ups and... not much more, right? Think again!

Throughout the years, Archie, Jughead, Betty, Veronica, Reggie and the whole Riverdale gang have gone beyond the borders of their hometown to have wild adventures and explorations—and we're not just talking about visiting other cities or countries—they've travelled through time, space, and even other dimensions!

What you'll find in this Big Book are a number of never-before-collected stories that see the beloved characters entering into the fun worlds of fantasy and sci-fi.

There's a fantasy story about a wizarding high school, a comic take on the classic fairy tale about a heroic outlaw and his very merry followers, a few of Sabrina's spells that go haywire, some supernatural beasts and monsters and even Betty and Veronica facing off as high-octane, action-loving spies! Plus, a few classic stories that cast the teens in their own versions of iconic films and plays.

This collection has everything a fantasy fan could wish for! So what are you waiting for?

Start reading!

CHAPTER ONE

Magic Mayhem

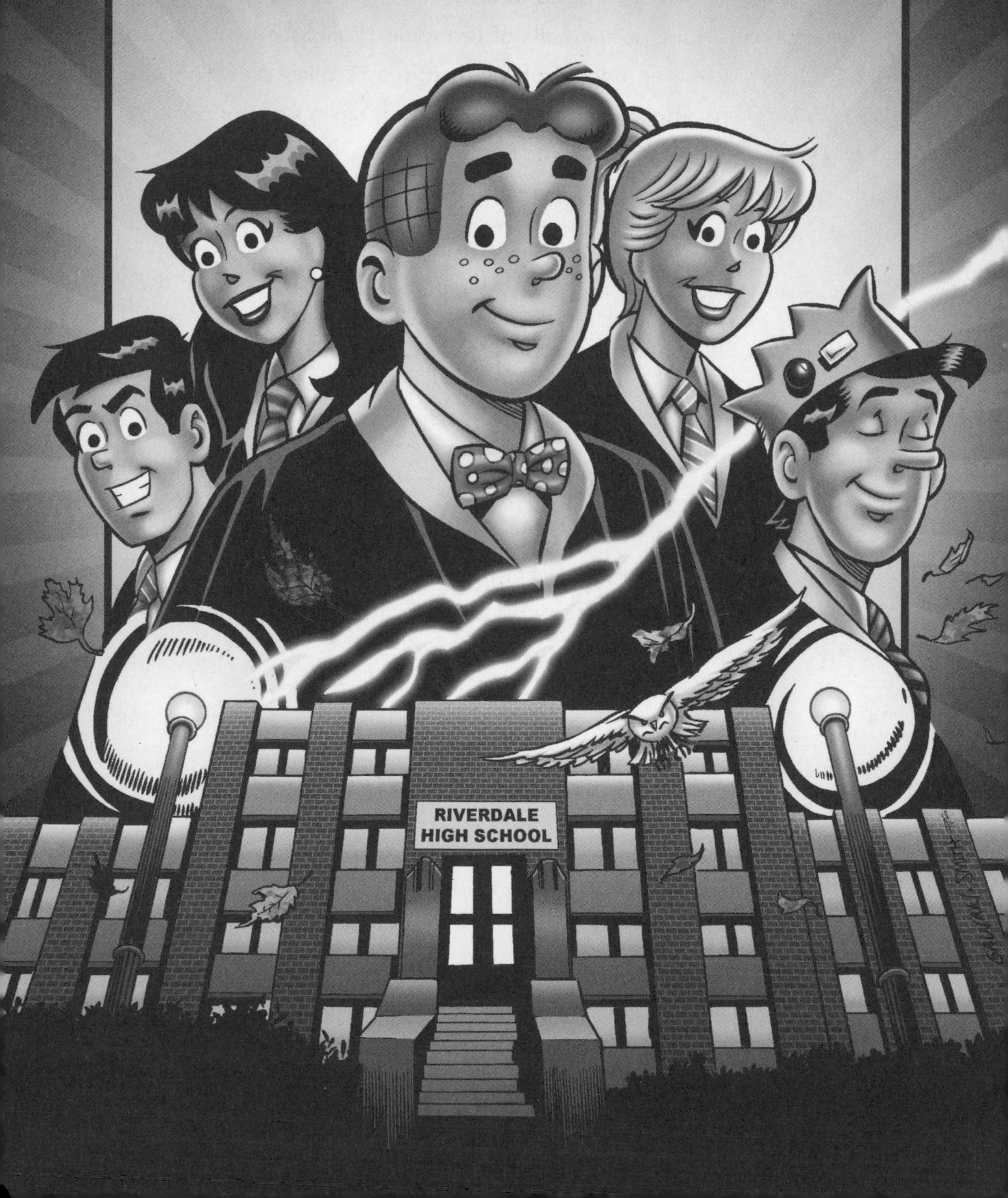
RIVERDALE
HIGH SCHOOL

INTRODUCING MAGIC MAYHEM

Originally printed in *Archie #649*

"Magic Mayhem" features Jughead as the star of this magical story! Things are getting very strange in the halls of Riverdale High School—or should we call it, Riverdale: The School of Witchcraft and Wizardry? With the UGAJ (United Girls Against Jughead) back in action, can Archie's crowned compadre manage to avoid having to take a date to the Fall Gala? When the usual suspects up their antics with some supernatural help, it's going to take some wizardry to make it out alive!

WRITER
TOM DEFALCO

PENCILS
BILL GALVAN

INKS
RICH KOSLOWSKI

LETTERS
JACK MORELLI

COLORS
DIGIKORE STUDIOS

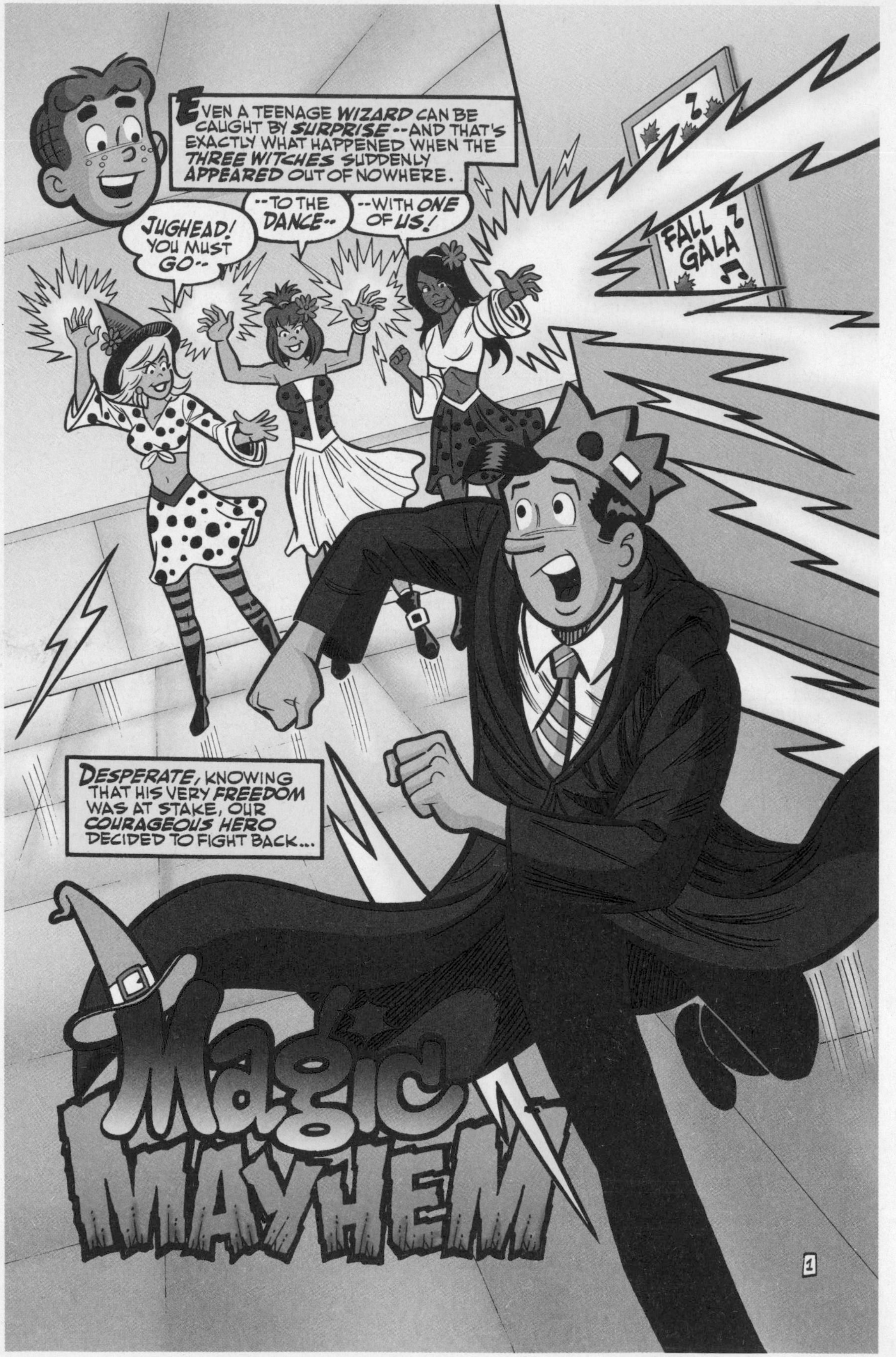
EVEN A TEENAGE WIZARD CAN BE CAUGHT BY SURPRISE --AND THAT'S EXACTLY WHAT HAPPENED WHEN THE THREE WITCHES SUDDENLY APPEARED OUT OF NOWHERE.
JUGHEAD! YOU MUST GO--
--TO THE DANCE--
--WITH ONE OF US!
FALL GALA
DESPERATE, KNOWING THAT HIS VERY FREEDOM WAS AT STAKE, OUR COURAGEOUS HERO DECIDED TO FIGHT BACK...
Magic MAYHEM
1

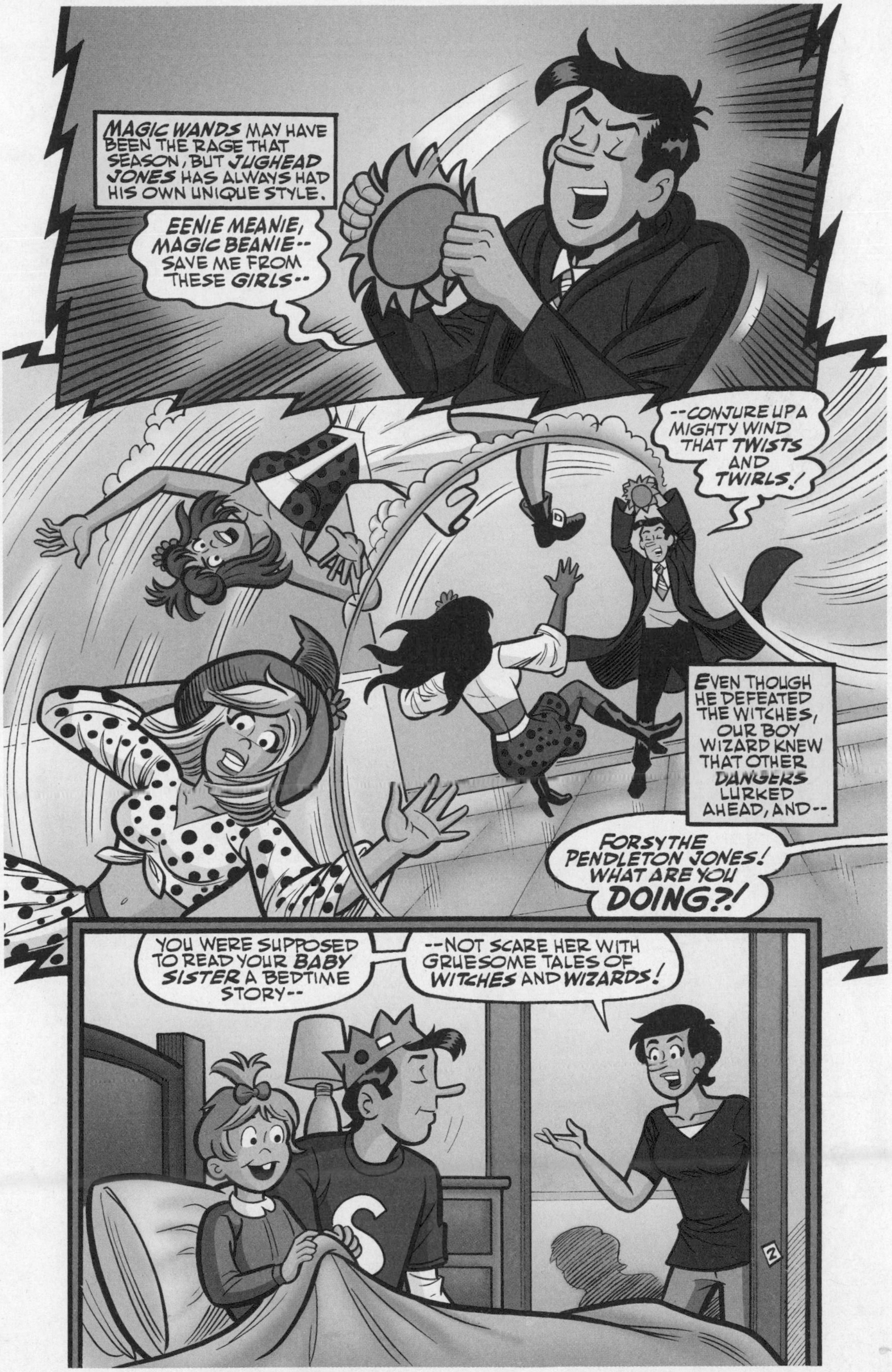
MAGIC WANDS MAY HAVE BEEN THE RAGE THAT SEASON, BUT JUGHEAD JONES HAS ALWAYS HAD HIS OWN UNIQUE STYLE.
EENIE MEANIE, MAGIC BEANIE-- SAVE ME FROM THESE GIRLS--
--CONJURE UP A MIGHTY WIND THAT TWISTS AND TWIRLS!
EVEN THOUGH HE DEFEATED THE WITCHES, OUR BOY WIZARD KNEW THAT OTHER DANGERS LURKED AHEAD, AND--
FORSYTHE PENDLETON JONES! WHAT ARE YOU DOING?!
YOU WERE SUPPOSED TO READ YOUR BABY SISTER A BEDTIME STORY--
--NOT SCARE HER WITH GRUESOME TALES OF WITCHES AND WIZARDS!

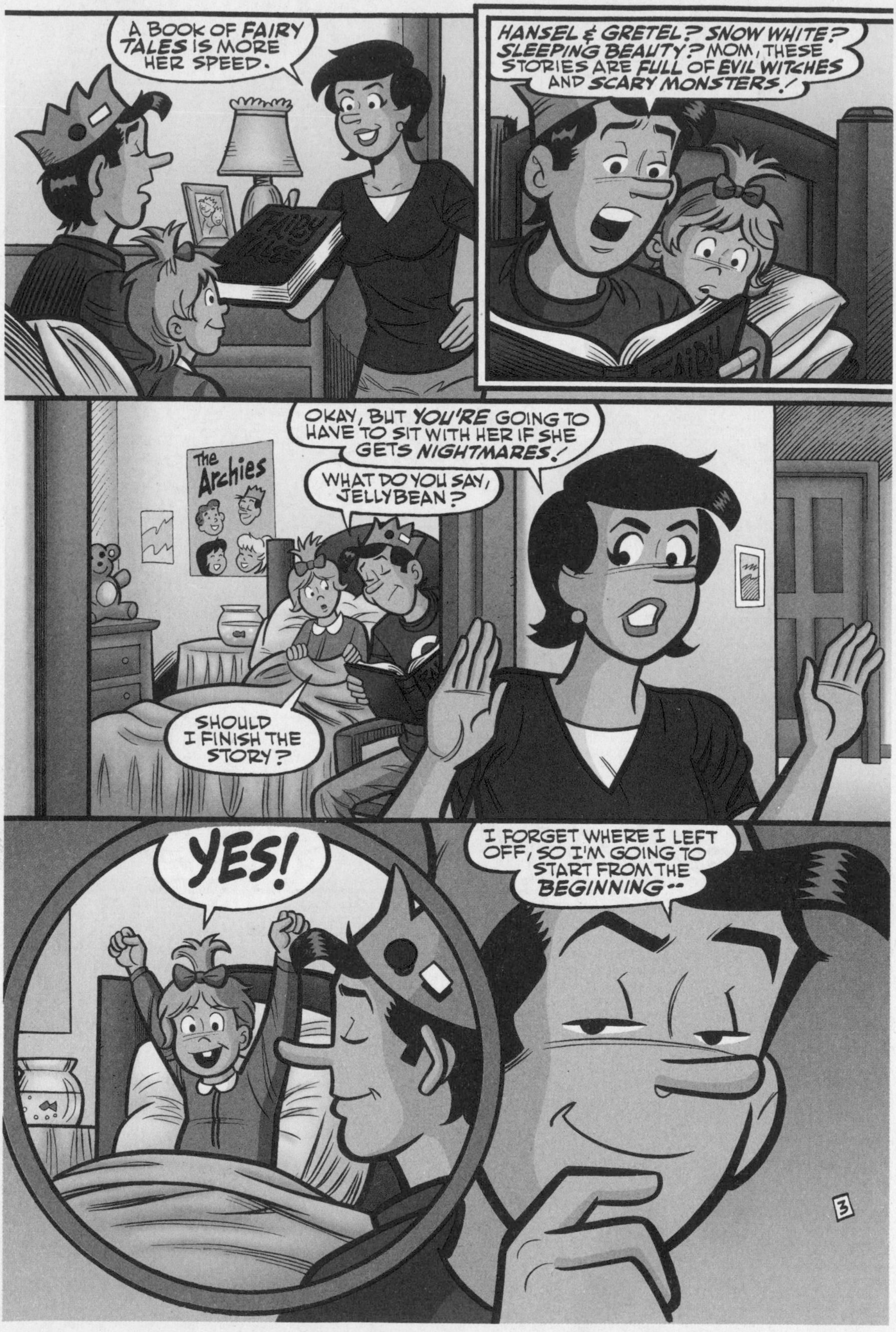
A BOOK OF FAIRY TALES IS MORE HER SPEED.
FAIRY TALES
HANSEL & GRETEL? SNOW WHITE? SLEEPING BEAUTY? MOM, THESE STORIES ARE FULL OF EVIL WITCHES AND SCARY MONSTERS!
OKAY, BUT YOU'RE GOING TO HAVE TO SIT WITH HER IF SHE GETS NIGHTMARES!
WHAT DO YOU SAY, JELLYBEAN?
The Archies
SHOULD I FINISH THE STORY?
YES!
I FORGET WHERE I LEFT OFF, SO I'M GOING TO START FROM THE BEGINNING--
3

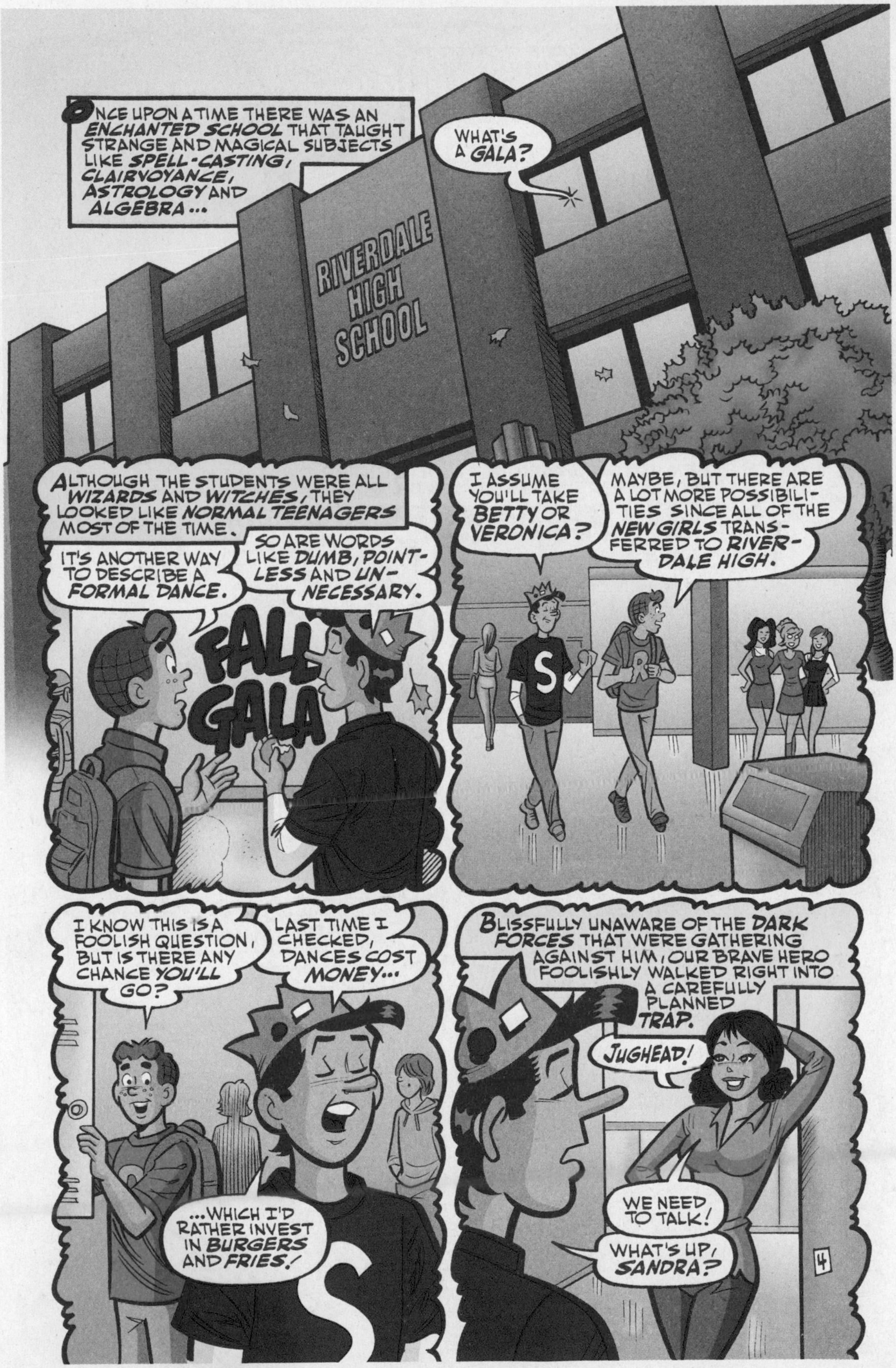
ONCE UPON A TIME THERE WAS AN ENCHANTED SCHOOL THAT TAUGHT STRANGE AND MAGICAL SUBJECTS LIKE SPELL-CASTING, CLAIRVOYANCE, ASTROLOGY AND ALGEBRA...
WHAT'S A GALA?
RIVERDALE HIGH SCHOOL
ALTHOUGH THE STUDENTS WERE ALL WIZARDS AND WITCHES, THEY LOOKED LIKE NORMAL TEENAGERS MOST OF THE TIME.
IT'S ANOTHER WAY TO DESCRIBE A FORMAL DANCE.
SO ARE WORDS LIKE DUMB, POINTLESS AND UNNECESSARY.
FALL GALA
I ASSUME YOU'LL TAKE BETTY OR VERONICA?
MAYBE, BUT THERE ARE A LOT MORE POSSIBILITIES SINCE ALL OF THE NEW GIRLS TRANSFERRED TO RIVERDALE HIGH.
I KNOW THIS IS A FOOLISH QUESTION, BUT IS THERE ANY CHANCE YOU'LL GO?
LAST TIME I CHECKED, DANCES COST MONEY...
...WHICH I'D RATHER INVEST IN BURGERS AND FRIES!
BLISSFULLY UNAWARE OF THE DARK FORCES THAT WERE GATHERING AGAINST HIM, OUR BRAVE HERO FOOLISHLY WALKED RIGHT INTO A CAREFULLY PLANNED TRAP.
JUGHEAD!
WE NEED TO TALK!
WHAT'S UP, SANDRA?
4

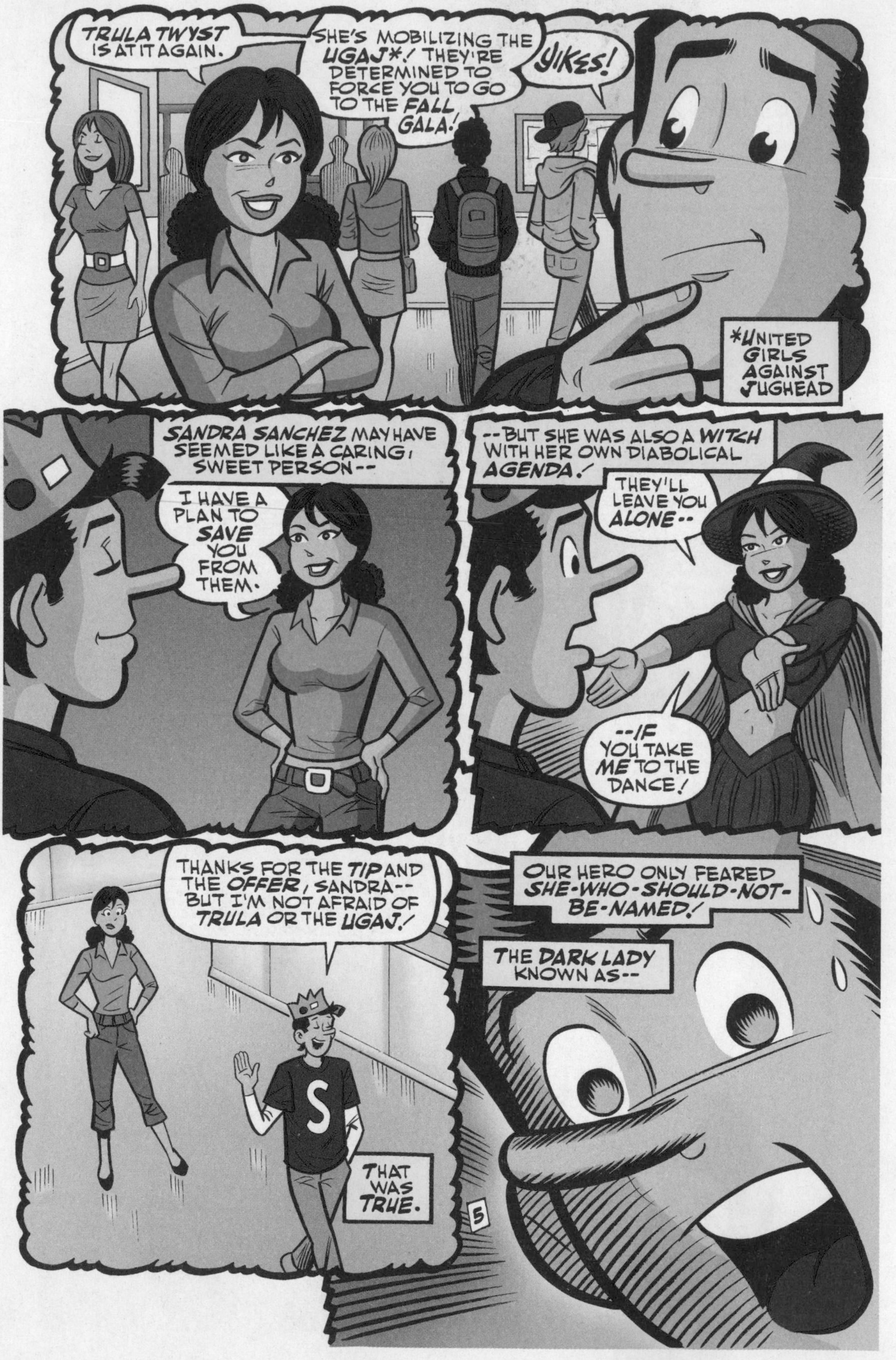
TRULA TWYST IS AT IT AGAIN.
SHE'S MOBILIZING THE UGAJ*! THEY'RE DETERMINED TO FORCE YOU TO GO TO THE FALL GALA!
YIKES!
*UNITED GIRLS AGAINST JUGHEAD
SANDRA SANCHEZ MAY HAVE SEEMED LIKE A CARING, SWEET PERSON--
I HAVE A PLAN TO SAVE YOU FROM THEM.
--BUT SHE WAS ALSO A WITCH WITH HER OWN DIABOLICAL AGENDA!
THEY'LL LEAVE YOU ALONE--
--IF YOU TAKE ME TO THE DANCE!
THANKS FOR THE TIP AND THE OFFER, SANDRA-- BUT I'M NOT AFRAID OF TRULA OR THE UGAJ!
THAT WAS TRUE.
5
OUR HERO ONLY FEARED SHE-WHO-SHOULD-NOT-BE-NAMED!
THE DARK LADY KNOWN AS--

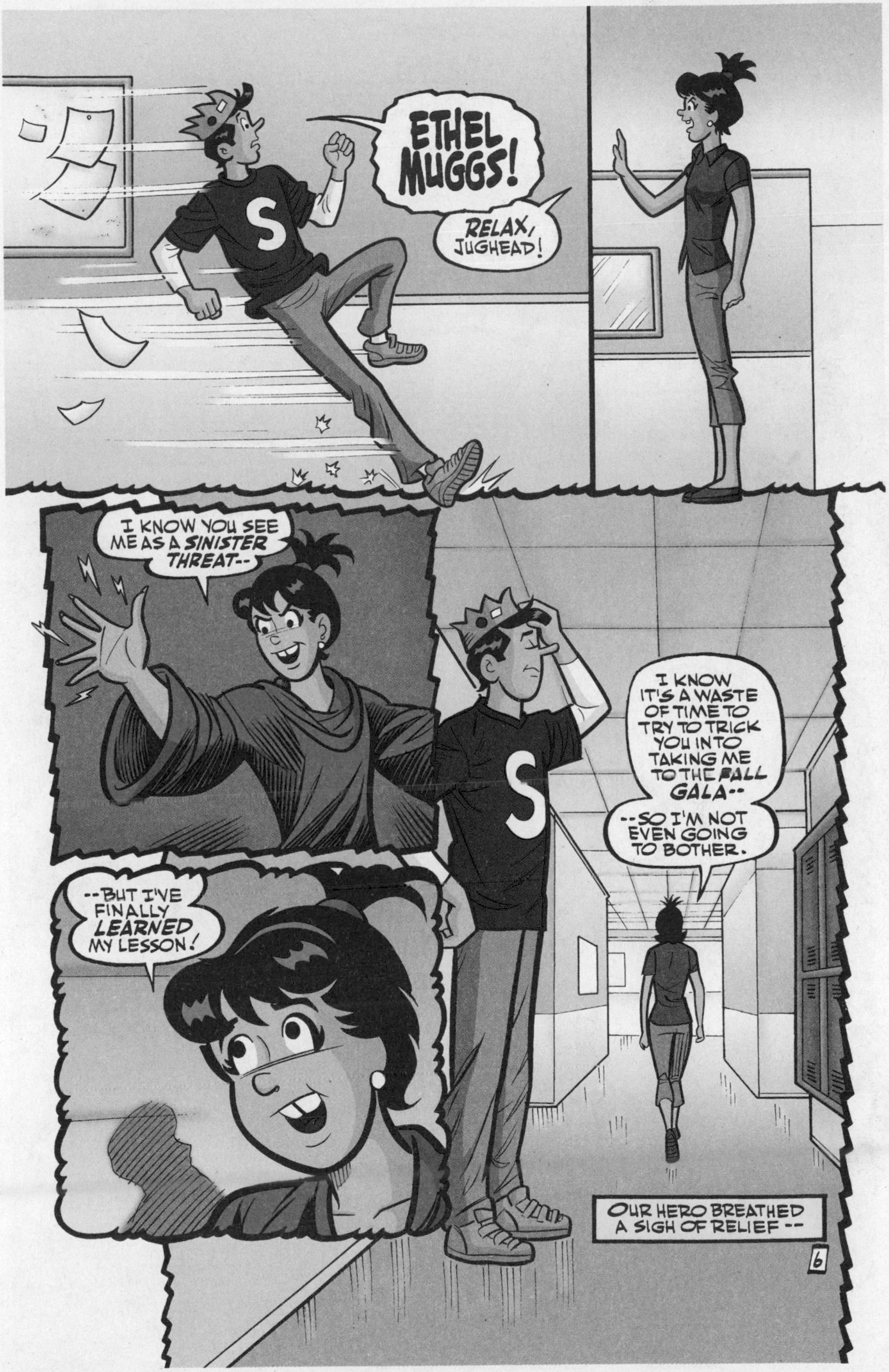
ETHEL MUGGS!
RELAX, JUGHEAD!
I KNOW YOU SEE ME AS A SINISTER THREAT--
--BUT I'VE FINALLY LEARNED MY LESSON!
I KNOW IT'S A WASTE OF TIME TO TRY TO TRICK YOU INTO TAKING ME TO THE FALL GALA--
--SO I'M NOT EVEN GOING TO BOTHER.
OUR HERO BREATHED A SIGH OF RELIEF --
6

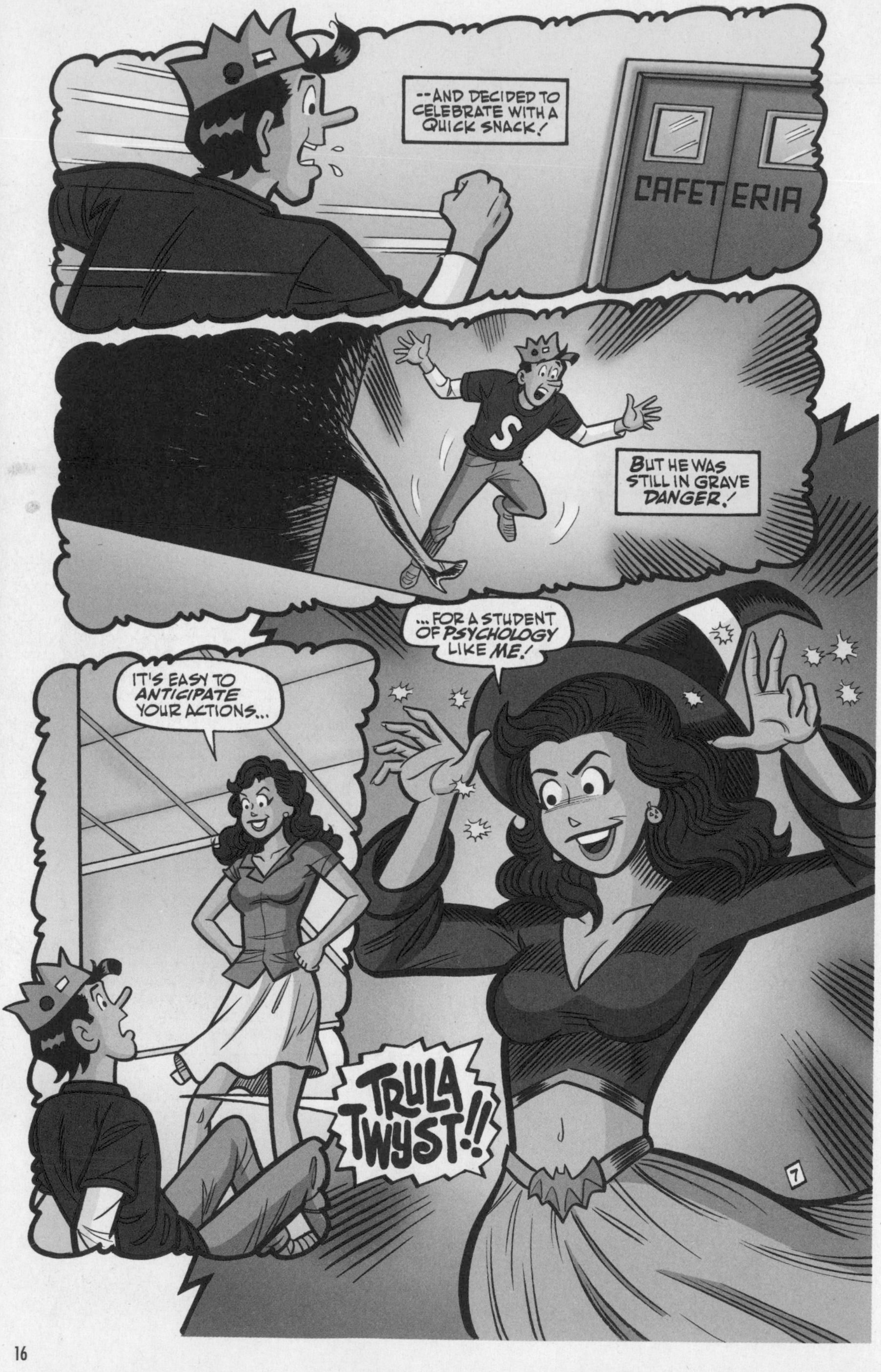
--AND DECIDED TO CELEBRATE WITH A QUICK SNACK!
CAFETERIA
BUT HE WAS STILL IN GRAVE DANGER!
IT'S EASY TO ANTICIPATE YOUR ACTIONS...
...FOR A STUDENT OF PSYCHOLOGY LIKE ME!
TRULA TWYST!!
7

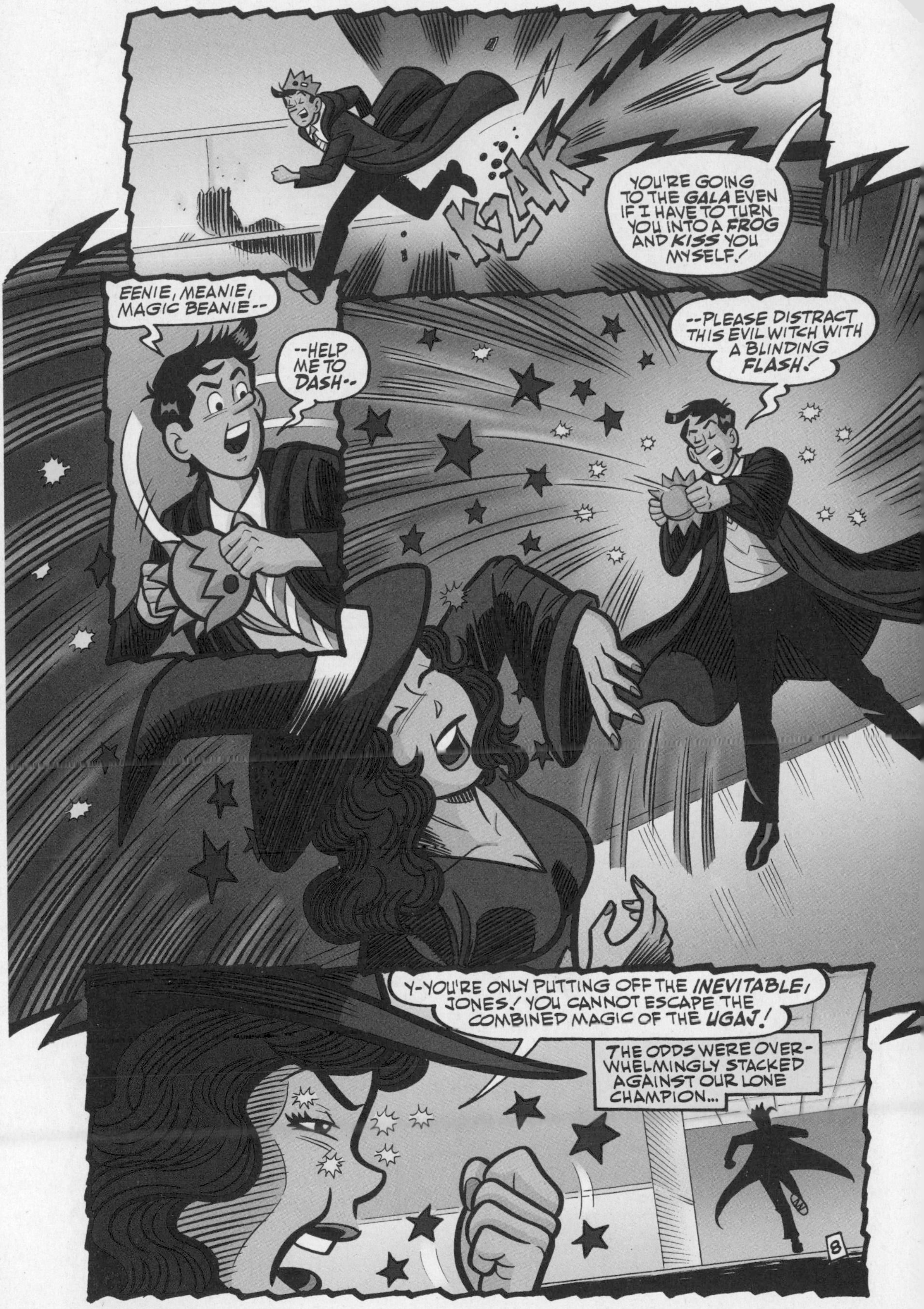
KZAK
YOU'RE GOING TO THE GALA EVEN IF I HAVE TO TURN YOU INTO A FROG AND KISS YOU MYSELF!
EENIE, MEANIE, MAGIC BEANIE--
--HELP ME TO DASH--
--PLEASE DISTRACT THIS EVIL WITCH WITH A BLINDING FLASH!
Y-YOU'RE ONLY PUTTING OFF THE INEVITABLE, JONES! YOU CANNOT ESCAPE THE COMBINED MAGIC OF THE UGAJ!
THE ODDS WERE OVER-WHELMINGLY STACKED AGAINST OUR LONE CHAMPION...
8

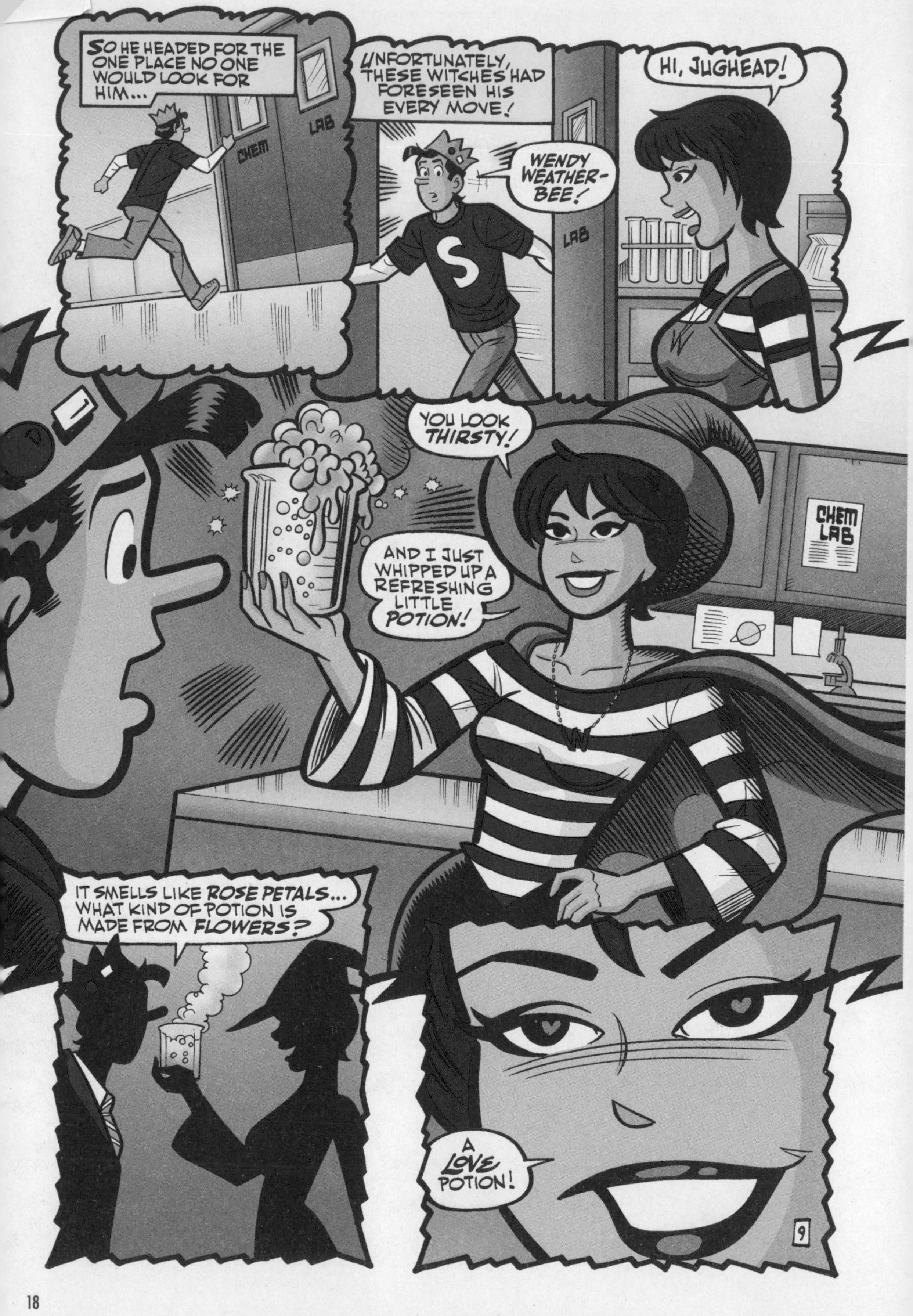
SO HE HEADED FOR THE ONE PLACE NO ONE WOULD LOOK FOR HIM...
CHEM
LAB
UNFORTUNATELY, THESE WITCHES HAD FORESEEN HIS EVERY MOVE!
WENDY WEATHER-BEE!
LAB
HI, JUGHEAD!
YOU LOOK THIRSTY!
AND I JUST WHIPPED UP A REFRESHING LITTLE POTION!
CHEM LAB
IT SMELLS LIKE ROSE PETALS... WHAT KIND OF POTION IS MADE FROM FLOWERS?
A LOVE POTION!
9

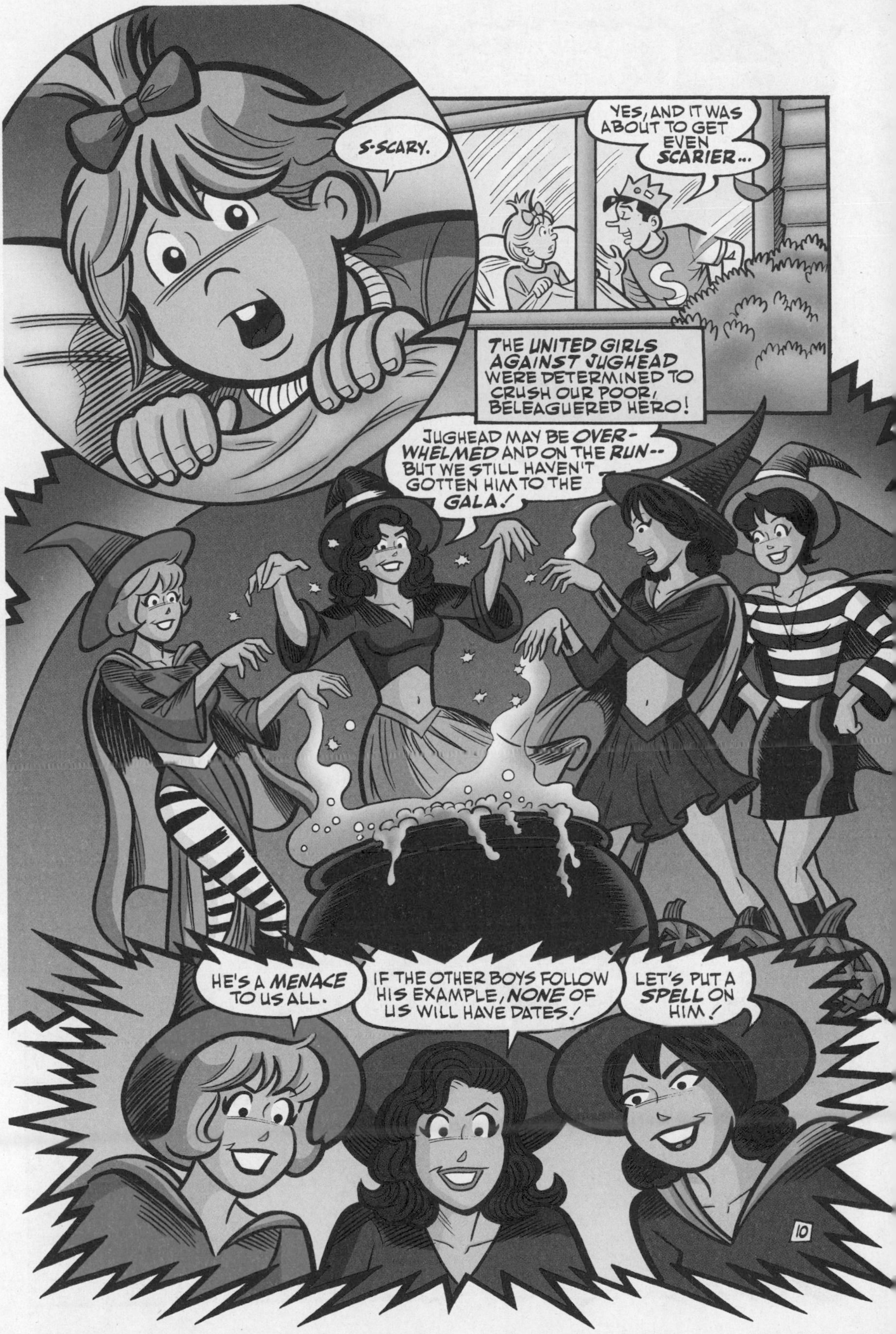
S-SCARY.
YES, AND IT WAS ABOUT TO GET EVEN SCARIER...
THE UNITED GIRLS AGAINST JUGHEAD WERE DETERMINED TO CRUSH OUR POOR, BELEAGUERED HERO!
JUGHEAD MAY BE OVER-WHELMED AND ON THE RUN-- BUT WE STILL HAVEN'T GOTTEN HIM TO THE GALA!
HE'S A MENACE TO US ALL.
IF THE OTHER BOYS FOLLOW HIS EXAMPLE, NONE OF US WILL HAVE DATES!
LET'S PUT A SPELL ON HIM!
10

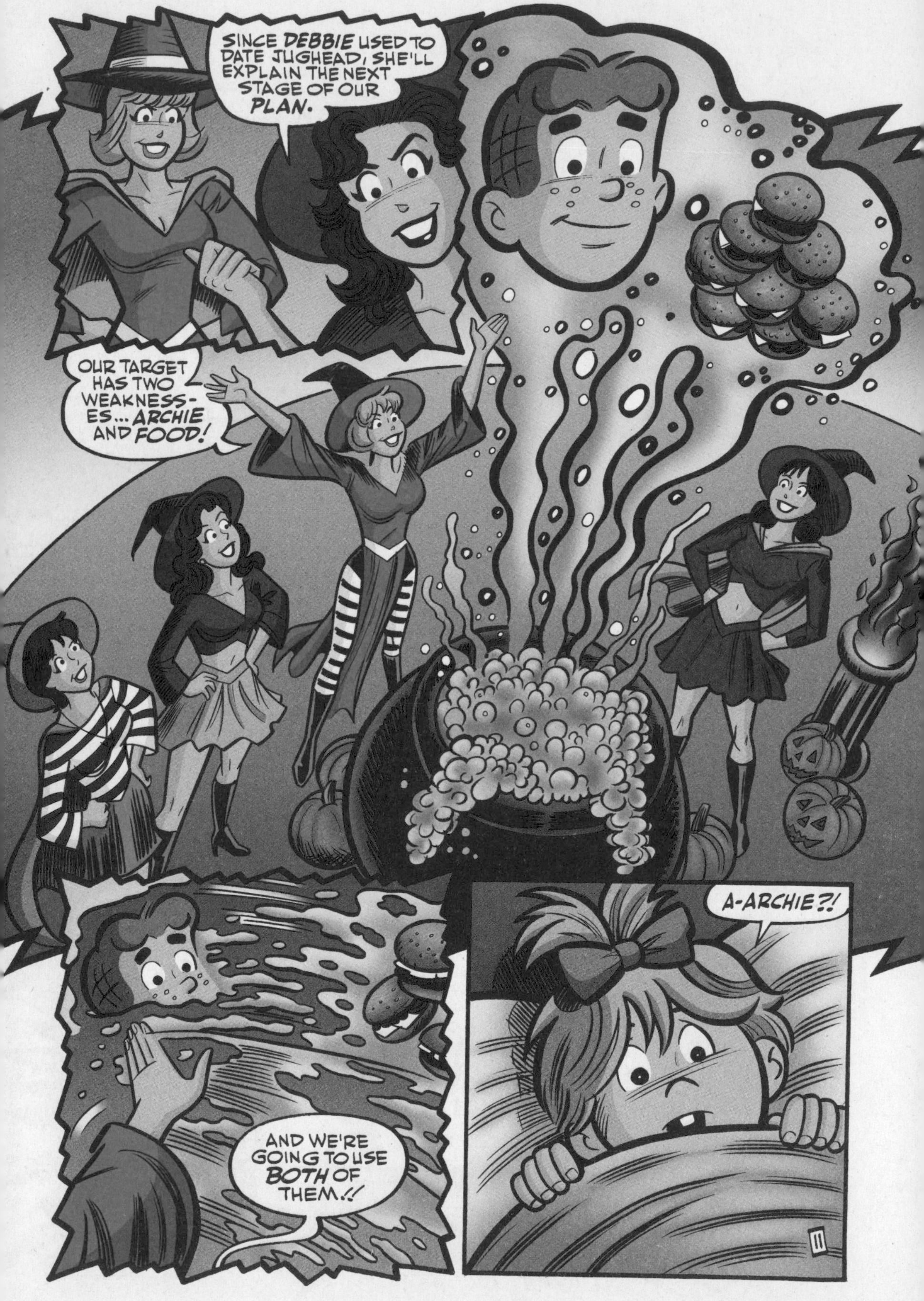
SINCE DEBBIE USED TO DATE JUGHEAD, SHE'LL EXPLAIN THE NEXT STAGE OF OUR PLAN.
OUR TARGET HAS TWO WEAKNESS-ES... ARCHIE AND FOOD!
AND WE'RE GOING TO USE BOTH OF THEM.!!
A-ARCHIE?!

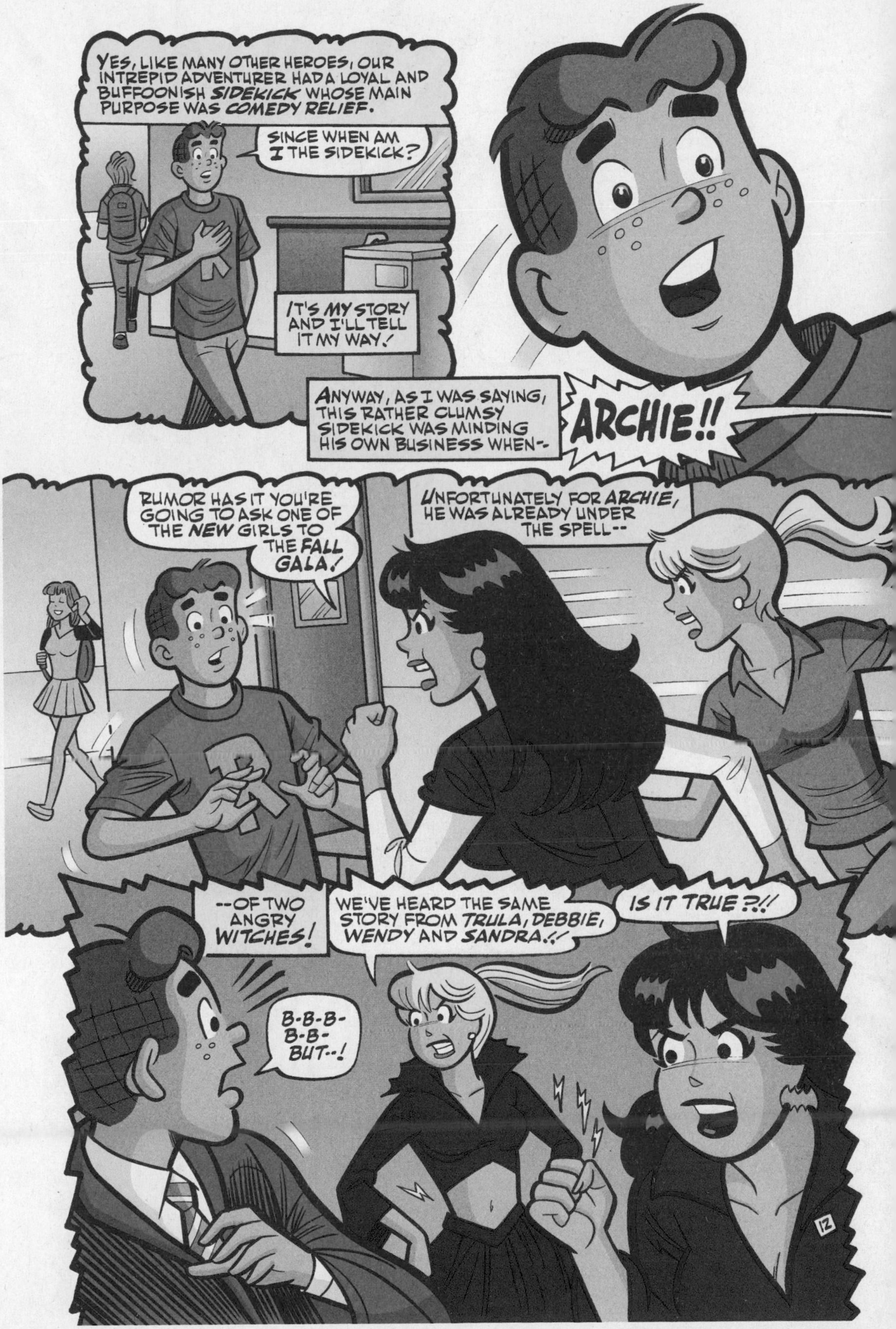
YES, LIKE MANY OTHER HEROES, OUR INTREPID ADVENTURER HAD A LOYAL AND BUFFOONISH SIDEKICK WHOSE MAIN PURPOSE WAS COMEDY RELIEF.
SINCE WHEN AM I THE SIDEKICK?
IT'S MY STORY AND I'LL TELL IT MY WAY!
ANYWAY, AS I WAS SAYING, THIS RATHER CLUMSY SIDEKICK WAS MINDING HIS OWN BUSINESS WHEN--
ARCHIE!!
RUMOR HAS IT YOU'RE GOING TO ASK ONE OF THE NEW GIRLS TO THE FALL GALA!
UNFORTUNATELY FOR ARCHIE, HE WAS ALREADY UNDER THE SPELL--
--OF TWO ANGRY WITCHES!
WE'VE HEARD THE SAME STORY FROM TRULA, DEBBIE, WENDY AND SANDRA!!
IS IT TRUE?!!
B-B-B-B-B-BUT--!
12

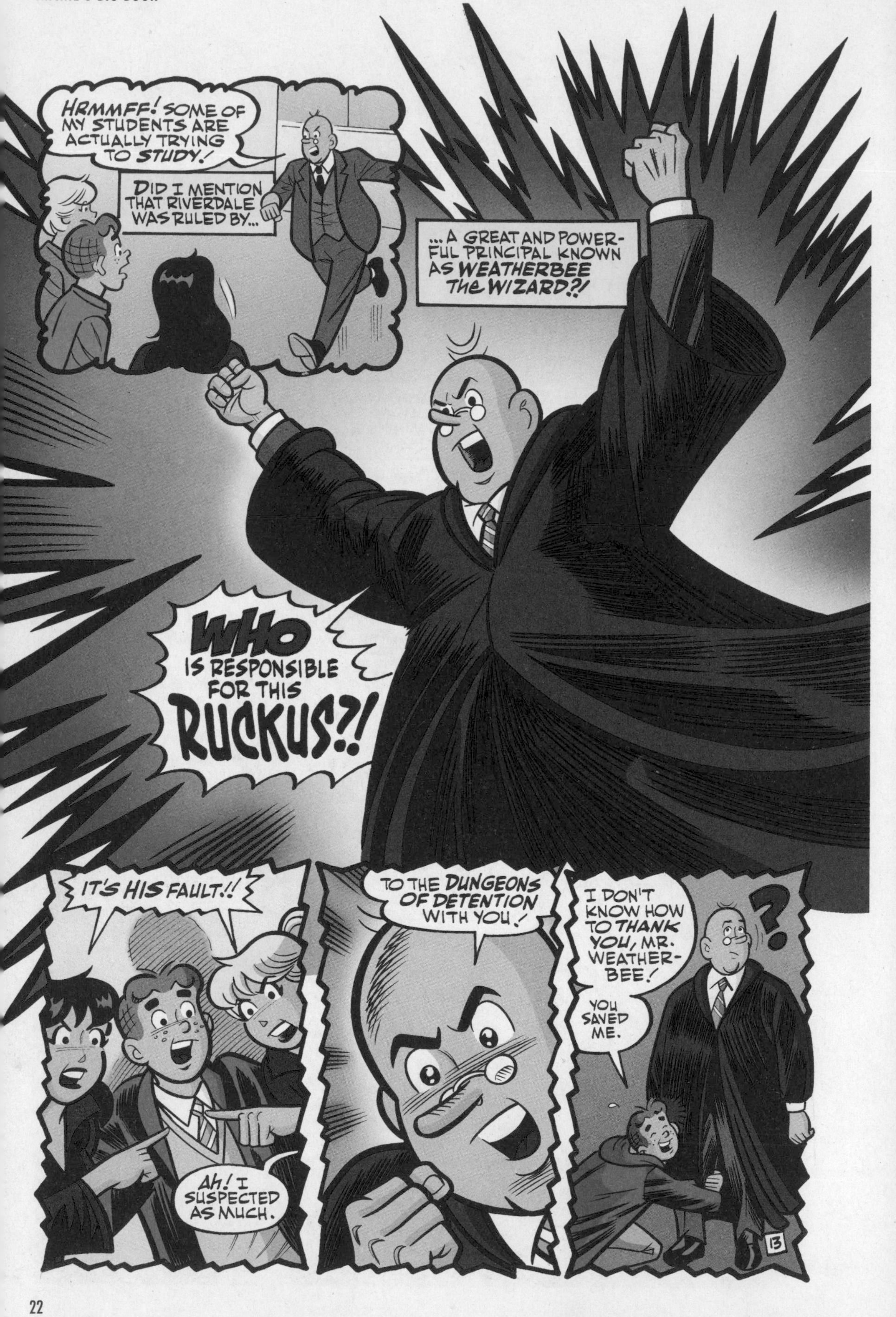
HRMMFF! SOME OF MY STUDENTS ARE ACTUALLY TRYING TO STUDY!
DID I MENTION THAT RIVERDALE WAS RULED BY...
...A GREAT AND POWERFUL PRINCIPAL KNOWN AS WEATHERBEE THE WIZARD?!
WHO IS RESPONSIBLE FOR THIS RUCKUS?!
IT'S HIS FAULT!!
AH! I SUSPECTED AS MUCH.
TO THE DUNGEONS OF DETENTION WITH YOU!
I DON'T KNOW HOW TO THANK YOU, MR. WEATHERBEE!
YOU SAVED ME.
?
13

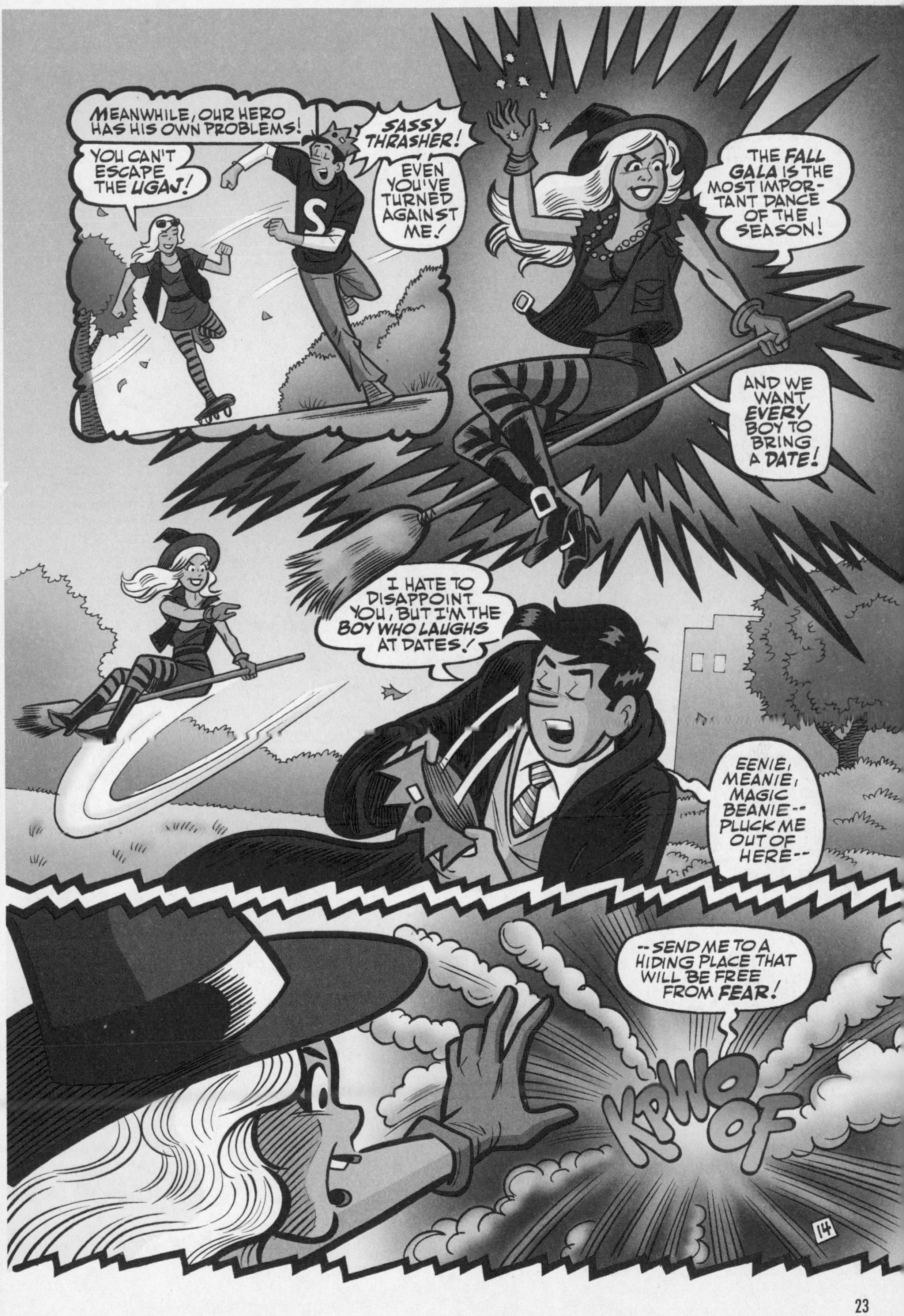
MEANWHILE, OUR HERO HAS HIS OWN PROBLEMS!
YOU CAN'T ESCAPE THE UGAJ!
SASSY THRASHER!
EVEN YOU'VE TURNED AGAINST ME!
THE FALL GALA IS THE MOST IMPORTANT DANCE OF THE SEASON!
AND WE WANT EVERY BOY TO BRING A DATE!
I HATE TO DISAPPOINT YOU, BUT I'M THE BOY WHO LAUGHS AT DATES!
EENIE, MEANIE, MAGIC BEANIE-- PLUCK ME OUT OF HERE--
--SEND ME TO A HIDING PLACE THAT WILL BE FREE FROM FEAR!
KPWOOF
14

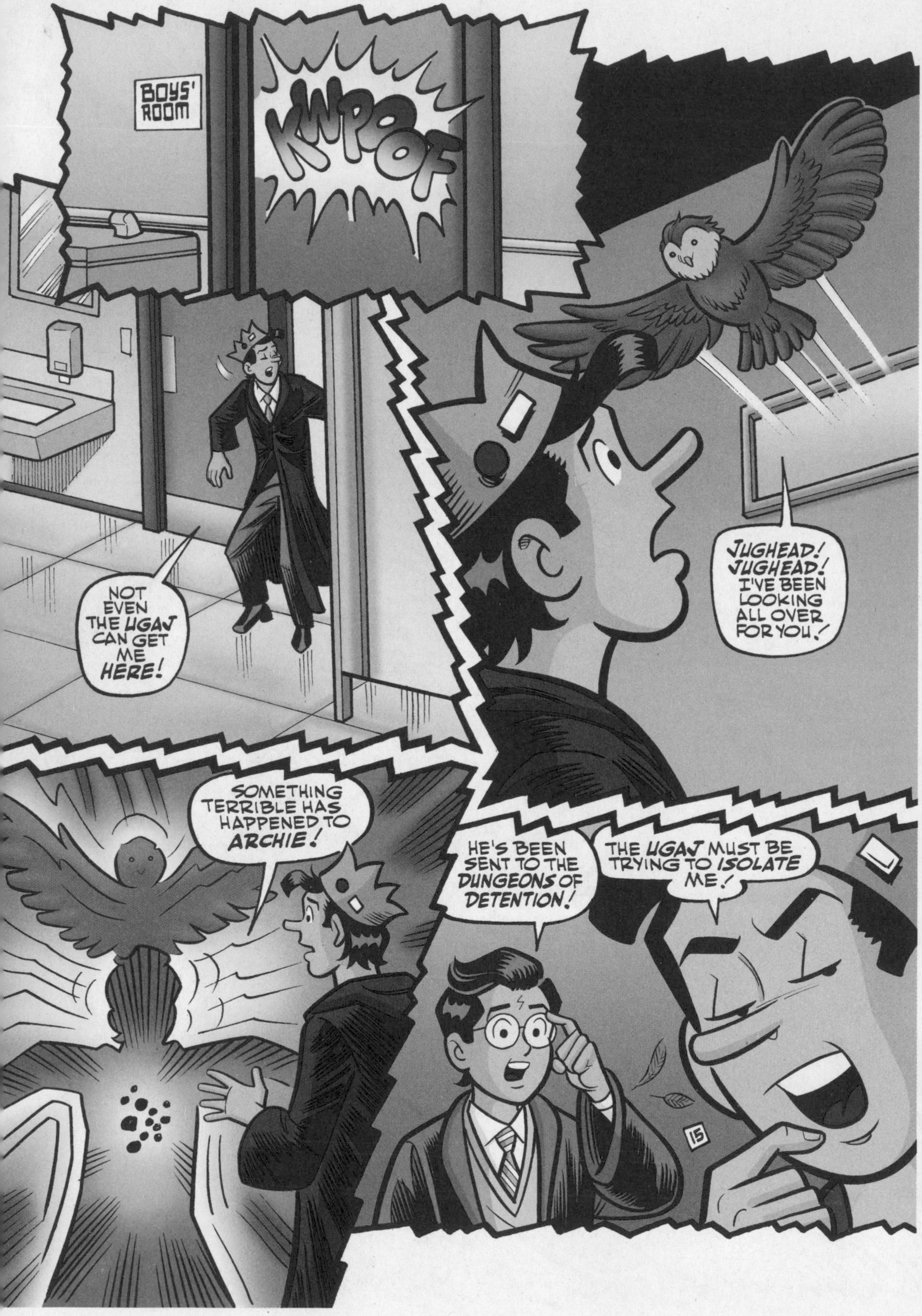
BOYS' ROOM
KINPOOF
NOT EVEN THE UGAJ CAN GET ME HERE!
JUGHEAD! JUGHEAD! I'VE BEEN LOOKING ALL OVER FOR YOU!
SOMETHING TERRIBLE HAS HAPPENED TO ARCHIE!
HE'S BEEN SENT TO THE DUNGEONS OF DETENTION!
THE UGAJ MUST BE TRYING TO ISOLATE ME!
15

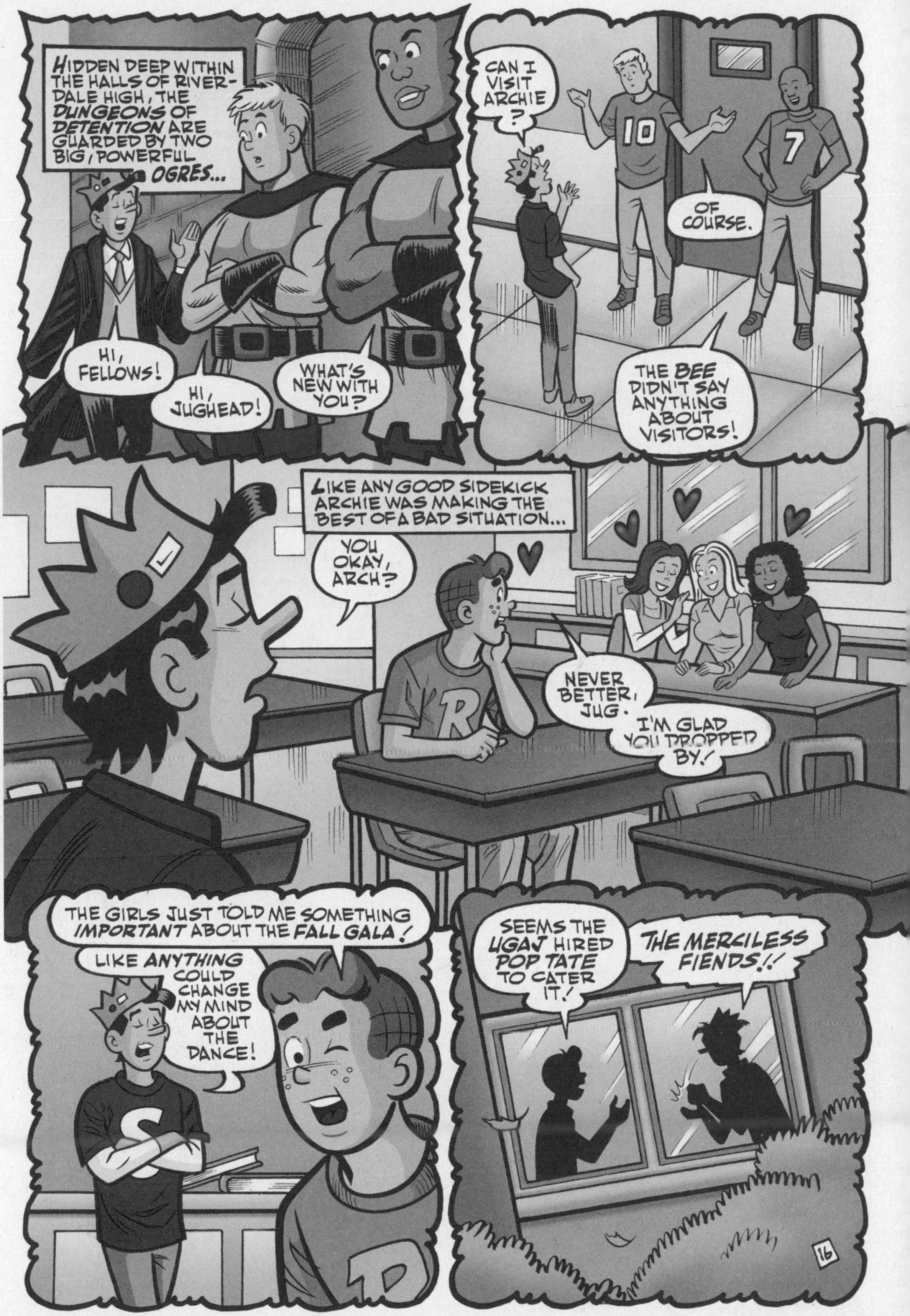
HIDDEN DEEP WITHIN THE HALLS OF RIVERDALE HIGH, THE DUNGEONS OF DETENTION ARE GUARDED BY TWO BIG, POWERFUL OGRES...
HI, FELLOWS!
HI, JUGHEAD!
WHAT'S NEW WITH YOU?
CAN I VISIT ARCHIE?
OF COURSE.
THE BEE DIDN'T SAY ANYTHING ABOUT VISITORS!
LIKE ANY GOOD SIDEKICK ARCHIE WAS MAKING THE BEST OF A BAD SITUATION...
YOU OKAY, ARCH?
NEVER BETTER, JUG.
I'M GLAD YOU DROPPED BY!
THE GIRLS JUST TOLD ME SOMETHING IMPORTANT ABOUT THE FALL GALA!
LIKE ANYTHING COULD CHANGE MY MIND ABOUT THE DANCE!
SEEMS THE UGAJ HIRED POP TATE TO CATER IT!
THE MERCILESS FIENDS!!
16

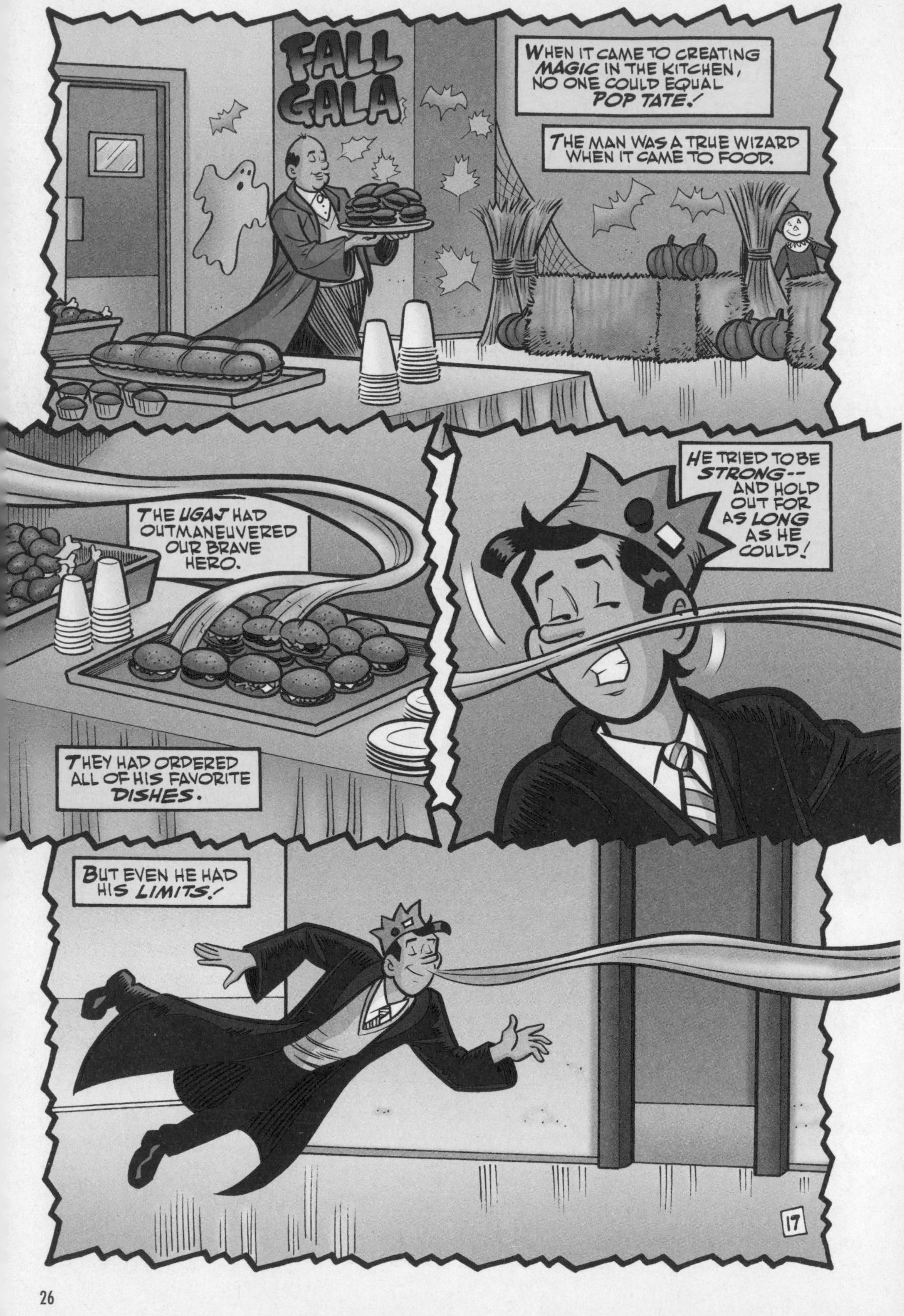
FALL GALA
WHEN IT CAME TO CREATING MAGIC IN THE KITCHEN, NO ONE COULD EQUAL POP TATE!
THE MAN WAS A TRUE WIZARD WHEN IT CAME TO FOOD.
THE UGAJ HAD OUTMANEUVERED OUR BRAVE HERO.
THEY HAD ORDERED ALL OF HIS FAVORITE DISHES.
HE TRIED TO BE STRONG-- AND HOLD OUT FOR AS LONG AS HE COULD!
BUT EVEN HE HAD HIS LIMITS!
17

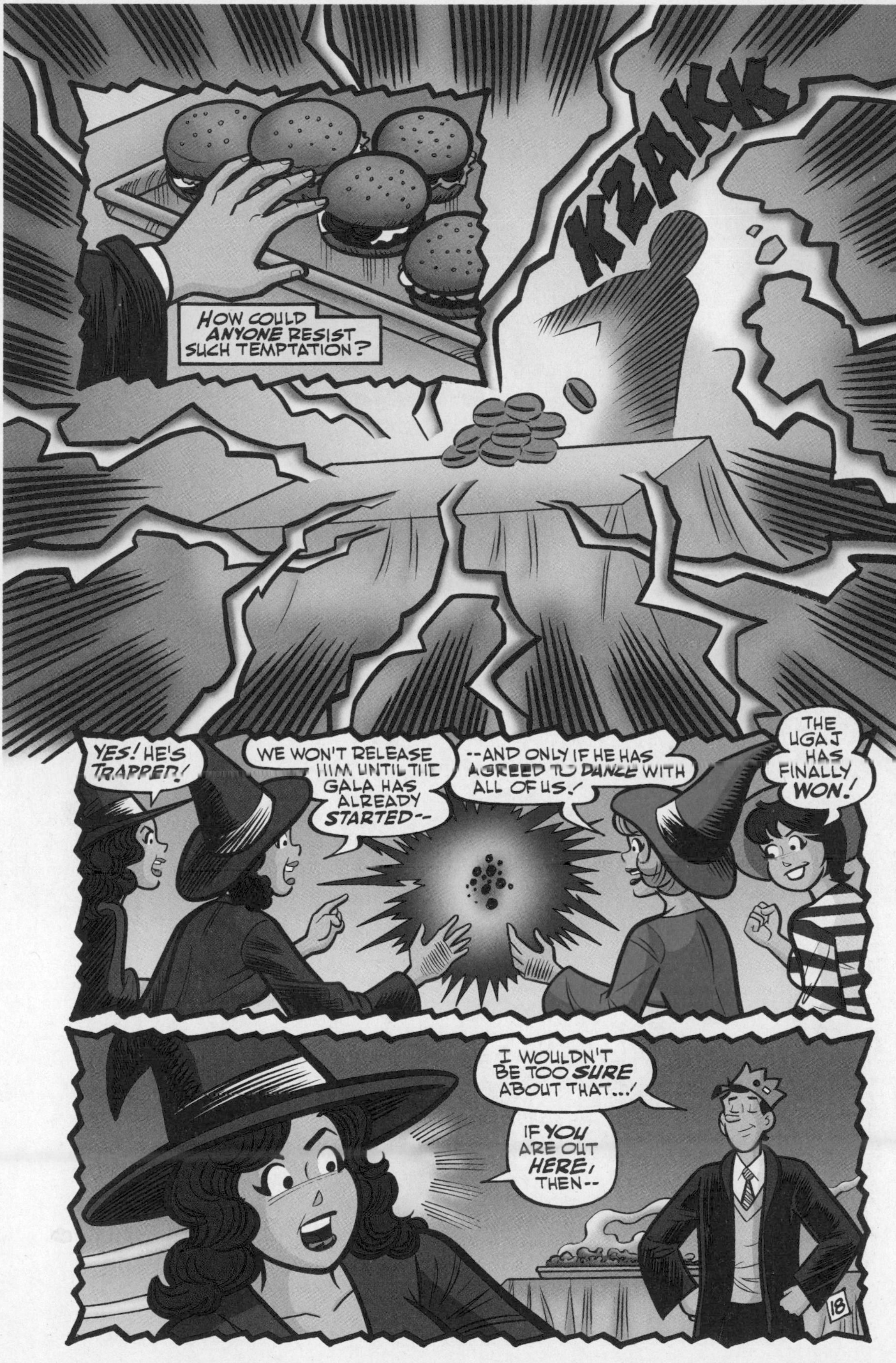
HOW COULD ANYONE RESIST SUCH TEMPTATION?
KZAKK
YES! HE'S TRAPPED!
WE WON'T RELEASE HIM UNTIL THE GALA HAS ALREADY STARTED--
--AND ONLY IF HE HAS AGREED TO DANCE WITH ALL OF US.!
THE UGAJ HAS FINALLY WON!
I WOULDN'T BE TOO SURE ABOUT THAT...!
IF YOU ARE OUT HERE, THEN--

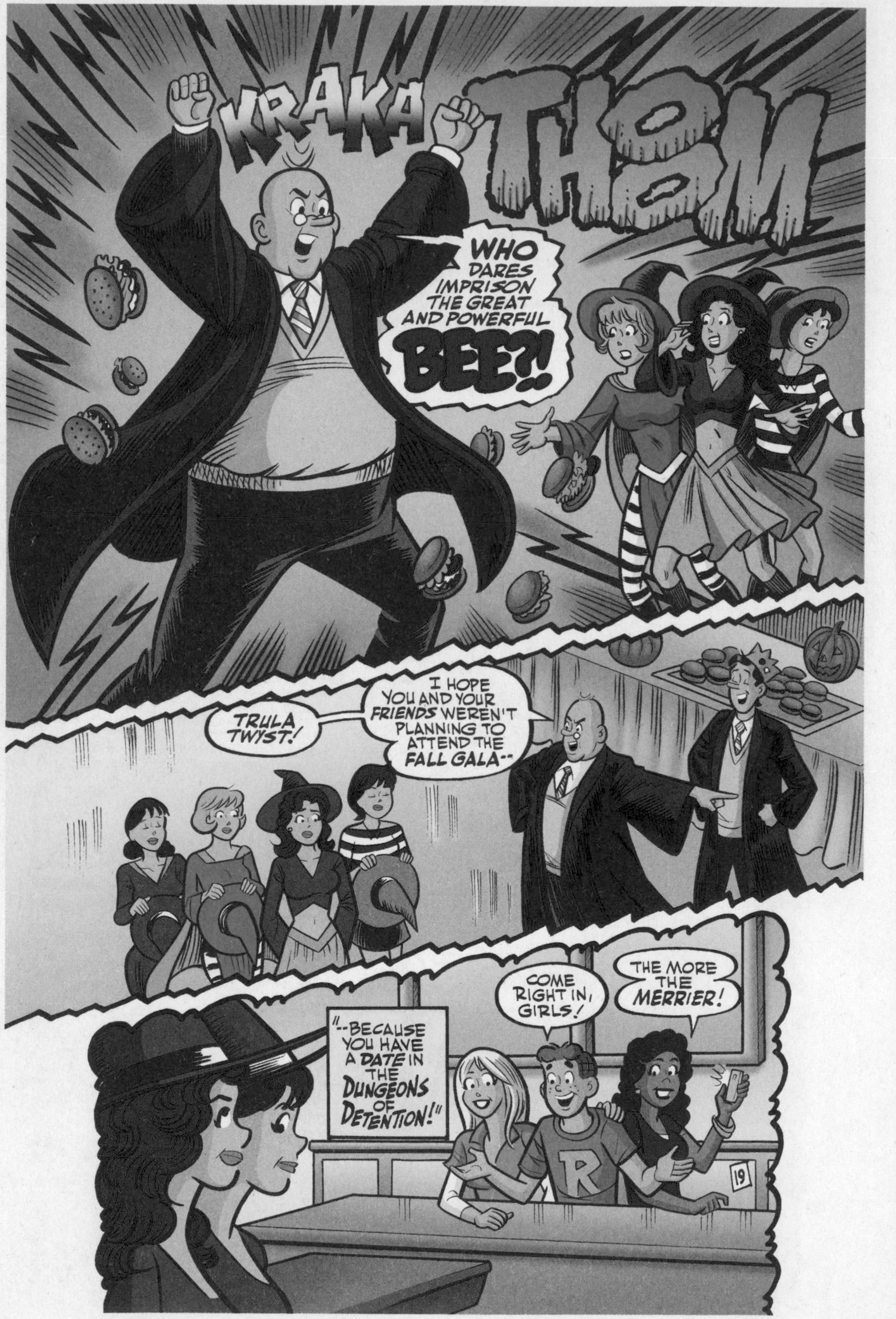
KRAKA THOOM
WHO DARES IMPRISON THE GREAT AND POWERFUL BEE?!
TRULA TWYST!
I HOPE YOU AND YOUR FRIENDS WEREN'T PLANNING TO ATTEND THE FALL GALA--
"--BECAUSE YOU HAVE A DATE IN THE DUNGEONS OF DETENTION!"
COME RIGHT IN, GIRLS!
THE MORE THE MERRIER!
19

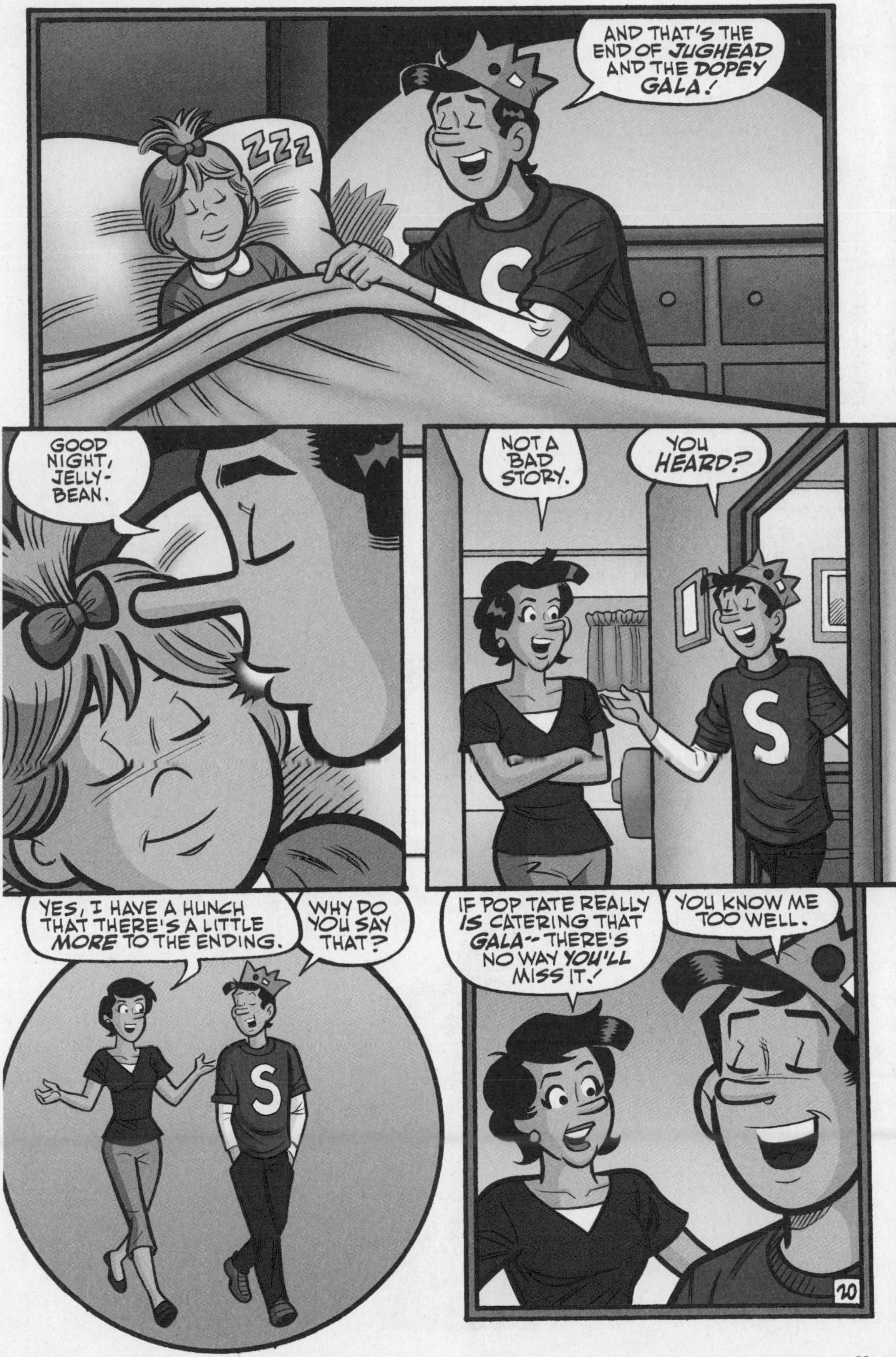
AND THAT'S THE END OF JUGHEAD AND THE DOPEY GALA!
ZZZ
GOOD NIGHT, JELLY-BEAN.
NOT A BAD STORY.
YOU HEARD?
YES, I HAVE A HUNCH THAT THERE'S A LITTLE MORE TO THE ENDING.
WHY DO YOU SAY THAT?
IF POP TATE REALLY IS CATERING THAT GALA-- THERE'S NO WAY YOU'LL MISS IT!
YOU KNOW ME TOO WELL.
20

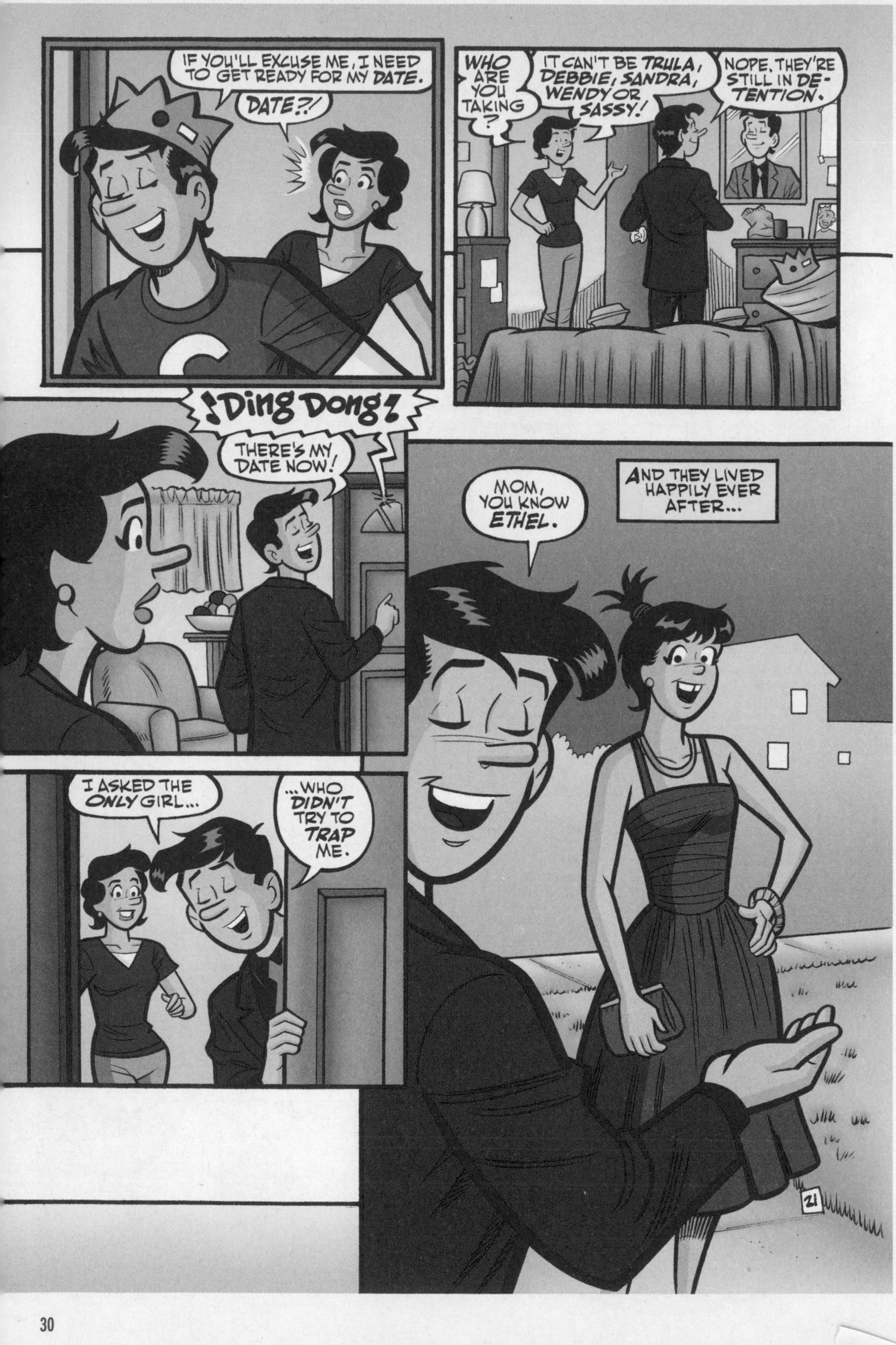
IF YOU'LL EXCUSE ME, I NEED TO GET READY FOR MY DATE.
DATE?!
WHO ARE YOU TAKING?
IT CAN'T BE TRULA, DEBBIE, SANDRA, WENDY OR SASSY!
NOPE. THEY'RE STILL IN DETENTION.
DING DONG
THERE'S MY DATE NOW!
MOM, YOU KNOW ETHEL.
AND THEY LIVED HAPPILY EVER AFTER...
I ASKED THE ONLY GIRL...
...WHO DIDN'T TRY TO TRAP ME.
21

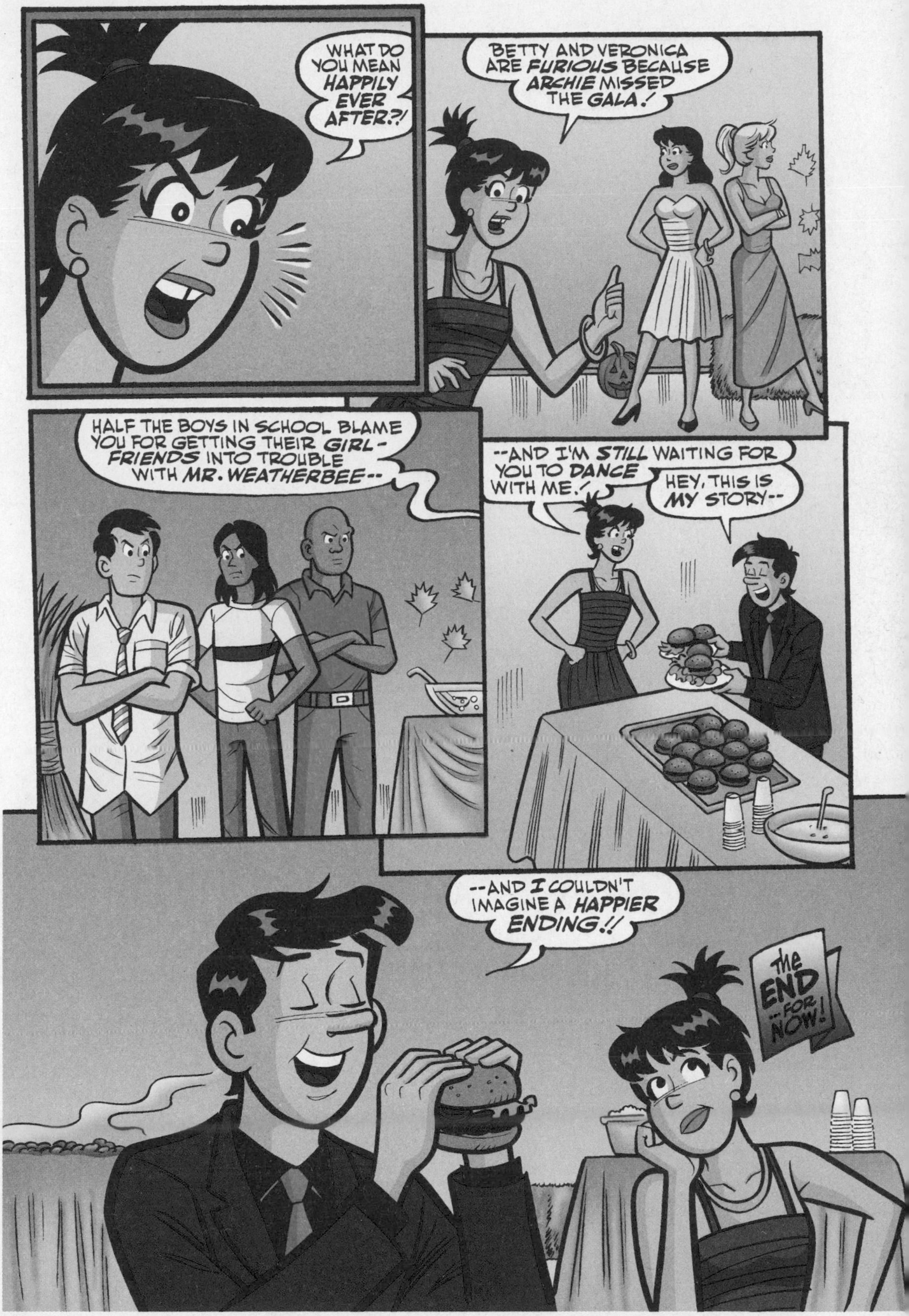
WHAT DO YOU MEAN HAPPILY EVER AFTER?!
BETTY AND VERONICA ARE FURIOUS BECAUSE ARCHIE MISSED THE GALA!
HALF THE BOYS IN SCHOOL BLAME YOU FOR GETTING THEIR GIRL-FRIENDS INTO TROUBLE WITH MR. WEATHERBEE--
--AND I'M STILL WAITING FOR YOU TO DANCE WITH ME.!
HEY, THIS IS MY STORY--
--AND I COULDN'T IMAGINE A HAPPIER ENDING.!!
the END ...FOR NOW!

CHAPTER TWO

Clod of Thunder

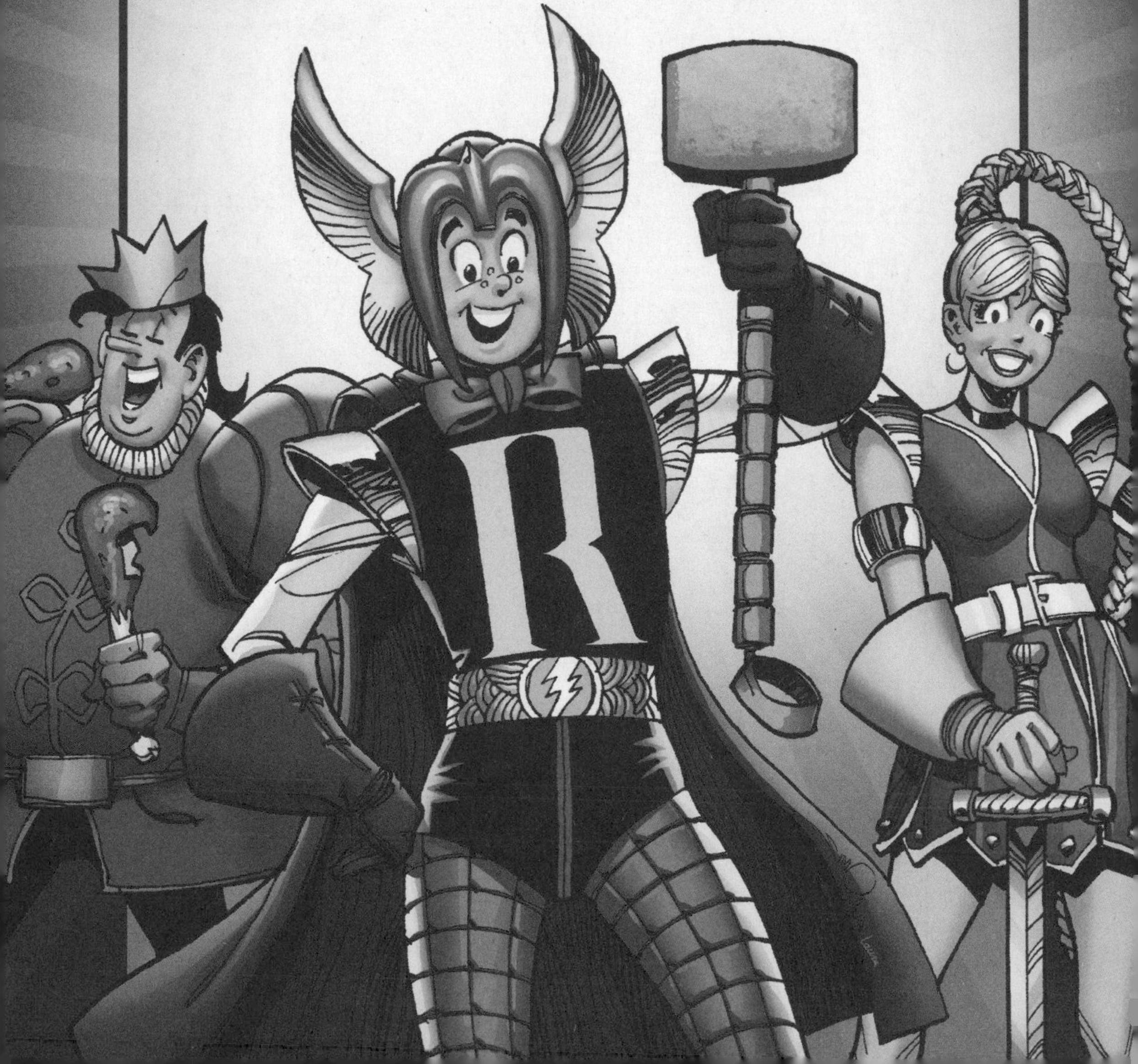

INTRODUCING CLOD OF THUNDER

Originally printed in *Archie #648*

It's Archie in "Clod of Thunder!" Archie resides in Allgood, an honorable city over the Rainbow Bridge, where the food is plentiful, the girls are heavenly, and everything is absolutely... boring! Turns out that being an immortal warrior isn't as fun as people might think. When Archie finds himself in trouble, thanks to a prank of his brother Reggie the Wicked, his father banishes Archie to Planet Earth—to the town of Riverdale, USA to be exact! Will Archie be able to dutifully serve out his punishment? Or will he find life on Earth to be just the excitement he was looking for?

WRITER
TOM DEFALCO

PENCILS
FERNANDO RUIZ

INKS
RICH KOSLOWSKI

LETTERS
JOHN WORKMAN

COLORS
DIGIKORE STUDIOS

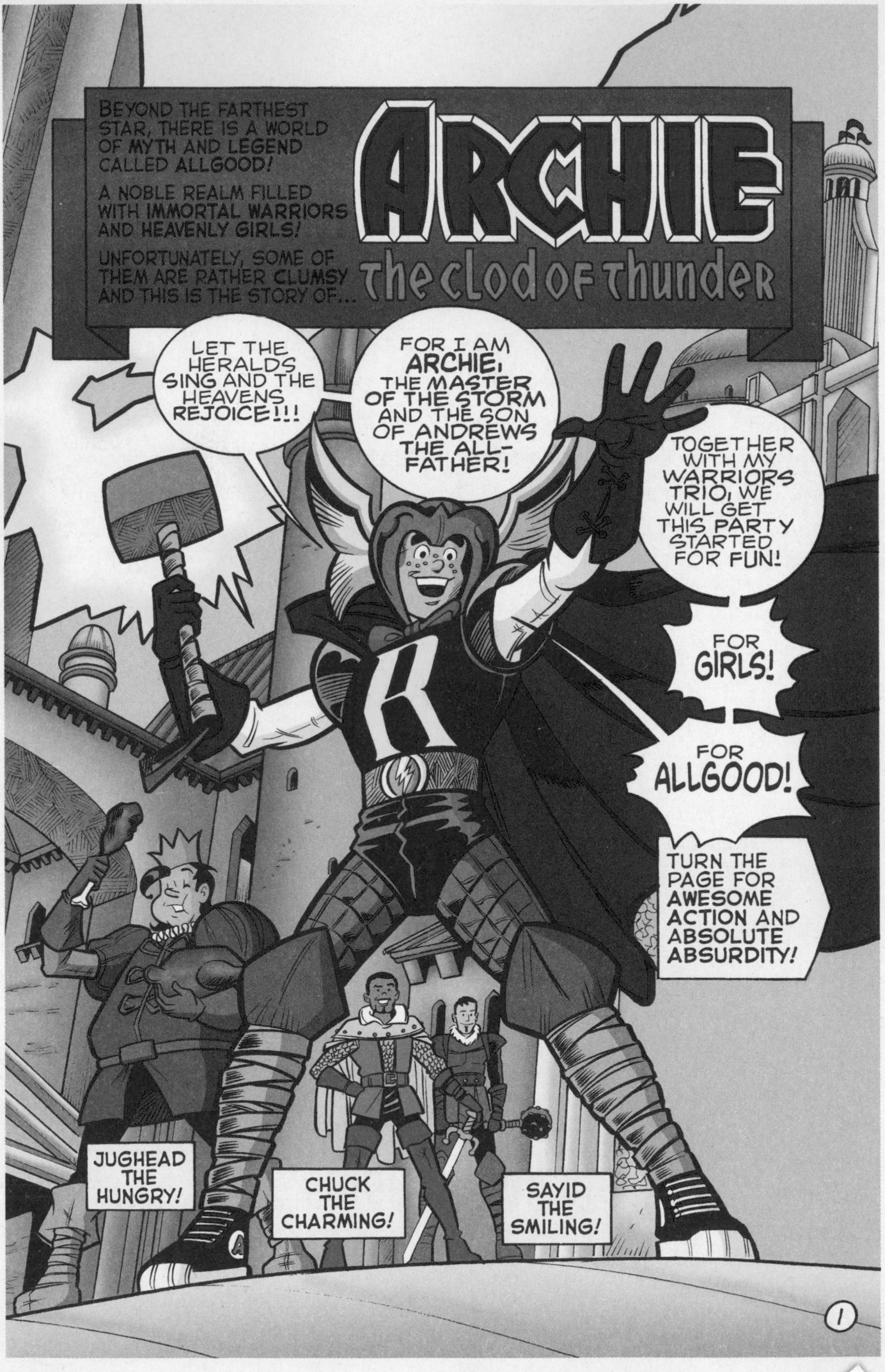
BEYOND THE FARTHEST STAR, THERE IS A WORLD OF MYTH AND LEGEND CALLED ALLGOOD!
A NOBLE REALM FILLED WITH IMMORTAL WARRIORS AND HEAVENLY GIRLS!
UNFORTUNATELY, SOME OF THEM ARE RATHER CLUMSY AND THIS IS THE STORY OF...
ARCHIE
the clod of thunder
LET THE HERALDS SING AND THE HEAVENS REJOICE!!!
FOR I AM ARCHIE, THE MASTER OF THE STORM AND THE SON OF ANDREWS THE ALL-FATHER!
TOGETHER WITH MY WARRIORS TRIO, WE WILL GET THIS PARTY STARTED FOR FUN!
FOR GIRLS!
FOR ALLGOOD!
TURN THE PAGE FOR AWESOME ACTION AND ABSOLUTE ABSURDITY!
JUGHEAD THE HUNGRY!
CHUCK THE CHARMING!
SAYID THE SMILING!
1

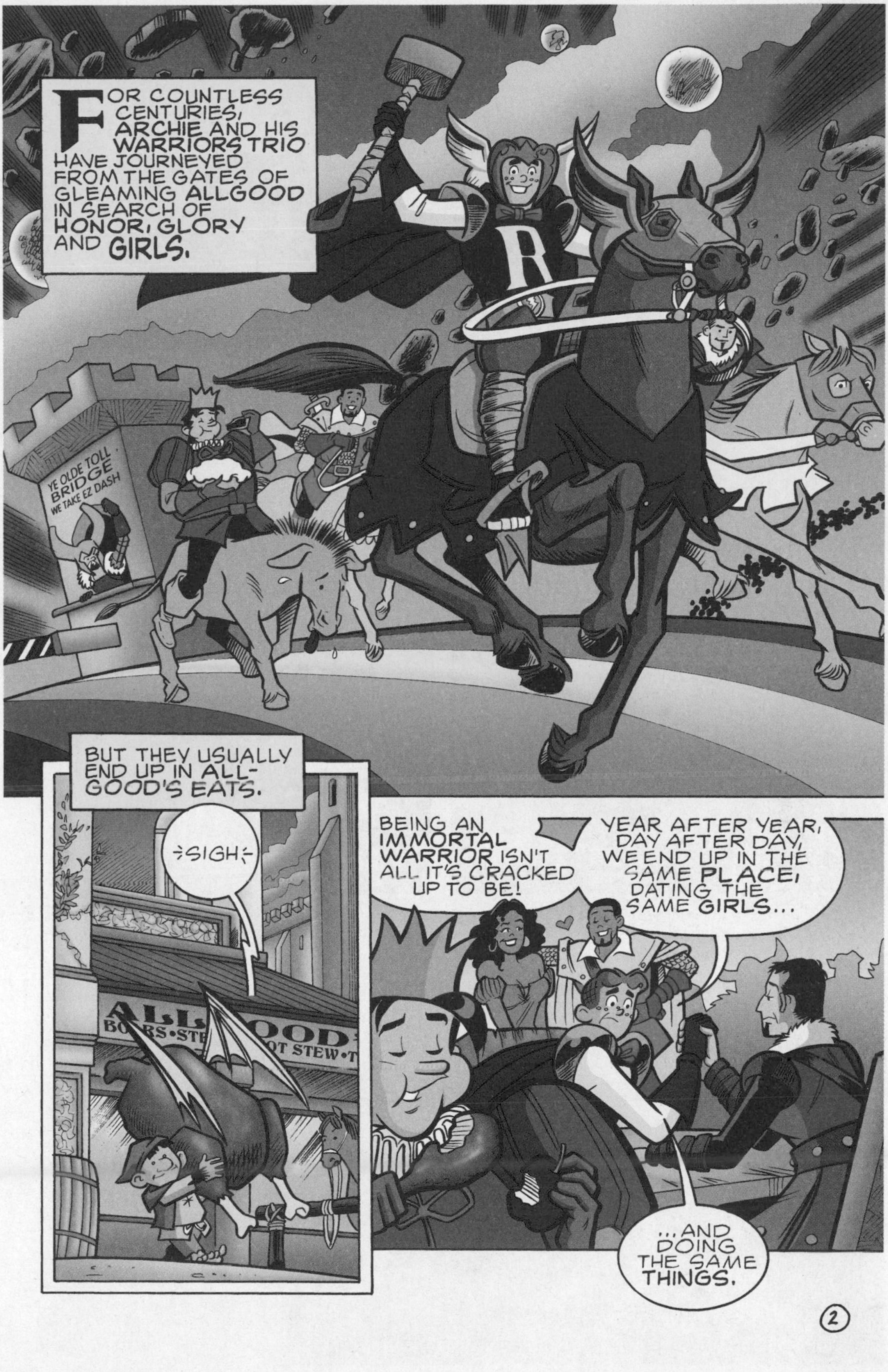
FOR COUNTLESS CENTURIES, ARCHIE AND HIS WARRIORS TRIO HAVE JOURNEYED FROM THE GATES OF GLEAMING ALLGOOD IN SEARCH OF HONOR, GLORY AND GIRLS.
YE OLDE TOLL BRIDGE WE TAKE EZ DASH
BUT THEY USUALLY END UP IN ALL-GOOD'S EATS.
SIGH
BEING AN IMMORTAL WARRIOR ISN'T ALL IT'S CRACKED UP TO BE!
YEAR AFTER YEAR, DAY AFTER DAY, WE END UP IN THE SAME PLACE, DATING THE SAME GIRLS...
...AND DOING THE SAME THINGS.
2

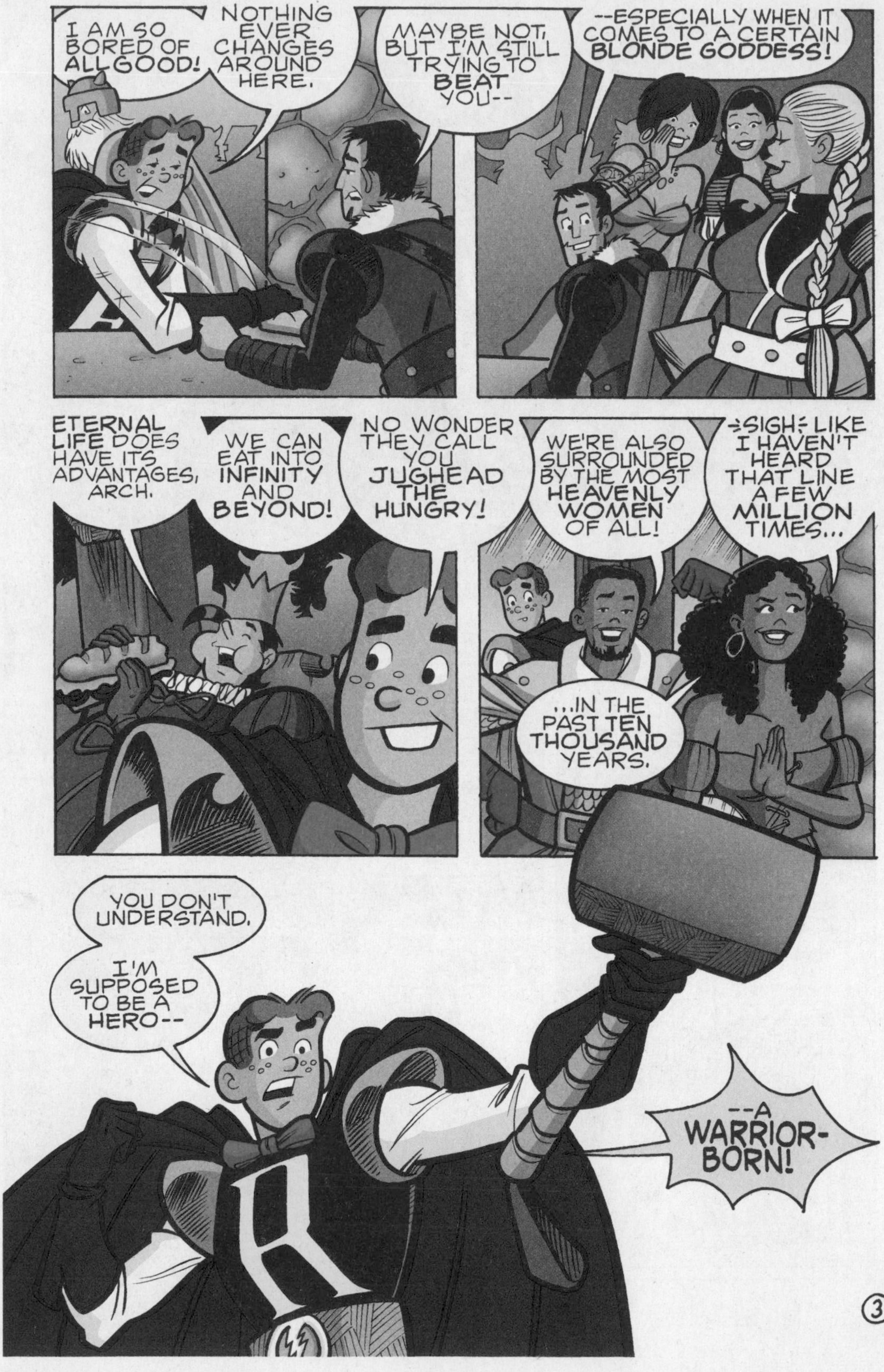
I AM SO BORED OF ALLGOOD!
NOTHING EVER CHANGES AROUND HERE.
MAYBE NOT, BUT I'M STILL TRYING TO BEAT YOU--
--ESPECIALLY WHEN IT COMES TO A CERTAIN BLONDE GODDESS!
ETERNAL LIFE DOES HAVE ITS ADVANTAGES, ARCH.
WE CAN EAT INTO INFINITY AND BEYOND!
NO WONDER THEY CALL YOU JUGHEAD THE HUNGRY!
WE'RE ALSO SURROUNDED BY THE MOST HEAVENLY WOMEN OF ALL!
=SIGH= LIKE I HAVEN'T HEARD THAT LINE A FEW MILLION TIMES...
...IN THE PAST TEN THOUSAND YEARS.
YOU DON'T UNDERSTAND.
I'M SUPPOSED TO BE A HERO--
--A WARRIOR-BORN!
3

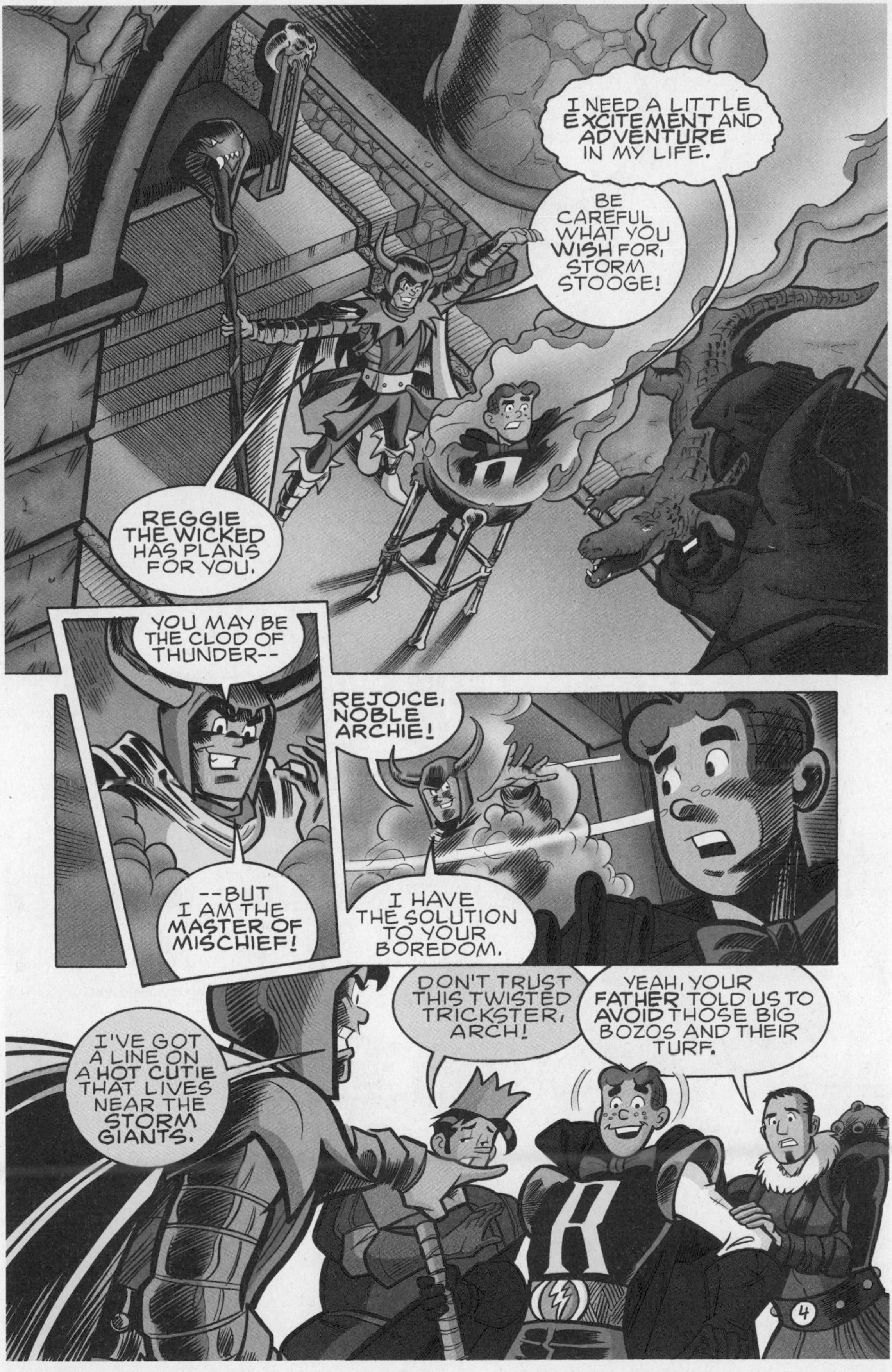
I NEED A LITTLE EXCITEMENT AND ADVENTURE IN MY LIFE.
BE CAREFUL WHAT YOU WISH FOR, STORM STOOGE!
REGGIE THE WICKED HAS PLANS FOR YOU.
YOU MAY BE THE CLOD OF THUNDER--
--BUT I AM THE MASTER OF MISCHIEF!
REJOICE, NOBLE ARCHIE!
I HAVE THE SOLUTION TO YOUR BOREDOM.
I'VE GOT A LINE ON A HOT CUTIE THAT LIVES NEAR THE STORM GIANTS.
DON'T TRUST THIS TWISTED TRICKSTER, ARCH!
YEAH, YOUR FATHER TOLD US TO AVOID THOSE BIG BOZOS AND THEIR TURF.

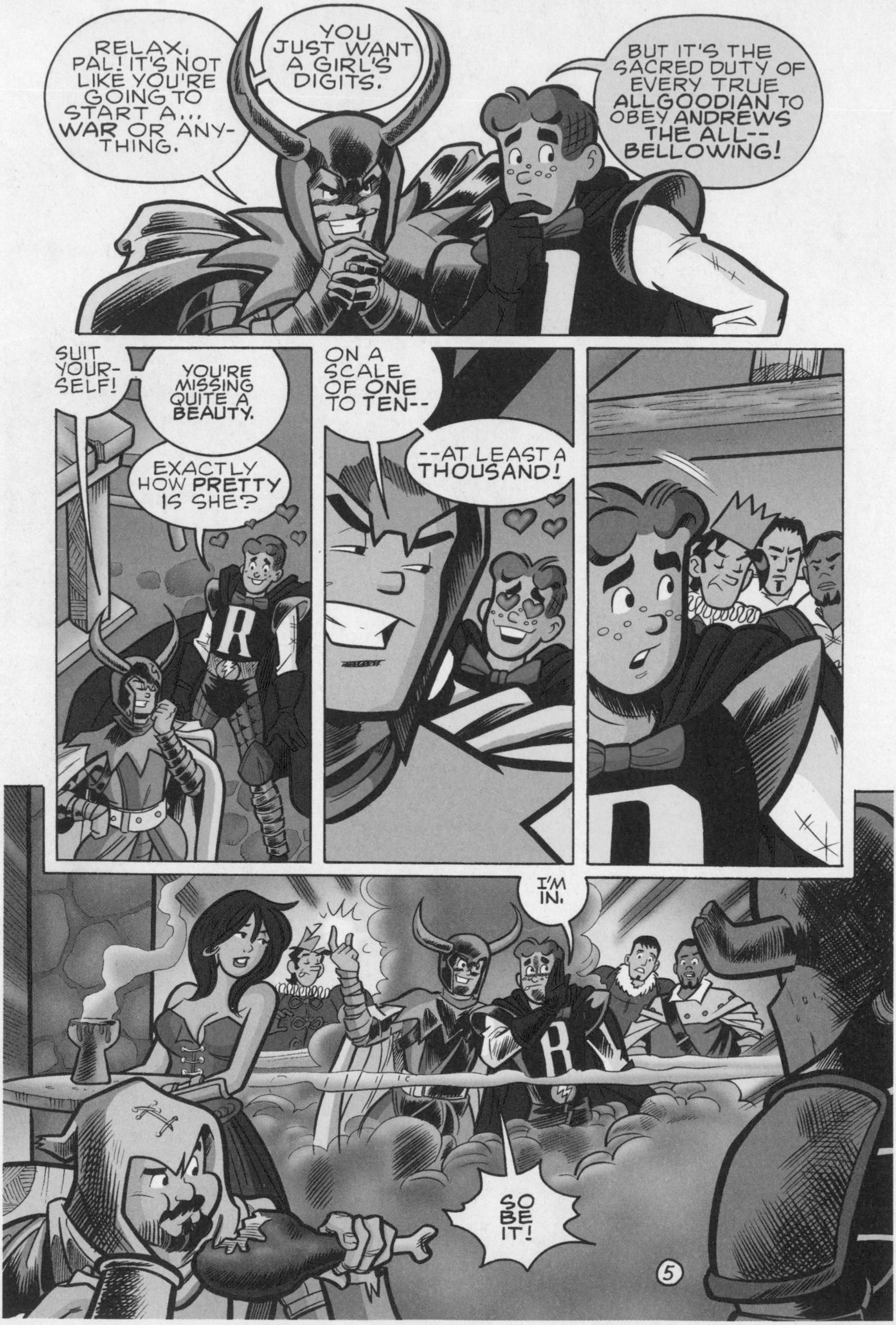
RELAX, PAL! IT'S NOT LIKE YOU'RE GOING TO START A... WAR OR ANY-THING.
YOU JUST WANT A GIRL'S DIGITS.
BUT IT'S THE SACRED DUTY OF EVERY TRUE ALLGOODIAN TO OBEY ANDREWS THE ALL--BELLOWING!
SUIT YOUR-SELF!
YOU'RE MISSING QUITE A BEAUTY.
EXACTLY HOW PRETTY IS SHE?
ON A SCALE OF ONE TO TEN--
--AT LEAST A THOUSAND!
I'M IN.
SO BE IT!
5

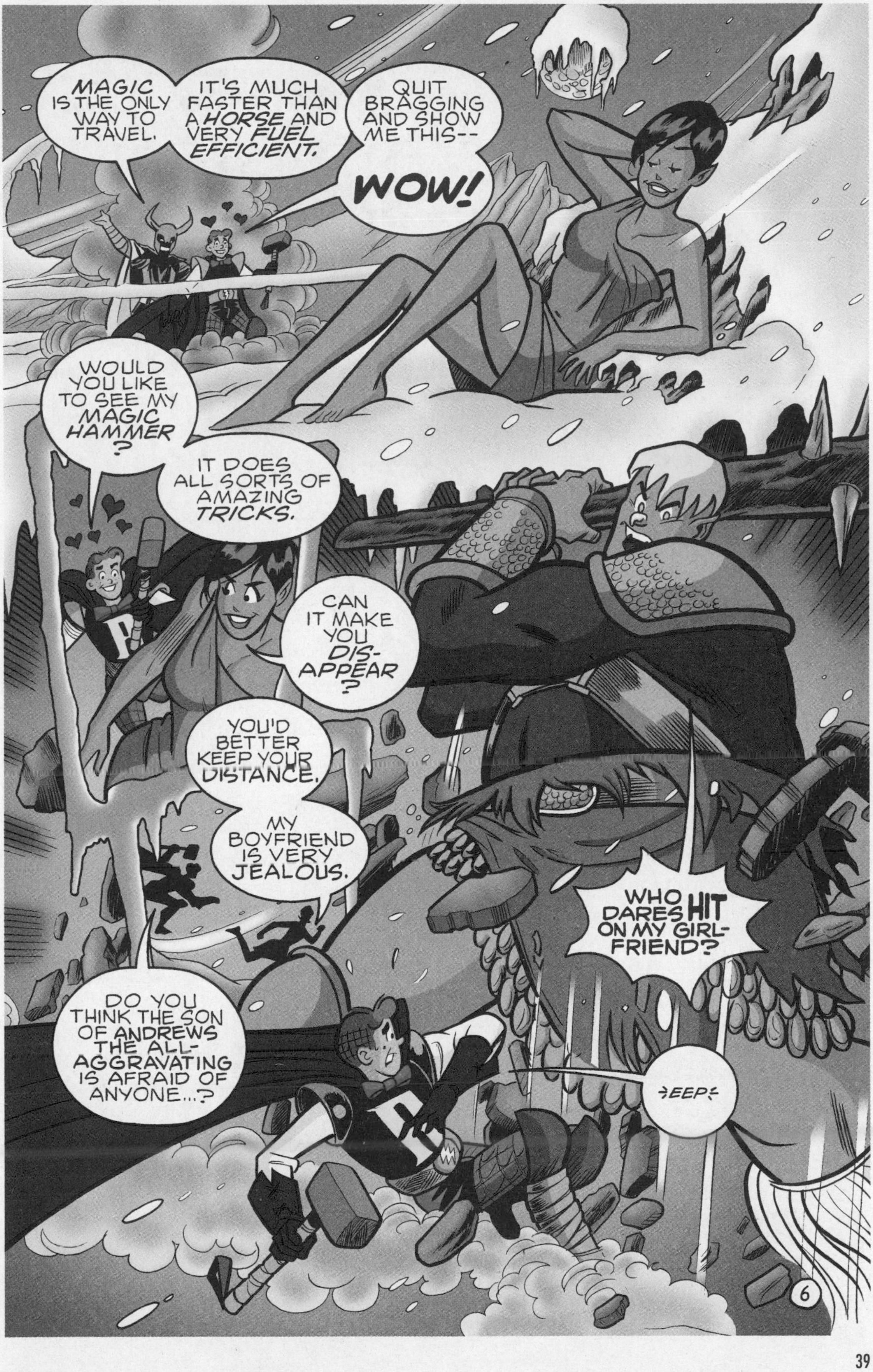
MAGIC IS THE ONLY WAY TO TRAVEL.
IT'S MUCH FASTER THAN A HORSE AND VERY FUEL EFFICIENT.
QUIT BRAGGING AND SHOW ME THIS--
WOW!
WOULD YOU LIKE TO SEE MY MAGIC HAMMER?
IT DOES ALL SORTS OF AMAZING TRICKS.
CAN IT MAKE YOU DIS-APPEAR?
YOU'D BETTER KEEP YOUR DISTANCE.
MY BOYFRIEND IS VERY JEALOUS.
WHO DARES HIT ON MY GIRL-FRIEND?
DO YOU THINK THE SON OF ANDREWS THE ALL-AGGRAVATING IS AFRAID OF ANYONE...?
EEP
6

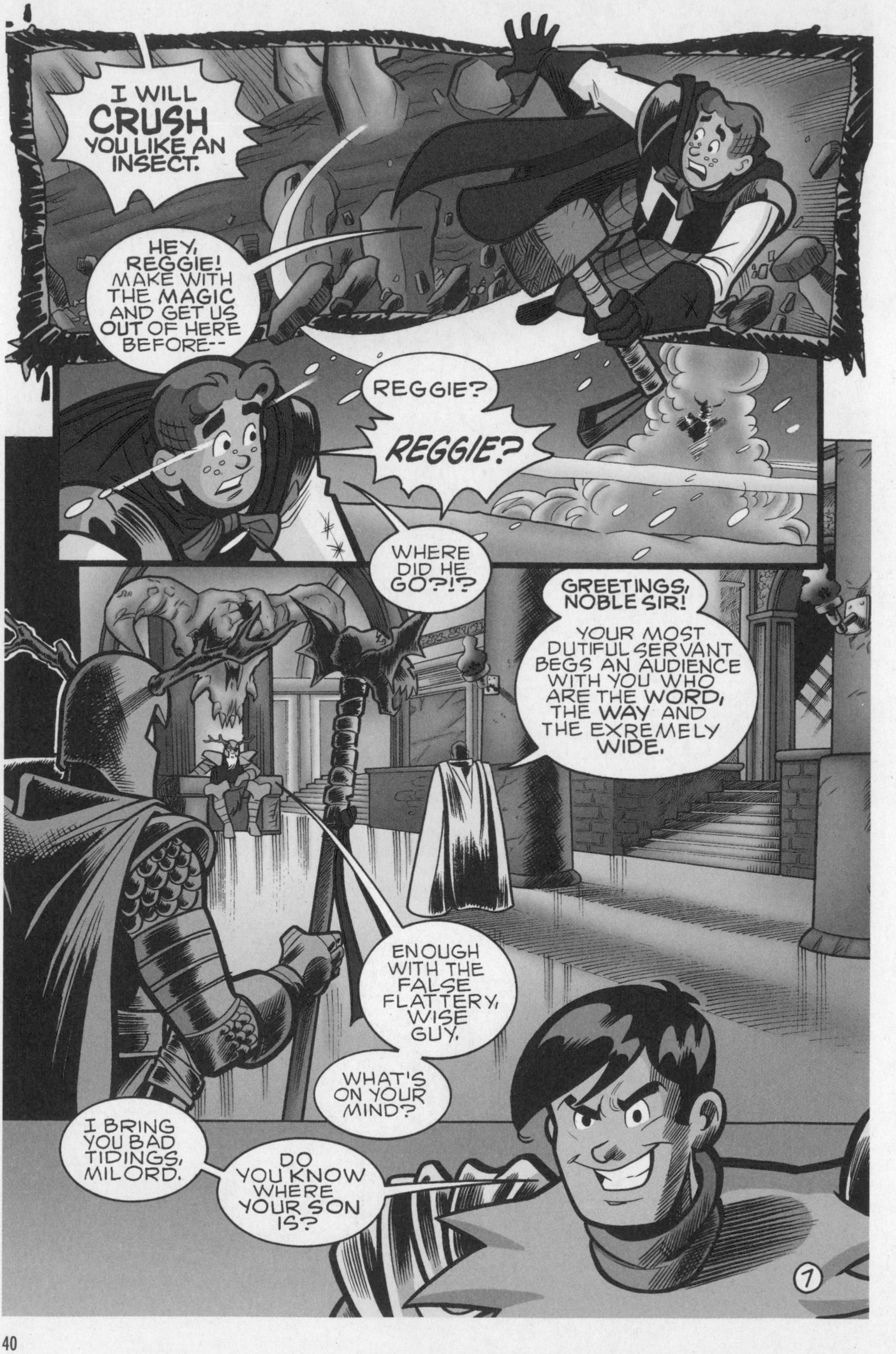
I WILL CRUSH YOU LIKE AN INSECT.
HEY, REGGIE! MAKE WITH THE MAGIC AND GET US OUT OF HERE BEFORE--
REGGIE?
REGGIE?
WHERE DID HE GO?!?
GREETINGS, NOBLE SIR!
YOUR MOST DUTIFUL SERVANT BEGS AN AUDIENCE WITH YOU WHO ARE THE WORD, THE WAY AND THE EXREMELY WIDE.
ENOUGH WITH THE FALSE FLATTERY, WISE GUY.
WHAT'S ON YOUR MIND?
I BRING YOU BAD TIDINGS, MILORD.
DO YOU KNOW WHERE YOUR SON IS?
7

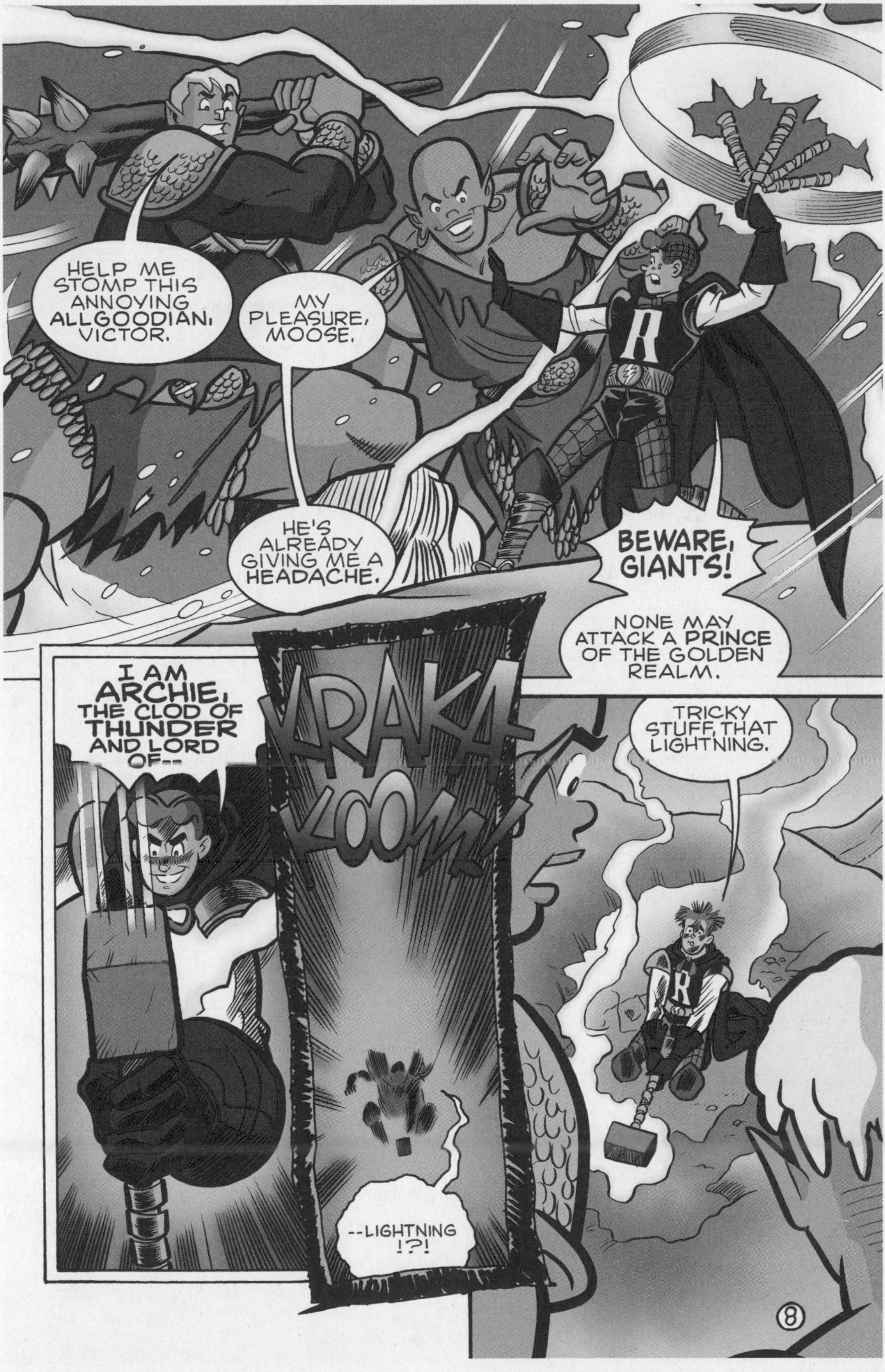
HELP ME STOMP THIS ANNOYING ALLGOODIAN, VICTOR.
MY PLEASURE, MOOSE.
HE'S ALREADY GIVING ME A HEADACHE.
BEWARE, GIANTS!
NONE MAY ATTACK A PRINCE OF THE GOLDEN REALM.
I AM ARCHIE, THE CLOD OF THUNDER AND LORD OF--
KRAKA KOOM!
--LIGHTNING !?!
TRICKY STUFF, THAT LIGHTNING.
8

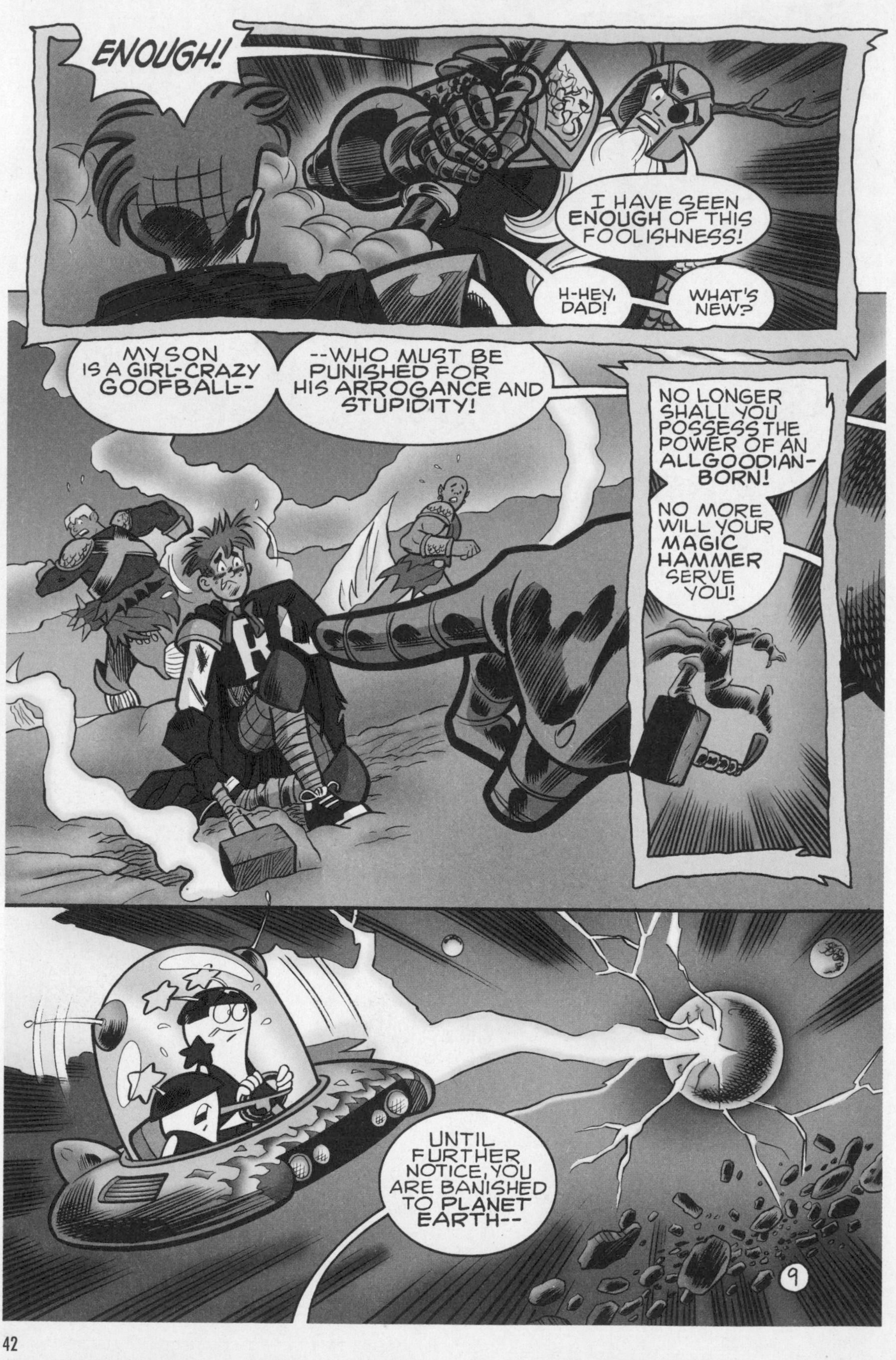
ENOUGH!
I HAVE SEEN ENOUGH OF THIS FOOLISHNESS!
H-HEY, DAD!
WHAT'S NEW?
MY SON IS A GIRL-CRAZY GOOFBALL--
--WHO MUST BE PUNISHED FOR HIS ARROGANCE AND STUPIDITY!
NO LONGER SHALL YOU POSSESS THE POWER OF AN ALLGOODIAN-BORN!
NO MORE WILL YOUR MAGIC HAMMER SERVE YOU!
UNTIL FURTHER NOTICE, YOU ARE BANISHED TO PLANET EARTH--
9

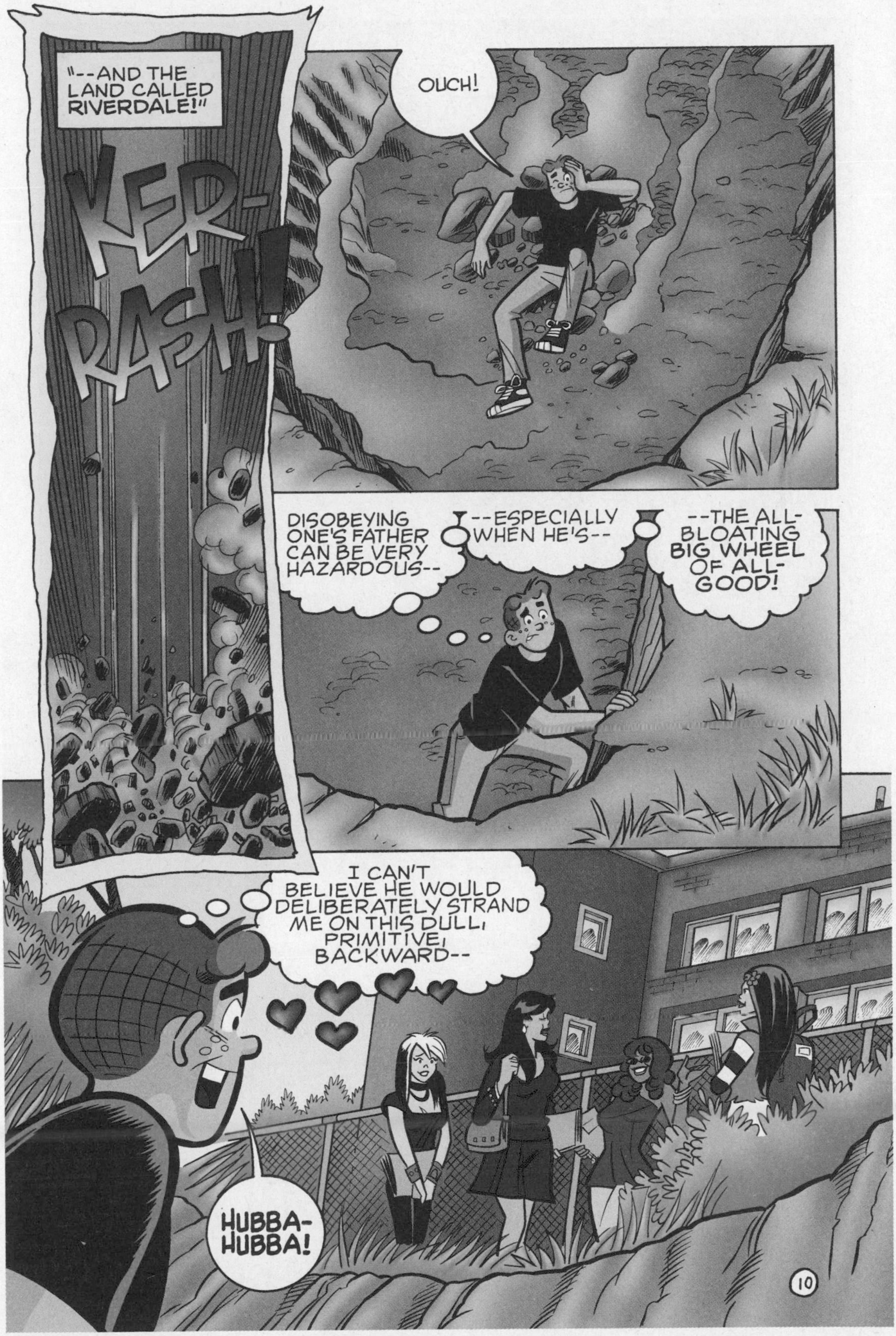
"--AND THE LAND CALLED RIVERDALE!"
KER-RASH!!
OUCH!
DISOBEYING ONE'S FATHER CAN BE VERY HAZARDOUS--
--ESPECIALLY WHEN HE'S--
--THE ALL-BLOATING BIG WHEEL OF ALL-GOOD!
I CAN'T BELIEVE HE WOULD DELIBERATELY STRAND ME ON THIS DULL, PRIMITIVE, BACKWARD--
HUBBA-HUBBA!
10

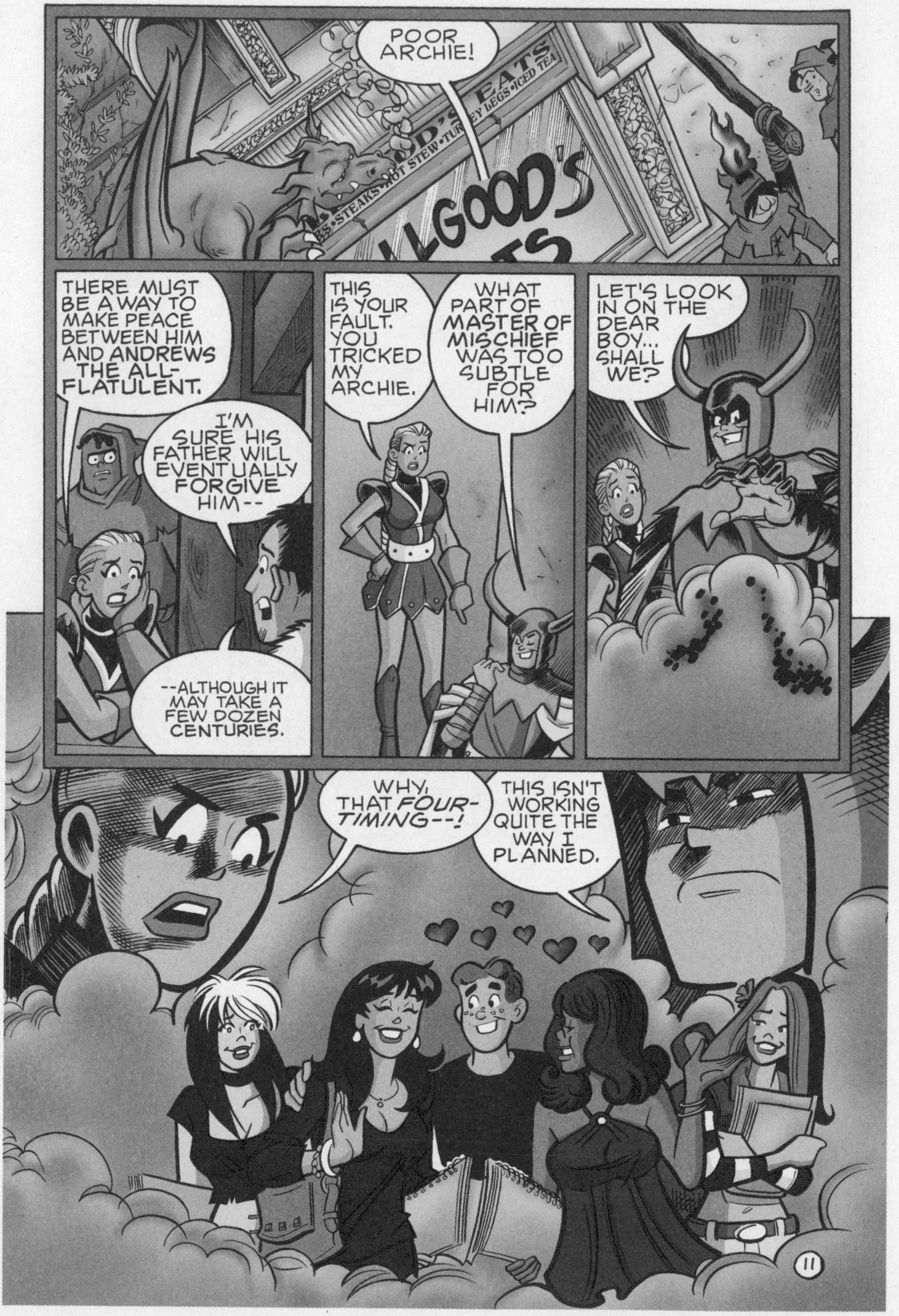
POOR ARCHIE!
...D'S EATS
STEAKS • HOT STEW • TURKEY LEGS • ICED TEA
...LLGOOD'S
THERE MUST BE A WAY TO MAKE PEACE BETWEEN HIM AND ANDREWS THE ALL-FLATULENT.
I'M SURE HIS FATHER WILL EVENTUALLY FORGIVE HIM--
--ALTHOUGH IT MAY TAKE A FEW DOZEN CENTURIES.
THIS IS YOUR FAULT. YOU TRICKED MY ARCHIE.
WHAT PART OF MASTER OF MISCHIEF WAS TOO SUBTLE FOR HIM?
LET'S LOOK IN ON THE DEAR BOY... SHALL WE?
WHY, THAT FOUR-TIMING--!
THIS ISN'T WORKING QUITE THE WAY I PLANNED.
11

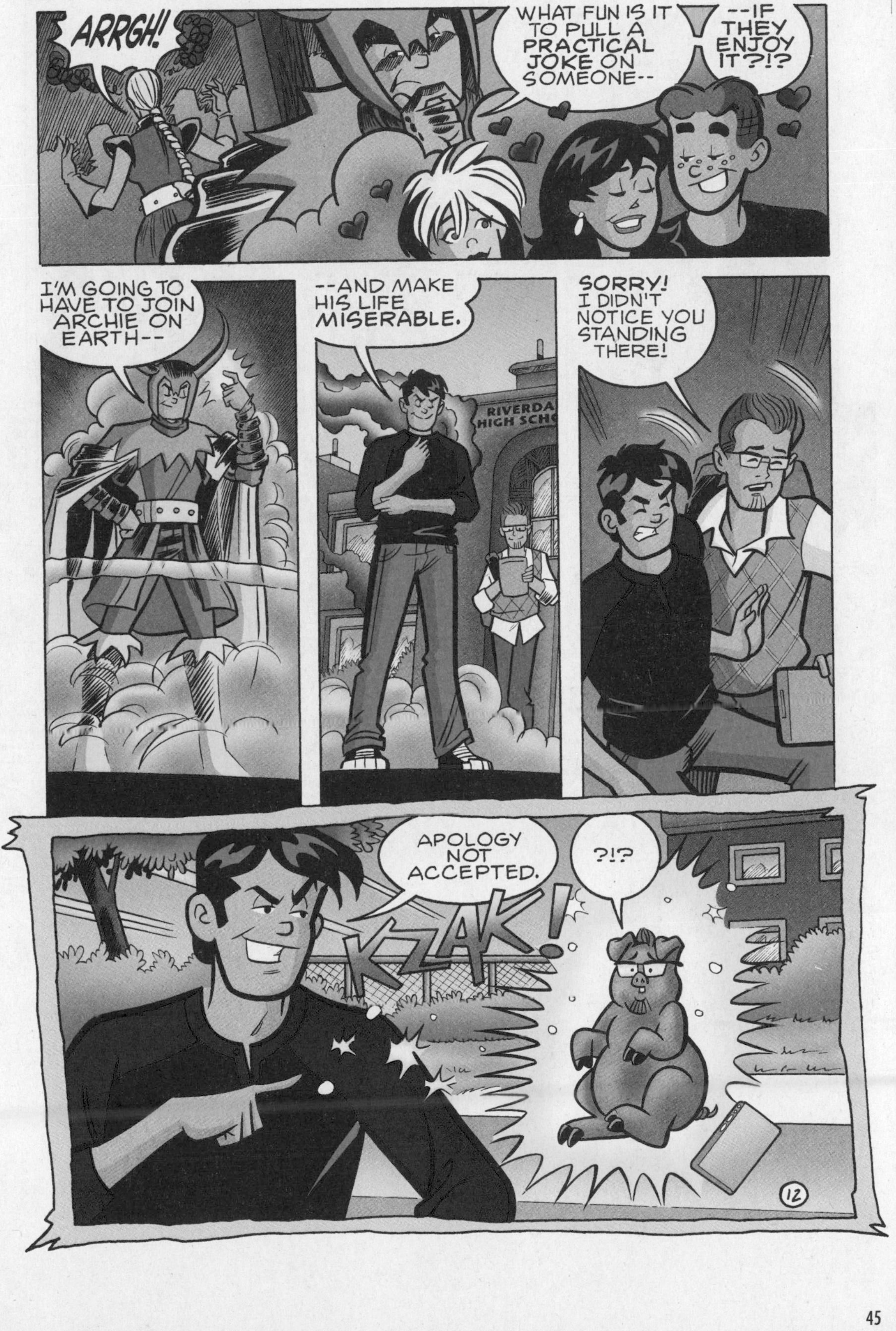
ARRGH!
WHAT FUN IS IT TO PULL A PRACTICAL JOKE ON SOMEONE--
--IF THEY ENJOY IT?!?
I'M GOING TO HAVE TO JOIN ARCHIE ON EARTH--
--AND MAKE HIS LIFE MISERABLE.
RIVERDA HIGH SCHO
SORRY! I DIDN'T NOTICE YOU STANDING THERE!
APOLOGY NOT ACCEPTED.
?!?
KZZAK!
12

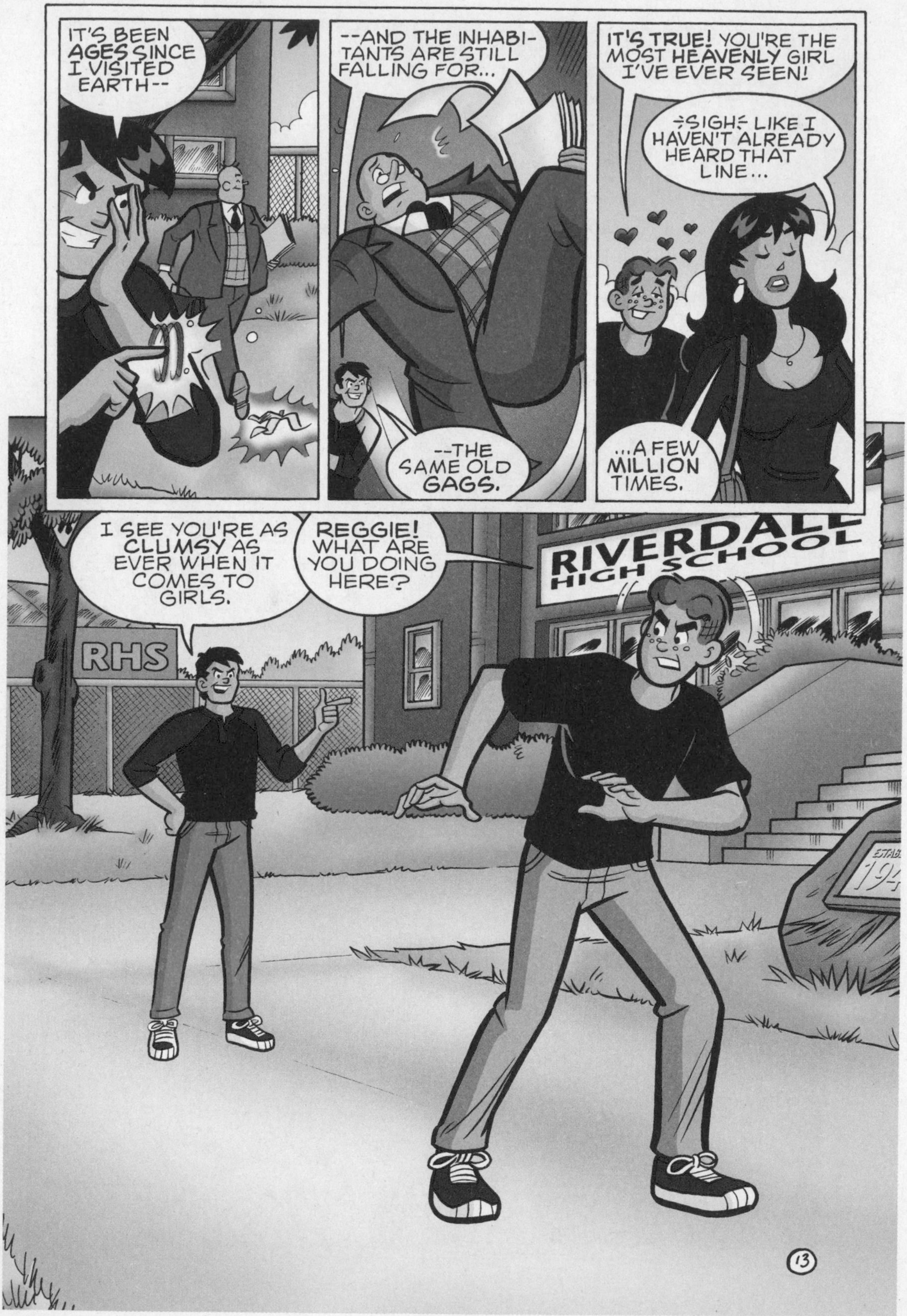
IT'S BEEN AGES SINCE I VISITED EARTH--
--AND THE INHABITANTS ARE STILL FALLING FOR...
--THE SAME OLD GAGS.
IT'S TRUE! YOU'RE THE MOST HEAVENLY GIRL I'VE EVER SEEN!
=SIGH= LIKE I HAVEN'T ALREADY HEARD THAT LINE...
...A FEW MILLION TIMES.
I SEE YOU'RE AS CLUMSY AS EVER WHEN IT COMES TO GIRLS.
REGGIE! WHAT ARE YOU DOING HERE?
RIVERDALE HIGH SCHOOL
RHS
13

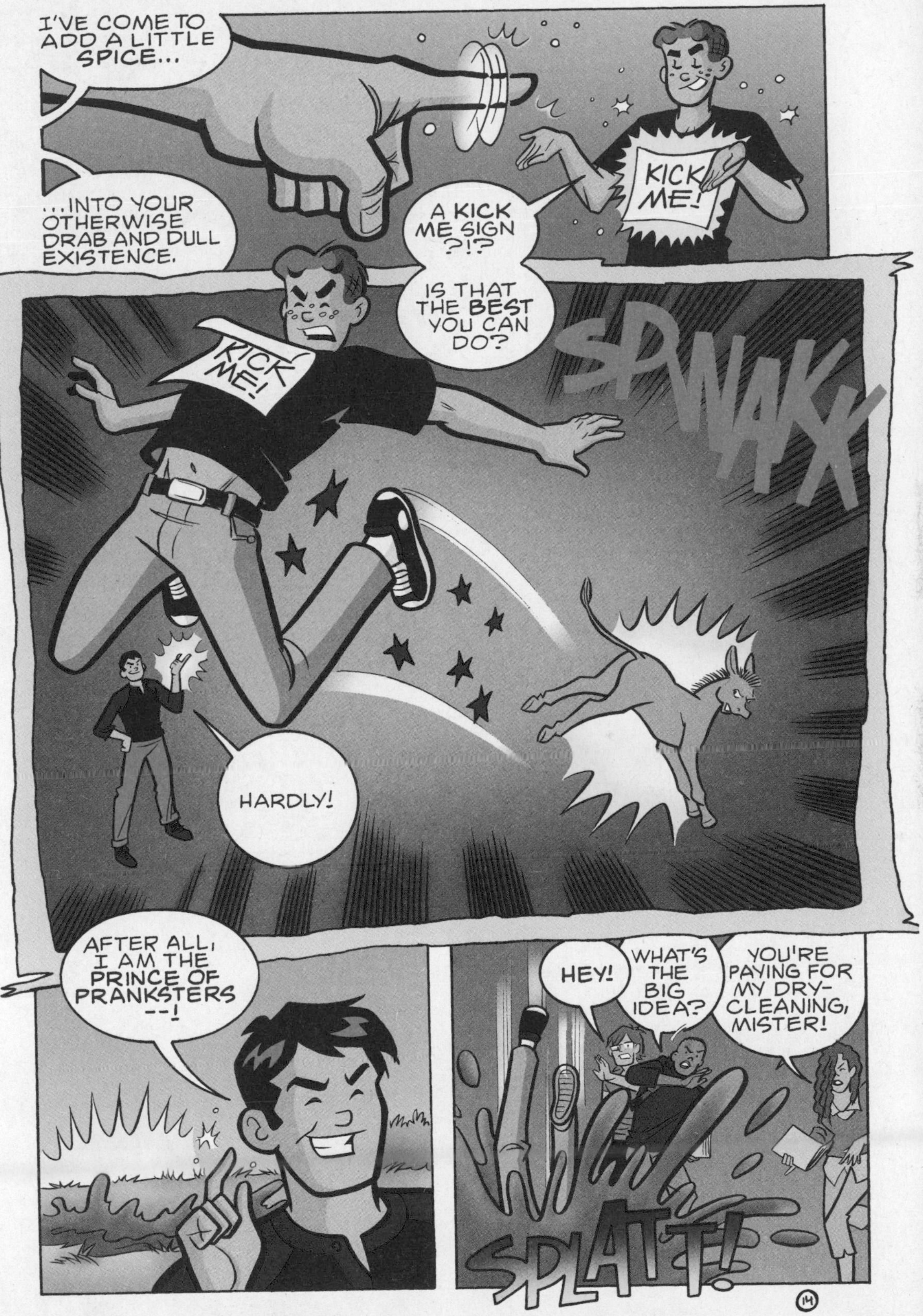
I'VE COME TO ADD A LITTLE SPICE...
...INTO YOUR OTHERWISE DRAB AND DULL EXISTENCE.
KICK ME!
A KICK ME SIGN ?!?
IS THAT THE BEST YOU CAN DO?
KICK ME!
SPWAKK
HARDLY!
AFTER ALL, I AM THE PRINCE OF PRANKSTERS --!
HEY!
WHAT'S THE BIG IDEA?
YOU'RE PAYING FOR MY DRY-CLEANING, MISTER!
SPLATT!
14

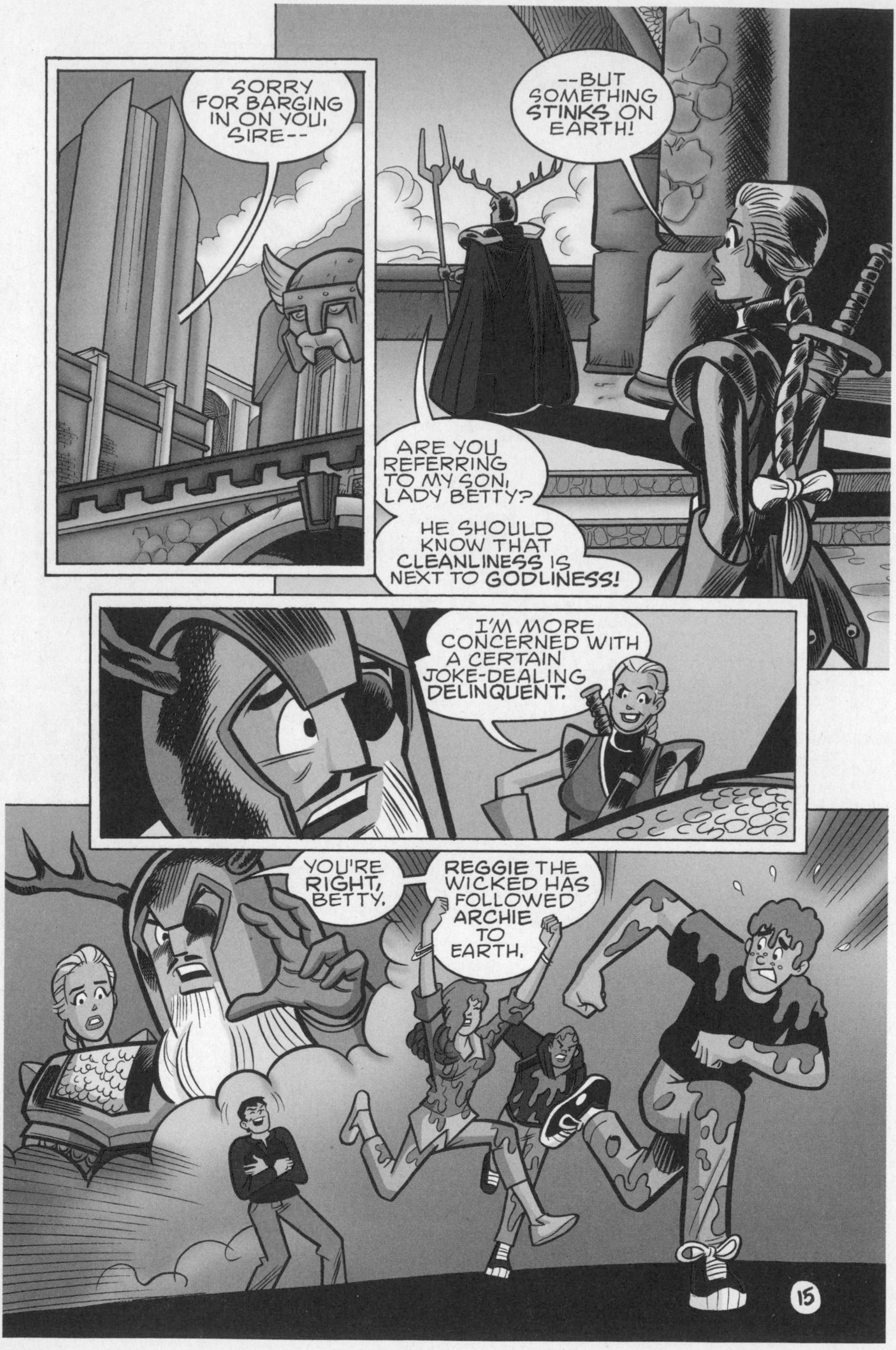
SORRY FOR BARGING IN ON YOU, SIRE--
--BUT SOMETHING STINKS ON EARTH!
ARE YOU REFERRING TO MY SON, LADY BETTY?
HE SHOULD KNOW THAT CLEANLINESS IS NEXT TO GODLINESS!
I'M MORE CONCERNED WITH A CERTAIN JOKE-DEALING DELINQUENT.
YOU'RE RIGHT, BETTY.
REGGIE THE WICKED HAS FOLLOWED ARCHIE TO EARTH.
15

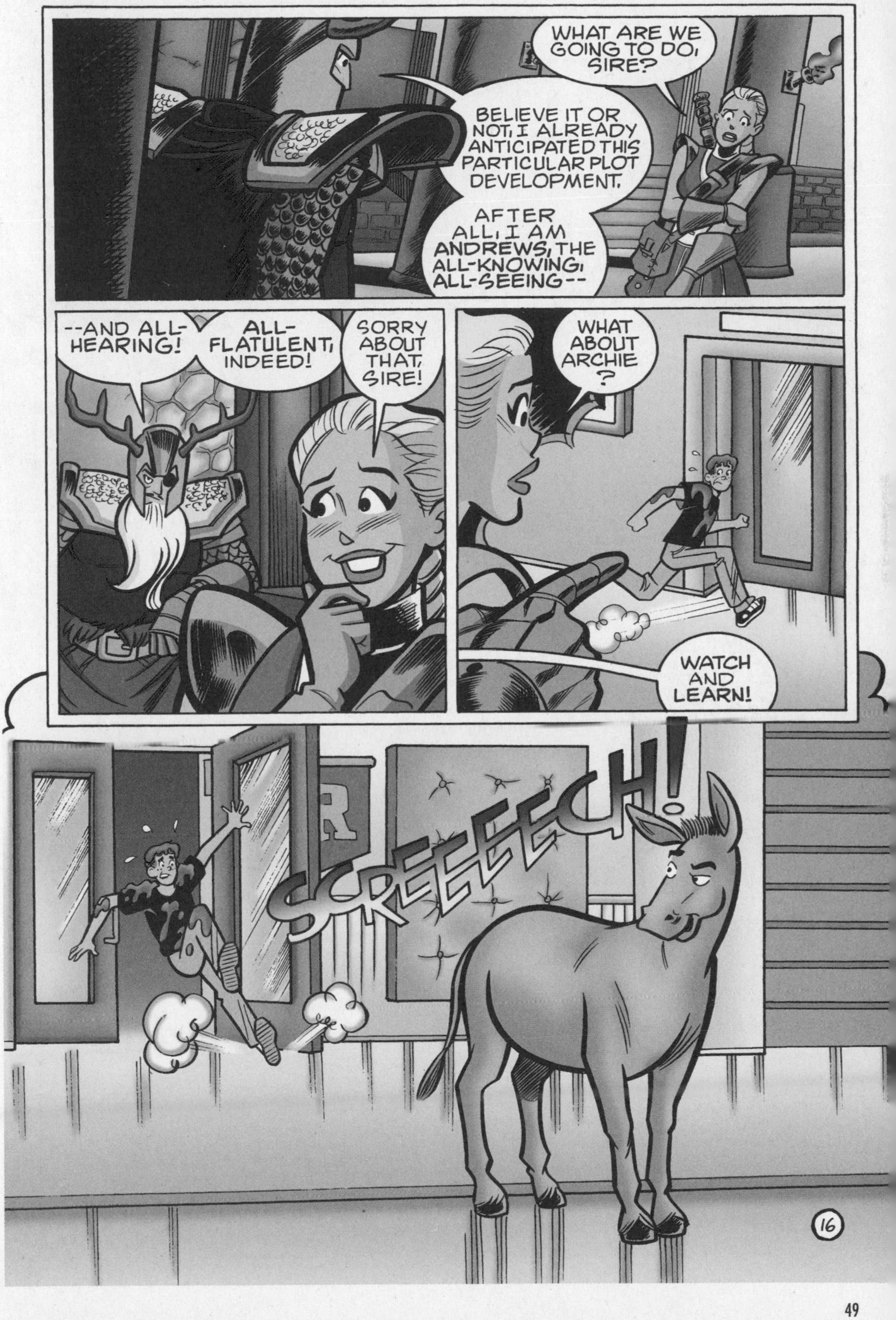
WHAT ARE WE GOING TO DO, SIRE?
BELIEVE IT OR NOT, I ALREADY ANTICIPATED THIS PARTICULAR PLOT DEVELOPMENT.
AFTER ALL, I AM ANDREWS, THE ALL-KNOWING, ALL-SEEING--
--AND ALL-HEARING!
ALL-FLATULENT, INDEED!
SORRY ABOUT THAT, SIRE!
WHAT ABOUT ARCHIE?
WATCH AND LEARN!
R
SCREEEECH!
16

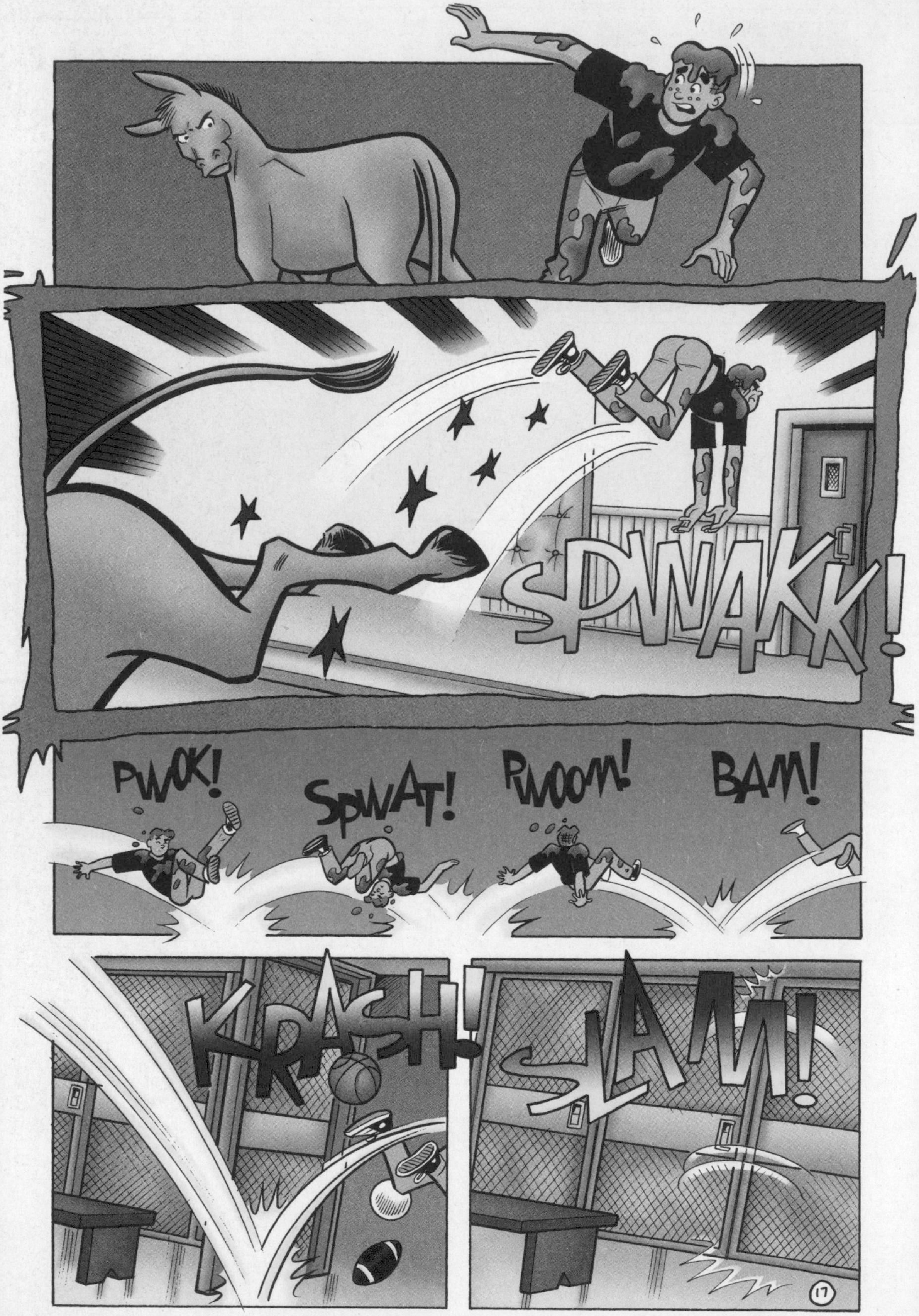
SPWAKK!
PWOK!
SPWAT!
PWOOM!
BAM!
KRASH!
SLAM!
17

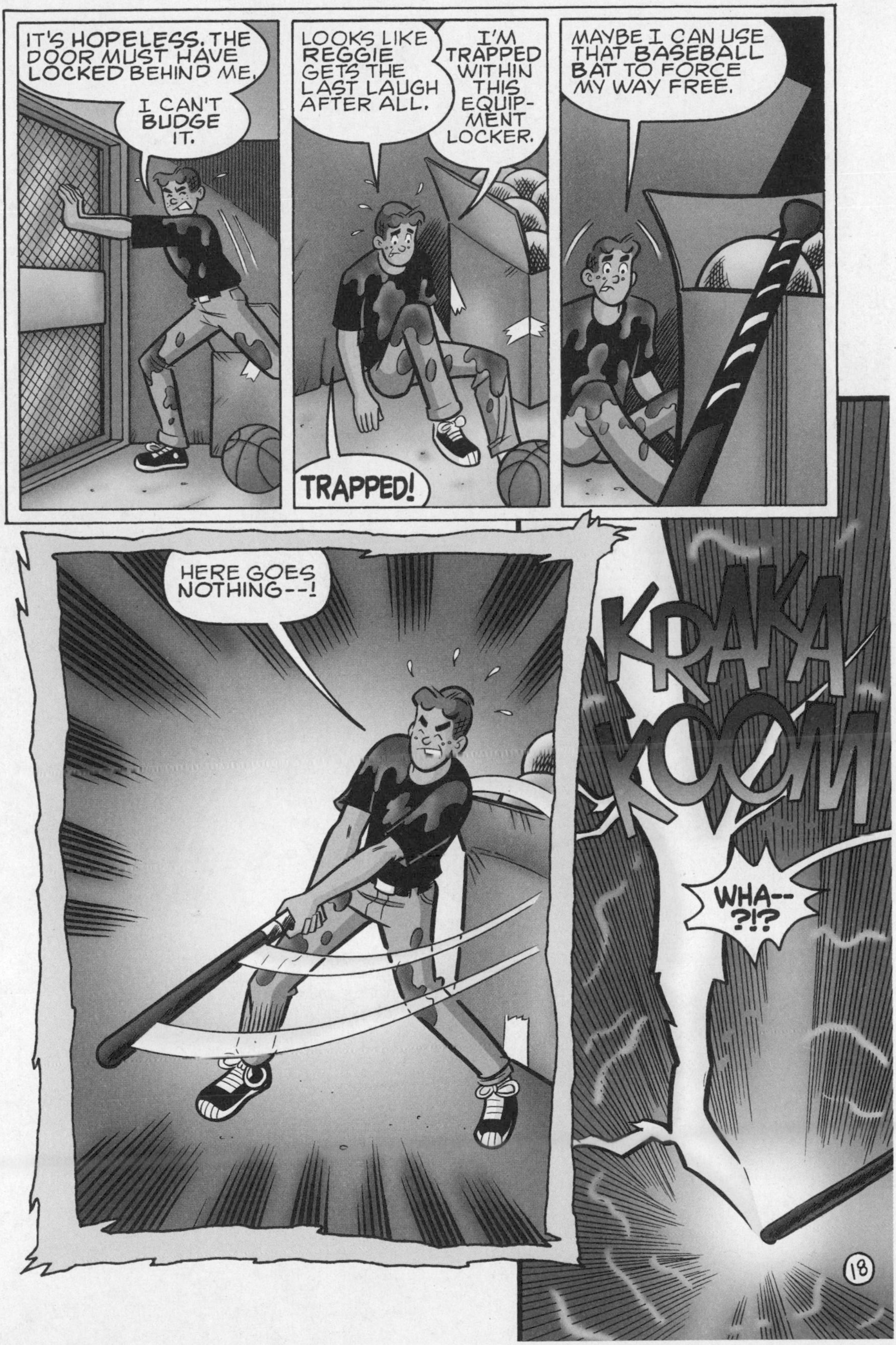
IT'S HOPELESS. THE DOOR MUST HAVE LOCKED BEHIND ME.
I CAN'T BUDGE IT.
LOOKS LIKE REGGIE GETS THE LAST LAUGH AFTER ALL.
I'M TRAPPED WITHIN THIS EQUIPMENT LOCKER.
TRAPPED!
MAYBE I CAN USE THAT BASEBALL BAT TO FORCE MY WAY FREE.
HERE GOES NOTHING--!
KRAKA KOOM
WHA-- ?!?
18

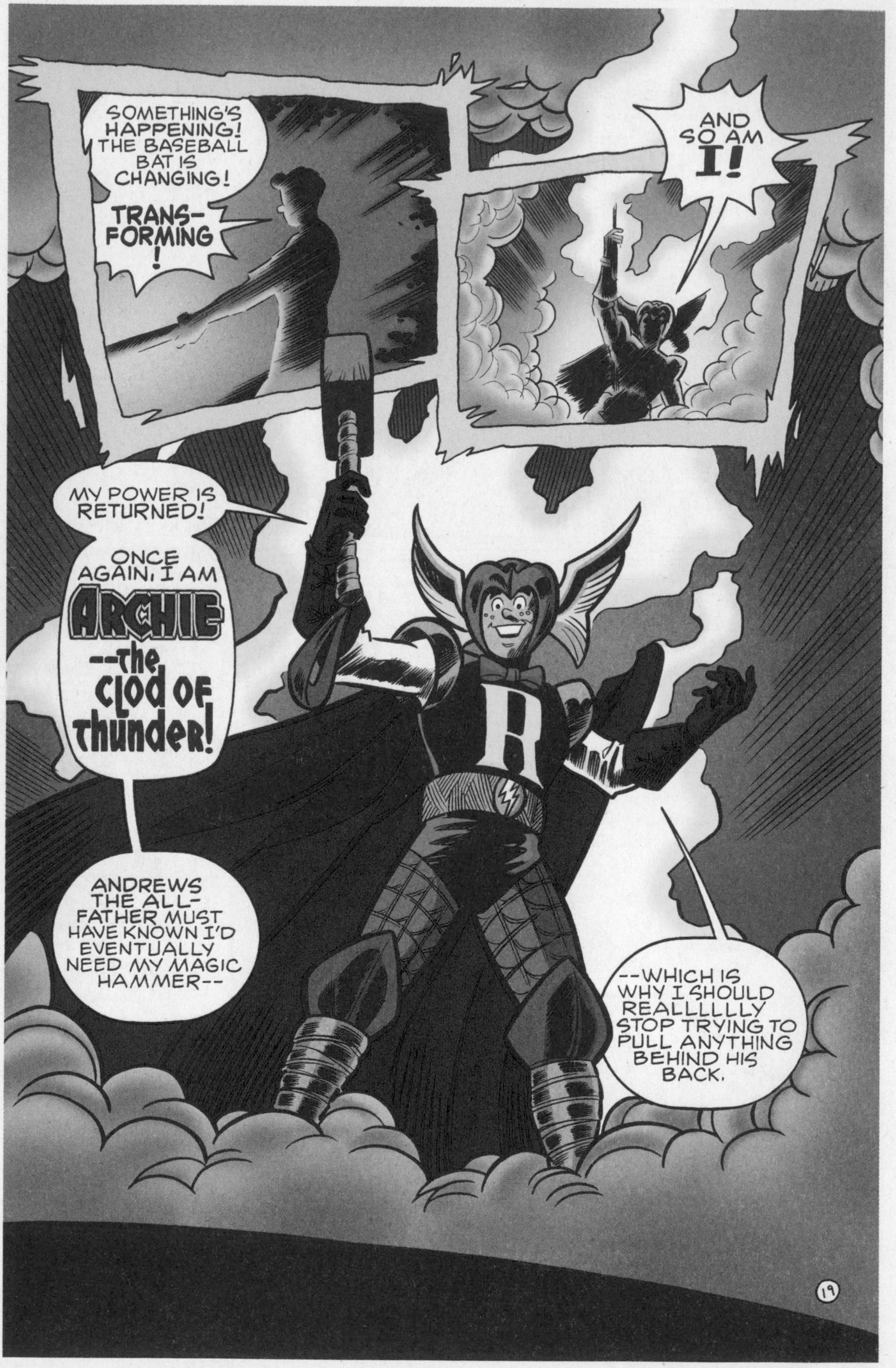
SOMETHING'S HAPPENING! THE BASEBALL BAT IS CHANGING!
TRANS-FORMING!
AND SO AM I!
MY POWER IS RETURNED!
ONCE AGAIN, I AM ARCHIE --the clod of thunder!
ANDREWS THE ALL-FATHER MUST HAVE KNOWN I'D EVENTUALLY NEED MY MAGIC HAMMER--
--WHICH IS WHY I SHOULD REALLLLLLY STOP TRYING TO PULL ANYTHING BEHIND HIS BACK.
19

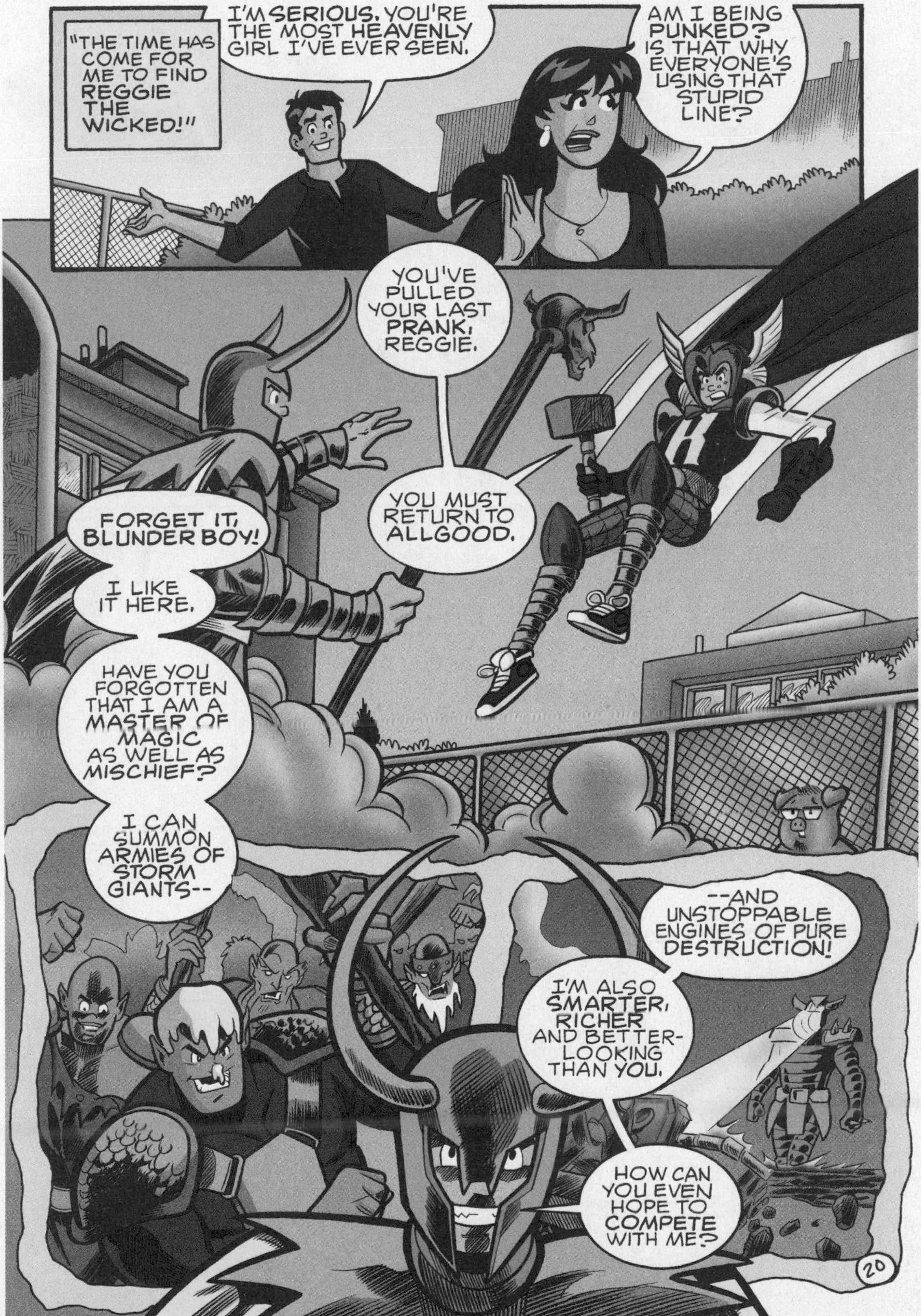
"THE TIME HAS COME FOR ME TO FIND REGGIE THE WICKED!"
I'M SERIOUS. YOU'RE THE MOST HEAVENLY GIRL I'VE EVER SEEN.
AM I BEING PUNKED? IS THAT WHY EVERYONE'S USING THAT STUPID LINE?
YOU'VE PULLED YOUR LAST PRANK, REGGIE.
YOU MUST RETURN TO ALLGOOD.
FORGET IT, BLUNDER BOY!
I LIKE IT HERE.
HAVE YOU FORGOTTEN THAT I AM A MASTER OF MAGIC AS WELL AS MISCHIEF?
I CAN SUMMON ARMIES OF STORM GIANTS--
--AND UNSTOPPABLE ENGINES OF PURE DESTRUCTION!
I'M ALSO SMARTER, RICHER AND BETTER-LOOKING THAN YOU.
HOW CAN YOU EVEN HOPE TO COMPETE WITH ME?
20

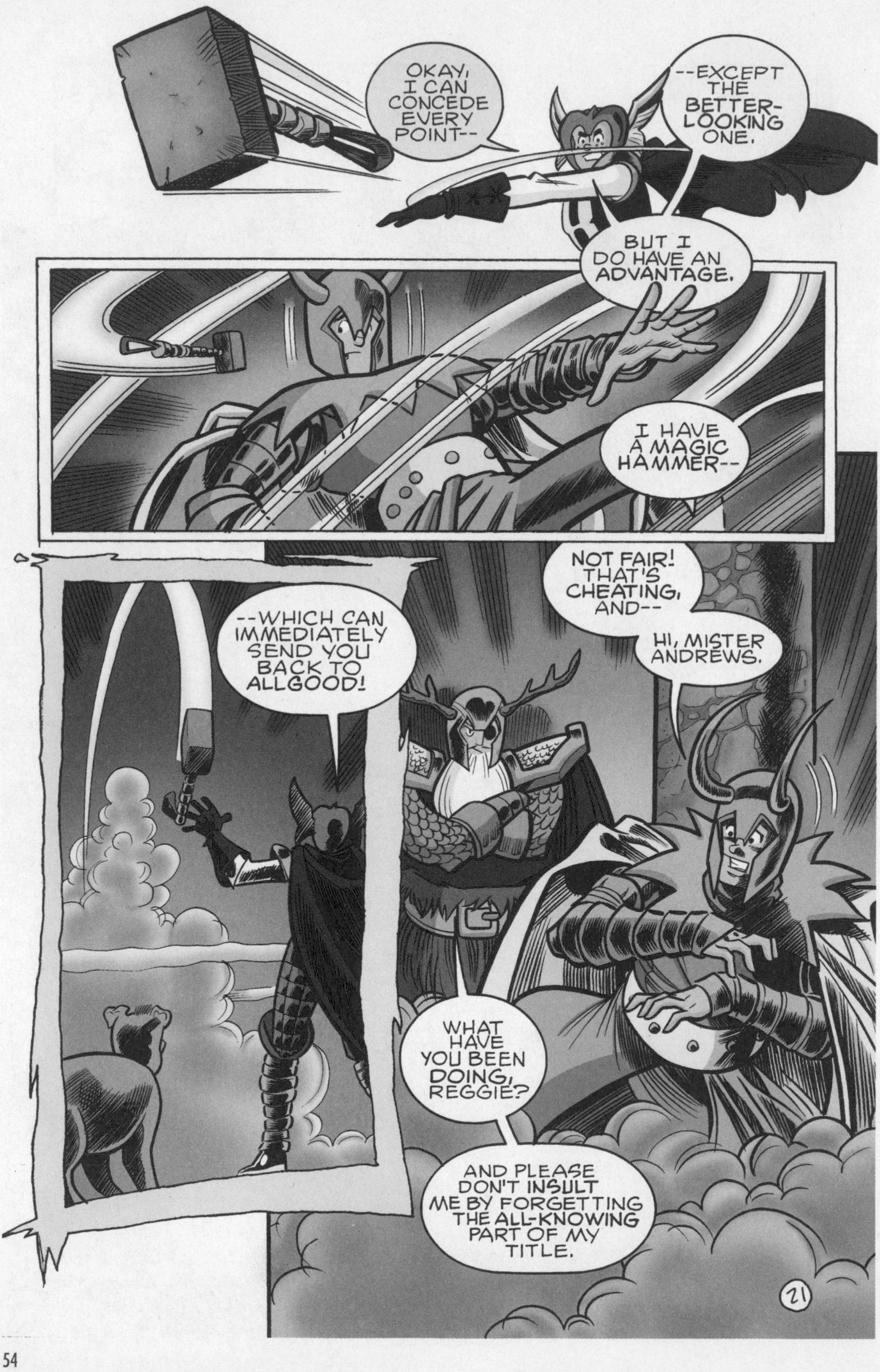
OKAY, I CAN CONCEDE EVERY POINT--
--EXCEPT THE BETTER-LOOKING ONE.
BUT I DO HAVE AN ADVANTAGE.
I HAVE A MAGIC HAMMER--
--WHICH CAN IMMEDIATELY SEND YOU BACK TO ALLGOOD!
NOT FAIR! THAT'S CHEATING, AND--
HI, MISTER ANDREWS.
WHAT HAVE YOU BEEN DOING, REGGIE?
AND PLEASE DON'T INSULT ME BY FORGETTING THE ALL-KNOWING PART OF MY TITLE.
21

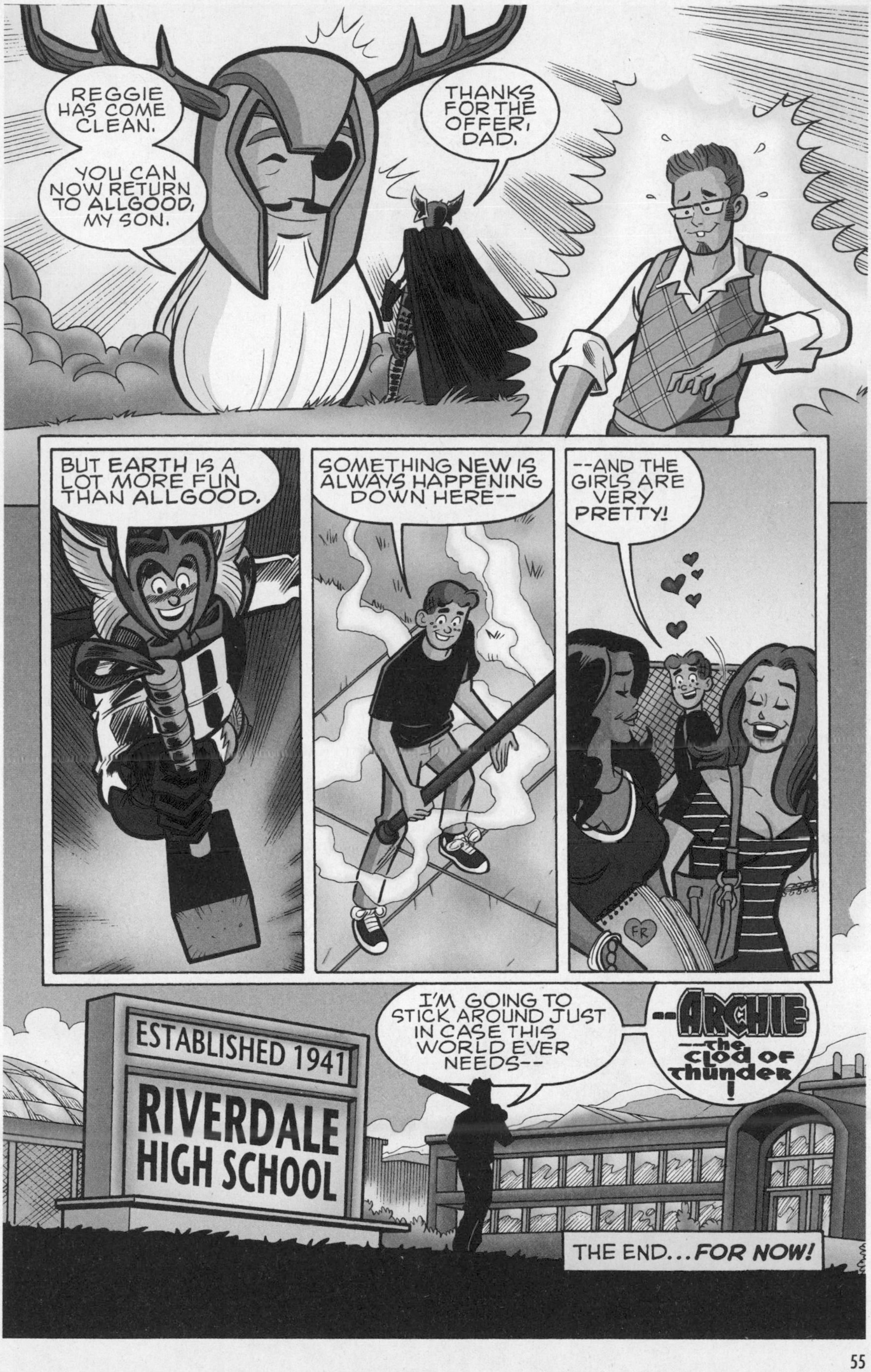
REGGIE HAS COME CLEAN.
YOU CAN NOW RETURN TO ALLGOOD, MY SON.
THANKS FOR THE OFFER, DAD.
BUT EARTH IS A LOT MORE FUN THAN ALLGOOD.
SOMETHING NEW IS ALWAYS HAPPENING DOWN HERE--
--AND THE GIRLS ARE VERY PRETTY!
FR
ESTABLISHED 1941
RIVERDALE HIGH SCHOOL
I'M GOING TO STICK AROUND JUST IN CASE THIS WORLD EVER NEEDS--
--ARCHIE --the clod of thunder!
THE END... FOR NOW!

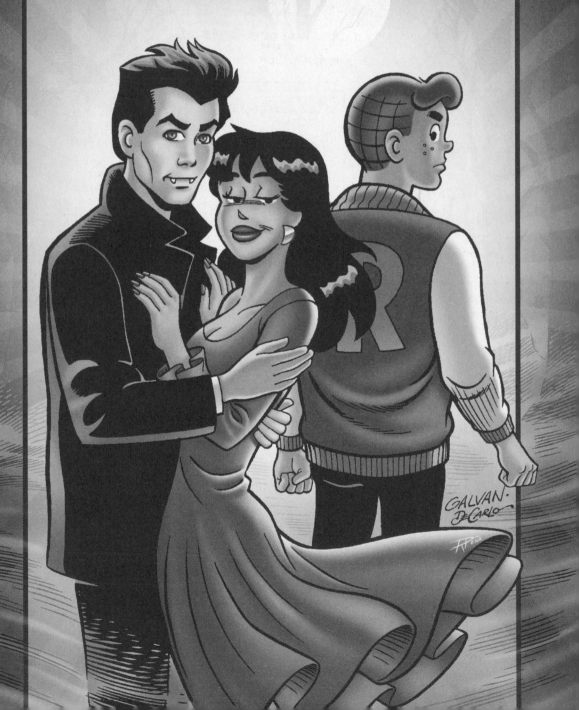

CHAPTER THREE
Twilite
PART ONE

INTRODUCING TWILITE

Originally printed in *Archie & Friends* #146 and #147

It's love at first bite in "Twilite," when two new students arrive in Riverdale. Betty and Veronica feel a frisson of fascination by the smoldering-hot Ivan, but Jared is warning everyone who'll listen that Ivan is really a vampire! Reggie volunteers to help Jared expose Ivan as a bloodsucker, but love, or maybe Ivan, is clouding the girls' judgment. Can the girls be saved before romance sinks its teeth in? And will mere mortals like Archie and Reggie be able to compete against these supernatural Casanovas?

WRITER
ANGELO DECESARE

PENCILS
BILL GALVAN

INKS
AL MILGROM

LETTERS
JACK MORELLI

COLORS
DIGIKORE STUDIOS

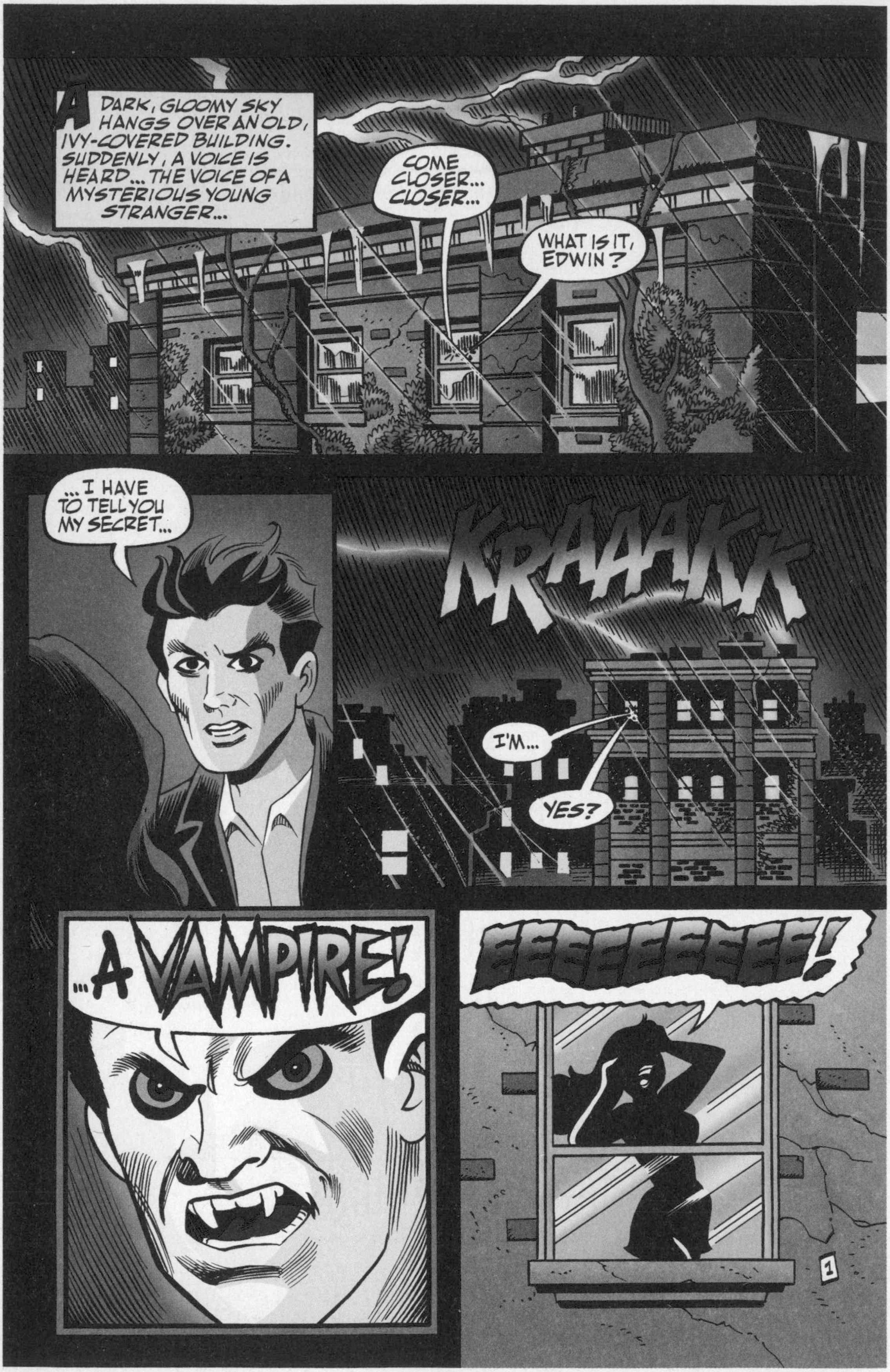
A DARK, GLOOMY SKY HANGS OVER AN OLD, IVY-COVERED BUILDING. SUDDENLY, A VOICE IS HEARD... THE VOICE OF A MYSTERIOUS YOUNG STRANGER...
COME CLOSER... CLOSER...
WHAT IS IT, EDWIN?
...I HAVE TO TELL YOU MY SECRET...
KRAAAKK
I'M...
YES?
...A VAMPIRE!
EEEEEEEEEE!
1

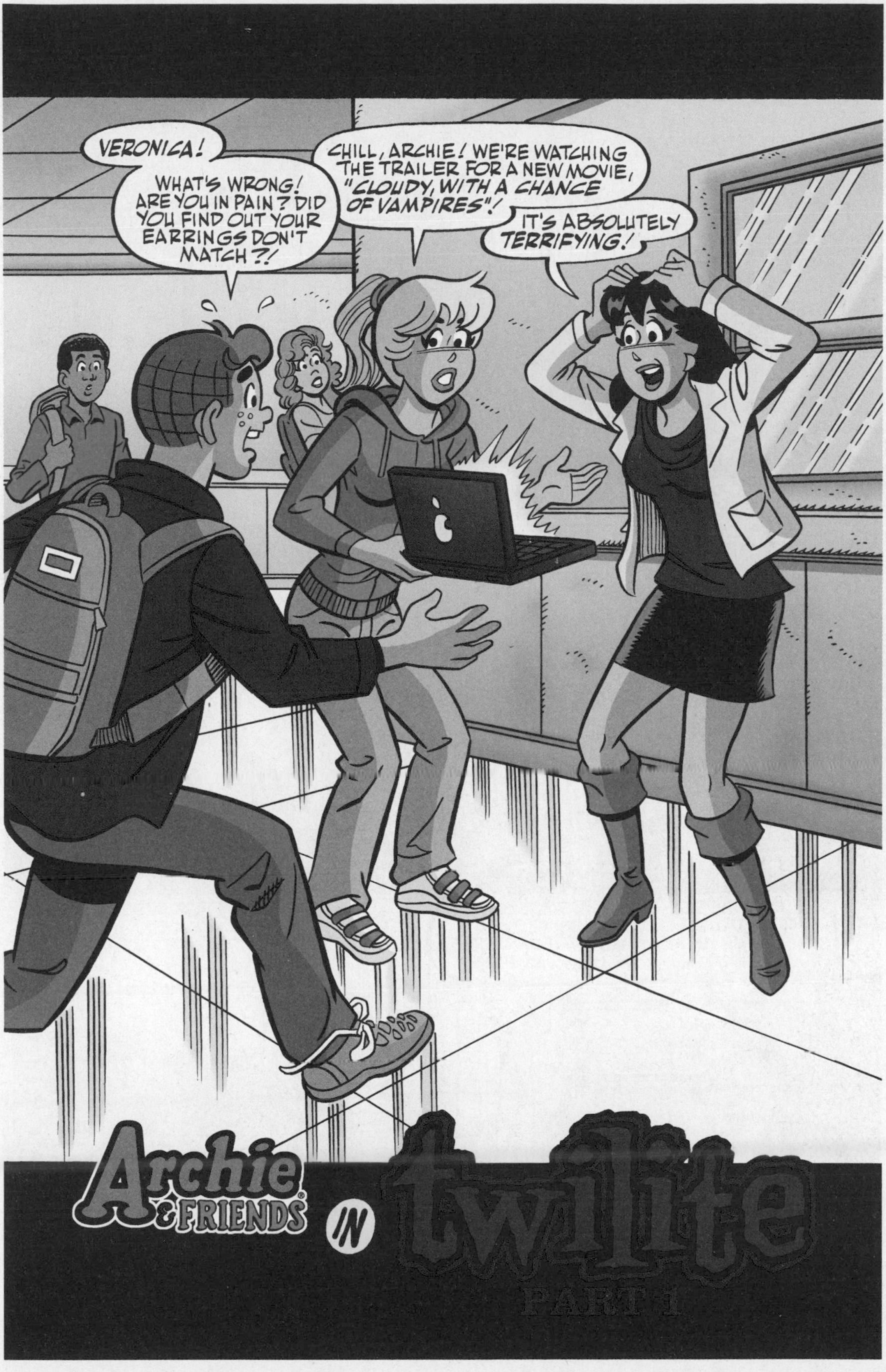
VERONICA!
WHAT'S WRONG! ARE YOU IN PAIN? DID YOU FIND OUT YOUR EARRINGS DON'T MATCH?!
CHILL, ARCHIE! WE'RE WATCHING THE TRAILER FOR A NEW MOVIE, "CLOUDY, WITH A CHANCE OF VAMPIRES"!
IT'S ABSOLUTELY TERRIFYING!
Archie & FRIENDS IN twilite
PART 1

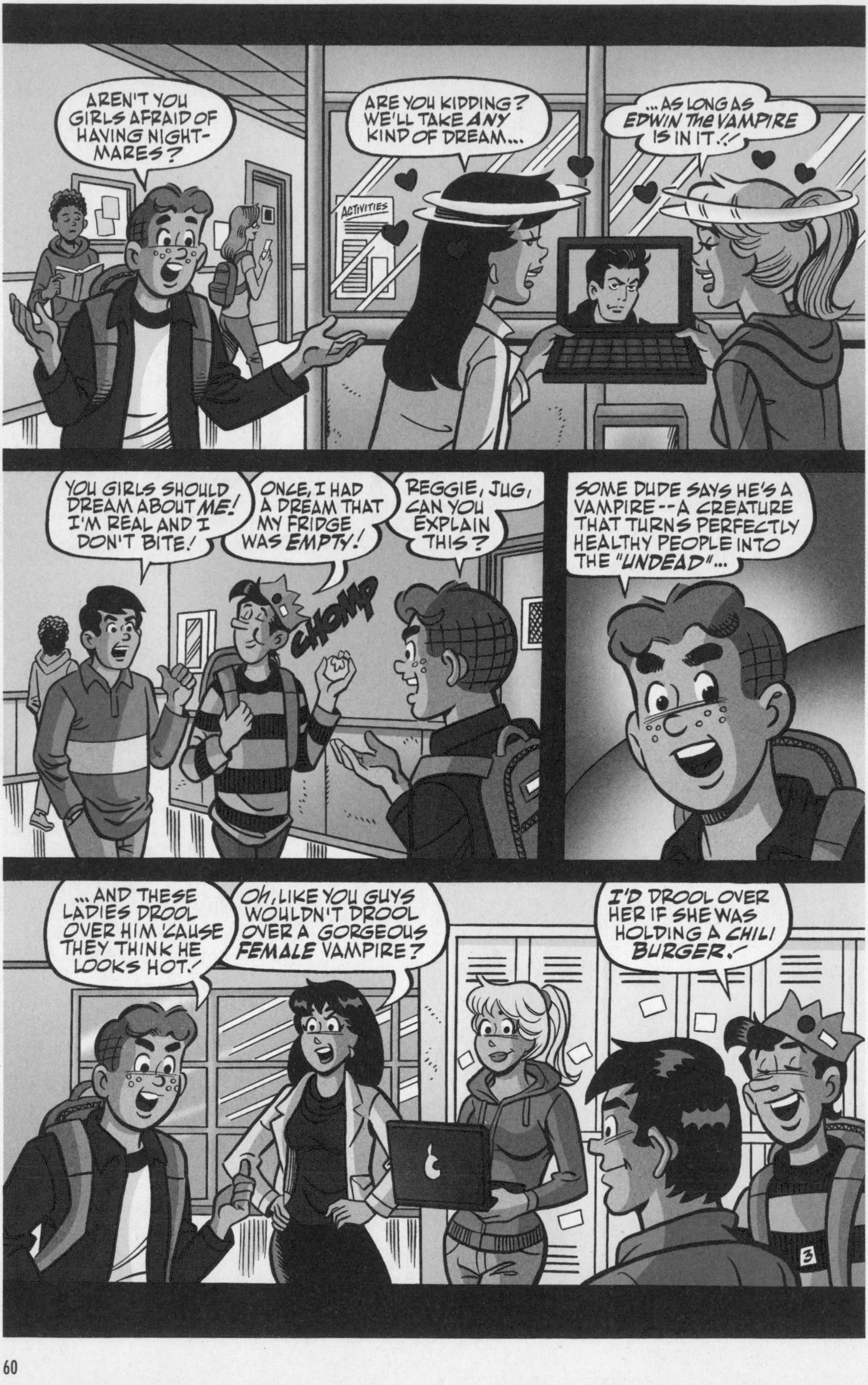
AREN'T YOU GIRLS AFRAID OF HAVING NIGHT-MARES?
ARE YOU KIDDING? WE'LL TAKE ANY KIND OF DREAM...
...AS LONG AS EDWIN THE VAMPIRE IS IN IT.!!
ACTIVITIES
YOU GIRLS SHOULD DREAM ABOUT ME! I'M REAL AND I DON'T BITE!
ONCE, I HAD A DREAM THAT MY FRIDGE WAS EMPTY!
CHOMP
REGGIE, JUG, CAN YOU EXPLAIN THIS?
SOME DUDE SAYS HE'S A VAMPIRE--A CREATURE THAT TURNS PERFECTLY HEALTHY PEOPLE INTO THE "UNDEAD"...
...AND THESE LADIES DROOL OVER HIM 'CAUSE THEY THINK HE LOOKS HOT!
Oh, LIKE YOU GUYS WOULDN'T DROOL OVER A GORGEOUS FEMALE VAMPIRE?
I'D DROOL OVER HER IF SHE WAS HOLDING A CHILI BURGER!
3

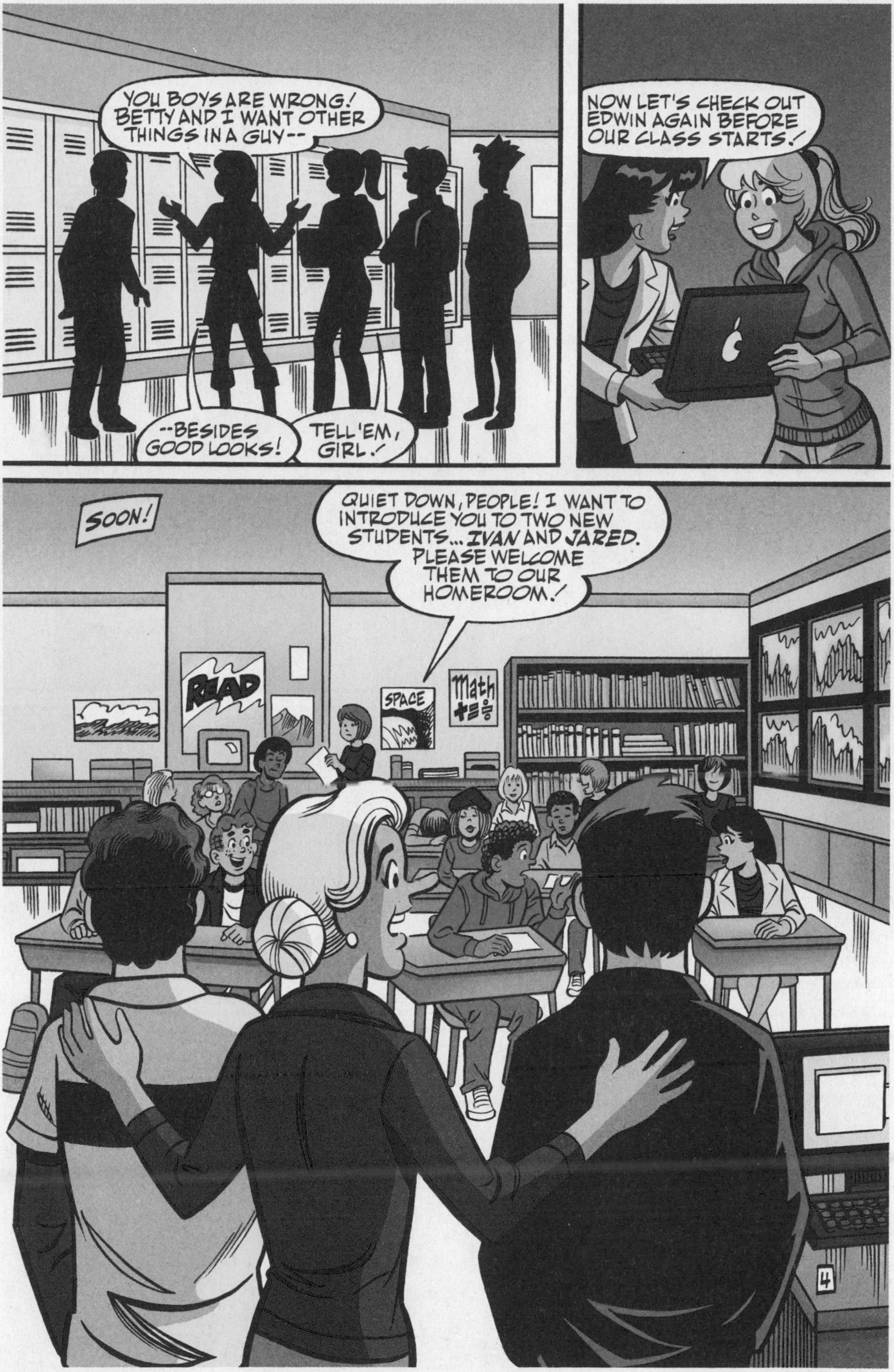
YOU BOYS ARE WRONG! BETTY AND I WANT OTHER THINGS IN A GUY--
--BESIDES GOOD LOOKS!
TELL'EM, GIRL!
NOW LET'S CHECK OUT EDWIN AGAIN BEFORE OUR CLASS STARTS!
SOON!
QUIET DOWN, PEOPLE! I WANT TO INTRODUCE YOU TO TWO NEW STUDENTS... IVAN AND JARED. PLEASE WELCOME THEM TO OUR HOMEROOM!
READ
SPACE
Math
4

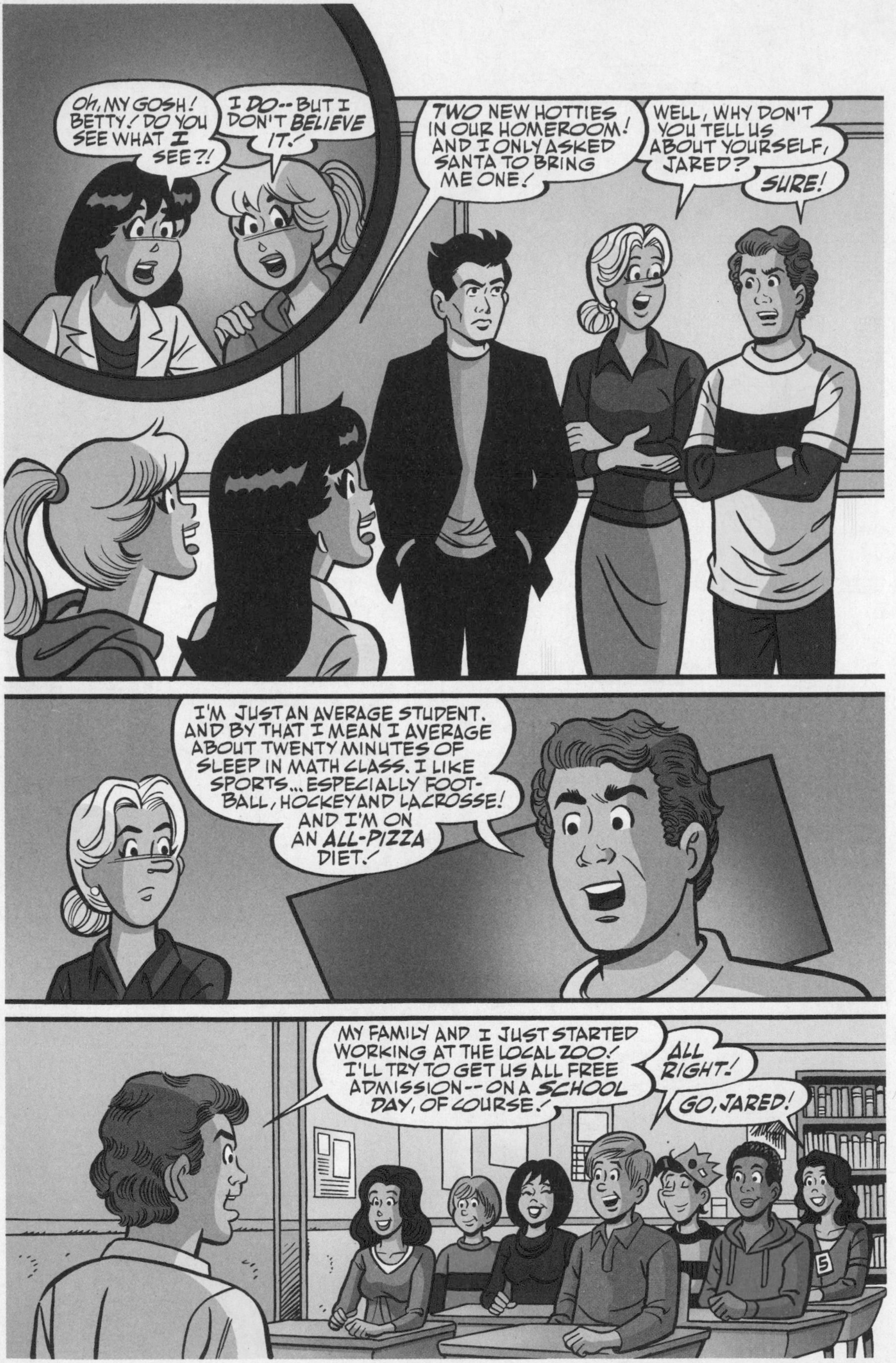
OH, MY GOSH! BETTY! DO YOU SEE WHAT I SEE?!
I DO--BUT I DON'T BELIEVE IT!
TWO NEW HOTTIES IN OUR HOMEROOM! AND I ONLY ASKED SANTA TO BRING ME ONE!
WELL, WHY DON'T YOU TELL US ABOUT YOURSELF, JARED?
SURE!
I'M JUST AN AVERAGE STUDENT. AND BY THAT I MEAN I AVERAGE ABOUT TWENTY MINUTES OF SLEEP IN MATH CLASS. I LIKE SPORTS... ESPECIALLY FOOT-BALL, HOCKEY AND LACROSSE! AND I'M ON AN ALL-PIZZA DIET!
MY FAMILY AND I JUST STARTED WORKING AT THE LOCAL ZOO! I'LL TRY TO GET US ALL FREE ADMISSION--ON A SCHOOL DAY, OF COURSE!
ALL RIGHT!
GO, JARED!

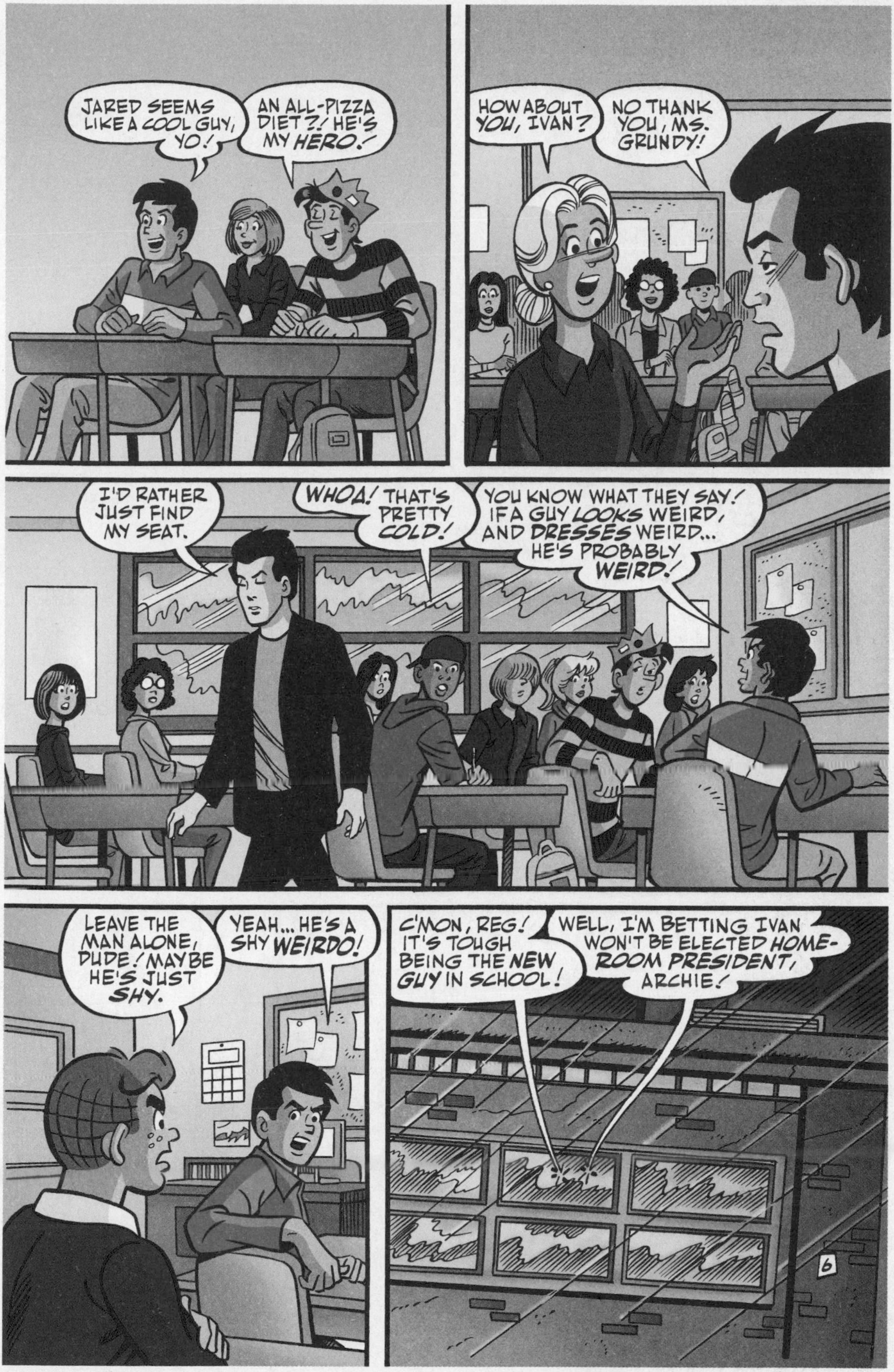
JARED SEEMS LIKE A COOL GUY, YO!
AN ALL-PIZZA DIET?! HE'S MY HERO!
HOW ABOUT YOU, IVAN?
NO THANK YOU, MS. GRUNDY!
I'D RATHER JUST FIND MY SEAT.
WHOA! THAT'S PRETTY COLD!
YOU KNOW WHAT THEY SAY! IF A GUY LOOKS WEIRD, AND DRESSES WEIRD... HE'S PROBABLY WEIRD!
LEAVE THE MAN ALONE, DUDE! MAYBE HE'S JUST SHY.
YEAH... HE'S A SHY WEIRDO!
C'MON, REG! IT'S TOUGH BEING THE NEW GUY IN SCHOOL!
WELL, I'M BETTING IVAN WON'T BE ELECTED HOME-ROOM PRESIDENT, ARCHIE!
6

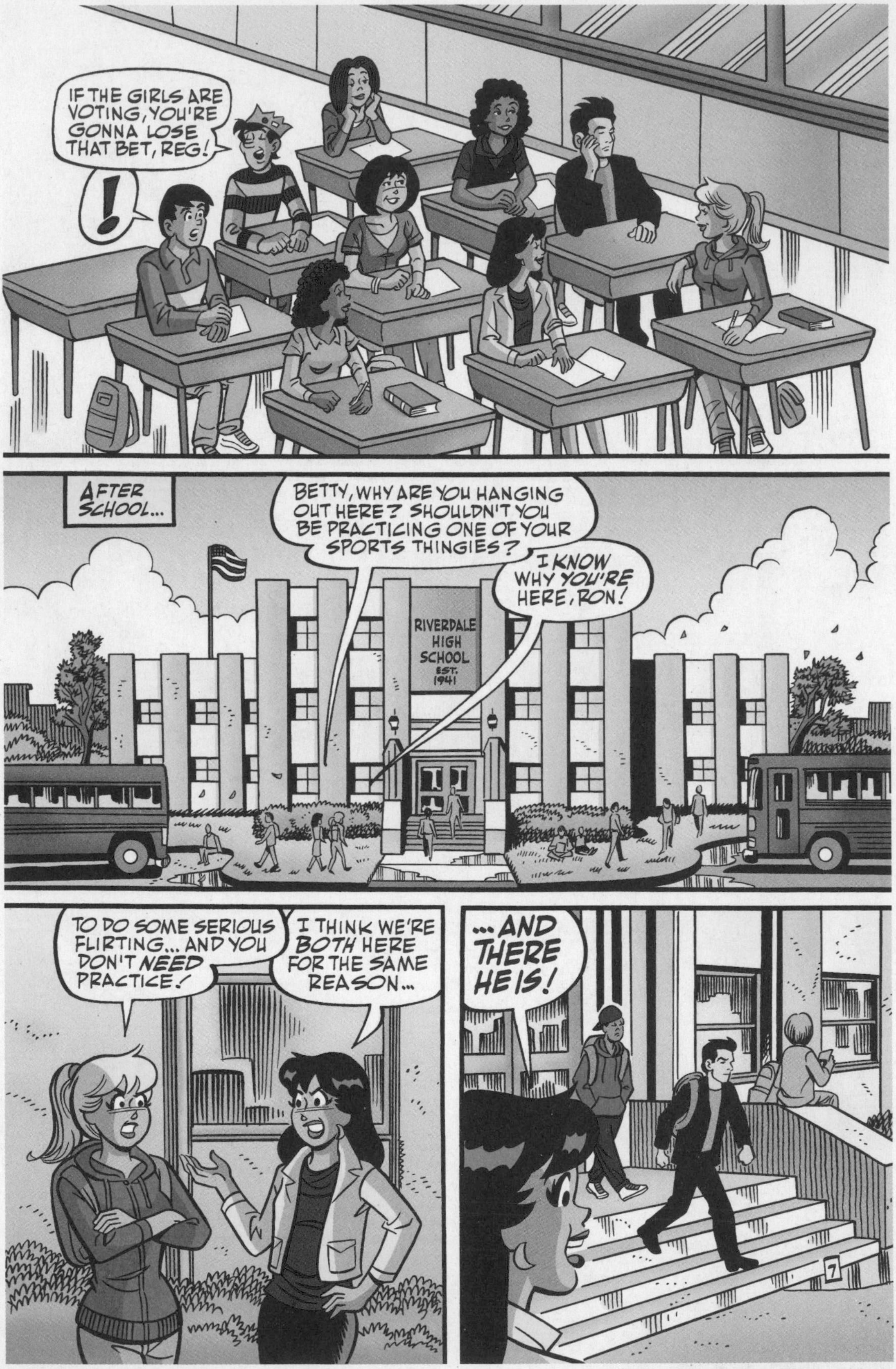
IF THE GIRLS ARE VOTING, YOU'RE GONNA LOSE THAT BET, REG!
!
AFTER SCHOOL...
BETTY, WHY ARE YOU HANGING OUT HERE? SHOULDN'T YOU BE PRACTICING ONE OF YOUR SPORTS THINGIES?
I KNOW WHY YOU'RE HERE, RON!
RIVERDALE HIGH SCHOOL EST. 1941
TO DO SOME SERIOUS FLIRTING... AND YOU DON'T NEED PRACTICE!
I THINK WE'RE BOTH HERE FOR THE SAME REASON...
...AND THERE HE IS!
7

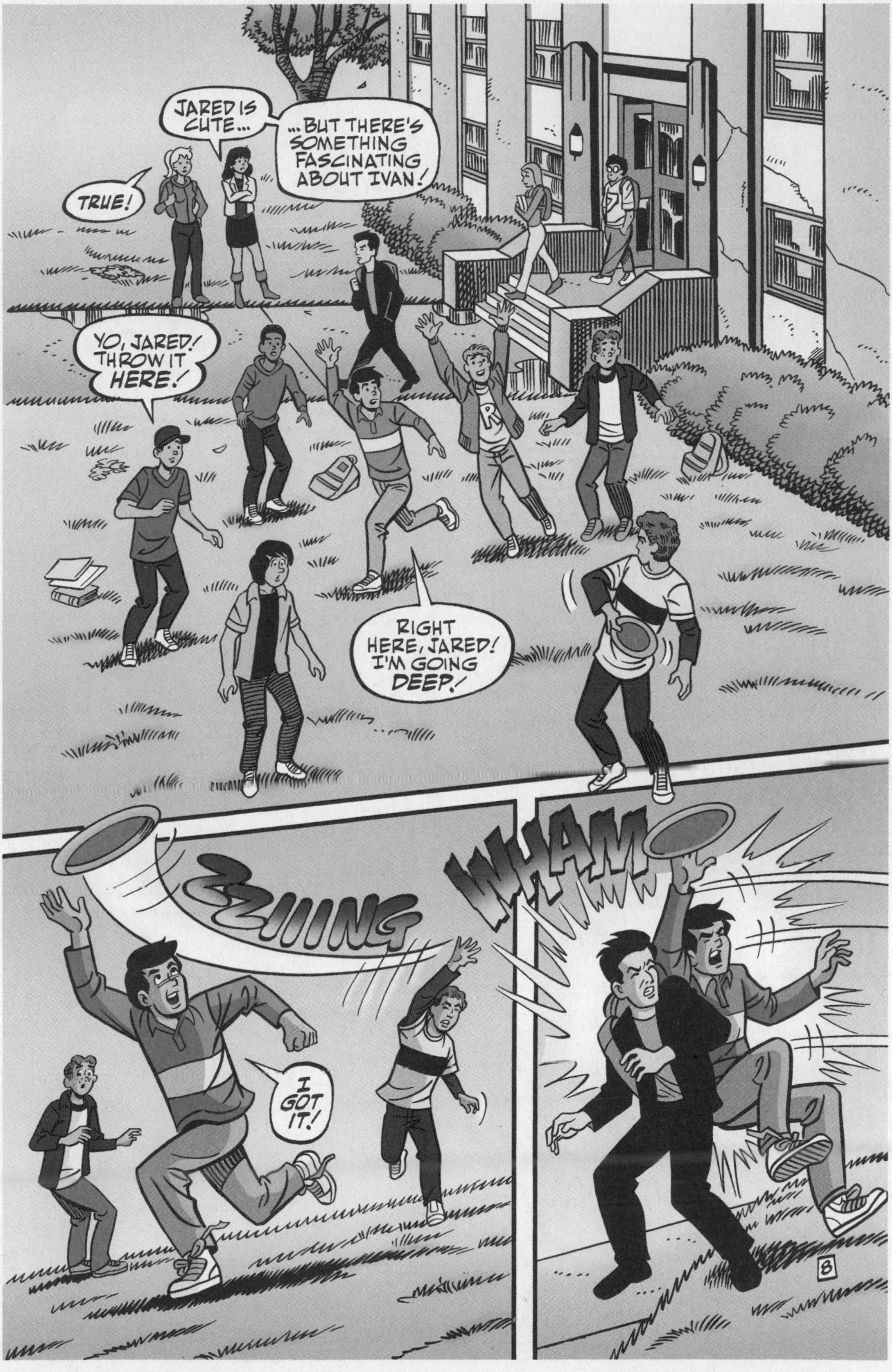
JARED IS CUTE...
...BUT THERE'S SOMETHING FASCINATING ABOUT IVAN!
TRUE!
YO, JARED! THROW IT HERE!
RIGHT HERE, JARED! I'M GOING DEEP!
ZZIIING
I GOT IT!
WHAM
8

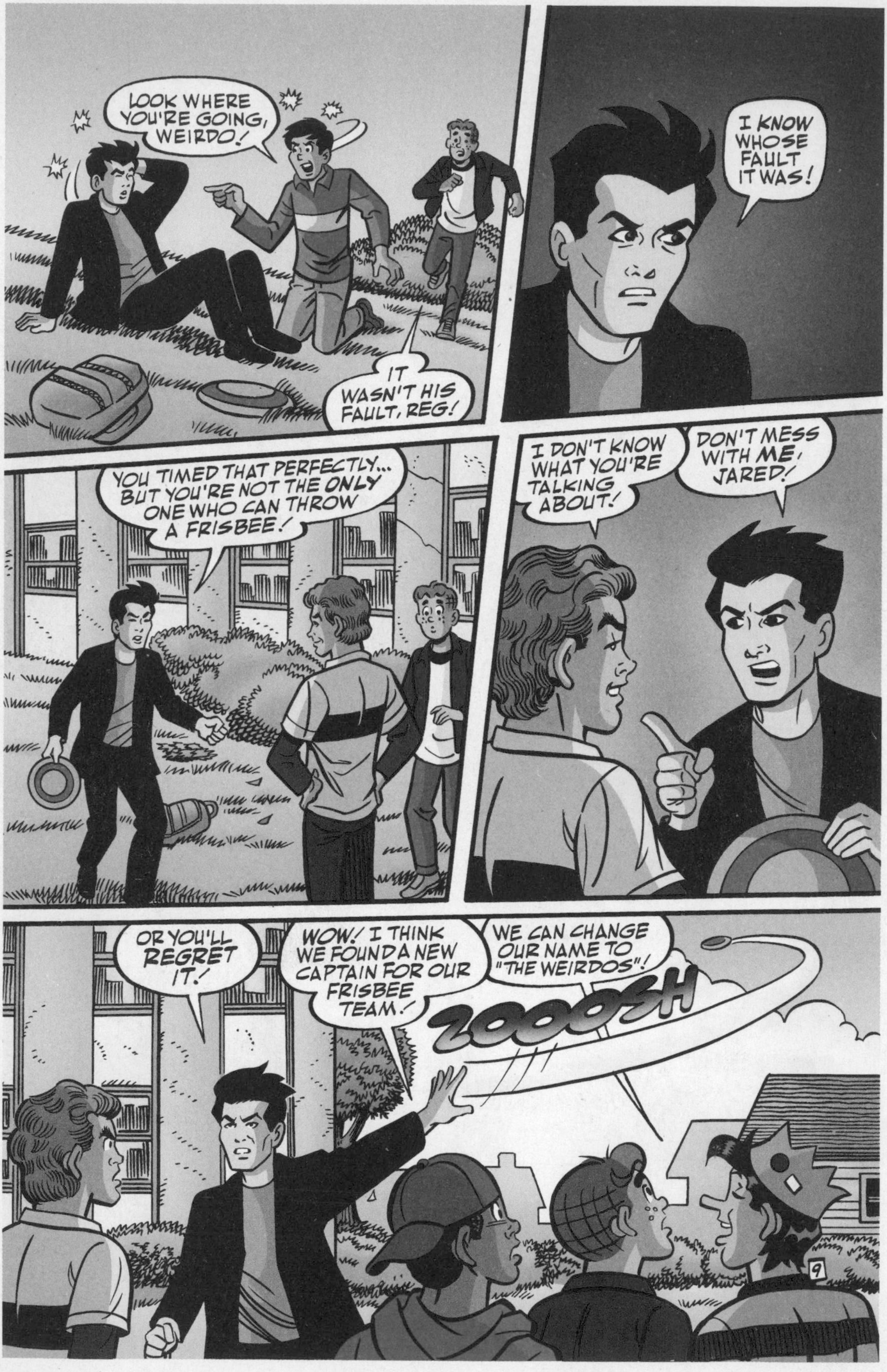
LOOK WHERE YOU'RE GOING, WEIRDO!
IT WASN'T HIS FAULT, REG!
I KNOW WHOSE FAULT IT WAS!
YOU TIMED THAT PERFECTLY... BUT YOU'RE NOT THE ONLY ONE WHO CAN THROW A FRISBEE!
I DON'T KNOW WHAT YOU'RE TALKING ABOUT!
DON'T MESS WITH ME, JARED!
OR YOU'LL REGRET IT!
WOW! I THINK WE FOUND A NEW CAPTAIN FOR OUR FRISBEE TEAM!
WE CAN CHANGE OUR NAME TO "THE WEIRDOS"!
ZOOOOSH
9

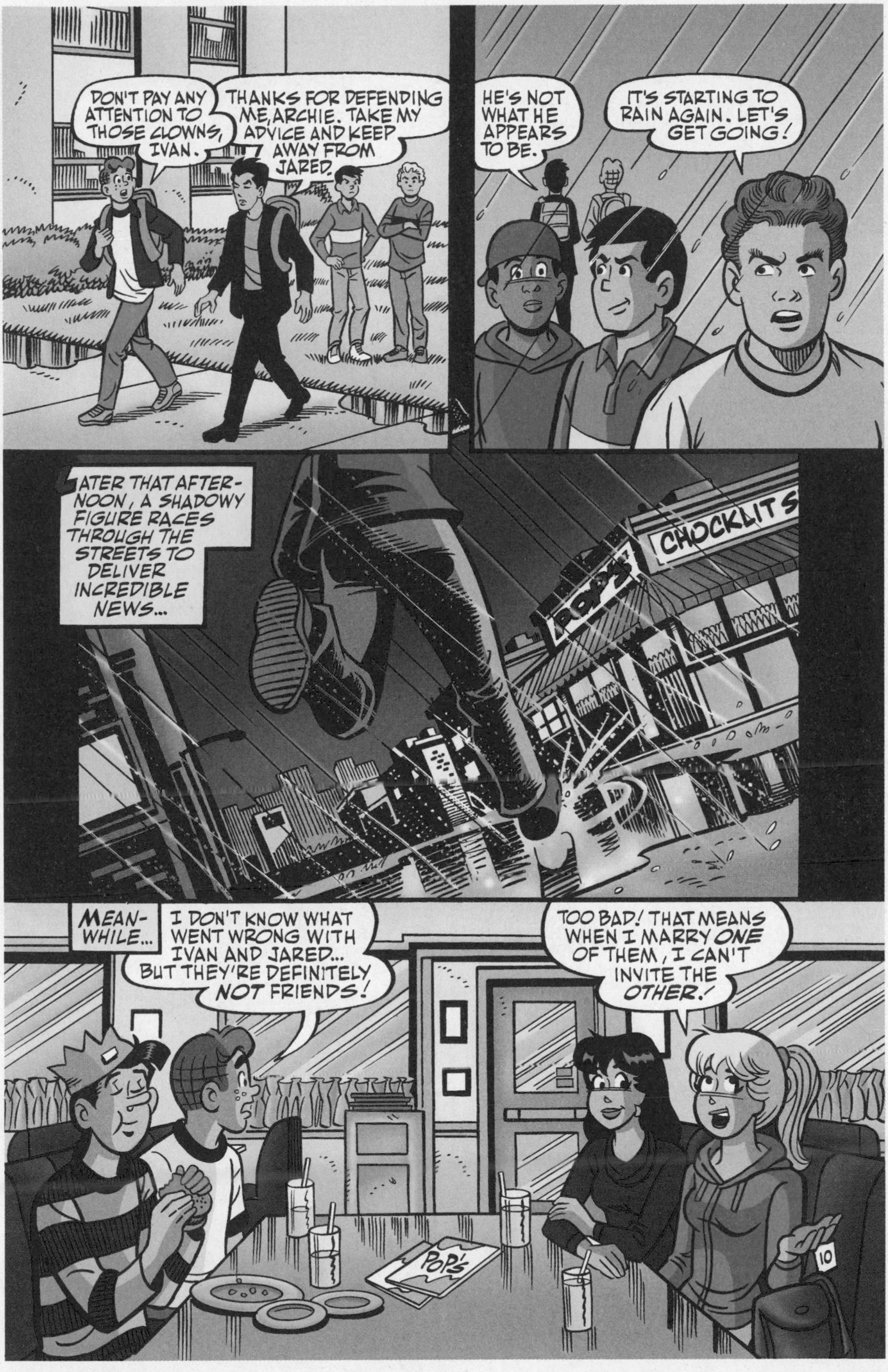
DON'T PAY ANY ATTENTION TO THOSE CLOWNS, IVAN.
THANKS FOR DEFENDING ME, ARCHIE. TAKE MY ADVICE AND KEEP AWAY FROM JARED.
HE'S NOT WHAT HE APPEARS TO BE.
IT'S STARTING TO RAIN AGAIN. LET'S GET GOING!
LATER THAT AFTERNOON, A SHADOWY FIGURE RACES THROUGH THE STREETS TO DELIVER INCREDIBLE NEWS...
CHOCKLIT S
POP'S
MEANWHILE...
I DON'T KNOW WHAT WENT WRONG WITH IVAN AND JARED... BUT THEY'RE DEFINITELY NOT FRIENDS!
TOO BAD! THAT MEANS WHEN I MARRY ONE OF THEM, I CAN'T INVITE THE OTHER!
POP'S
10

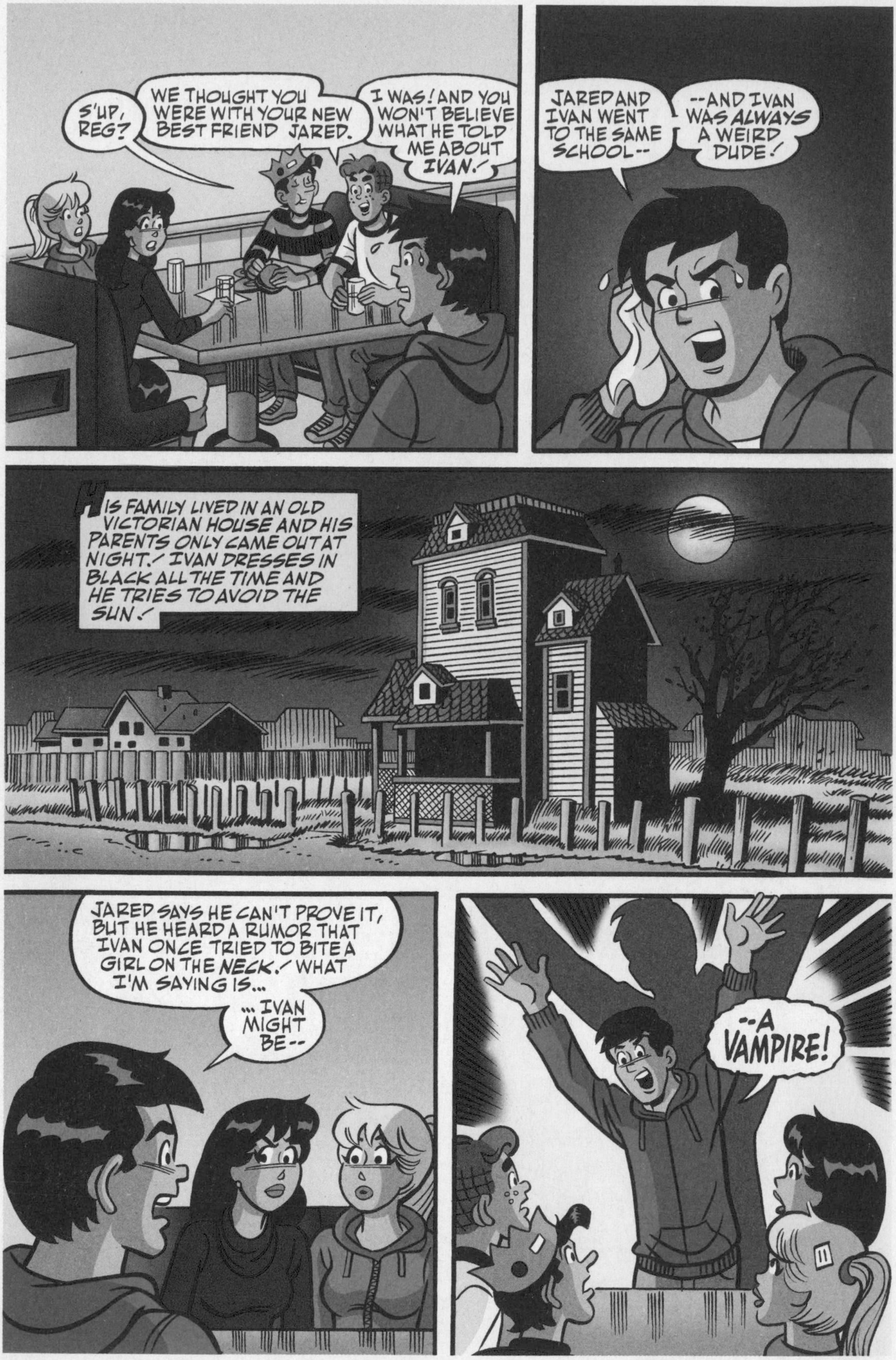
S'UP, REG?
WE THOUGHT YOU WERE WITH YOUR NEW BEST FRIEND JARED.
I WAS! AND YOU WON'T BELIEVE WHAT HE TOLD ME ABOUT IVAN!
JARED AND IVAN WENT TO THE SAME SCHOOL--
--AND IVAN WAS ALWAYS A WEIRD DUDE!
HIS FAMILY LIVED IN AN OLD VICTORIAN HOUSE AND HIS PARENTS ONLY CAME OUT AT NIGHT! IVAN DRESSES IN BLACK ALL THE TIME AND HE TRIES TO AVOID THE SUN!
JARED SAYS HE CAN'T PROVE IT, BUT HE HEARD A RUMOR THAT IVAN ONCE TRIED TO BITE A GIRL ON THE NECK! WHAT I'M SAYING IS...
...IVAN MIGHT BE--
--A VAMPIRE!

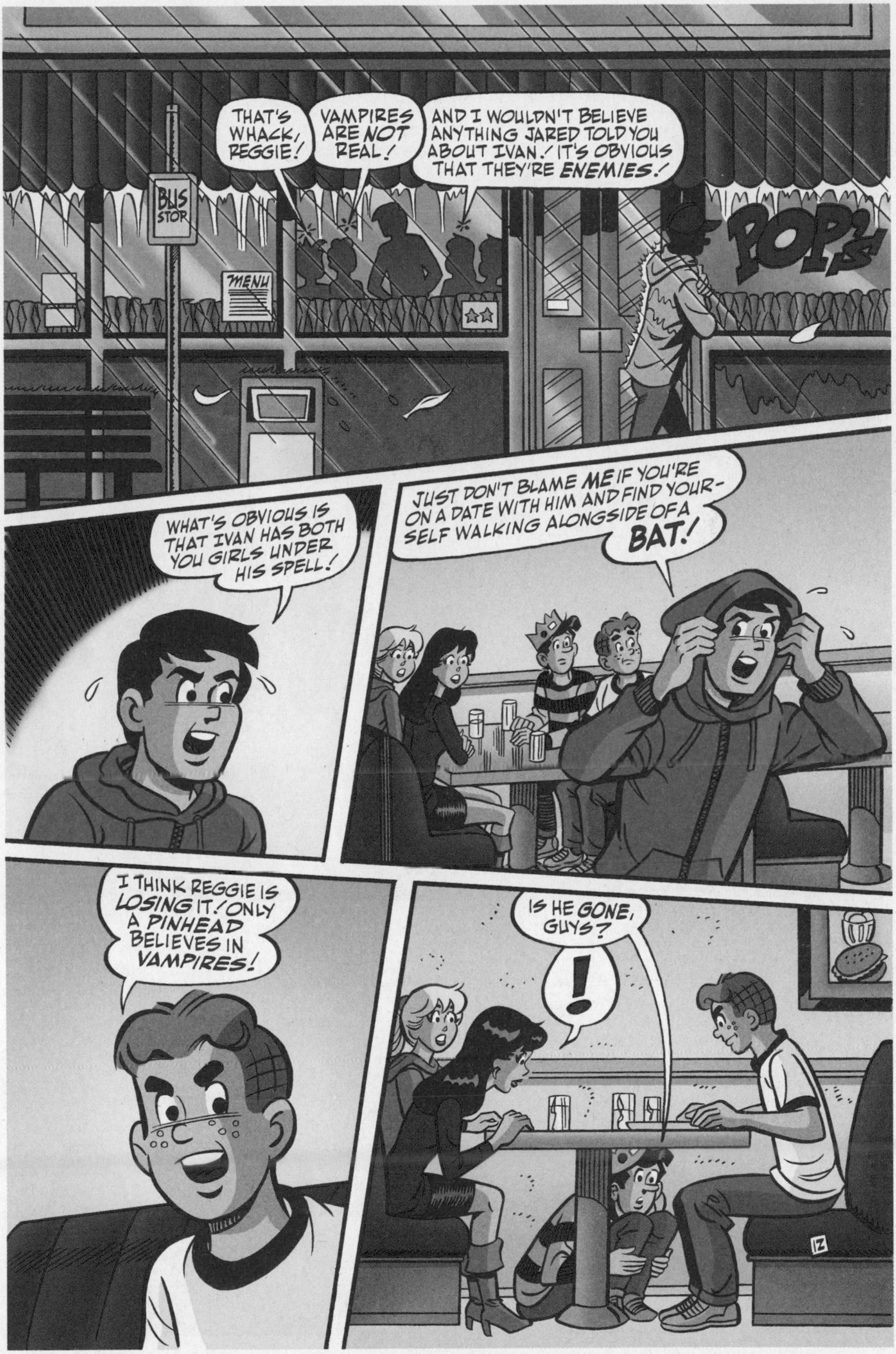
THAT'S WHACK, REGGIE!
VAMPIRES ARE NOT REAL!
AND I WOULDN'T BELIEVE ANYTHING JARED TOLD YOU ABOUT IVAN! IT'S OBVIOUS THAT THEY'RE ENEMIES!
BUS STOP
MENU
POP'S
WHAT'S OBVIOUS IS THAT IVAN HAS BOTH YOU GIRLS UNDER HIS SPELL!
JUST DON'T BLAME ME IF YOU'RE ON A DATE WITH HIM AND FIND YOURSELF WALKING ALONGSIDE OF A BAT!
I THINK REGGIE IS LOSING IT! ONLY A PINHEAD BELIEVES IN VAMPIRES!
IS HE GONE, GUYS?
!

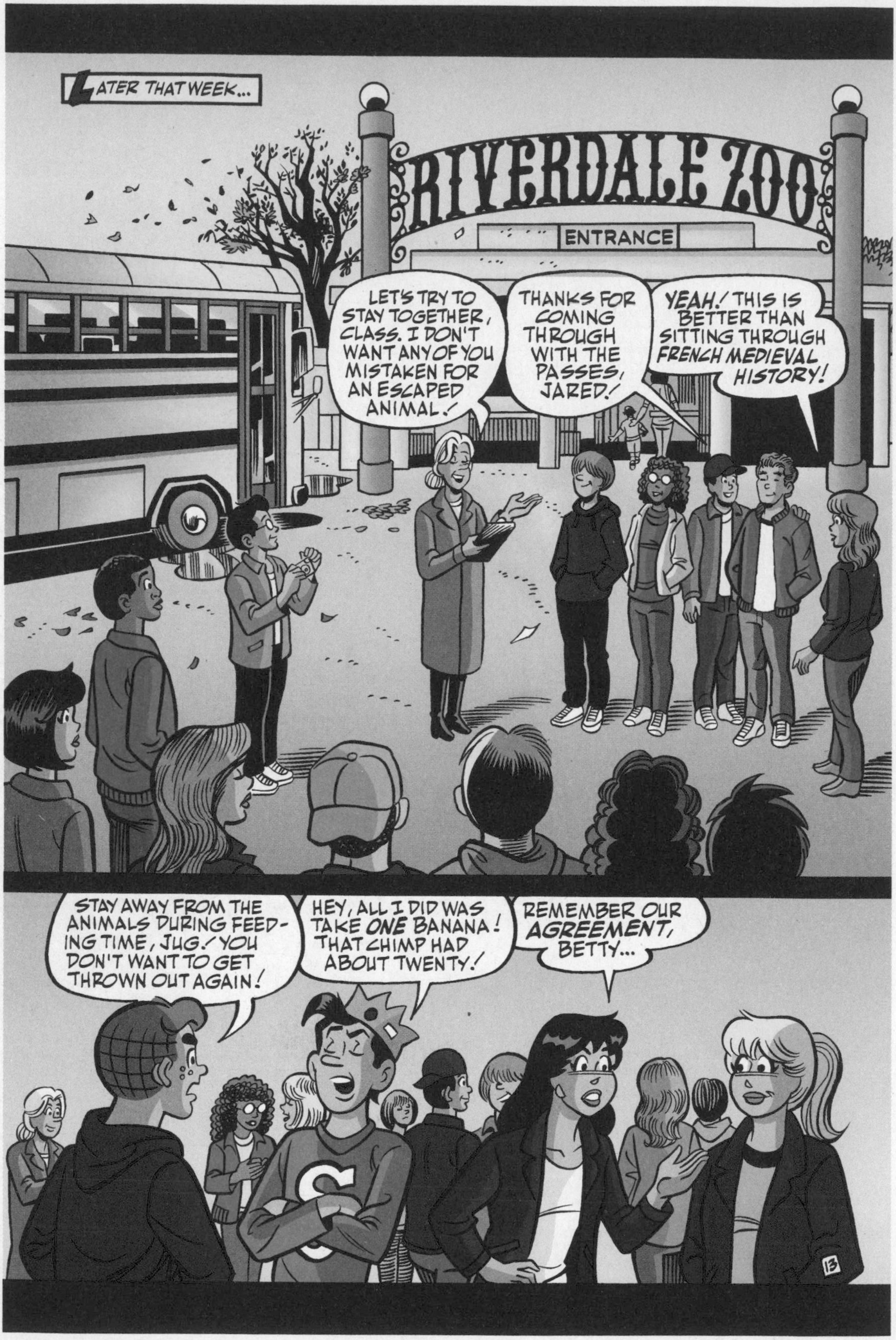
LATER THAT WEEK...
RIVERDALE ZOO
ENTRANCE
LET'S TRY TO STAY TOGETHER, CLASS. I DON'T WANT ANY OF YOU MISTAKEN FOR AN ESCAPED ANIMAL!
THANKS FOR COMING THROUGH WITH THE PASSES, JARED!
YEAH! THIS IS BETTER THAN SITTING THROUGH FRENCH MEDIEVAL HISTORY!
STAY AWAY FROM THE ANIMALS DURING FEEDING TIME, JUG! YOU DON'T WANT TO GET THROWN OUT AGAIN!
HEY, ALL I DID WAS TAKE ONE BANANA! THAT CHIMP HAD ABOUT TWENTY!
REMEMBER OUR AGREEMENT, BETTY...

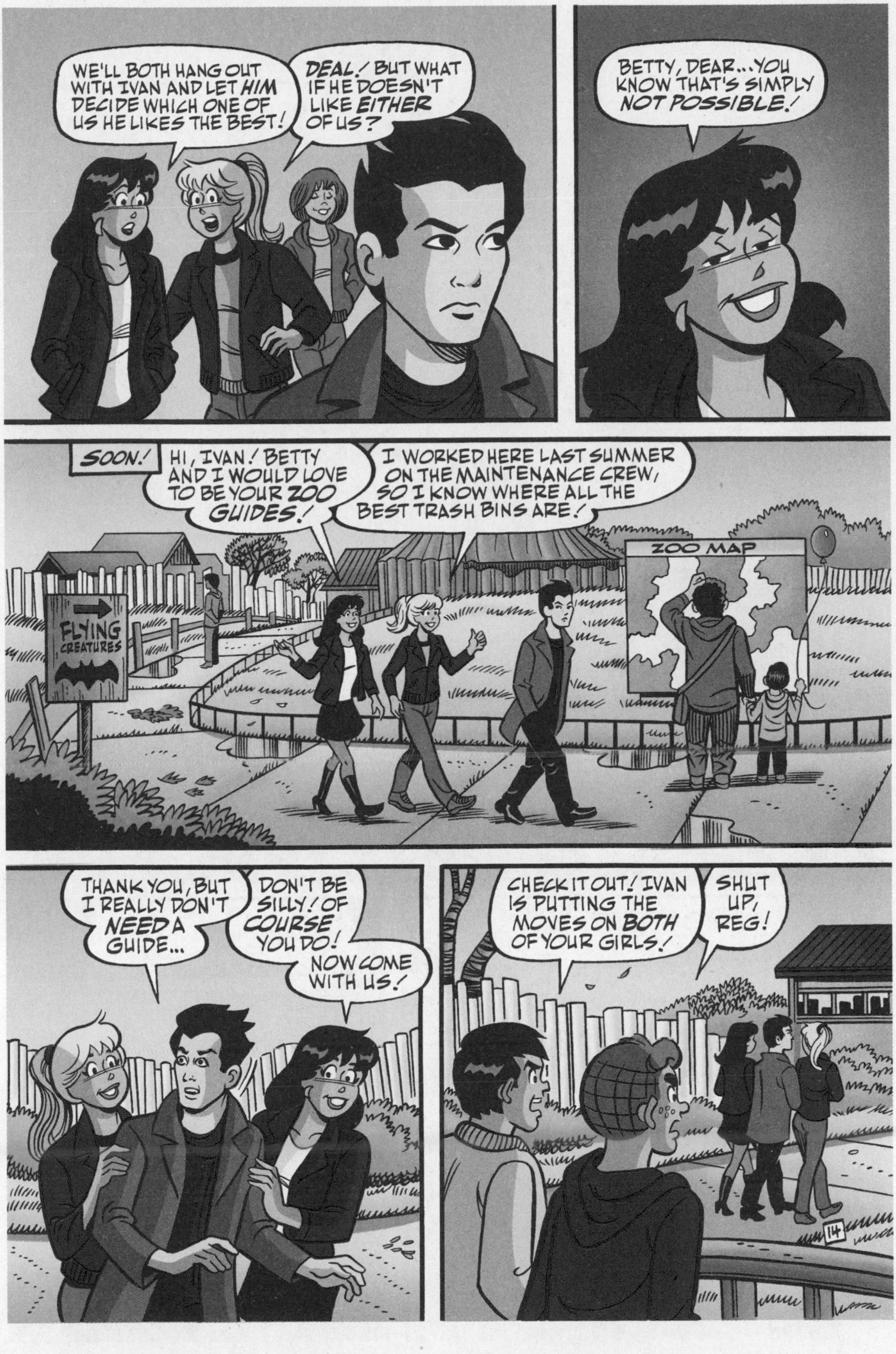
WE'LL BOTH HANG OUT WITH IVAN AND LET HIM DECIDE WHICH ONE OF US HE LIKES THE BEST!
DEAL! BUT WHAT IF HE DOESN'T LIKE EITHER OF US?
BETTY, DEAR... YOU KNOW THAT'S SIMPLY NOT POSSIBLE!
SOON!
HI, IVAN! BETTY AND I WOULD LOVE TO BE YOUR ZOO GUIDES!
I WORKED HERE LAST SUMMER ON THE MAINTENANCE CREW, SO I KNOW WHERE ALL THE BEST TRASH BINS ARE!
FLYING CREATURES
ZOO MAP
THANK YOU, BUT I REALLY DON'T NEED A GUIDE...
DON'T BE SILLY! OF COURSE YOU DO!
NOW COME WITH US!
CHECK IT OUT! IVAN IS PUTTING THE MOVES ON BOTH OF YOUR GIRLS!
SHUT UP, REG!
14

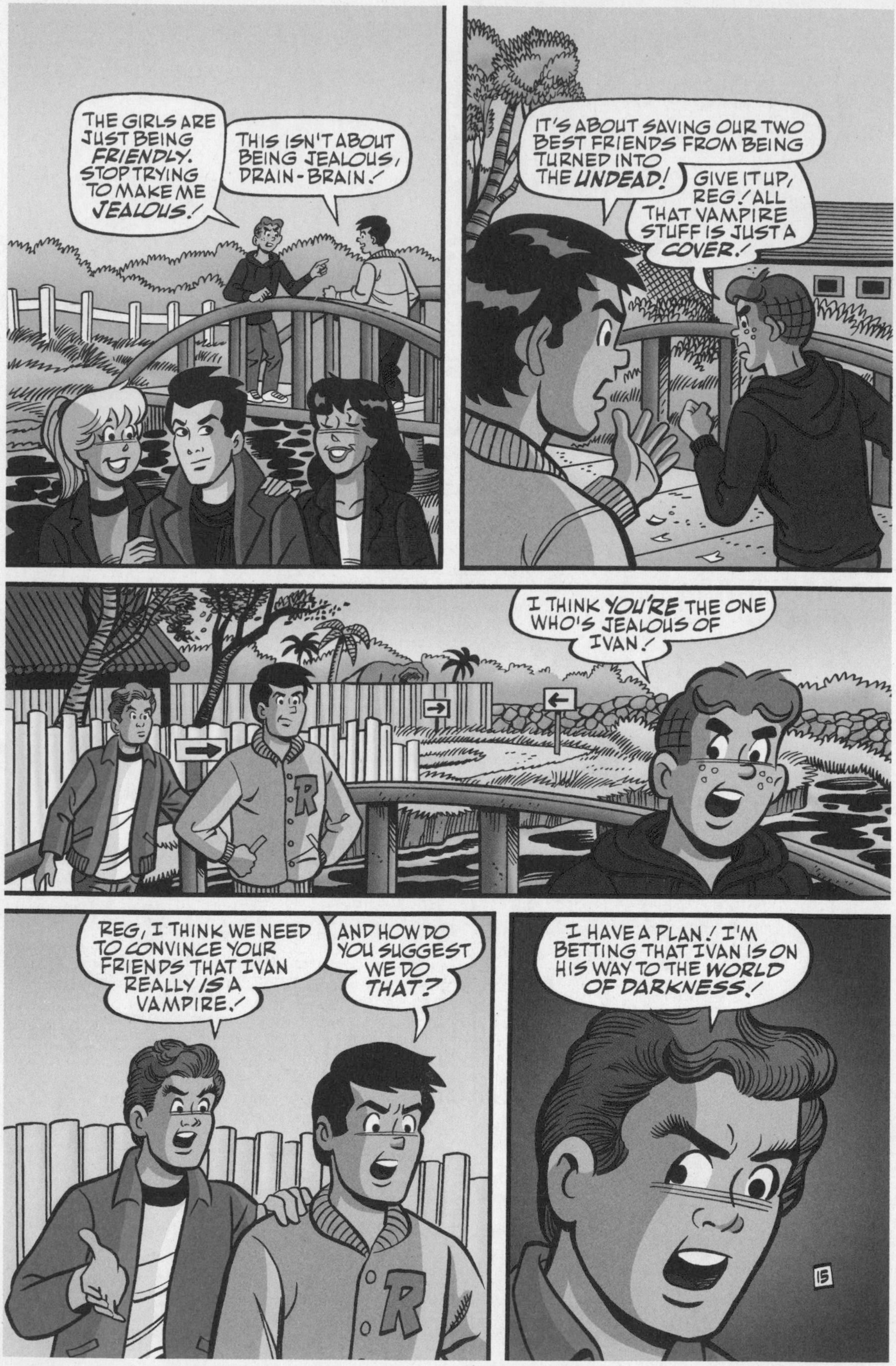
THE GIRLS ARE JUST BEING FRIENDLY. STOP TRYING TO MAKE ME JEALOUS!
THIS ISN'T ABOUT BEING JEALOUS, DRAIN-BRAIN!
IT'S ABOUT SAVING OUR TWO BEST FRIENDS FROM BEING TURNED INTO THE UNDEAD!
GIVE IT UP, REG! ALL THAT VAMPIRE STUFF IS JUST A COVER!
I THINK YOU'RE THE ONE WHO'S JEALOUS OF IVAN!
R
REG, I THINK WE NEED TO CONVINCE YOUR FRIENDS THAT IVAN REALLY IS A VAMPIRE!
AND HOW DO YOU SUGGEST WE DO THAT?
R
I HAVE A PLAN! I'M BETTING THAT IVAN IS ON HIS WAY TO THE WORLD OF DARKNESS!
15

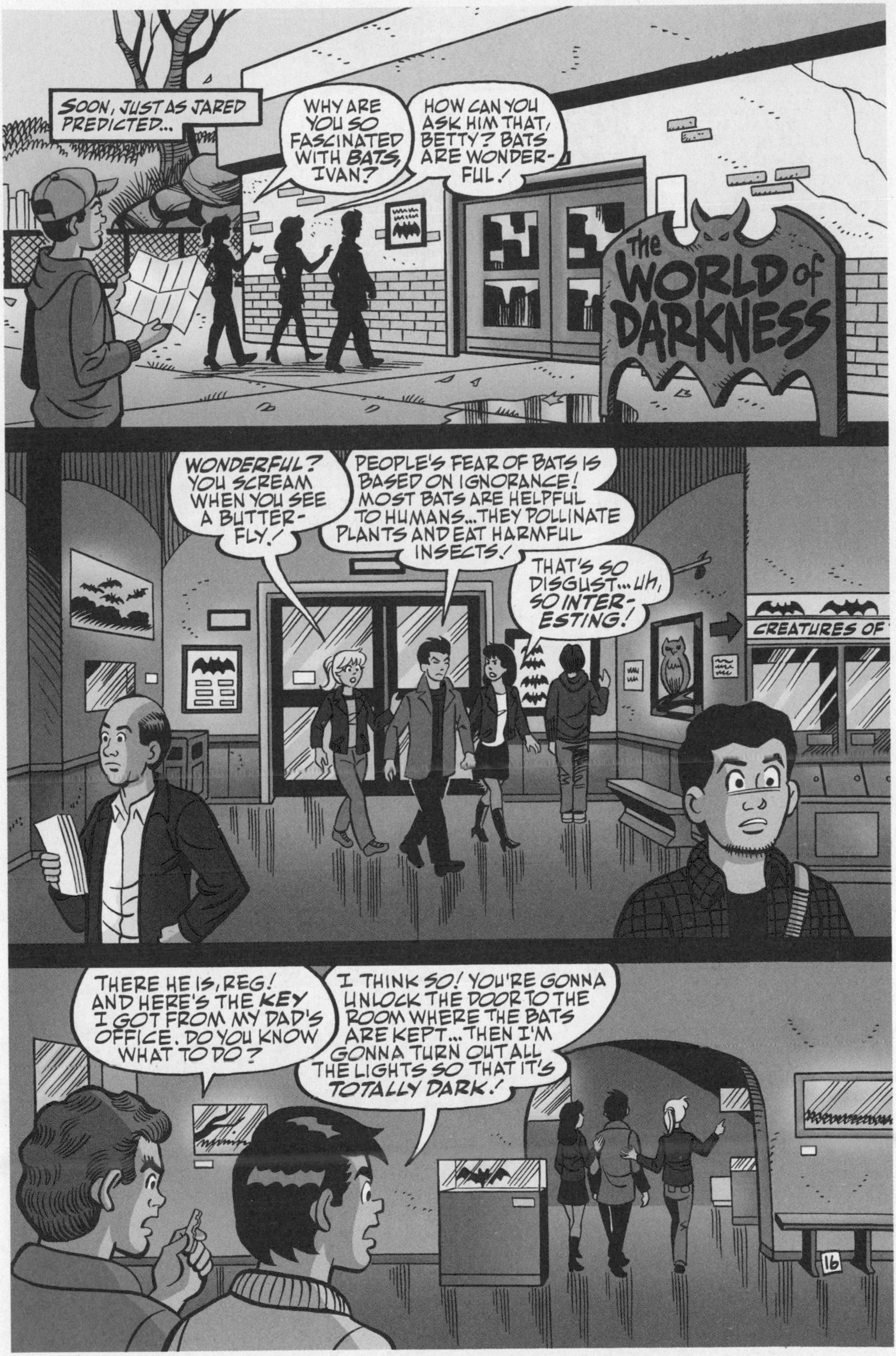
SOON, JUST AS JARED PREDICTED...
WHY ARE YOU SO FASCINATED WITH BATS, IVAN?
HOW CAN YOU ASK HIM THAT, BETTY? BATS ARE WONDER-FUL!
The WORLD of DARKNESS
WONDERFUL? YOU SCREAM WHEN YOU SEE A BUTTER-FLY!
PEOPLE'S FEAR OF BATS IS BASED ON IGNORANCE! MOST BATS ARE HELPFUL TO HUMANS...THEY POLLINATE PLANTS AND EAT HARMFUL INSECTS!
THAT'S SO DISGUST...uh, SO INTER-ESTING!
CREATURES OF
THERE HE IS, REG! AND HERE'S THE KEY I GOT FROM MY DAD'S OFFICE. DO YOU KNOW WHAT TO DO?
I THINK SO! YOU'RE GONNA UNLOCK THE DOOR TO THE ROOM WHERE THE BATS ARE KEPT... THEN I'M GONNA TURN OUT ALL THE LIGHTS SO THAT IT'S TOTALLY DARK!
16

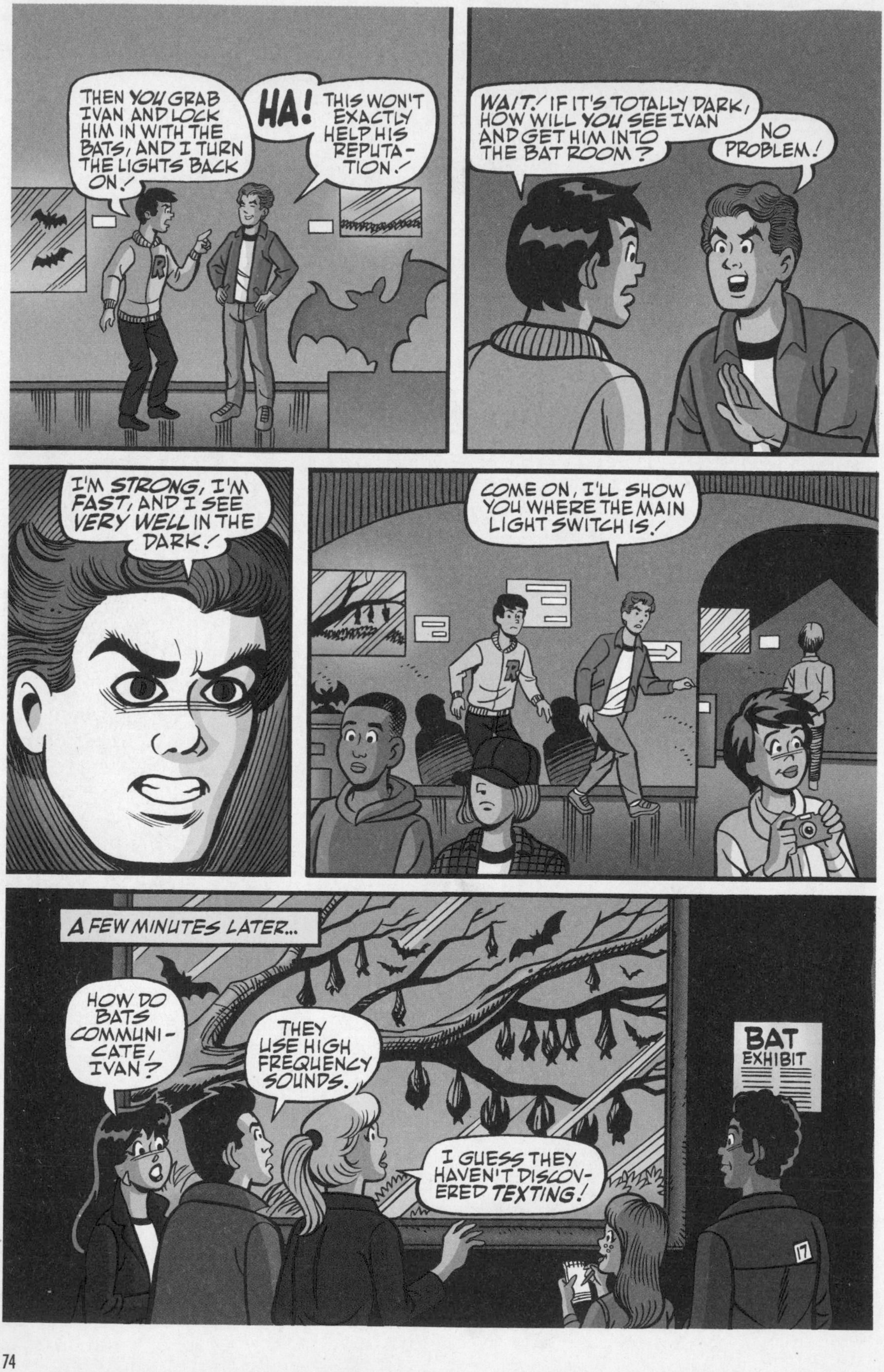
THEN YOU GRAB IVAN AND LOCK HIM IN WITH THE BATS, AND I TURN THE LIGHTS BACK ON!
HA! THIS WON'T EXACTLY HELP HIS REPUTATION!
WAIT! IF IT'S TOTALLY DARK, HOW WILL YOU SEE IVAN AND GET HIM INTO THE BAT ROOM?
NO PROBLEM!
I'M STRONG, I'M FAST, AND I SEE VERY WELL IN THE DARK!
COME ON, I'LL SHOW YOU WHERE THE MAIN LIGHT SWITCH IS!
A FEW MINUTES LATER...
HOW DO BATS COMMUNICATE, IVAN?
THEY USE HIGH FREQUENCY SOUNDS.
I GUESS THEY HAVEN'T DISCOVERED TEXTING!
BAT EXHIBIT
17

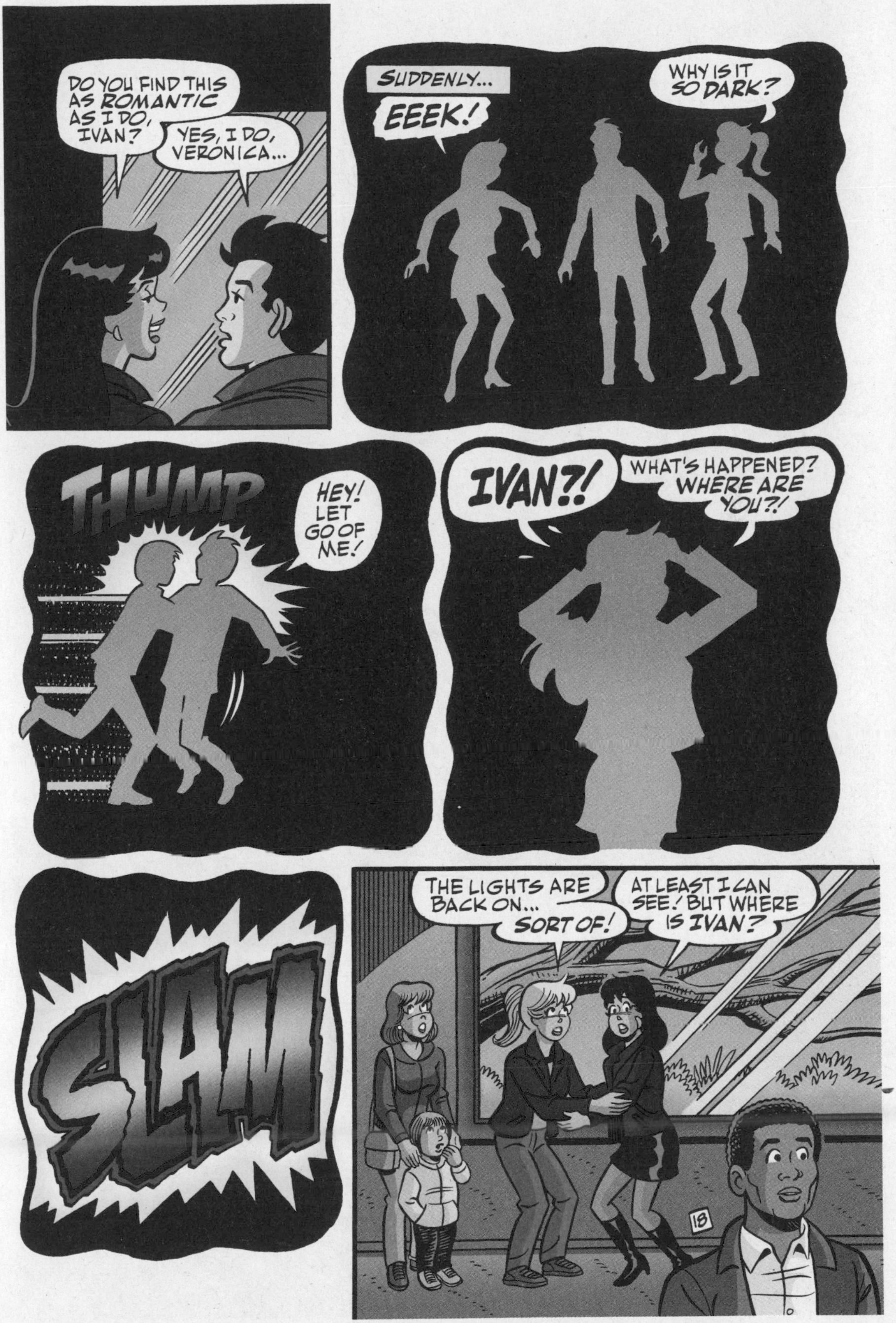

DO YOU FIND THIS AS ROMANTIC AS I DO, IVAN?
YES, I DO, VERONICA...
SUDDENLY...
EEEK!
WHY IS IT SO DARK?
THUMP
HEY! LET GO OF ME!
IVAN?!
WHAT'S HAPPENED? WHERE ARE YOU?!
SLAM
THE LIGHTS ARE BACK ON... SORT OF!
AT LEAST I CAN SEE! BUT WHERE IS IVAN?
18

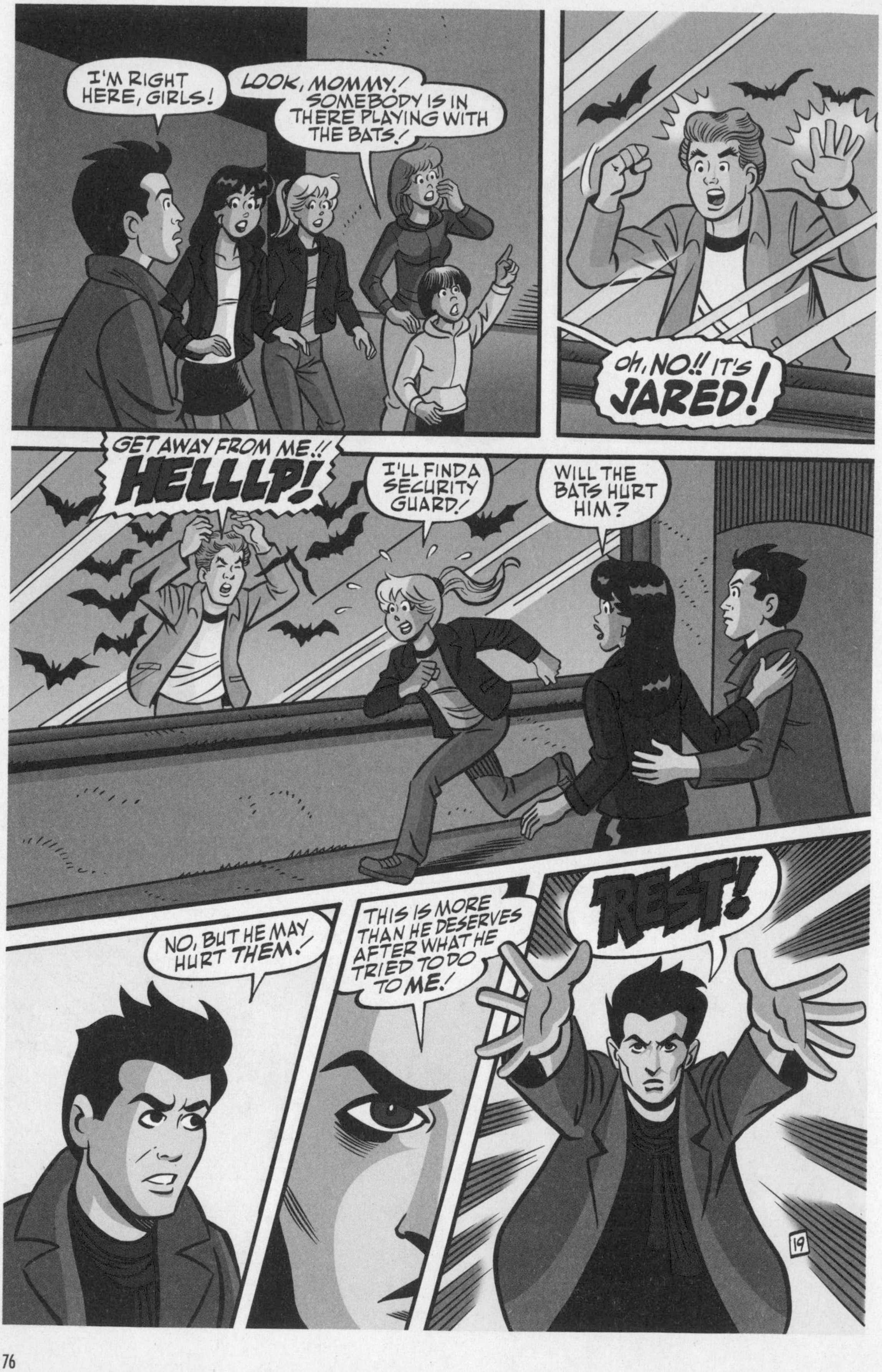
I'M RIGHT HERE, GIRLS!
LOOK, MOMMY! SOMEBODY IS IN THERE PLAYING WITH THE BATS!
OH, NO!! IT'S JARED!
GET AWAY FROM ME!! HELLLP!
I'LL FIND A SECURITY GUARD!
WILL THE BATS HURT HIM?
NO, BUT HE MAY HURT THEM!
THIS IS MORE THAN HE DESERVES AFTER WHAT HE TRIED TO DO TO ME!
REST!
19

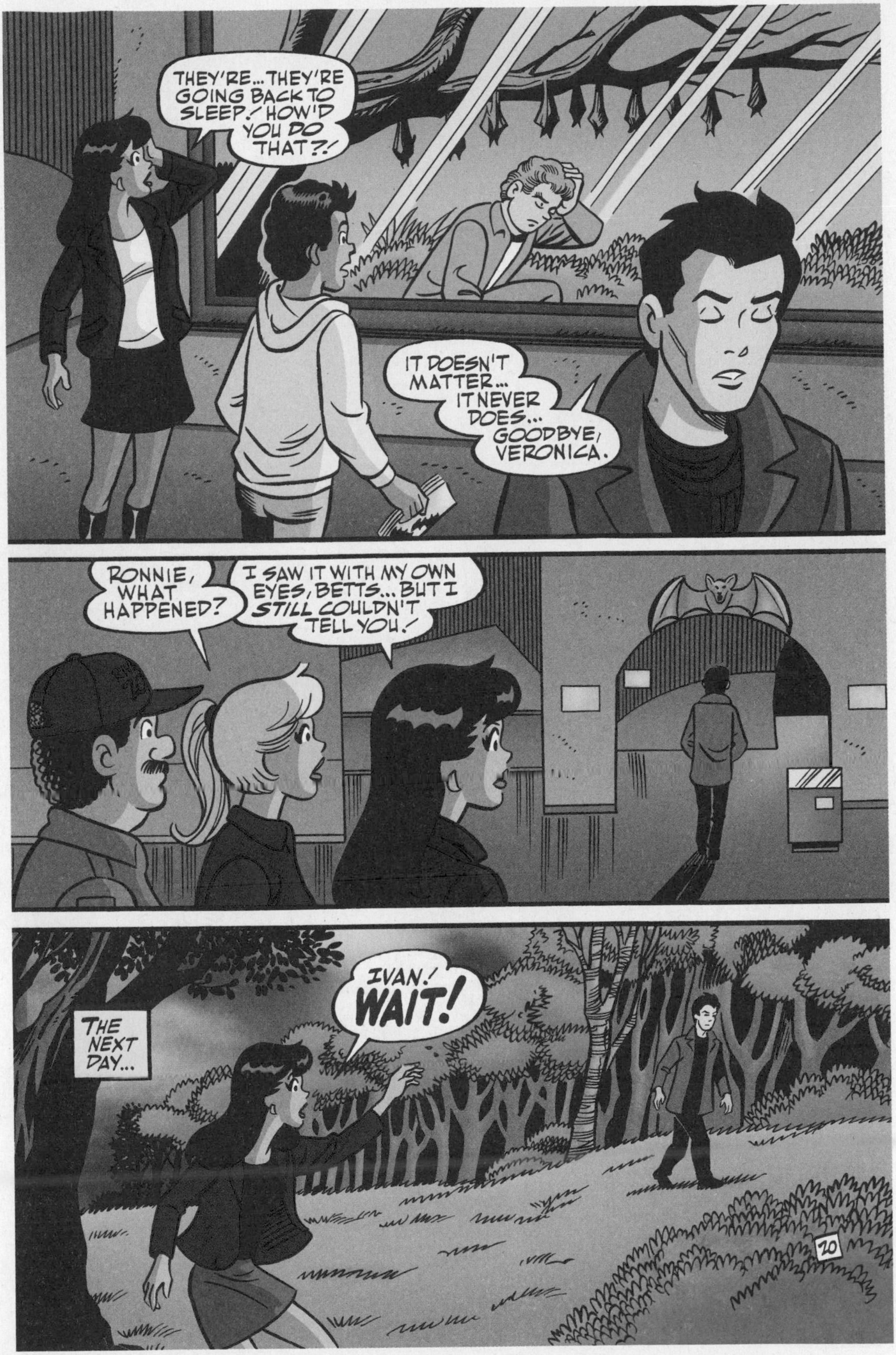
THEY'RE... THEY'RE GOING BACK TO SLEEP! HOW'D YOU DO THAT?!
IT DOESN'T MATTER... IT NEVER DOES... GOODBYE, VERONICA.
RONNIE, WHAT HAPPENED?
I SAW IT WITH MY OWN EYES, BETTS... BUT I STILL COULDN'T TELL YOU!
THE NEXT DAY...
IVAN! WAIT!
20

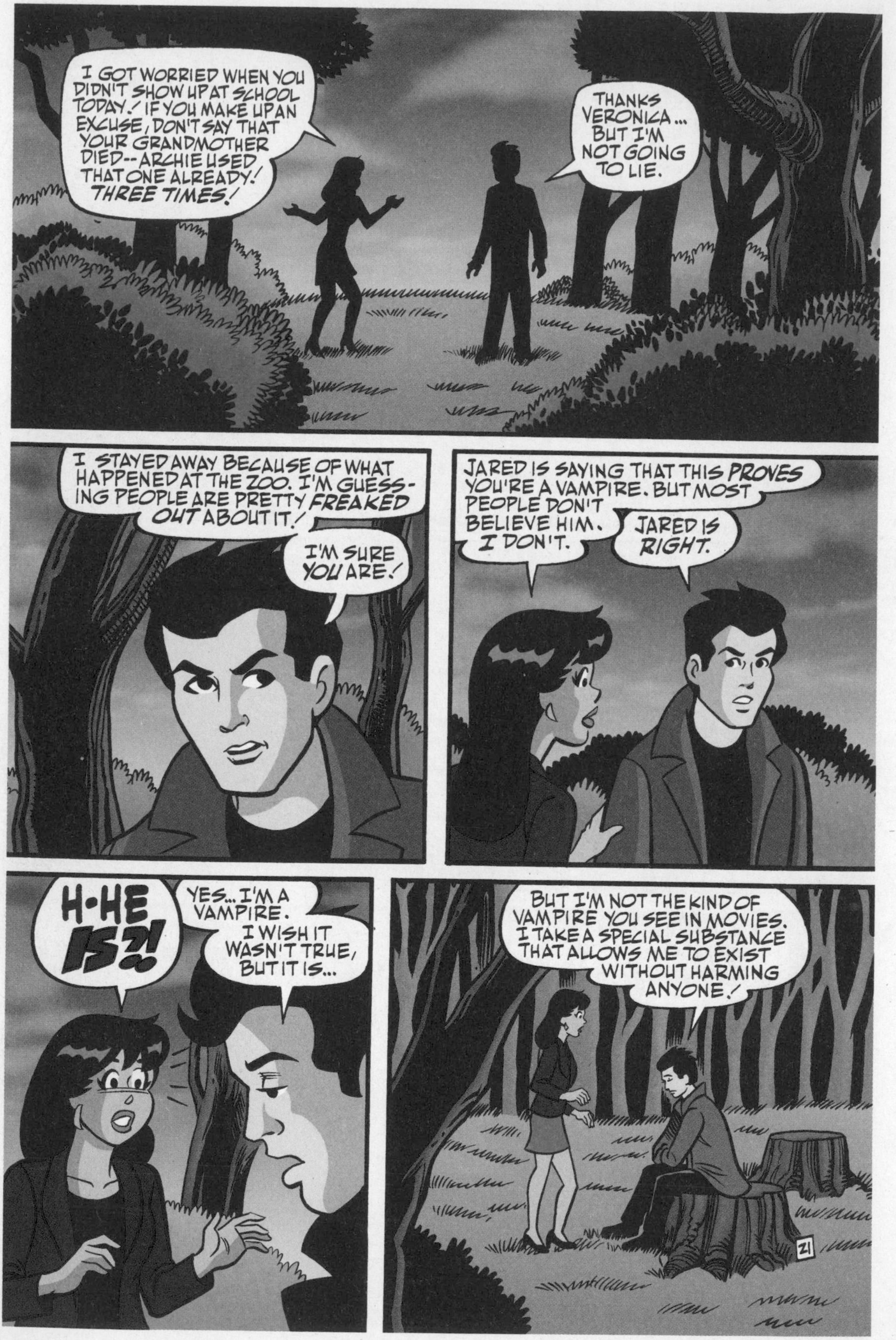
I GOT WORRIED WHEN YOU DIDN'T SHOW UP AT SCHOOL TODAY! IF YOU MAKE UP AN EXCUSE, DON'T SAY THAT YOUR GRANDMOTHER DIED--ARCHIE USED THAT ONE ALREADY! THREE TIMES!
THANKS VERONICA... BUT I'M NOT GOING TO LIE.
I STAYED AWAY BECAUSE OF WHAT HAPPENED AT THE ZOO. I'M GUESSING PEOPLE ARE PRETTY FREAKED OUT ABOUT IT!
I'M SURE YOU ARE!
JARED IS SAYING THAT THIS PROVES YOU'RE A VAMPIRE. BUT MOST PEOPLE DON'T BELIEVE HIM. I DON'T.
JARED IS RIGHT.
H-HE IS?!
YES... I'M A VAMPIRE.
I WISH IT WASN'T TRUE, BUT IT IS...
BUT I'M NOT THE KIND OF VAMPIRE YOU SEE IN MOVIES. I TAKE A SPECIAL SUBSTANCE THAT ALLOWS ME TO EXIST WITHOUT HARMING ANYONE!
21

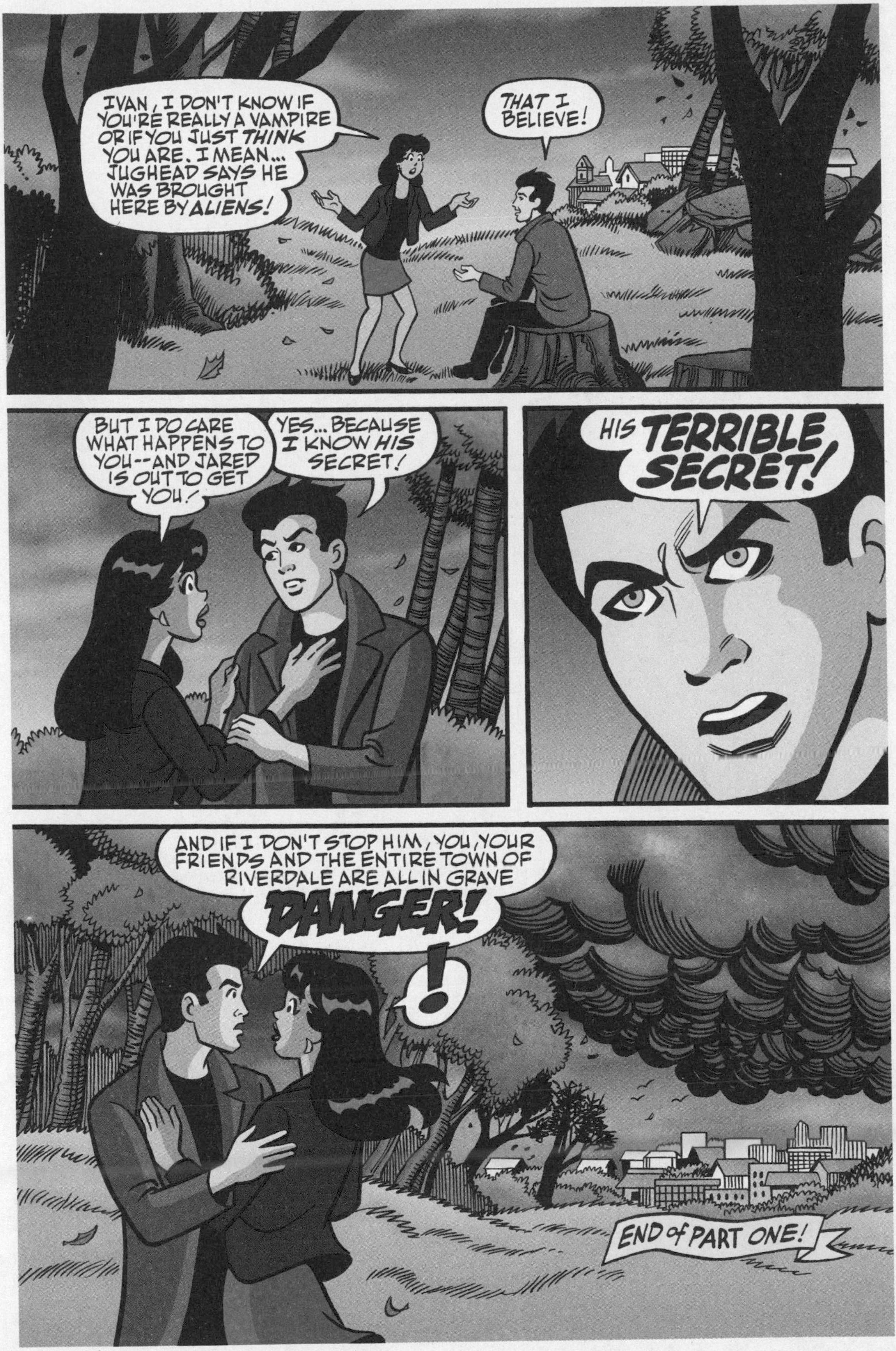
IVAN, I DON'T KNOW IF YOU'RE REALLY A VAMPIRE OR IF YOU JUST THINK YOU ARE. I MEAN... JUGHEAD SAYS HE WAS BROUGHT HERE BY ALIENS!
THAT I BELIEVE!
BUT I DO CARE WHAT HAPPENS TO YOU--AND JARED IS OUT TO GET YOU!
YES... BECAUSE I KNOW HIS SECRET!
HIS TERRIBLE SECRET!
AND IF I DON'T STOP HIM, YOU, YOUR FRIENDS AND THE ENTIRE TOWN OF RIVERDALE ARE ALL IN GRAVE DANGER!
!
END of PART ONE!

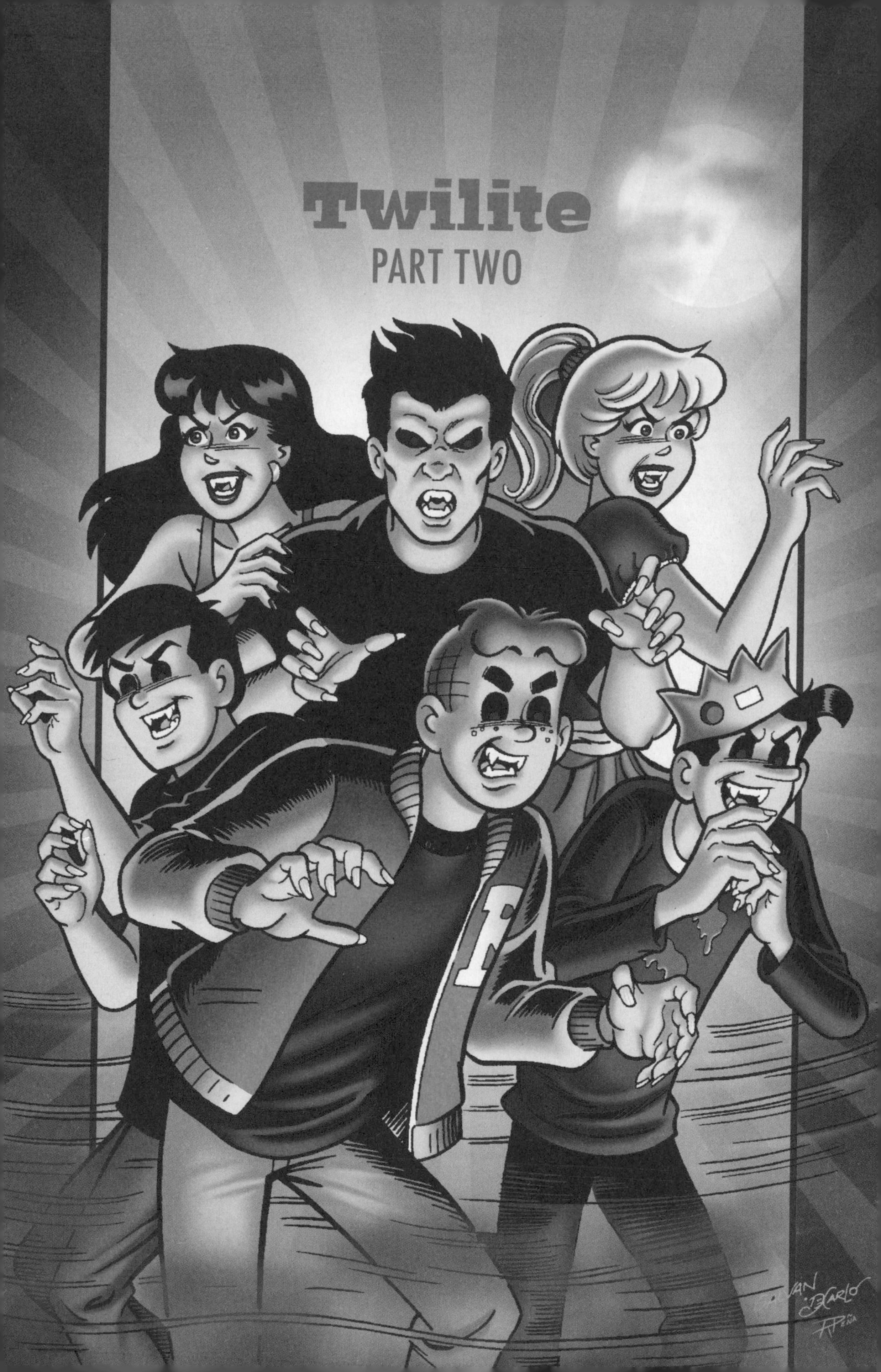
Twilite
PART TWO

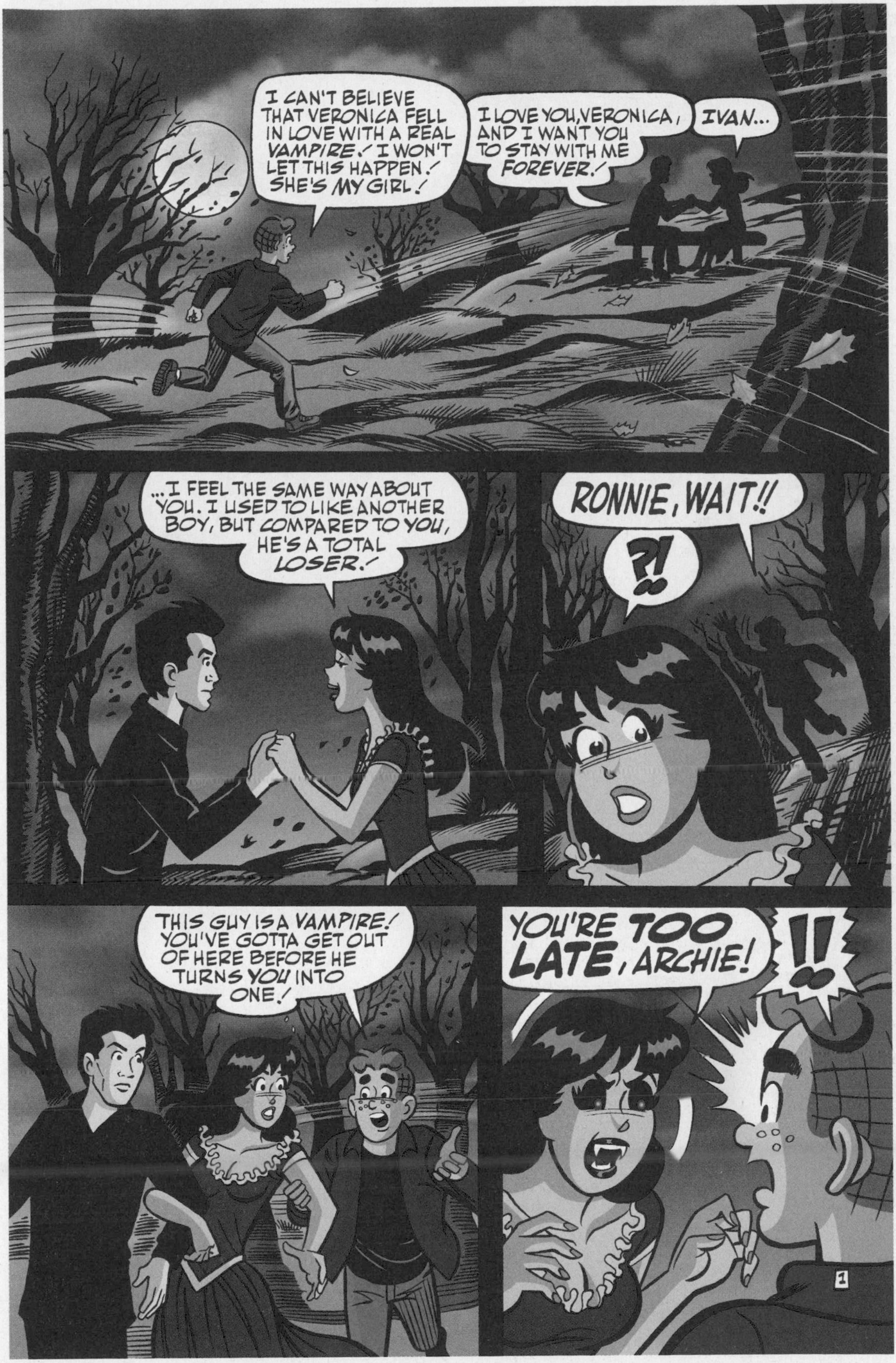
I CAN'T BELIEVE THAT VERONICA FELL IN LOVE WITH A REAL VAMPIRE! I WON'T LET THIS HAPPEN! SHE'S MY GIRL!
I LOVE YOU, VERONICA, AND I WANT YOU TO STAY WITH ME FOREVER!
IVAN...
...I FEEL THE SAME WAY ABOUT YOU. I USED TO LIKE ANOTHER BOY, BUT COMPARED TO YOU, HE'S A TOTAL LOSER!
RONNIE, WAIT!!
?!
THIS GUY IS A VAMPIRE! YOU'VE GOTTA GET OUT OF HERE BEFORE HE TURNS YOU INTO ONE!
YOU'RE TOO LATE, ARCHIE!
!!

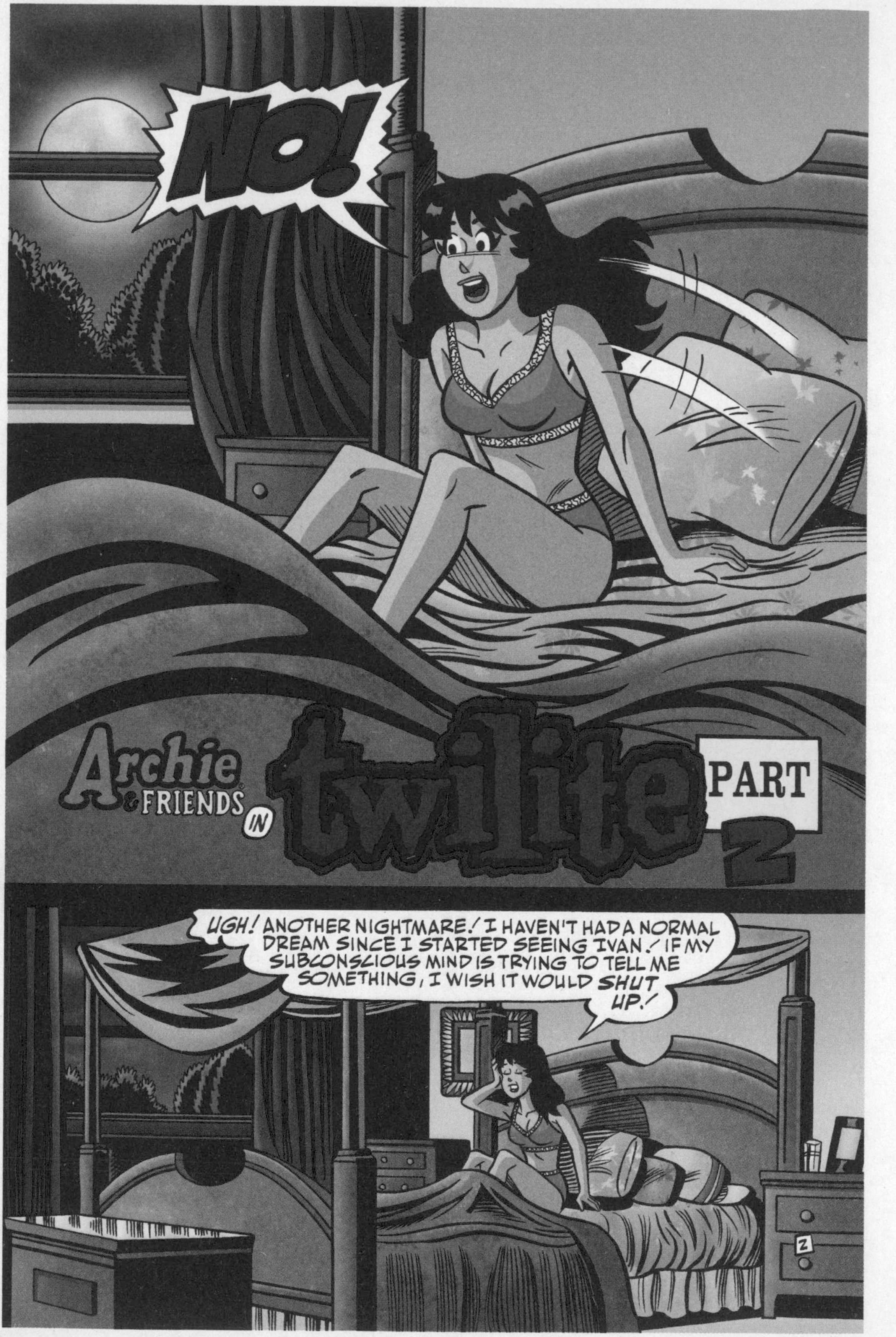
NO!
Archie & FRIENDS IN twilite PART 2
UGH! ANOTHER NIGHTMARE! I HAVEN'T HAD A NORMAL DREAM SINCE I STARTED SEEING IVAN! IF MY SUBCONSCIOUS MIND IS TRYING TO TELL ME SOMETHING, I WISH IT WOULD SHUT UP!

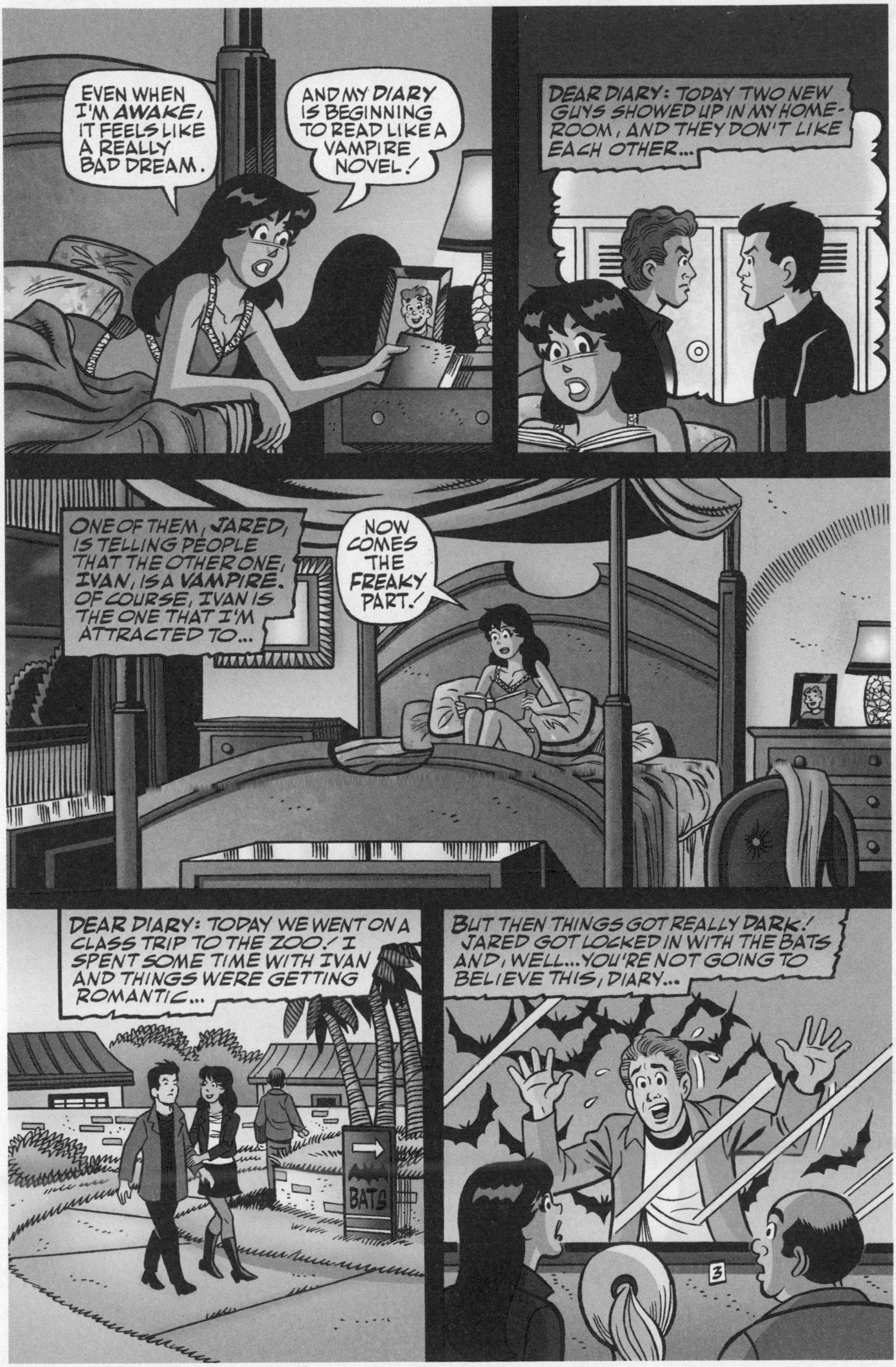
EVEN WHEN I'M AWAKE, IT FEELS LIKE A REALLY BAD DREAM.
AND MY DIARY IS BEGINNING TO READ LIKE A VAMPIRE NOVEL!
DEAR DIARY: TODAY TWO NEW GUYS SHOWED UP IN MY HOME-ROOM, AND THEY DON'T LIKE EACH OTHER...
ONE OF THEM, JARED, IS TELLING PEOPLE THAT THE OTHER ONE, IVAN, IS A VAMPIRE. OF COURSE, IVAN IS THE ONE THAT I'M ATTRACTED TO...
NOW COMES THE FREAKY PART!
DEAR DIARY: TODAY WE WENT ON A CLASS TRIP TO THE ZOO! I SPENT SOME TIME WITH IVAN AND THINGS WERE GETTING ROMANTIC...
BATS
BUT THEN THINGS GOT REALLY DARK! JARED GOT LOCKED IN WITH THE BATS AND, WELL... YOU'RE NOT GOING TO BELIEVE THIS, DIARY...
3

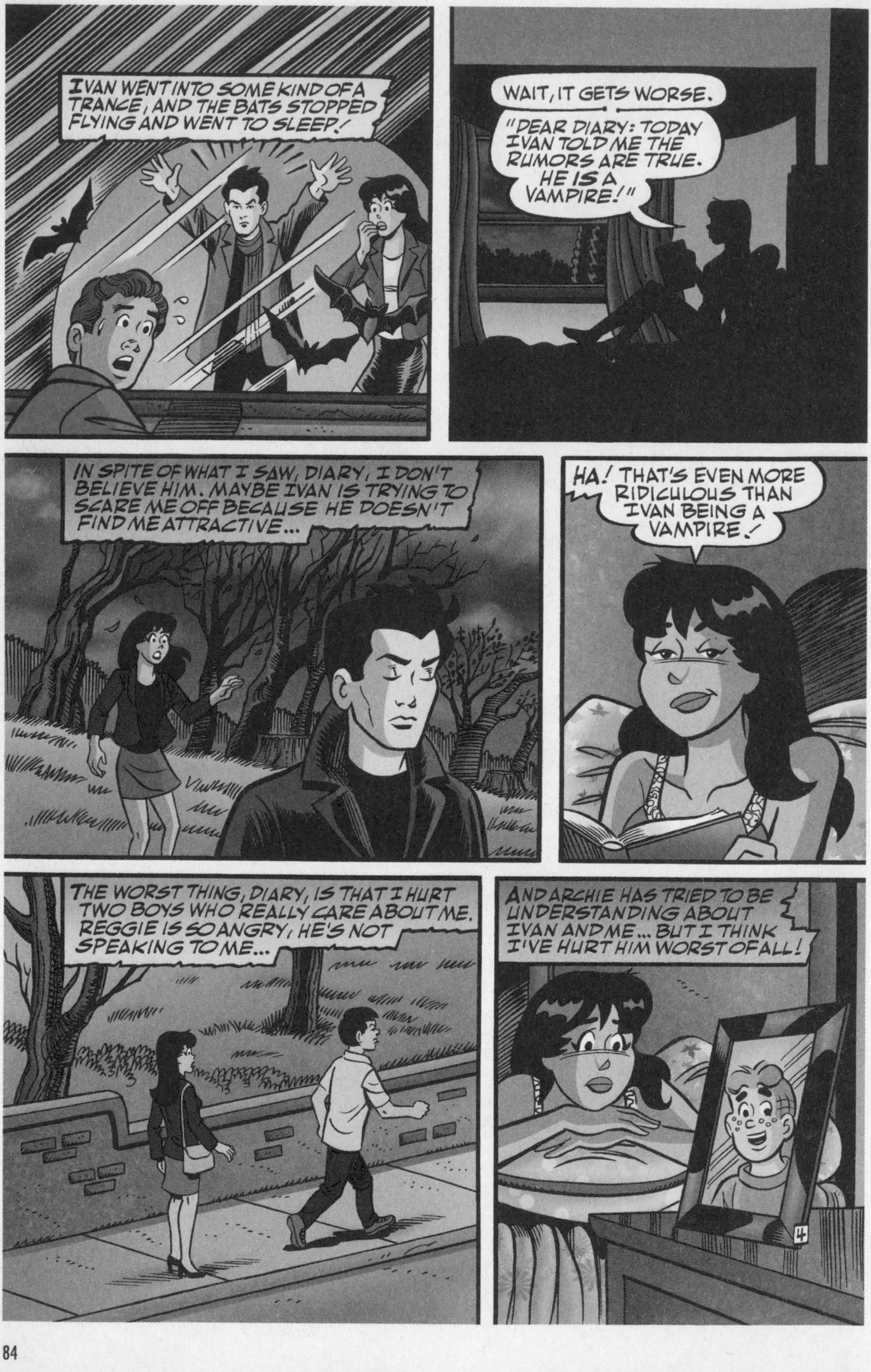
IVAN WENT INTO SOME KIND OF A TRANCE, AND THE BATS STOPPED FLYING AND WENT TO SLEEP!
WAIT, IT GETS WORSE.
"DEAR DIARY: TODAY IVAN TOLD ME THE RUMORS ARE TRUE. HE IS A VAMPIRE!"
IN SPITE OF WHAT I SAW, DIARY, I DON'T BELIEVE HIM. MAYBE IVAN IS TRYING TO SCARE ME OFF BECAUSE HE DOESN'T FIND ME ATTRACTIVE...
HA! THAT'S EVEN MORE RIDICULOUS THAN IVAN BEING A VAMPIRE!
THE WORST THING, DIARY, IS THAT I HURT TWO BOYS WHO REALLY CARE ABOUT ME. REGGIE IS SO ANGRY, HE'S NOT SPEAKING TO ME...
AND ARCHIE HAS TRIED TO BE UNDERSTANDING ABOUT IVAN AND ME... BUT I THINK I'VE HURT HIM WORST OF ALL!
4

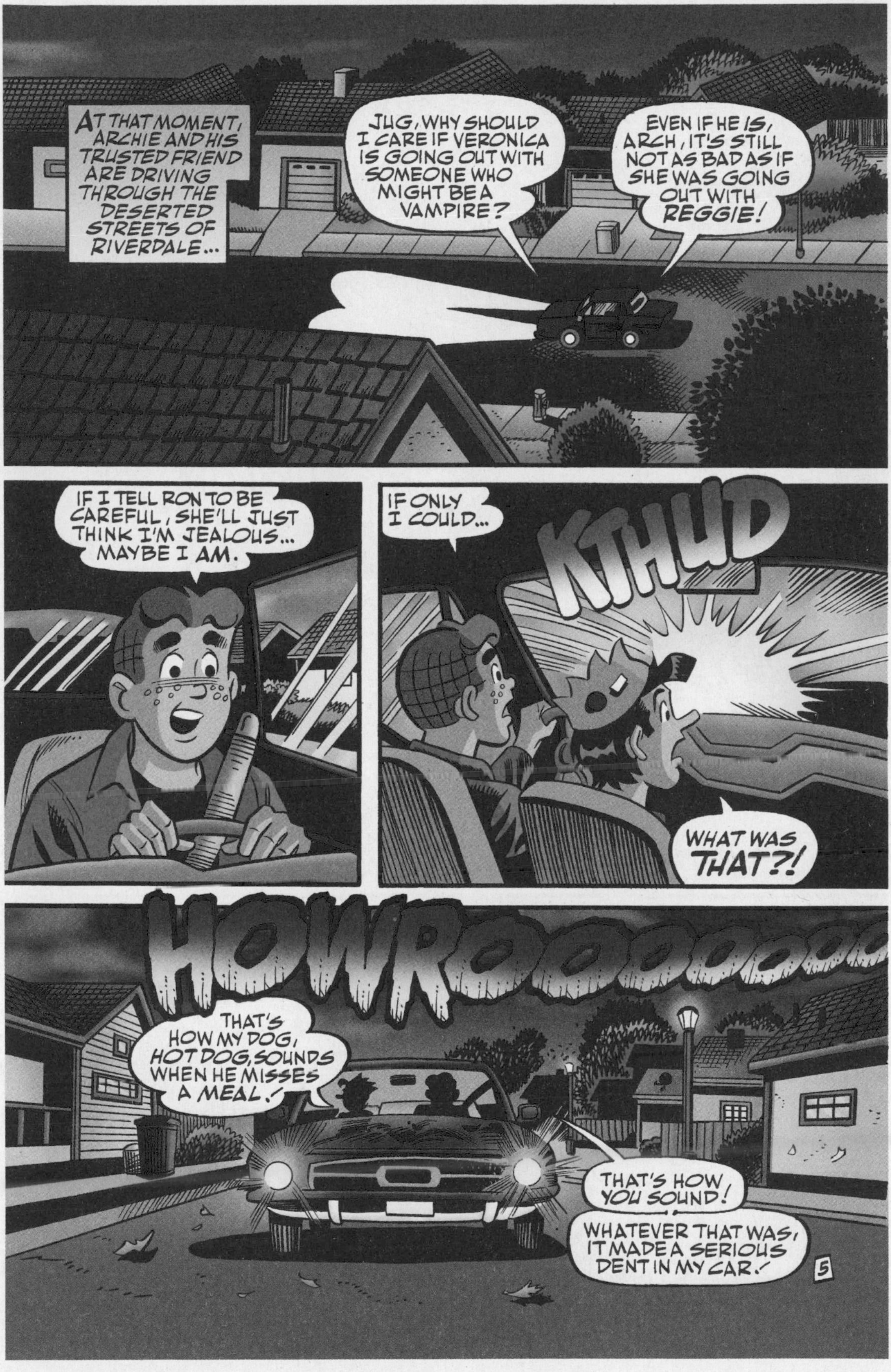
AT THAT MOMENT, ARCHIE AND HIS TRUSTED FRIEND ARE DRIVING THROUGH THE DESERTED STREETS OF RIVERDALE...
JUG, WHY SHOULD I CARE IF VERONICA IS GOING OUT WITH SOMEONE WHO MIGHT BE A VAMPIRE?
EVEN IF HE IS, ARCH, IT'S STILL NOT AS BAD AS IF SHE WAS GOING OUT WITH REGGIE!
IF I TELL RON TO BE CAREFUL, SHE'LL JUST THINK I'M JEALOUS... MAYBE I AM.
IF ONLY I COULD...
KTHUD
WHAT WAS THAT?!
HOWROOOOOOO
THAT'S HOW MY DOG, HOT DOG, SOUNDS WHEN HE MISSES A MEAL!
THAT'S HOW YOU SOUND!
WHATEVER THAT WAS, IT MADE A SERIOUS DENT IN MY CAR!
5

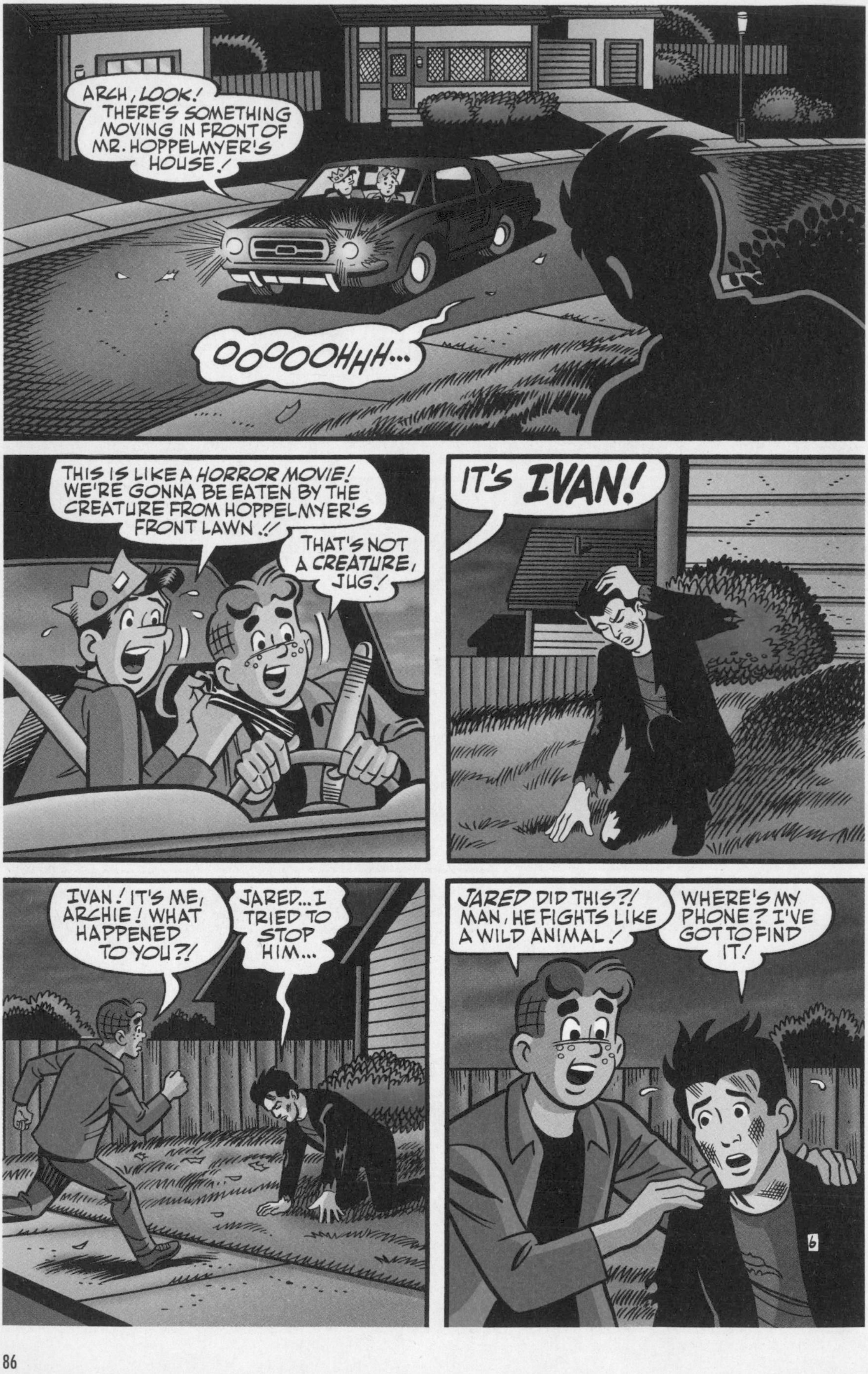
ARCH, LOOK! THERE'S SOMETHING MOVING IN FRONT OF MR. HOPPELMYER'S HOUSE!
OOOOOOHHH...
THIS IS LIKE A HORROR MOVIE! WE'RE GONNA BE EATEN BY THE CREATURE FROM HOPPELMYER'S FRONT LAWN!!
THAT'S NOT A CREATURE, JUG!
IT'S IVAN!
IVAN! IT'S ME, ARCHIE! WHAT HAPPENED TO YOU?!
JARED... I TRIED TO STOP HIM...
JARED DID THIS?! MAN, HE FIGHTS LIKE A WILD ANIMAL!
WHERE'S MY PHONE? I'VE GOT TO FIND IT!
6

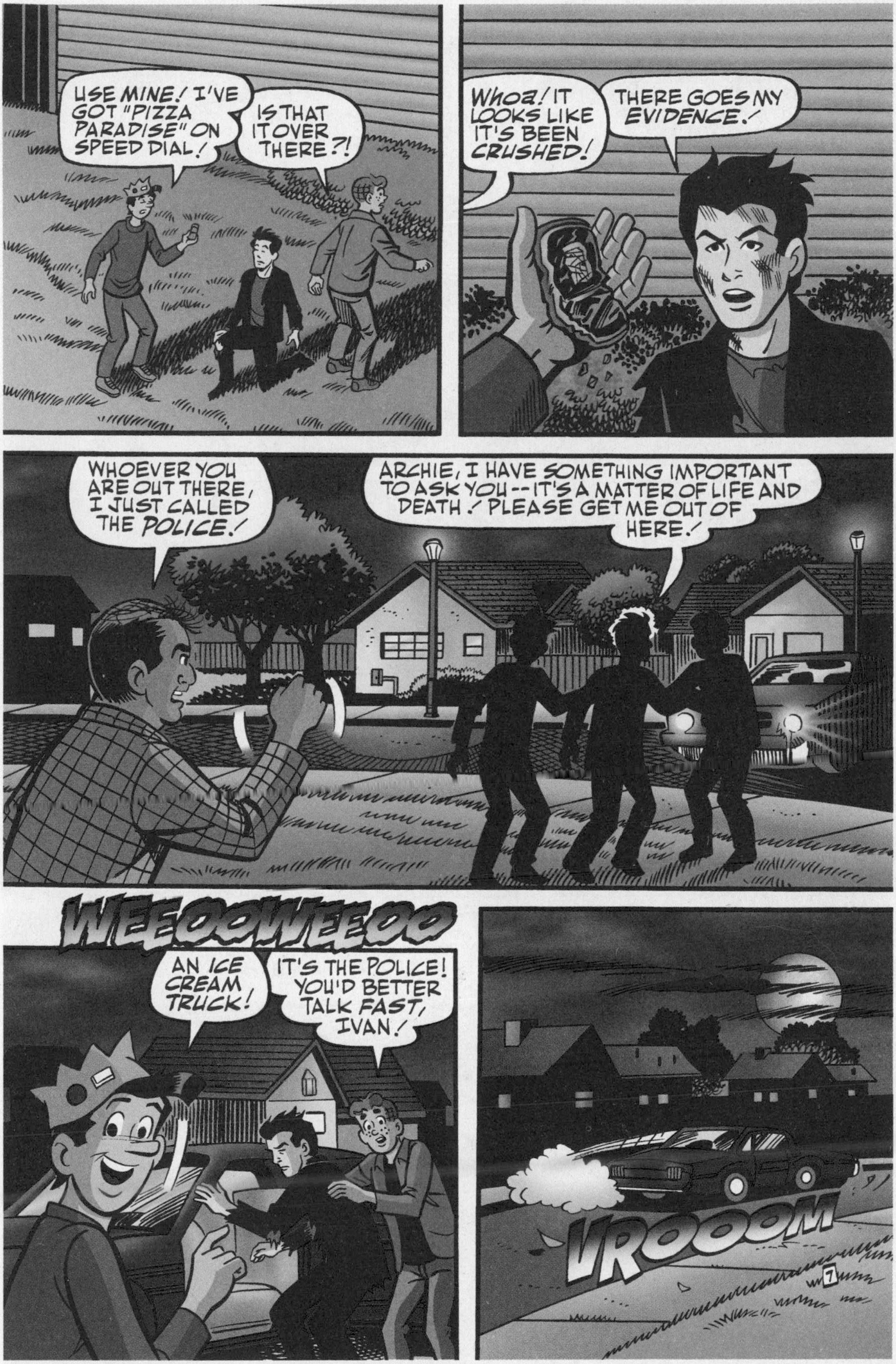
USE MINE! I'VE GOT "PIZZA PARADISE" ON SPEED DIAL!
IS THAT IT OVER THERE?!
Whoa! IT LOOKS LIKE IT'S BEEN CRUSHED!
THERE GOES MY EVIDENCE!
WHOEVER YOU ARE OUT THERE, I JUST CALLED THE POLICE!
ARCHIE, I HAVE SOMETHING IMPORTANT TO ASK YOU -- IT'S A MATTER OF LIFE AND DEATH! PLEASE GET ME OUT OF HERE!
WEEOOWEEOO
AN ICE CREAM TRUCK!
IT'S THE POLICE! YOU'D BETTER TALK FAST, IVAN!
VROOOOM
7

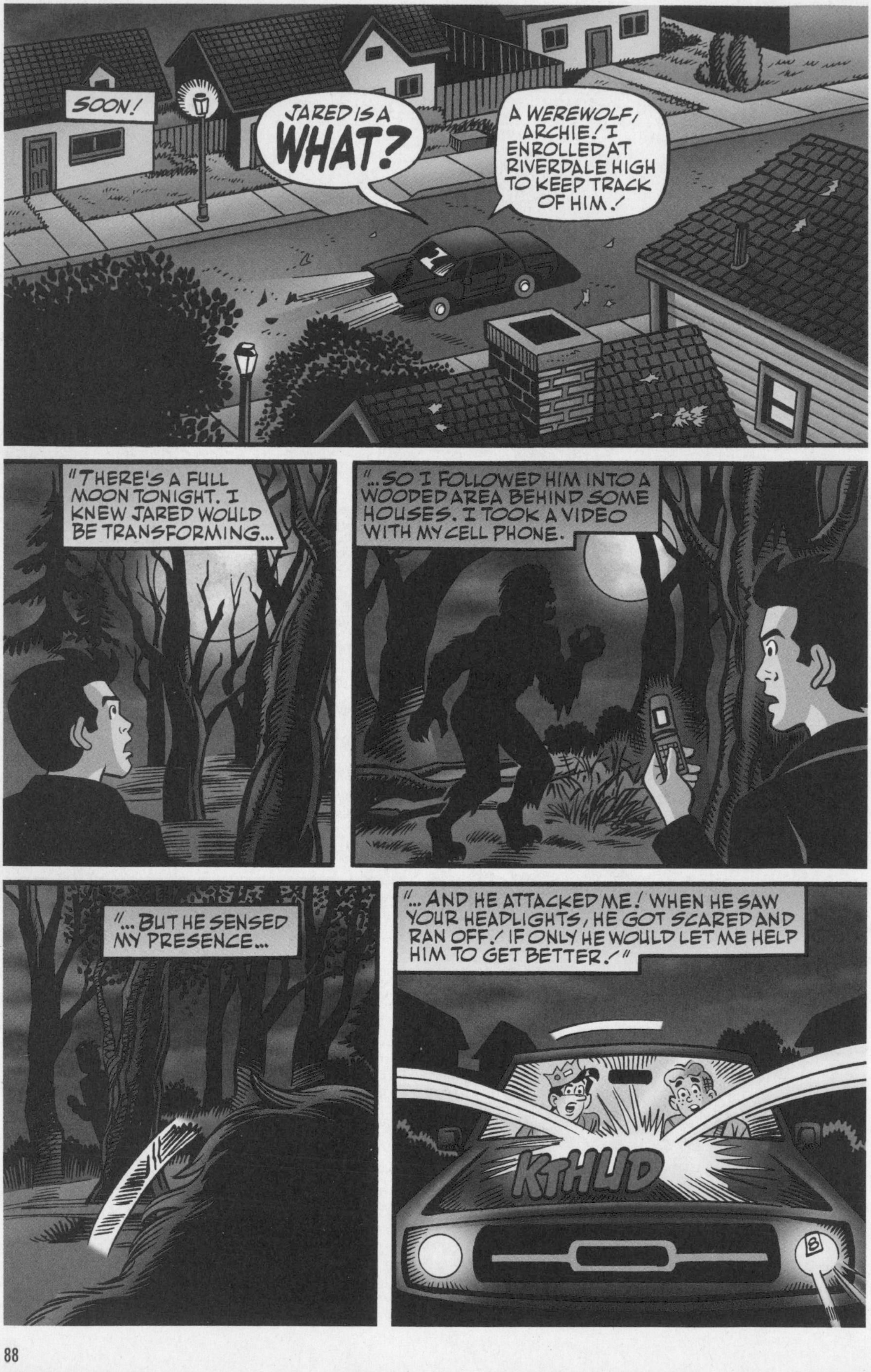
SOON!
JARED IS A WHAT?
A WEREWOLF, ARCHIE! I ENROLLED AT RIVERDALE HIGH TO KEEP TRACK OF HIM!
"THERE'S A FULL MOON TONIGHT. I KNEW JARED WOULD BE TRANSFORMING...
"...SO I FOLLOWED HIM INTO A WOODED AREA BEHIND SOME HOUSES. I TOOK A VIDEO WITH MY CELL PHONE.
"...BUT HE SENSED MY PRESENCE...
"...AND HE ATTACKED ME! WHEN HE SAW YOUR HEADLIGHTS, HE GOT SCARED AND RAN OFF! IF ONLY HE WOULD LET ME HELP HIM TO GET BETTER!"
KTHUD

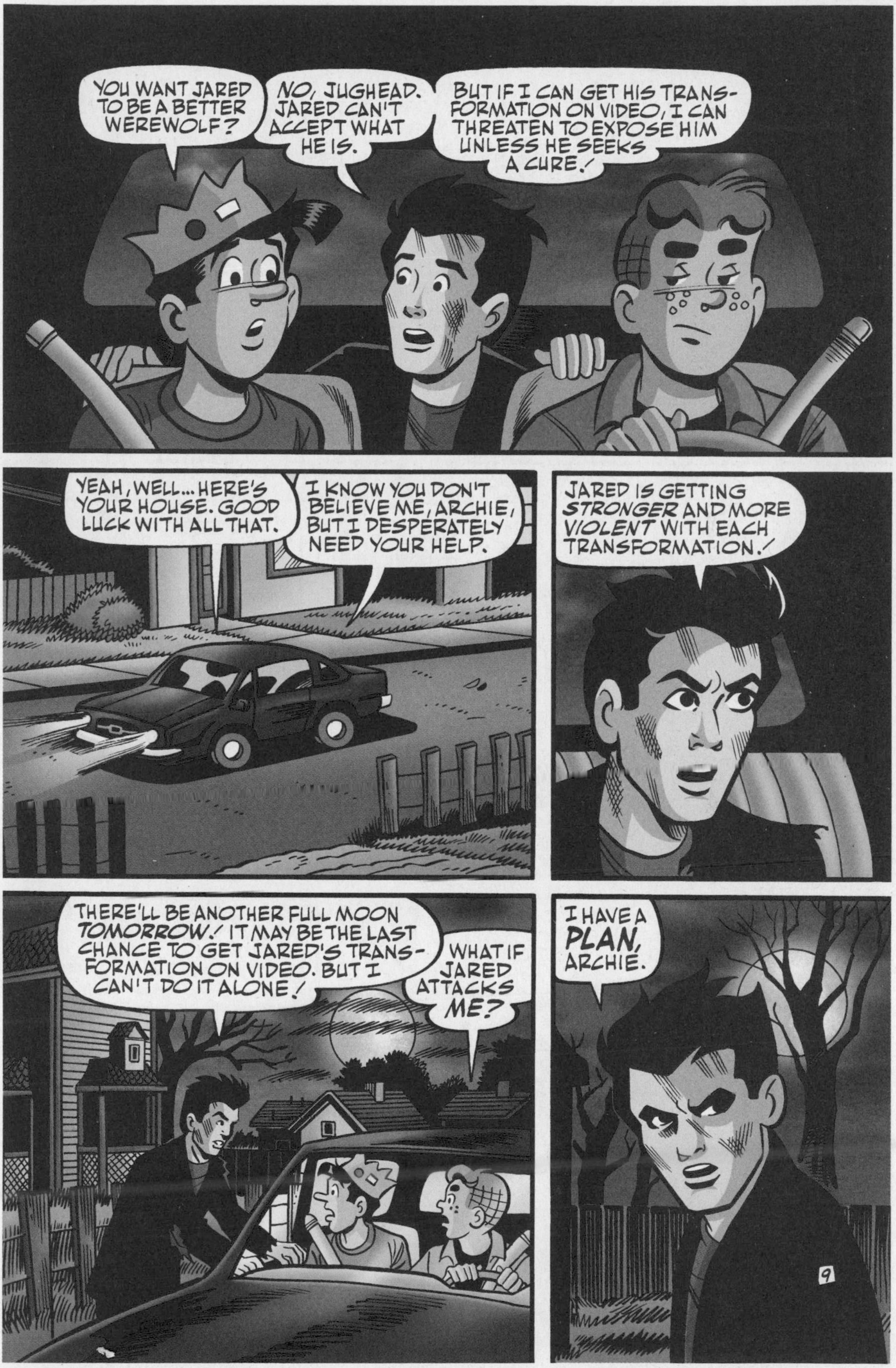
YOU WANT JARED TO BE A BETTER WEREWOLF?
NO, JUGHEAD. JARED CAN'T ACCEPT WHAT HE IS.
BUT IF I CAN GET HIS TRANSFORMATION ON VIDEO, I CAN THREATEN TO EXPOSE HIM UNLESS HE SEEKS A CURE!
YEAH, WELL... HERE'S YOUR HOUSE. GOOD LUCK WITH ALL THAT.
I KNOW YOU DON'T BELIEVE ME, ARCHIE, BUT I DESPERATELY NEED YOUR HELP.
JARED IS GETTING STRONGER AND MORE VIOLENT WITH EACH TRANSFORMATION!
THERE'LL BE ANOTHER FULL MOON TOMORROW! IT MAY BE THE LAST CHANCE TO GET JARED'S TRANSFORMATION ON VIDEO. BUT I CAN'T DO IT ALONE!
WHAT IF JARED ATTACKS ME?
I HAVE A PLAN, ARCHIE.
9

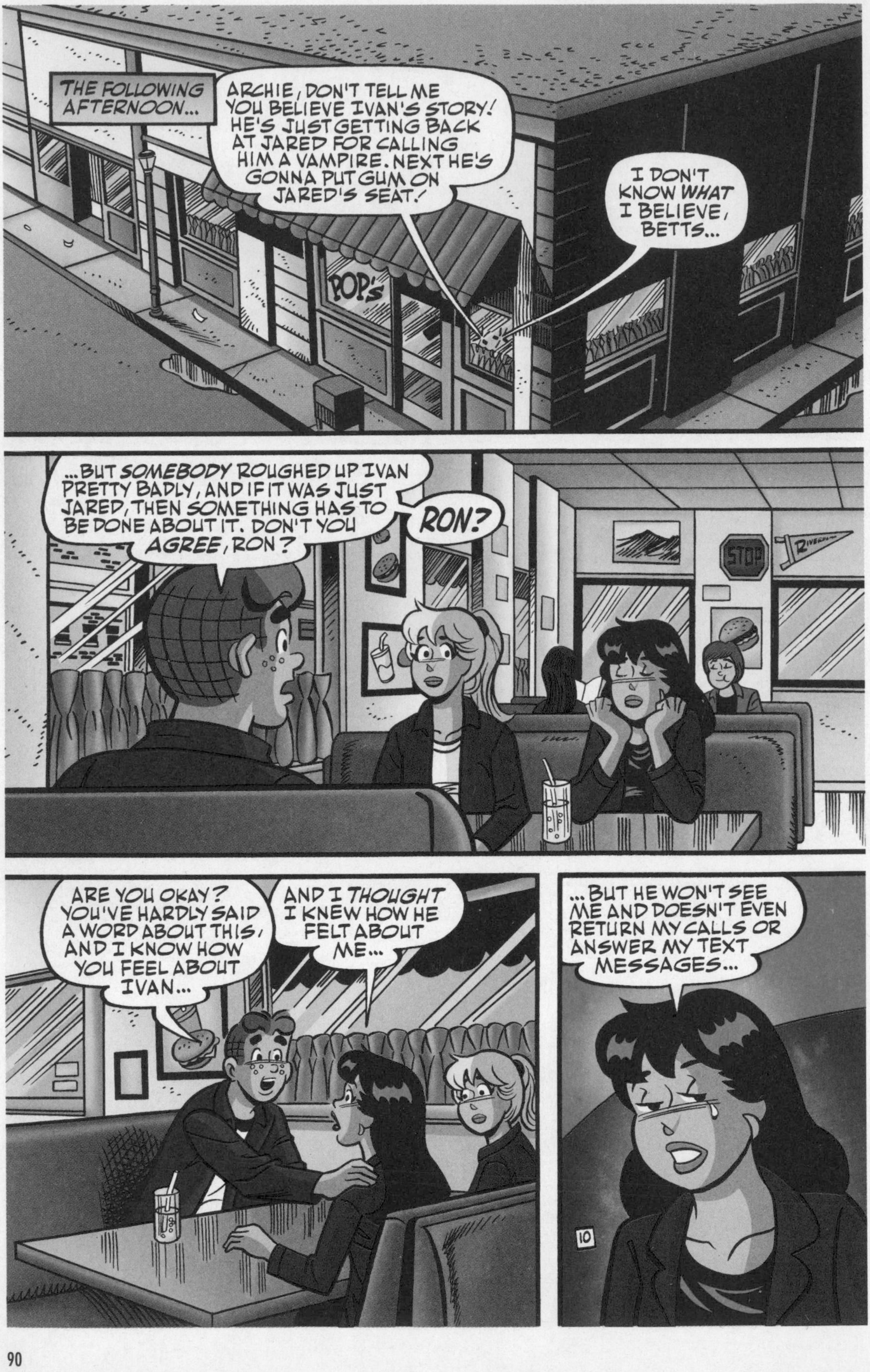
THE FOLLOWING AFTERNOON...
ARCHIE, DON'T TELL ME YOU BELIEVE IVAN'S STORY! HE'S JUST GETTING BACK AT JARED FOR CALLING HIM A VAMPIRE. NEXT HE'S GONNA PUT GUM ON JARED'S SEAT!
POP'S
I DON'T KNOW WHAT I BELIEVE, BETTS...
...BUT SOMEBODY ROUGHED UP IVAN PRETTY BADLY, AND IF IT WAS JUST JARED, THEN SOMETHING HAS TO BE DONE ABOUT IT. DON'T YOU AGREE, RON?
RON?
STOP
ARE YOU OKAY? YOU'VE HARDLY SAID A WORD ABOUT THIS, AND I KNOW HOW YOU FEEL ABOUT IVAN...
AND I THOUGHT I KNEW HOW HE FELT ABOUT ME...
...BUT HE WON'T SEE ME AND DOESN'T EVEN RETURN MY CALLS OR ANSWER MY TEXT MESSAGES...
10

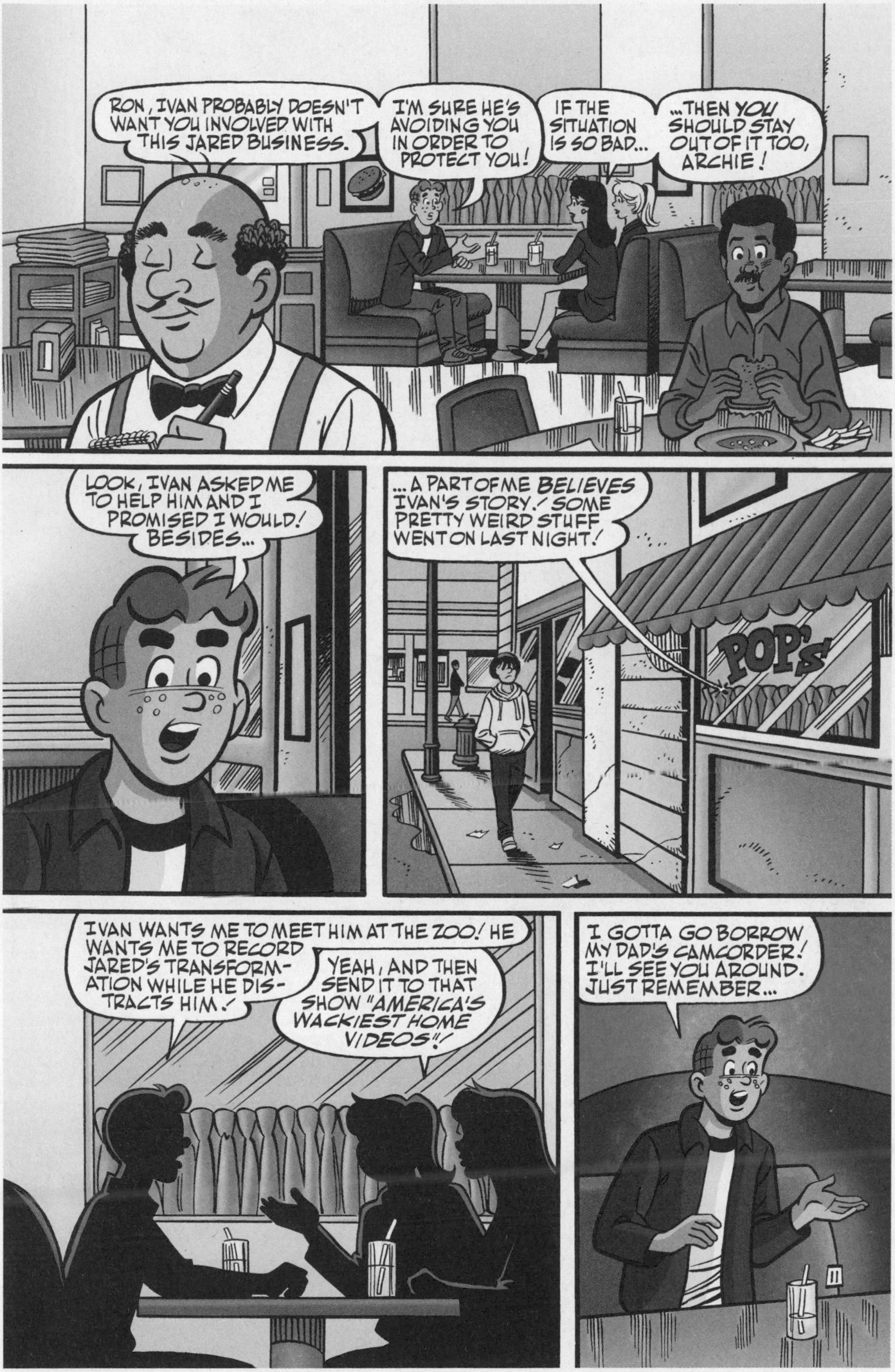
RON, IVAN PROBABLY DOESN'T WANT YOU INVOLVED WITH THIS JARED BUSINESS.
I'M SURE HE'S AVOIDING YOU IN ORDER TO PROTECT YOU!
IF THE SITUATION IS SO BAD...
...THEN YOU SHOULD STAY OUT OF IT TOO, ARCHIE!
LOOK, IVAN ASKED ME TO HELP HIM AND I PROMISED I WOULD! BESIDES...
...A PART OF ME BELIEVES IVAN'S STORY! SOME PRETTY WEIRD STUFF WENT ON LAST NIGHT!
POP'S
IVAN WANTS ME TO MEET HIM AT THE ZOO! HE WANTS ME TO RECORD JARED'S TRANSFORM-ATION WHILE HE DIS-TRACTS HIM!
YEAH, AND THEN SEND IT TO THAT SHOW "AMERICA'S WACKIEST HOME VIDEOS"!
I GOTTA GO BORROW MY DAD'S CAMCORDER! I'LL SEE YOU AROUND. JUST REMEMBER...

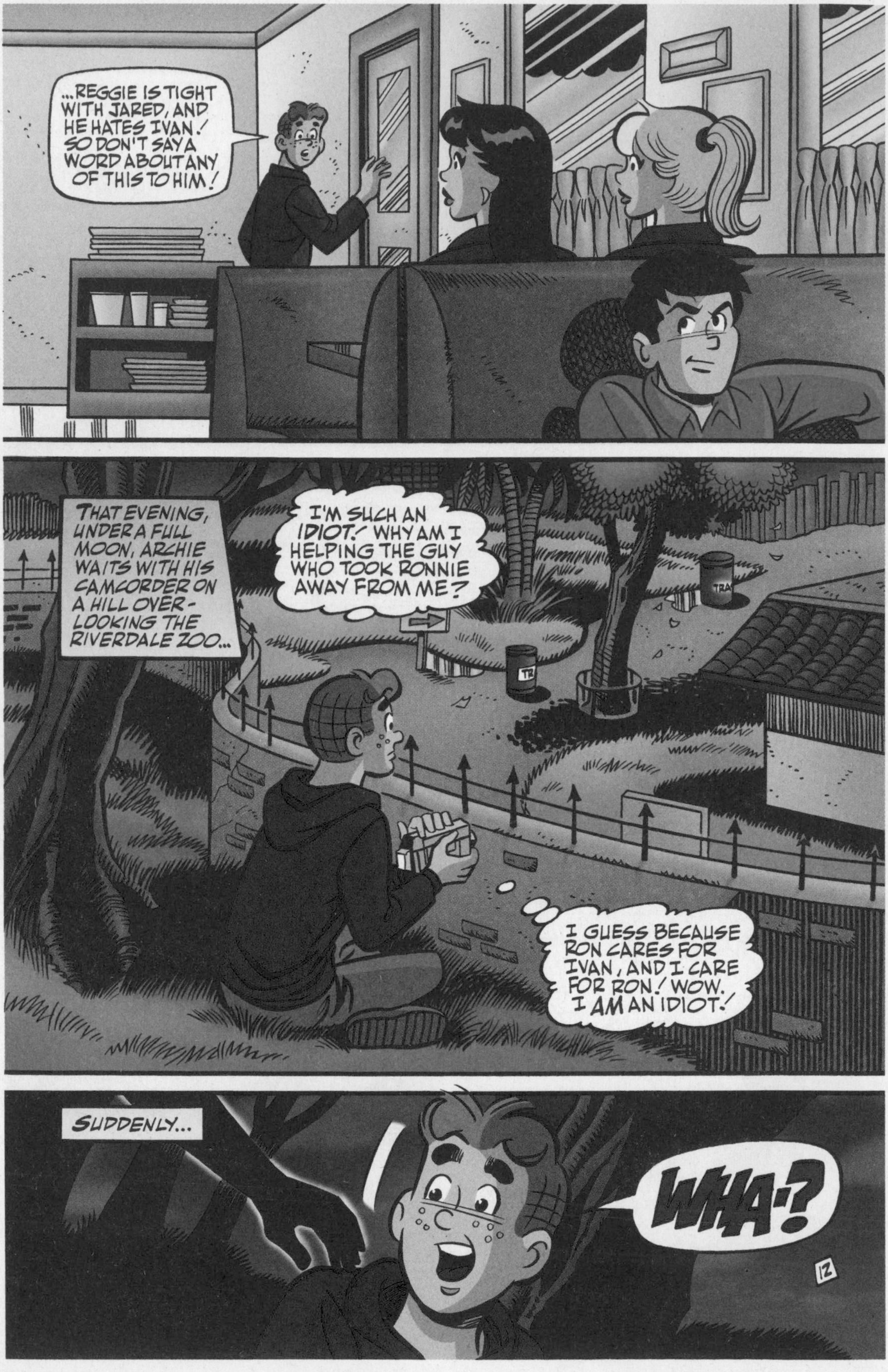
...REGGIE IS TIGHT WITH JARED, AND HE HATES IVAN! SO DON'T SAY A WORD ABOUT ANY OF THIS TO HIM!
THAT EVENING, UNDER A FULL MOON, ARCHIE WAITS WITH HIS CAMCORDER ON A HILL OVER-LOOKING THE RIVERDALE ZOO...
I'M SUCH AN IDIOT! WHY AM I HELPING THE GUY WHO TOOK RONNIE AWAY FROM ME?
I GUESS BECAUSE RON CARES FOR IVAN, AND I CARE FOR RON! WOW. I AM AN IDIOT!
SUDDENLY...
WHA-?
12

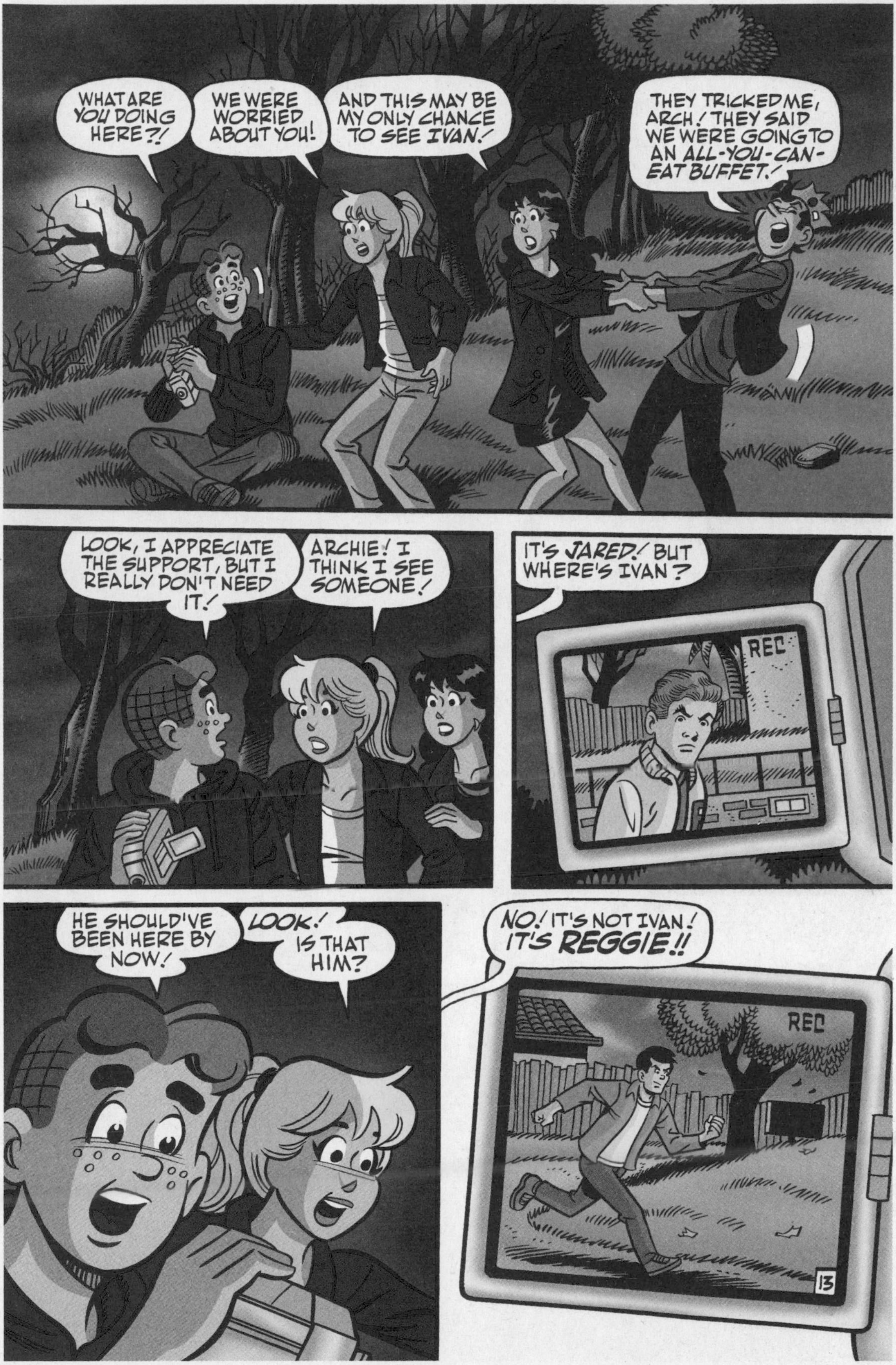
WHAT ARE YOU DOING HERE?!
WE WERE WORRIED ABOUT YOU!
AND THIS MAY BE MY ONLY CHANCE TO SEE IVAN!
THEY TRICKED ME, ARCH! THEY SAID WE WERE GOING TO AN ALL-YOU-CAN-EAT BUFFET!
LOOK, I APPRECIATE THE SUPPORT, BUT I REALLY DON'T NEED IT!
ARCHIE! I THINK I SEE SOMEONE!
IT'S JARED! BUT WHERE'S IVAN?
REC
HE SHOULD'VE BEEN HERE BY NOW!
LOOK! IS THAT HIM?
NO! IT'S NOT IVAN! IT'S REGGIE!!
REC
13

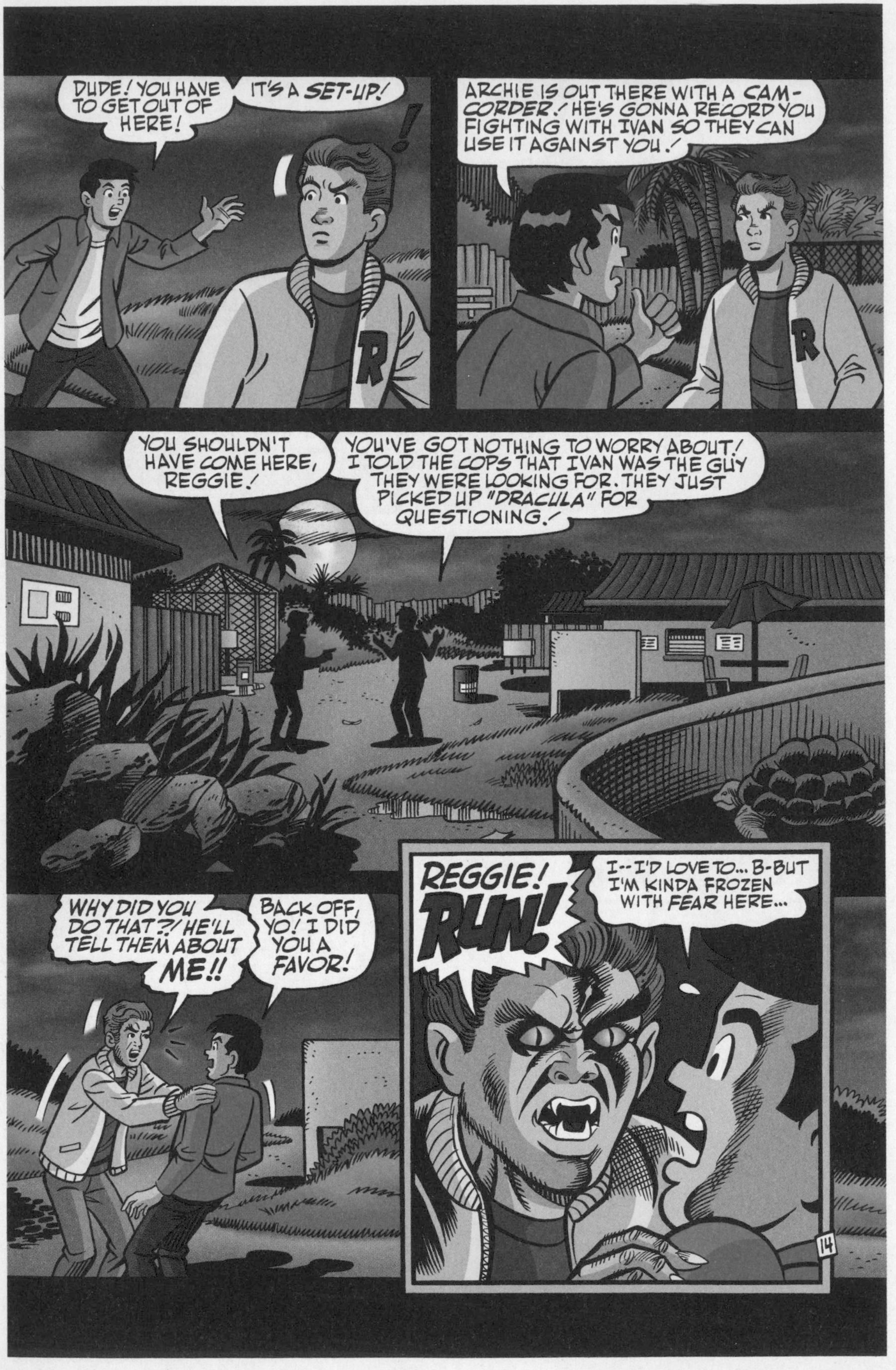
DUDE! YOU HAVE TO GET OUT OF HERE!
IT'S A SET-UP!
ARCHIE IS OUT THERE WITH A CAM-CORDER! HE'S GONNA RECORD YOU FIGHTING WITH IVAN SO THEY CAN USE IT AGAINST YOU!
YOU SHOULDN'T HAVE COME HERE, REGGIE!
YOU'VE GOT NOTHING TO WORRY ABOUT! I TOLD THE COPS THAT IVAN WAS THE GUY THEY WERE LOOKING FOR. THEY JUST PICKED UP "DRACULA" FOR QUESTIONING!
WHY DID YOU DO THAT?! HE'LL TELL THEM ABOUT ME!!
BACK OFF, YO! I DID YOU A FAVOR!
REGGIE! RUN!
I--I'D LOVE TO... B-BUT I'M KINDA FROZEN WITH FEAR HERE...
14

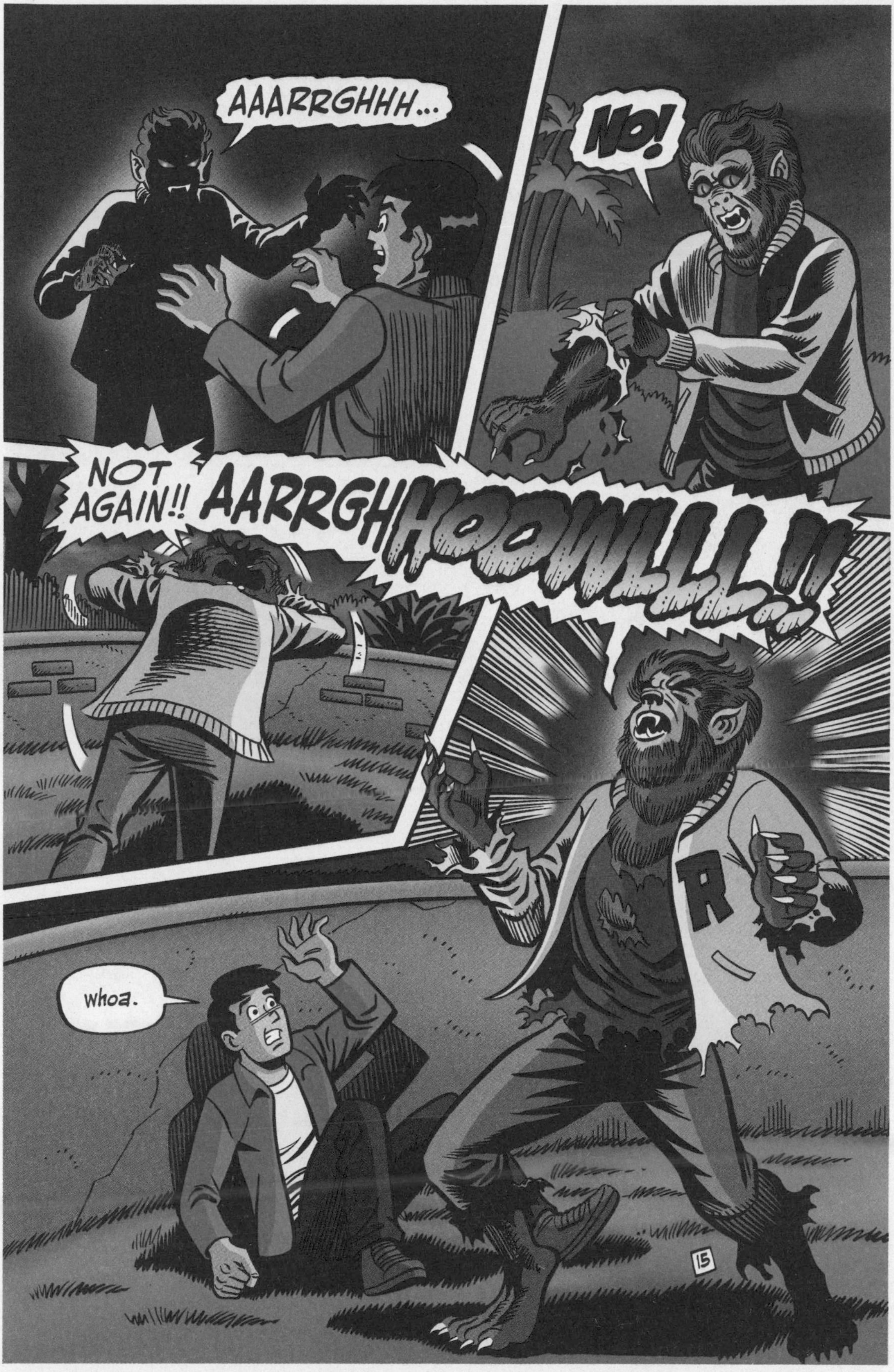
AAARRGHHH...
NO!
NOT AGAIN!! AARRGHHOOWLLL!!
whoa.
15

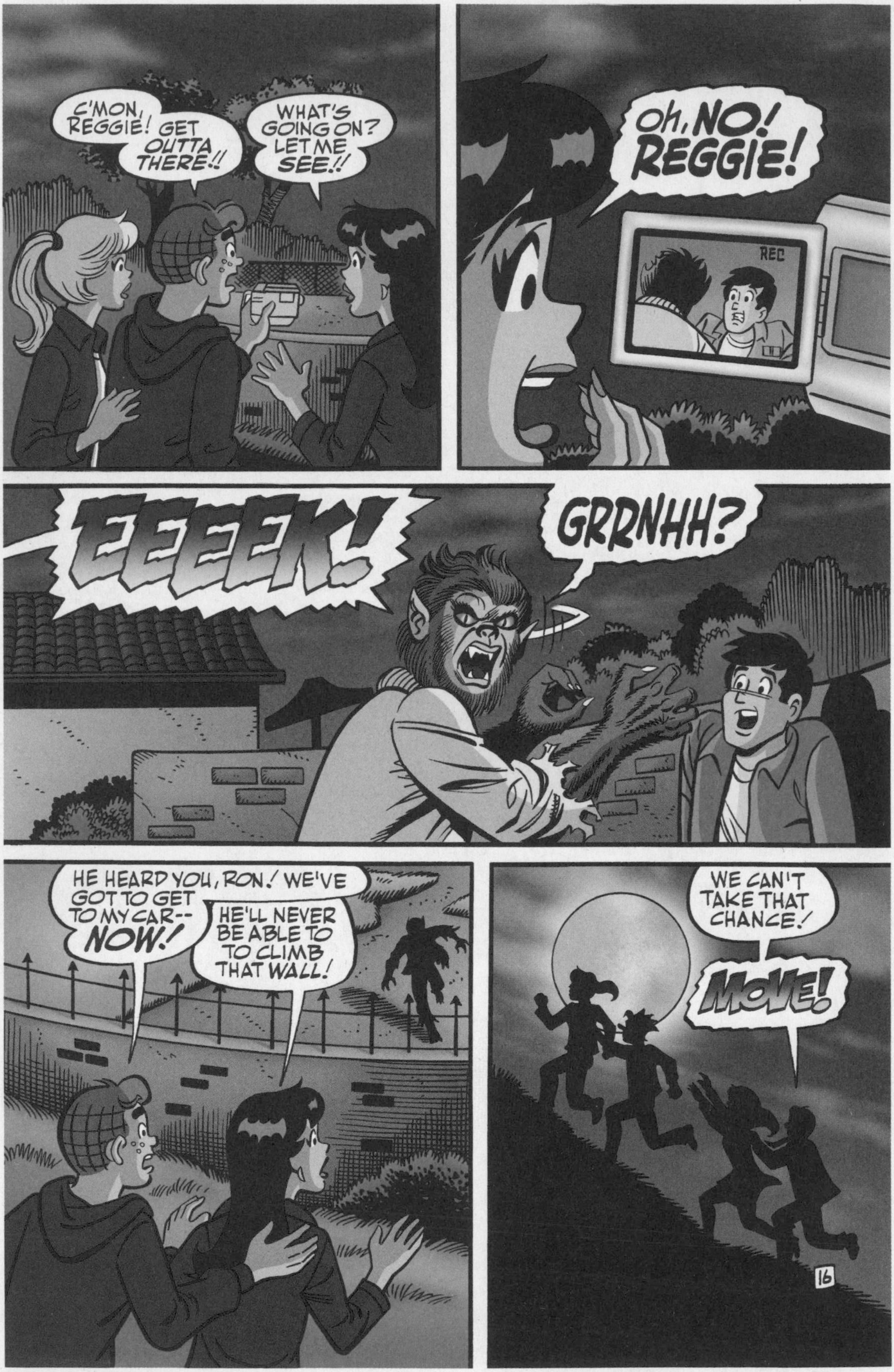
C'MON, REGGIE! GET OUTTA THERE!!
WHAT'S GOING ON? LET ME SEE!!
Oh, NO! REGGIE!
REC
EEEEK!
GRRNHH?
HE HEARD YOU, RON! WE'VE GOT TO GET TO MY CAR-- NOW!
HE'LL NEVER BE ABLE TO TO CLIMB THAT WALL!
WE CAN'T TAKE THAT CHANCE!
MOVE!
16

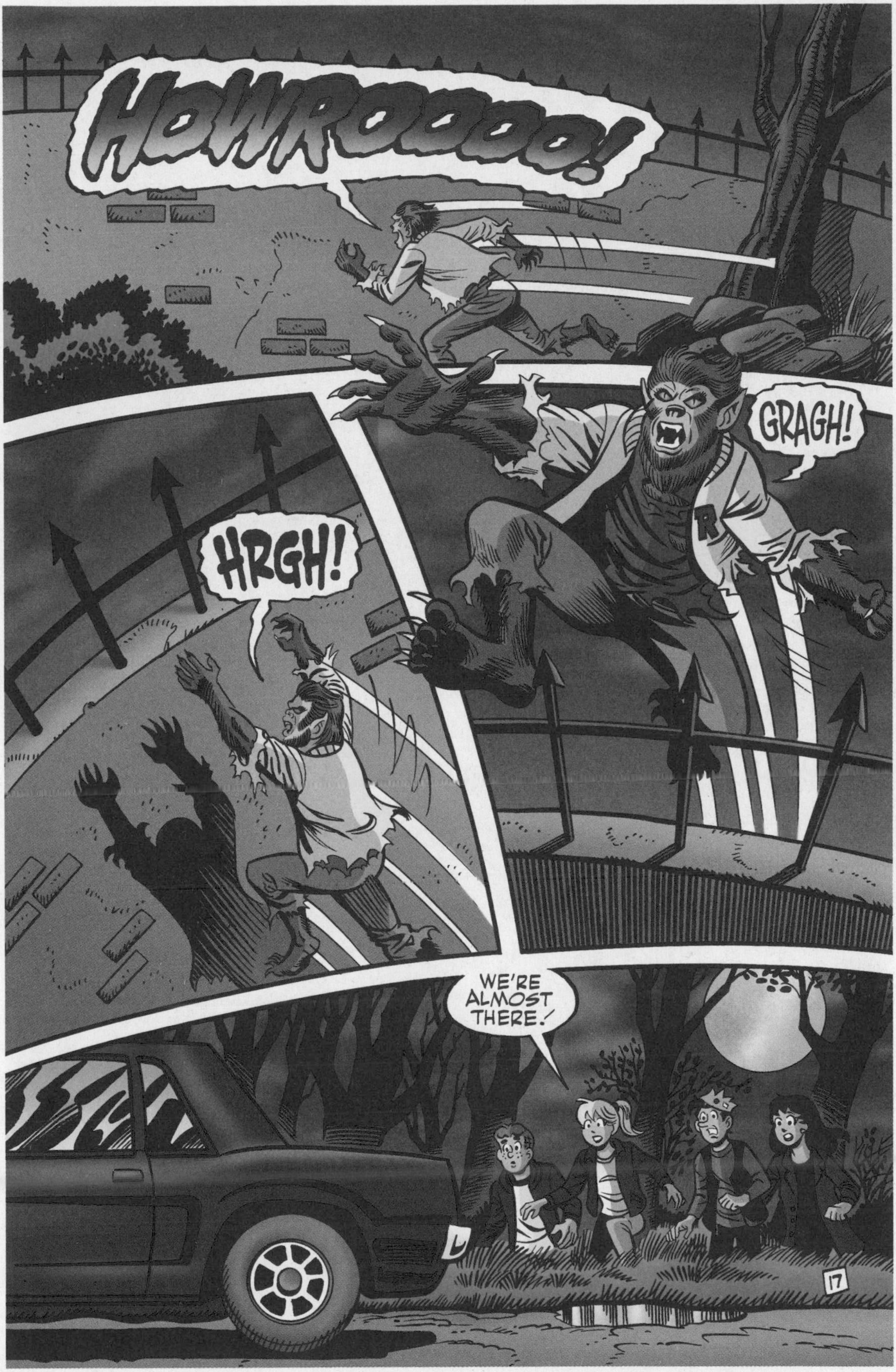
HOWROOOOO!
GRAGH!
HRGH!
WE'RE ALMOST THERE!
17

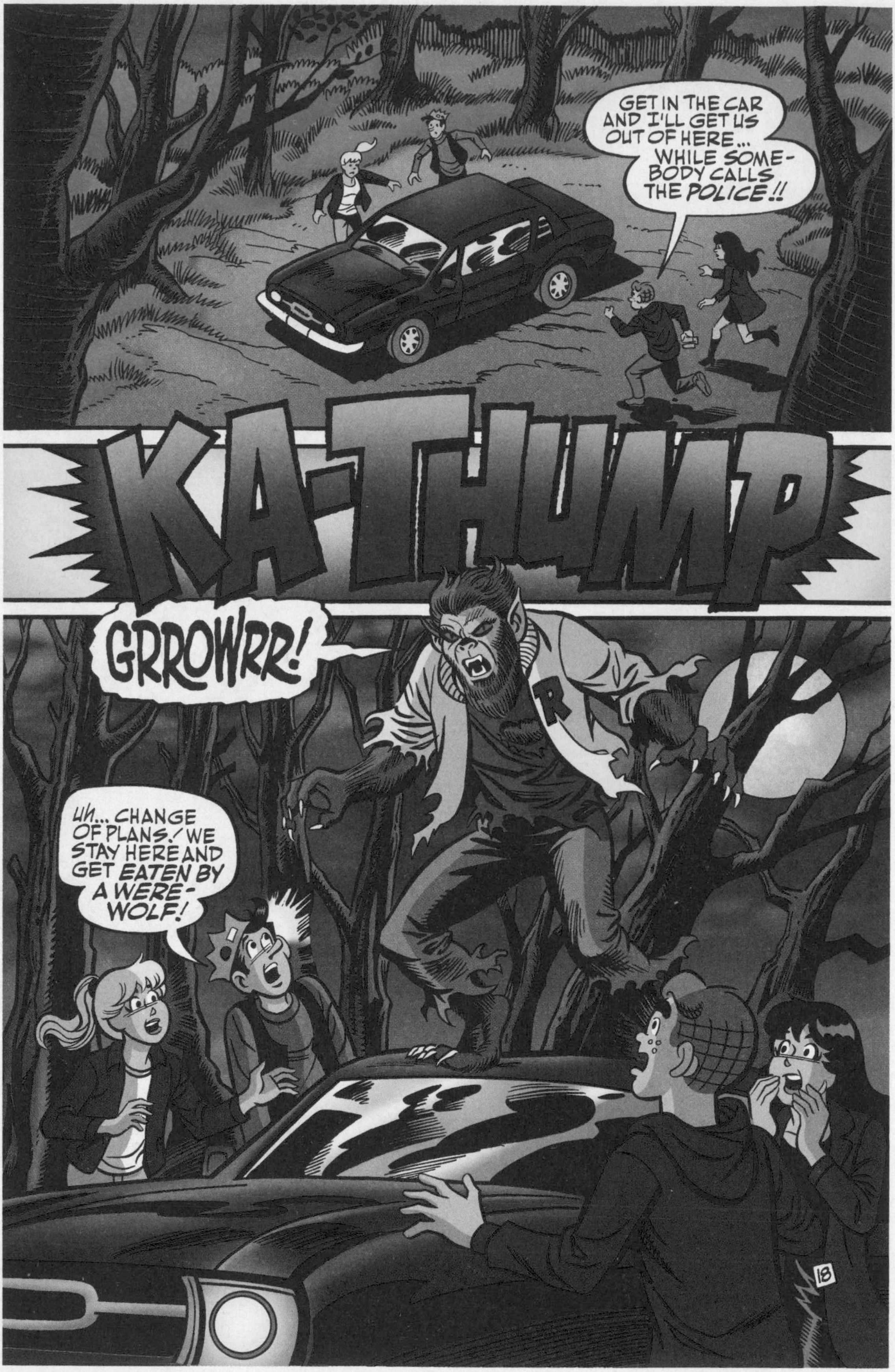
GET IN THE CAR AND I'LL GET US OUT OF HERE... WHILE SOMEBODY CALLS THE POLICE!!
KA-THUMP
GRROWRR!
UH... CHANGE OF PLANS! WE STAY HERE AND GET EATEN BY A WEREWOLF!

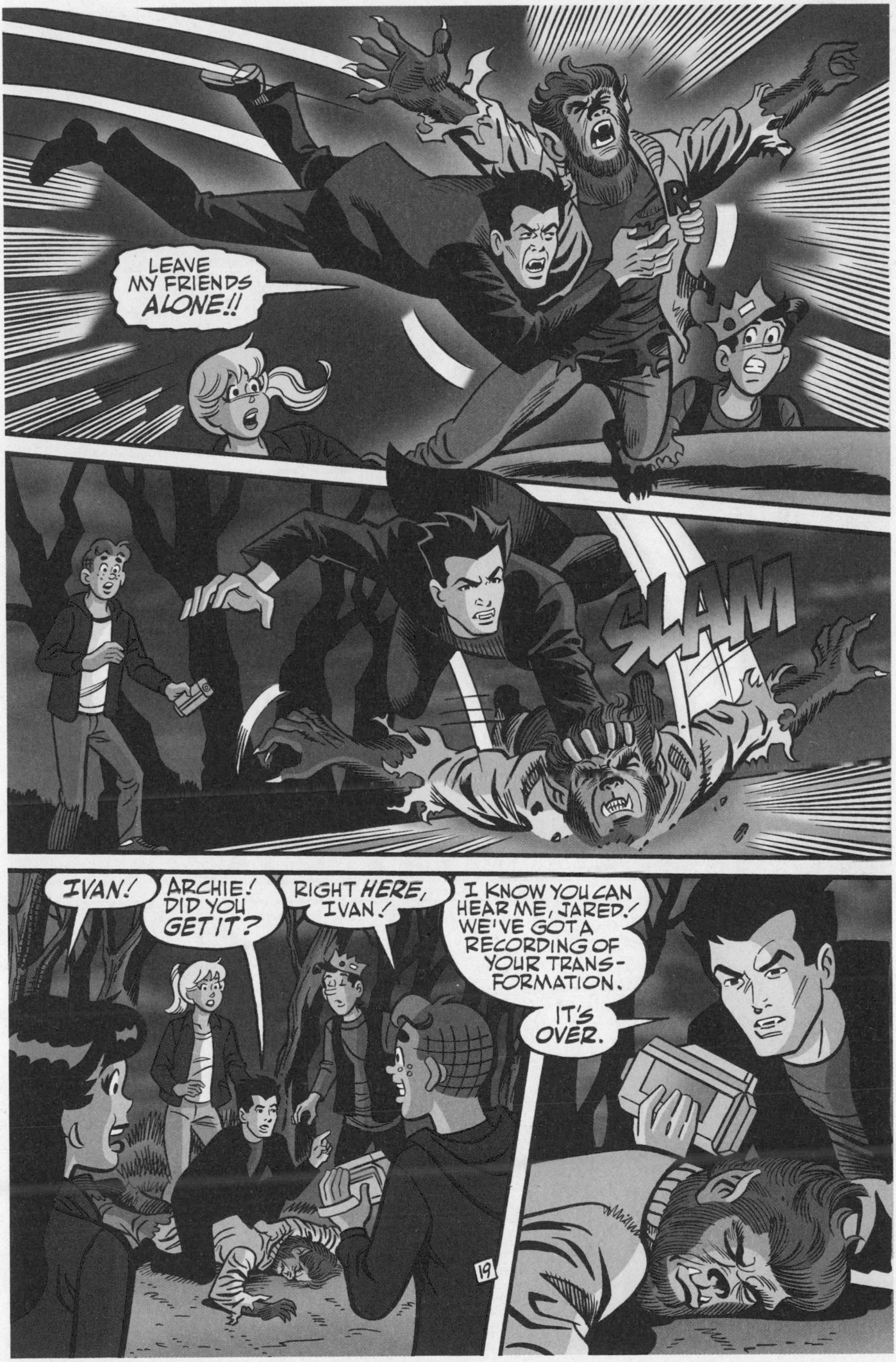
LEAVE MY FRIENDS ALONE!!
SLAM
IVAN!
ARCHIE! DID YOU GET IT?
RIGHT HERE, IVAN!
I KNOW YOU CAN HEAR ME, JARED! WE'VE GOT A RECORDING OF YOUR TRANS-FORMATION.
IT'S OVER.
19

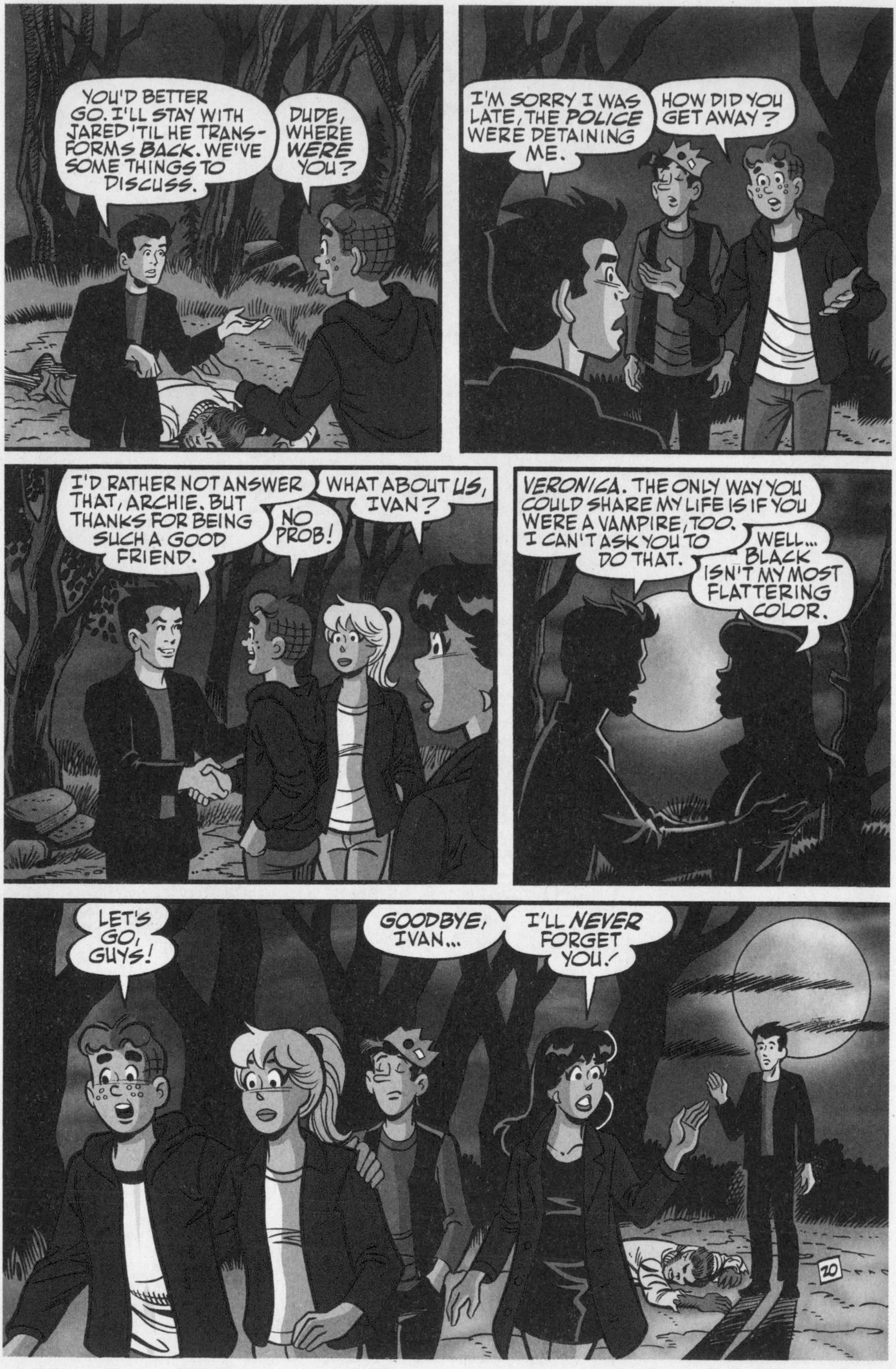
YOU'D BETTER GO. I'LL STAY WITH JARED 'TIL HE TRANS-FORMS BACK. WE'VE SOME THINGS TO DISCUSS.
DUDE, WHERE WERE YOU?
I'M SORRY I WAS LATE, THE POLICE WERE DETAINING ME.
HOW DID YOU GET AWAY?
I'D RATHER NOT ANSWER THAT, ARCHIE. BUT THANKS FOR BEING SUCH A GOOD FRIEND.
NO PROB!
WHAT ABOUT US, IVAN?
VERONICA. THE ONLY WAY YOU COULD SHARE MY LIFE IS IF YOU WERE A VAMPIRE, TOO. I CAN'T ASK YOU TO DO THAT.
WELL... BLACK ISN'T MY MOST FLATTERING COLOR.
LET'S GO, GUYS!
GOODBYE, IVAN...
I'LL NEVER FORGET YOU!
20

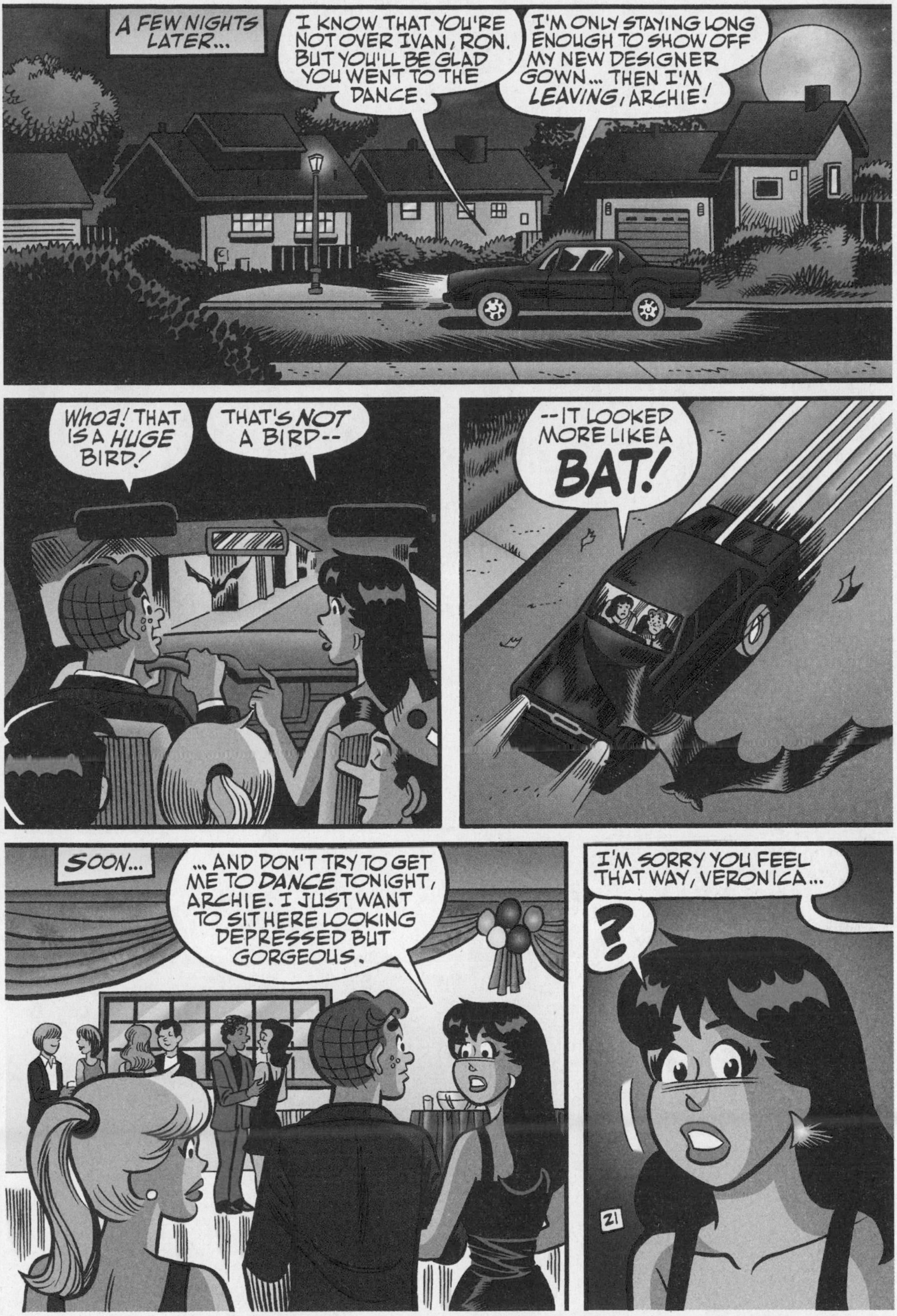
A FEW NIGHTS LATER...
I KNOW THAT YOU'RE NOT OVER IVAN, RON. BUT YOU'LL BE GLAD YOU WENT TO THE DANCE.
I'M ONLY STAYING LONG ENOUGH TO SHOW OFF MY NEW DESIGNER GOWN... THEN I'M LEAVING, ARCHIE!
Whoa! THAT IS A HUGE BIRD!
THAT'S NOT A BIRD--
--IT LOOKED MORE LIKE A BAT!
SOON...
... AND DON'T TRY TO GET ME TO DANCE TONIGHT, ARCHIE. I JUST WANT TO SIT HERE LOOKING DEPRESSED BUT GORGEOUS.
I'M SORRY YOU FEEL THAT WAY, VERONICA...
?
21

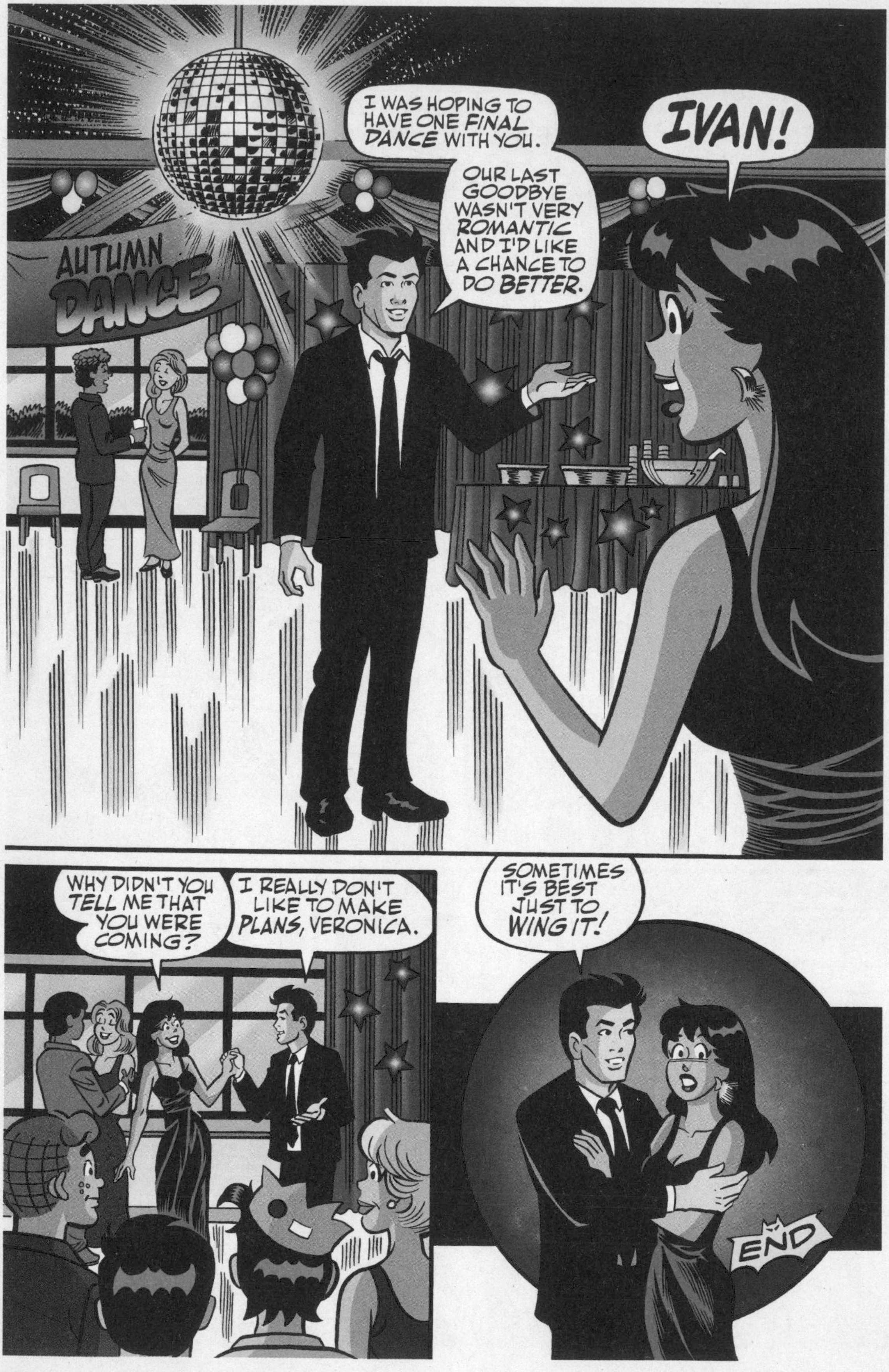
AUTUMN DANCE
I WAS HOPING TO HAVE ONE FINAL DANCE WITH YOU.
OUR LAST GOODBYE WASN'T VERY ROMANTIC AND I'D LIKE A CHANCE TO DO BETTER.
IVAN!
WHY DIDN'T YOU TELL ME THAT YOU WERE COMING?
I REALLY DON'T LIKE TO MAKE PLANS, VERONICA.
SOMETIMES IT'S BEST JUST TO WING IT!
END

CHAPTER FOUR

Mighty Archie Art Players

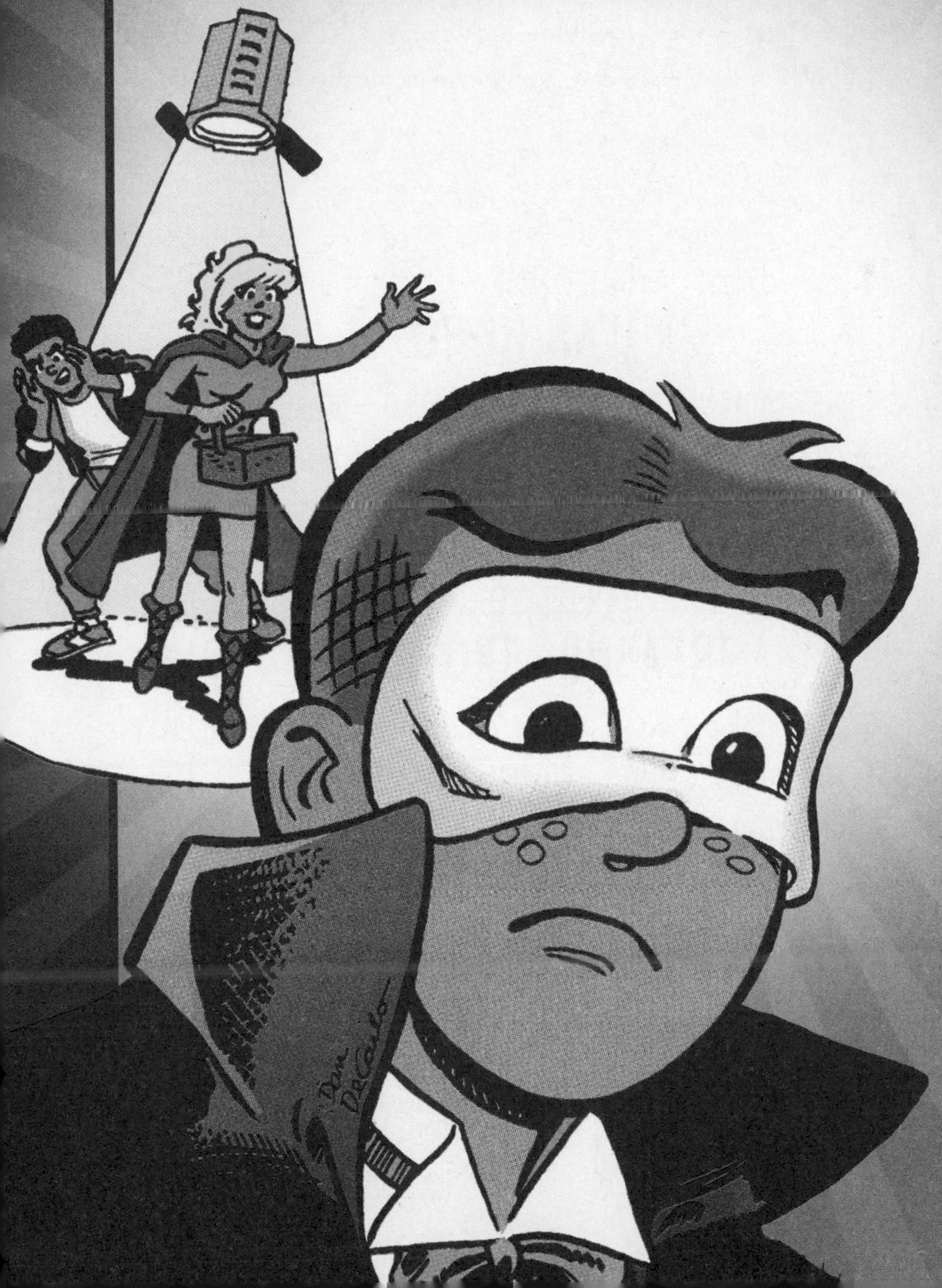

INTRODUCING MIGHTY ARCHIE ART PLAYERS

Originally printed in *Laugh* #7-#21

The Mighty Archie Art Players stories were a mainstay of several Archie titles throughout the years. Each story was a play put on by Archie and his friends, with all the characters taking on roles to tell tales set in various times and places. In the next three stories, you'll see Archie and the Gang go medieval, battle rowdy pirates and put their own spin on an iconic drama!

PART ONE
SIR IVAN HOHO

SCRIPT: GEORGE GLADIR **PENCILS: STAN GOLDBERG** **INKS: RUDY LAPICK**
LETTERS: BILL YOSHIDA **COLORS: BARRY GROSSMAN**

PART TWO
TREASURE TROVE

SCRIPT: GEORGE GLADIR **PENCILS: BOB BOLLING** **INKS: RICH KOSLOWSKI**
LETTERS: BILL YOSHIDA **COLORS: BARRY GROSSMAN**

PART THREE
PHANTOM OF THE BOPERA

SCRIPT: GEORGE GLADIR **PENCILS: STAN GOLDBERG** **INKS: RUDY LAPICK**
LETTERS: BILL YOSHIDA **COLORS: BARRY GROSSMAN**

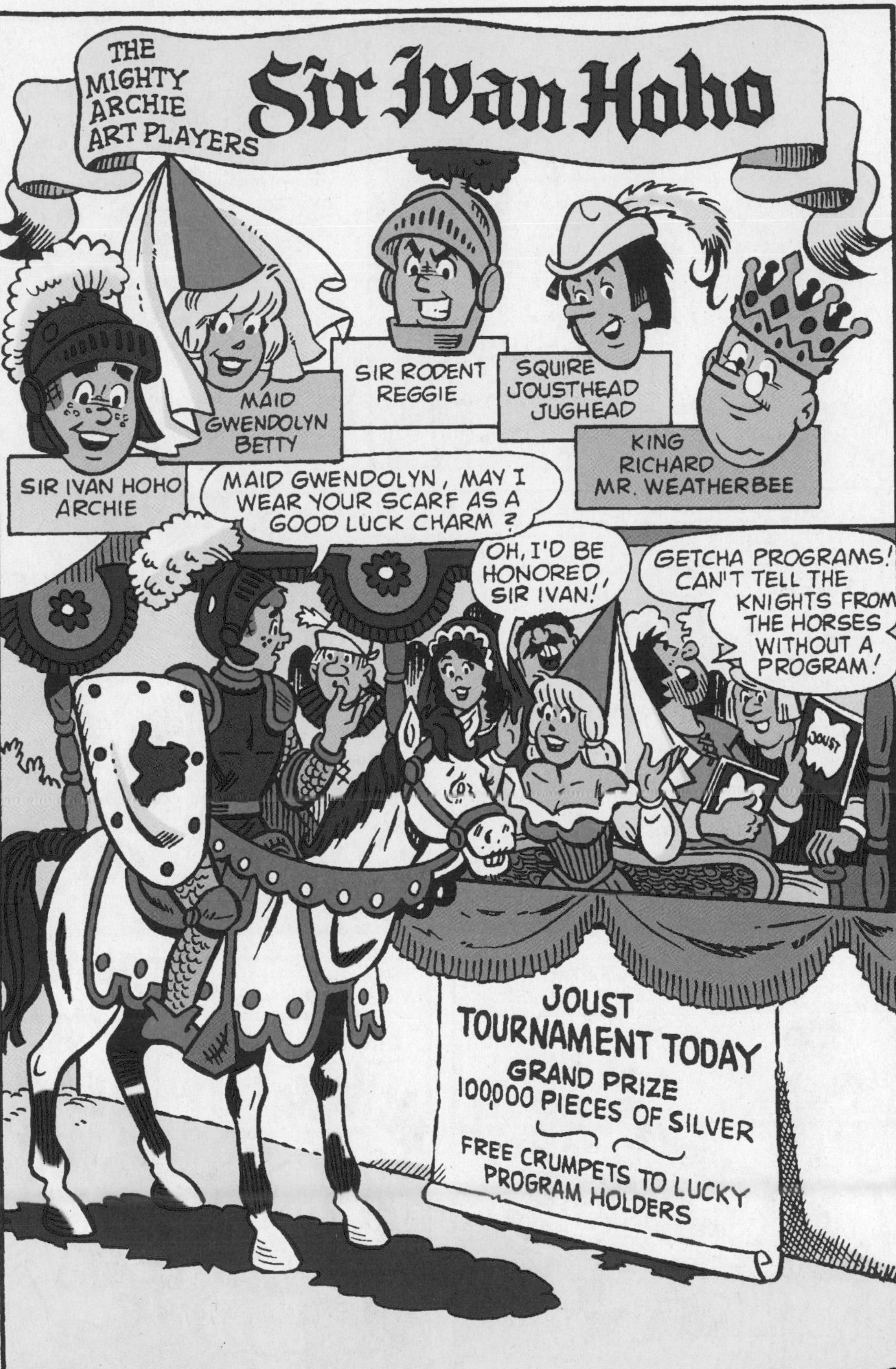
THE MIGHTY ARCHIE ART PLAYERS
Sir Ivan Hoho
SIR IVAN HOHO ARCHIE
MAID GWENDOLYN BETTY
SIR RODENT REGGIE
SQUIRE JOUSTHEAD JUGHEAD
KING RICHARD MR. WEATHERBEE
MAID GWENDOLYN, MAY I WEAR YOUR SCARF AS A GOOD LUCK CHARM?
OH, I'D BE HONORED, SIR IVAN!
GETCHA PROGRAMS! CAN'T TELL THE KNIGHTS FROM THE HORSES WITHOUT A PROGRAM!
JOUST
JOUST TOURNAMENT TODAY
GRAND PRIZE
100,000 PIECES OF SILVER
FREE CRUMPETS TO LUCKY PROGRAM HOLDERS
1

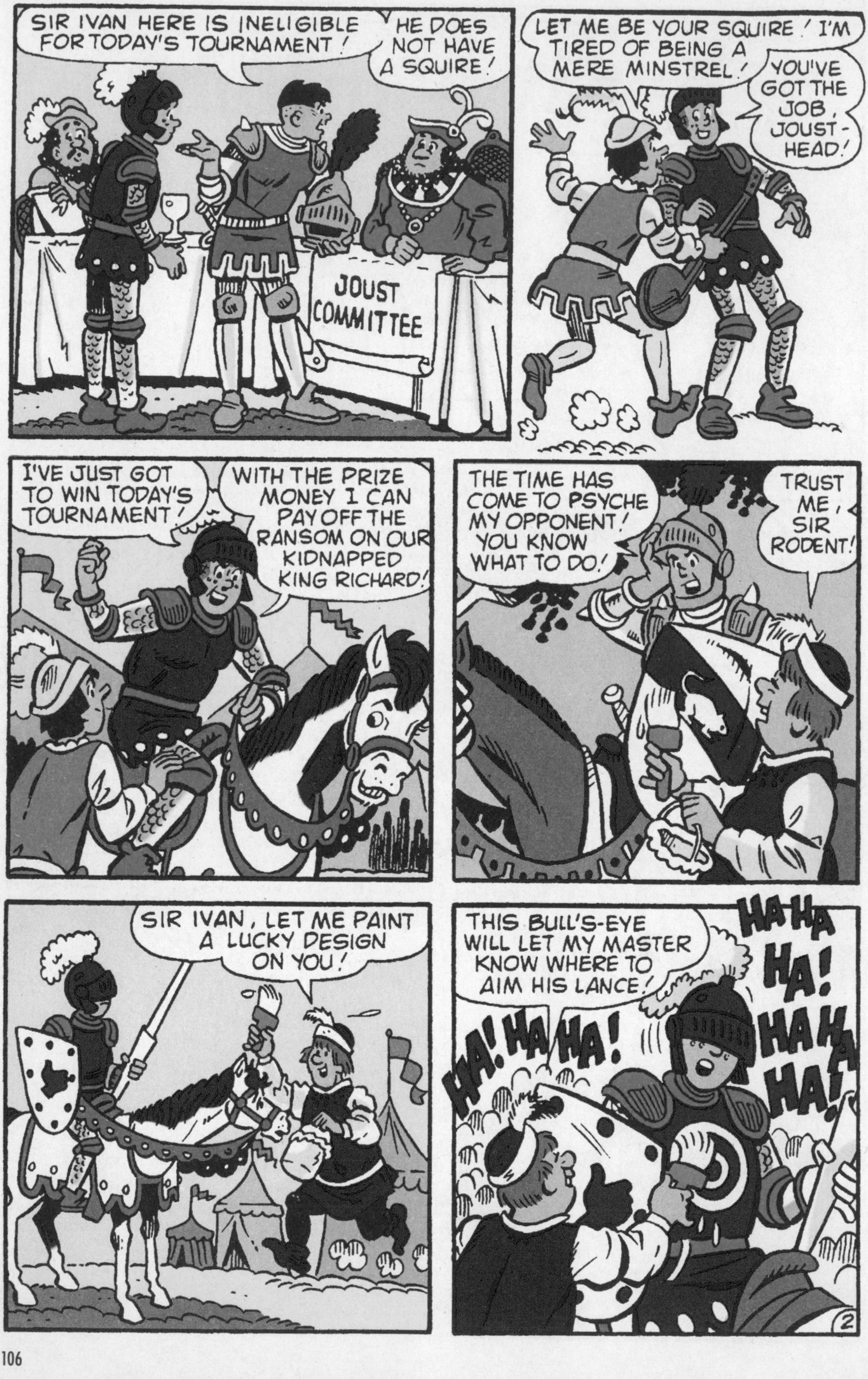
SIR IVAN HERE IS INELIGIBLE FOR TODAY'S TOURNAMENT!
HE DOES NOT HAVE A SQUIRE!
JOUST COMMITTEE
LET ME BE YOUR SQUIRE! I'M TIRED OF BEING A MERE MINSTREL!
YOU'VE GOT THE JOB, JOUST-HEAD!
I'VE JUST GOT TO WIN TODAY'S TOURNAMENT!
WITH THE PRIZE MONEY I CAN PAY OFF THE RANSOM ON OUR KIDNAPPED KING RICHARD!
THE TIME HAS COME TO PSYCHE MY OPPONENT! YOU KNOW WHAT TO DO!
TRUST ME, SIR RODENT!
SIR IVAN, LET ME PAINT A LUCKY DESIGN ON YOU!
THIS BULL'S-EYE WILL LET MY MASTER KNOW WHERE TO AIM HIS LANCE!
HA HA HA! HA HA HA!
HA! HA HA HA!
2

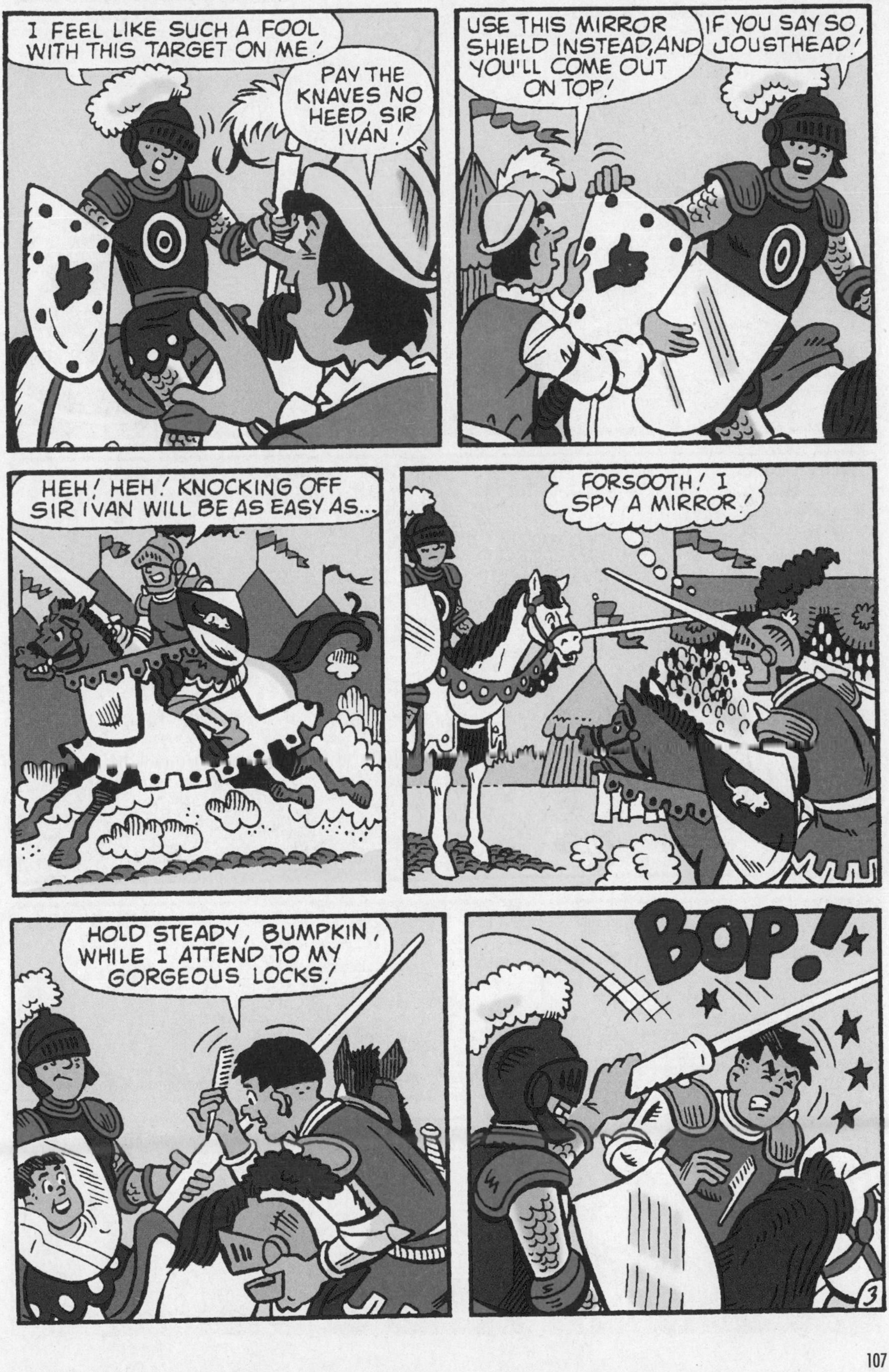
I FEEL LIKE SUCH A FOOL WITH THIS TARGET ON ME!
PAY THE KNAVES NO HEED, SIR IVÁN!
USE THIS MIRROR SHIELD INSTEAD, AND YOU'LL COME OUT ON TOP!
IF YOU SAY SO, JOUSTHEAD!
HEH! HEH! KNOCKING OFF SIR IVAN WILL BE AS EASY AS...
FORSOOTH! I SPY A MIRROR!
HOLD STEADY, BUMPKIN, WHILE I ATTEND TO MY GORGEOUS LOCKS!
BOP!
3

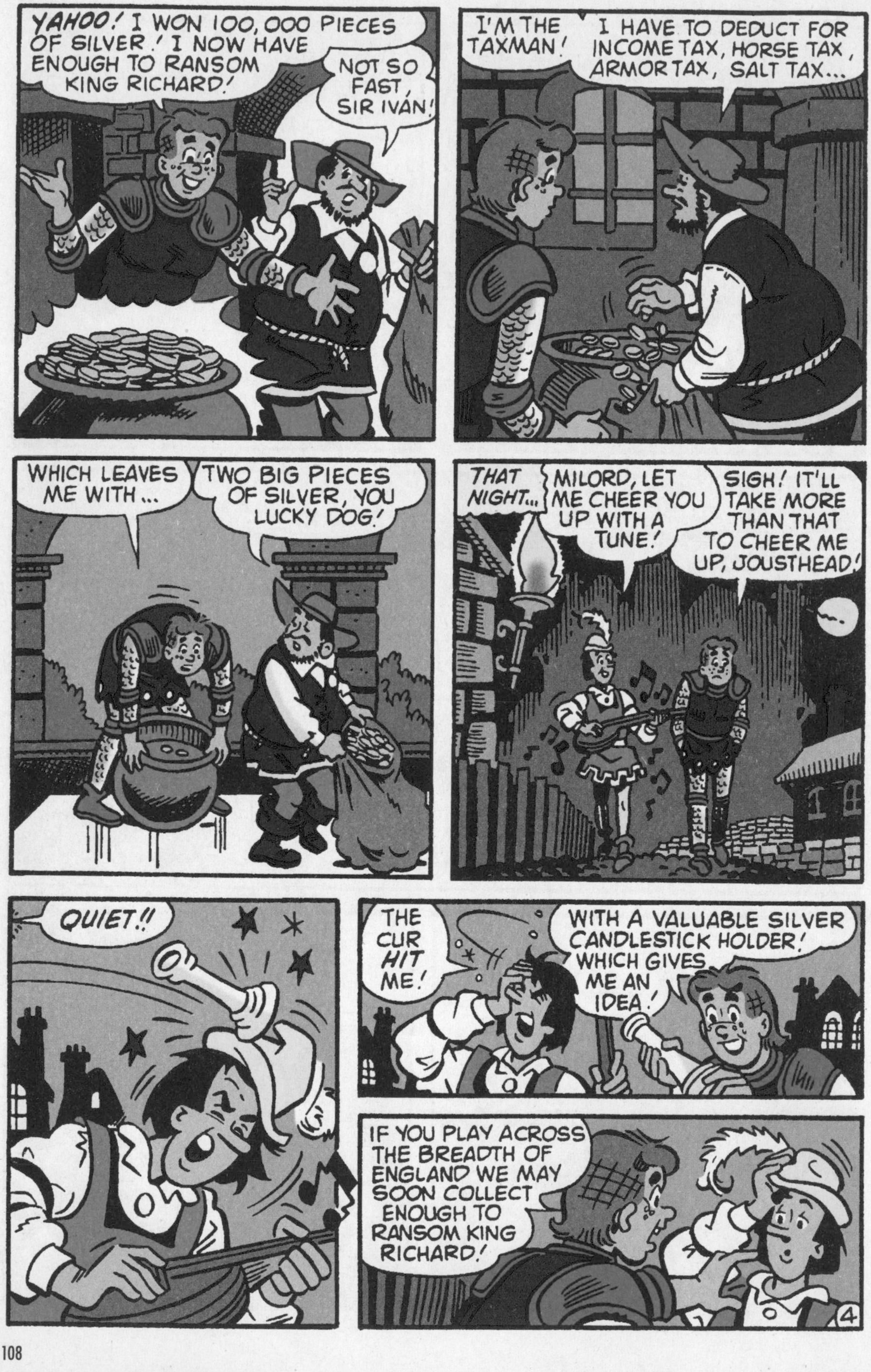
YAHOO! I WON 100,000 PIECES OF SILVER! I NOW HAVE ENOUGH TO RANSOM KING RICHARD!
NOT SO FAST, SIR IVÁN!
I'M THE TAXMAN!
I HAVE TO DEDUCT FOR INCOME TAX, HORSE TAX, ARMOR TAX, SALT TAX...
WHICH LEAVES ME WITH ...
TWO BIG PIECES OF SILVER, YOU LUCKY DOG!
THAT NIGHT...
MILORD, LET ME CHEER YOU UP WITH A TUNE!
SIGH! IT'LL TAKE MORE THAN THAT TO CHEER ME UP, JOUSTHEAD!
QUIET!!
THE CUR HIT ME!
WITH A VALUABLE SILVER CANDLESTICK HOLDER! WHICH GIVES ME AN IDEA!
IF YOU PLAY ACROSS THE BREADTH OF ENGLAND WE MAY SOON COLLECT ENOUGH TO RANSOM KING RICHARD!
4

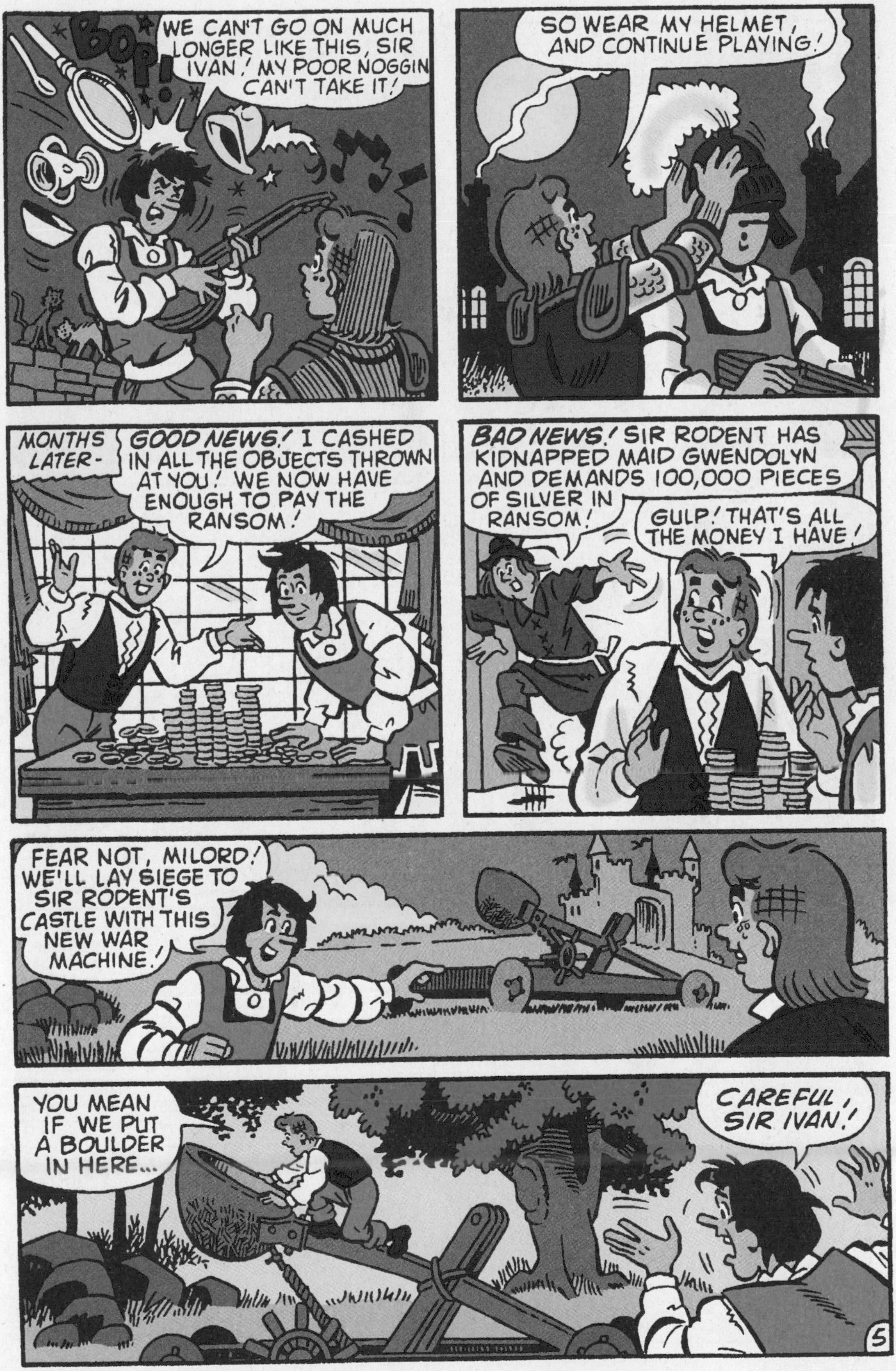
BOP!
WE CAN'T GO ON MUCH LONGER LIKE THIS, SIR IVAN! MY POOR NOGGIN CAN'T TAKE IT!
SO WEAR MY HELMET, AND CONTINUE PLAYING!
MONTHS LATER-
GOOD NEWS! I CASHED IN ALL THE OBJECTS THROWN AT YOU! WE NOW HAVE ENOUGH TO PAY THE RANSOM!
BAD NEWS! SIR RODENT HAS KIDNAPPED MAID GWENDOLYN AND DEMANDS 100,000 PIECES OF SILVER IN RANSOM!
GULP! THAT'S ALL THE MONEY I HAVE!
FEAR NOT, MILORD! WE'LL LAY SIEGE TO SIR RODENT'S CASTLE WITH THIS NEW WAR MACHINE!
YOU MEAN IF WE PUT A BOULDER IN HERE...
CAREFUL, SIR IVAN!
5

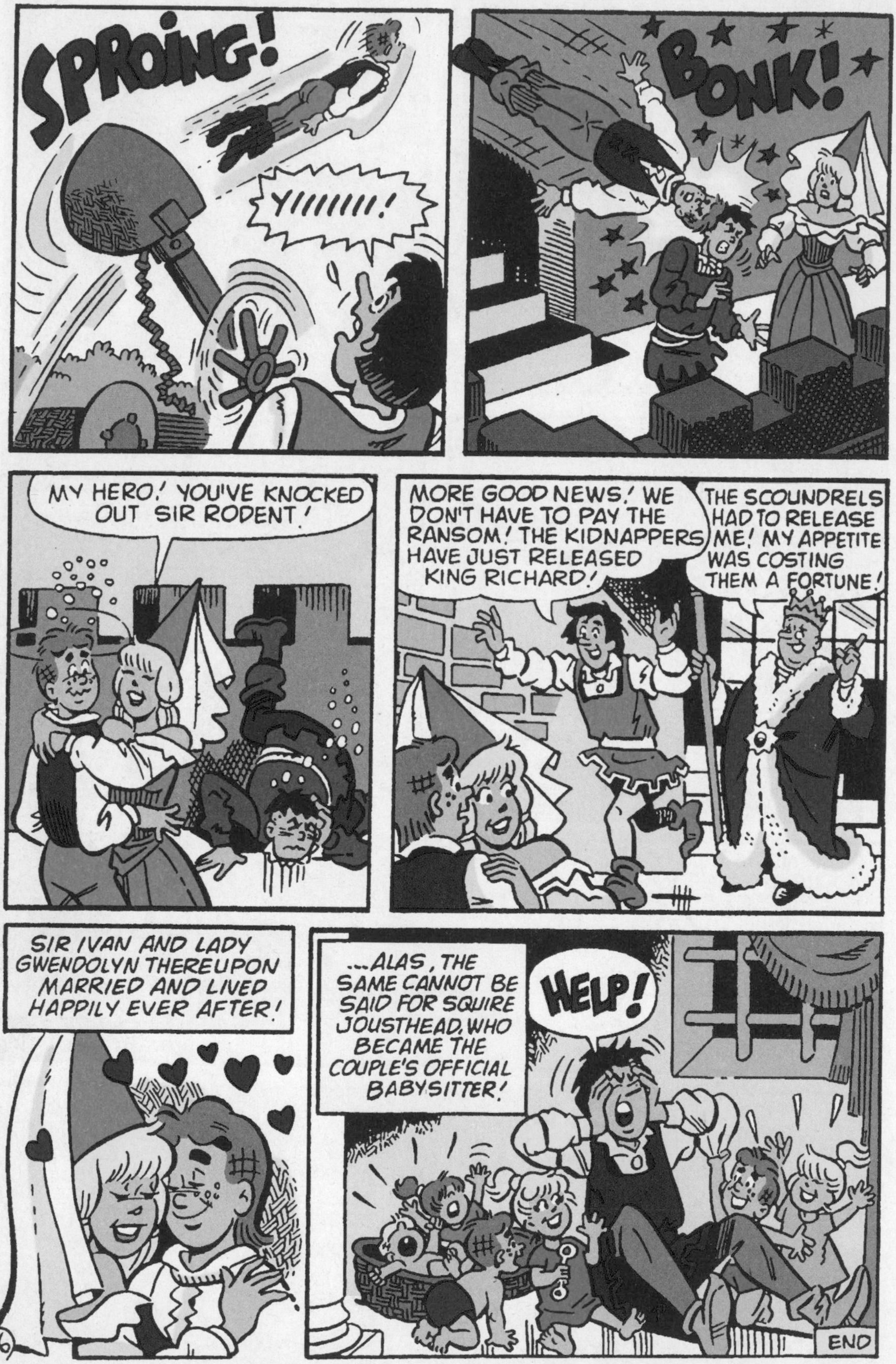
SPROING!
Y!!!!!!!!
BONK!
MY HERO! YOU'VE KNOCKED OUT SIR RODENT!
MORE GOOD NEWS! WE DON'T HAVE TO PAY THE RANSOM! THE KIDNAPPERS HAVE JUST RELEASED KING RICHARD!
THE SCOUNDRELS HAD TO RELEASE ME! MY APPETITE WAS COSTING THEM A FORTUNE!
SIR IVAN AND LADY GWENDOLYN THEREUPON MARRIED AND LIVED HAPPILY EVER AFTER!
...ALAS, THE SAME CANNOT BE SAID FOR SQUIRE JOUSTHEAD, WHO BECAME THE COUPLE'S OFFICIAL BABYSITTER!
HELP!
END

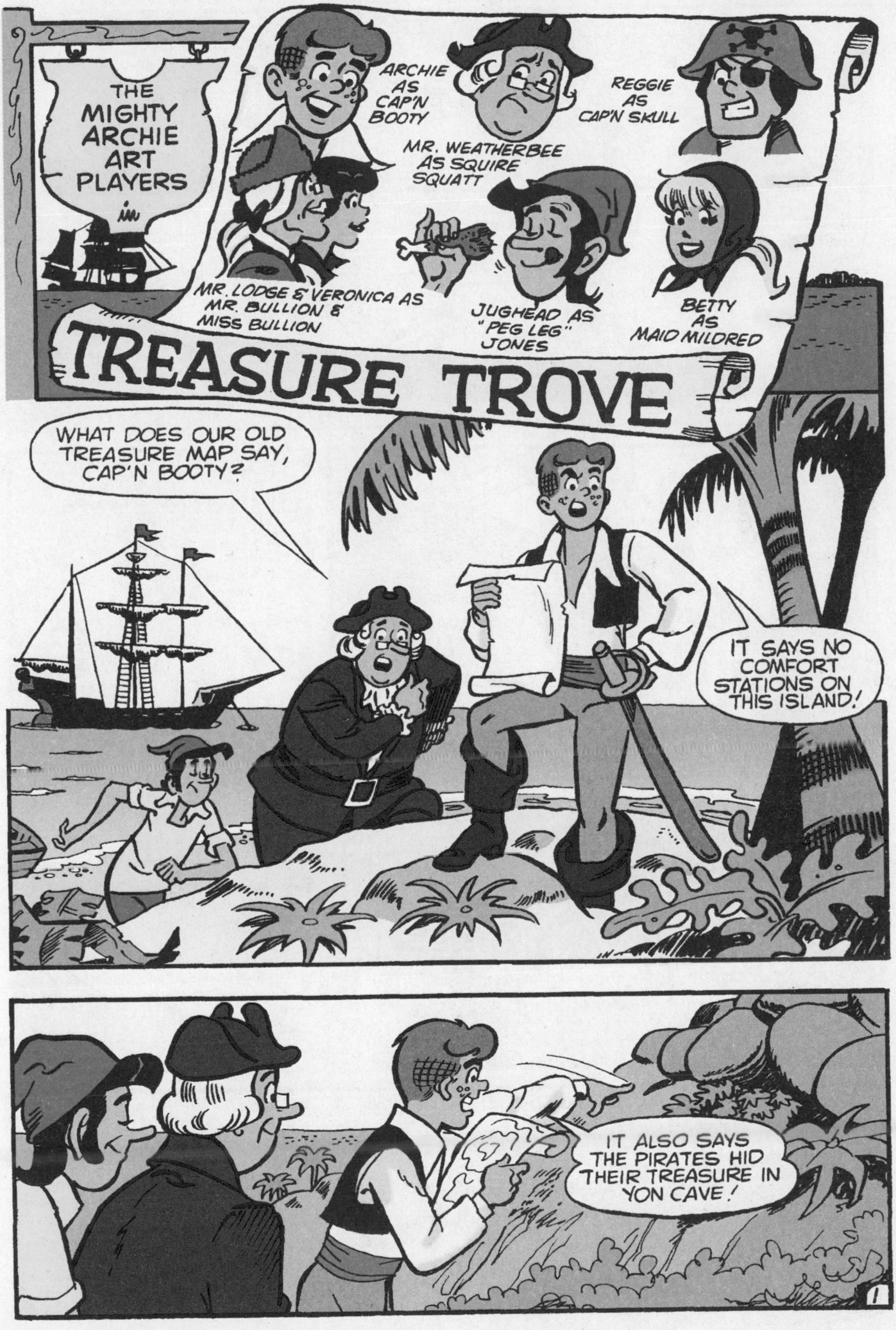
THE MIGHTY ARCHIE ART PLAYERS in
ARCHIE AS CAP'N BOOTY
MR. WEATHERBEE AS SQUIRE SQUATT
REGGIE AS CAP'N SKULL
MR. LODGE & VERONICA AS MR. BULLION & MISS BULLION
JUGHEAD AS "PEG LEG" JONES
BETTY AS MAID MILDRED
TREASURE TROVE
WHAT DOES OUR OLD TREASURE MAP SAY, CAP'N BOOTY?
IT SAYS NO COMFORT STATIONS ON THIS ISLAND!
IT ALSO SAYS THE PIRATES HID THEIR TREASURE IN YON CAVE!
1

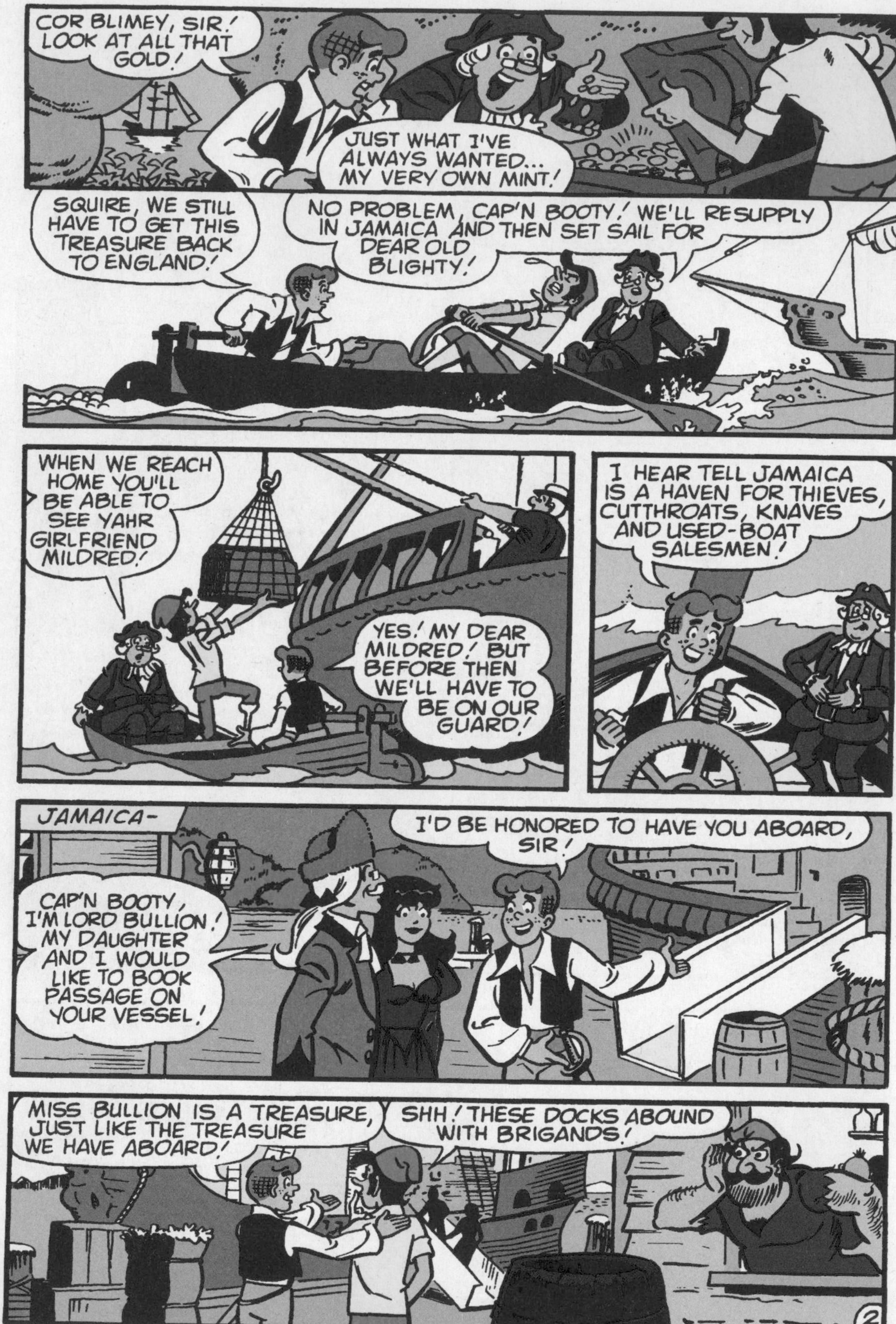
COR BLIMEY, SIR! LOOK AT ALL THAT GOLD!
JUST WHAT I'VE ALWAYS WANTED... MY VERY OWN MINT!
SQUIRE, WE STILL HAVE TO GET THIS TREASURE BACK TO ENGLAND!
NO PROBLEM, CAP'N BOOTY! WE'LL RESUPPLY IN JAMAICA AND THEN SET SAIL FOR DEAR OLD BLIGHTY!
WHEN WE REACH HOME YOU'LL BE ABLE TO SEE YAHR GIRLFRIEND MILDRED!
YES! MY DEAR MILDRED! BUT BEFORE THEN WE'LL HAVE TO BE ON OUR GUARD!
I HEAR TELL JAMAICA IS A HAVEN FOR THIEVES, CUTTHROATS, KNAVES AND USED-BOAT SALESMEN!
JAMAICA-
CAP'N BOOTY, I'M LORD BULLION! MY DAUGHTER AND I WOULD LIKE TO BOOK PASSAGE ON YOUR VESSEL!
I'D BE HONORED TO HAVE YOU ABOARD, SIR!
MISS BULLION IS A TREASURE, JUST LIKE THE TREASURE WE HAVE ABOARD!
SHH! THESE DOCKS ABOUND WITH BRIGANDS!
2

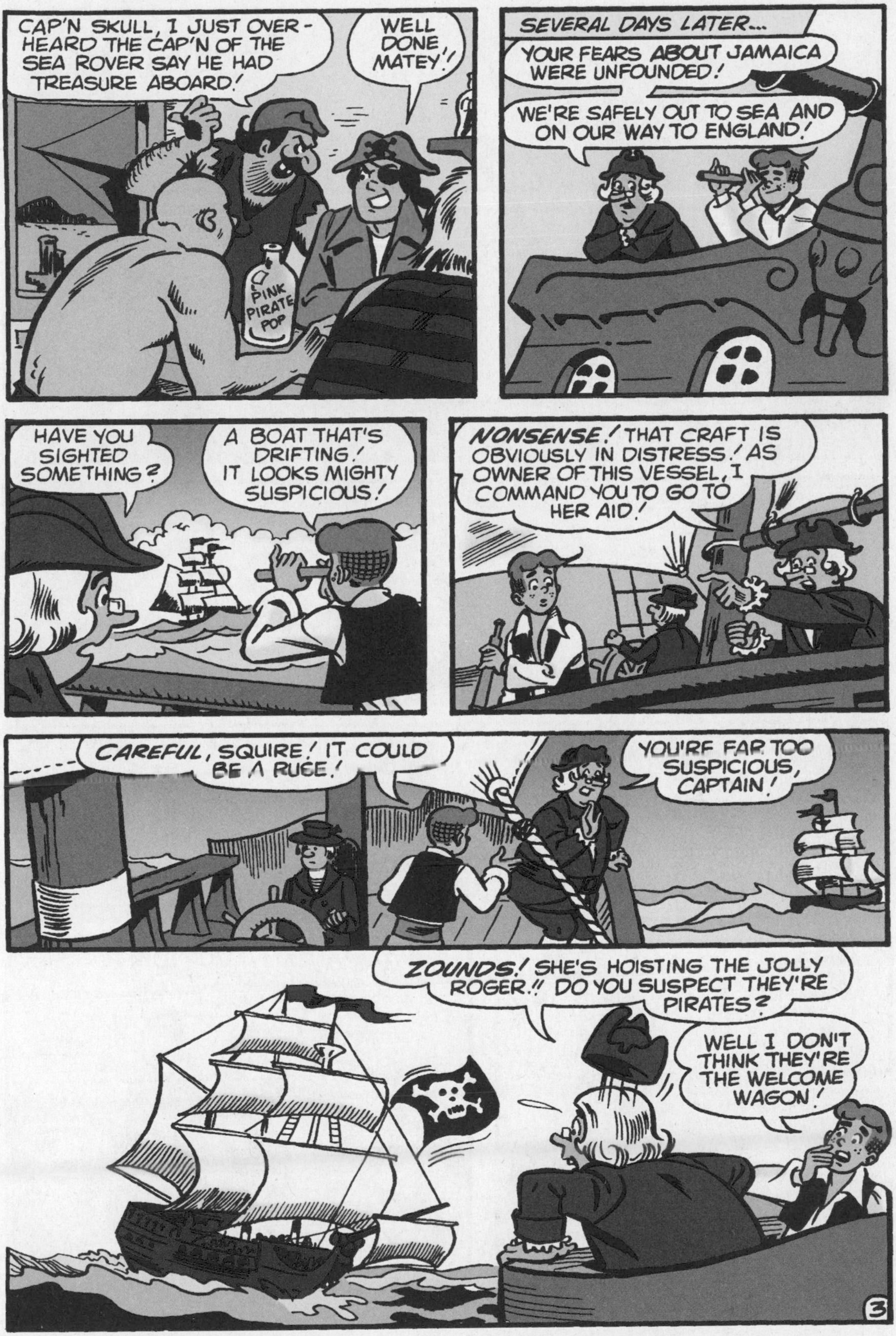
CAP'N SKULL, I JUST OVER-HEARD THE CAP'N OF THE SEA ROVER SAY HE HAD TREASURE ABOARD!
WELL DONE, MATEY!!
PINK PIRATE POP
SEVERAL DAYS LATER...
YOUR FEARS ABOUT JAMAICA WERE UNFOUNDED!
WE'RE SAFELY OUT TO SEA AND ON OUR WAY TO ENGLAND!
HAVE YOU SIGHTED SOMETHING?
A BOAT THAT'S DRIFTING! IT LOOKS MIGHTY SUSPICIOUS!
NONSENSE! THAT CRAFT IS OBVIOUSLY IN DISTRESS! AS OWNER OF THIS VESSEL, I COMMAND YOU TO GO TO HER AID!
CAREFUL, SQUIRE! IT COULD BE A RUSE!
YOU'RE FAR TOO SUSPICIOUS, CAPTAIN!
ZOUNDS! SHE'S HOISTING THE JOLLY ROGER!! DO YOU SUSPECT THEY'RE PIRATES?
WELL I DON'T THINK THEY'RE THE WELCOME WAGON!
3

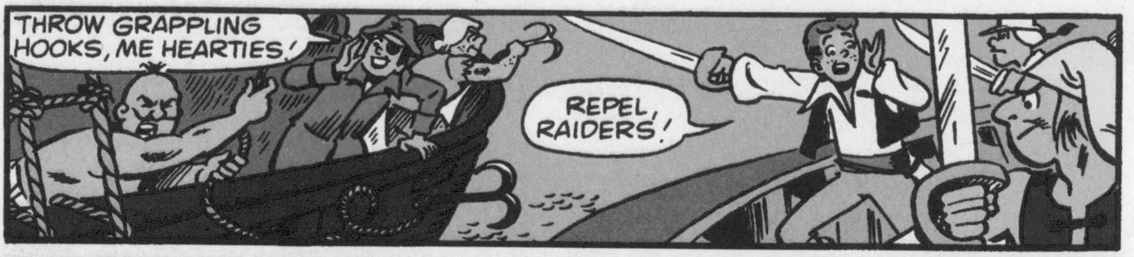
THROW GRAPPLING HOOKS, ME HEARTIES!
REPEL RAIDERS!

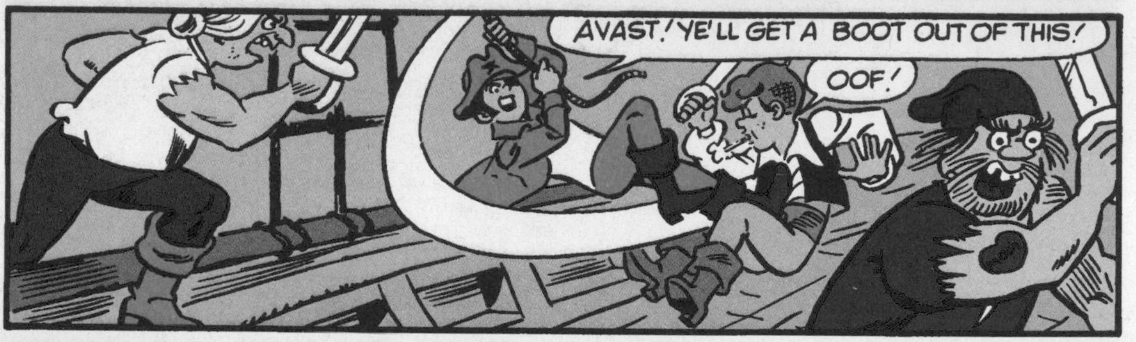
AVAST! YE'LL GET A BOOT OUT OF THIS!
OOF!

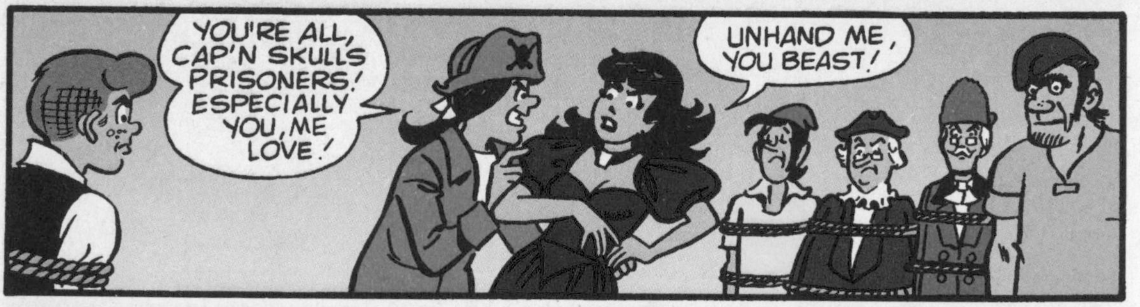
YOU'RE ALL, CAP'N SKULL'S PRISONERS! ESPECIALLY YOU, ME LOVE!
UNHAND ME, YOU BEAST!

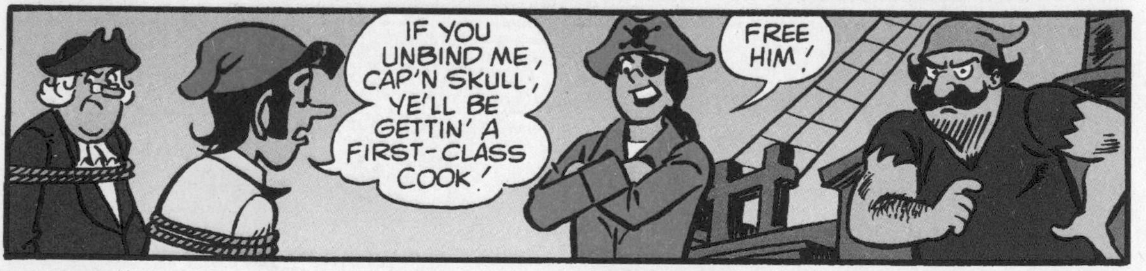
IF YOU UNBIND ME, CAP'N SKULL, YE'LL BE GETTIN' A FIRST-CLASS COOK!
FREE HIM!

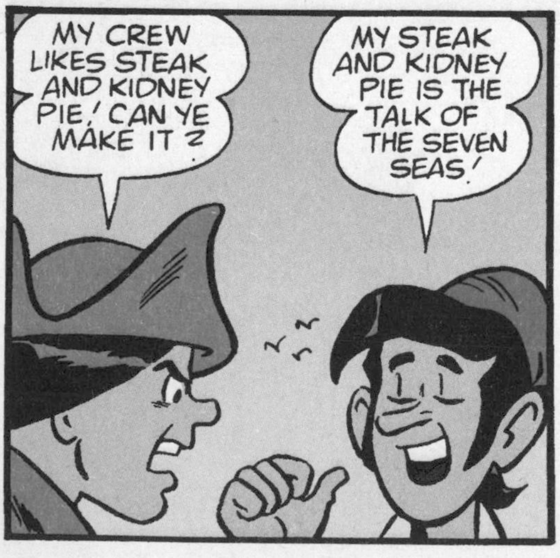
MY CREW LIKES STEAK AND KIDNEY PIE! CAN YE MAKE IT?
MY STEAK AND KIDNEY PIE IS THE TALK OF THE SEVEN SEAS!

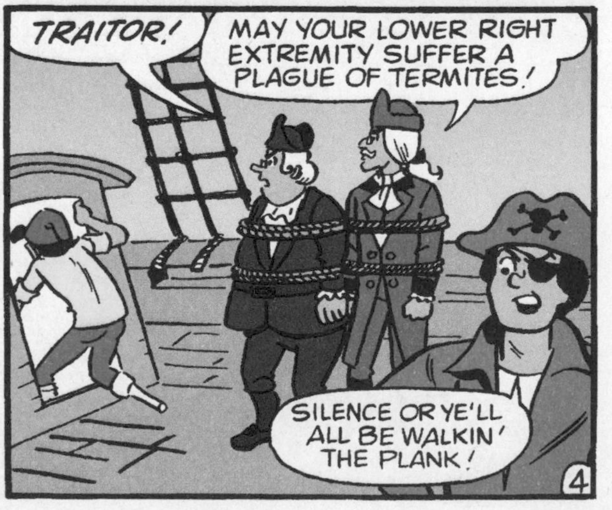
TRAITOR!
MAY YOUR LOWER RIGHT EXTREMITY SUFFER A PLAGUE OF TERMITES!
SILENCE OR YE'LL ALL BE WALKIN' THE PLANK!
4

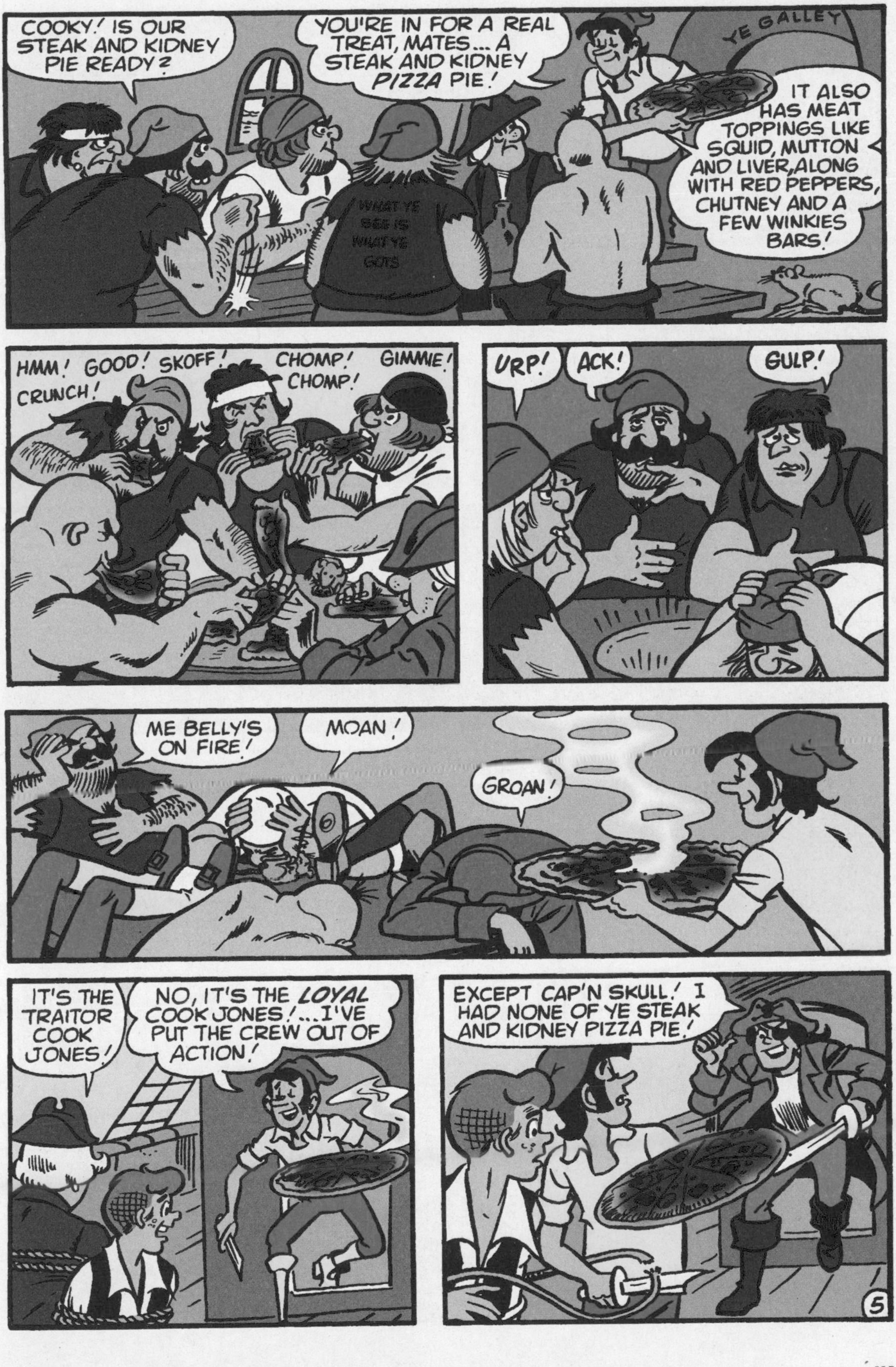
COOKY! IS OUR STEAK AND KIDNEY PIE READY?
YOU'RE IN FOR A REAL TREAT, MATES... A STEAK AND KIDNEY PIZZA PIE!
YE GALLEY
IT ALSO HAS MEAT TOPPINGS LIKE SQUID, MUTTON AND LIVER, ALONG WITH RED PEPPERS, CHUTNEY AND A FEW WINKIES BARS!
WHAT YE SEE IS WHAT YE GOTS
HMM! GOOD! SKOFF! CHOMP! GIMMIE!
CRUNCH! CHOMP!
URP!
ACK!
GULP!
ME BELLY'S ON FIRE!
MOAN!
GROAN!
IT'S THE TRAITOR COOK JONES!
NO, IT'S THE LOYAL COOK JONES!...I'VE PUT THE CREW OUT OF ACTION!
EXCEPT CAP'N SKULL! I HAD NONE OF YE STEAK AND KIDNEY PIZZA PIE!
5

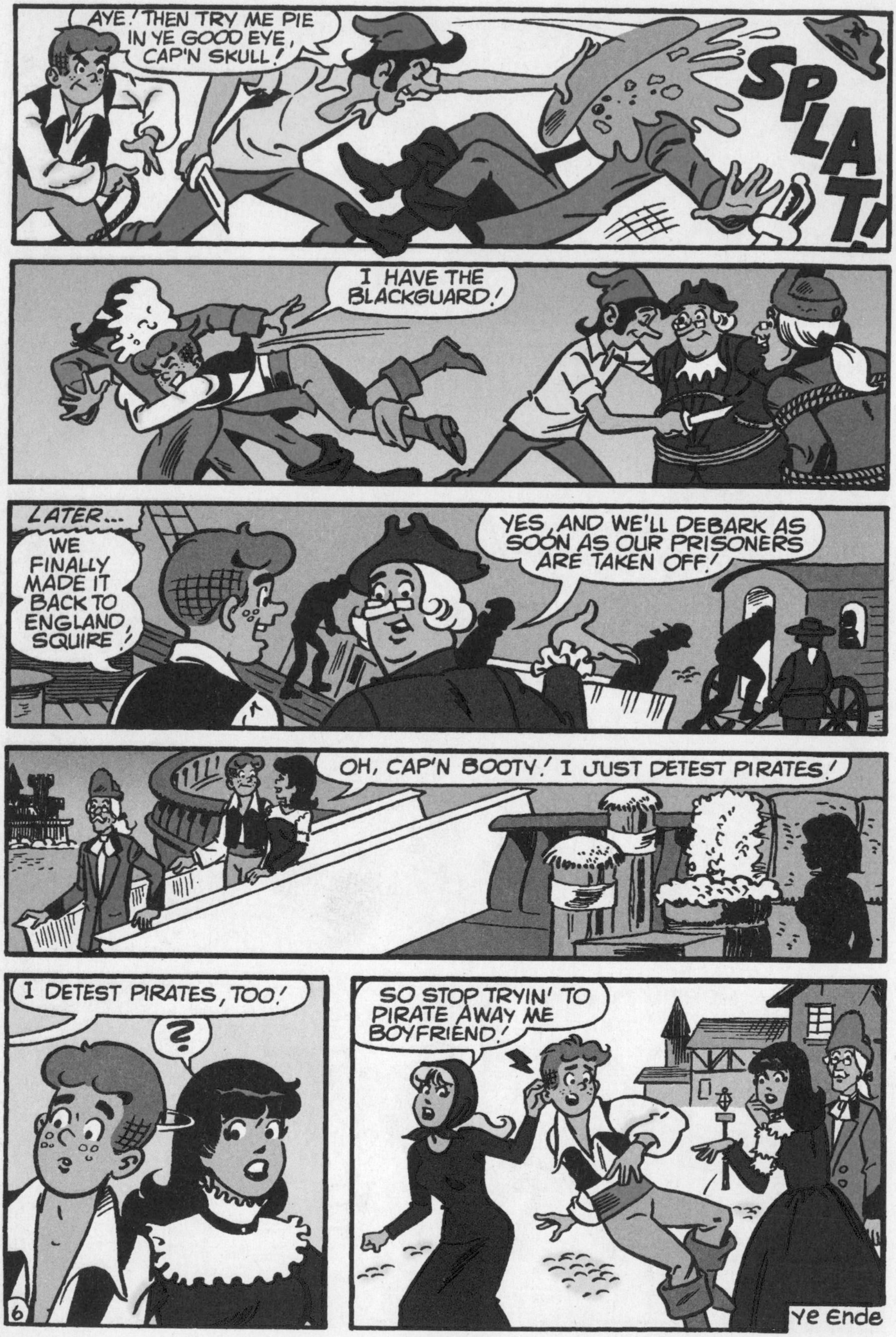
AYE! THEN TRY ME PIE IN YE GOOD EYE, CAP'N SKULL!
SPLAT!
I HAVE THE BLACKGUARD!
LATER...
WE FINALLY MADE IT BACK TO ENGLAND, SQUIRE!
YES, AND WE'LL DEBARK AS SOON AS OUR PRISONERS ARE TAKEN OFF!
OH, CAP'N BOOTY! I JUST DETEST PIRATES!
I DETEST PIRATES, TOO!
?
SO STOP TRYIN' TO PIRATE AWAY ME BOYFRIEND!
6
Ye Ende

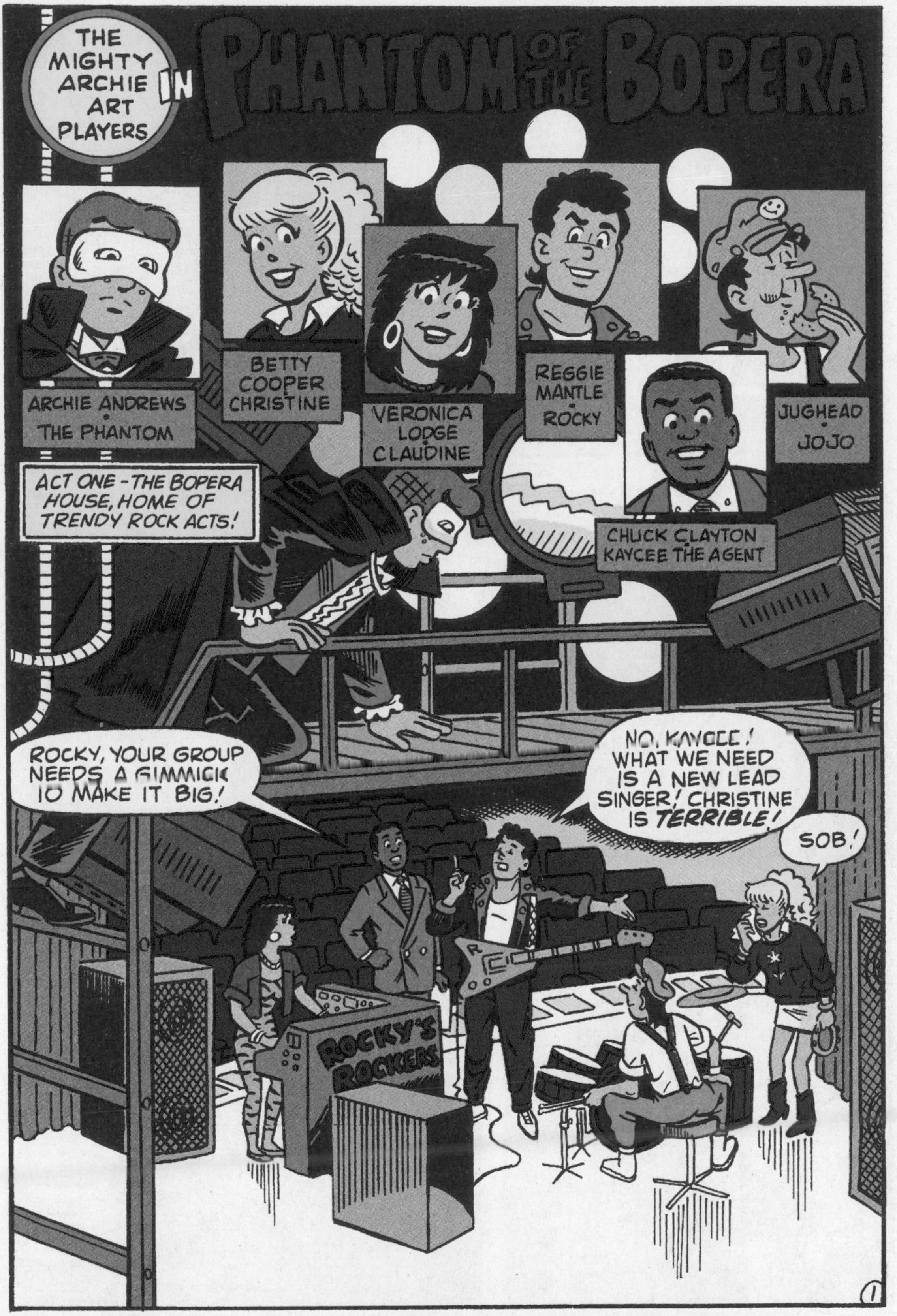
THE MIGHTY ARCHIE ART PLAYERS IN
PHANTOM OF THE BOPERA
ARCHIE ANDREWS • THE PHANTOM
BETTY COOPER • CHRISTINE
VERONICA LODGE • CLAUDINE
REGGIE MANTLE • ROCKY
CHUCK CLAYTON • KAYCEE THE AGENT
JUGHEAD • JOJO
ACT ONE - THE BOPERA HOUSE, HOME OF TRENDY ROCK ACTS!
ROCKY, YOUR GROUP NEEDS A GIMMICK TO MAKE IT BIG!
NO, KAYCEE! WHAT WE NEED IS A NEW LEAD SINGER! CHRISTINE IS TERRIBLE!
SOB!
ROCKY'S ROCKERS
1

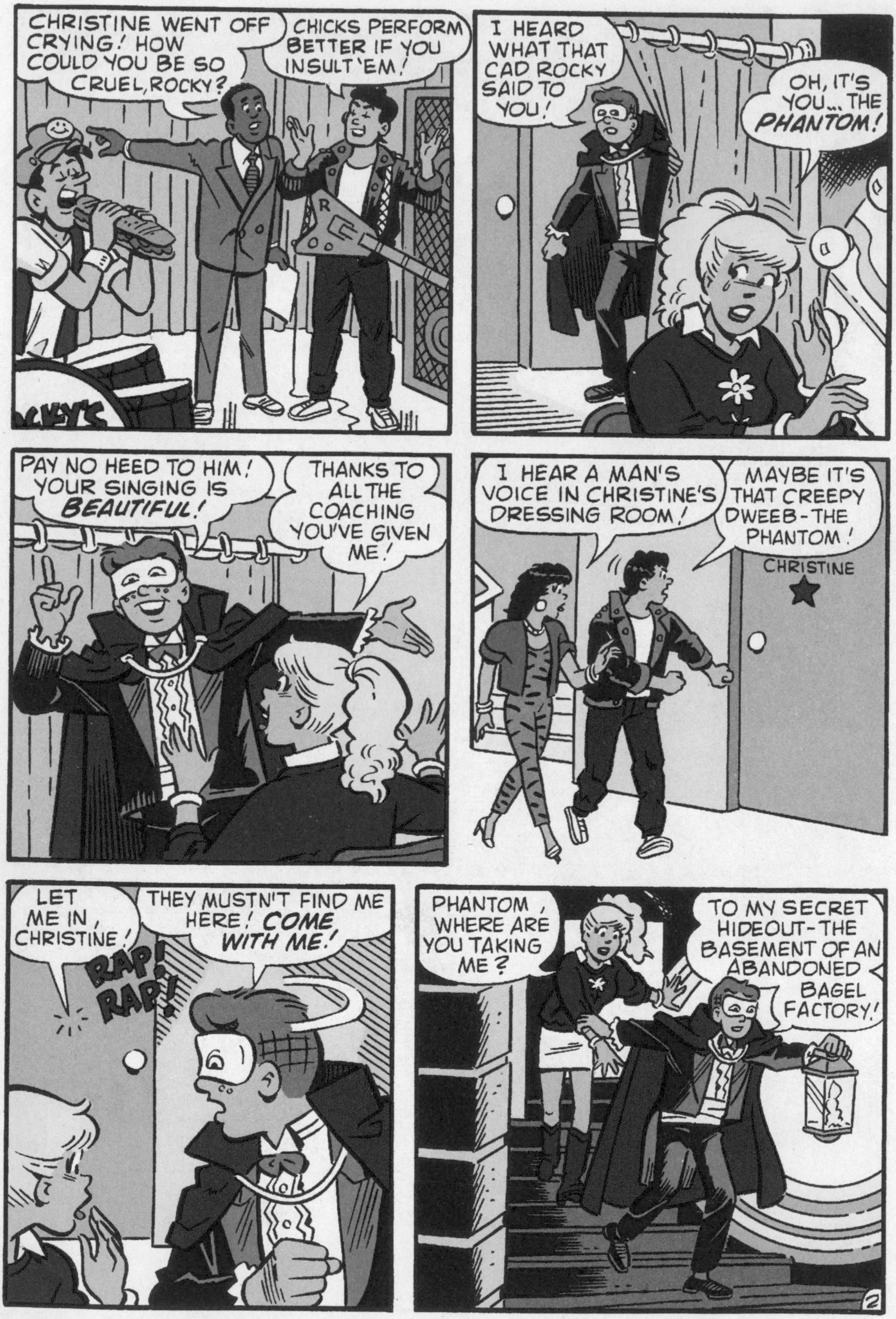
CHRISTINE WENT OFF CRYING! HOW COULD YOU BE SO CRUEL, ROCKY?
CHICKS PERFORM BETTER IF YOU INSULT 'EM!
I HEARD WHAT THAT CAD ROCKY SAID TO YOU!
OH, IT'S YOU... THE PHANTOM!
PAY NO HEED TO HIM! YOUR SINGING IS BEAUTIFUL!
THANKS TO ALL THE COACHING YOU'VE GIVEN ME!
I HEAR A MAN'S VOICE IN CHRISTINE'S DRESSING ROOM!
MAYBE IT'S THAT CREEPY DWEEB-THE PHANTOM!
CHRISTINE
LET ME IN, CHRISTINE!
RAP! RAP!
THEY MUSTN'T FIND ME HERE! COME WITH ME!
PHANTOM, WHERE ARE YOU TAKING ME?
TO MY SECRET HIDEOUT-THE BASEMENT OF AN ABANDONED BAGEL FACTORY!
2

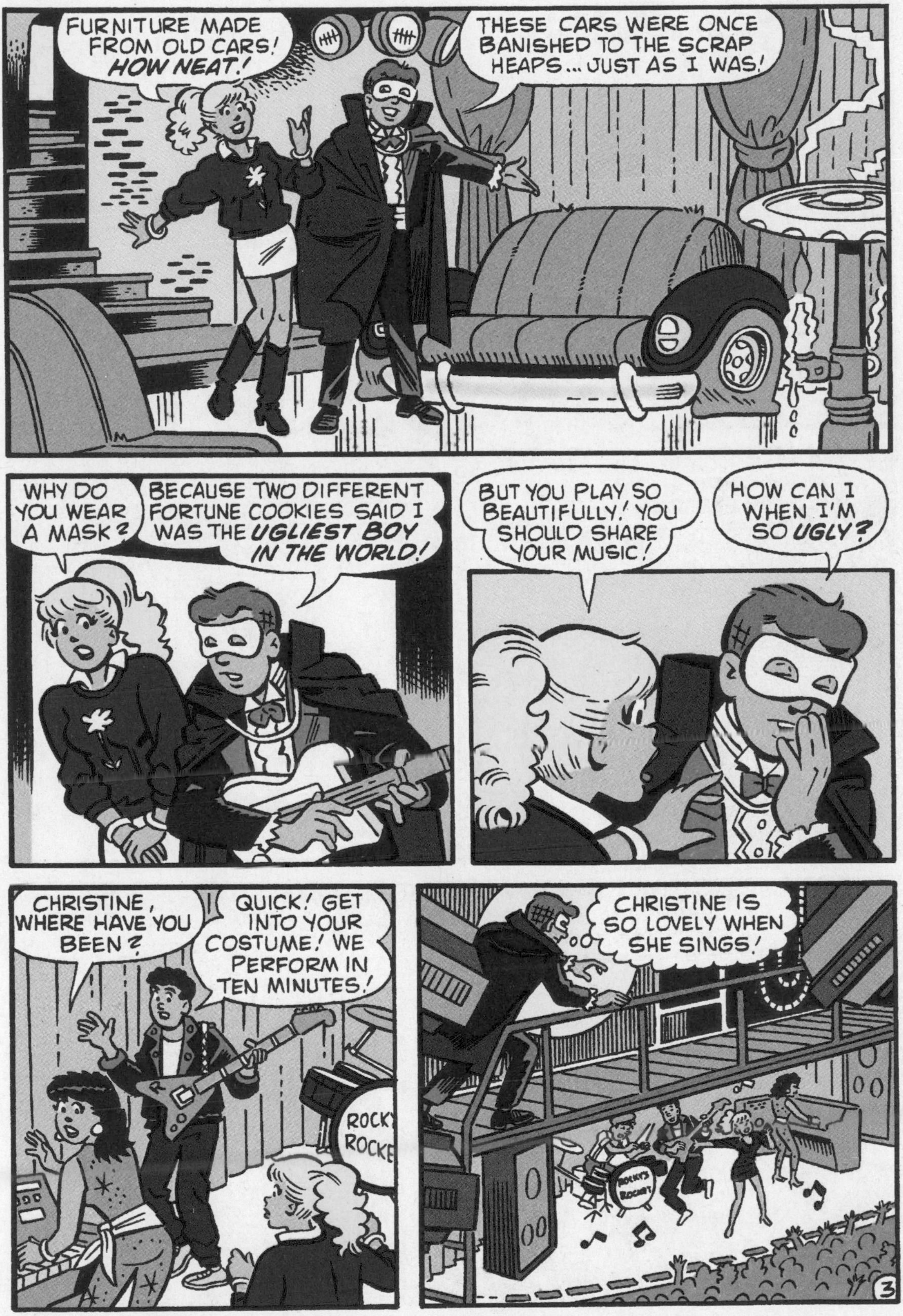
FURNITURE MADE FROM OLD CARS! HOW NEAT!
THESE CARS WERE ONCE BANISHED TO THE SCRAP HEAPS... JUST AS I WAS!
WHY DO YOU WEAR A MASK?
BECAUSE TWO DIFFERENT FORTUNE COOKIES SAID I WAS THE UGLIEST BOY IN THE WORLD!
BUT YOU PLAY SO BEAUTIFULLY! YOU SHOULD SHARE YOUR MUSIC!
HOW CAN I WHEN I'M SO UGLY?
CHRISTINE, WHERE HAVE YOU BEEN?
QUICK! GET INTO YOUR COSTUME! WE PERFORM IN TEN MINUTES!
ROCKY ROCKE
CHRISTINE IS SO LOVELY WHEN SHE SINGS!
3

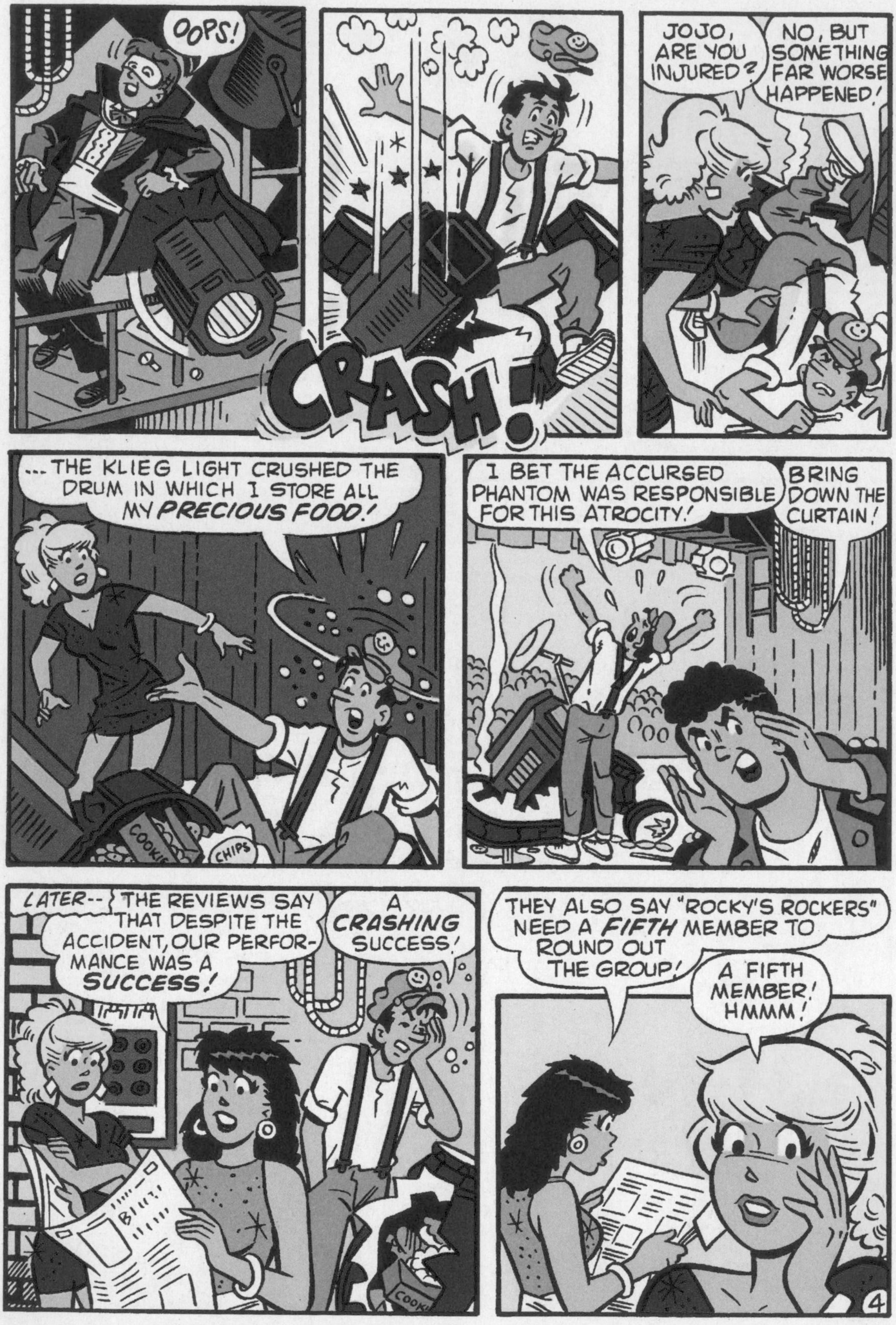
OOPS!
CRASH!
JOJO, ARE YOU INJURED?
NO, BUT SOMETHING FAR WORSE HAPPENED!
...THE KLIEG LIGHT CRUSHED THE DRUM IN WHICH I STORE ALL MY PRECIOUS FOOD!
COOKIES
CHIPS
I BET THE ACCURSED PHANTOM WAS RESPONSIBLE FOR THIS ATROCITY!
BRING DOWN THE CURTAIN!
LATER--
THE REVIEWS SAY THAT DESPITE THE ACCIDENT, OUR PERFORMANCE WAS A SUCCESS!
A CRASHING SUCCESS!
THEY ALSO SAY "ROCKY'S ROCKERS" NEED A FIFTH MEMBER TO ROUND OUT THE GROUP!
A FIFTH MEMBER! HMMM!
4

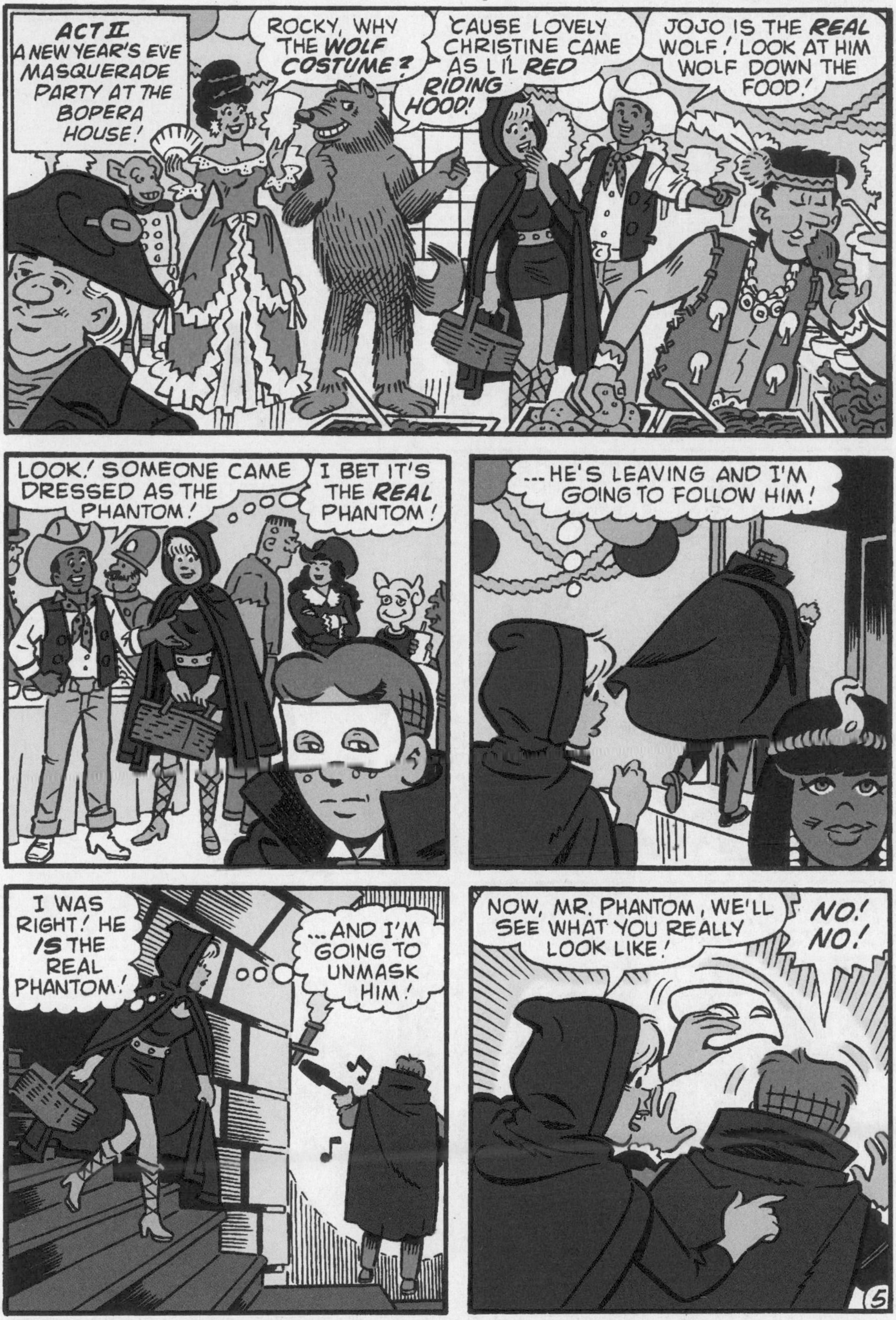
ACT II A NEW YEAR'S EVE MASQUERADE PARTY AT THE BOPERA HOUSE!
ROCKY, WHY THE WOLF COSTUME?
'CAUSE LOVELY CHRISTINE CAME AS L'IL RED RIDING HOOD!
JOJO IS THE REAL WOLF! LOOK AT HIM WOLF DOWN THE FOOD!
LOOK! SOMEONE CAME DRESSED AS THE PHANTOM!
I BET IT'S THE REAL PHANTOM!
...HE'S LEAVING AND I'M GOING TO FOLLOW HIM!
I WAS RIGHT! HE IS THE REAL PHANTOM!
...AND I'M GOING TO UNMASK HIM!
NOW, MR. PHANTOM, WE'LL SEE WHAT YOU REALLY LOOK LIKE!
NO! NO!
5

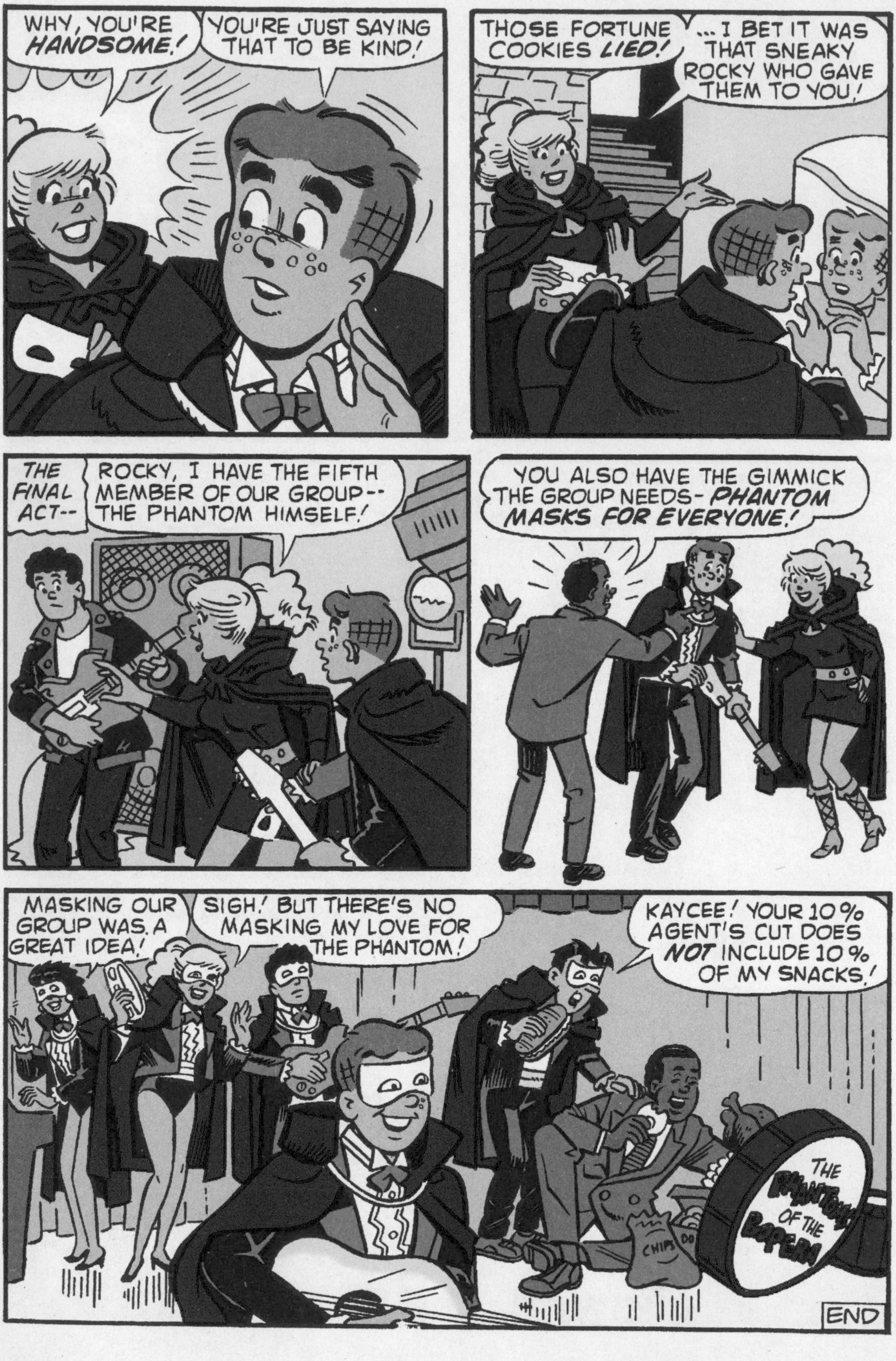
WHY, YOU'RE HANDSOME!
YOU'RE JUST SAYING THAT TO BE KIND!
THOSE FORTUNE COOKIES LIED!
...I BET IT WAS THAT SNEAKY ROCKY WHO GAVE THEM TO YOU!
THE FINAL ACT--
ROCKY, I HAVE THE FIFTH MEMBER OF OUR GROUP-- THE PHANTOM HIMSELF!
YOU ALSO HAVE THE GIMMICK THE GROUP NEEDS- PHANTOM MASKS FOR EVERYONE!
MASKING OUR GROUP WAS A GREAT IDEA!
SIGH! BUT THERE'S NO MASKING MY LOVE FOR THE PHANTOM!
KAYCEE! YOUR 10% AGENT'S CUT DOES NOT INCLUDE 10% OF MY SNACKS!
CHIPS
END

CHAPTER FIVE

Spy Girlz

PART ONE

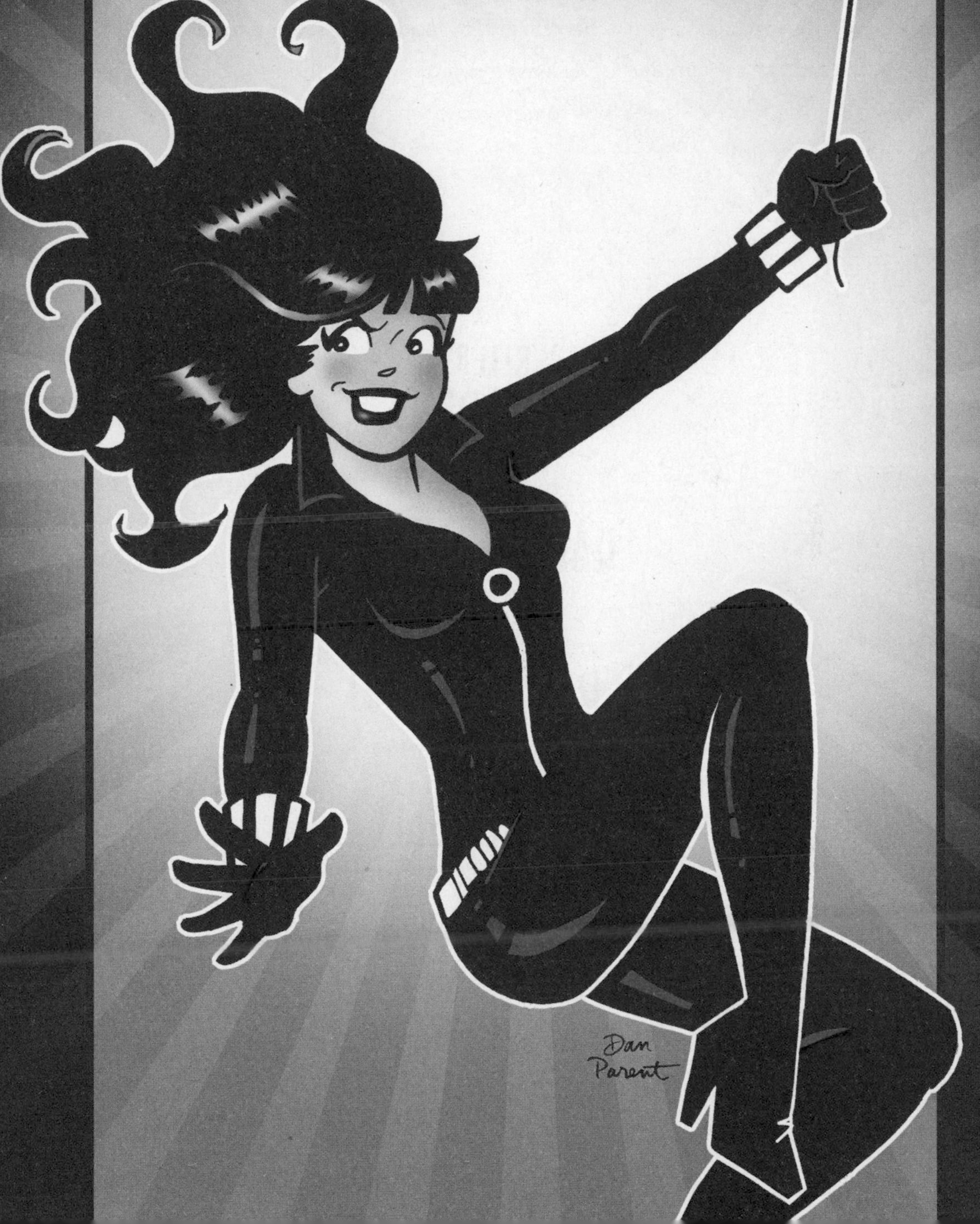
Dan Parent

INTRODUCING SPY GIRLZ

Originally printed in *Veronica #206* and *Betty #192*

"Spy Girlz: Back in Action," is a two-part spy crossover! Pranks and bad behavior are running wild in Riverdale! Agents Betty and Veronica soon discover the problems could be caused by coded messages hidden on the popular kids show *Funtime USA*! And the main culprit looks to be a lovable clown named Klutzy. Things look to get worse when *Funtime USA* makes a live stop in Riverdale!

WRITER
DAN PARENT

PENCILS
DAN PARENT

INKS
RICH KOSLOWSKI

LETTERS
JACK MORELLI

COLORS
DIGIKORE STUDIOS

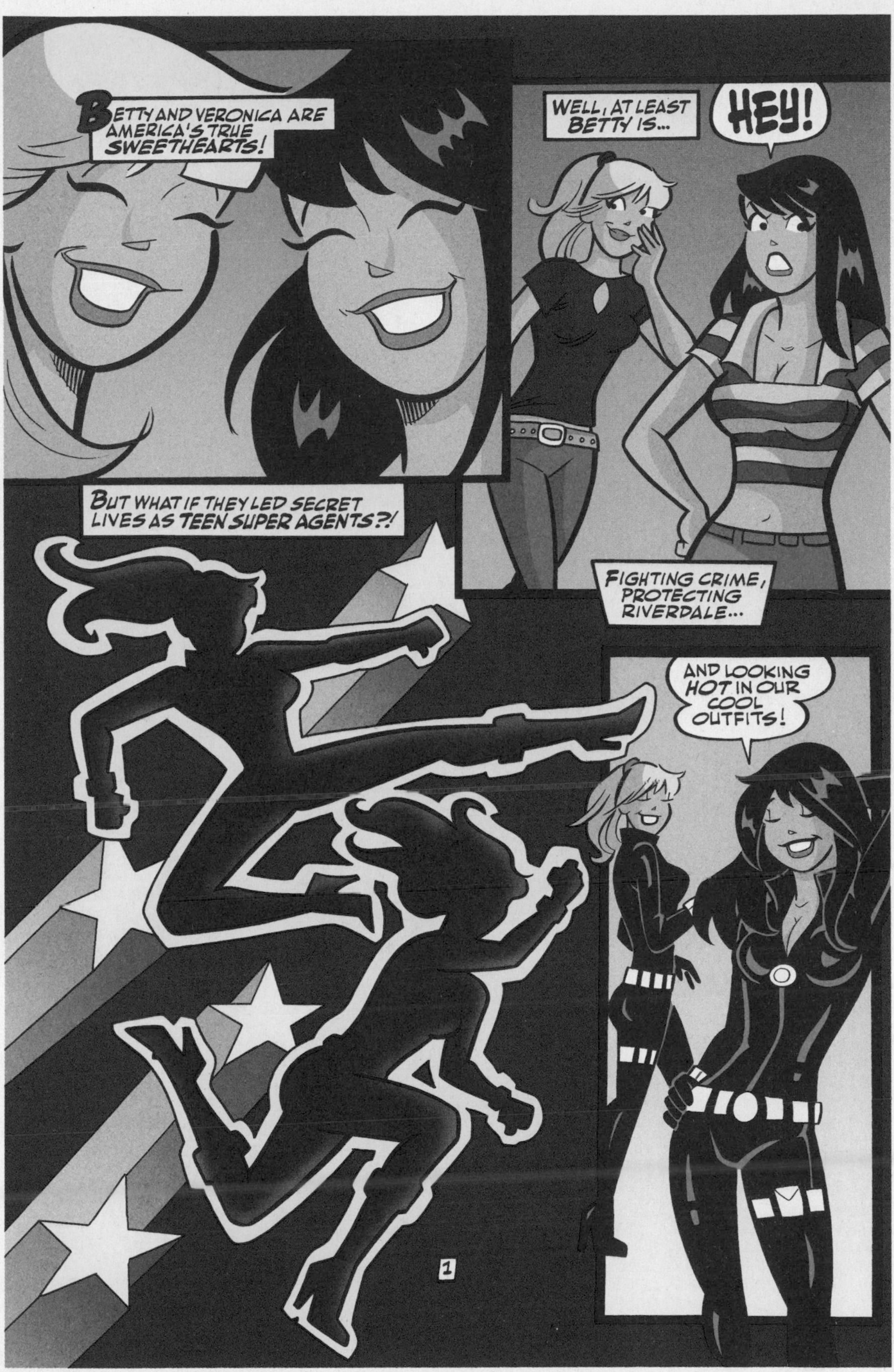
BETTY AND VERONICA ARE AMERICA'S TRUE SWEETHEARTS!
WELL, AT LEAST BETTY IS...
HEY!
BUT WHAT IF THEY LED SECRET LIVES AS TEEN SUPER AGENTS?!
FIGHTING CRIME, PROTECTING RIVERDALE...
AND LOOKING HOT IN OUR COOL OUTFITS!
1

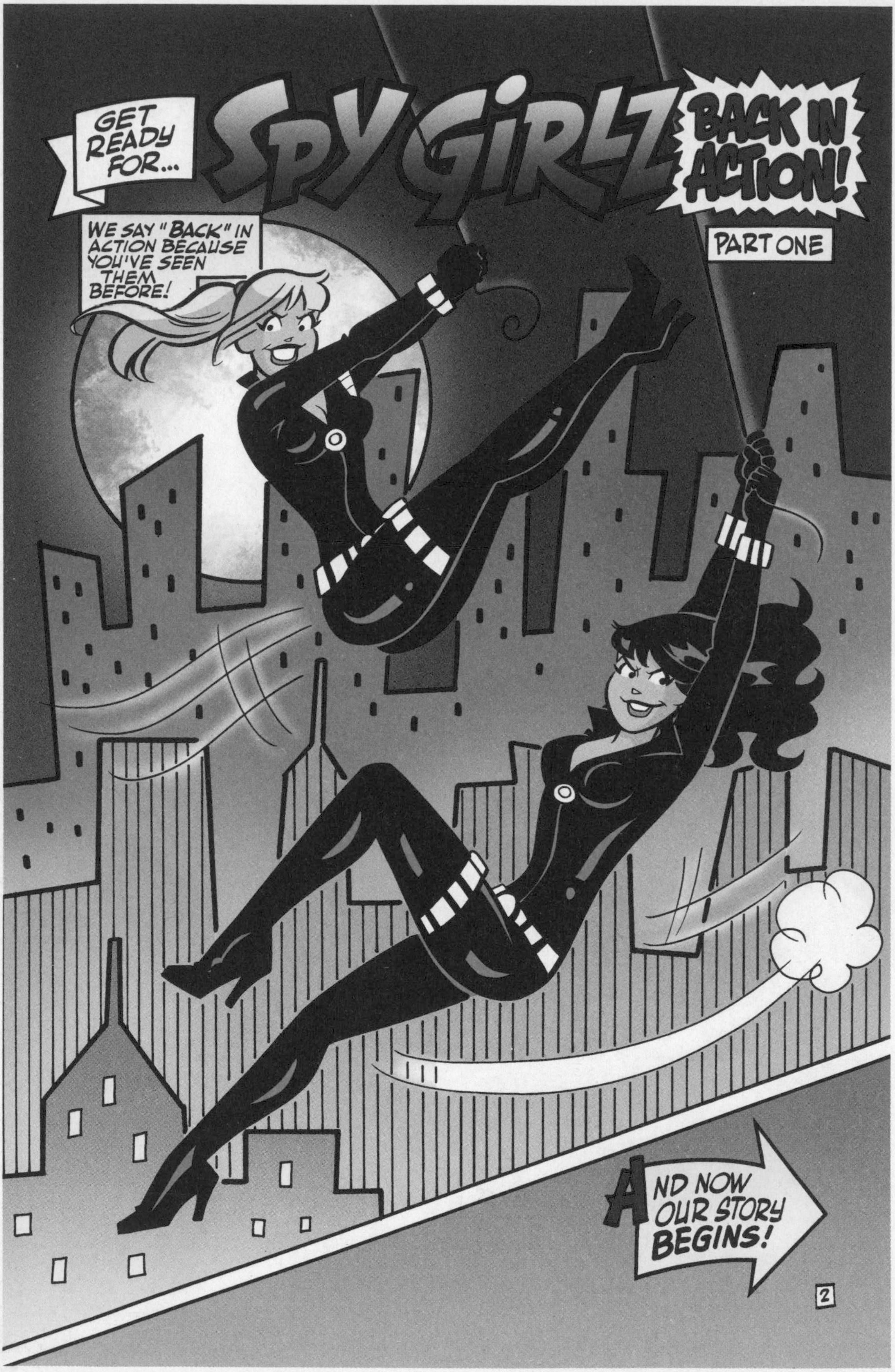
GET READY FOR...
SPY GIRLZ
BACK IN ACTION!
PART ONE
WE SAY "BACK" IN ACTION BECAUSE YOU'VE SEEN THEM BEFORE!
AND NOW OUR STORY BEGINS!
2

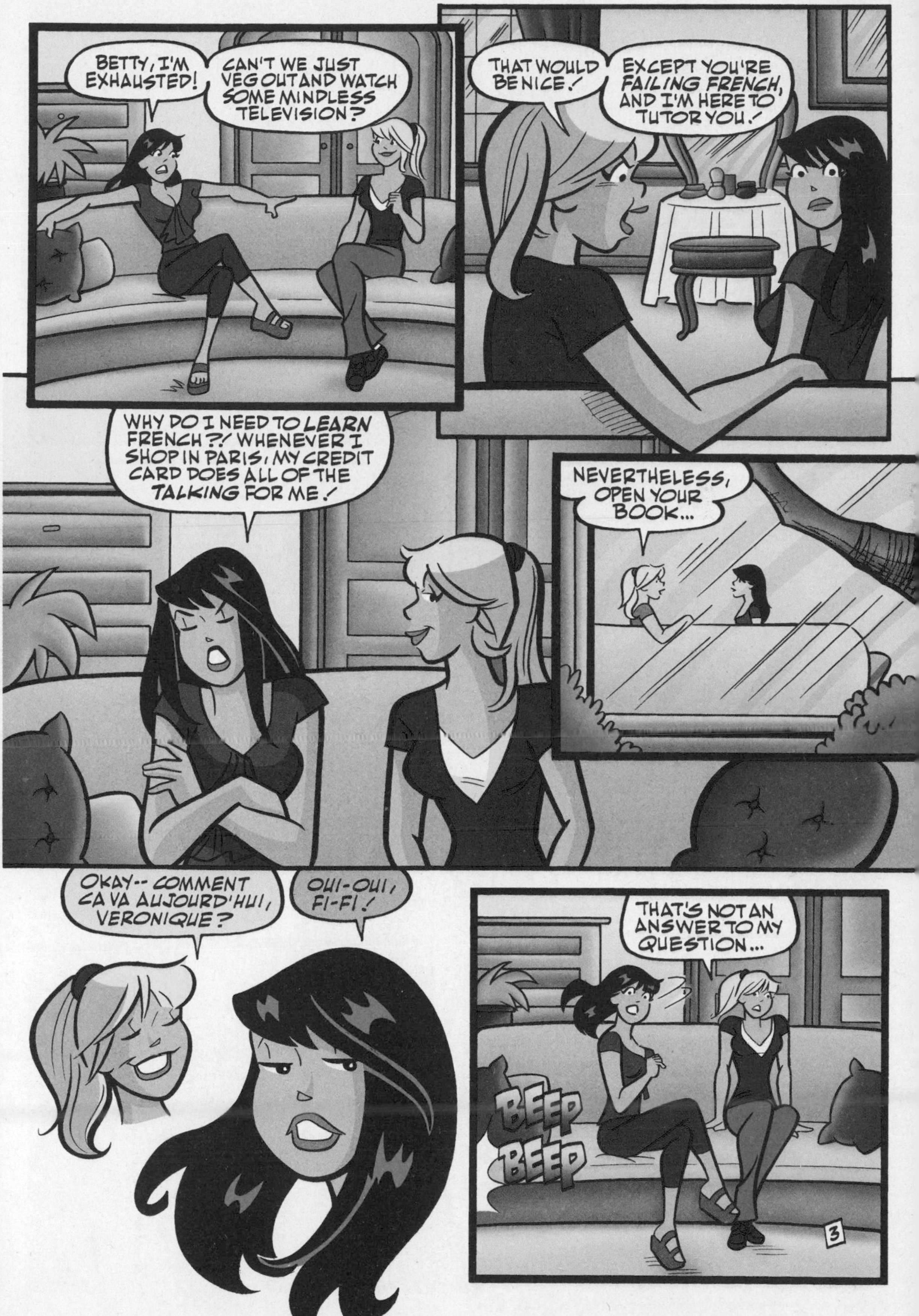
BETTY, I'M EXHAUSTED!
CAN'T WE JUST VEG OUT AND WATCH SOME MINDLESS TELEVISION?
THAT WOULD BE NICE!
EXCEPT YOU'RE FAILING FRENCH, AND I'M HERE TO TUTOR YOU!
WHY DO I NEED TO LEARN FRENCH?! WHENEVER I SHOP IN PARIS, MY CREDIT CARD DOES ALL OF THE TALKING FOR ME!
NEVERTHELESS, OPEN YOUR BOOK...
OKAY-- COMMENT CA VA AUJOURD'HUI, VERONIQUE?
OUI-OUI, FI-FI!
THAT'S NOT AN ANSWER TO MY QUESTION...
BEEP BEEP
3

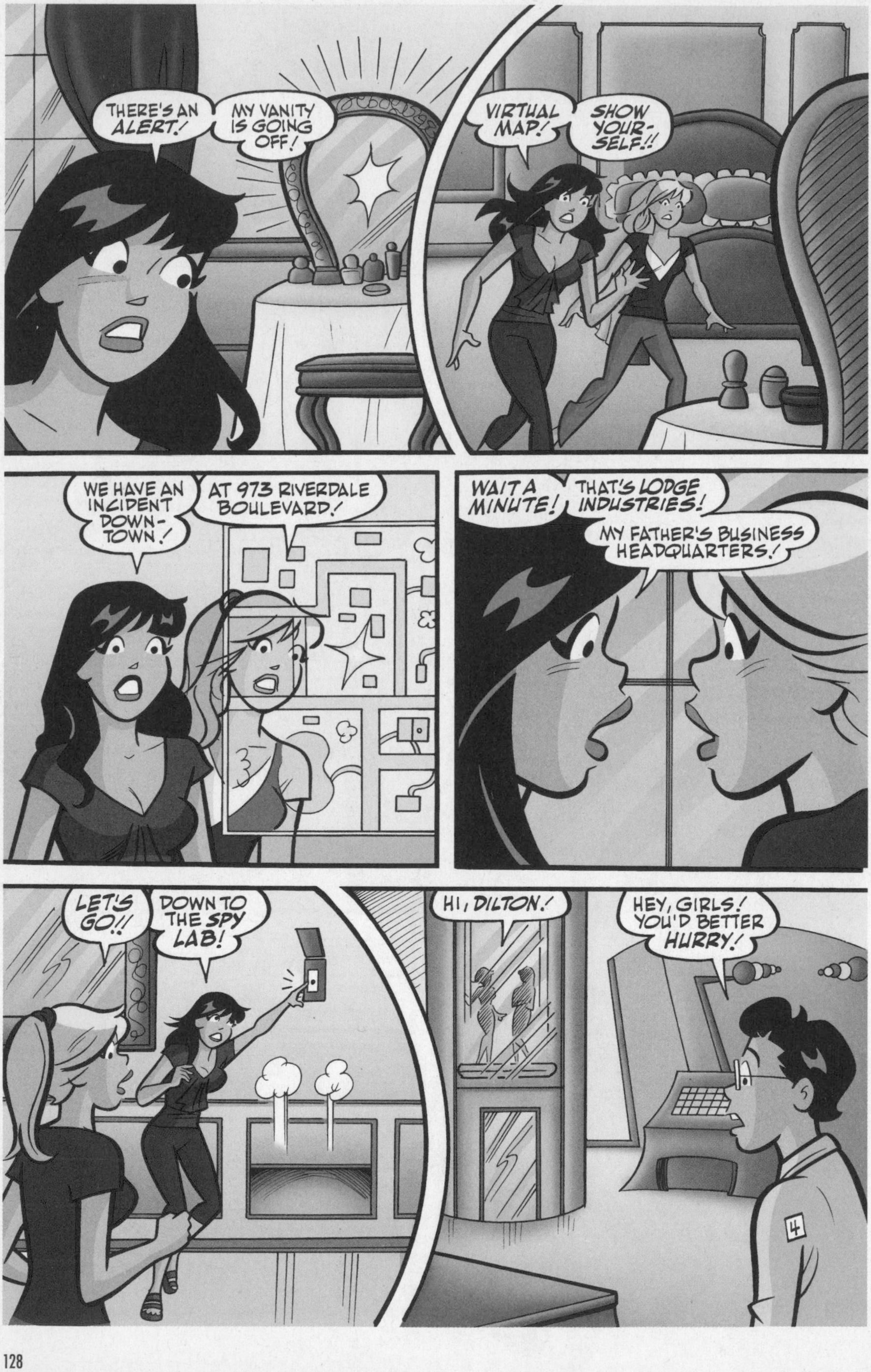
THERE'S AN ALERT!
MY VANITY IS GOING OFF!
VIRTUAL MAP!
SHOW YOURSELF!!
WE HAVE AN INCIDENT DOWNTOWN!
AT 973 RIVERDALE BOULEVARD!
WAIT A MINUTE!
THAT'S LODGE INDUSTRIES!
MY FATHER'S BUSINESS HEADQUARTERS!
LET'S GO!!
DOWN TO THE SPY LAB!
HI, DILTON!
HEY, GIRLS! YOU'D BETTER HURRY!
4

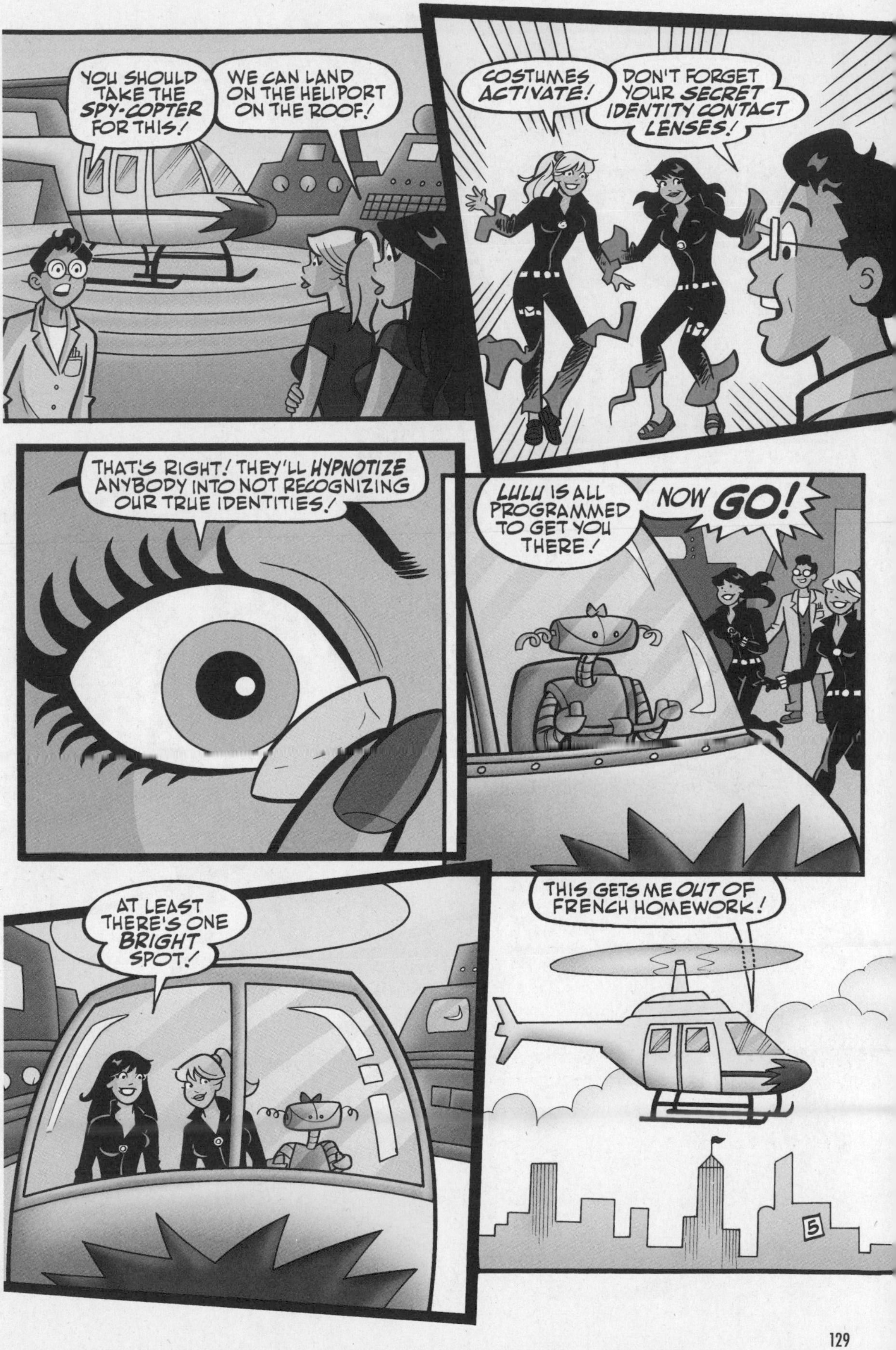
YOU SHOULD TAKE THE SPY-COPTER FOR THIS!
WE CAN LAND ON THE HELIPORT ON THE ROOF!
COSTUMES ACTIVATE!
DON'T FORGET YOUR SECRET IDENTITY CONTACT LENSES!
THAT'S RIGHT! THEY'LL HYPNOTIZE ANYBODY INTO NOT RECOGNIZING OUR TRUE IDENTITIES!
LULU IS ALL PROGRAMMED TO GET YOU THERE!
NOW GO!
AT LEAST THERE'S ONE BRIGHT SPOT!
THIS GETS ME OUT OF FRENCH HOMEWORK!
5

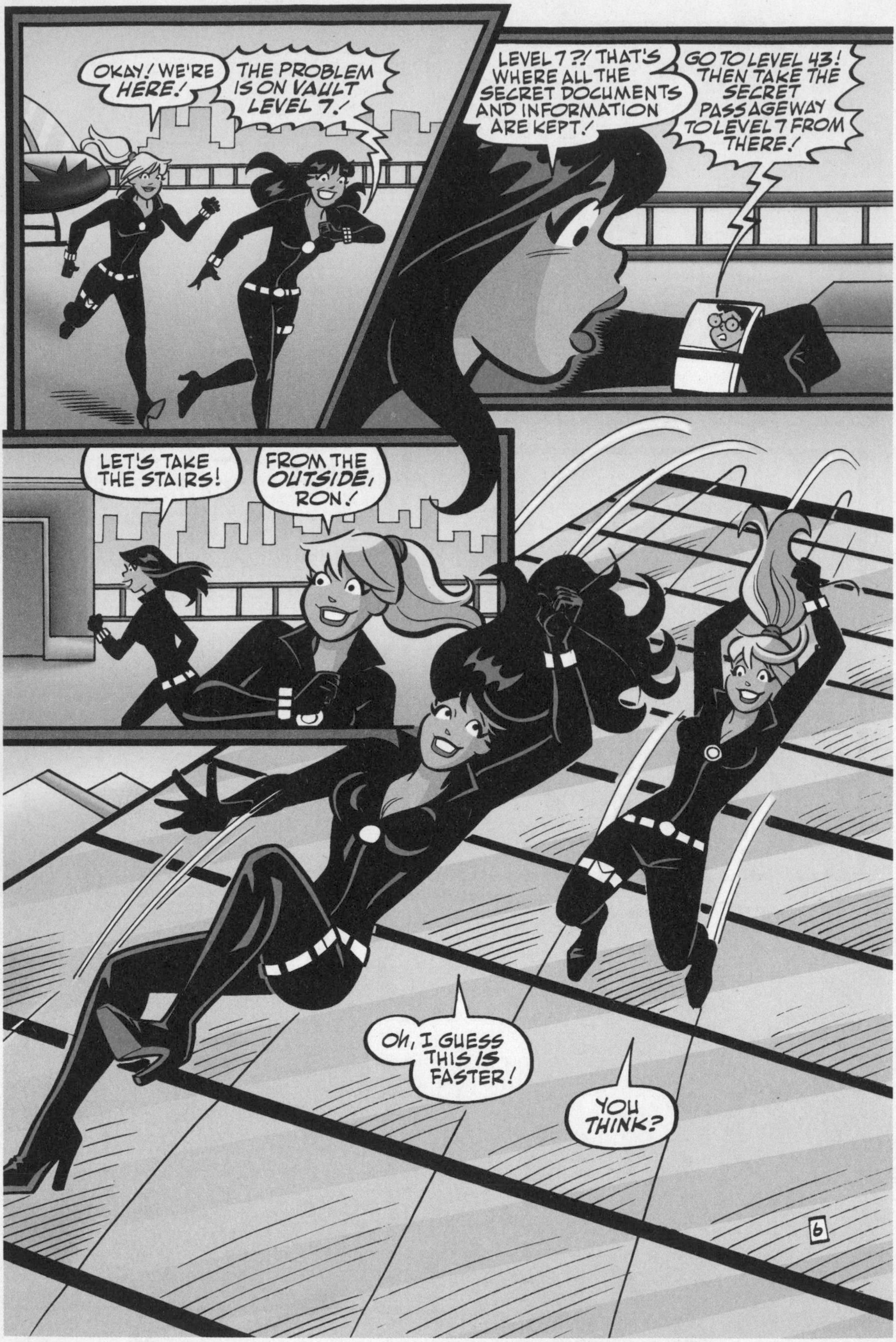
OKAY! WE'RE HERE!
THE PROBLEM IS ON VAULT LEVEL 7!
LEVEL 7?! THAT'S WHERE ALL THE SECRET DOCUMENTS AND INFORMATION ARE KEPT!
GO TO LEVEL 43! THEN TAKE THE SECRET PASSAGEWAY TO LEVEL 7 FROM THERE!
LET'S TAKE THE STAIRS!
FROM THE OUTSIDE, RON!
Oh, I GUESS THIS IS FASTER!
YOU THINK?
6

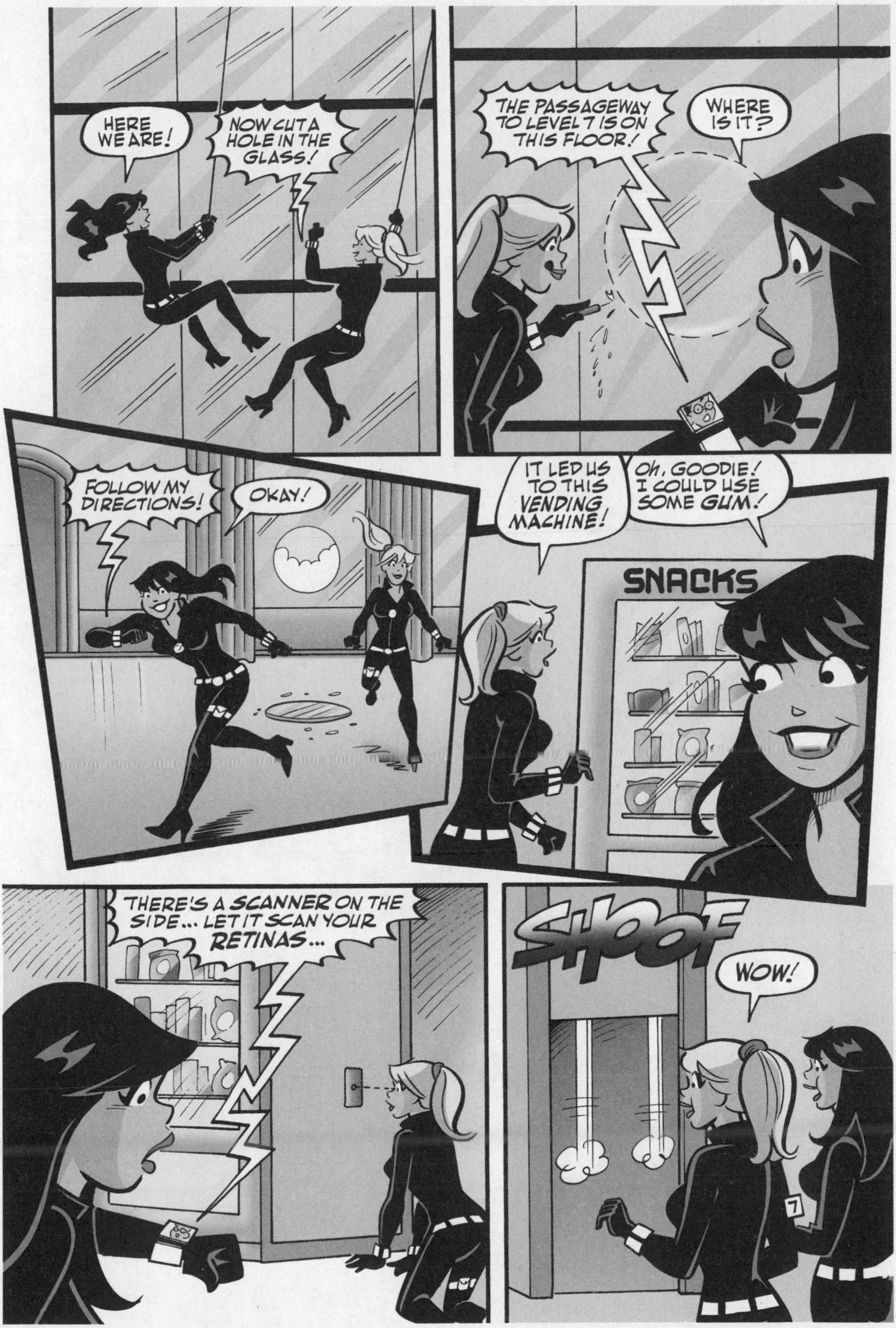
HERE WE ARE!
NOW CUT A HOLE IN THE GLASS!
THE PASSAGEWAY TO LEVEL 7 IS ON THIS FLOOR!
WHERE IS IT?
FOLLOW MY DIRECTIONS!
OKAY!
IT LED US TO THIS VENDING MACHINE!
Oh, GOODIE! I COULD USE SOME GUM!
SNACKS
THERE'S A SCANNER ON THE SIDE... LET IT SCAN YOUR RETINAS...
SHOOF
WOW!
7

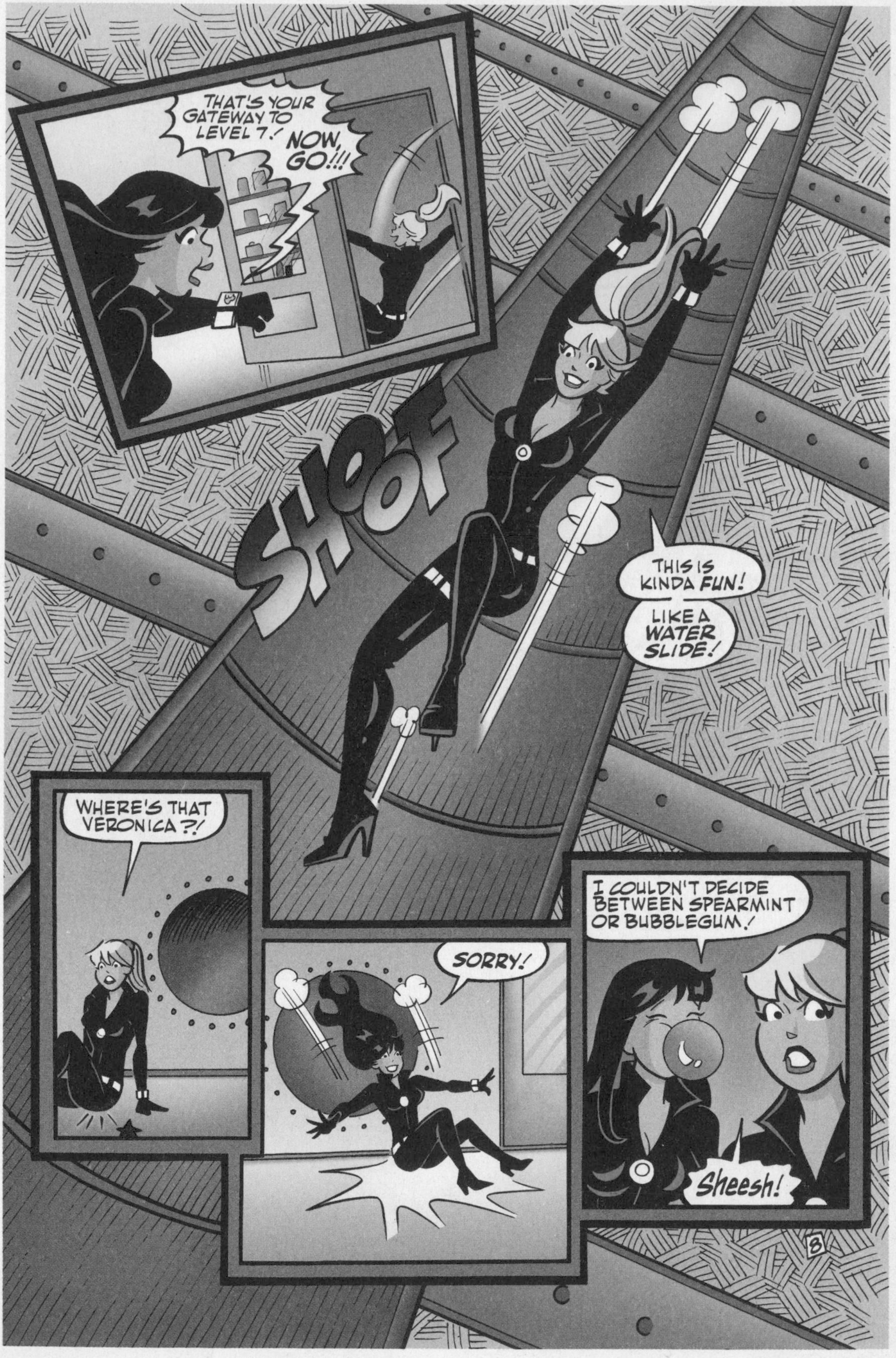
THAT'S YOUR GATEWAY TO LEVEL 7.! NOW, GO!!!
SHOOF
THIS IS KINDA FUN!
LIKE A WATER SLIDE!
WHERE'S THAT VERONICA ?!
SORRY!
I COULDN'T DECIDE BETWEEN SPEARMINT OR BUBBLEGUM.!
Sheesh!
8

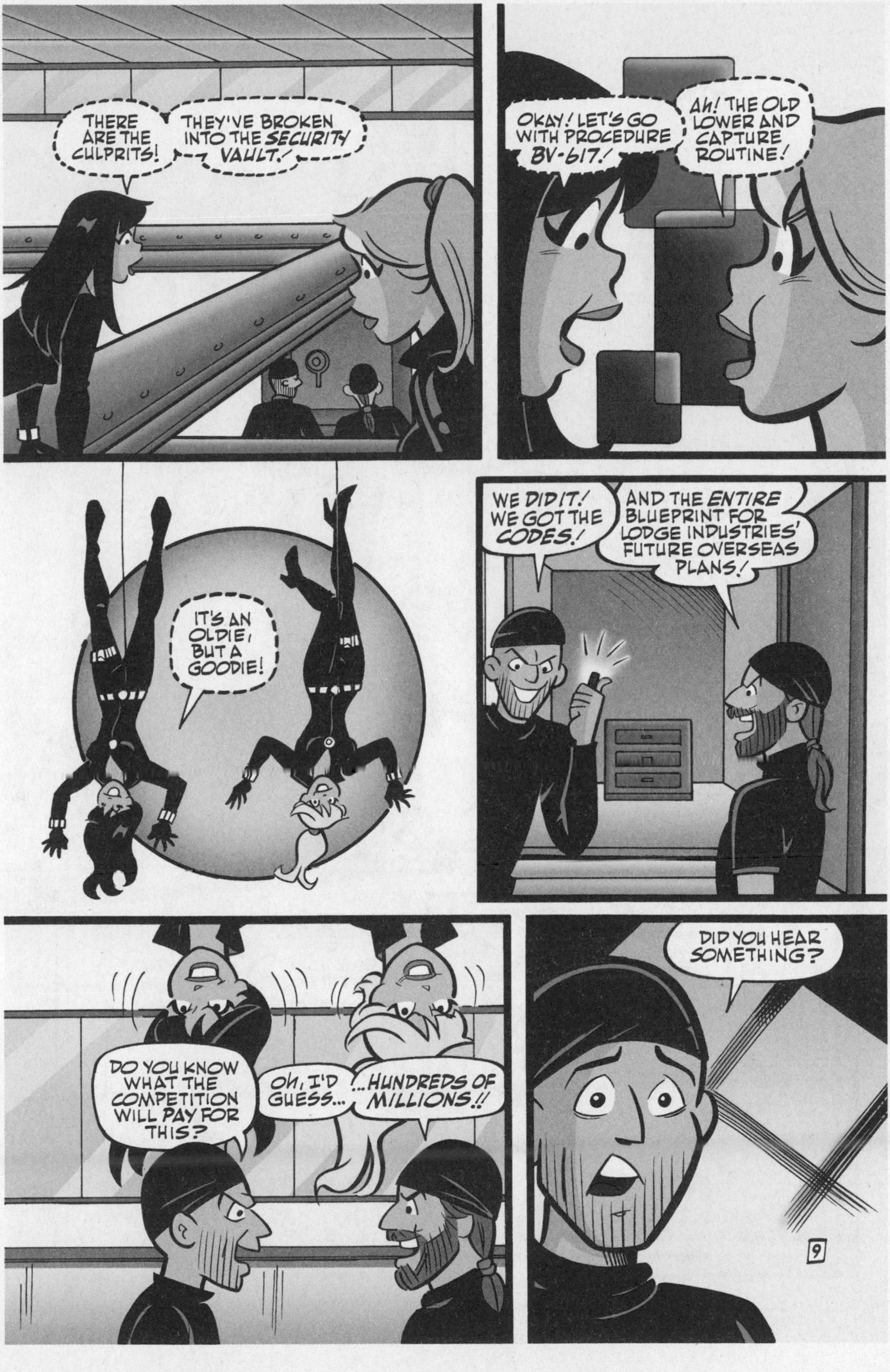
THERE ARE THE CULPRITS!
THEY'VE BROKEN INTO THE SECURITY VAULT!
OKAY! LET'S GO WITH PROCEDURE BV-617!
AH! THE OLD LOWER AND CAPTURE ROUTINE!
IT'S AN OLDIE, BUT A GOODIE!
WE DID IT! WE GOT THE CODES!
AND THE ENTIRE BLUEPRINT FOR LODGE INDUSTRIES' FUTURE OVERSEAS PLANS!
DO YOU KNOW WHAT THE COMPETITION WILL PAY FOR THIS?
OH, I'D GUESS...
...HUNDREDS OF MILLIONS!!
DID YOU HEAR SOMETHING?
9

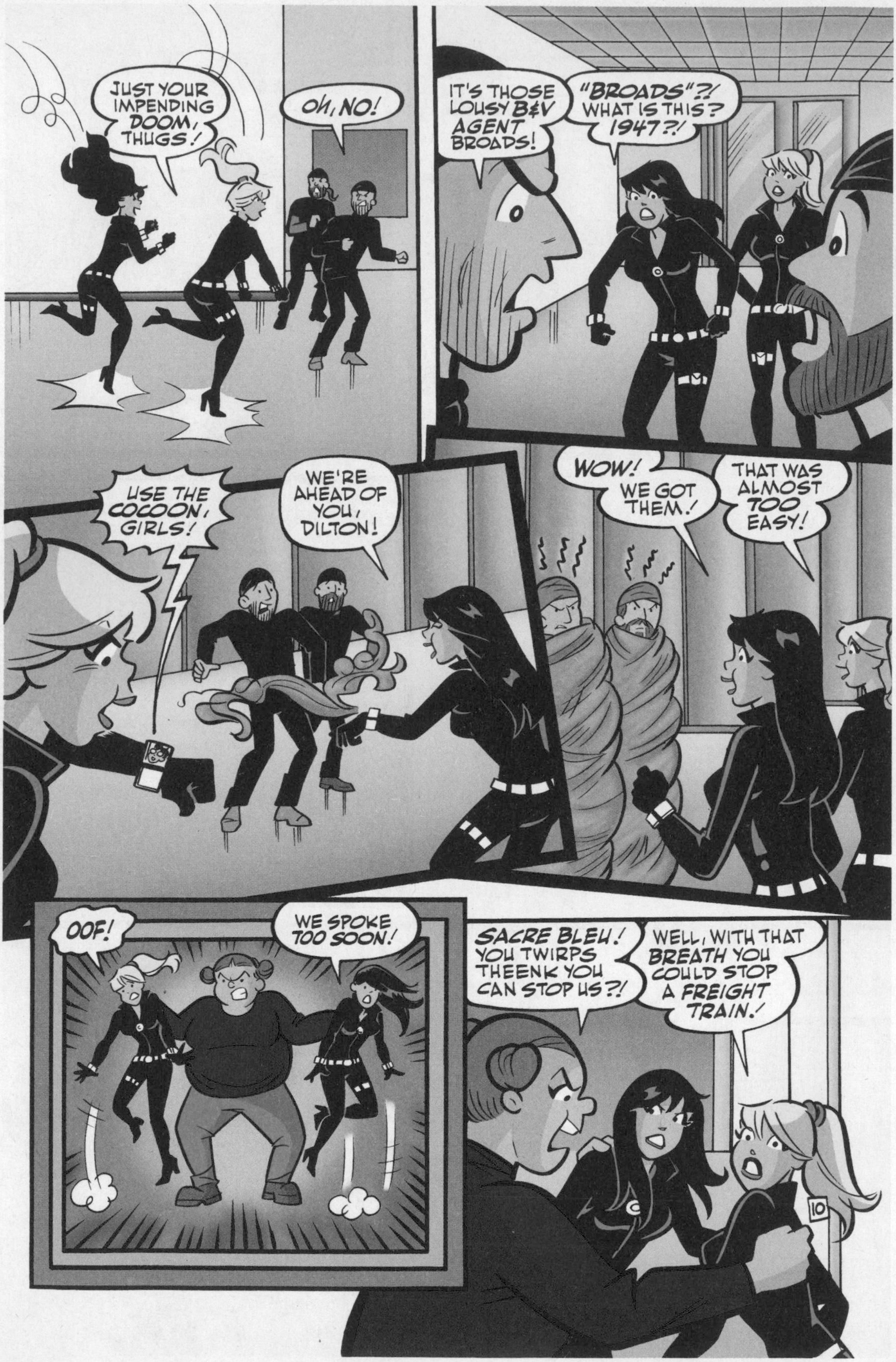
JUST YOUR IMPENDING DOOM, THUGS!
OH, NO!
IT'S THOSE LOUSY B&V AGENT BROADS!
"BROADS"?! WHAT IS THIS? 1947?!
USE THE COCOON, GIRLS!
WE'RE AHEAD OF YOU, DILTON!
WOW! WE GOT THEM!
THAT WAS ALMOST TOO EASY!
OOF!
WE SPOKE TOO SOON!
SACRE BLEU! YOU TWIRPS THEENK YOU CAN STOP US?!
WELL, WITH THAT BREATH YOU COULD STOP A FREIGHT TRAIN!
10

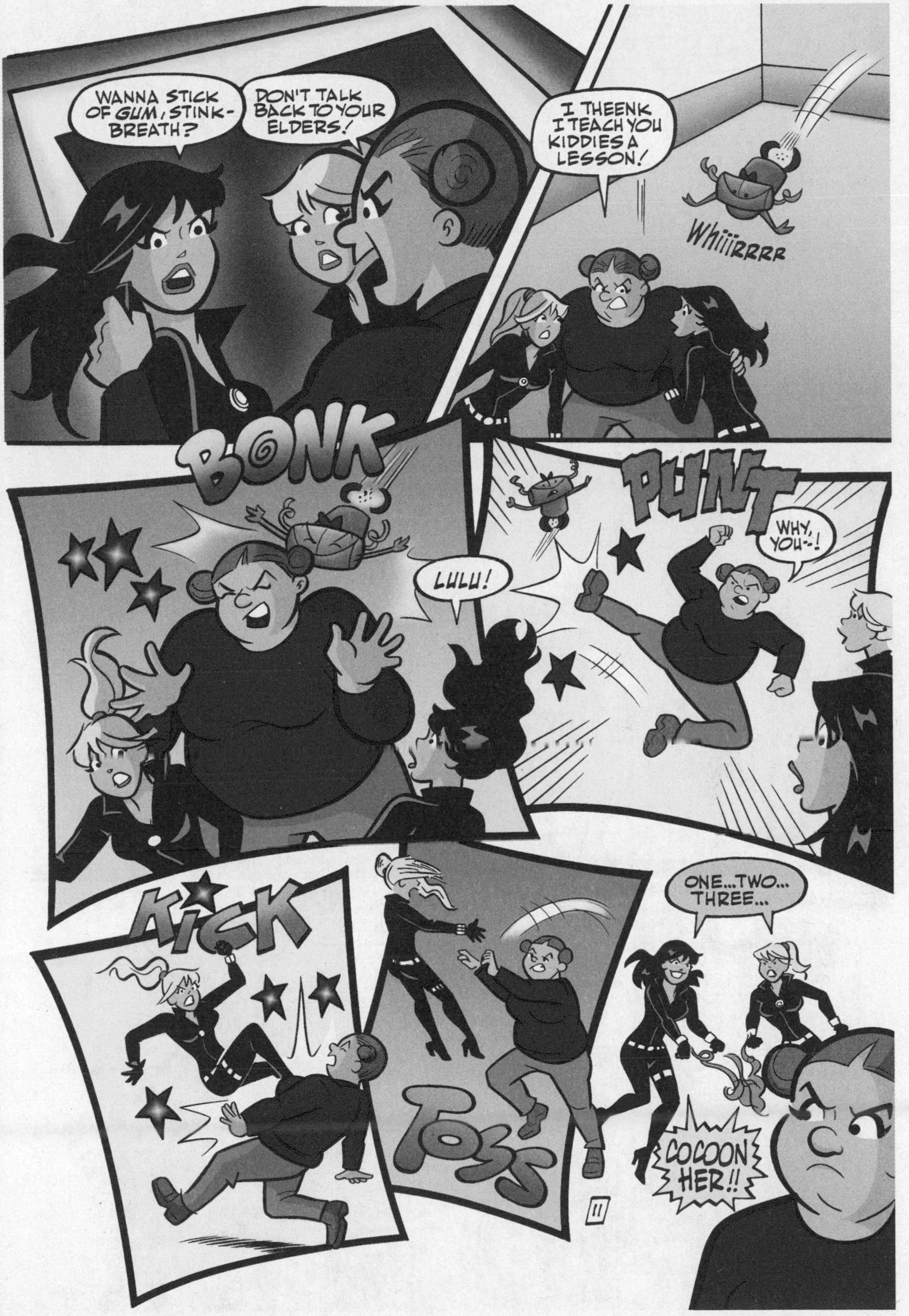
WANNA STICK OF GUM, STINK-BREATH?
DON'T TALK BACK TO YOUR ELDERS!
I THEENK I TEACH YOU KIDDIES A LESSON!
Whiiirrrr
BONK
LULU!
PUNT
WHY, YOU--!
KICK
TOSS
ONE...TWO... THREE...
COCOON HER!!

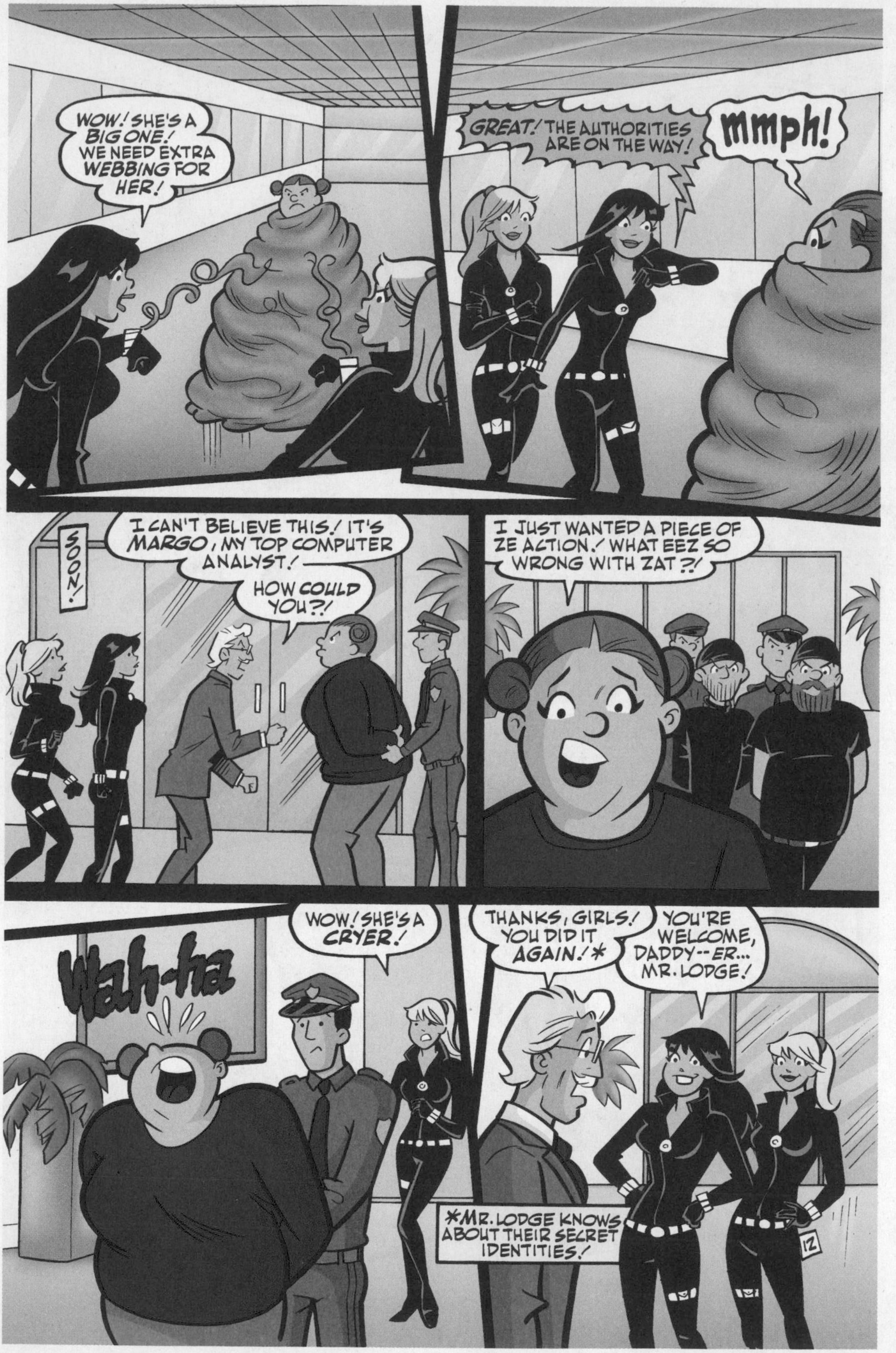
WOW! SHE'S A BIG ONE! WE NEED EXTRA WEBBING FOR HER!
GREAT! THE AUTHORITIES ARE ON THE WAY!
mmph!
SOON!
I CAN'T BELIEVE THIS! IT'S MARGO, MY TOP COMPUTER ANALYST!
HOW COULD YOU?!
I JUST WANTED A PIECE OF ZE ACTION! WHAT EEZ SO WRONG WITH ZAT?!
Wah-ha
WOW! SHE'S A CRYER!
THANKS, GIRLS! YOU DID IT AGAIN!*
YOU'RE WELCOME, DADDY--ER... MR. LODGE!
*MR. LODGE KNOWS ABOUT THEIR SECRET IDENTITIES!
12

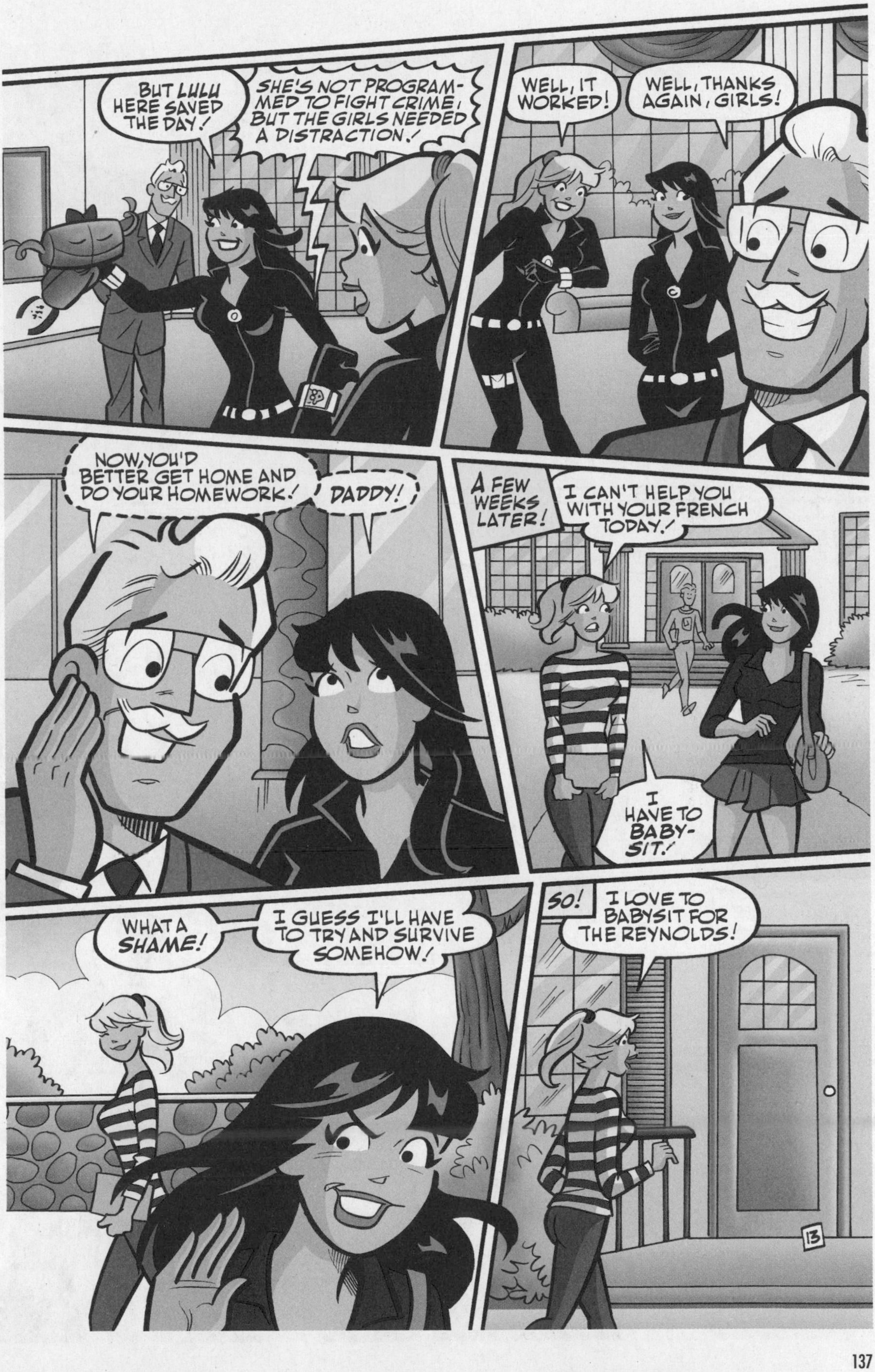
BUT LULU HERE SAVED THE DAY!
SHE'S NOT PROGRAMMED TO FIGHT CRIME, BUT THE GIRLS NEEDED A DISTRACTION!
WELL, IT WORKED!
WELL, THANKS AGAIN, GIRLS!
NOW, YOU'D BETTER GET HOME AND DO YOUR HOMEWORK!
DADDY!
A FEW WEEKS LATER!
I CAN'T HELP YOU WITH YOUR FRENCH TODAY!
I HAVE TO BABY-SIT!
WHAT A SHAME!
I GUESS I'LL HAVE TO TRY AND SURVIVE SOMEHOW!
SO!
I LOVE TO BABYSIT FOR THE REYNOLDS!
13

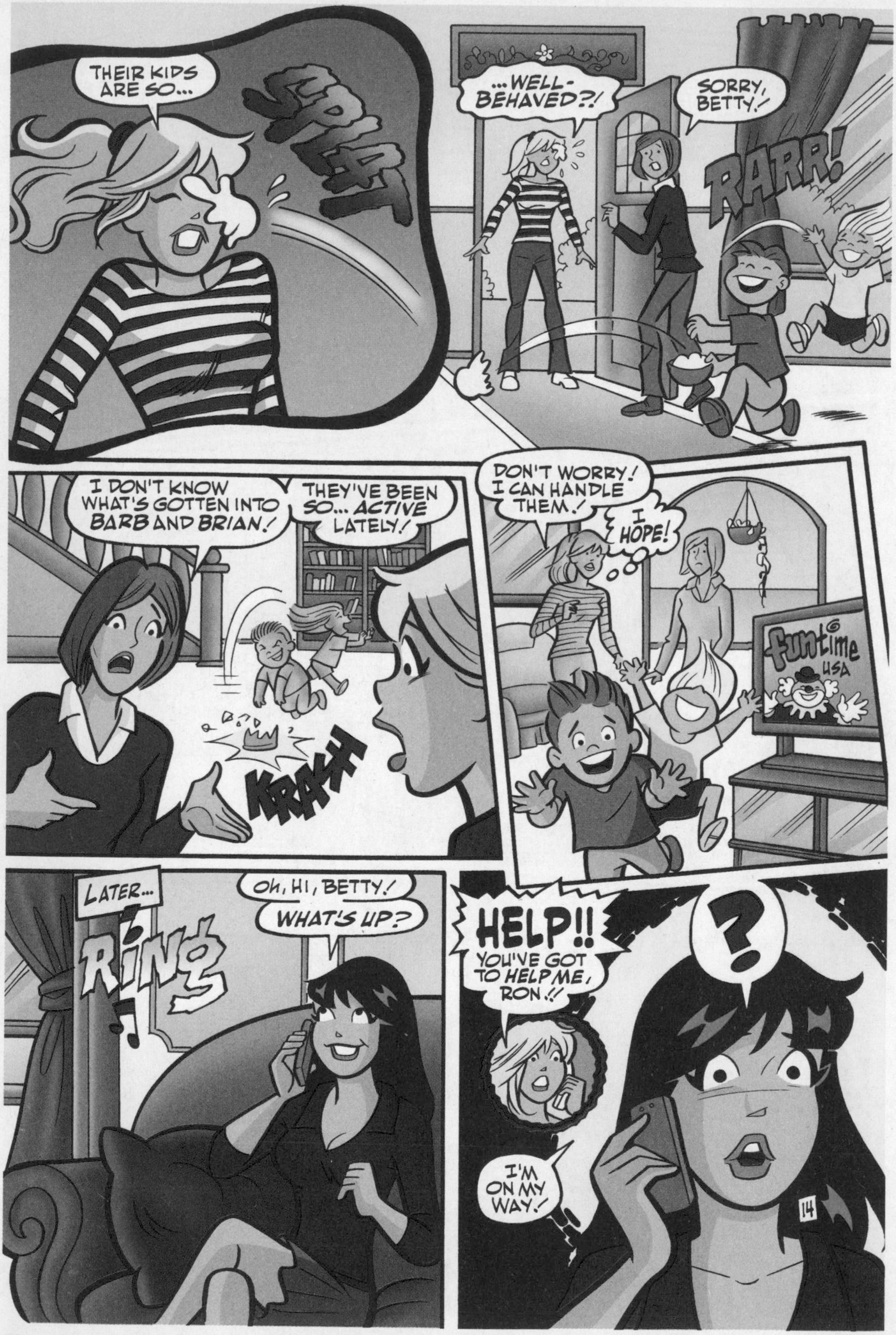
THEIR KIDS ARE SO...
SPLAT
...WELL-BEHAVED?!
SORRY, BETTY!
RARR!
I DON'T KNOW WHAT'S GOTTEN INTO BARB AND BRIAN!
THEY'VE BEEN SO... ACTIVE LATELY!
KRASH
DON'T WORRY! I CAN HANDLE THEM!
I HOPE!
funtime USA
LATER...
RING
Oh, HI, BETTY!
WHAT'S UP?
HELP!!
YOU'VE GOT TO HELP ME, RON!!
?
I'M ON MY WAY!
14

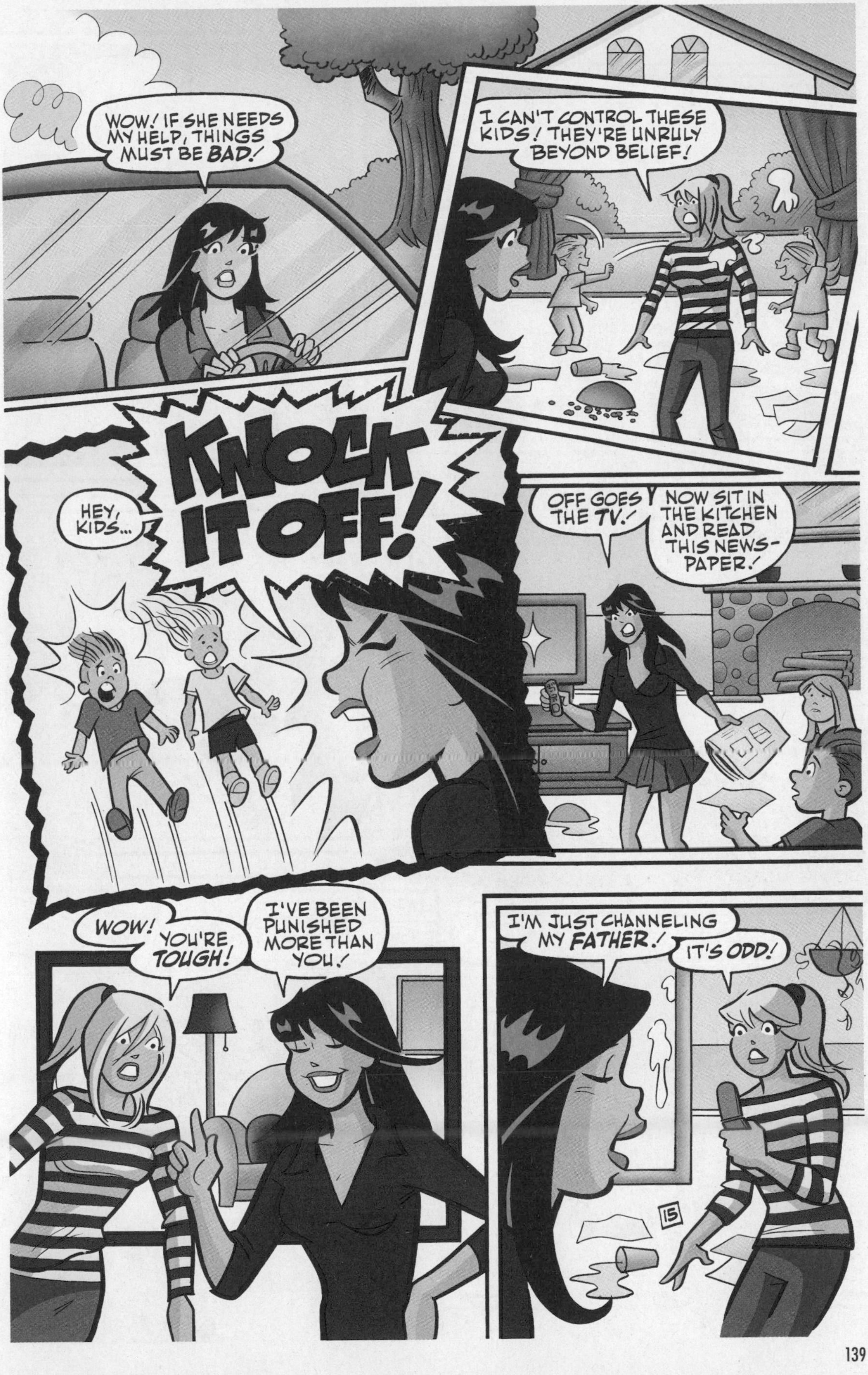
WOW! IF SHE NEEDS MY HELP, THINGS MUST BE BAD!
I CAN'T CONTROL THESE KIDS! THEY'RE UNRULY BEYOND BELIEF!
HEY, KIDS...
KNOCK IT OFF!
OFF GOES THE TV!
NOW SIT IN THE KITCHEN AND READ THIS NEWS-PAPER!
WOW!
YOU'RE TOUGH!
I'VE BEEN PUNISHED MORE THAN YOU!
I'M JUST CHANNELING MY FATHER!
IT'S ODD!
15

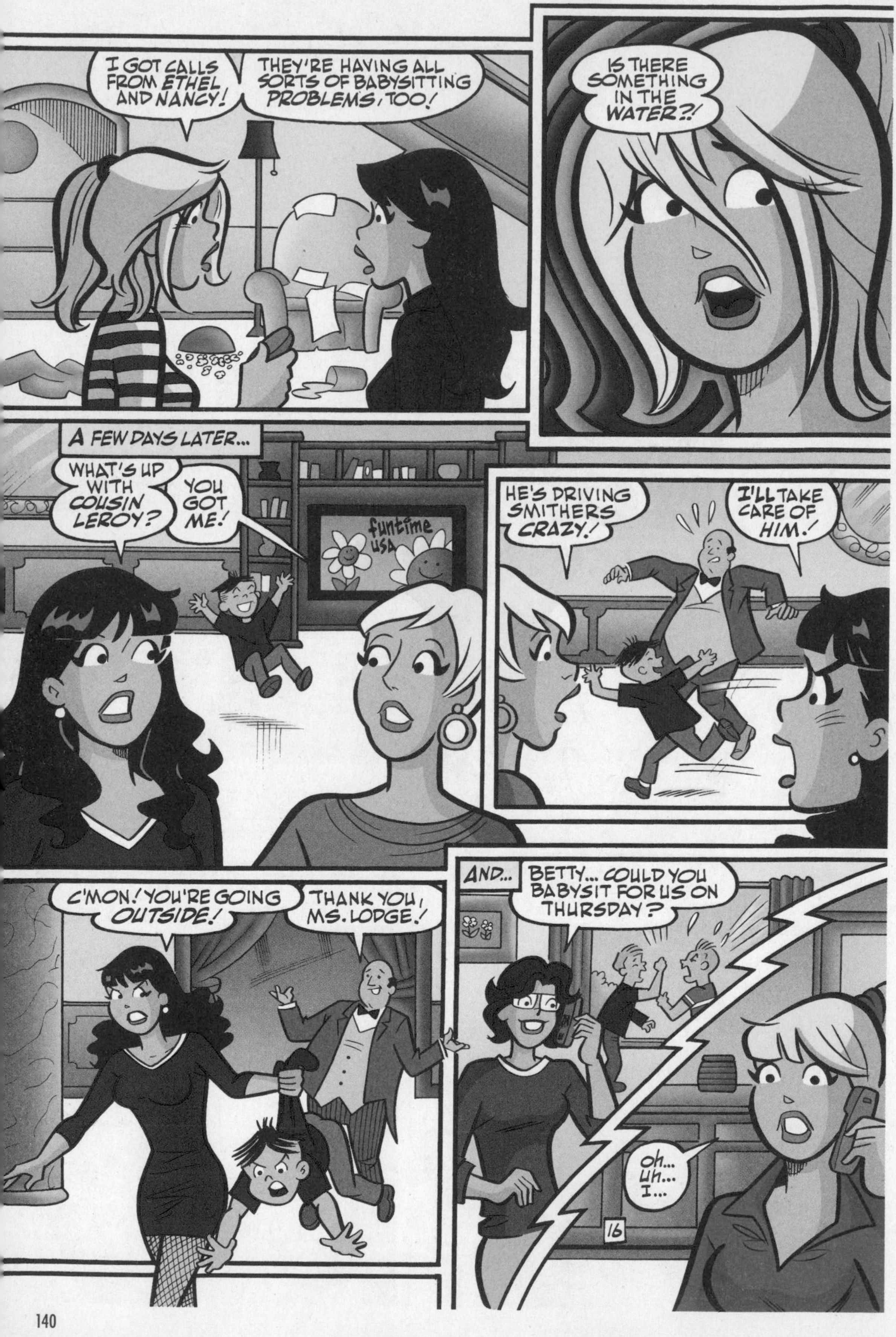
I GOT CALLS FROM ETHEL AND NANCY!
THEY'RE HAVING ALL SORTS OF BABYSITTING PROBLEMS, TOO!
IS THERE SOMETHING IN THE WATER?!
A FEW DAYS LATER...
WHAT'S UP WITH COUSIN LEROY?
YOU GOT ME!
funtime usa
HE'S DRIVING SMITHERS CRAZY!
I'LL TAKE CARE OF HIM!
C'MON! YOU'RE GOING OUTSIDE!
THANK YOU, MS. LODGE!
AND...
BETTY... COULD YOU BABYSIT FOR US ON THURSDAY?
OH... UH... I...
16

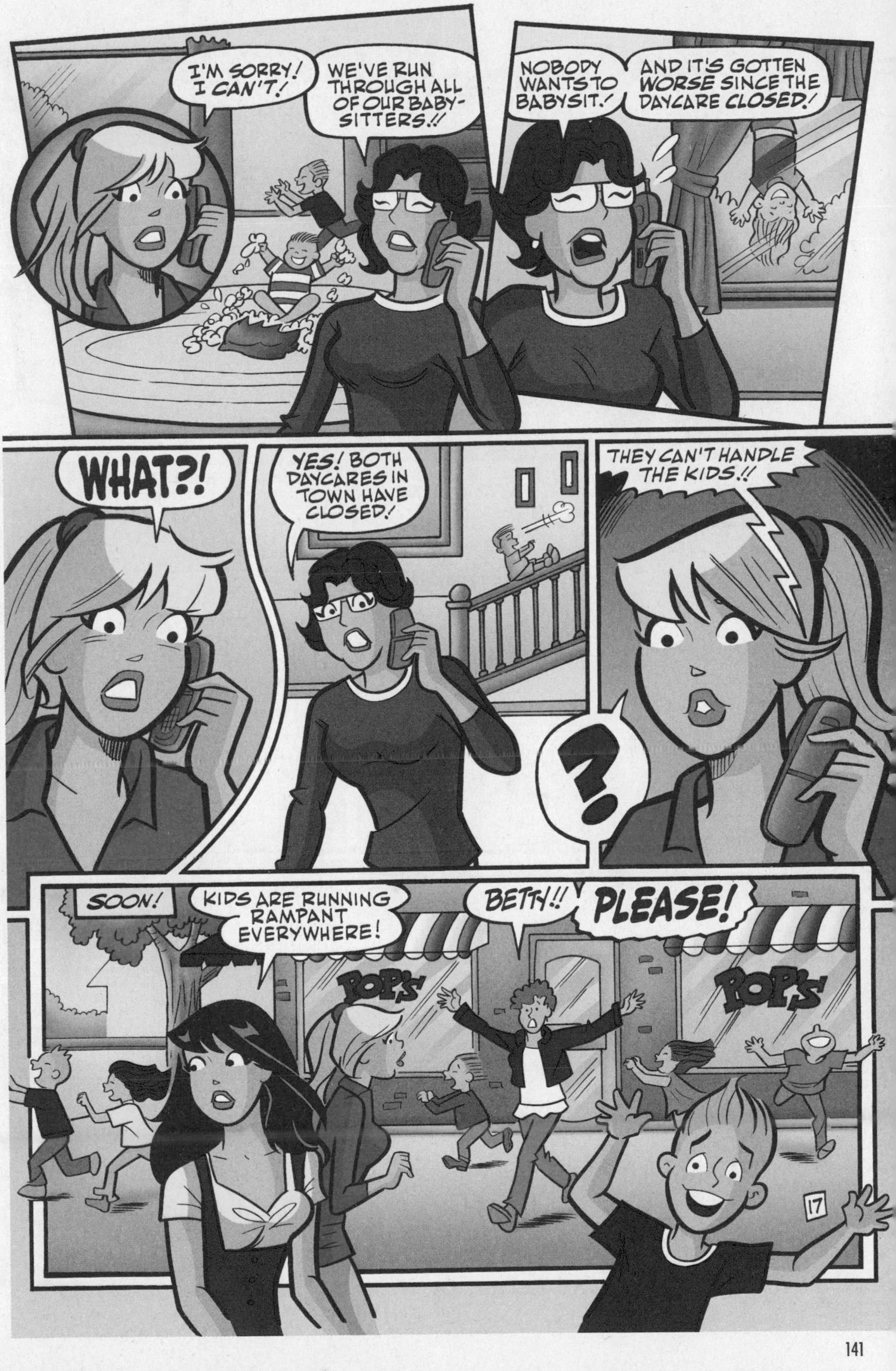
I'M SORRY! I CAN'T!
WE'VE RUN THROUGH ALL OF OUR BABY-SITTERS!!
NOBODY WANTS TO BABYSIT.!
AND IT'S GOTTEN WORSE SINCE THE DAYCARE CLOSED!
WHAT?!
YES! BOTH DAYCARES IN TOWN HAVE CLOSED!
THEY CAN'T HANDLE THE KIDS!!
?
SOON!
KIDS ARE RUNNING RAMPANT EVERYWHERE!
BETTY!!
PLEASE!
POP'S
POP'S
17

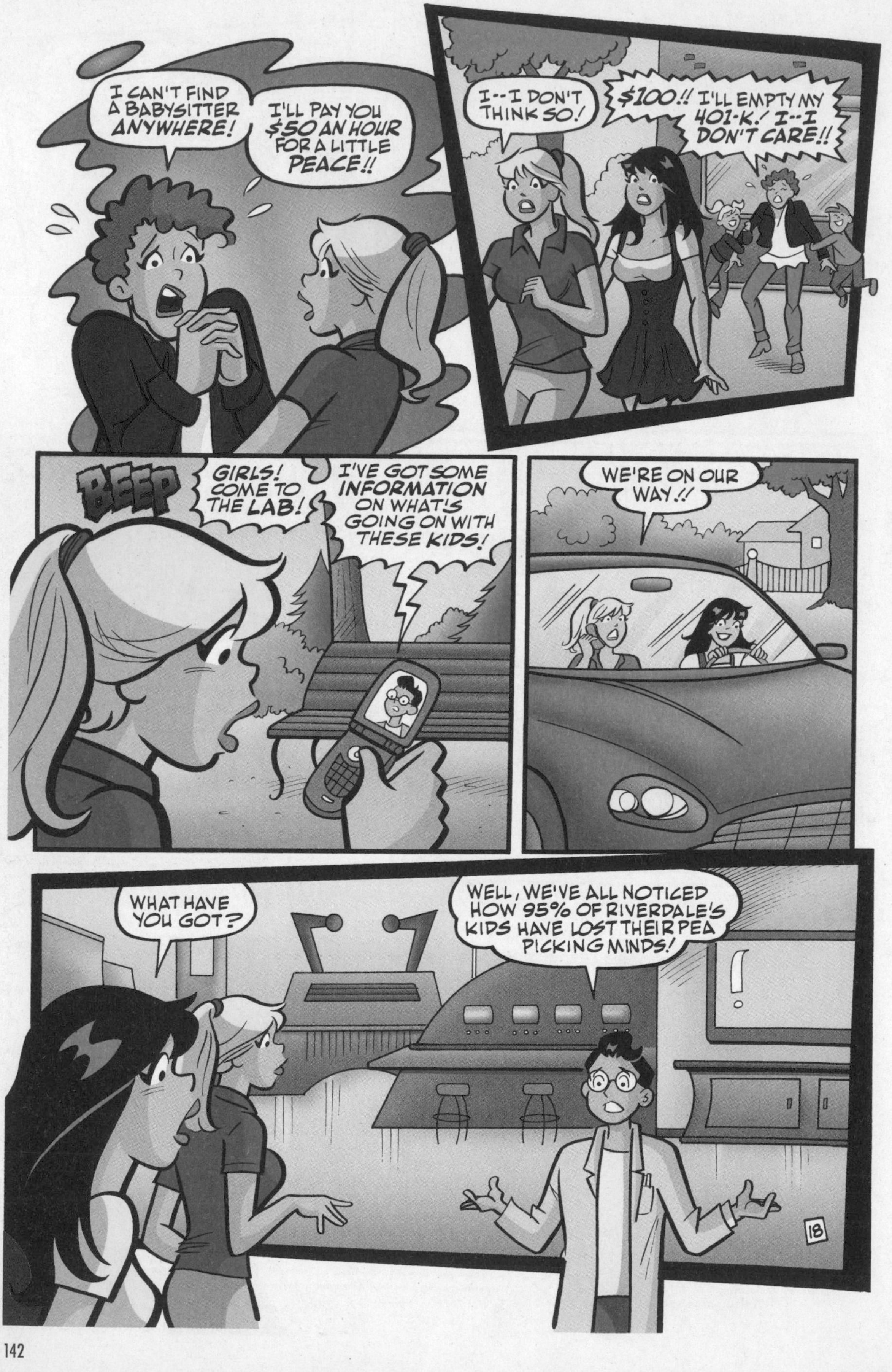
I CAN'T FIND A BABYSITTER ANYWHERE!
I'LL PAY YOU $50 AN HOUR FOR A LITTLE PEACE!!
I--I DON'T THINK SO!
$100!! I'LL EMPTY MY 401-K! I--I DON'T CARE!!
BEEP
GIRLS! COME TO THE LAB!
I'VE GOT SOME INFORMATION ON WHAT'S GOING ON WITH THESE KIDS!
WE'RE ON OUR WAY!!
WHAT HAVE YOU GOT?
WELL, WE'VE ALL NOTICED HOW 95% OF RIVERDALE'S KIDS HAVE LOST THEIR PEA PICKING MINDS!
18

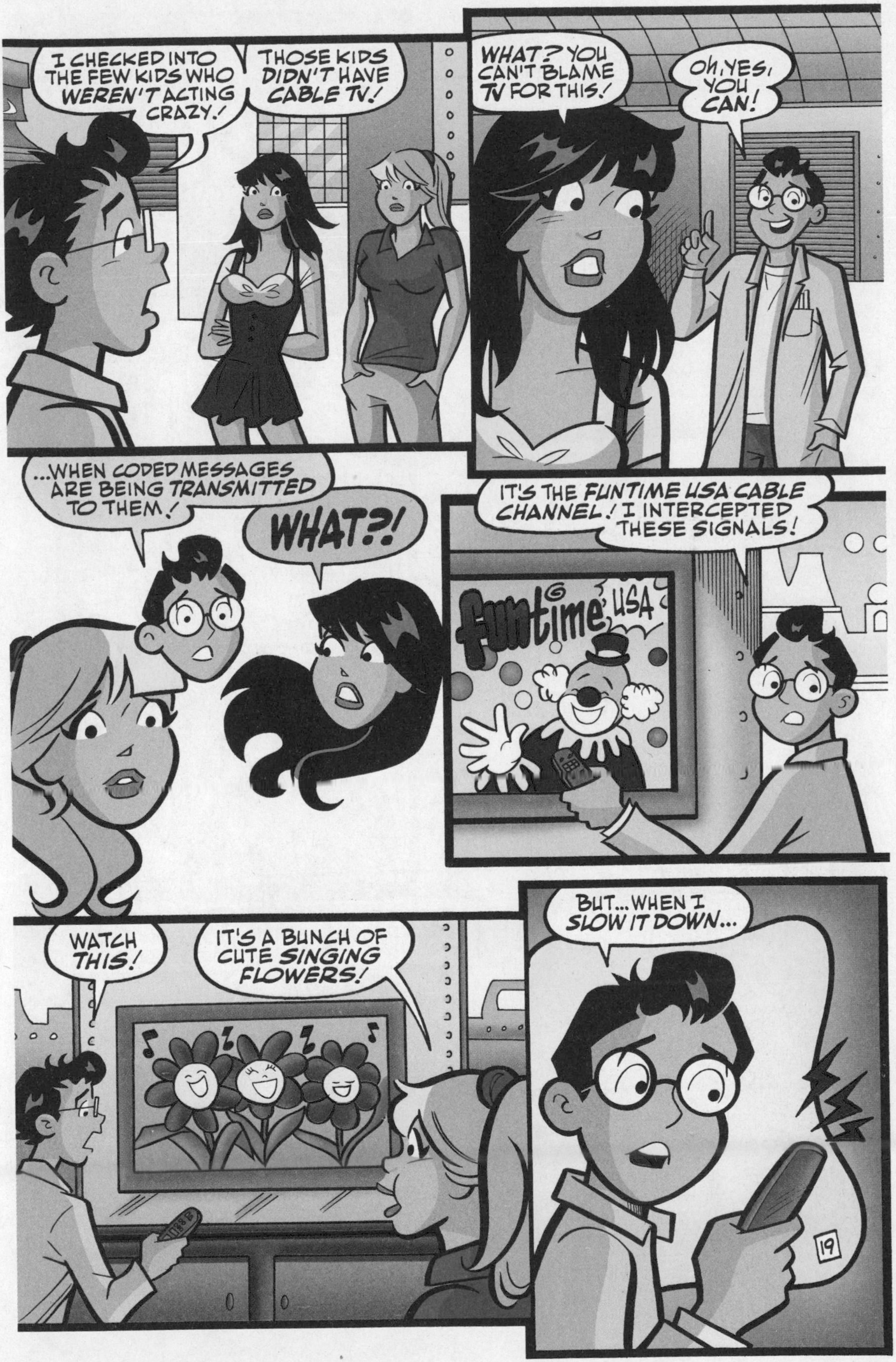

I CHECKED INTO THE FEW KIDS WHO WEREN'T ACTING CRAZY!
THOSE KIDS DIDN'T HAVE CABLE TV!
WHAT? YOU CAN'T BLAME TV FOR THIS!
Oh, YES, YOU CAN!
...WHEN CODED MESSAGES ARE BEING TRANSMITTED TO THEM!
WHAT?!
IT'S THE FUNTIME USA CABLE CHANNEL! I INTERCEPTED THESE SIGNALS!
funtime USA
WATCH THIS!
IT'S A BUNCH OF CUTE SINGING FLOWERS!
BUT...WHEN I SLOW IT DOWN...
19

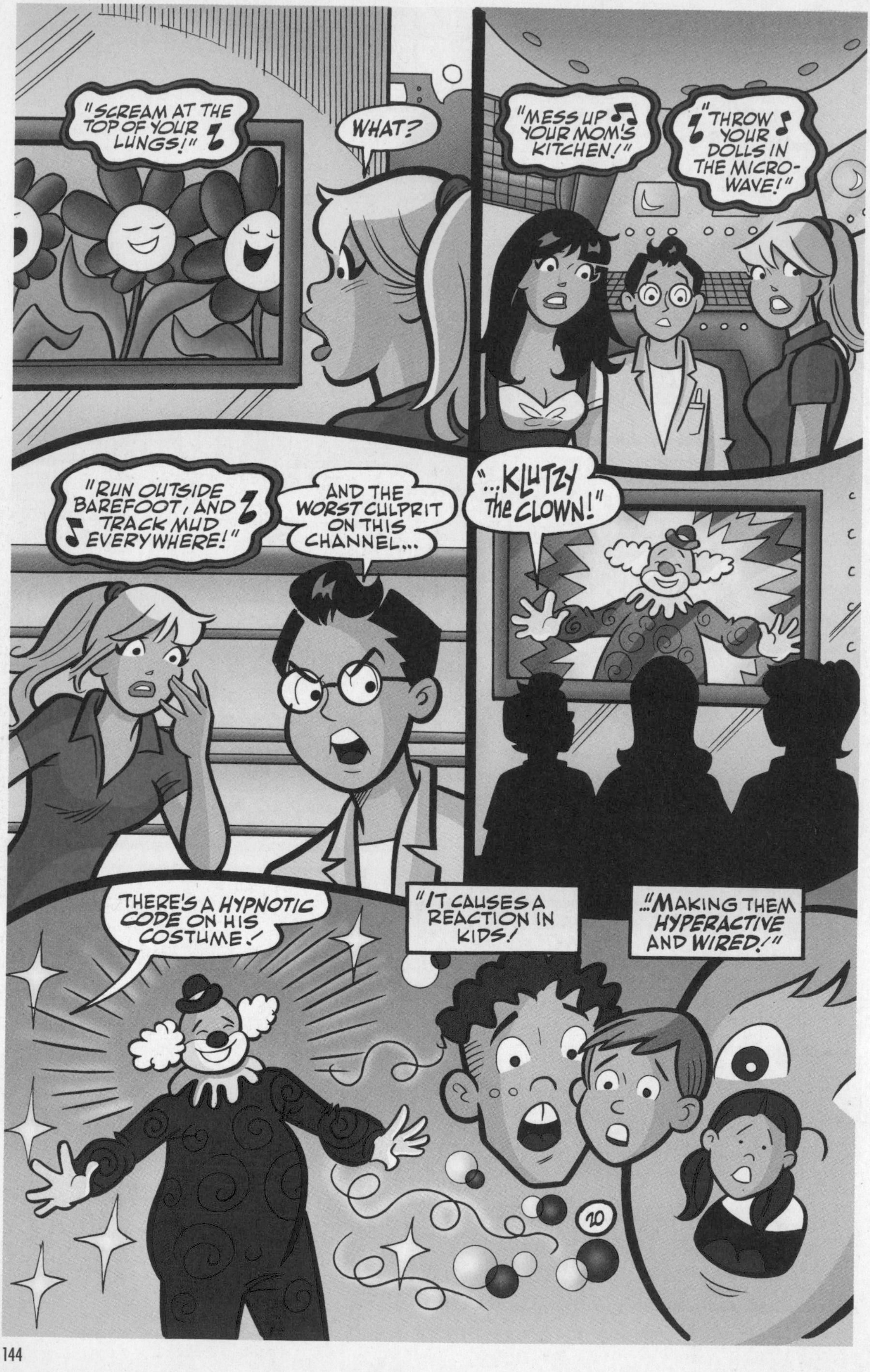
"SCREAM AT THE TOP OF YOUR LUNGS!"
WHAT?
"MESS UP YOUR MOM'S KITCHEN!"
"THROW YOUR DOLLS IN THE MICRO-WAVE!"
"RUN OUTSIDE BAREFOOT, AND TRACK MUD EVERYWHERE!"
AND THE WORST CULPRIT ON THIS CHANNEL...
"...KLUTZY the CLOWN!"
THERE'S A HYPNOTIC CODE ON HIS COSTUME!
"IT CAUSES A REACTION IN KIDS!
..."MAKING THEM HYPERACTIVE AND WIRED!"
20

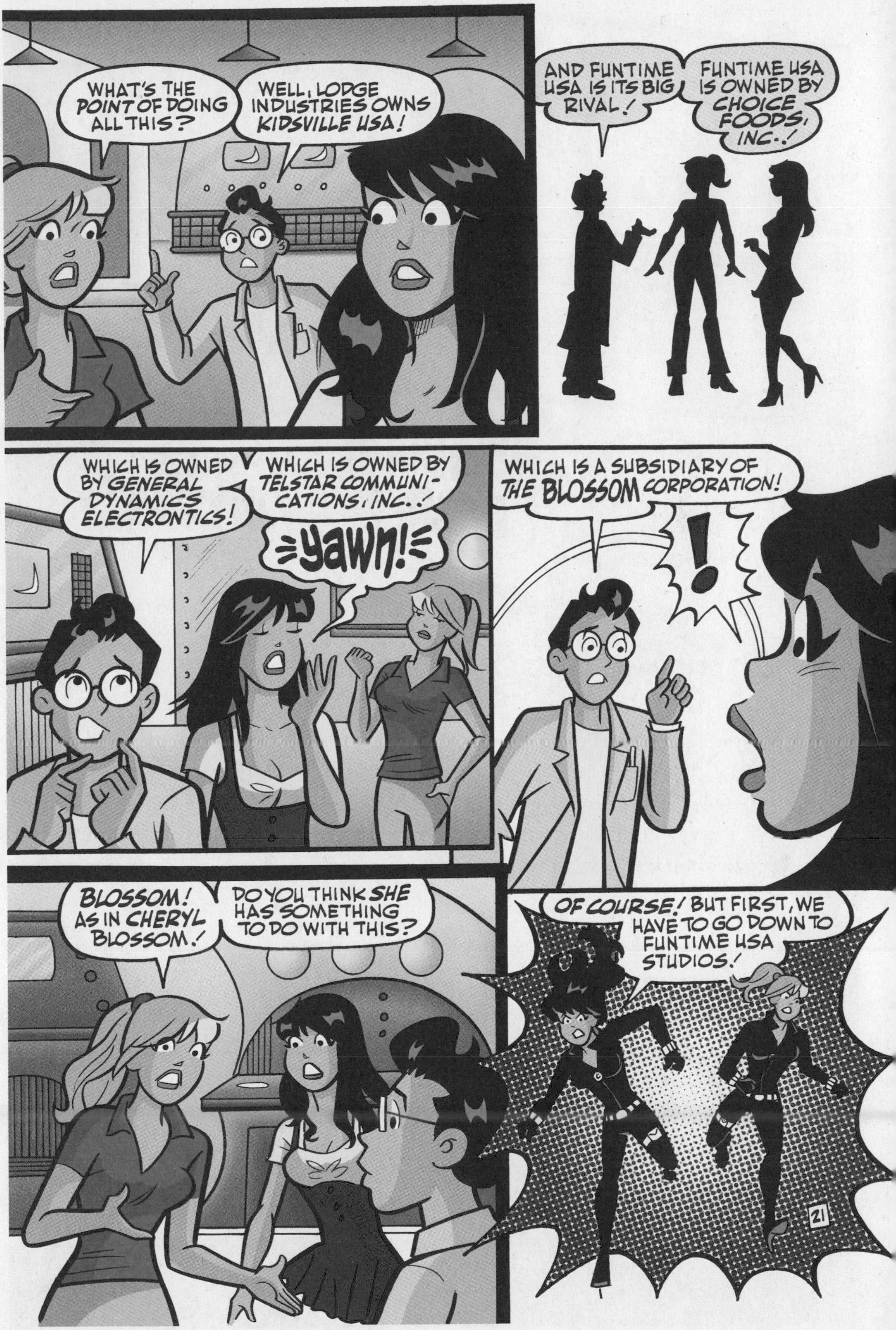
WHAT'S THE POINT OF DOING ALL THIS?
WELL, LODGE INDUSTRIES OWNS KIDSVILLE USA!
AND FUNTIME USA IS ITS BIG RIVAL!
FUNTIME USA IS OWNED BY CHOICE FOODS, INC.!
WHICH IS OWNED BY GENERAL DYNAMICS ELECTRONTICS!
WHICH IS OWNED BY TELSTAR COMMUNICATIONS, INC.!
YAWN!
WHICH IS A SUBSIDIARY OF THE BLOSSOM CORPORATION!
!
BLOSSOM! AS IN CHERYL BLOSSOM!
DO YOU THINK SHE HAS SOMETHING TO DO WITH THIS?
OF COURSE! BUT FIRST, WE HAVE TO GO DOWN TO FUNTIME USA STUDIOS!
21

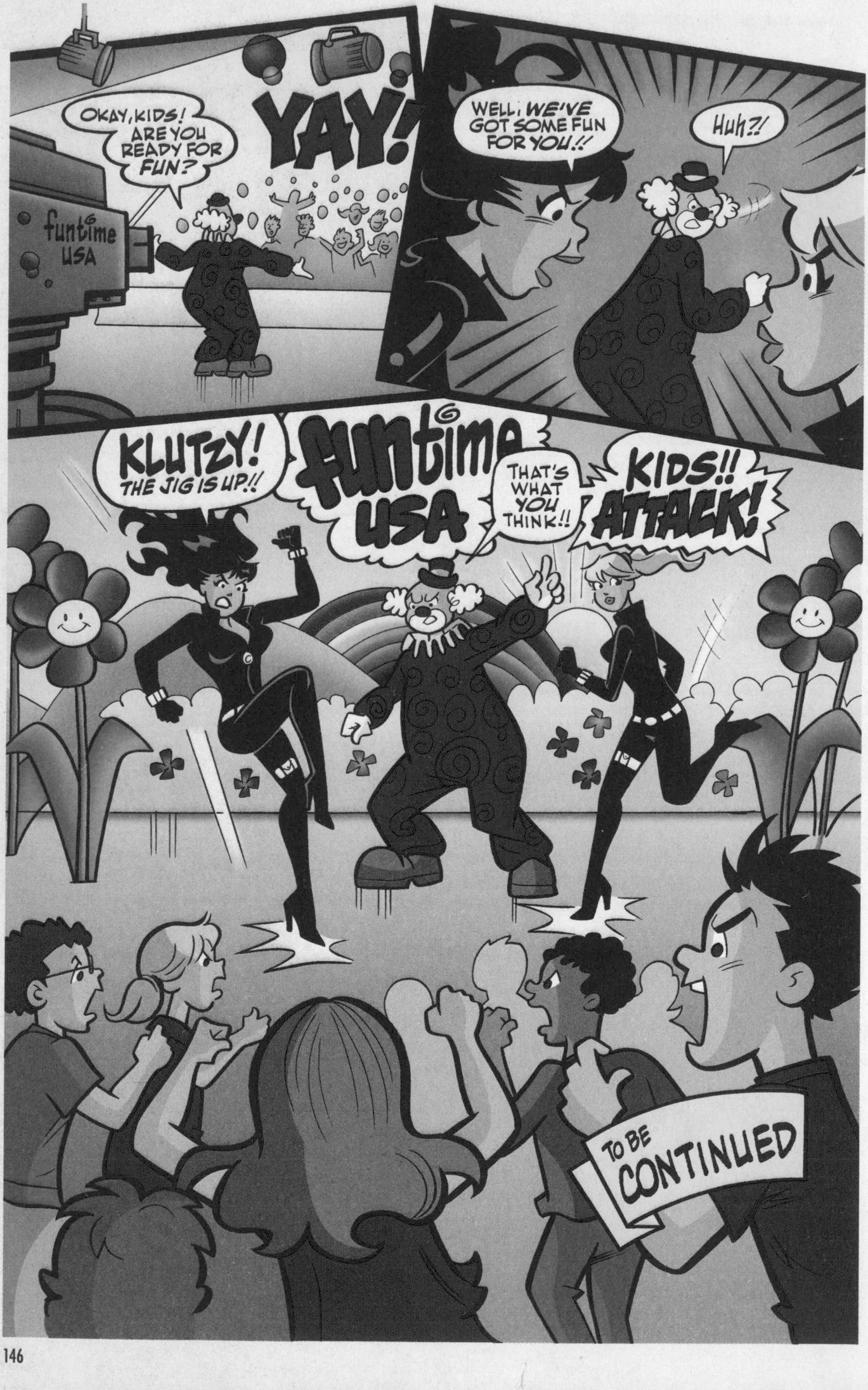
OKAY, KIDS! ARE YOU READY FOR FUN?
YAY!
funtime USA
WELL, WE'VE GOT SOME FUN FOR YOU!!
Huh?!
KLUTZY! THE JIG IS UP!!
funtime USA
THAT'S WHAT YOU THINK!!
KIDS!! ATTACK!
TO BE CONTINUED

Spy Girlz

PART TWO

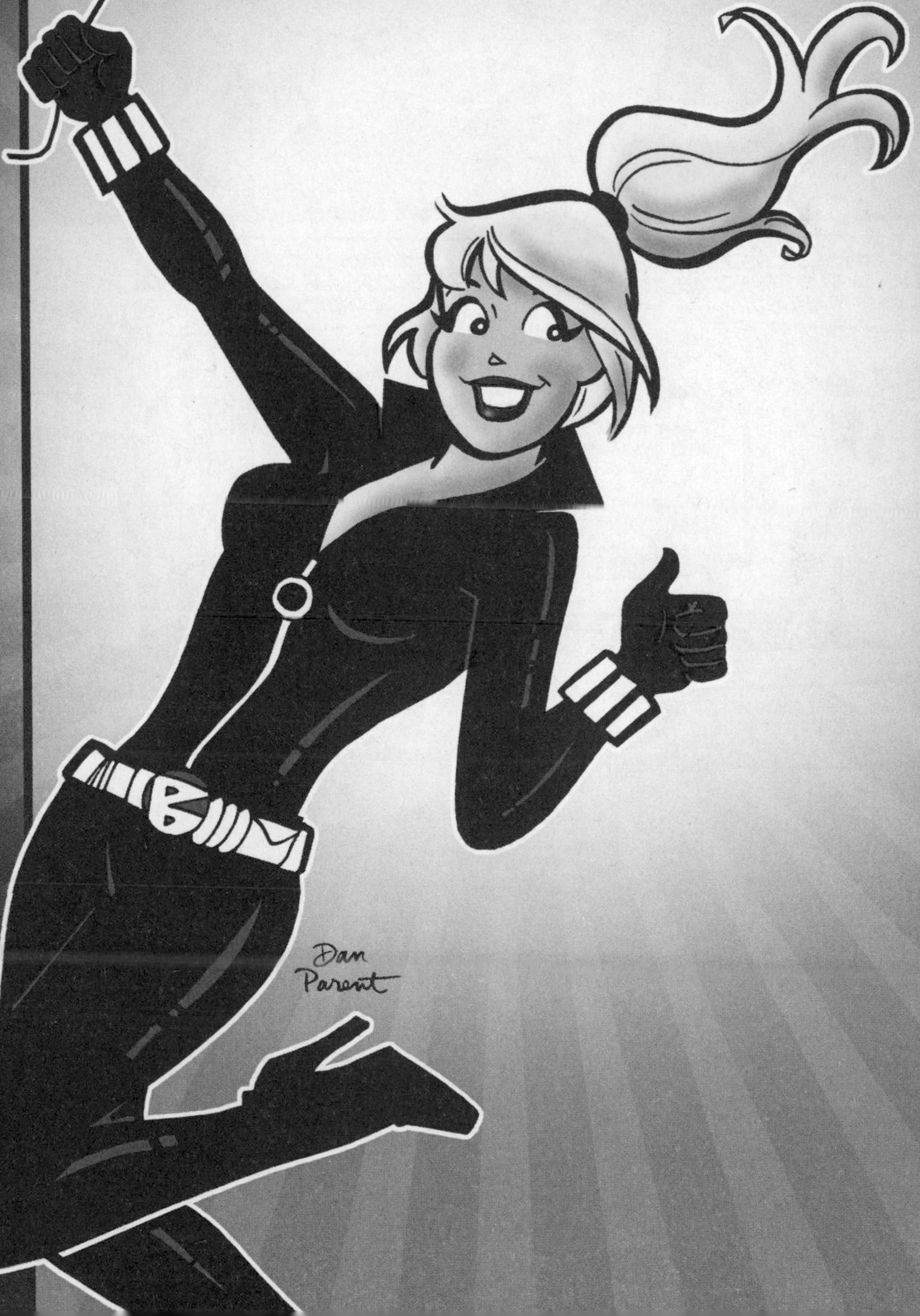

Dan Parent

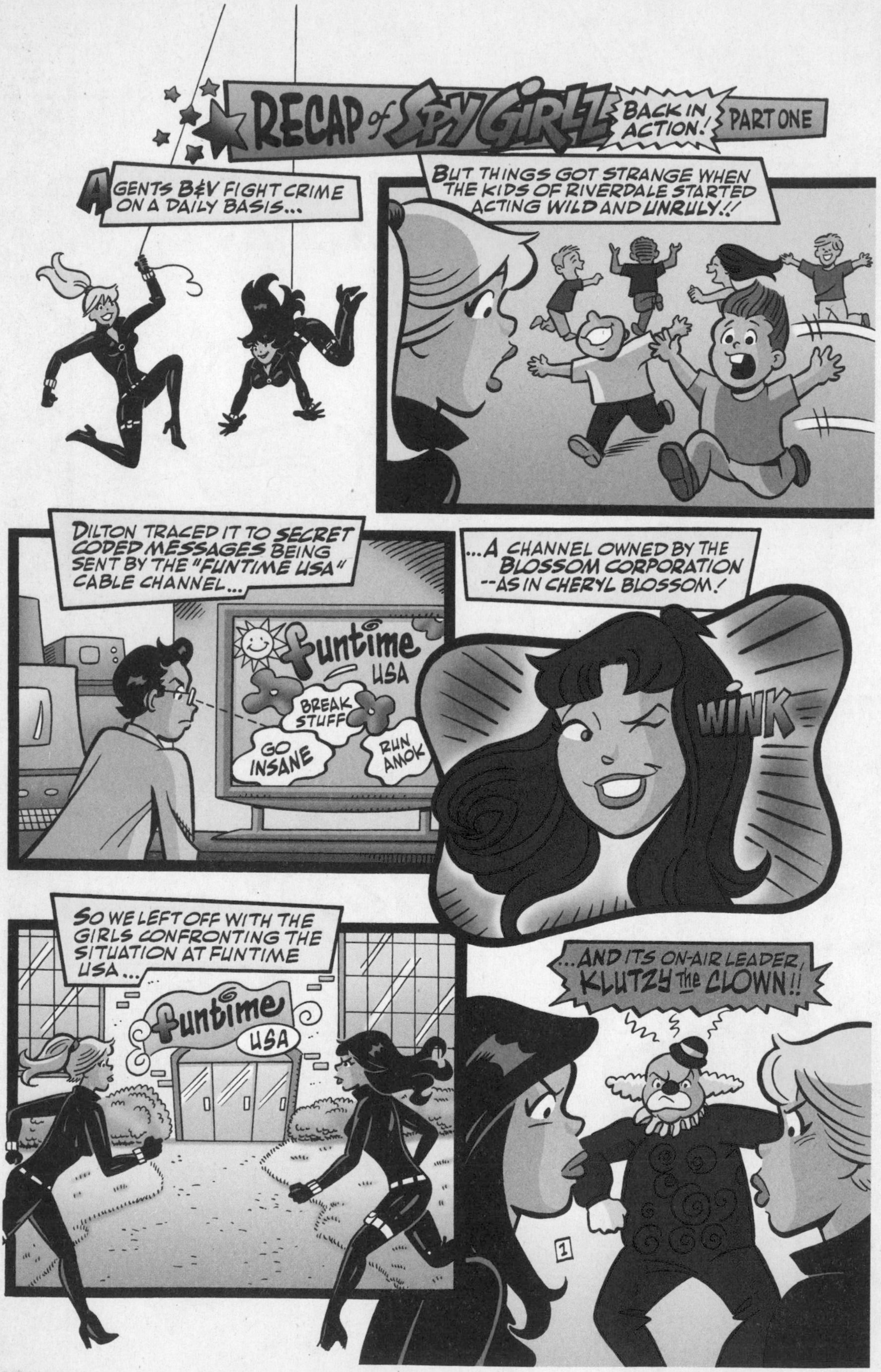
RECAP of SPY GIRLZ BACK IN ACTION! PART ONE
AGENTS B&V FIGHT CRIME ON A DAILY BASIS...
BUT THINGS GOT STRANGE WHEN THE KIDS OF RIVERDALE STARTED ACTING WILD AND UNRULY!!
DILTON TRACED IT TO SECRET CODED MESSAGES BEING SENT BY THE "FUNTIME USA" CABLE CHANNEL...
funtime USA
BREAK STUFF
GO INSANE
RUN AMOK
...A CHANNEL OWNED BY THE BLOSSOM CORPORATION --AS IN CHERYL BLOSSOM!
WINK
SO WE LEFT OFF WITH THE GIRLS CONFRONTING THE SITUATION AT FUNTIME USA...
funtime USA
...AND ITS ON-AIR LEADER, KLUTZY the CLOWN!!
1

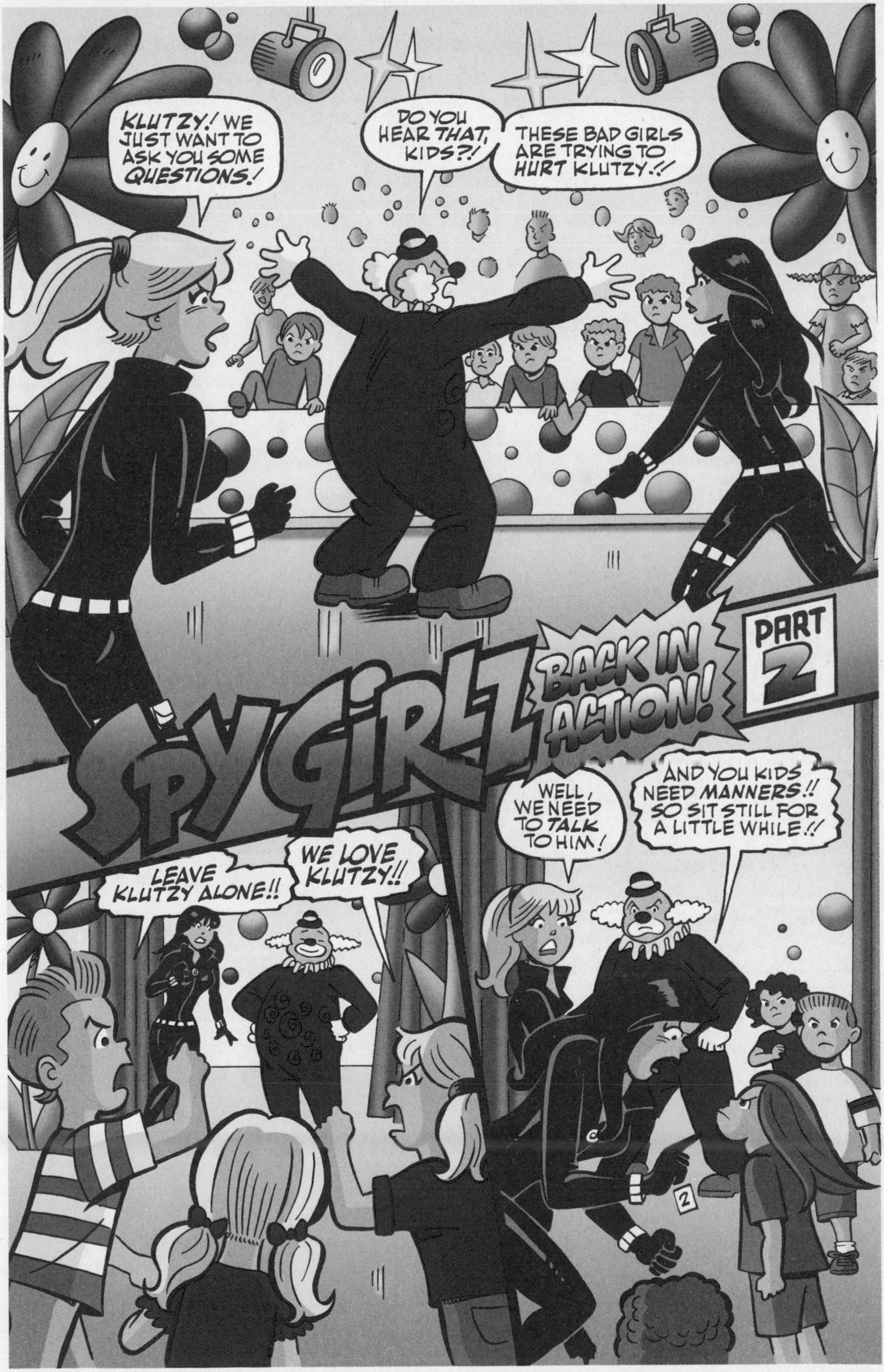
KLUTZY! WE JUST WANT TO ASK YOU SOME QUESTIONS!
DO YOU HEAR THAT, KIDS?!
THESE BAD GIRLS ARE TRYING TO HURT KLUTZY!!
SPY GIRLZ BACK IN ACTION! PART 2
LEAVE KLUTZY ALONE!!
WE LOVE KLUTZY!!
WELL, WE NEED TO TALK TO HIM!
AND YOU KIDS NEED MANNERS!! SO SIT STILL FOR A LITTLE WHILE!!
2

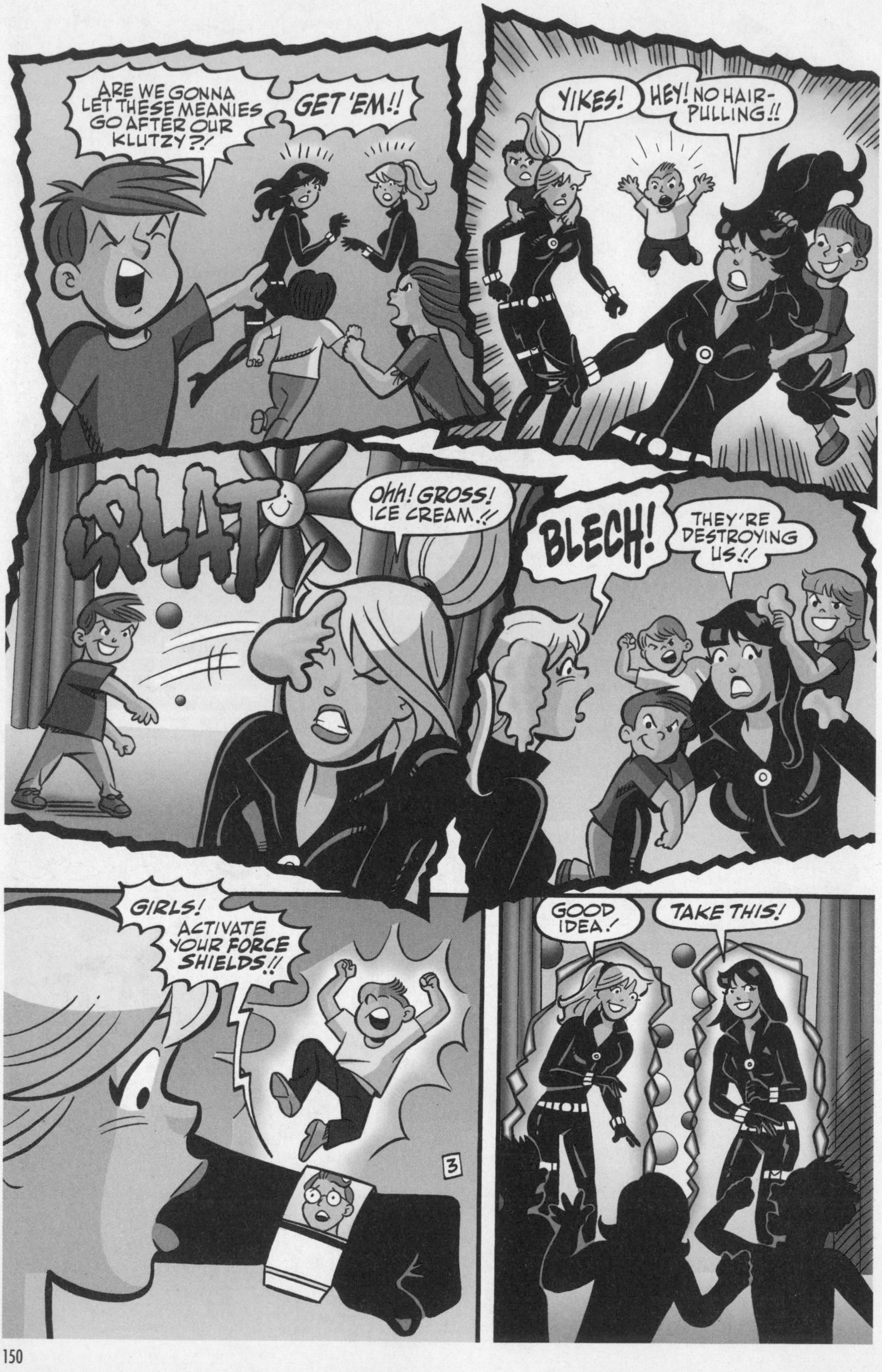
ARE WE GONNA LET THESE MEANIES GO AFTER OUR KLUTZY?!
GET 'EM!!
YIKES!
HEY! NO HAIR-PULLING!!
SPLAT
Ohh! GROSS! ICE CREAM!!
BLECH!
THEY'RE DESTROYING US!!
GIRLS! ACTIVATE YOUR FORCE SHIELDS!!
3
GOOD IDEA!
TAKE THIS!

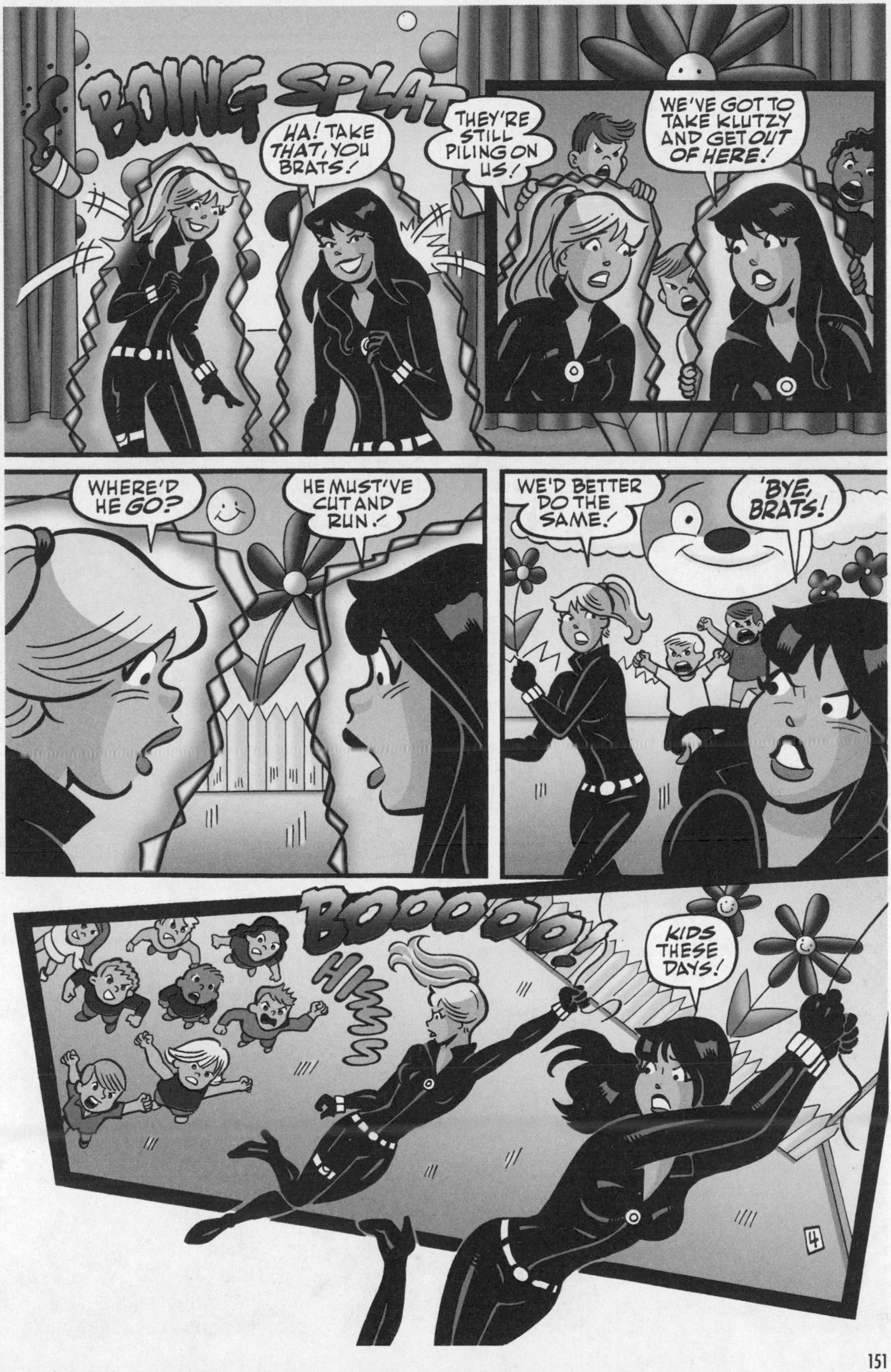
BOING
SPLAT
HA! TAKE THAT, YOU BRATS!
THEY'RE STILL PILING ON US!
WE'VE GOT TO TAKE KLUTZY AND GET OUT OF HERE!
WHERE'D HE GO?
HE MUST'VE CUT AND RUN!
WE'D BETTER DO THE SAME!
'BYE, BRATS!
BOOOOOO!
HISSS
KIDS THESE DAYS!
4

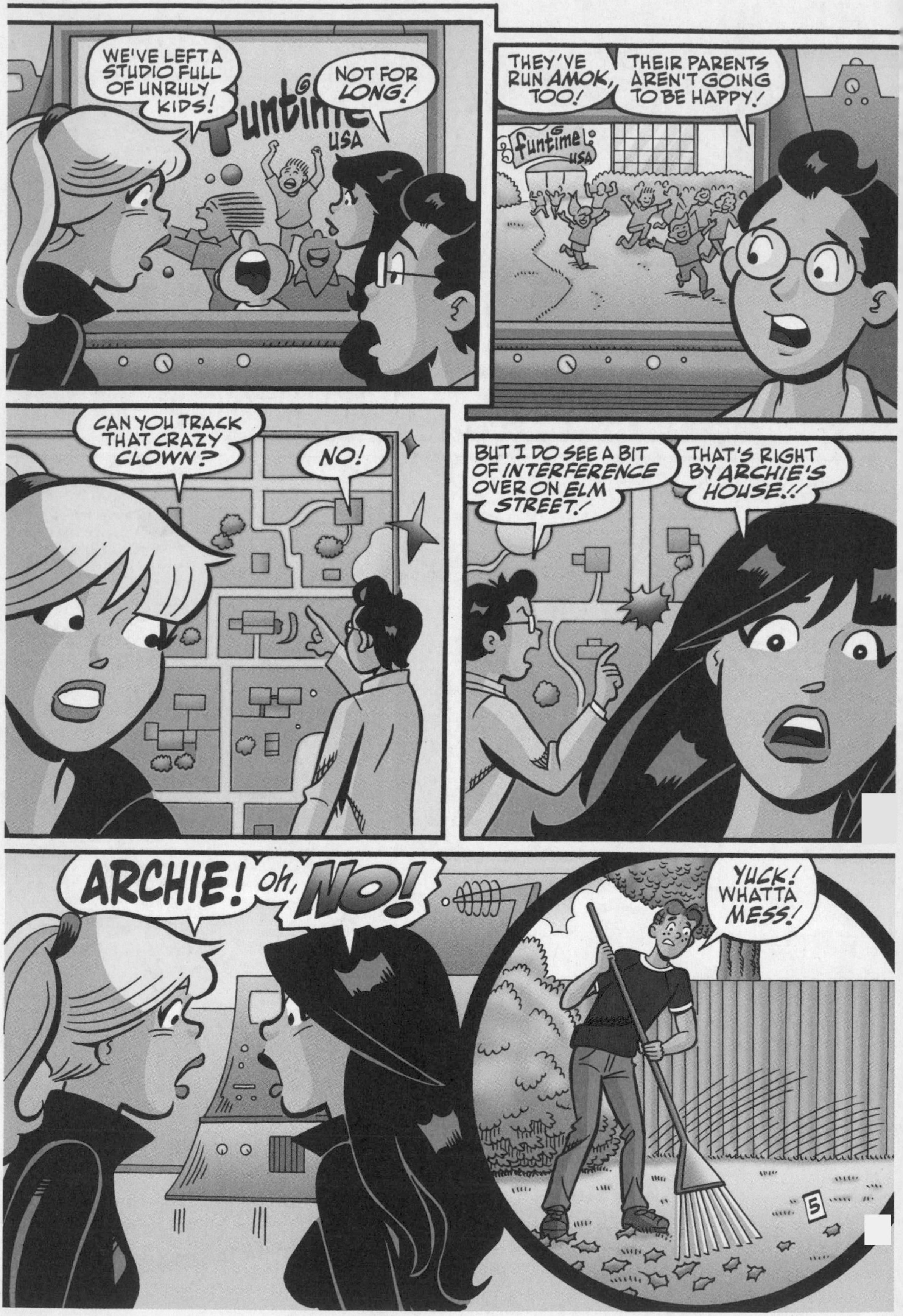
WE'VE LEFT A STUDIO FULL OF UNRULY KIDS!
NOT FOR LONG!
funtime USA
THEY'VE RUN AMOK, TOO!
THEIR PARENTS AREN'T GOING TO BE HAPPY!
funtime USA
CAN YOU TRACK THAT CRAZY CLOWN?
NO!
BUT I DO SEE A BIT OF INTERFERENCE OVER ON ELM STREET.!
THAT'S RIGHT BY ARCHIE'S HOUSE.!!
ARCHIE! oh, NO!
YUCK! WHATTA MESS!

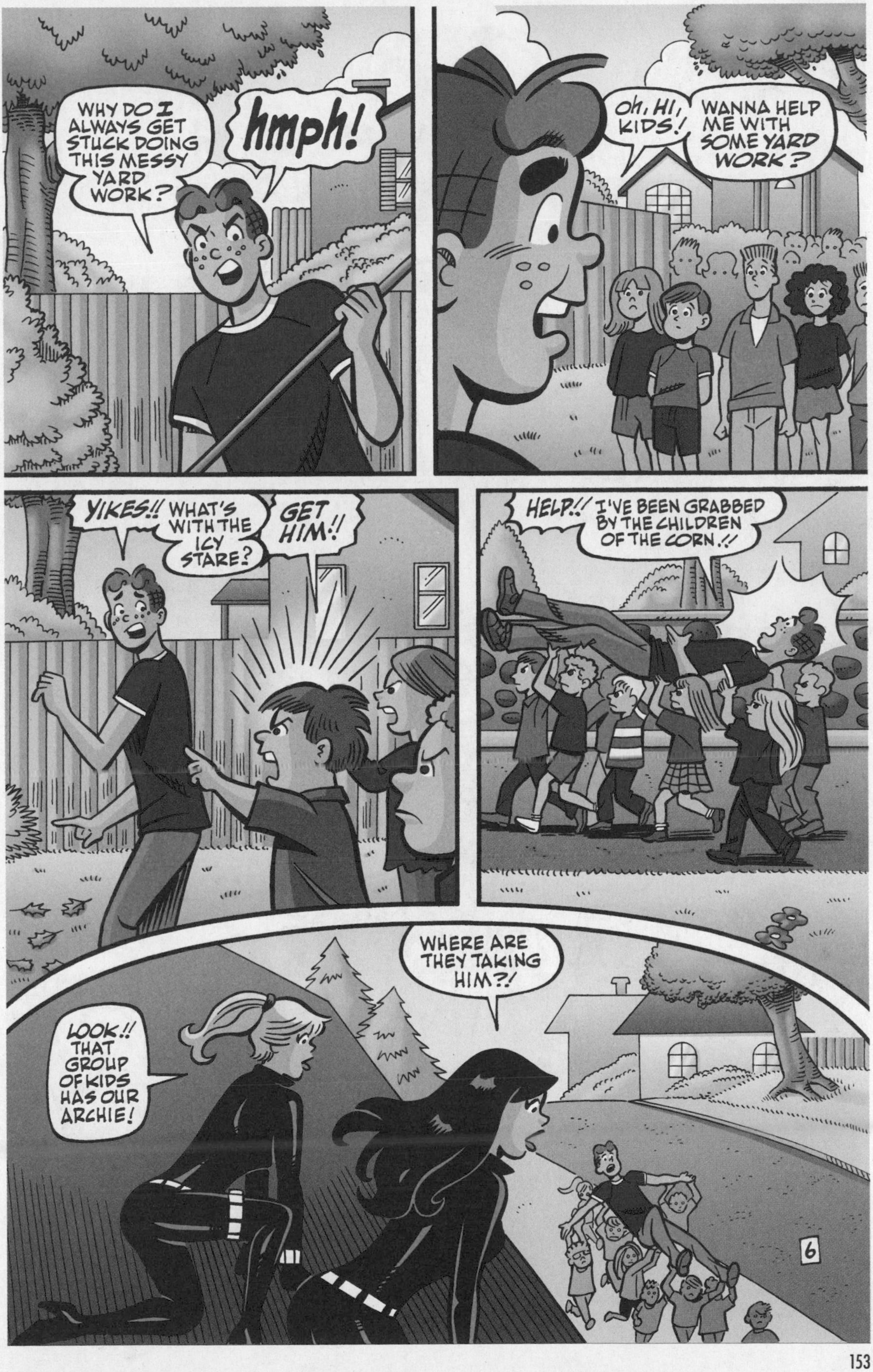
WHY DO I ALWAYS GET STUCK DOING THIS MESSY YARD WORK?
hmph!
OH, HI, KIDS!
WANNA HELP ME WITH SOME YARD WORK?
YIKES!!
WHAT'S WITH THE ICY STARE?
GET HIM!!
HELP!! I'VE BEEN GRABBED BY THE CHILDREN OF THE CORN!!
WHERE ARE THEY TAKING HIM?!
LOOK!! THAT GROUP OF KIDS HAS OUR ARCHIE!
6

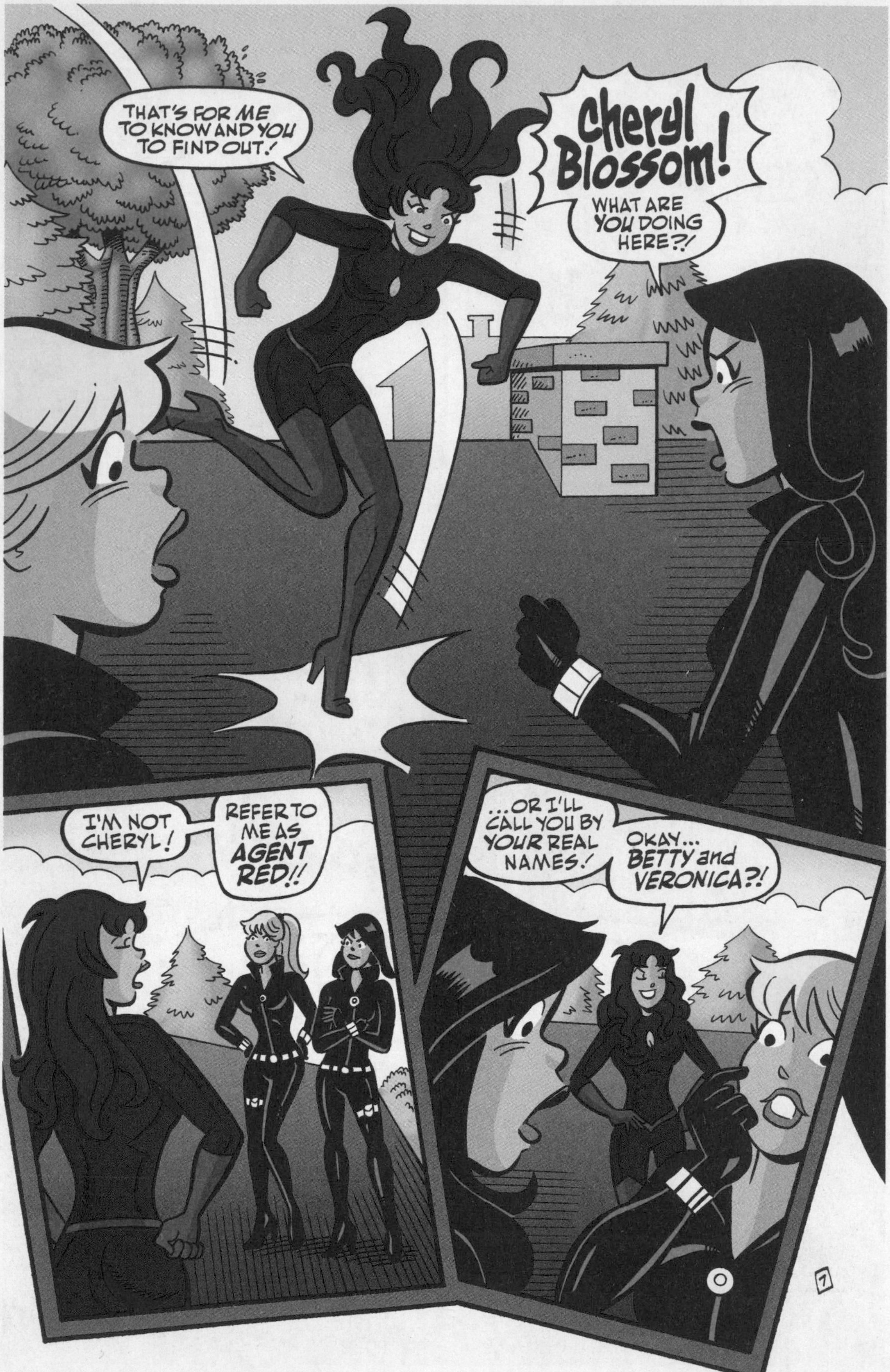
THAT'S FOR ME TO KNOW AND YOU TO FIND OUT!
Cheryl Blossom! WHAT ARE YOU DOING HERE?!
I'M NOT CHERYL!
REFER TO ME AS AGENT RED!!
...OR I'LL CALL YOU BY YOUR REAL NAMES!
OKAY... BETTY and VERONICA?!
7

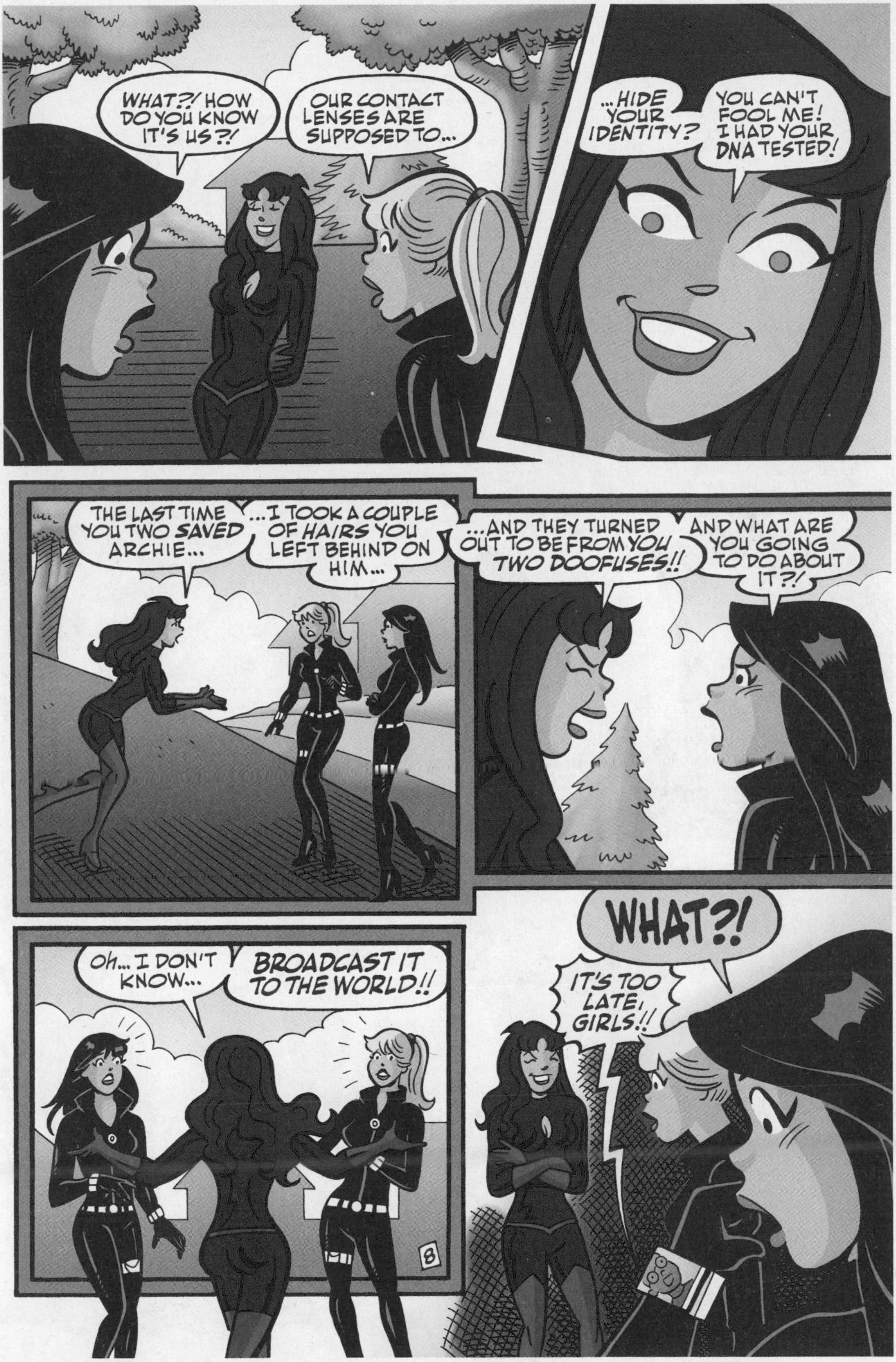
WHAT?! HOW DO YOU KNOW IT'S US?!
OUR CONTACT LENSES ARE SUPPOSED TO...
...HIDE YOUR IDENTITY?
YOU CAN'T FOOL ME! I HAD YOUR DNA TESTED!
THE LAST TIME YOU TWO SAVED ARCHIE...
...I TOOK A COUPLE OF HAIRS YOU LEFT BEHIND ON HIM...
...AND THEY TURNED OUT TO BE FROM YOU TWO DOOFUSES!!
AND WHAT ARE YOU GOING TO DO ABOUT IT?!
Oh... I DON'T KNOW...
BROADCAST IT TO THE WORLD!!
8
WHAT?!
IT'S TOO LATE, GIRLS!!

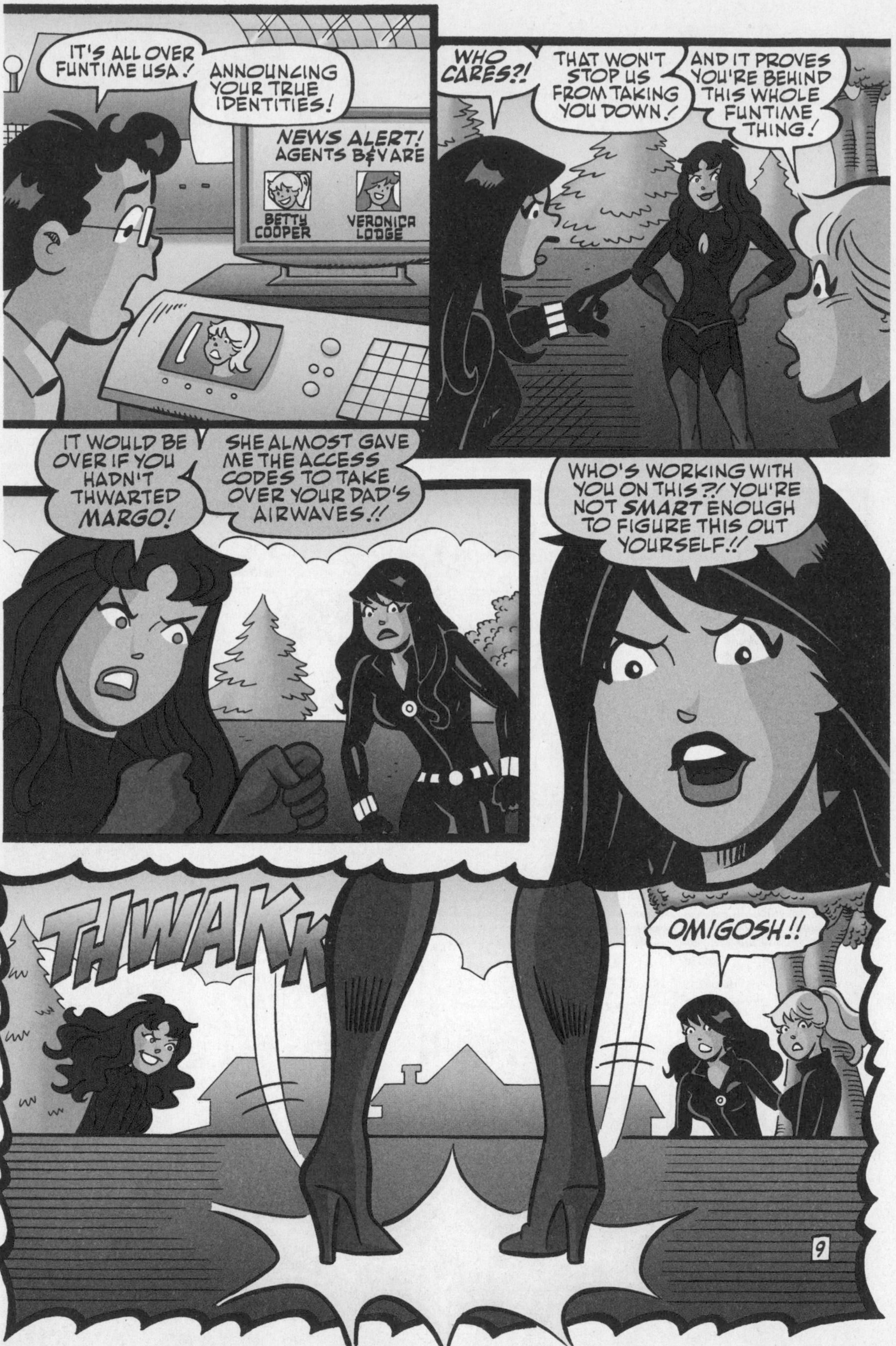
IT'S ALL OVER FUNTIME USA!
ANNOUNCING YOUR TRUE IDENTITIES!
NEWS ALERT! AGENTS B&V ARE
BETTY COOPER
VERONICA LODGE
WHO CARES?!
THAT WON'T STOP US FROM TAKING YOU DOWN!
AND IT PROVES YOU'RE BEHIND THIS WHOLE FUNTIME THING!
IT WOULD BE OVER IF YOU HADN'T THWARTED MARGO!
SHE ALMOST GAVE ME THE ACCESS CODES TO TAKE OVER YOUR DAD'S AIRWAVES!!
WHO'S WORKING WITH YOU ON THIS?! YOU'RE NOT SMART ENOUGH TO FIGURE THIS OUT YOURSELF!!
THWAKK
OMIGOSH!!
9

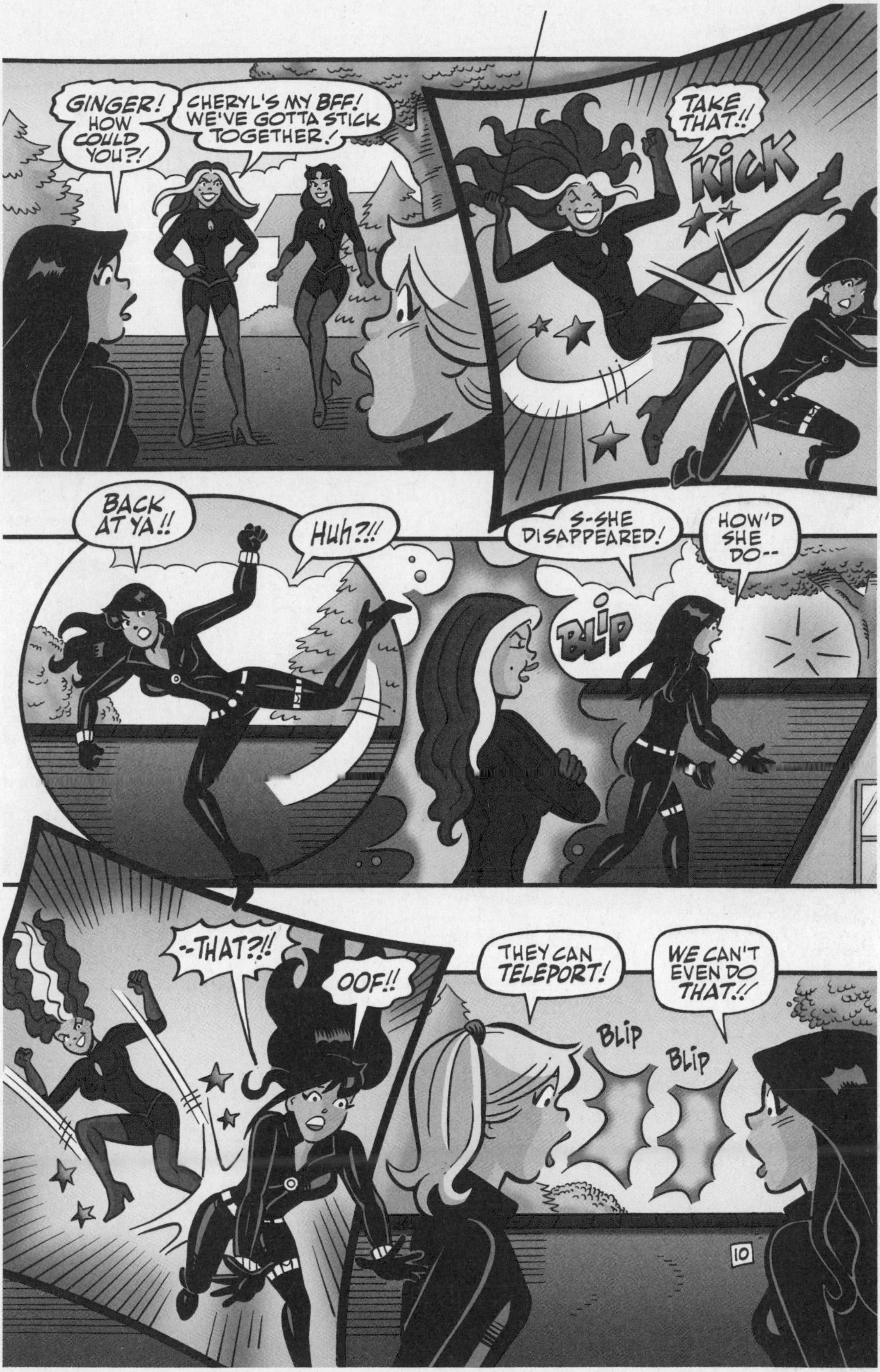
GINGER! HOW COULD YOU?!
CHERYL'S MY BFF! WE'VE GOTTA STICK TOGETHER!
TAKE THAT!!
KICK
BACK AT YA!!
Huh?!!
S-SHE DISAPPEARED!
HOW'D SHE DO--
BLIP
--THAT?!!
OOF!!
THEY CAN TELEPORT!
WE CAN'T EVEN DO THAT!!
BLIP
BLIP
10

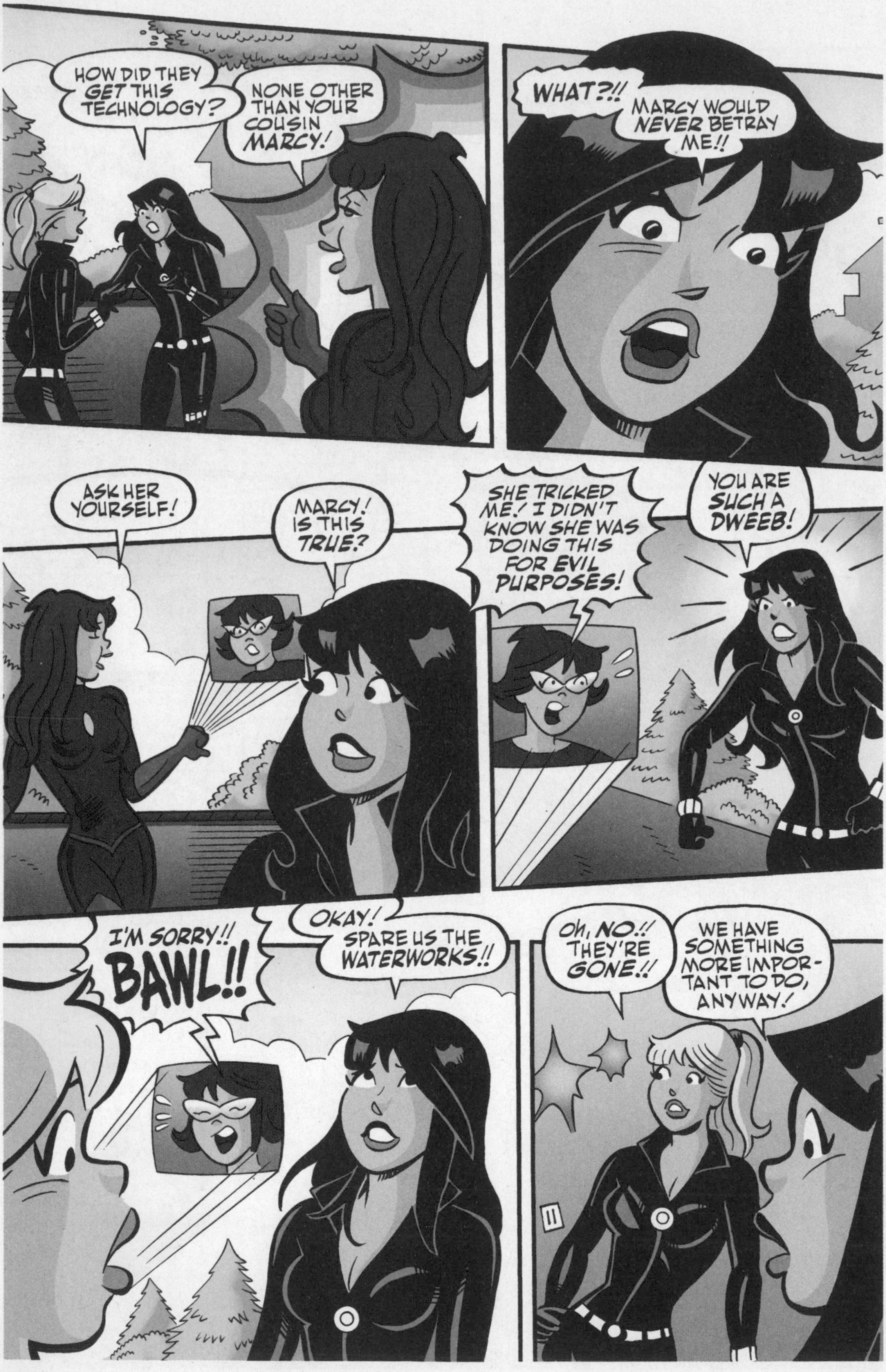
HOW DID THEY GET THIS TECHNOLOGY?
NONE OTHER THAN YOUR COUSIN MARCY!
WHAT?!!
MARCY WOULD NEVER BETRAY ME!!
ASK HER YOURSELF!
MARCY! IS THIS TRUE?
SHE TRICKED ME! I DIDN'T KNOW SHE WAS DOING THIS FOR EVIL PURPOSES!
YOU ARE SUCH A DWEEB!
I'M SORRY!! BAWL!!
OKAY! SPARE US THE WATERWORKS!!
Oh, NO!! THEY'RE GONE!!
WE HAVE SOMETHING MORE IMPOR-TANT TO DO, ANYWAY!

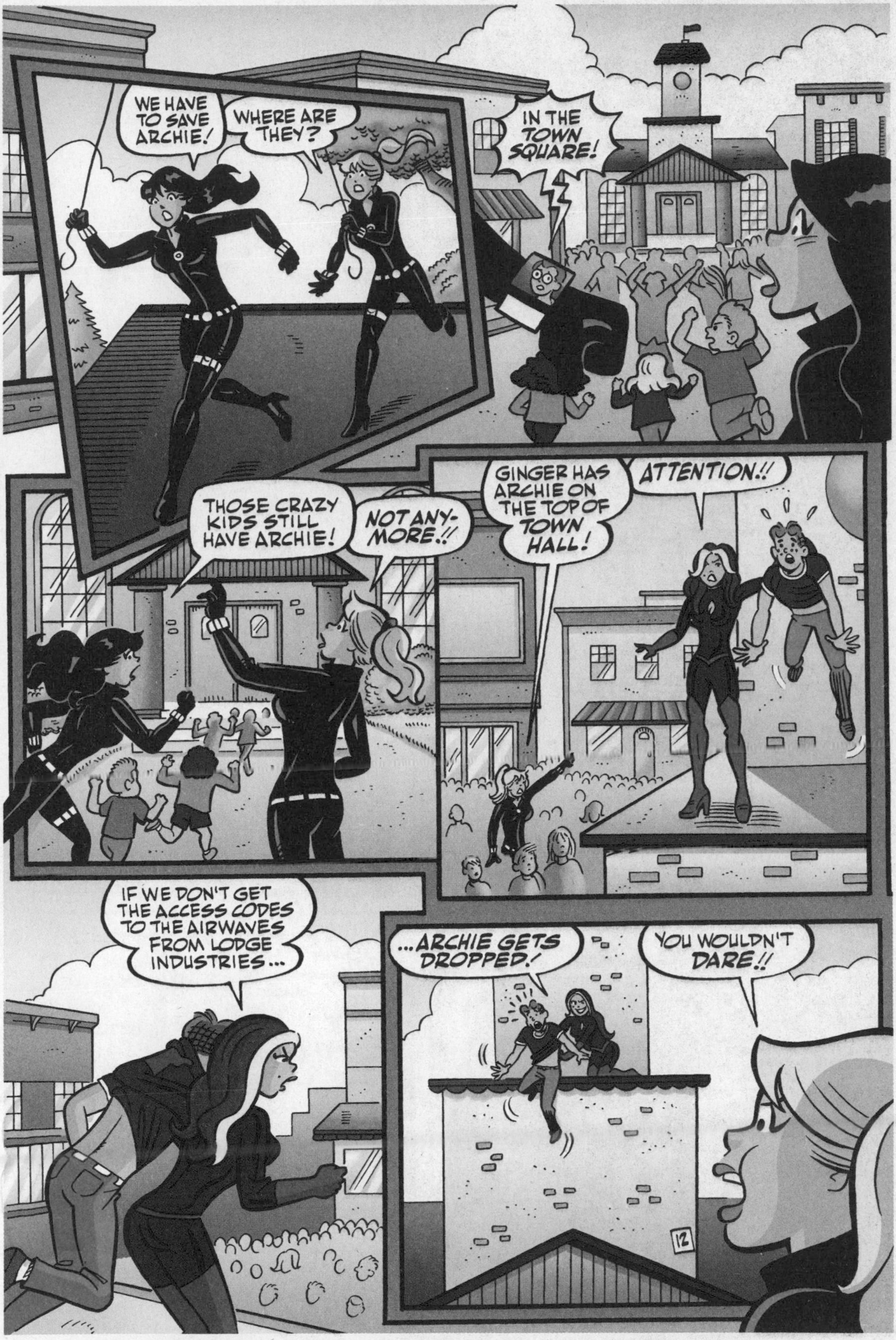
WE HAVE TO SAVE ARCHIE!
WHERE ARE THEY?
IN THE TOWN SQUARE!
THOSE CRAZY KIDS STILL HAVE ARCHIE!
NOT ANY-MORE.!!
GINGER HAS ARCHIE ON THE TOP OF TOWN HALL!
ATTENTION!!
IF WE DON'T GET THE ACCESS CODES TO THE AIRWAVES FROM LODGE INDUSTRIES...
...ARCHIE GETS DROPPED!
YOU WOULDN'T DARE!!
12

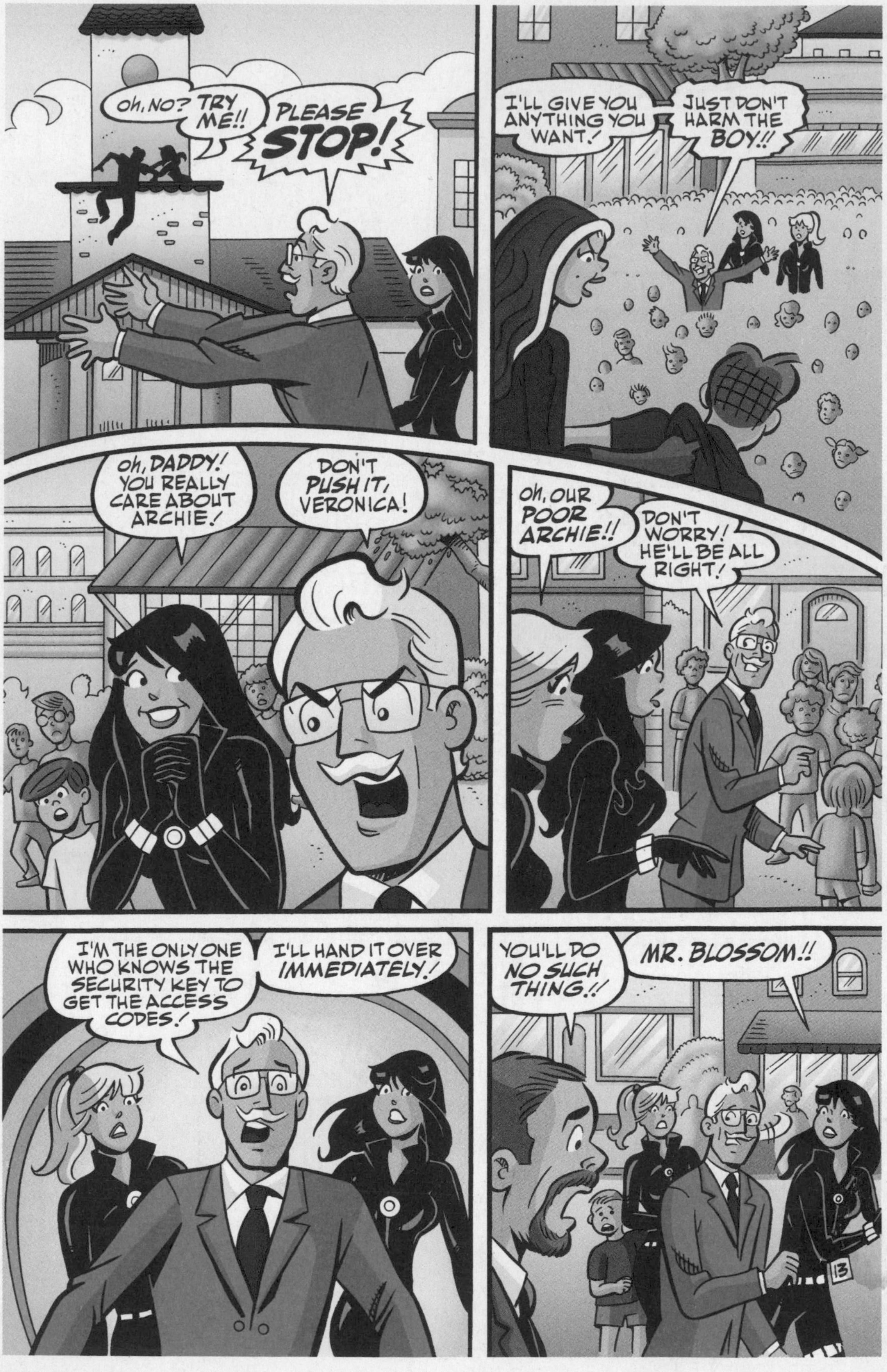
OH, NO? TRY ME!!
PLEASE STOP!
I'LL GIVE YOU ANYTHING YOU WANT!
JUST DON'T HARM THE BOY!!
OH, DADDY! YOU REALLY CARE ABOUT ARCHIE!
DON'T PUSH IT, VERONICA!
OH, OUR POOR ARCHIE!!
DON'T WORRY! HE'LL BE ALL RIGHT!
I'M THE ONLY ONE WHO KNOWS THE SECURITY KEY TO GET THE ACCESS CODES!
I'LL HAND IT OVER IMMEDIATELY!
YOU'LL DO NO SUCH THING!!
MR. BLOSSOM!!
13

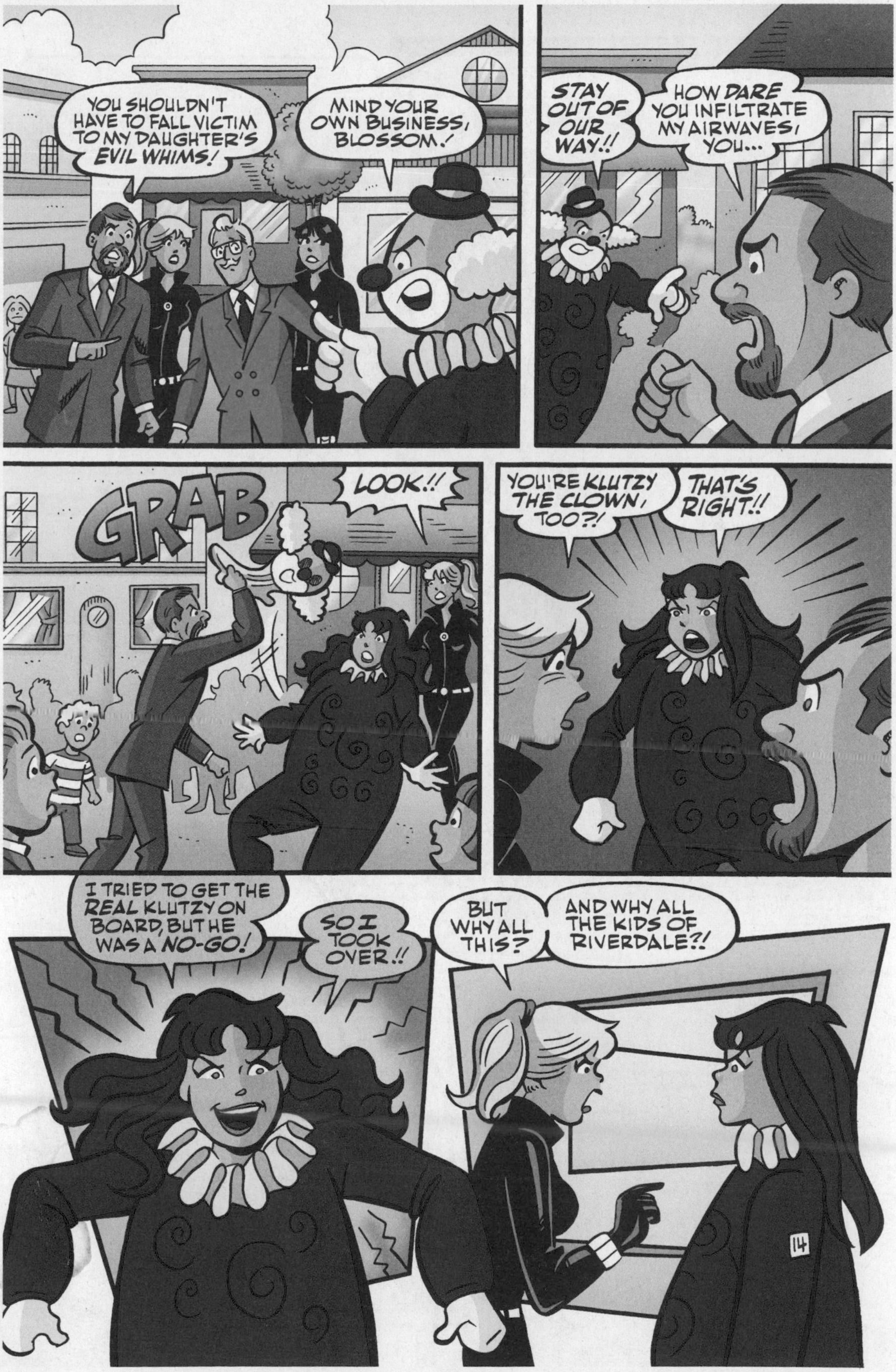
YOU SHOULDN'T HAVE TO FALL VICTIM TO MY DAUGHTER'S EVIL WHIMS!
MIND YOUR OWN BUSINESS, BLOSSOM!
STAY OUT OF OUR WAY!!
HOW DARE YOU INFILTRATE MY AIRWAVES, YOU...
GRAB
LOOK!!
YOU'RE KLUTZY THE CLOWN, TOO?!
THAT'S RIGHT!!
I TRIED TO GET THE REAL KLUTZY ON BOARD, BUT HE WAS A NO-GO!
SO I TOOK OVER!!
BUT WHY ALL THIS?
AND WHY ALL THE KIDS OF RIVERDALE?!
14

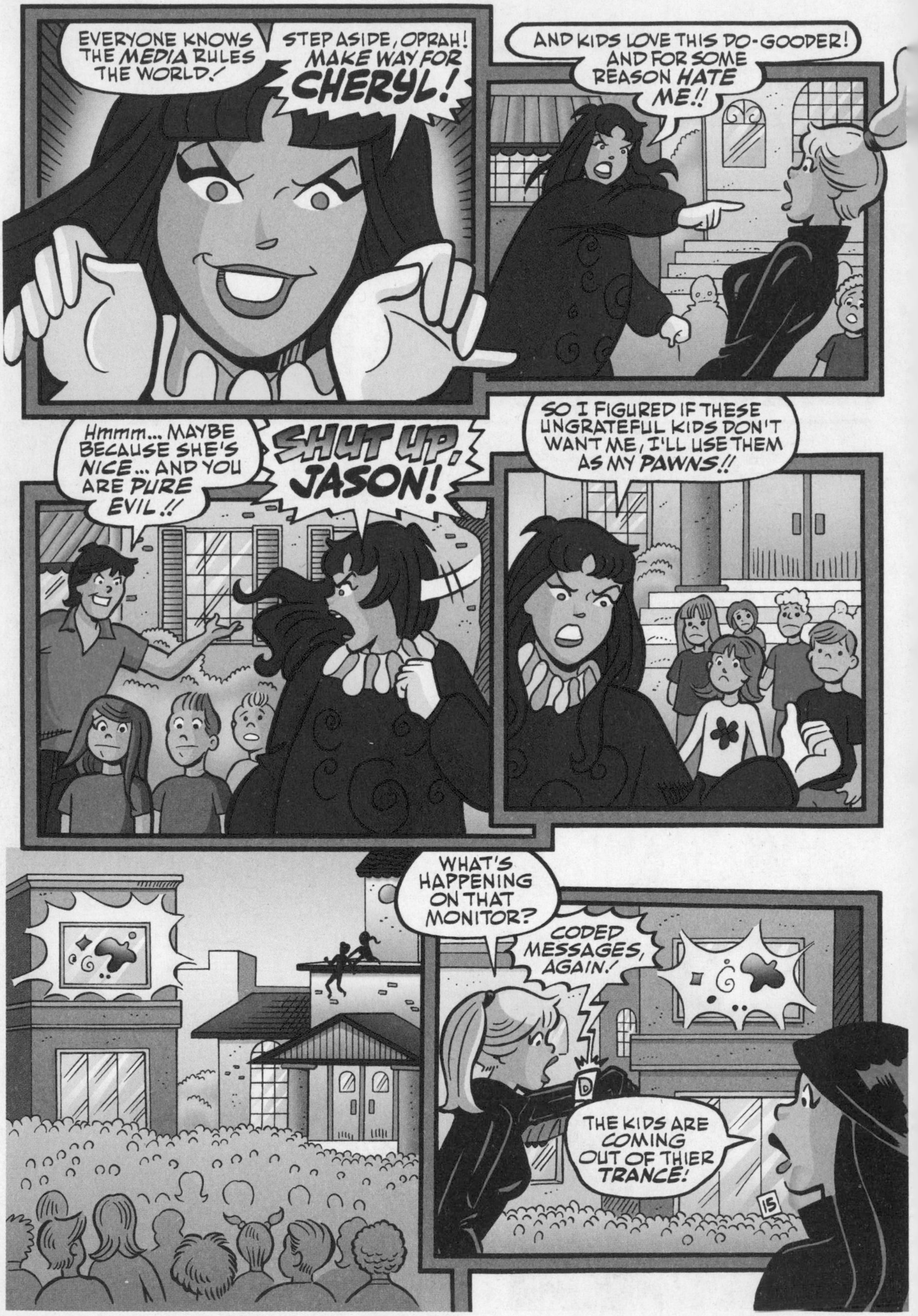
EVERYONE KNOWS THE MEDIA RULES THE WORLD!
STEP ASIDE, OPRAH! MAKE WAY FOR CHERYL!
AND KIDS LOVE THIS DO-GOODER! AND FOR SOME REASON HATE ME!!
Hmmm... MAYBE BECAUSE SHE'S NICE... AND YOU ARE PURE EVIL!!
SHUT UP, JASON!
SO I FIGURED IF THESE UNGRATEFUL KIDS DON'T WANT ME, I'LL USE THEM AS MY PAWNS!!
WHAT'S HAPPENING ON THAT MONITOR?
CODED MESSAGES, AGAIN!
THE KIDS ARE COMING OUT OF THIER TRANCE!
15

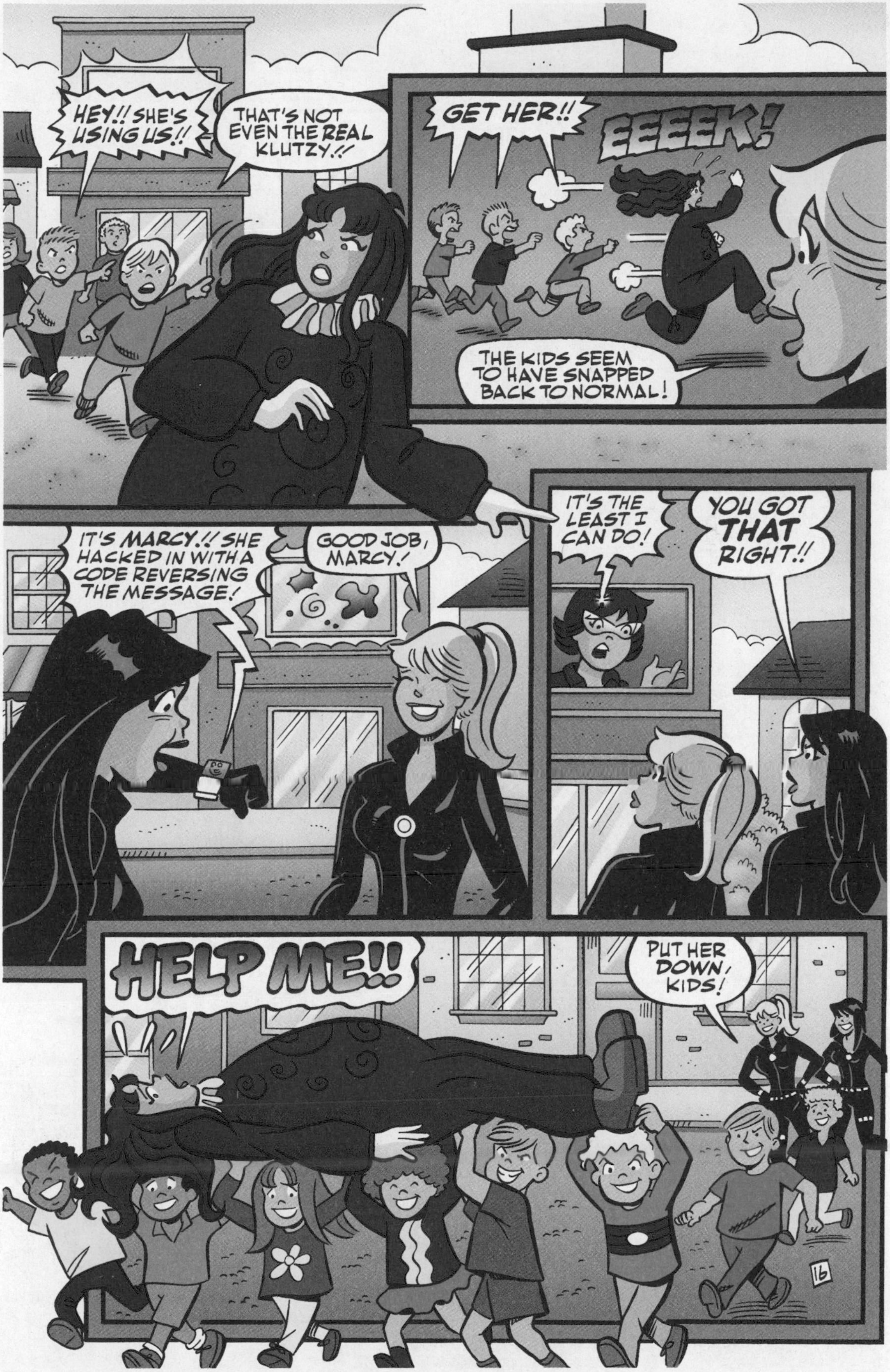
HEY!! SHE'S USING US!!
THAT'S NOT EVEN THE REAL KLUTZY!!
GET HER!!
EEEEK!
THE KIDS SEEM TO HAVE SNAPPED BACK TO NORMAL!
IT'S MARCY!! SHE HACKED IN WITH A CODE REVERSING THE MESSAGE!
GOOD JOB, MARCY!
IT'S THE LEAST I CAN DO!
YOU GOT THAT RIGHT!!
HELP ME!!
PUT HER DOWN, KIDS!
16

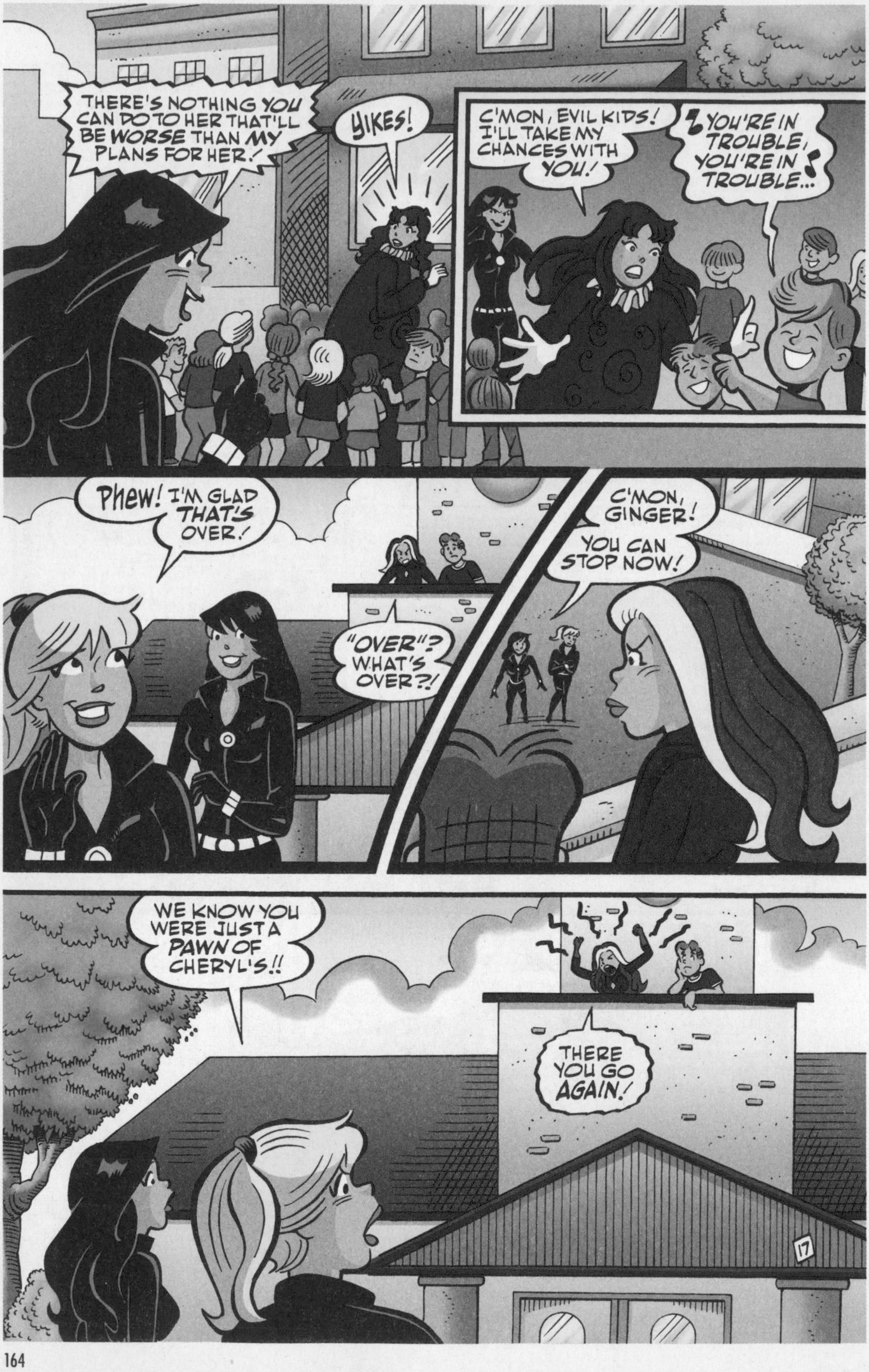
THERE'S NOTHING YOU CAN DO TO HER THAT'LL BE WORSE THAN MY PLANS FOR HER!
YIKES!
C'MON, EVIL KIDS! I'LL TAKE MY CHANCES WITH YOU!
YOU'RE IN TROUBLE, YOU'RE IN TROUBLE...
Phew! I'M GLAD THAT'S OVER!
"OVER"? WHAT'S OVER?!
C'MON, GINGER!
YOU CAN STOP NOW!
WE KNOW YOU WERE JUST A PAWN OF CHERYL'S!!
THERE YOU GO AGAIN!
17

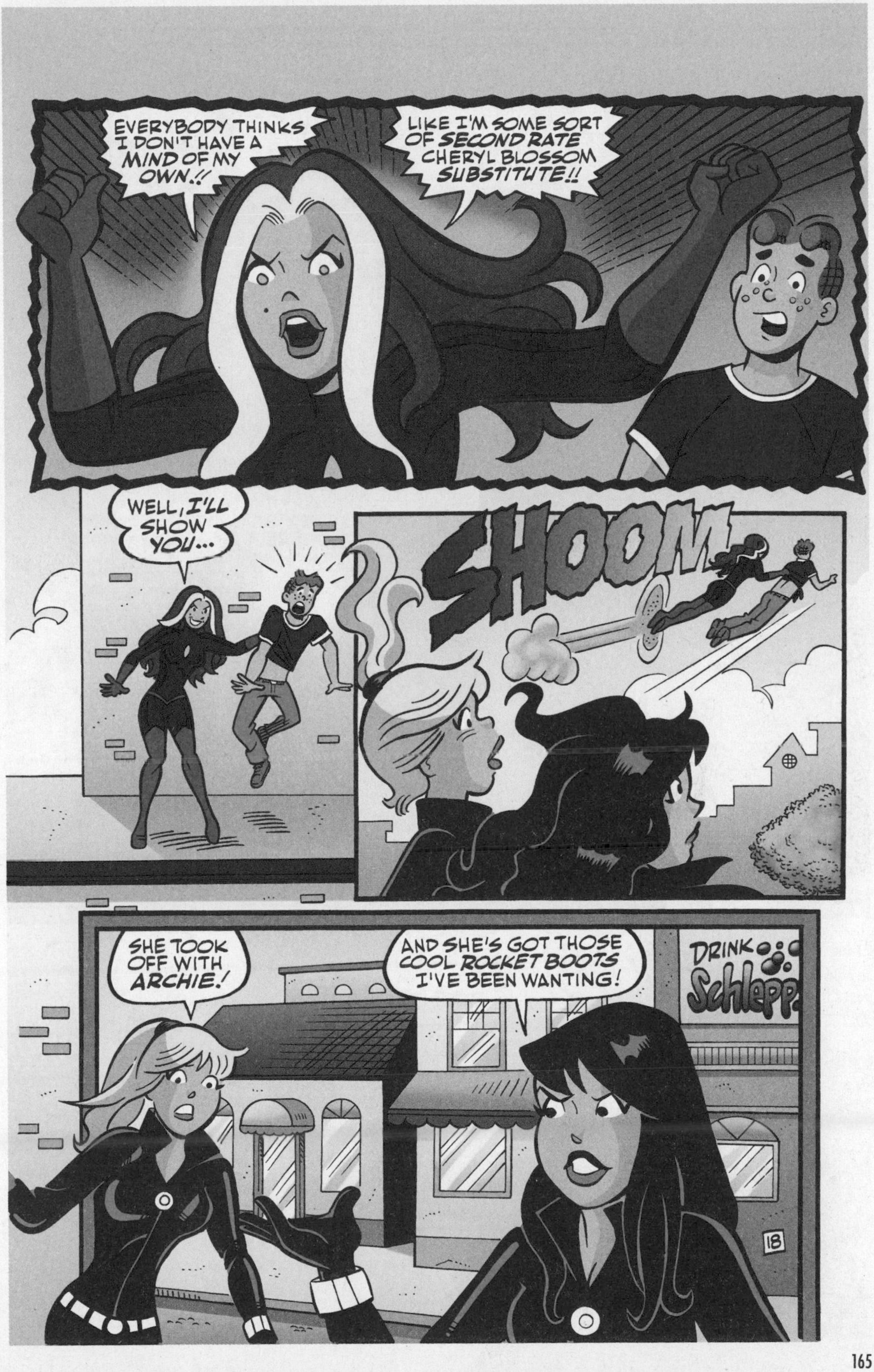
EVERYBODY THINKS I DON'T HAVE A MIND OF MY OWN.!!
LIKE I'M SOME SORT OF SECOND RATE CHERYL BLOSSOM SUBSTITUTE!!
WELL, I'LL SHOW YOU...
SHOOM
SHE TOOK OFF WITH ARCHIE!
AND SHE'S GOT THOSE COOL ROCKET BOOTS I'VE BEEN WANTING!
DRINK Schlepp
18

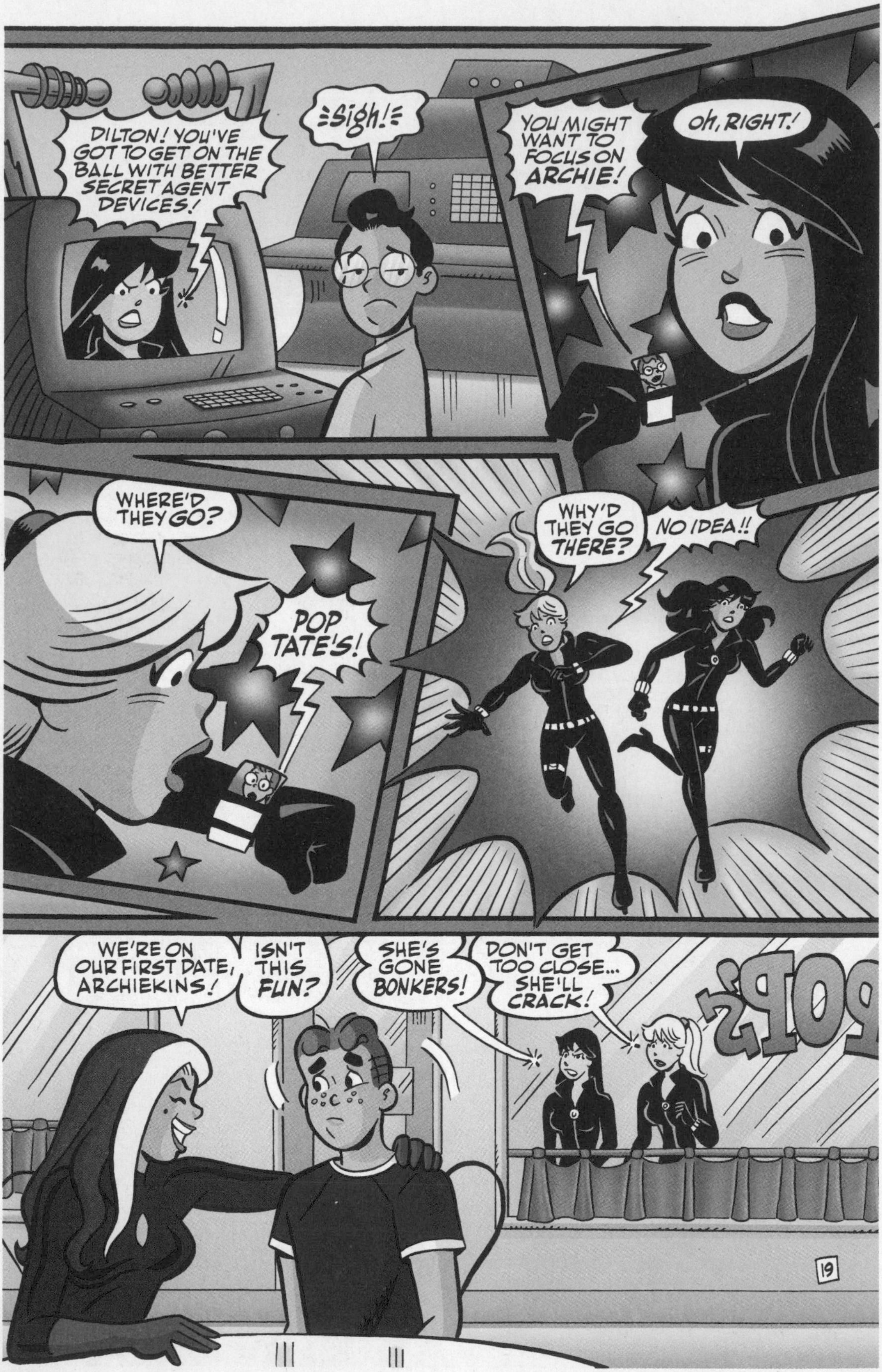
DILTON! YOU'VE GOT TO GET ON THE BALL WITH BETTER SECRET AGENT DEVICES!
SIGH!
YOU MIGHT WANT TO FOCUS ON ARCHIE!
OH, RIGHT!
WHERE'D THEY GO?
POP TATE'S!
WHY'D THEY GO THERE?
NO IDEA!!
WE'RE ON OUR FIRST DATE, ARCHIEKINS!
ISN'T THIS FUN?
SHE'S GONE BONKERS!
DON'T GET TOO CLOSE... SHE'LL CRACK!
POP'S
19

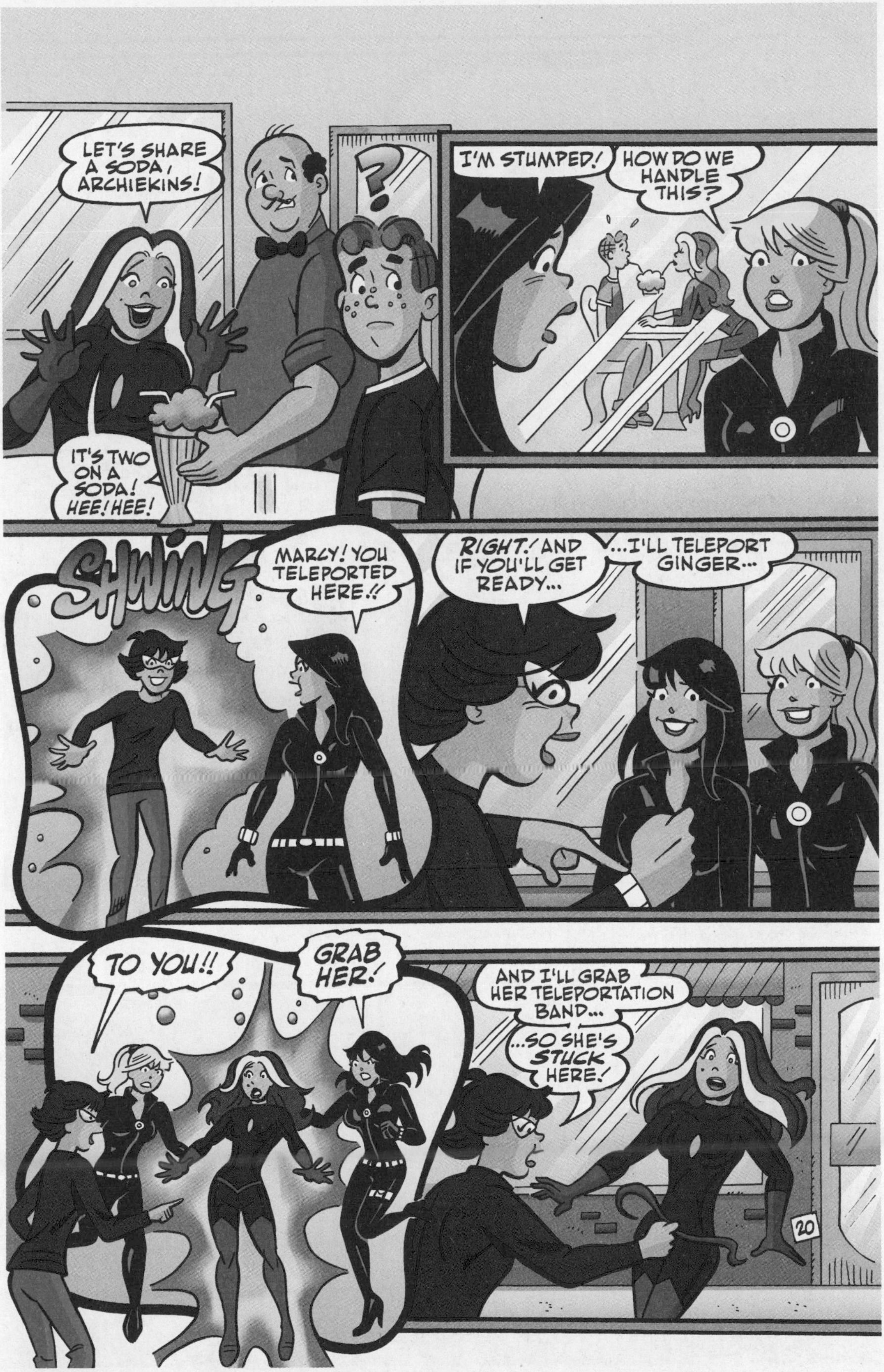
LET'S SHARE A SODA, ARCHIEKINS!
IT'S TWO ON A SODA! HEE! HEE!
I'M STUMPED!
HOW DO WE HANDLE THIS?
SHWING
MARCY! YOU TELEPORTED HERE!!
RIGHT! AND IF YOU'LL GET READY...
...I'LL TELEPORT GINGER...
TO YOU!!
GRAB HER!
AND I'LL GRAB HER TELEPORTATION BAND...
...SO SHE'S STUCK HERE!
20

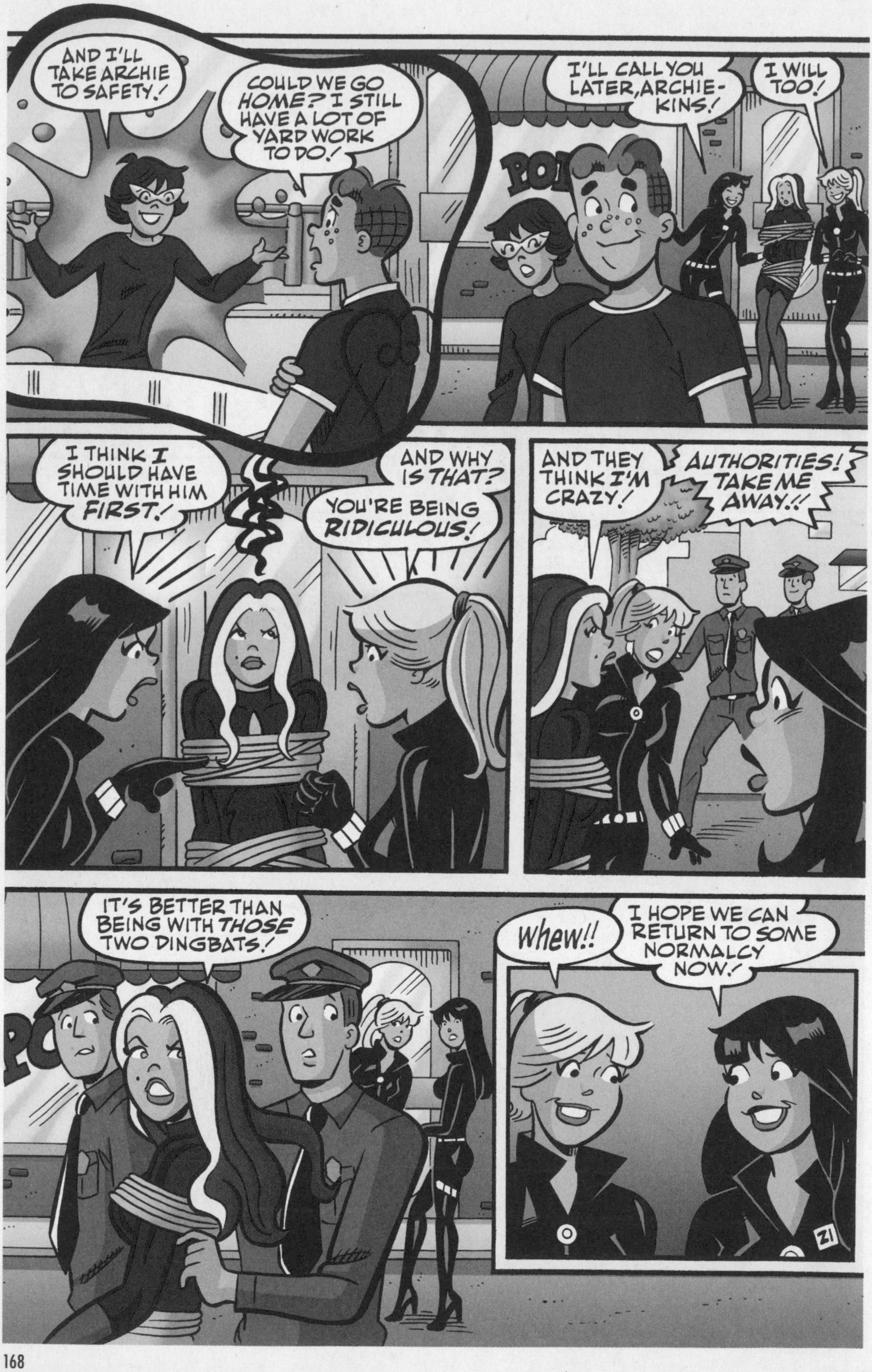
AND I'LL TAKE ARCHIE TO SAFETY!
COULD WE GO HOME? I STILL HAVE A LOT OF YARD WORK TO DO!
I'LL CALL YOU LATER, ARCHIE-KINS!
I WILL TOO!
POP
I THINK I SHOULD HAVE TIME WITH HIM FIRST!
AND WHY IS THAT?
YOU'RE BEING RIDICULOUS!
AND THEY THINK I'M CRAZY!
AUTHORITIES! TAKE ME AWAY!!
IT'S BETTER THAN BEING WITH THOSE TWO DINGBATS!
whew!!
I HOPE WE CAN RETURN TO SOME NORMALCY NOW!
ZI

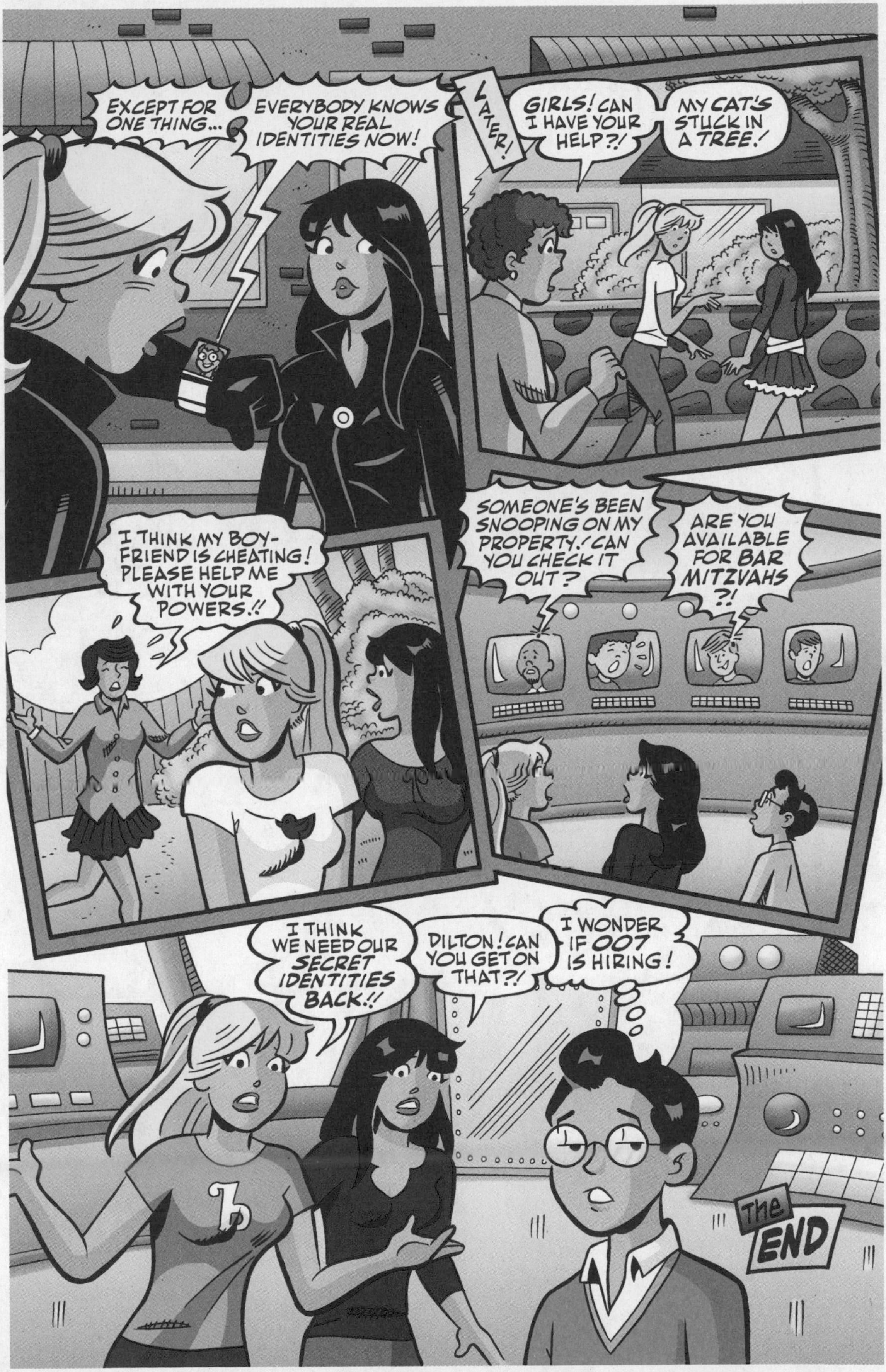
EXCEPT FOR ONE THING...
EVERYBODY KNOWS YOUR REAL IDENTITIES NOW!
LATER!
GIRLS! CAN I HAVE YOUR HELP?!
MY CAT'S STUCK IN A TREE!
I THINK MY BOY-FRIEND IS CHEATING! PLEASE HELP ME WITH YOUR POWERS!!
SOMEONE'S BEEN SNOOPING ON MY PROPERTY! CAN YOU CHECK IT OUT?
ARE YOU AVAILABLE FOR BAR MITZVAHS?!
I THINK WE NEED OUR SECRET IDENTITIES BACK!!
DILTON! CAN YOU GET ON THAT?!
I WONDER IF 007 IS HIRING!
The END

CHAPTER SIX

Robbing Arch

PART ONE

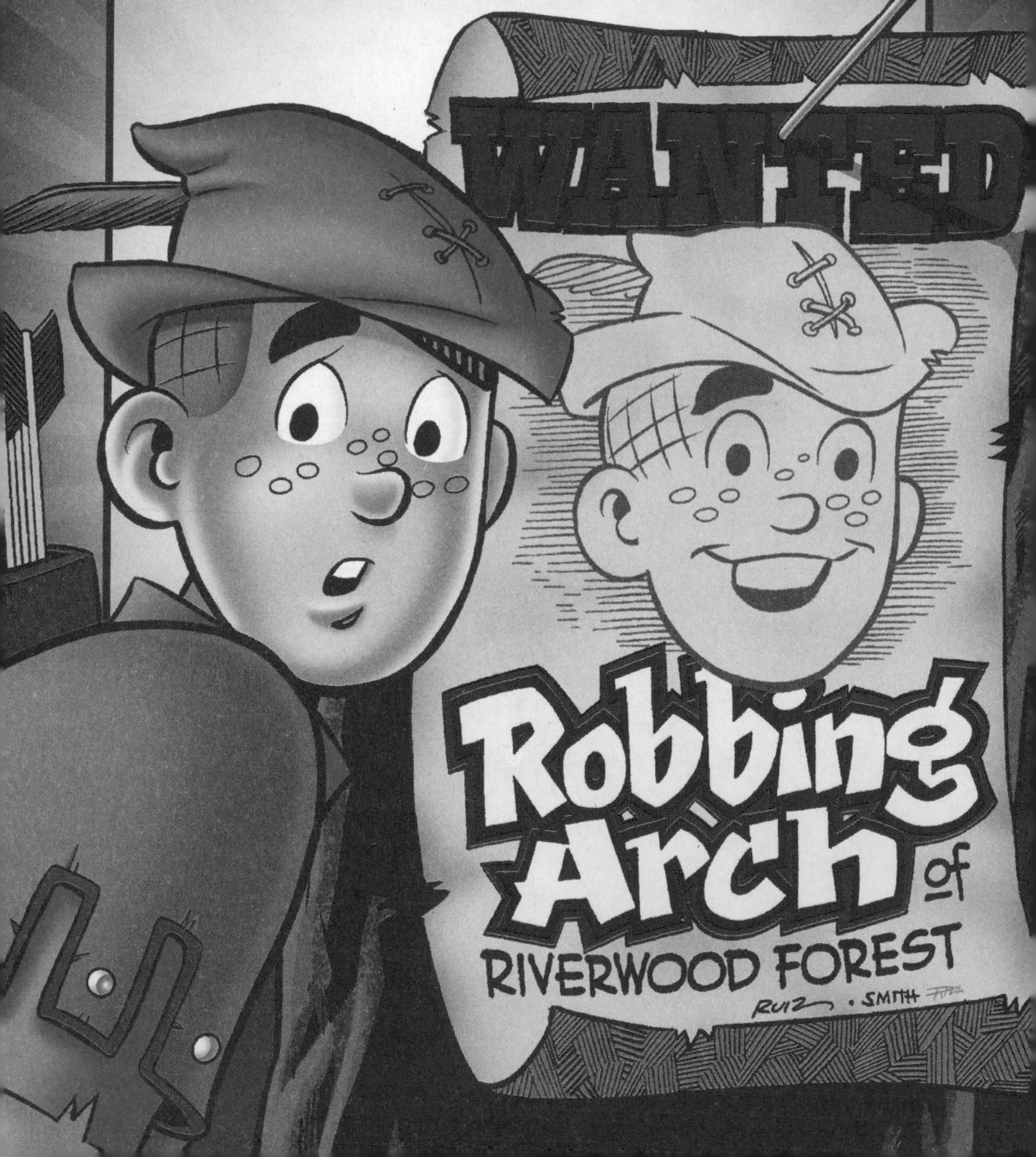
WANTED
Robbing Arch of
RIVERWOOD FOREST
RUIZ • SMITH

INTRODUCING ROBBING ARCH

Originally printed in *Archie* #618 and #619

Archie and Friends star as Robbing Arch and His Band of Merry Teens!
Archie and the gang must save Lord Lodge and Princess Veronica from the
evil clutches of the Mad Duke of Doom and his fiendish jester, Chester, in an
action-packed Robin Hood-inspired tale! Join Maid Betty, Juggie O'Dare,
Reggie the Red and Robbing Archie in their quest to save the Kingdom!

WRITER
TOM DEFALCO

PENCILS
FERNANDO RUIZ

INKS
RICH KOSLOWSKI

LETTERS
JACK MORELLI

COLORS
DIGIKORE STUDIOS

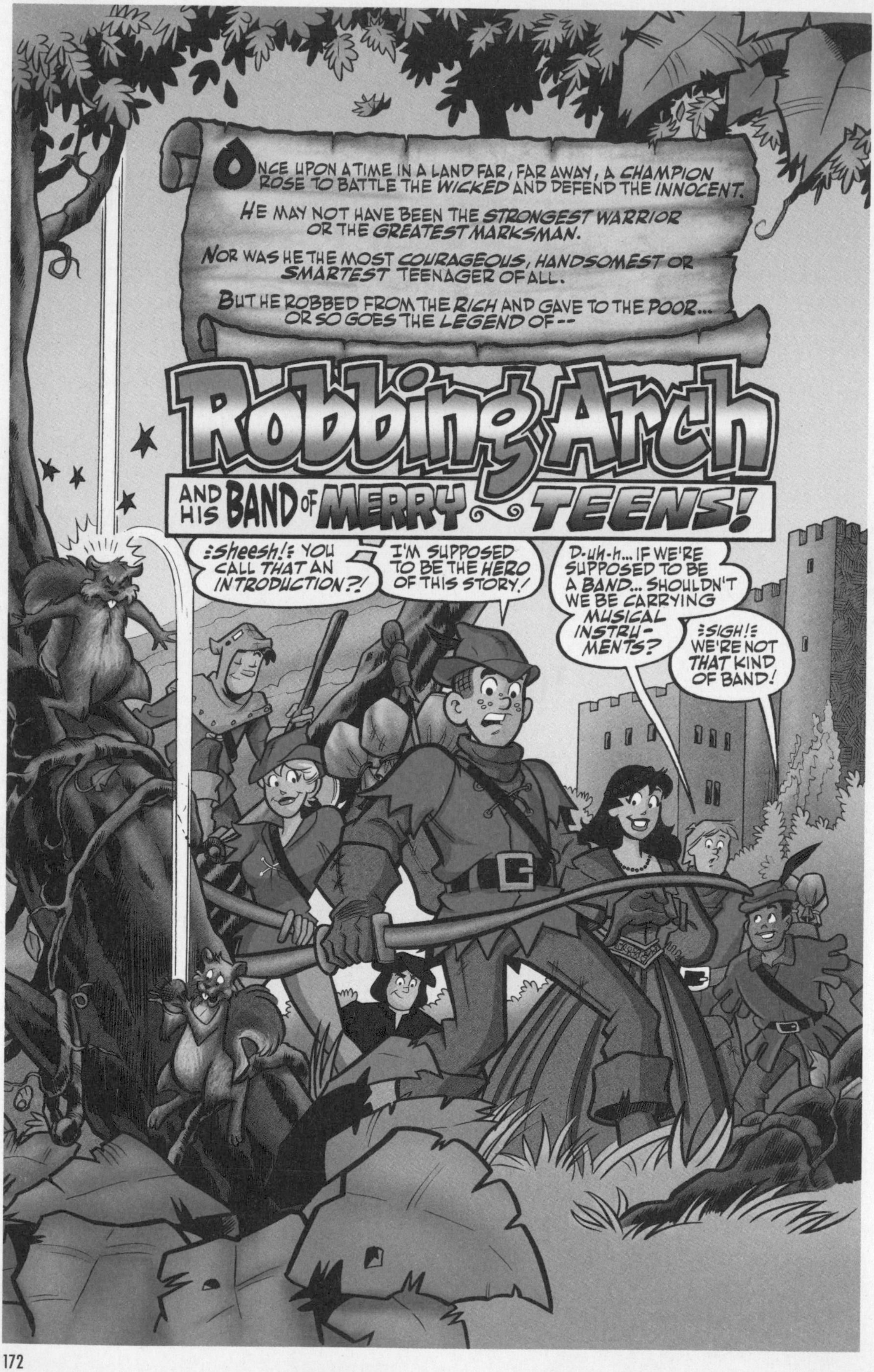
ONCE UPON A TIME IN A LAND FAR, FAR AWAY, A CHAMPION ROSE TO BATTLE THE WICKED AND DEFEND THE INNOCENT.
HE MAY NOT HAVE BEEN THE STRONGEST WARRIOR OR THE GREATEST MARKSMAN.
NOR WAS HE THE MOST COURAGEOUS, HANDSOMEST OR SMARTEST TEENAGER OF ALL.
BUT HE ROBBED FROM THE RICH AND GAVE TO THE POOR... OR SO GOES THE LEGEND OF --
Robbing Arch
AND HIS BAND OF MERRY TEENS!
SHEESH! YOU CALL THAT AN INTRODUCTION?!
I'M SUPPOSED TO BE THE HERO OF THIS STORY!
D-UH-H... IF WE'RE SUPPOSED TO BE A BAND... SHOULDN'T WE BE CARRYING MUSICAL INSTRU-MENTS?
SIGH! WE'RE NOT THAT KIND OF BAND!

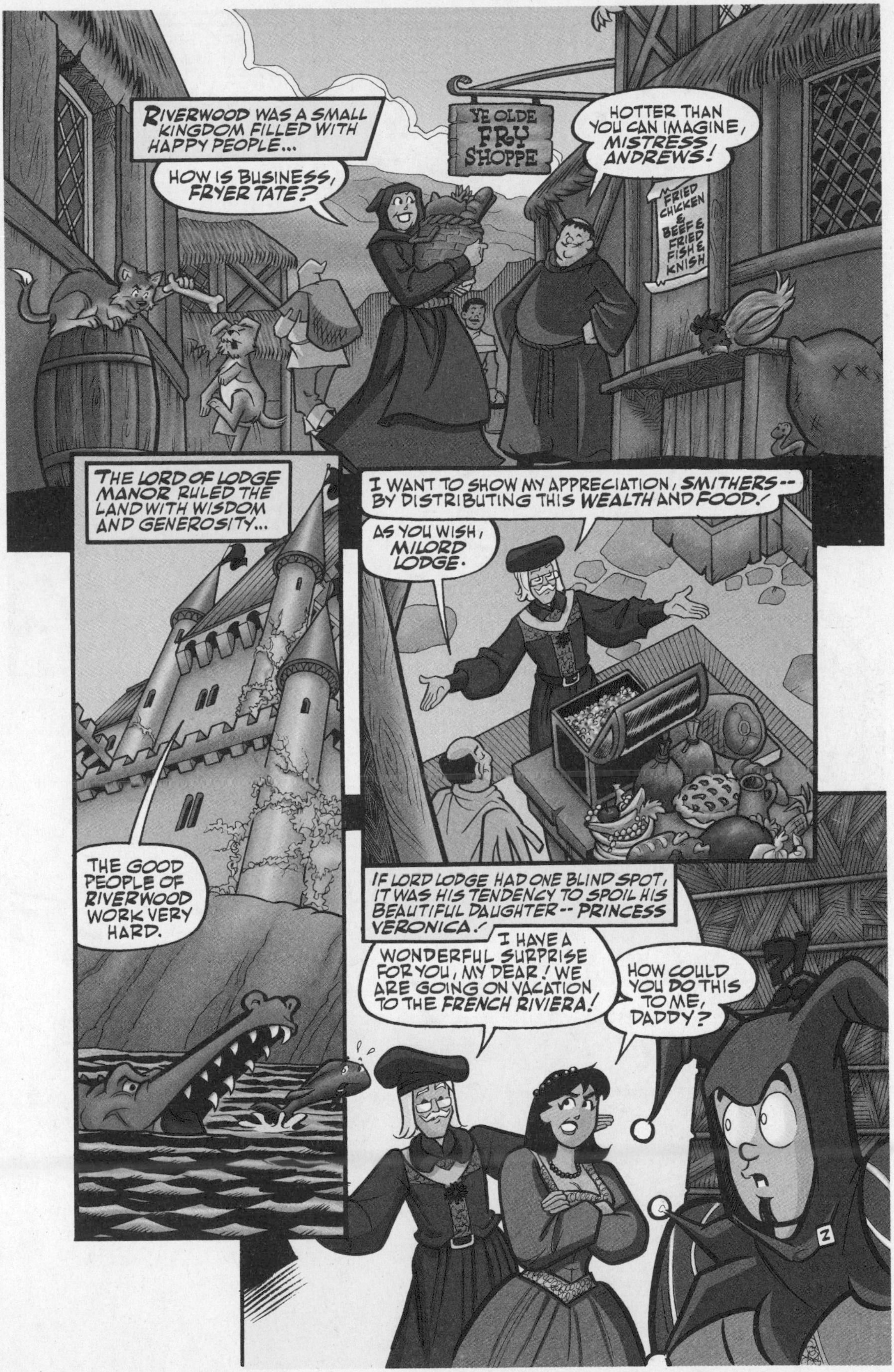
RIVERWOOD WAS A SMALL KINGDOM FILLED WITH HAPPY PEOPLE...
YE OLDE FRY SHOPPE
HOW IS BUSINESS, FRYER TATE?
HOTTER THAN YOU CAN IMAGINE, MISTRESS ANDREWS!
FRIED CHICKEN & BEEF & FRIED FISH & KNISH
THE LORD OF LODGE MANOR RULED THE LAND WITH WISDOM AND GENEROSITY...
I WANT TO SHOW MY APPRECIATION, SMITHERS -- BY DISTRIBUTING THIS WEALTH AND FOOD!
AS YOU WISH, MILORD LODGE.
THE GOOD PEOPLE OF RIVERWOOD WORK VERY HARD.
IF LORD LODGE HAD ONE BLIND SPOT, IT WAS HIS TENDENCY TO SPOIL HIS BEAUTIFUL DAUGHTER -- PRINCESS VERONICA!
I HAVE A WONDERFUL SURPRISE FOR YOU, MY DEAR! WE ARE GOING ON VACATION TO THE FRENCH RIVIERA!
HOW COULD YOU DO THIS TO ME, DADDY?
Z

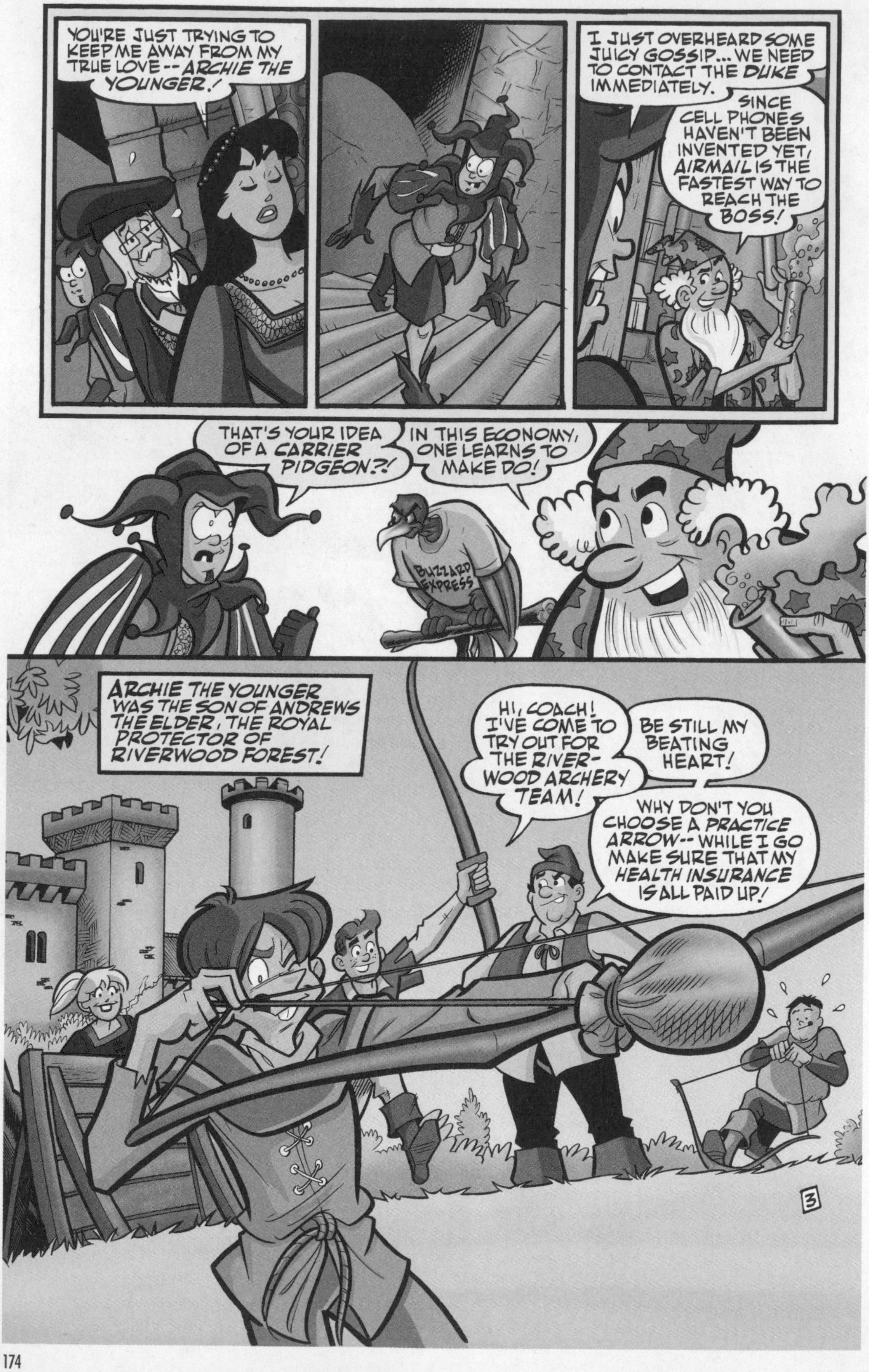
YOU'RE JUST TRYING TO KEEP ME AWAY FROM MY TRUE LOVE -- ARCHIE THE YOUNGER!
I JUST OVERHEARD SOME JUICY GOSSIP... WE NEED TO CONTACT THE DUKE IMMEDIATELY.
SINCE CELL PHONES HAVEN'T BEEN INVENTED YET, AIRMAIL IS THE FASTEST WAY TO REACH THE BOSS!
THAT'S YOUR IDEA OF A CARRIER PIDGEON?!
IN THIS ECONOMY, ONE LEARNS TO MAKE DO!
BUZZARD EXPRESS
ARCHIE THE YOUNGER WAS THE SON OF ANDREWS THE ELDER, THE ROYAL PROTECTOR OF RIVERWOOD FOREST!
HI, COACH! I'VE COME TO TRY OUT FOR THE RIVER-WOOD ARCHERY TEAM!
BE STILL MY BEATING HEART!
WHY DON'T YOU CHOOSE A PRACTICE ARROW-- WHILE I GO MAKE SURE THAT MY HEALTH INSURANCE IS ALL PAID UP!
3

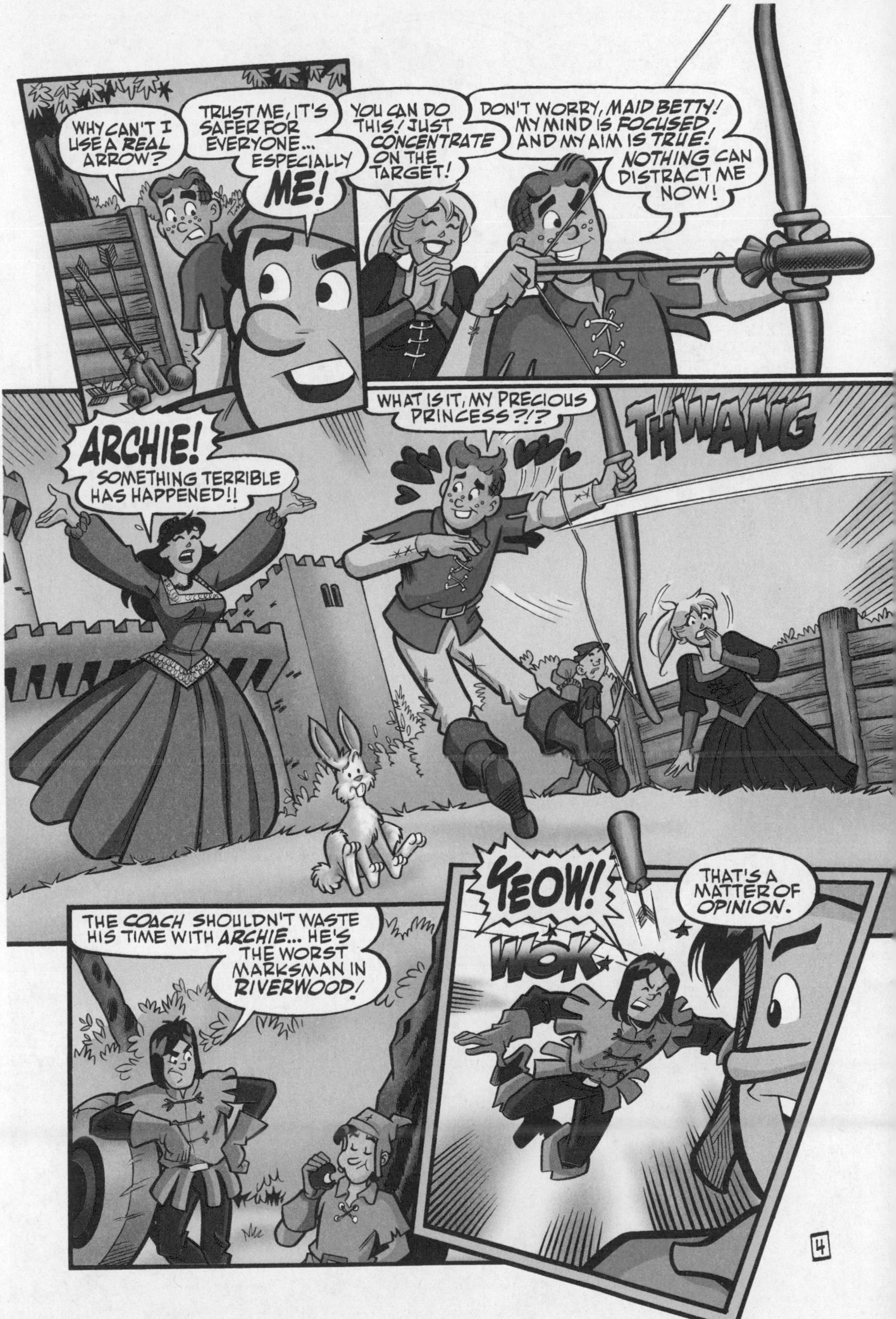
WHY CAN'T I USE A REAL ARROW?
TRUST ME, IT'S SAFER FOR EVERYONE... ESPECIALLY ME!
YOU CAN DO THIS! JUST CONCENTRATE ON THE TARGET!
DON'T WORRY, MAID BETTY! MY MIND IS FOCUSED AND MY AIM IS TRUE!
NOTHING CAN DISTRACT ME NOW!
ARCHIE! SOMETHING TERRIBLE HAS HAPPENED!!
WHAT IS IT, MY PRECIOUS PRINCESS?!?
THWANG
THE COACH SHOULDN'T WASTE HIS TIME WITH ARCHIE... HE'S THE WORST MARKSMAN IN RIVERWOOD!
YEOW!
WOK
THAT'S A MATTER OF OPINION.
4

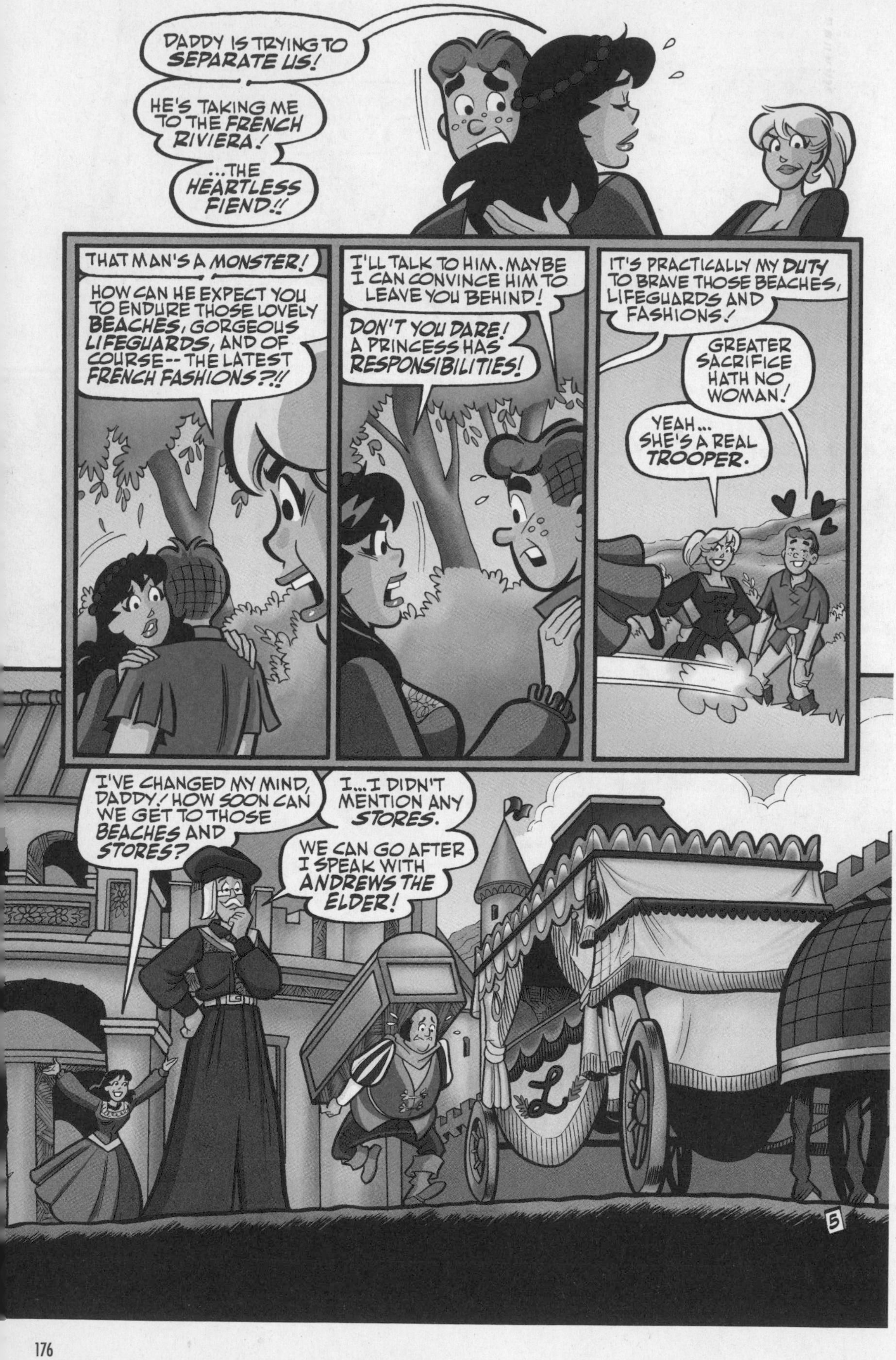
DADDY IS TRYING TO SEPARATE US!
HE'S TAKING ME TO THE FRENCH RIVIERA!
...THE HEARTLESS FIEND!!
THAT MAN'S A MONSTER!
HOW CAN HE EXPECT YOU TO ENDURE THOSE LOVELY BEACHES, GORGEOUS LIFEGUARDS, AND OF COURSE-- THE LATEST FRENCH FASHIONS?!!
I'LL TALK TO HIM. MAYBE I CAN CONVINCE HIM TO LEAVE YOU BEHIND!
DON'T YOU DARE! A PRINCESS HAS RESPONSIBILITIES!
IT'S PRACTICALLY MY DUTY TO BRAVE THOSE BEACHES, LIFEGUARDS AND FASHIONS!
GREATER SACRIFICE HATH NO WOMAN!
YEAH... SHE'S A REAL TROOPER.
I'VE CHANGED MY MIND, DADDY! HOW SOON CAN WE GET TO THOSE BEACHES AND STORES?
I...I DIDN'T MENTION ANY STORES.
WE CAN GO AFTER I SPEAK WITH ANDREWS THE ELDER!
5

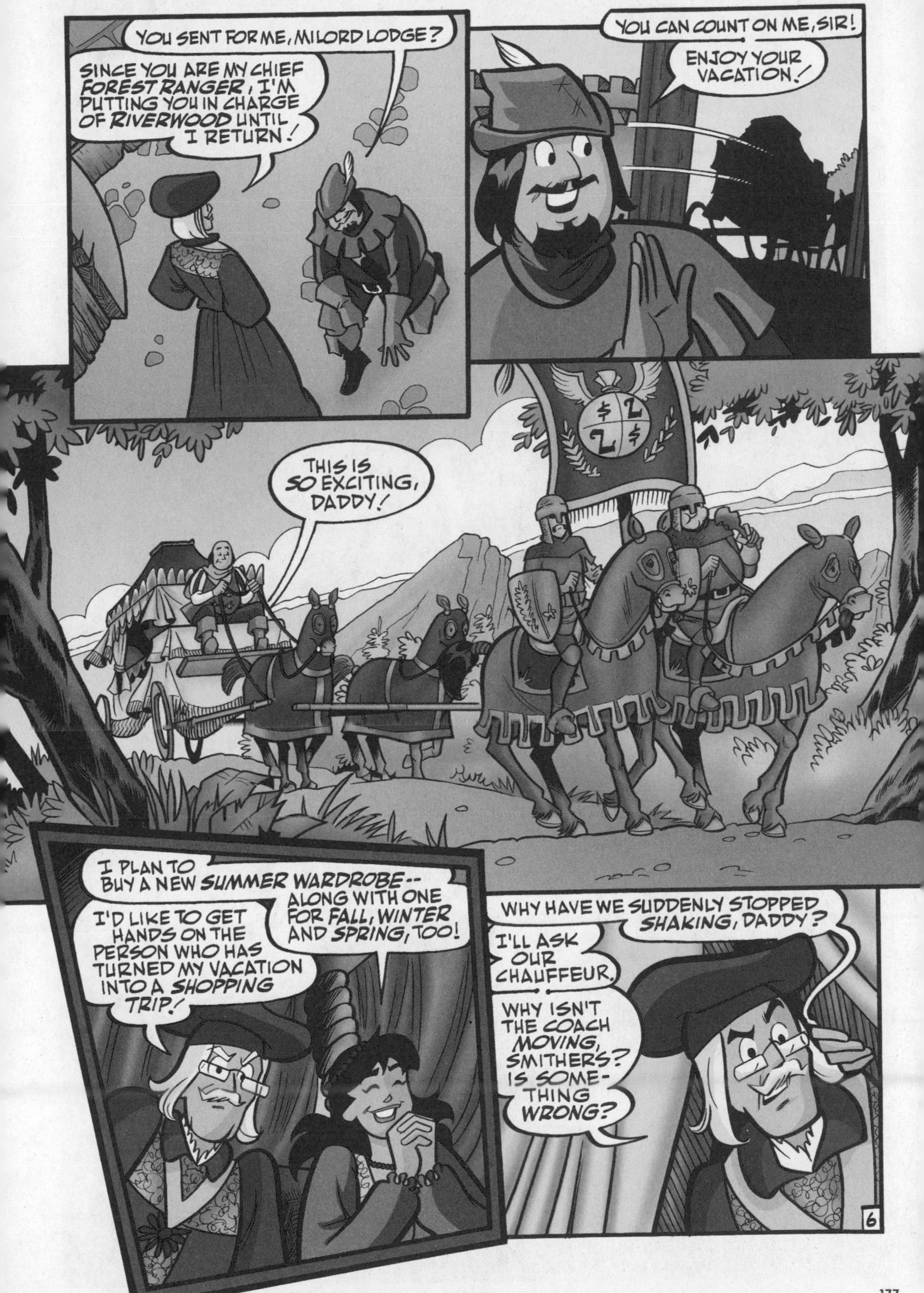
YOU SENT FOR ME, MILORD LODGE?
SINCE YOU ARE MY CHIEF FOREST RANGER, I'M PUTTING YOU IN CHARGE OF RIVERWOOD UNTIL I RETURN!
YOU CAN COUNT ON ME, SIR!
ENJOY YOUR VACATION!
THIS IS SO EXCITING, DADDY!
I PLAN TO BUY A NEW SUMMER WARDROBE--
ALONG WITH ONE FOR FALL, WINTER AND SPRING, TOO!
I'D LIKE TO GET HANDS ON THE PERSON WHO HAS TURNED MY VACATION INTO A SHOPPING TRIP!
WHY HAVE WE SUDDENLY STOPPED SHAKING, DADDY?
I'LL ASK OUR CHAUFFEUR.
WHY ISN'T THE COACH MOVING, SMITHERS? IS SOMETHING WRONG?
6

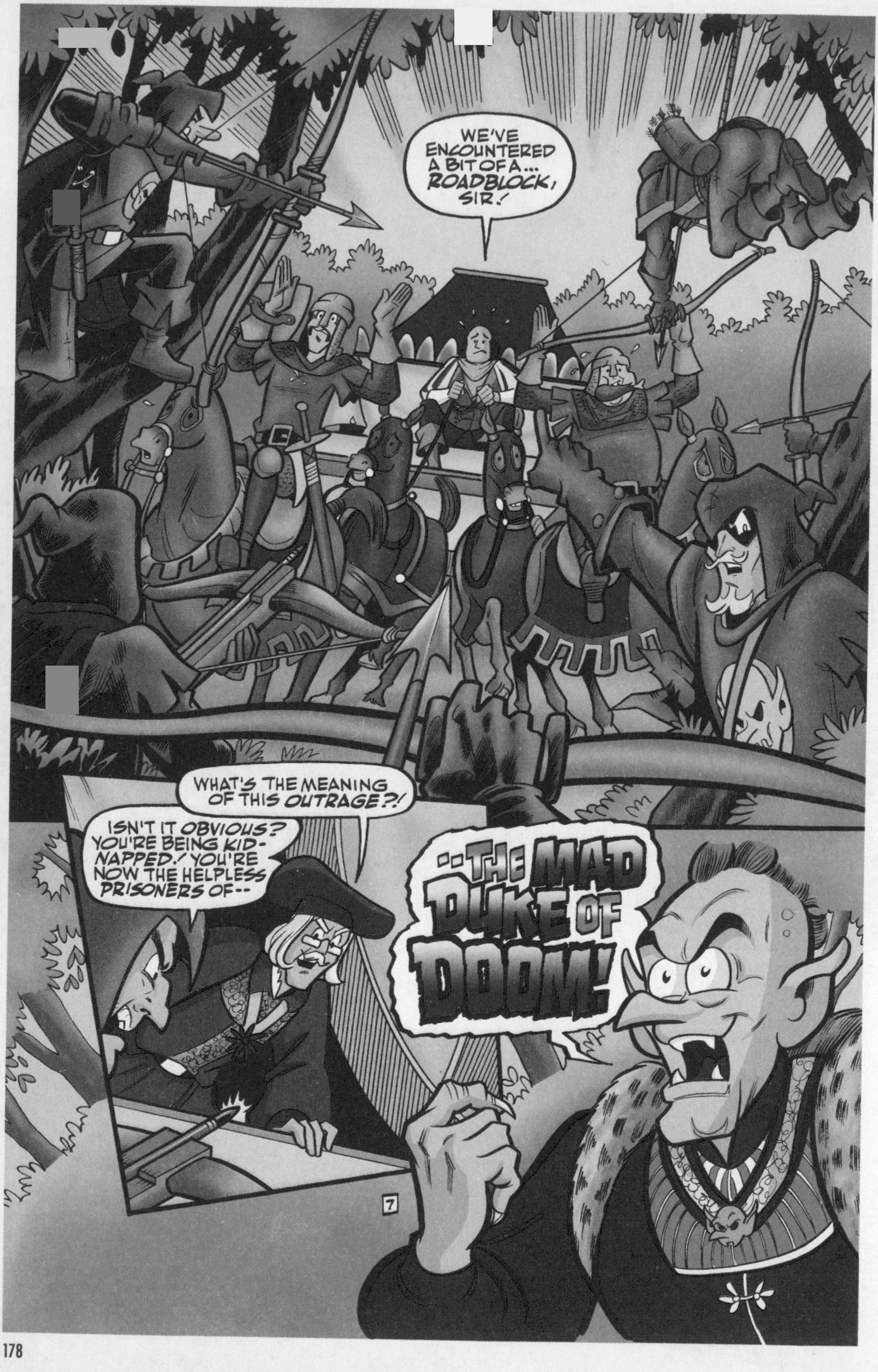
WE'VE ENCOUNTERED A BIT OF A... ROADBLOCK, SIR!
WHAT'S THE MEANING OF THIS OUTRAGE?!
ISN'T IT OBVIOUS? YOU'RE BEING KID-NAPPED! YOU'RE NOW THE HELPLESS PRISONERS OF--
--THE MAD DUKE OF DOOM!
7

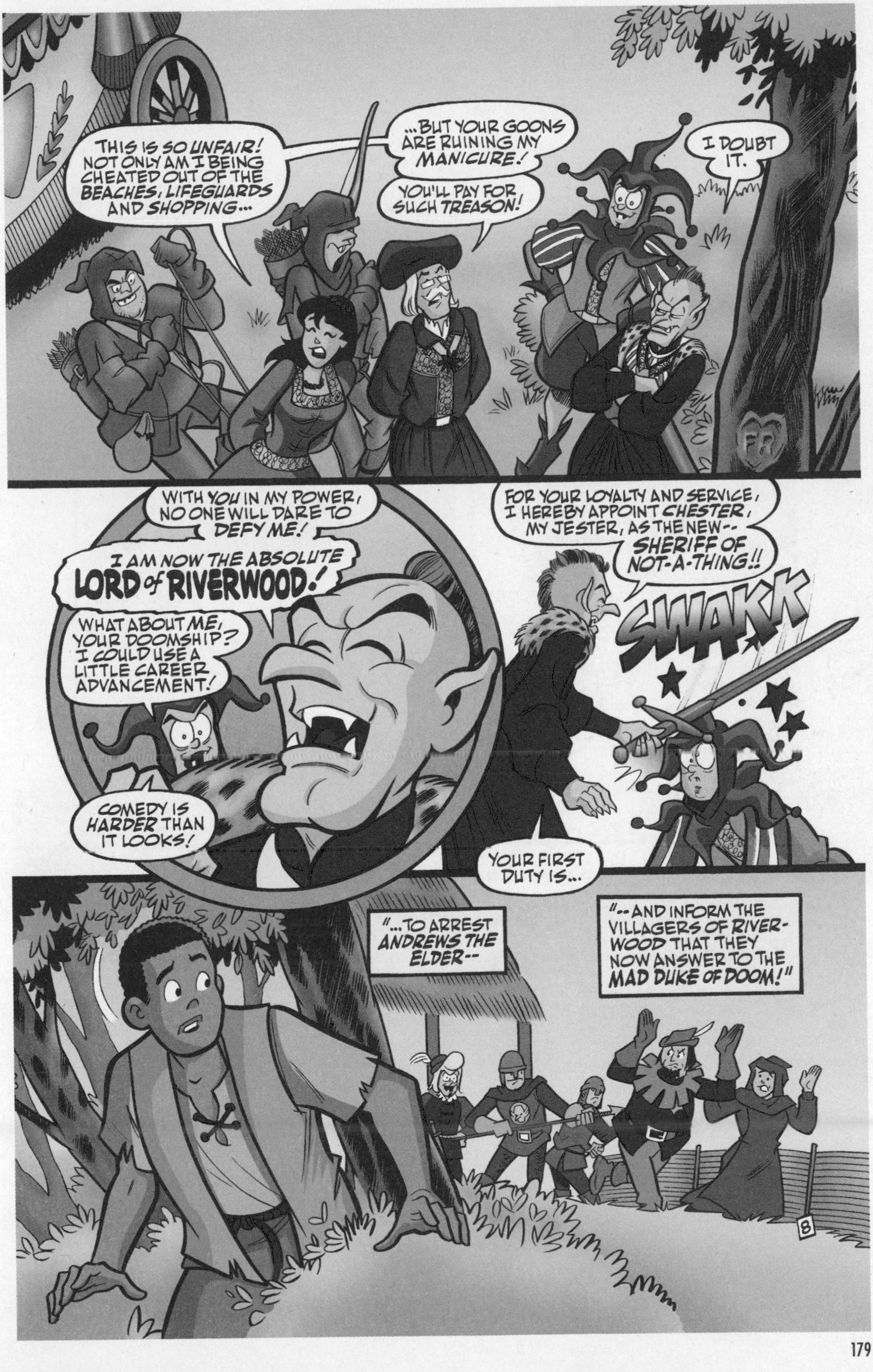
THIS IS SO UNFAIR! NOT ONLY AM I BEING CHEATED OUT OF THE BEACHES, LIFEGUARDS AND SHOPPING...
...BUT YOUR GOONS ARE RUINING MY MANICURE!
YOU'LL PAY FOR SUCH TREASON!
I DOUBT IT.
WITH YOU IN MY POWER, NO ONE WILL DARE TO DEFY ME!
I AM NOW THE ABSOLUTE LORD of RIVERWOOD!
WHAT ABOUT ME, YOUR DOOMSHIP? I COULD USE A LITTLE CAREER ADVANCEMENT!
COMEDY IS HARDER THAN IT LOOKS!
FOR YOUR LOYALTY AND SERVICE, I HEREBY APPOINT CHESTER, MY JESTER, AS THE NEW-- SHERIFF OF NOT-A-THING!!
SWAKK
YOUR FIRST DUTY IS...
"...TO ARREST ANDREWS THE ELDER--
"--AND INFORM THE VILLAGERS OF RIVER-WOOD THAT THEY NOW ANSWER TO THE MAD DUKE OF DOOM!"
8

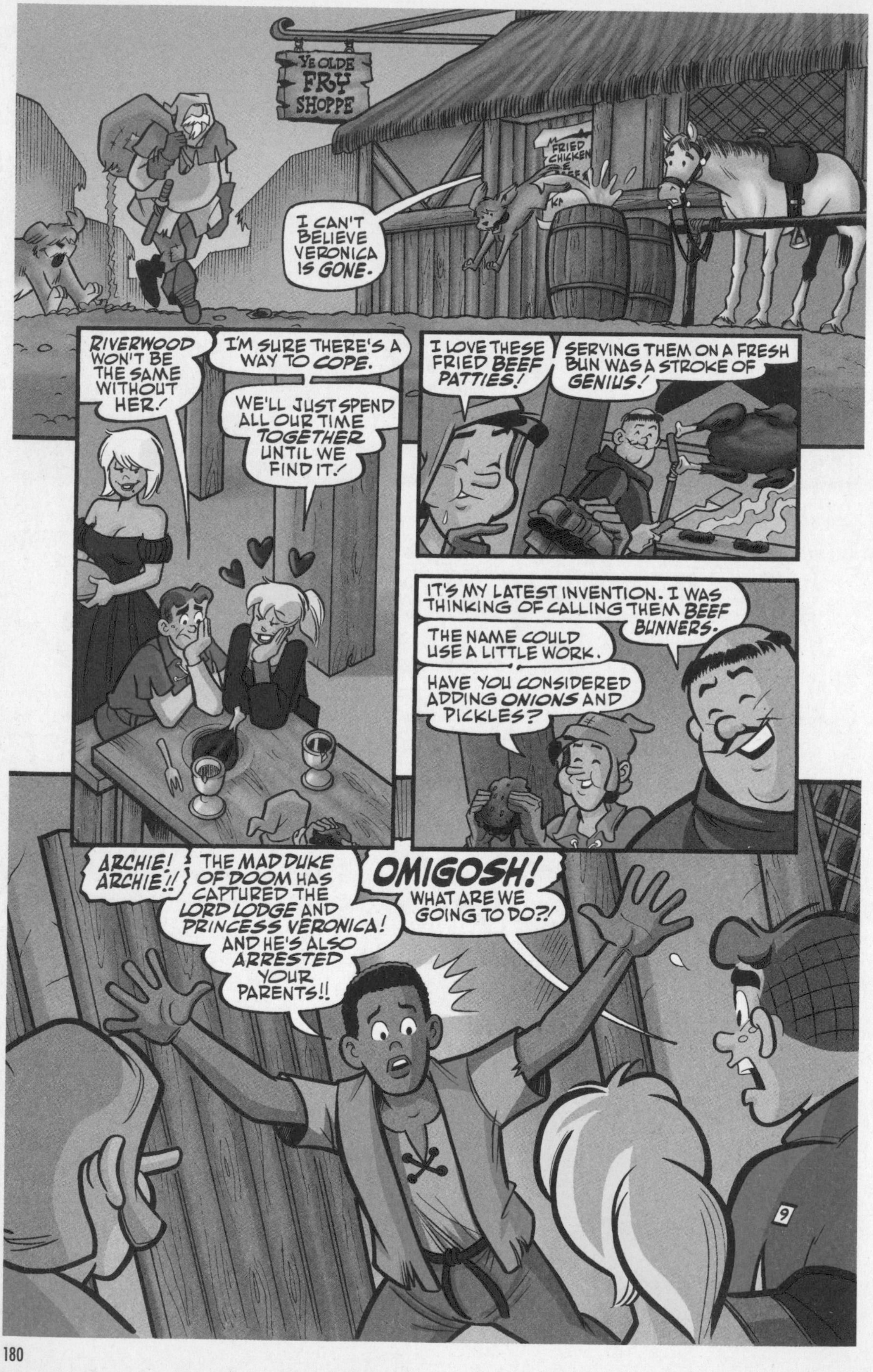
YE OLDE FRY SHOPPE
FRIED CHICKEN
I CAN'T BELIEVE VERONICA IS GONE.
RIVERWOOD WON'T BE THE SAME WITHOUT HER.!
I'M SURE THERE'S A WAY TO COPE.
WE'LL JUST SPEND ALL OUR TIME TOGETHER UNTIL WE FIND IT.!
I LOVE THESE FRIED BEEF PATTIES!
SERVING THEM ON A FRESH BUN WAS A STROKE OF GENIUS!
IT'S MY LATEST INVENTION. I WAS THINKING OF CALLING THEM BEEF BUNNERS.
THE NAME COULD USE A LITTLE WORK.
HAVE YOU CONSIDERED ADDING ONIONS AND PICKLES?
ARCHIE! ARCHIE!!
THE MAD DUKE OF DOOM HAS CAPTURED THE LORD LODGE AND PRINCESS VERONICA! AND HE'S ALSO ARRESTED YOUR PARENTS!!
OMIGOSH! WHAT ARE WE GOING TO DO?!
9

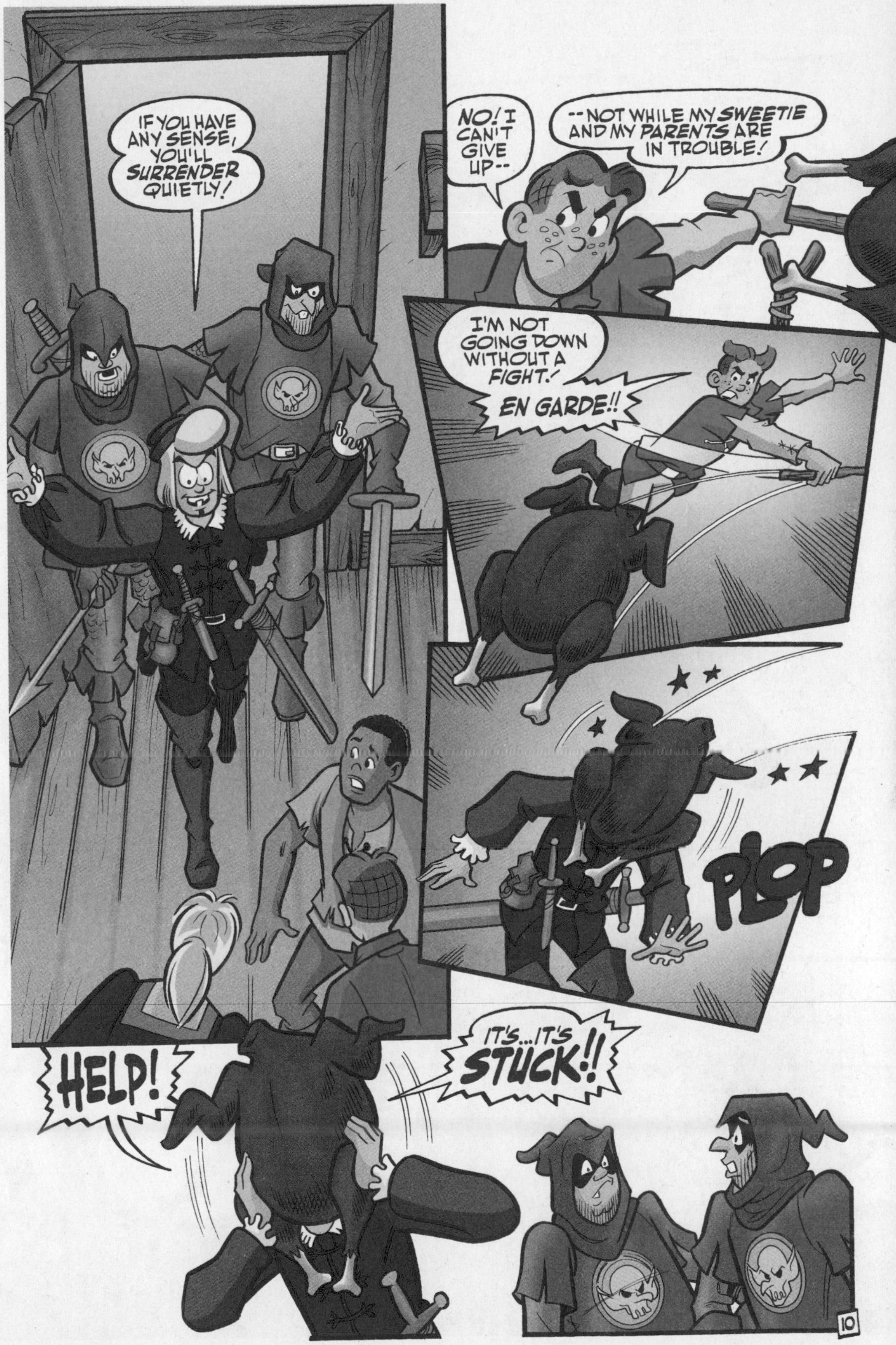
IF YOU HAVE ANY SENSE, YOU'LL SURRENDER QUIETLY!
NO! I CAN'T GIVE UP--
--NOT WHILE MY SWEETIE AND MY PARENTS ARE IN TROUBLE!
I'M NOT GOING DOWN WITHOUT A FIGHT!
EN GARDE!!
PLOP
HELP!
IT'S...IT'S STUCK!!
10

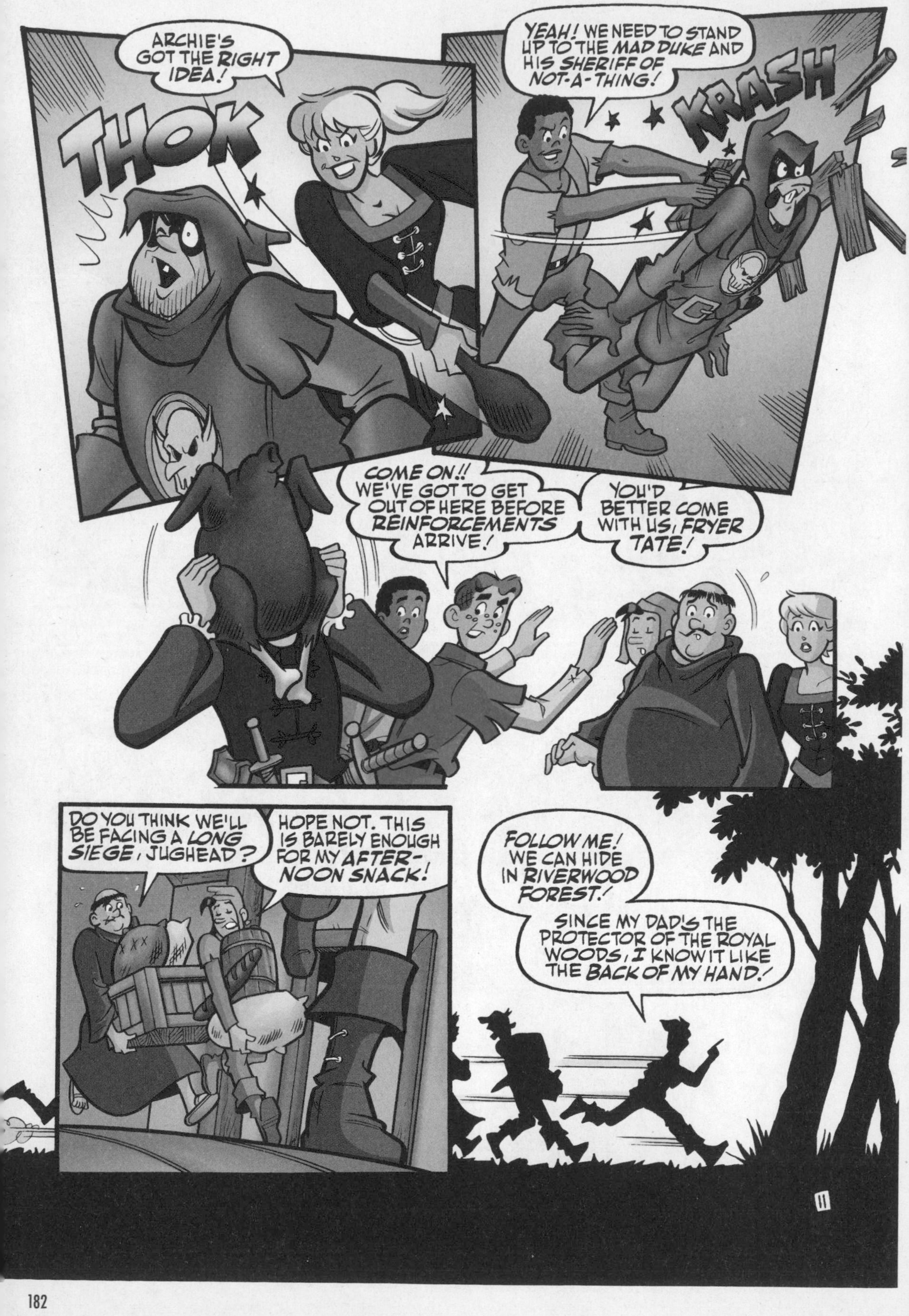
ARCHIE'S GOT THE RIGHT IDEA!
THOK
YEAH! WE NEED TO STAND UP TO THE MAD DUKE AND HIS SHERIFF OF NOT-A-THING!
KRASH
COME ON!! WE'VE GOT TO GET OUT OF HERE BEFORE REINFORCEMENTS ARRIVE!
YOU'D BETTER COME WITH US, FRYER TATE!
DO YOU THINK WE'LL BE FACING A LONG SIEGE, JUGHEAD?
HOPE NOT. THIS IS BARELY ENOUGH FOR MY AFTER-NOON SNACK!
FOLLOW ME! WE CAN HIDE IN RIVERWOOD FOREST!
SINCE MY DAD'S THE PROTECTOR OF THE ROYAL WOODS, I KNOW IT LIKE THE BACK OF MY HAND!
11

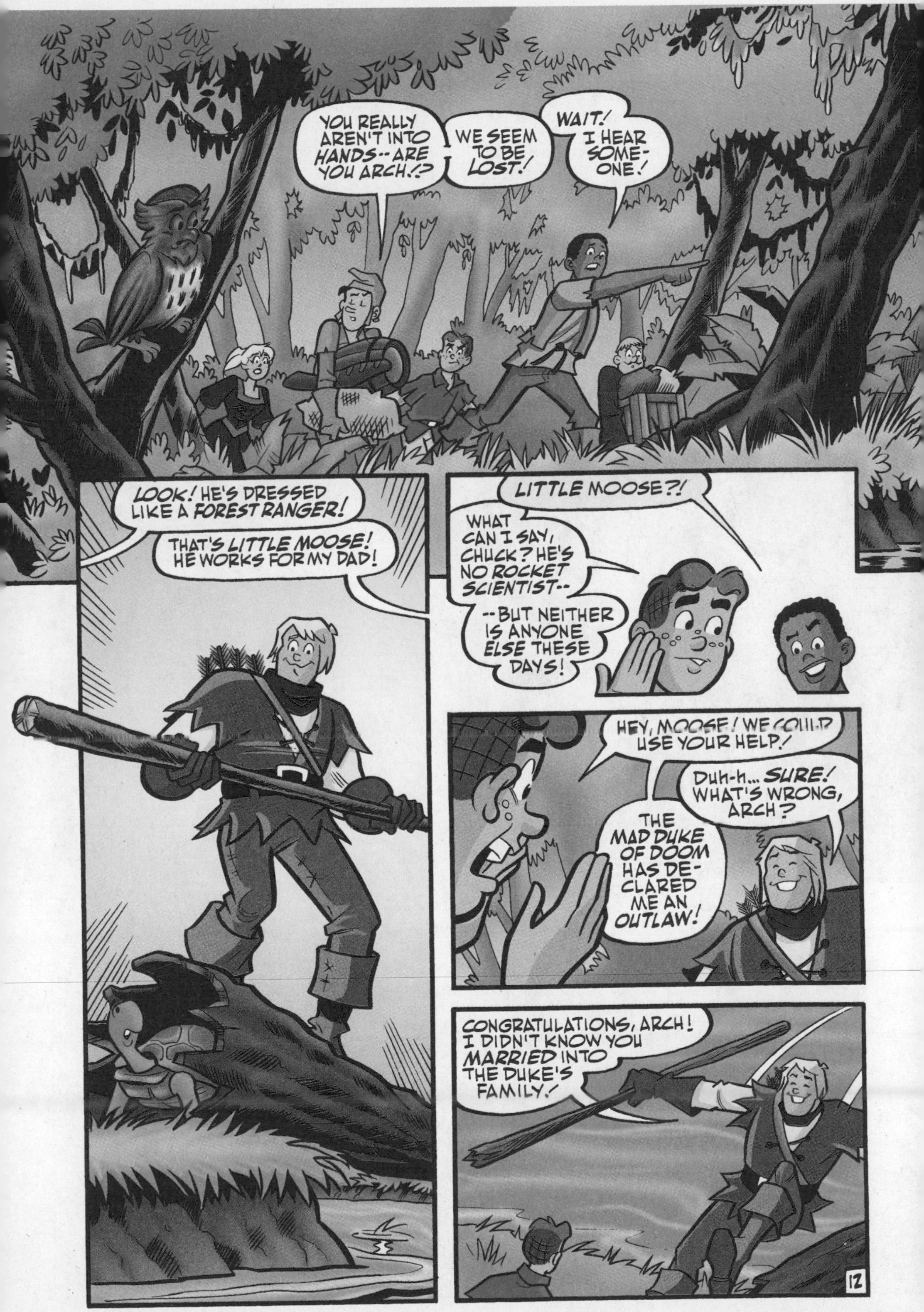
YOU REALLY AREN'T INTO HANDS--ARE YOU ARCH!?
WE SEEM TO BE LOST!
WAIT! I HEAR SOME-ONE!
LOOK! HE'S DRESSED LIKE A FOREST RANGER!
THAT'S LITTLE MOOSE! HE WORKS FOR MY DAD!
LITTLE MOOSE?!
WHAT CAN I SAY, CHUCK? HE'S NO ROCKET SCIENTIST--
--BUT NEITHER IS ANYONE ELSE THESE DAYS!
HEY, MOOSE! WE COULD USE YOUR HELP!
Duh-h... SURE! WHAT'S WRONG, ARCH?
THE MAD DUKE OF DOOM HAS DE-CLARED ME AN OUTLAW!
CONGRATULATIONS, ARCH! I DIDN'T KNOW YOU MARRIED INTO THE DUKE'S FAMILY!
12

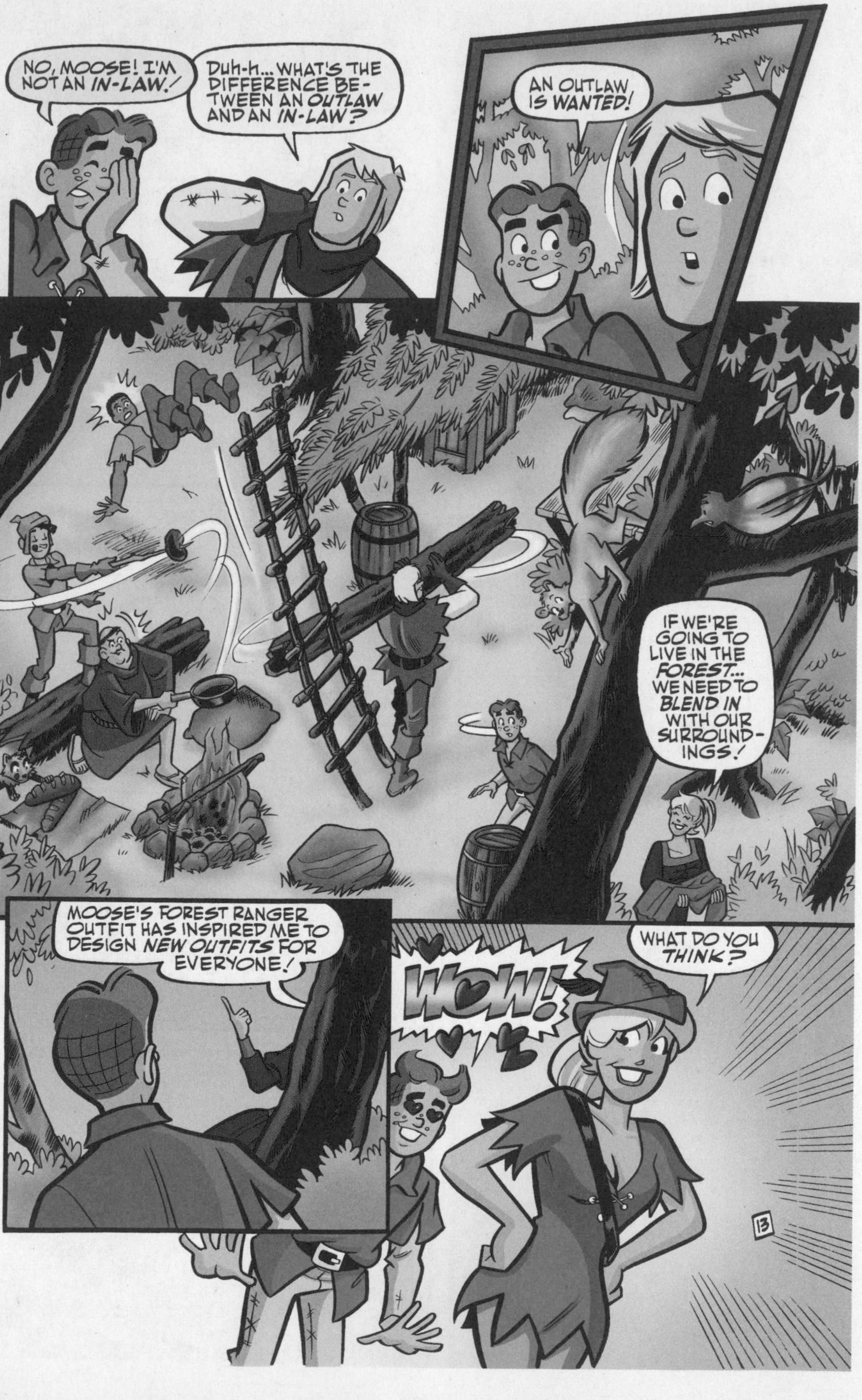
NO, MOOSE! I'M NOT AN IN-LAW!
Duh-h... WHAT'S THE DIFFERENCE BE-TWEEN AN OUTLAW AND AN IN-LAW?
AN OUTLAW IS WANTED!
IF WE'RE GOING TO LIVE IN THE FOREST... WE NEED TO BLEND IN WITH OUR SURROUND-INGS!
MOOSE'S FOREST RANGER OUTFIT HAS INSPIRED ME TO DESIGN NEW OUTFITS FOR EVERYONE!
WOW!
WHAT DO YOU THINK?
13

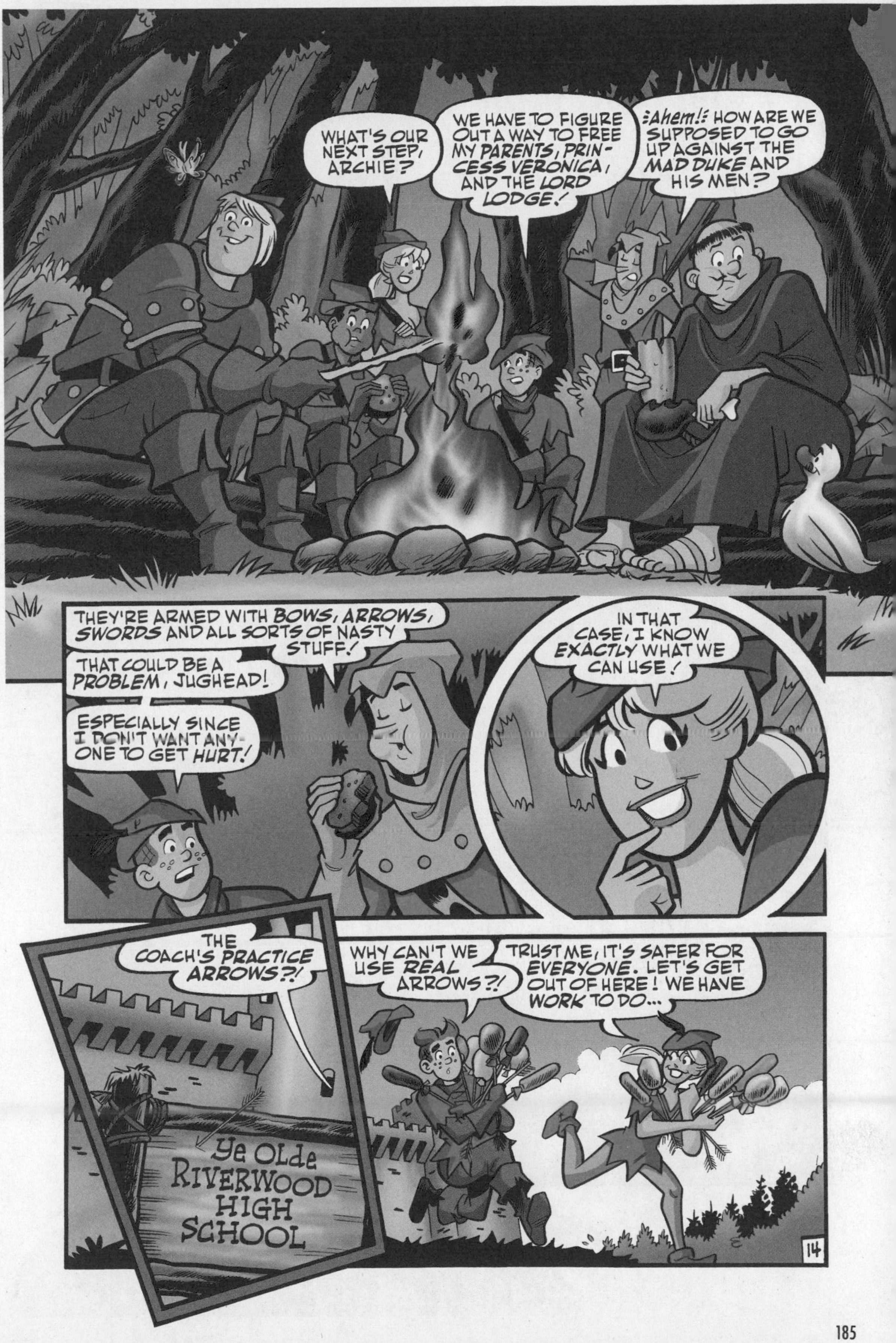
WHAT'S OUR NEXT STEP, ARCHIE?
WE HAVE TO FIGURE OUT A WAY TO FREE MY PARENTS, PRINCESS VERONICA, AND THE LORD LODGE!
AHEM! HOW ARE WE SUPPOSED TO GO UP AGAINST THE MAD DUKE AND HIS MEN?
THEY'RE ARMED WITH BOWS, ARROWS, SWORDS AND ALL SORTS OF NASTY STUFF!
THAT COULD BE A PROBLEM, JUGHEAD!
ESPECIALLY SINCE I DON'T WANT ANYONE TO GET HURT!
IN THAT CASE, I KNOW EXACTLY WHAT WE CAN USE!
THE COACH'S PRACTICE ARROWS?!
Ye Olde RIVERWOOD HIGH SCHOOL
WHY CAN'T WE USE REAL ARROWS?!
TRUST ME, IT'S SAFER FOR EVERYONE. LET'S GET OUT OF HERE! WE HAVE WORK TO DO...
14

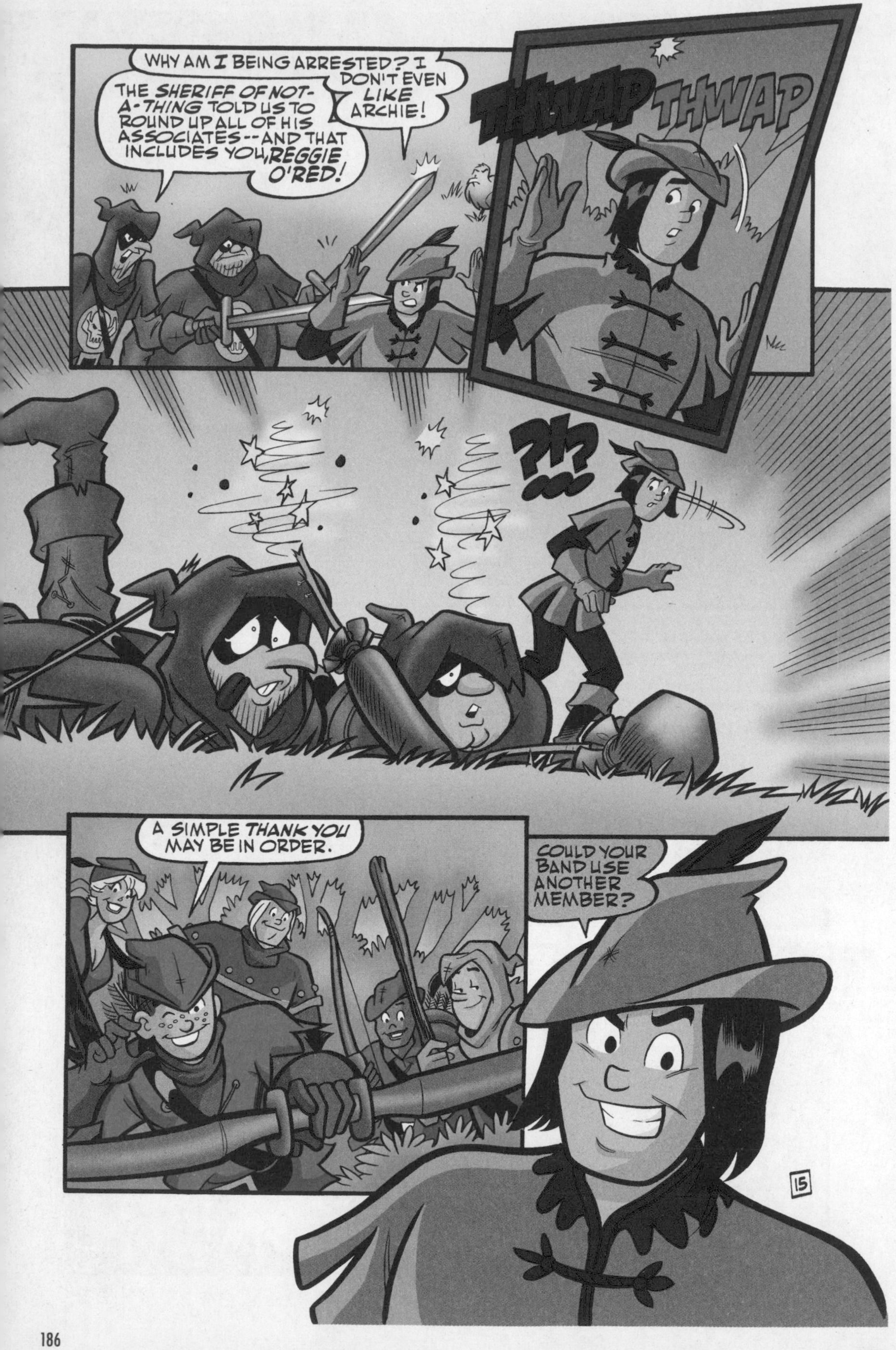
WHY AM I BEING ARRESTED? I DON'T EVEN LIKE ARCHIE!
THE SHERIFF OF NOT-A-THING TOLD US TO ROUND UP ALL OF HIS ASSOCIATES--AND THAT INCLUDES YOU, REGGIE O'RED!
THWAP THWAP
?!?...
A SIMPLE THANK YOU MAY BE IN ORDER.
COULD YOUR BAND USE ANOTHER MEMBER?
15

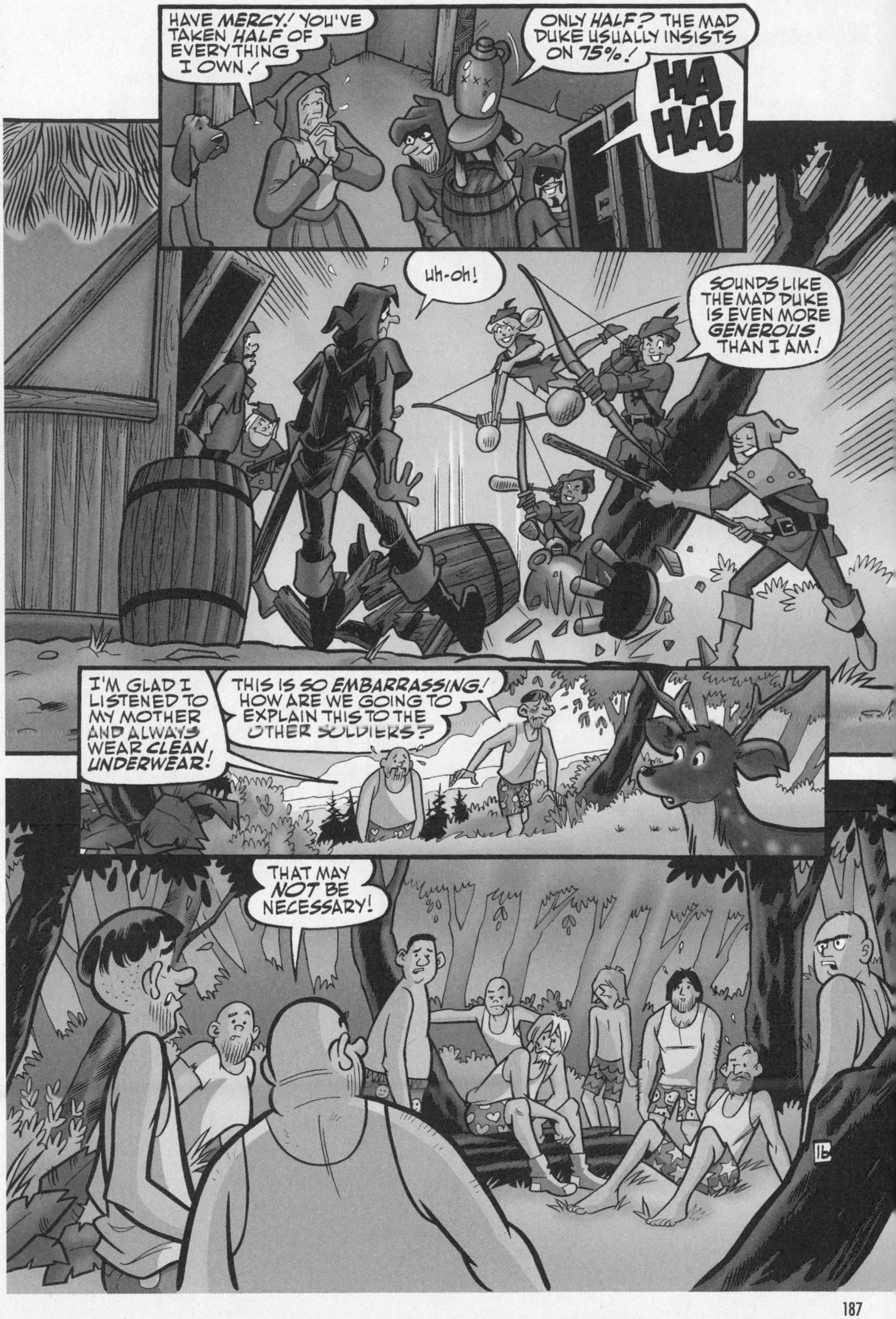
HAVE MERCY! YOU'VE TAKEN HALF OF EVERYTHING I OWN!
ONLY HALF? THE MAD DUKE USUALLY INSISTS ON 75%!
HA HA!
uh-oh!
SOUNDS LIKE THE MAD DUKE IS EVEN MORE GENEROUS THAN I AM!
I'M GLAD I LISTENED TO MY MOTHER AND ALWAYS WEAR CLEAN UNDERWEAR!
THIS IS SO EMBARRASSING! HOW ARE WE GOING TO EXPLAIN THIS TO THE OTHER SOLDIERS?
THAT MAY NOT BE NECESSARY!

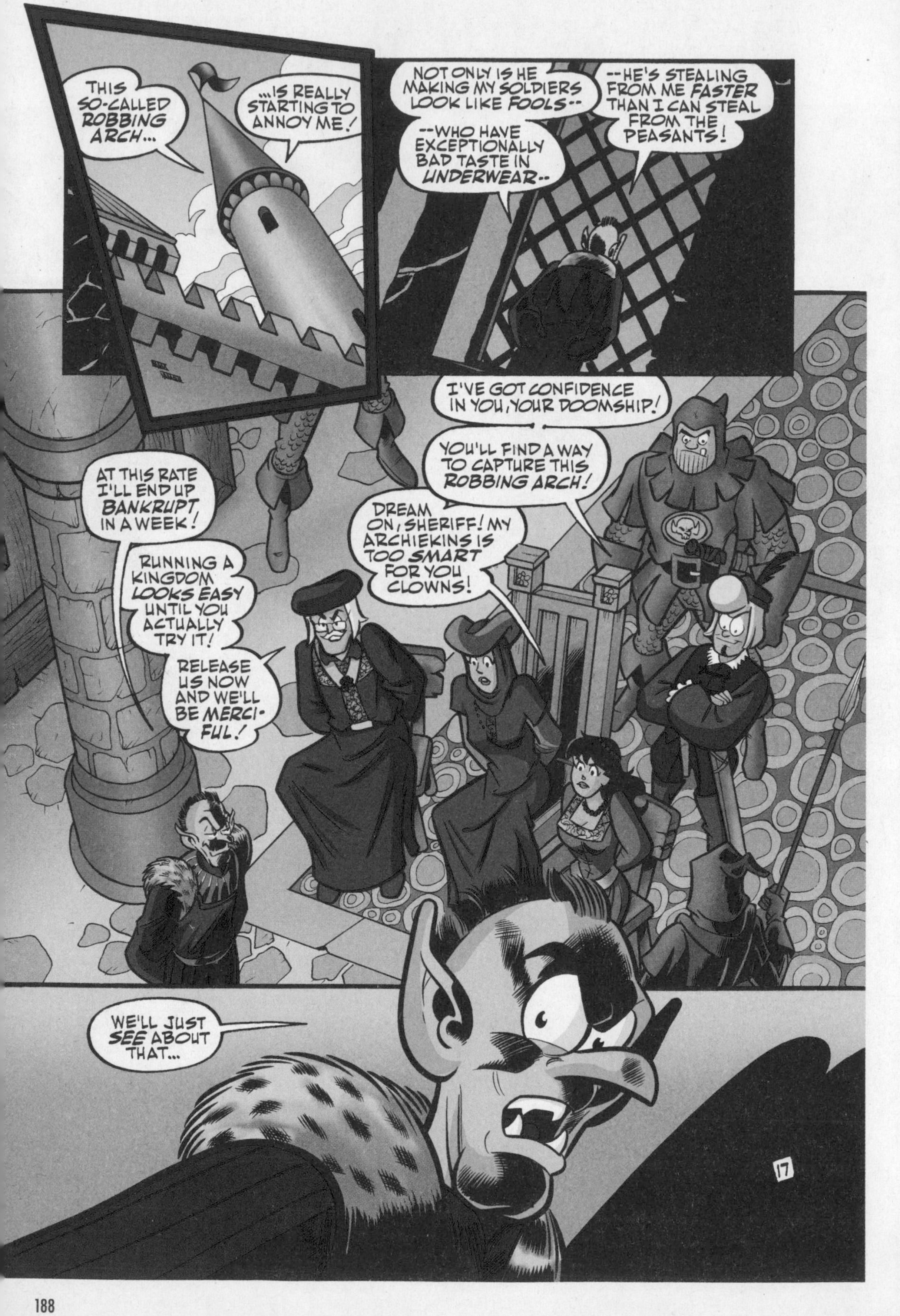
THIS SO-CALLED ROBBING ARCH...
...IS REALLY STARTING TO ANNOY ME!
NOT ONLY IS HE MAKING MY SOLDIERS LOOK LIKE FOOLS--
--WHO HAVE EXCEPTIONALLY BAD TASTE IN UNDERWEAR--
--HE'S STEALING FROM ME FASTER THAN I CAN STEAL FROM THE PEASANTS!
AT THIS RATE I'LL END UP BANKRUPT IN A WEEK!
RUNNING A KINGDOM LOOKS EASY UNTIL YOU ACTUALLY TRY IT!
RELEASE US NOW AND WE'LL BE MERCIFUL!
I'VE GOT CONFIDENCE IN YOU, YOUR DOOMSHIP!
YOU'LL FIND A WAY TO CAPTURE THIS ROBBING ARCH!
DREAM ON, SHERIFF! MY ARCHIEKINS IS TOO SMART FOR YOU CLOWNS!
WE'LL JUST SEE ABOUT THAT...
17

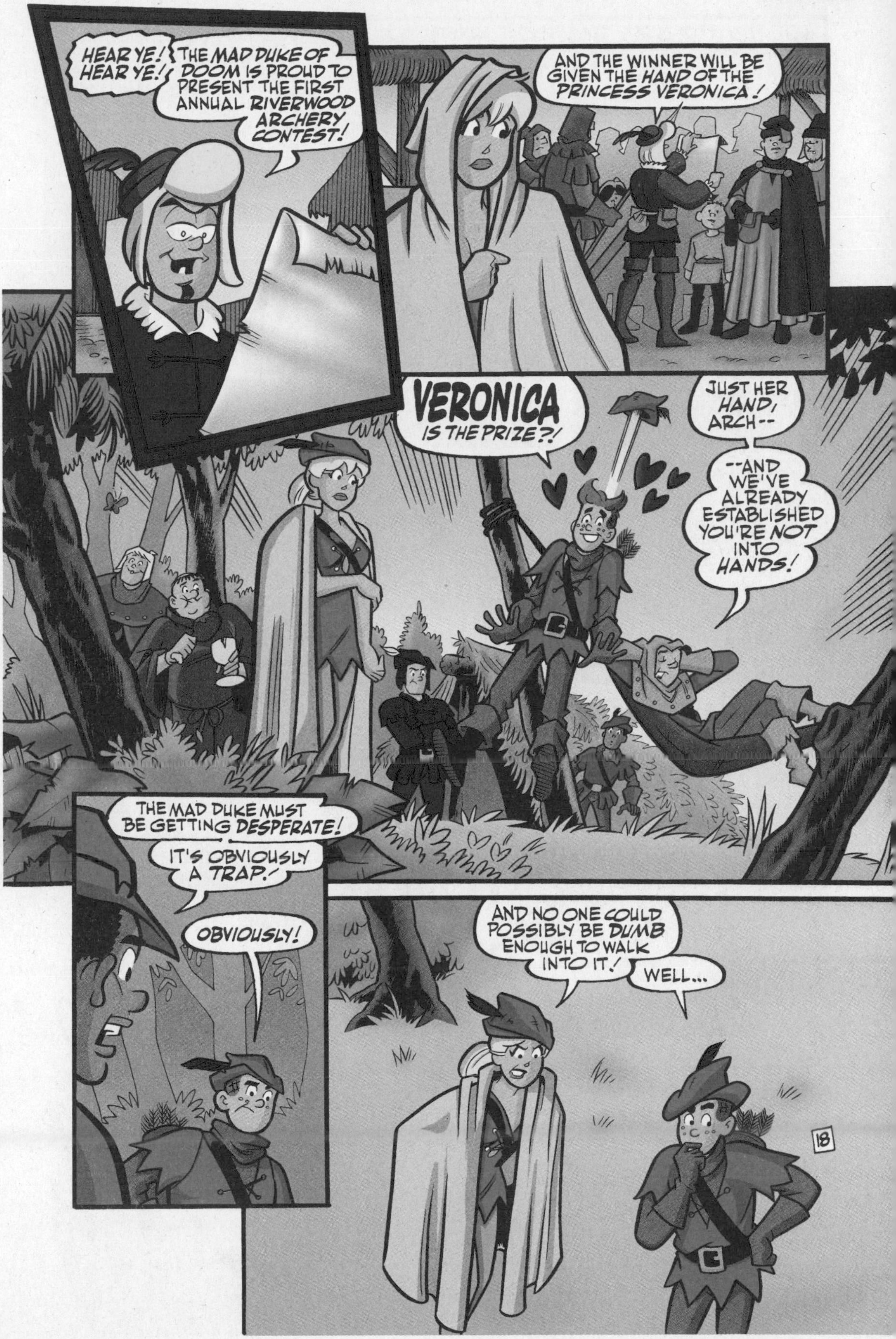
HEAR YE! HEAR YE!
THE MAD DUKE OF DOOM IS PROUD TO PRESENT THE FIRST ANNUAL RIVERWOOD ARCHERY CONTEST!
AND THE WINNER WILL BE GIVEN THE HAND OF THE PRINCESS VERONICA!
VERONICA IS THE PRIZE?!
JUST HER HAND, ARCH--
--AND WE'VE ALREADY ESTABLISHED YOU'RE NOT INTO HANDS!
THE MAD DUKE MUST BE GETTING DESPERATE!
IT'S OBVIOUSLY A TRAP!
OBVIOUSLY!
AND NO ONE COULD POSSIBLY BE DUMB ENOUGH TO WALK INTO IT!
WELL...
18

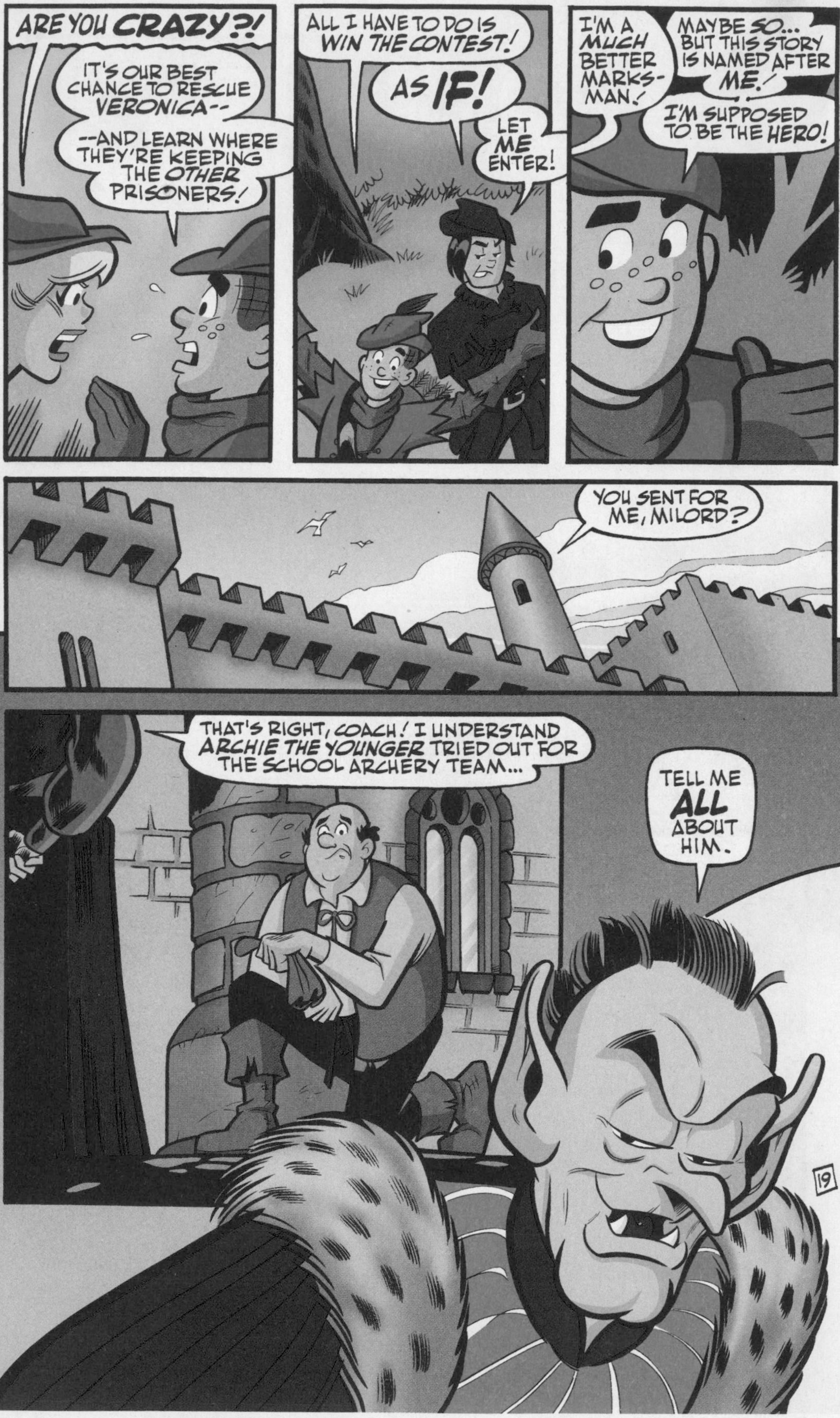
ARE YOU CRAZY?!
IT'S OUR BEST CHANCE TO RESCUE VERONICA--
--AND LEARN WHERE THEY'RE KEEPING THE OTHER PRISONERS!
ALL I HAVE TO DO IS WIN THE CONTEST!
AS IF!
LET ME ENTER!
I'M A MUCH BETTER MARKS-MAN!
MAYBE SO... BUT THIS STORY IS NAMED AFTER ME!
I'M SUPPOSED TO BE THE HERO!
YOU SENT FOR ME, MILORD?
THAT'S RIGHT, COACH! I UNDERSTAND ARCHIE THE YOUNGER TRIED OUT FOR THE SCHOOL ARCHERY TEAM...
TELL ME ALL ABOUT HIM.
19

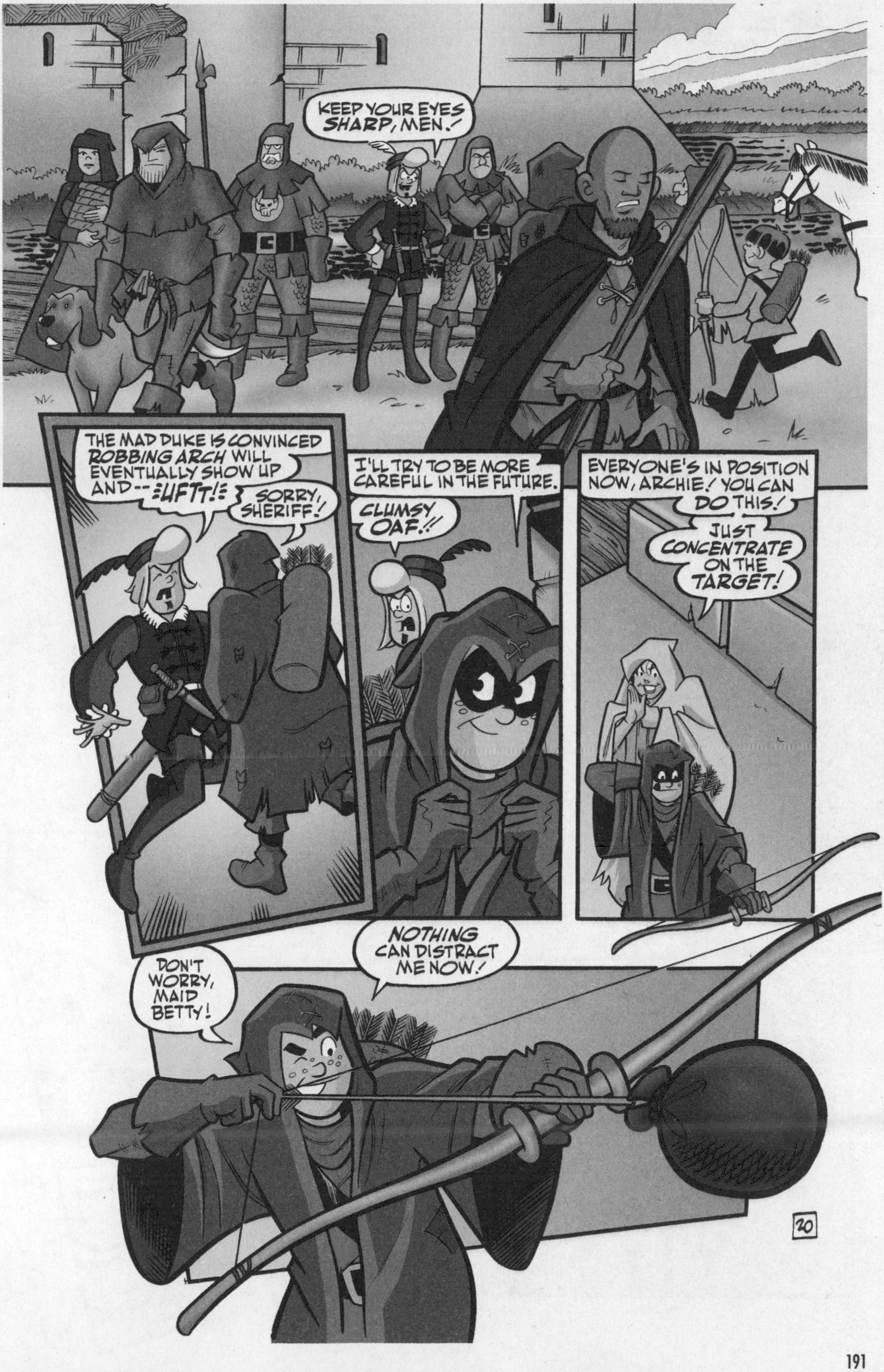
KEEP YOUR EYES SHARP, MEN.!
THE MAD DUKE IS CONVINCED ROBBING ARCH WILL EVENTUALLY SHOW UP AND-- UFTT!
SORRY, SHERIFF!
I'LL TRY TO BE MORE CAREFUL IN THE FUTURE.
CLUMSY OAF!!
EVERYONE'S IN POSITION NOW, ARCHIE! YOU CAN DO THIS!
JUST CONCENTRATE ON THE TARGET!
DON'T WORRY, MAID BETTY!
NOTHING CAN DISTRACT ME NOW!
20

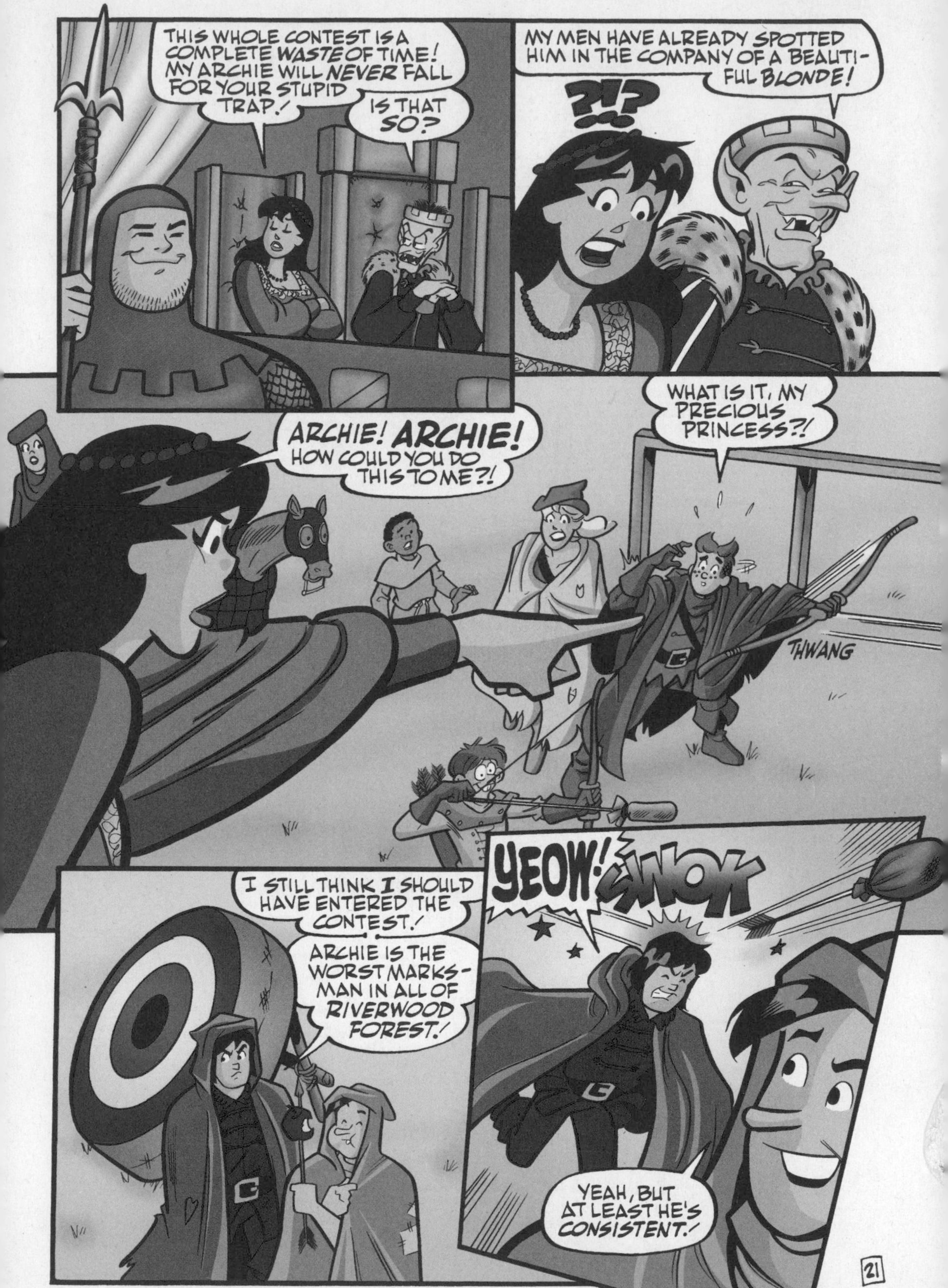
THIS WHOLE CONTEST IS A COMPLETE WASTE OF TIME! MY ARCHIE WILL NEVER FALL FOR YOUR STUPID TRAP!
IS THAT SO?
MY MEN HAVE ALREADY SPOTTED HIM IN THE COMPANY OF A BEAUTIFUL BLONDE!
?!?
ARCHIE! ARCHIE! HOW COULD YOU DO THIS TO ME?!
WHAT IS IT, MY PRECIOUS PRINCESS?!
THWANG
I STILL THINK I SHOULD HAVE ENTERED THE CONTEST!
ARCHIE IS THE WORST MARKSMAN IN ALL OF RIVERWOOD FOREST!
YEOW!
YEAH, BUT AT LEAST HE'S CONSISTENT!
21

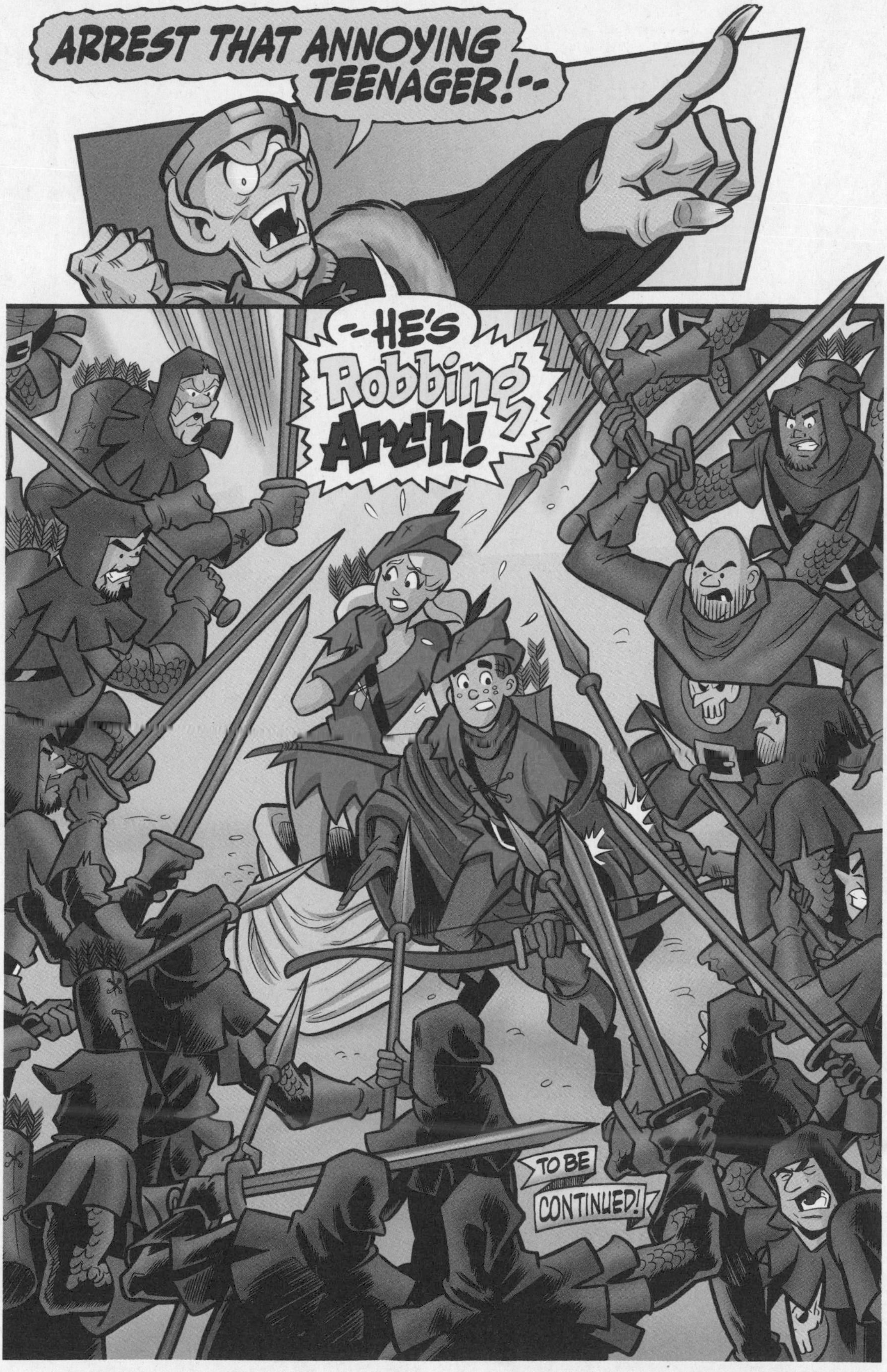
ARREST THAT ANNOYING TEENAGER!--
--HE'S Robbing Arch!
TO BE CONTINUED!

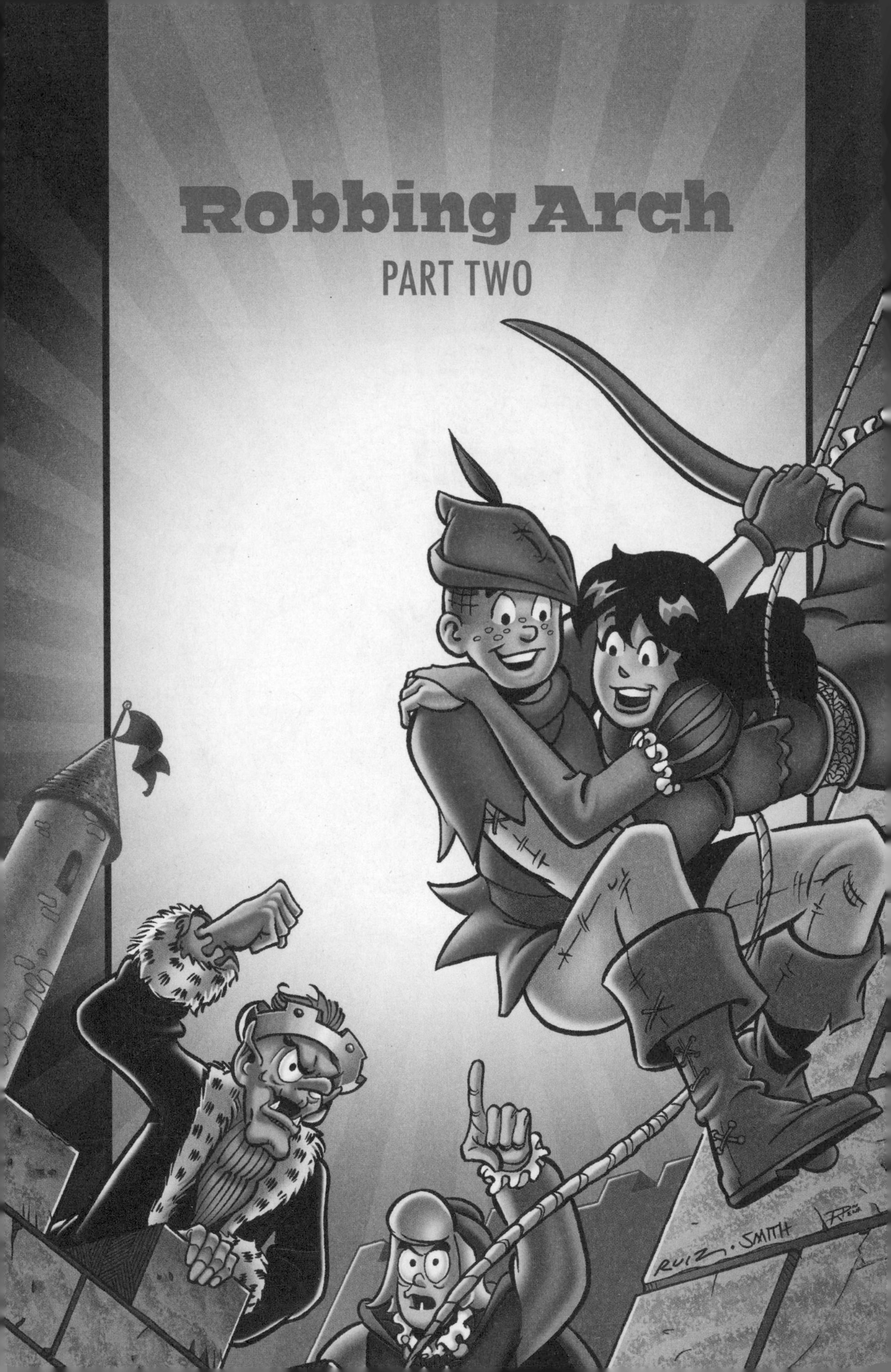
Robbing Arch
PART TWO
RUIZ . SMITH

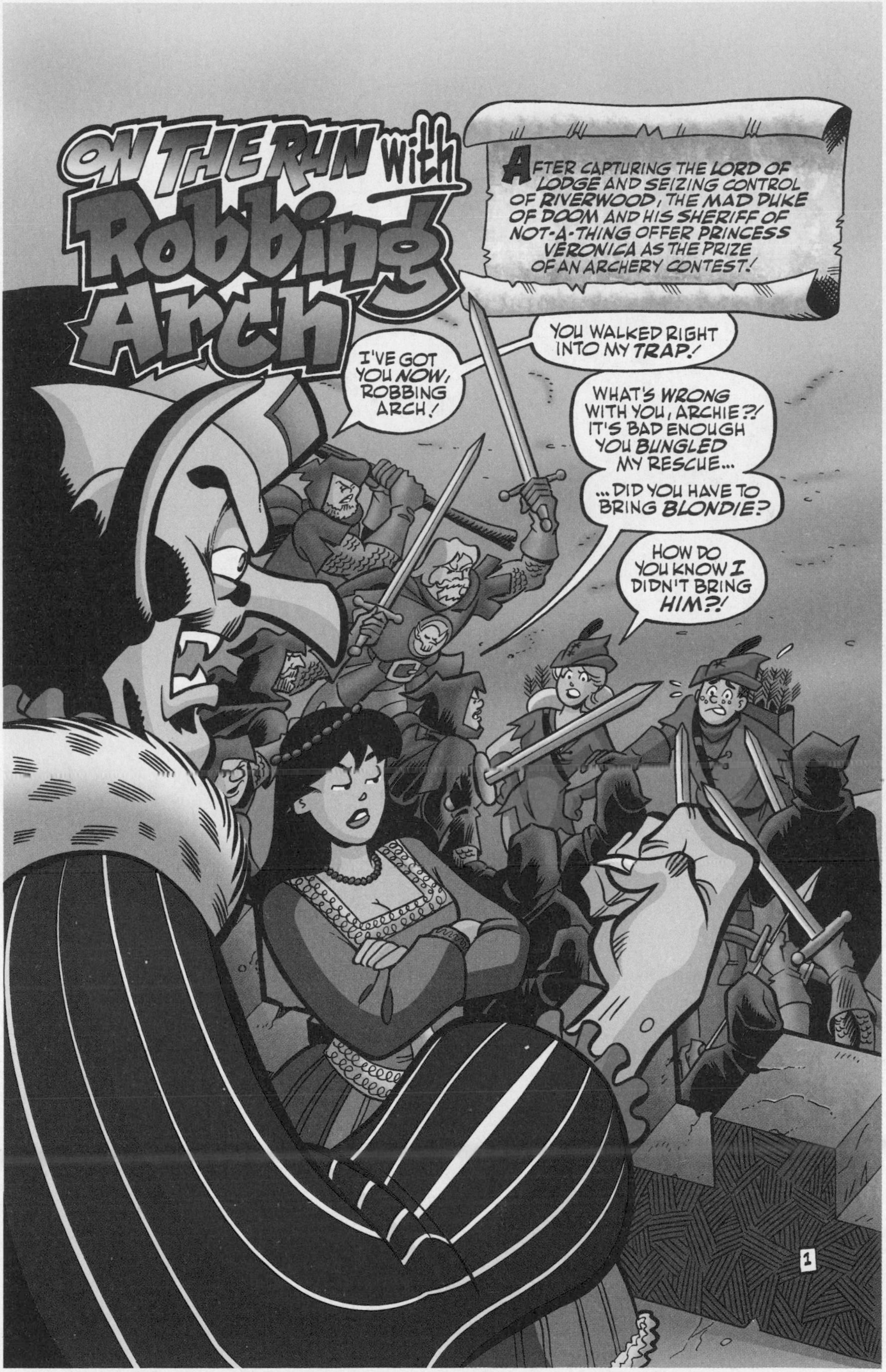
ON THE RUN with Robbing Arch
AFTER CAPTURING THE LORD OF LODGE AND SEIZING CONTROL OF RIVERWOOD, THE MAD DUKE OF DOOM AND HIS SHERIFF OF NOT-A-THING OFFER PRINCESS VERONICA AS THE PRIZE OF AN ARCHERY CONTEST!
I'VE GOT YOU NOW, ROBBING ARCH!
YOU WALKED RIGHT INTO MY TRAP!
WHAT'S WRONG WITH YOU, ARCHIE?! IT'S BAD ENOUGH YOU BUNGLED MY RESCUE...
...DID YOU HAVE TO BRING BLONDIE?
HOW DO YOU KNOW I DIDN'T BRING HIM?!
1

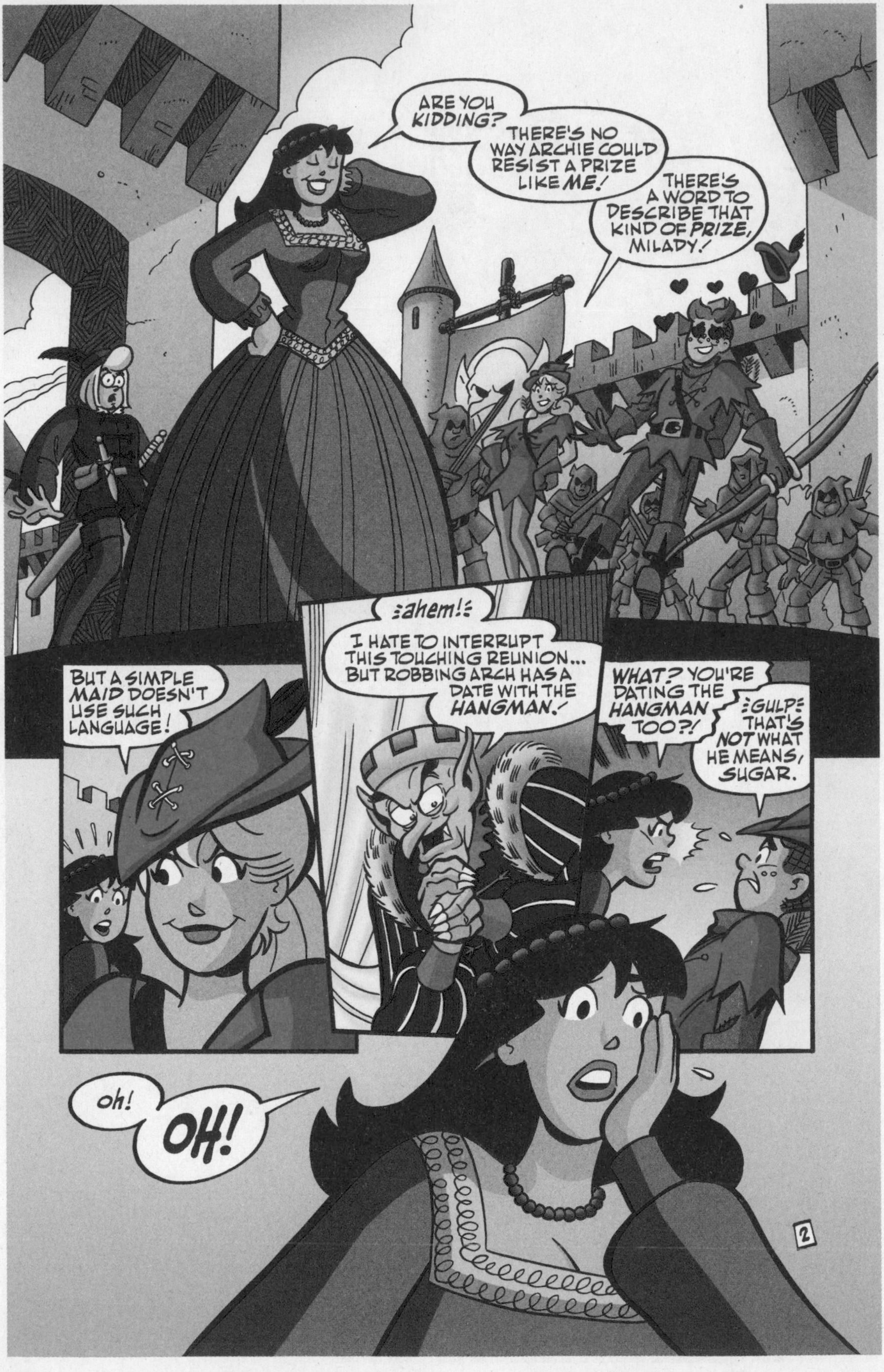
ARE YOU KIDDING? THERE'S NO WAY ARCHIE COULD RESIST A PRIZE LIKE ME!
THERE'S A WORD TO DESCRIBE THAT KIND OF PRIZE, MILADY!
BUT A SIMPLE MAID DOESN'T USE SUCH LANGUAGE!
:ahem!:
I HATE TO INTERRUPT THIS TOUCHING REUNION... BUT ROBBING ARCH HAS A DATE WITH THE HANGMAN!
WHAT? YOU'RE DATING THE HANGMAN TOO?!
:GULP: THAT'S NOT WHAT HE MEANS, SUGAR.
oh! OH!
2

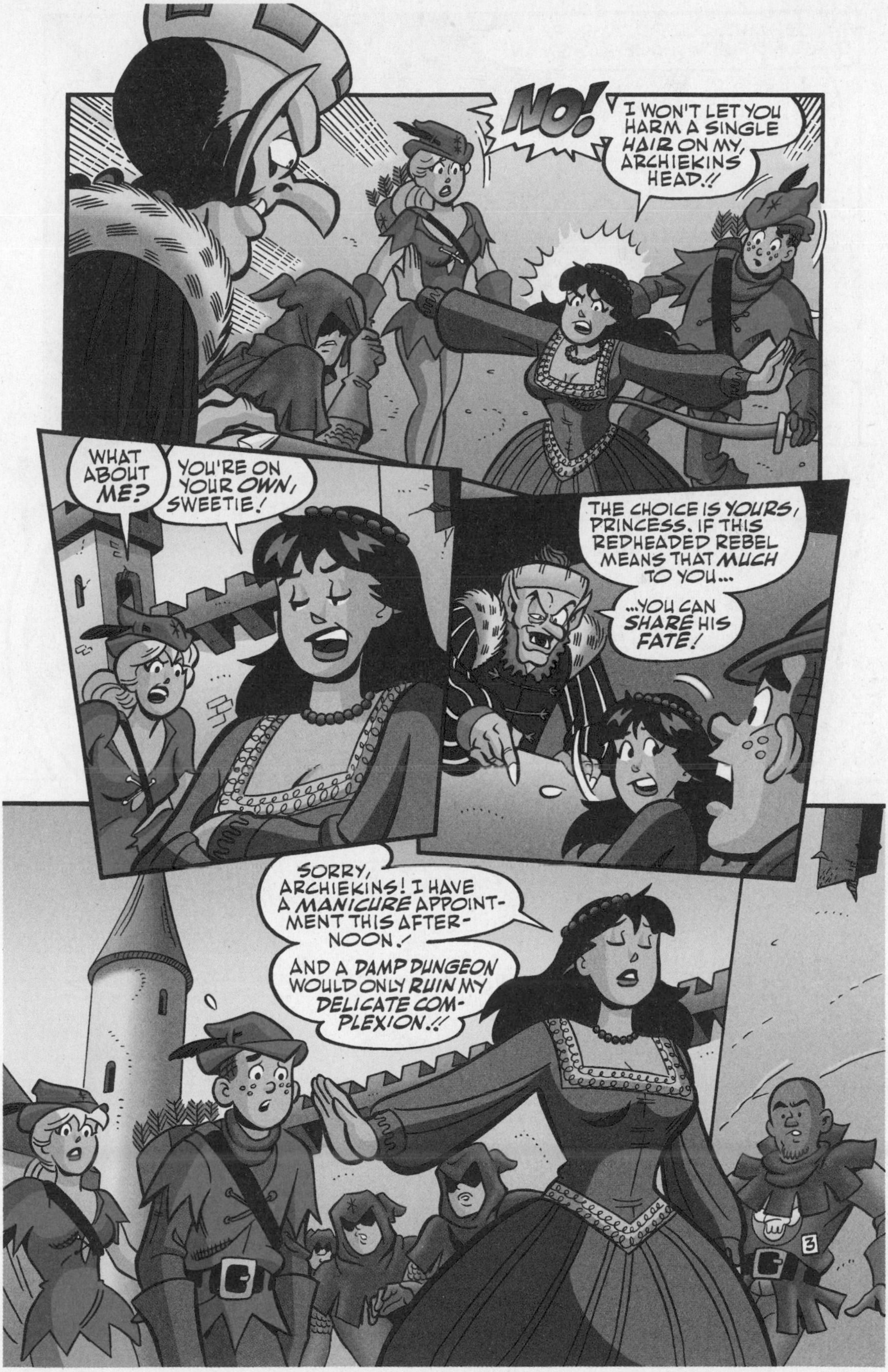
NO!
I WON'T LET YOU HARM A SINGLE HAIR ON MY ARCHIEKINS' HEAD!!
WHAT ABOUT ME?
YOU'RE ON YOUR OWN, SWEETIE!
THE CHOICE IS YOURS, PRINCESS. IF THIS REDHEADED REBEL MEANS THAT MUCH TO YOU...
...YOU CAN SHARE HIS FATE!
SORRY, ARCHIEKINS! I HAVE A MANICURE APPOINTMENT THIS AFTERNOON!
AND A DAMP DUNGEON WOULD ONLY RUIN MY DELICATE COMPLEXION!!

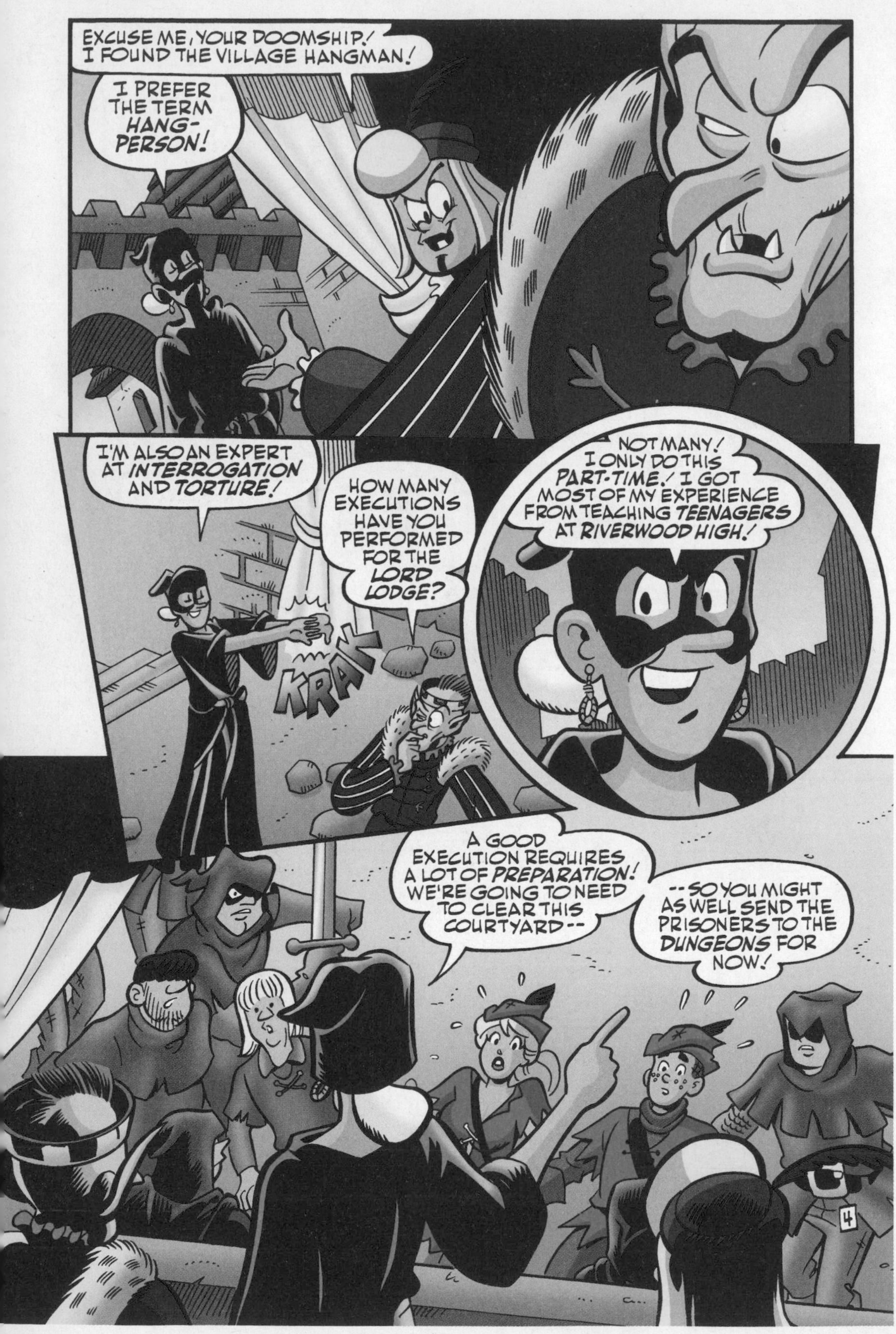
EXCUSE ME, YOUR DOOMSHIP! I FOUND THE VILLAGE HANGMAN!
I PREFER THE TERM HANG-PERSON!
I'M ALSO AN EXPERT AT INTERROGATION AND TORTURE!
HOW MANY EXECUTIONS HAVE YOU PERFORMED FOR THE LORD LODGE?
KRAK
NOT MANY! I ONLY DO THIS PART-TIME! I GOT MOST OF MY EXPERIENCE FROM TEACHING TEENAGERS AT RIVERWOOD HIGH!
A GOOD EXECUTION REQUIRES A LOT OF PREPARATION! WE'RE GOING TO NEED TO CLEAR THIS COURTYARD --
-- SO YOU MIGHT AS WELL SEND THE PRISONERS TO THE DUNGEONS FOR NOW!
4

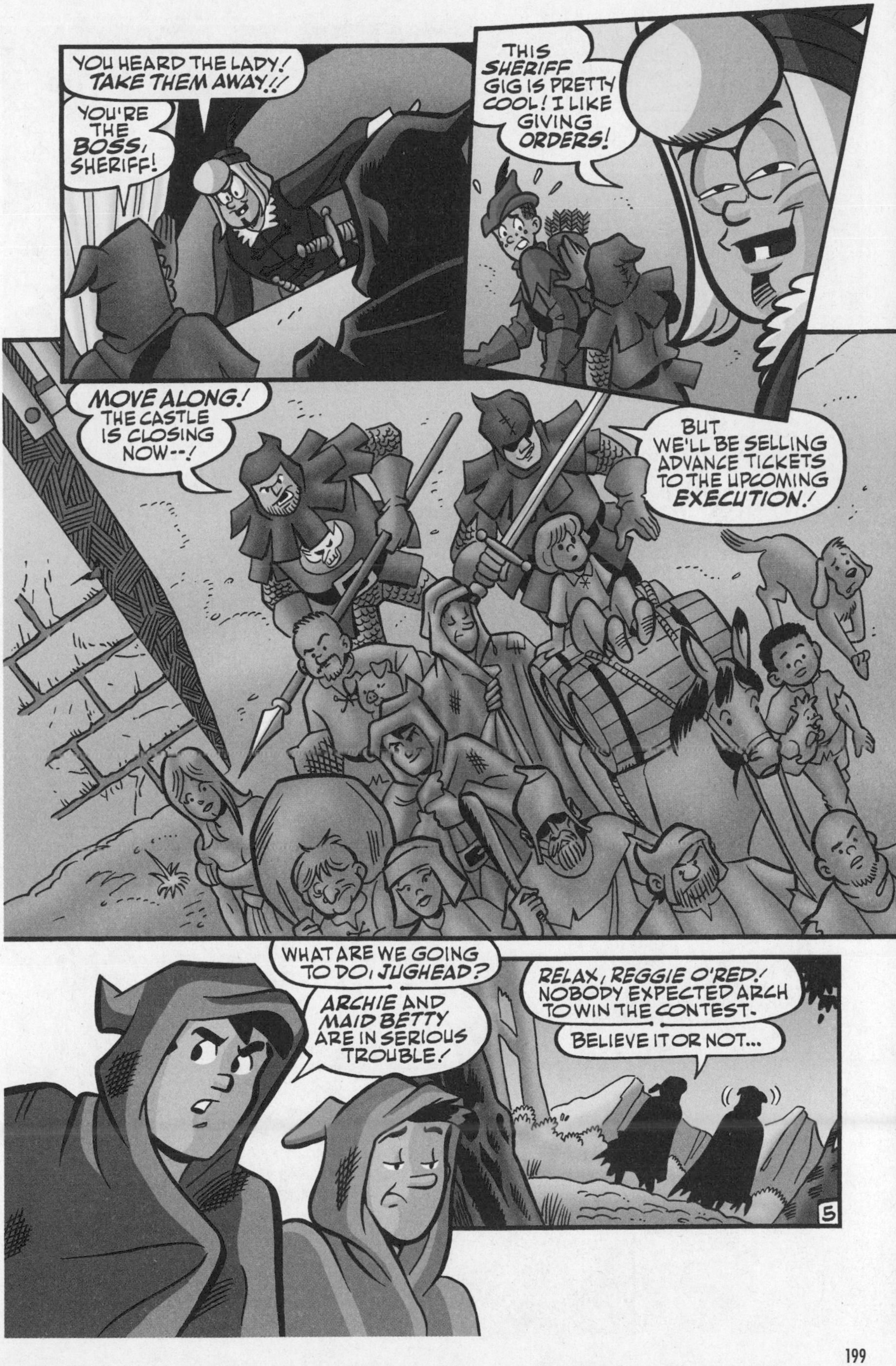
YOU HEARD THE LADY! TAKE THEM AWAY!!
YOU'RE THE BOSS, SHERIFF!
THIS SHERIFF GIG IS PRETTY COOL! I LIKE GIVING ORDERS!
MOVE ALONG! THE CASTLE IS CLOSING NOW--!
BUT WE'LL BE SELLING ADVANCE TICKETS TO THE UPCOMING EXECUTION!
WHAT ARE WE GOING TO DO, JUGHEAD?
ARCHIE AND MAID BETTY ARE IN SERIOUS TROUBLE!
RELAX, REGGIE O'RED! NOBODY EXPECTED ARCH TO WIN THE CONTEST.
BELIEVE IT OR NOT...
5

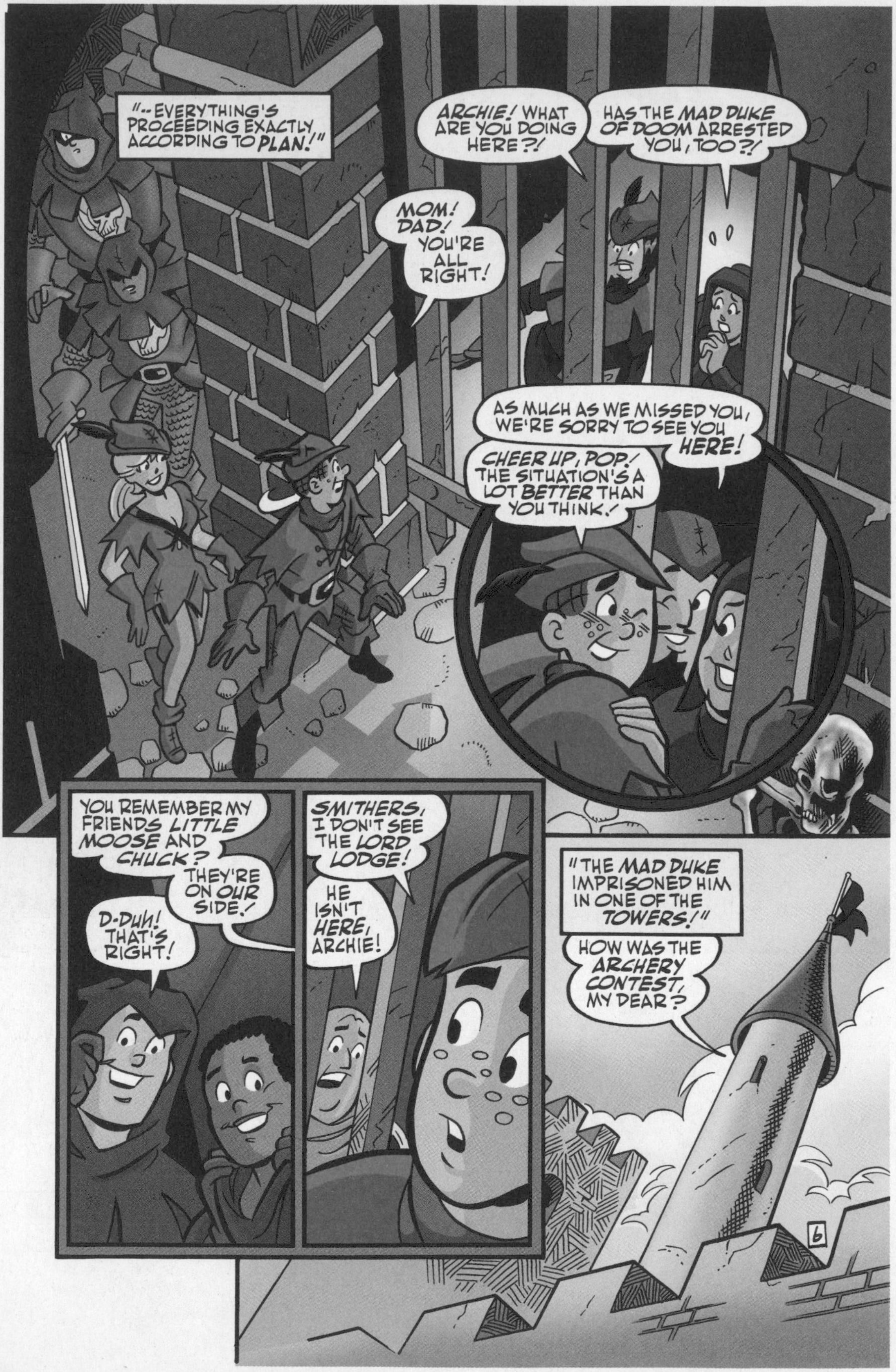
"--EVERYTHING'S PROCEEDING EXACTLY ACCORDING TO PLAN!"
ARCHIE! WHAT ARE YOU DOING HERE?!
HAS THE MAD DUKE OF DOOM ARRESTED YOU, TOO?!
MOM! DAD! YOU'RE ALL RIGHT!
AS MUCH AS WE MISSED YOU, WE'RE SORRY TO SEE YOU HERE!
CHEER UP, POP! THE SITUATION'S A LOT BETTER THAN YOU THINK!
YOU REMEMBER MY FRIENDS LITTLE MOOSE AND CHUCK?
THEY'RE ON OUR SIDE!
D-DUH! THAT'S RIGHT!
SMITHERS, I DON'T SEE THE LORD LODGE!
HE ISN'T HERE, ARCHIE!
"THE MAD DUKE IMPRISONED HIM IN ONE OF THE TOWERS!"
HOW WAS THE ARCHERY CONTEST, MY DEAR?
6

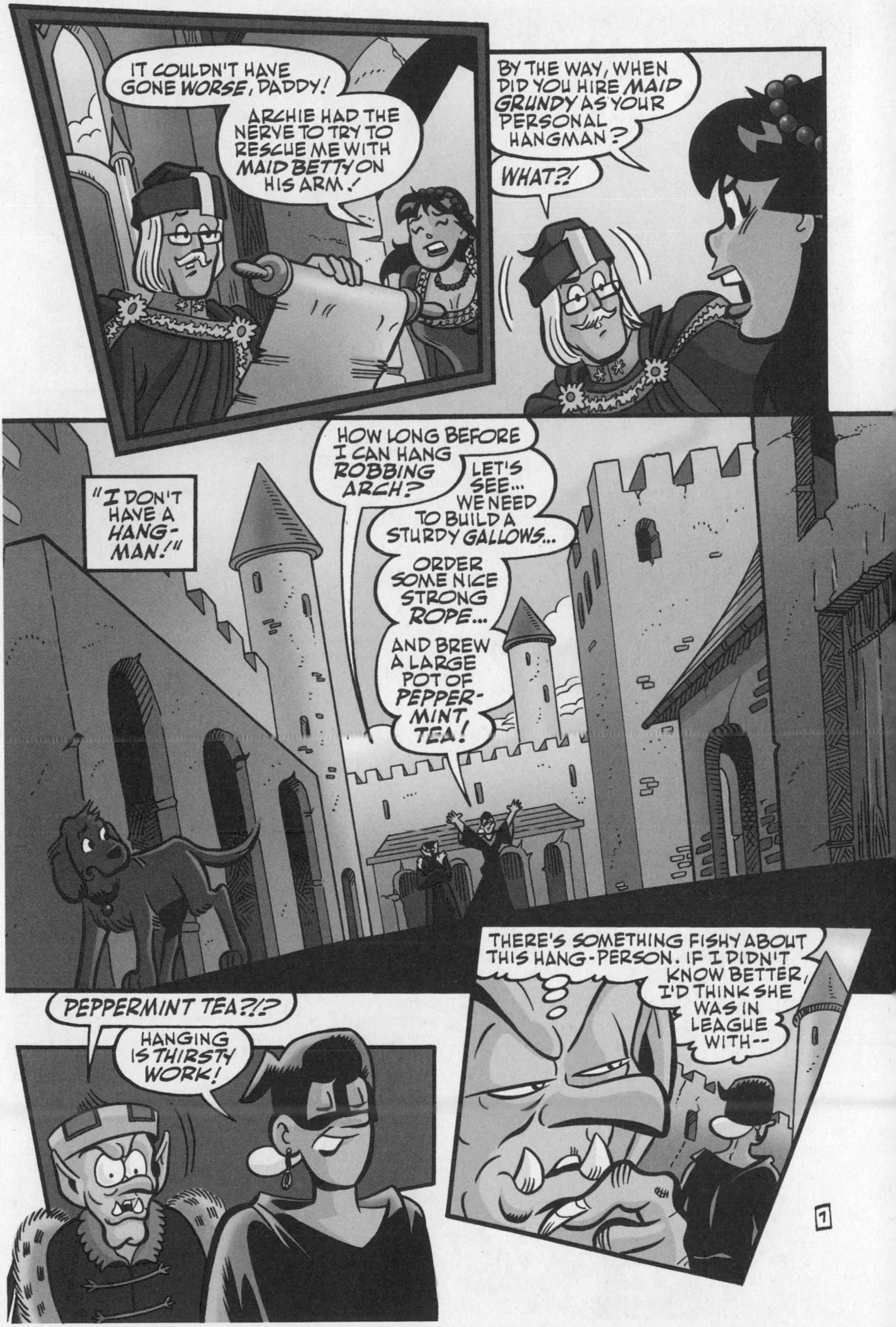
IT COULDN'T HAVE GONE WORSE, DADDY!
ARCHIE HAD THE NERVE TO TRY TO RESCUE ME WITH MAID BETTY ON HIS ARM!
BY THE WAY, WHEN DID YOU HIRE MAID GRUNDY AS YOUR PERSONAL HANGMAN?
WHAT?!
"I DON'T HAVE A HANG-MAN!"
HOW LONG BEFORE I CAN HANG ROBBING ARCH?
LET'S SEE... WE NEED TO BUILD A STURDY GALLOWS...
ORDER SOME NICE STRONG ROPE...
AND BREW A LARGE POT OF PEPPER-MINT TEA!
PEPPERMINT TEA?!?
HANGING IS THIRSTY WORK!
THERE'S SOMETHING FISHY ABOUT THIS HANG-PERSON. IF I DIDN'T KNOW BETTER, I'D THINK SHE WAS IN LEAGUE WITH--
7

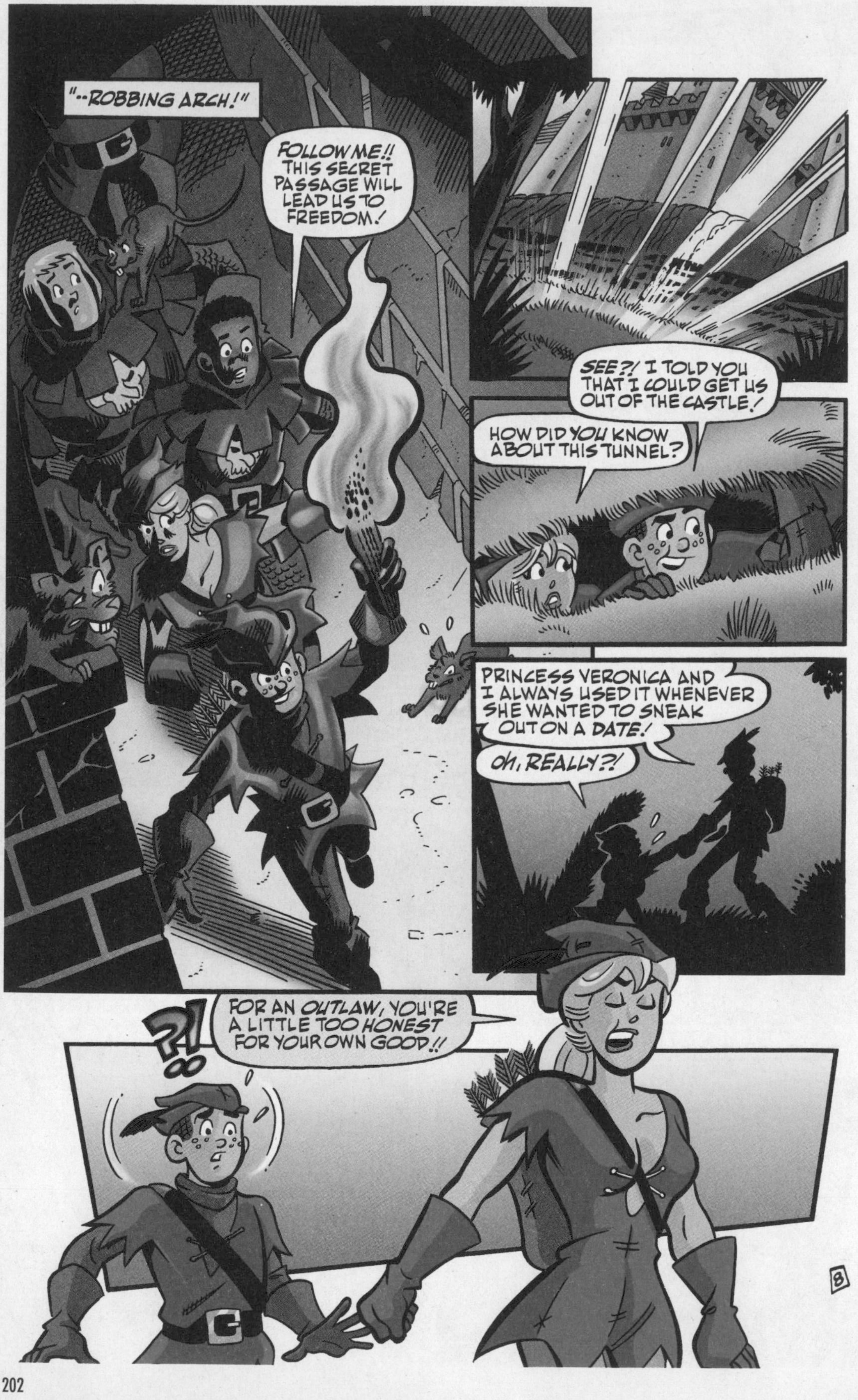
"--ROBBING ARCH!"
FOLLOW ME!! THIS SECRET PASSAGE WILL LEAD US TO FREEDOM!
SEE?! I TOLD YOU THAT I COULD GET US OUT OF THE CASTLE!
HOW DID YOU KNOW ABOUT THIS TUNNEL?
PRINCESS VERONICA AND I ALWAYS USED IT WHENEVER SHE WANTED TO SNEAK OUT ON A DATE!
oh, REALLY?!
FOR AN OUTLAW, YOU'RE A LITTLE TOO HONEST FOR YOUR OWN GOOD!!
?!
8

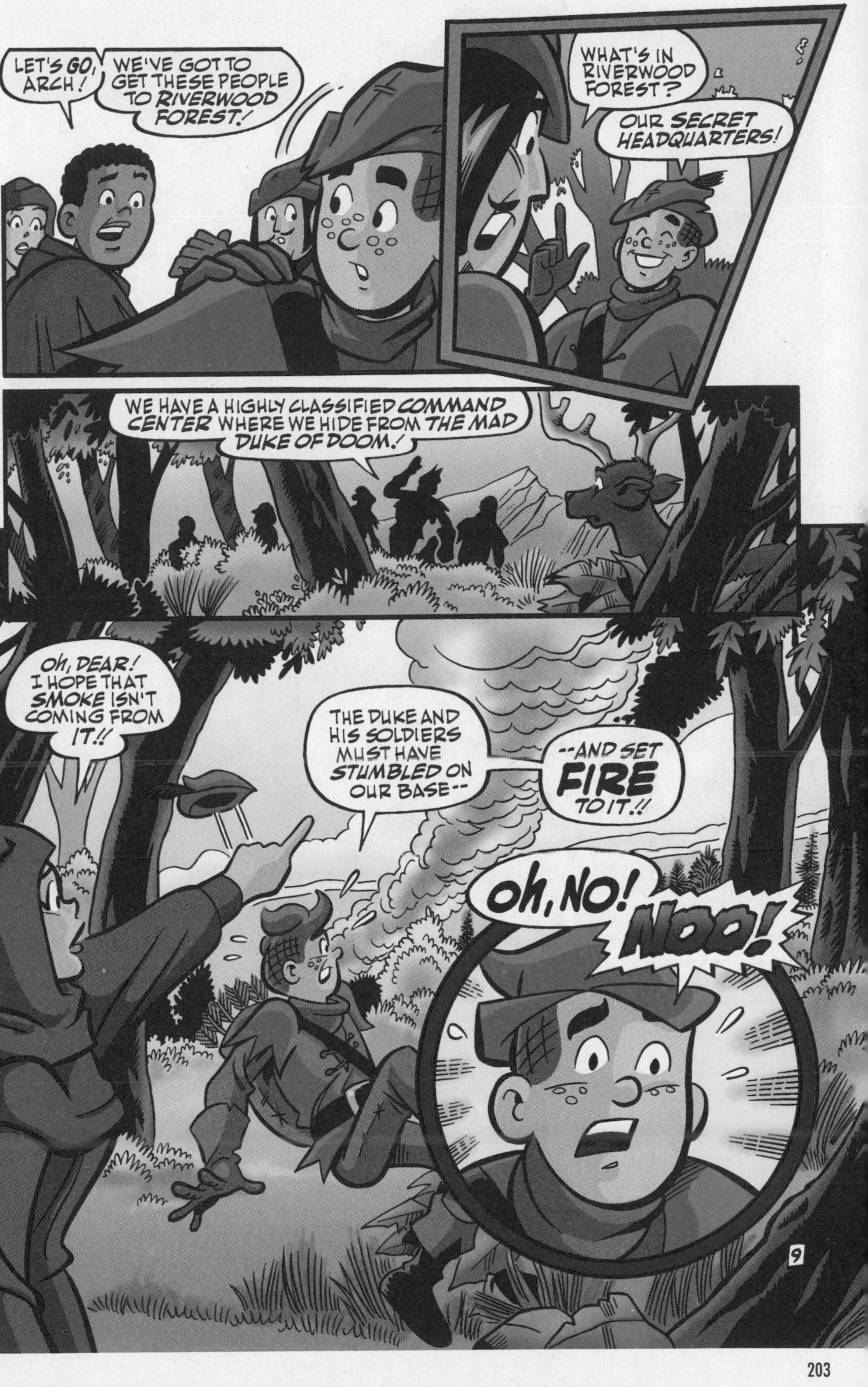
LET'S GO, ARCH!
WE'VE GOT TO GET THESE PEOPLE TO RIVERWOOD FOREST!
WHAT'S IN RIVERWOOD FOREST?
OUR SECRET HEADQUARTERS!
WE HAVE A HIGHLY CLASSIFIED COMMAND CENTER WHERE WE HIDE FROM THE MAD DUKE OF DOOM!
Oh, DEAR! I HOPE THAT SMOKE ISN'T COMING FROM IT!!
THE DUKE AND HIS SOLDIERS MUST HAVE STUMBLED ON OUR BASE--
--AND SET FIRE TO IT!!
Oh, NO! NOO!
9

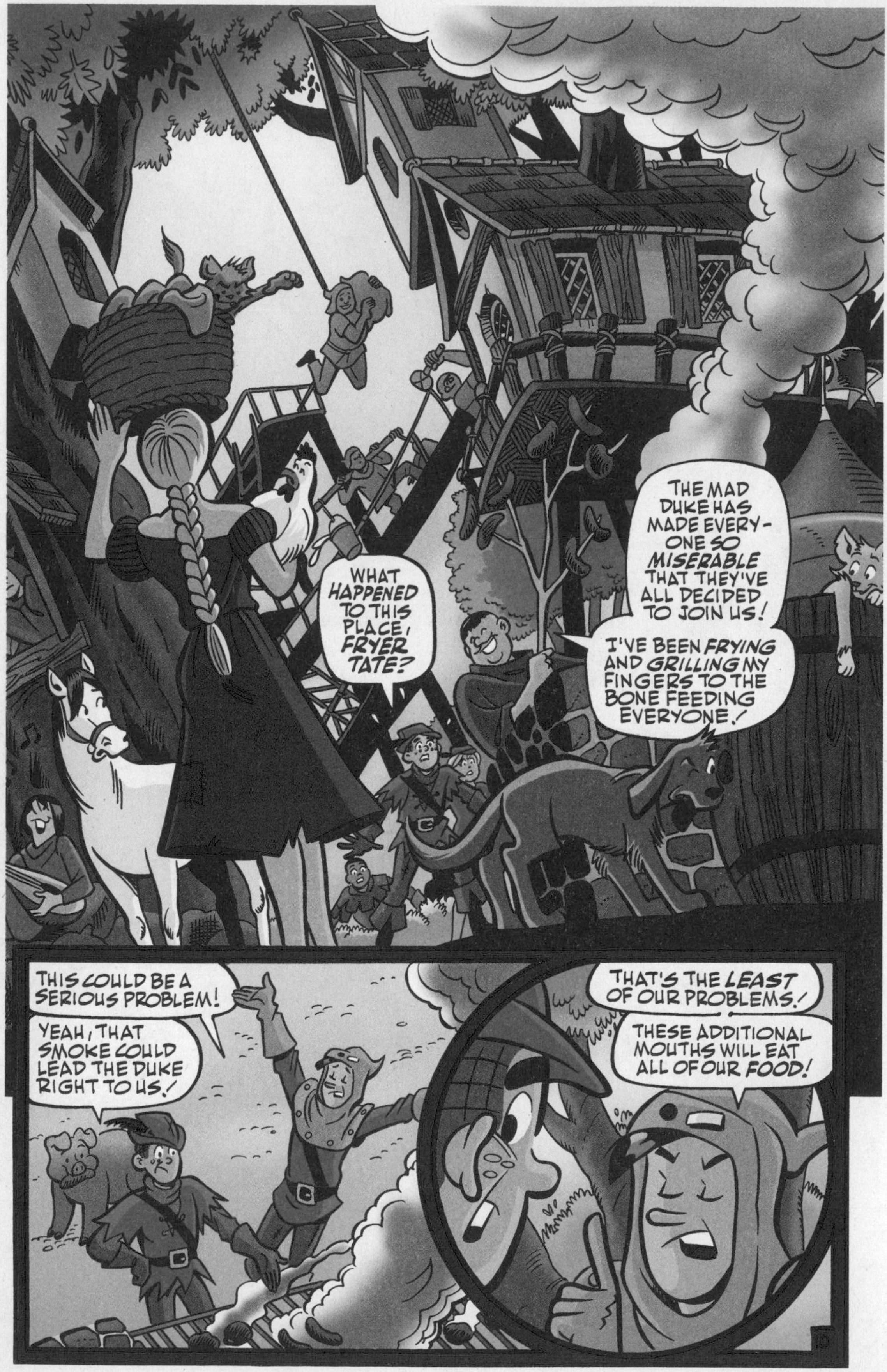
WHAT HAPPENED TO THIS PLACE, FRYER TATE?
THE MAD DUKE HAS MADE EVERY-ONE SO MISERABLE THAT THEY'VE ALL DECIDED TO JOIN US!
I'VE BEEN FRYING AND GRILLING MY FINGERS TO THE BONE FEEDING EVERYONE!
THIS COULD BE A SERIOUS PROBLEM!
YEAH, THAT SMOKE COULD LEAD THE DUKE RIGHT TO US!
THAT'S THE LEAST OF OUR PROBLEMS!
THESE ADDITIONAL MOUTHS WILL EAT ALL OF OUR FOOD!

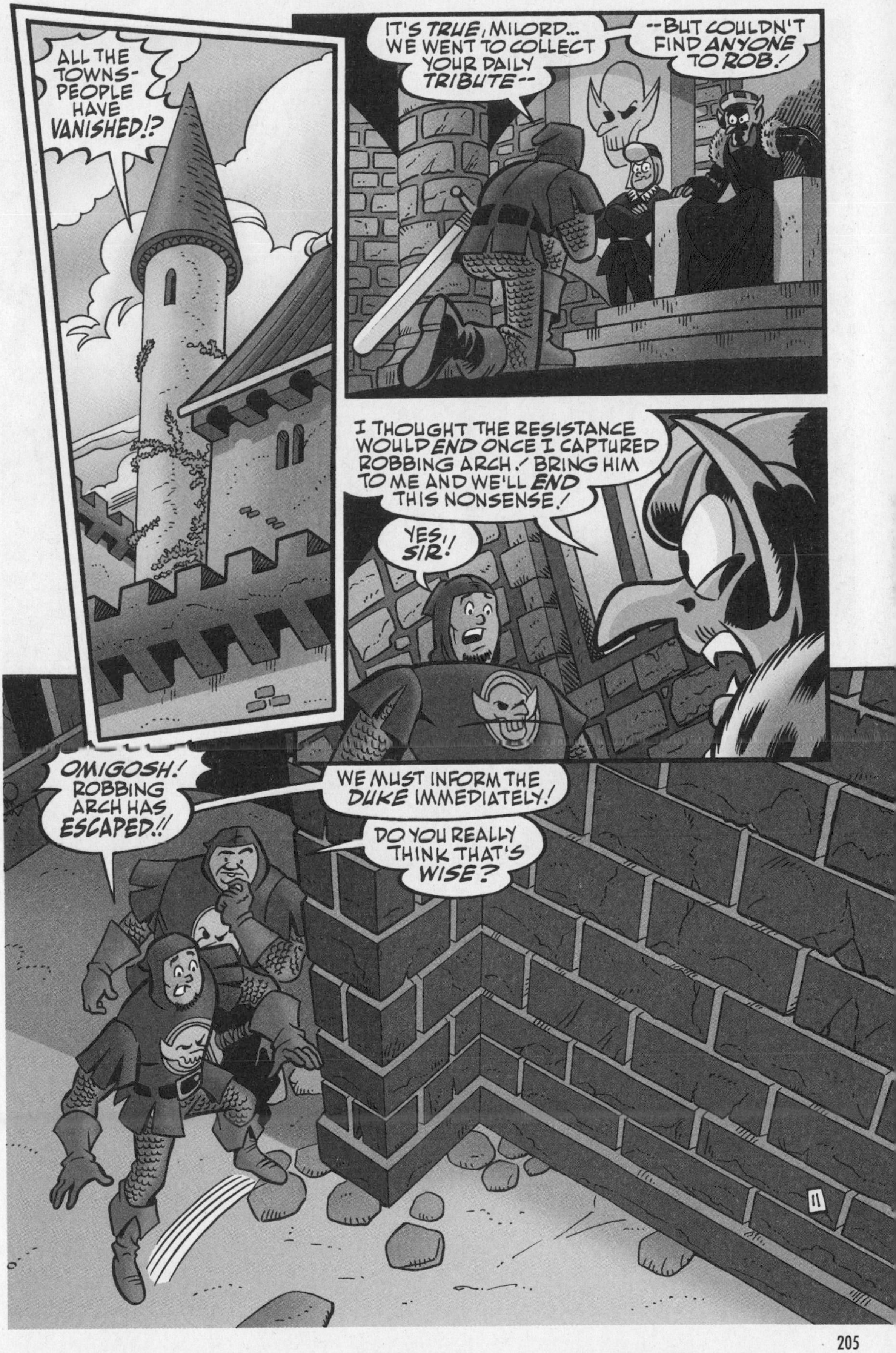

ALL THE TOWNSPEOPLE HAVE VANISHED!?
IT'S TRUE, MILORD... WE WENT TO COLLECT YOUR DAILY TRIBUTE--
--BUT COULDN'T FIND ANYONE TO ROB!
I THOUGHT THE RESISTANCE WOULD END ONCE I CAPTURED ROBBING ARCH! BRING HIM TO ME AND WE'LL END THIS NONSENSE!
YES, SIR!
OMIGOSH! ROBBING ARCH HAS ESCAPED!!
WE MUST INFORM THE DUKE IMMEDIATELY!
DO YOU REALLY THINK THAT'S WISE?
11

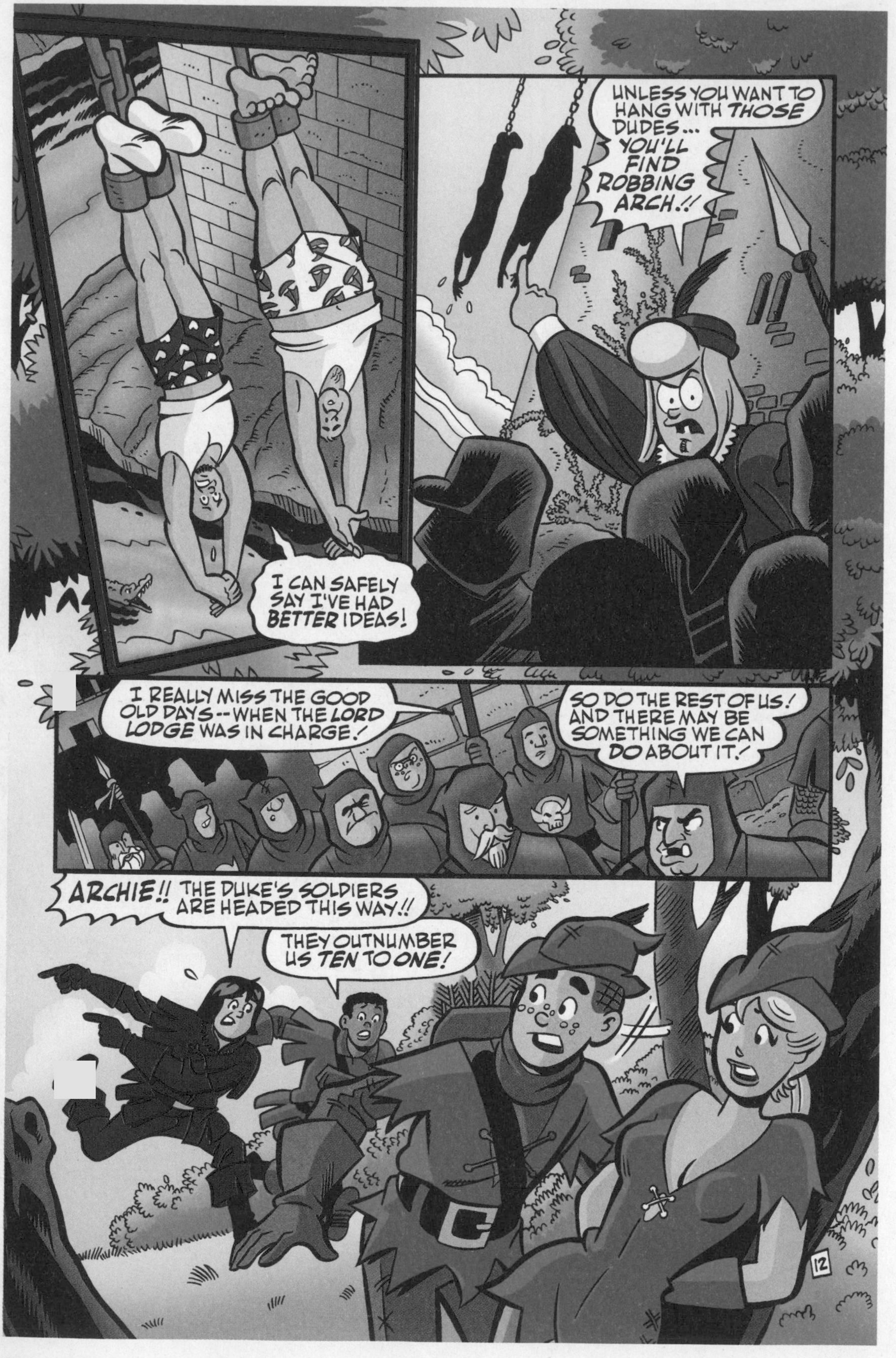
UNLESS YOU WANT TO HANG WITH THOSE DUDES... YOU'LL FIND ROBBING ARCH.!!
I CAN SAFELY SAY I'VE HAD BETTER IDEAS!
I REALLY MISS THE GOOD OLD DAYS--WHEN THE LORD LODGE WAS IN CHARGE!
SO DO THE REST OF US! AND THERE MAY BE SOMETHING WE CAN DO ABOUT IT!
ARCHIE!! THE DUKE'S SOLDIERS ARE HEADED THIS WAY!!
THEY OUTNUMBER US TEN TO ONE!
12

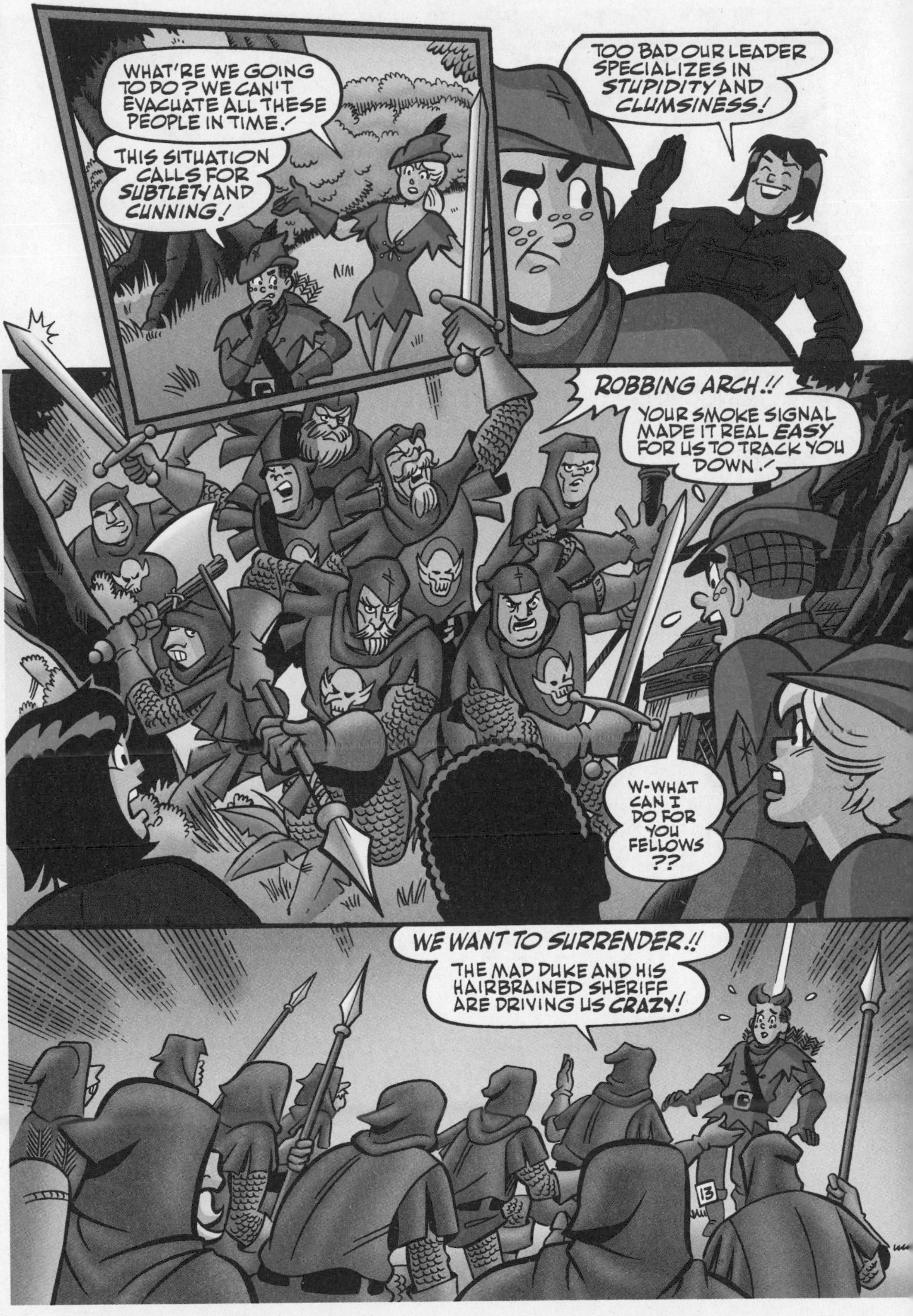
WHAT'RE WE GOING TO DO? WE CAN'T EVACUATE ALL THESE PEOPLE IN TIME!
THIS SITUATION CALLS FOR SUBTLETY AND CUNNING!
TOO BAD OUR LEADER SPECIALIZES IN STUPIDITY AND CLUMSINESS!
ROBBING ARCH!!
YOUR SMOKE SIGNAL MADE IT REAL EASY FOR US TO TRACK YOU DOWN!
W-WHAT CAN I DO FOR YOU FELLOWS??
WE WANT TO SURRENDER!!
THE MAD DUKE AND HIS HAIRBRAINED SHERIFF ARE DRIVING US CRAZY!
13

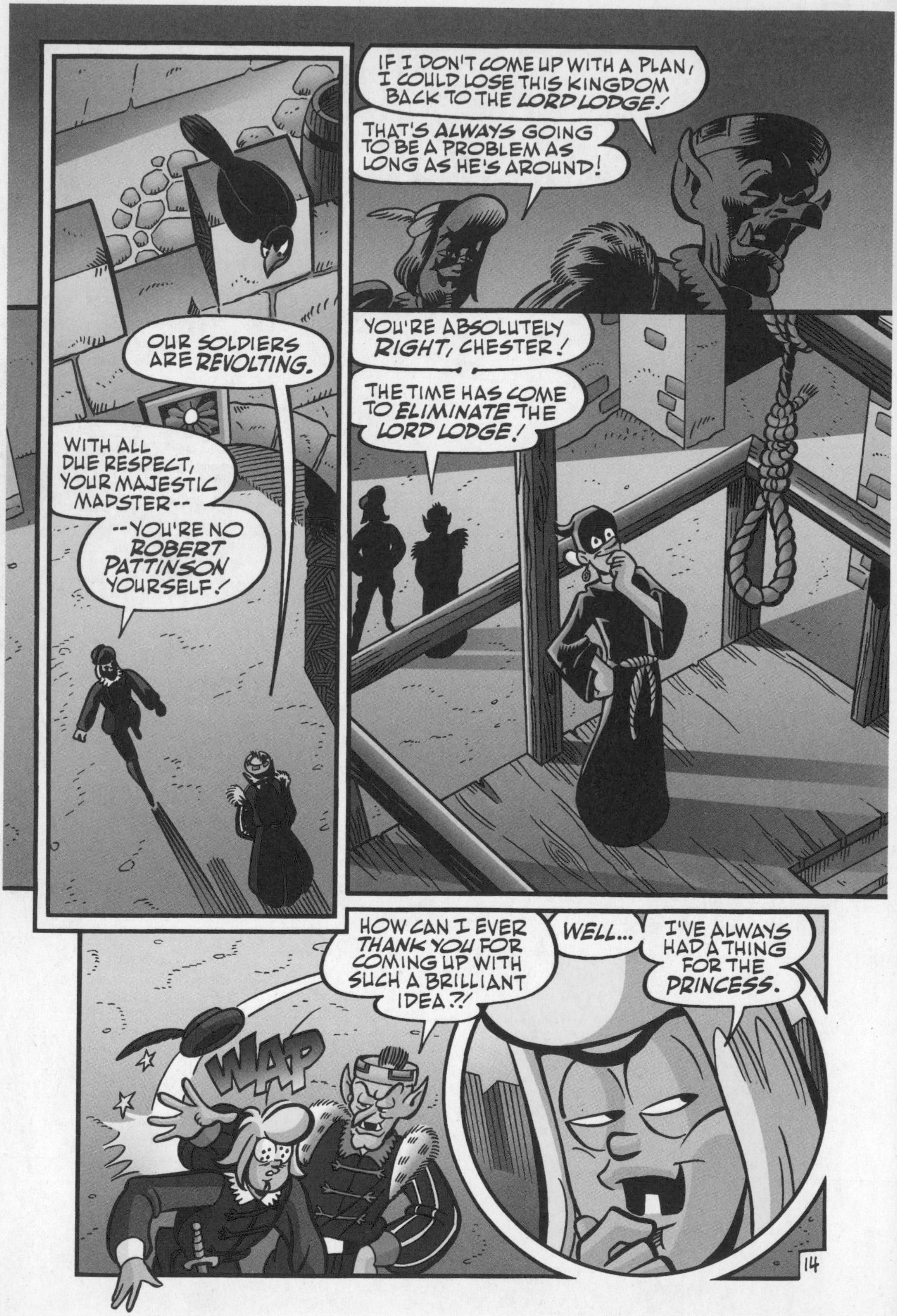
IF I DON'T COME UP WITH A PLAN, I COULD LOSE THIS KINGDOM BACK TO THE LORD LODGE!
THAT'S ALWAYS GOING TO BE A PROBLEM AS LONG AS HE'S AROUND!
OUR SOLDIERS ARE REVOLTING.
WITH ALL DUE RESPECT, YOUR MAJESTIC MADSTER--
--YOU'RE NO ROBERT PATTINSON YOURSELF!
YOU'RE ABSOLUTELY RIGHT, CHESTER!
THE TIME HAS COME TO ELIMINATE THE LORD LODGE!
HOW CAN I EVER THANK YOU FOR COMING UP WITH SUCH A BRILLIANT IDEA?!
WAP
WELL...
I'VE ALWAYS HAD A THING FOR THE PRINCESS.
14

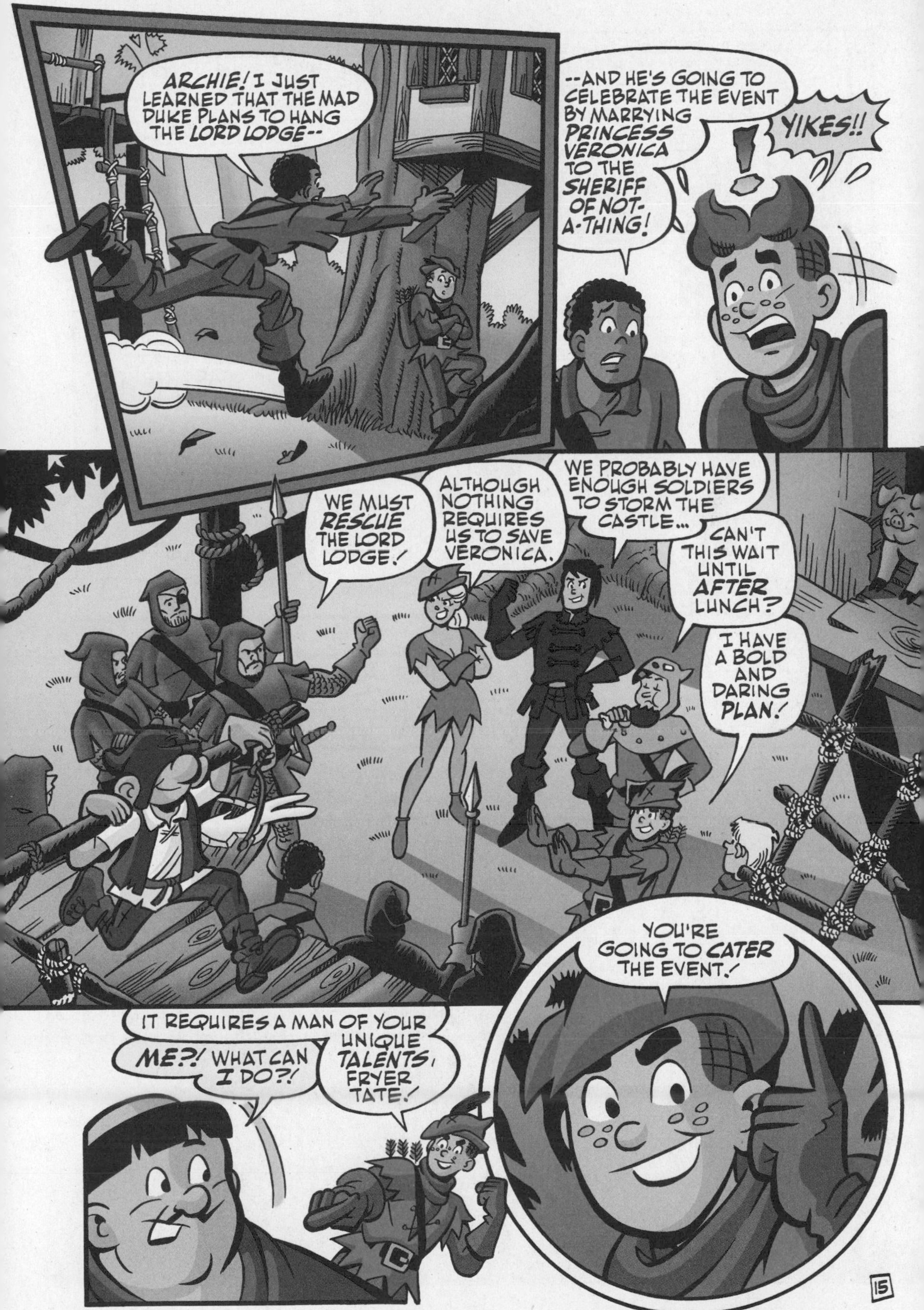
ARCHIE! I JUST LEARNED THAT THE MAD DUKE PLANS TO HANG THE LORD LODGE--
--AND HE'S GOING TO CELEBRATE THE EVENT BY MARRYING PRINCESS VERONICA TO THE SHERIFF OF NOT-A-THING!
YIKES!!
WE MUST RESCUE THE LORD LODGE!
ALTHOUGH NOTHING REQUIRES US TO SAVE VERONICA.
WE PROBABLY HAVE ENOUGH SOLDIERS TO STORM THE CASTLE...
CAN'T THIS WAIT UNTIL AFTER LUNCH?
I HAVE A BOLD AND DARING PLAN!
YOU'RE GOING TO CATER THE EVENT!
ME?! WHAT CAN I DO?!
IT REQUIRES A MAN OF YOUR UNIQUE TALENTS, FRYER TATE!
15

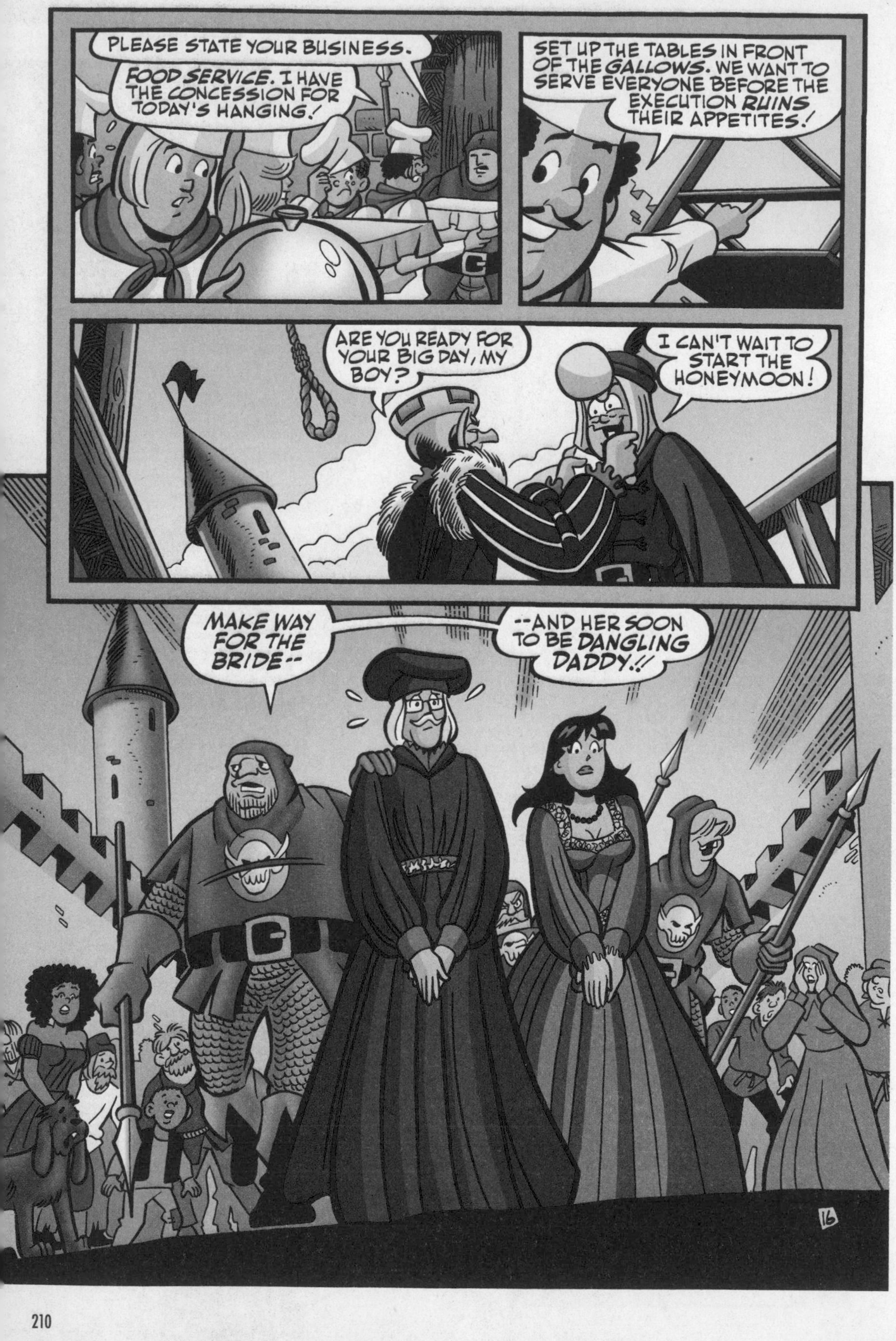
PLEASE STATE YOUR BUSINESS.
FOOD SERVICE. I HAVE THE CONCESSION FOR TODAY'S HANGING!
SET UP THE TABLES IN FRONT OF THE GALLOWS. WE WANT TO SERVE EVERYONE BEFORE THE EXECUTION RUINS THEIR APPETITES!
ARE YOU READY FOR YOUR BIG DAY, MY BOY?
I CAN'T WAIT TO START THE HONEYMOON!
MAKE WAY FOR THE BRIDE--
--AND HER SOON TO BE DANGLING DADDY!!
16

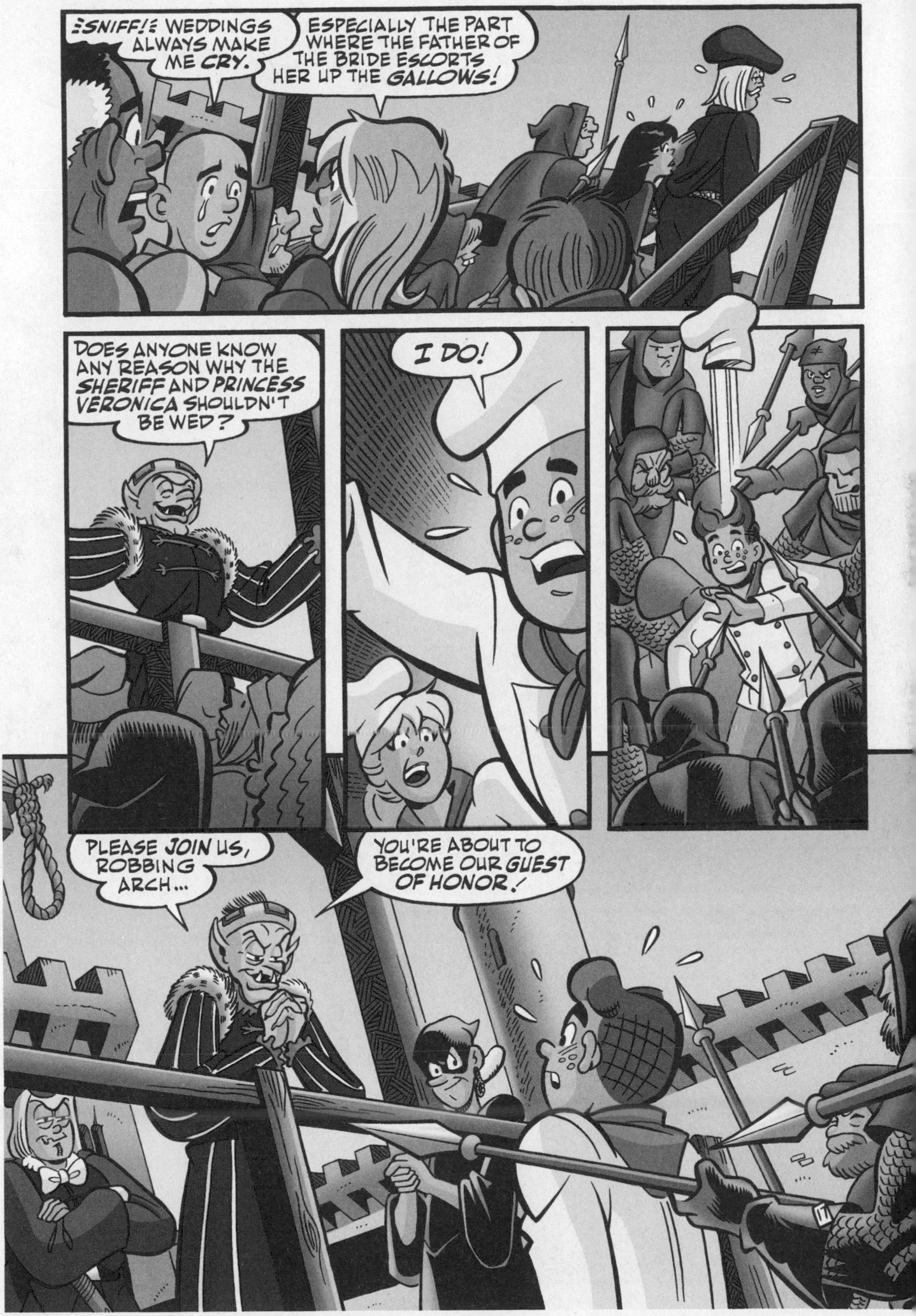

:SNIFF!: WEDDINGS ALWAYS MAKE ME CRY.
ESPECIALLY THE PART WHERE THE FATHER OF THE BRIDE ESCORTS HER UP THE GALLOWS!
DOES ANYONE KNOW ANY REASON WHY THE SHERIFF AND PRINCESS VERONICA SHOULDN'T BE WED?
I DO!
PLEASE JOIN US, ROBBING ARCH...
YOU'RE ABOUT TO BECOME OUR GUEST OF HONOR!

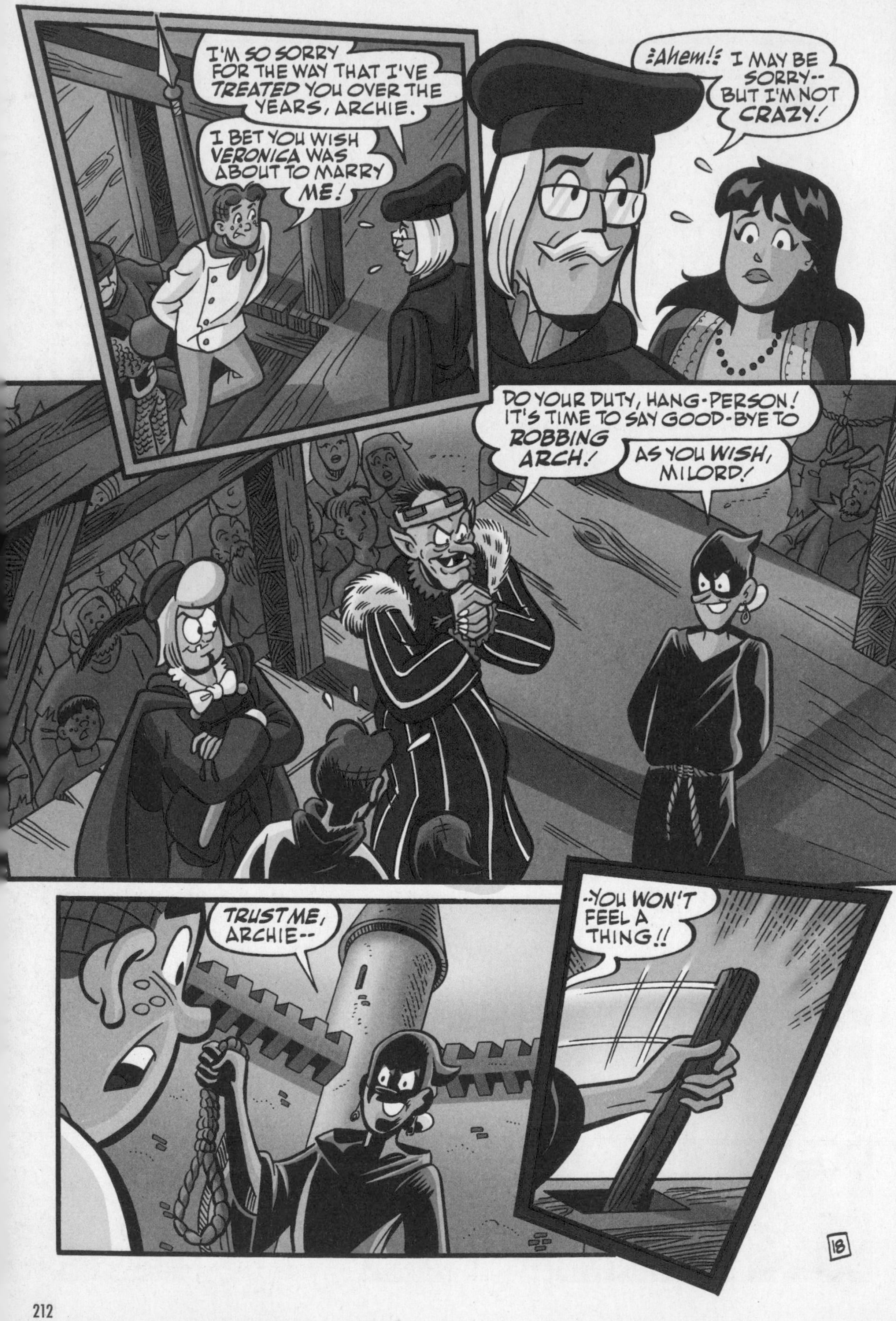
I'M SO SORRY FOR THE WAY THAT I'VE TREATED YOU OVER THE YEARS, ARCHIE.
I BET YOU WISH VERONICA WAS ABOUT TO MARRY ME!
:Ahem!: I MAY BE SORRY-- BUT I'M NOT CRAZY!
DO YOUR DUTY, HANG-PERSON! IT'S TIME TO SAY GOOD-BYE TO ROBBING ARCH!
AS YOU WISH, MILORD!
TRUST ME, ARCHIE--
--YOU WON'T FEEL A THING!!
18

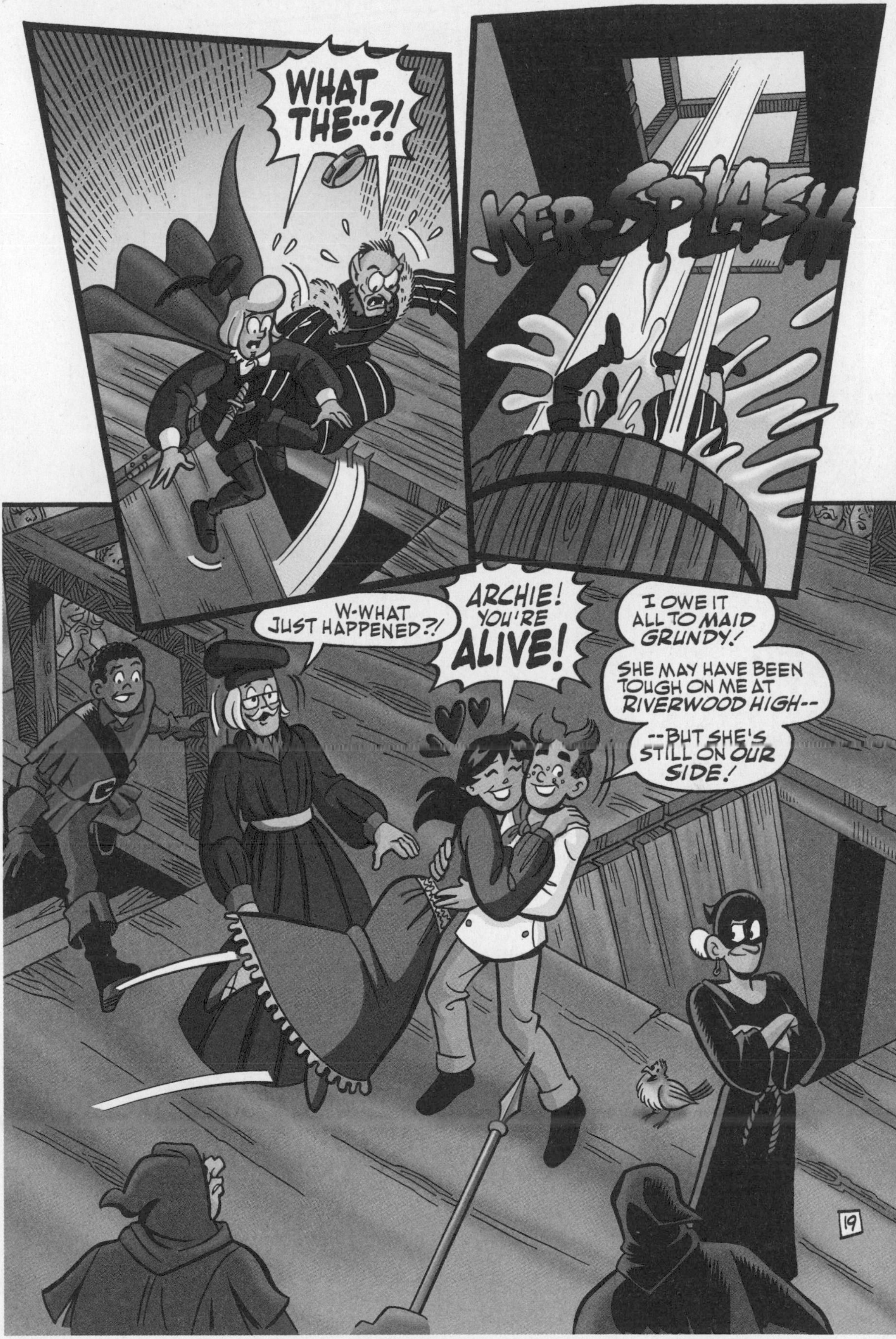
WHAT THE..?!
KER-SPLASH
W-WHAT JUST HAPPENED?!
ARCHIE! YOU'RE ALIVE!
I OWE IT ALL TO MAID GRUNDY!
SHE MAY HAVE BEEN TOUGH ON ME AT RIVERWOOD HIGH--
--BUT SHE'S STILL ON OUR SIDE!
19

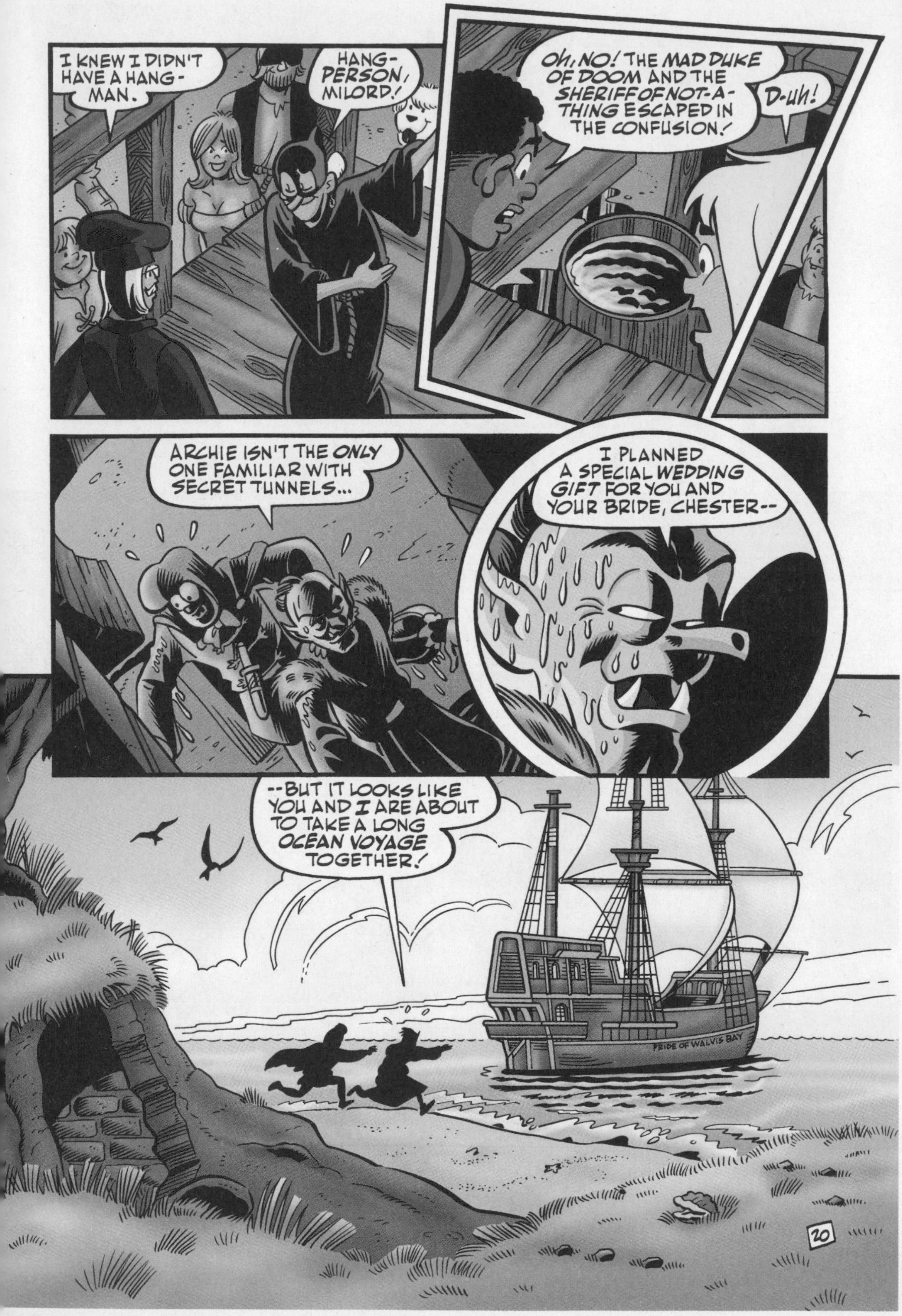
I KNEW I DIDN'T HAVE A HANG-MAN.
HANG-PERSON, MILORD!
OH, NO! THE MAD DUKE OF DOOM AND THE SHERIFF OF NOT-A-THING ESCAPED IN THE CONFUSION!
D-uh!
ARCHIE ISN'T THE ONLY ONE FAMILIAR WITH SECRET TUNNELS...
I PLANNED A SPECIAL WEDDING GIFT FOR YOU AND YOUR BRIDE, CHESTER--
--BUT IT LOOKS LIKE YOU AND I ARE ABOUT TO TAKE A LONG OCEAN VOYAGE TOGETHER!
PRIDE OF WALVIS BAY
20

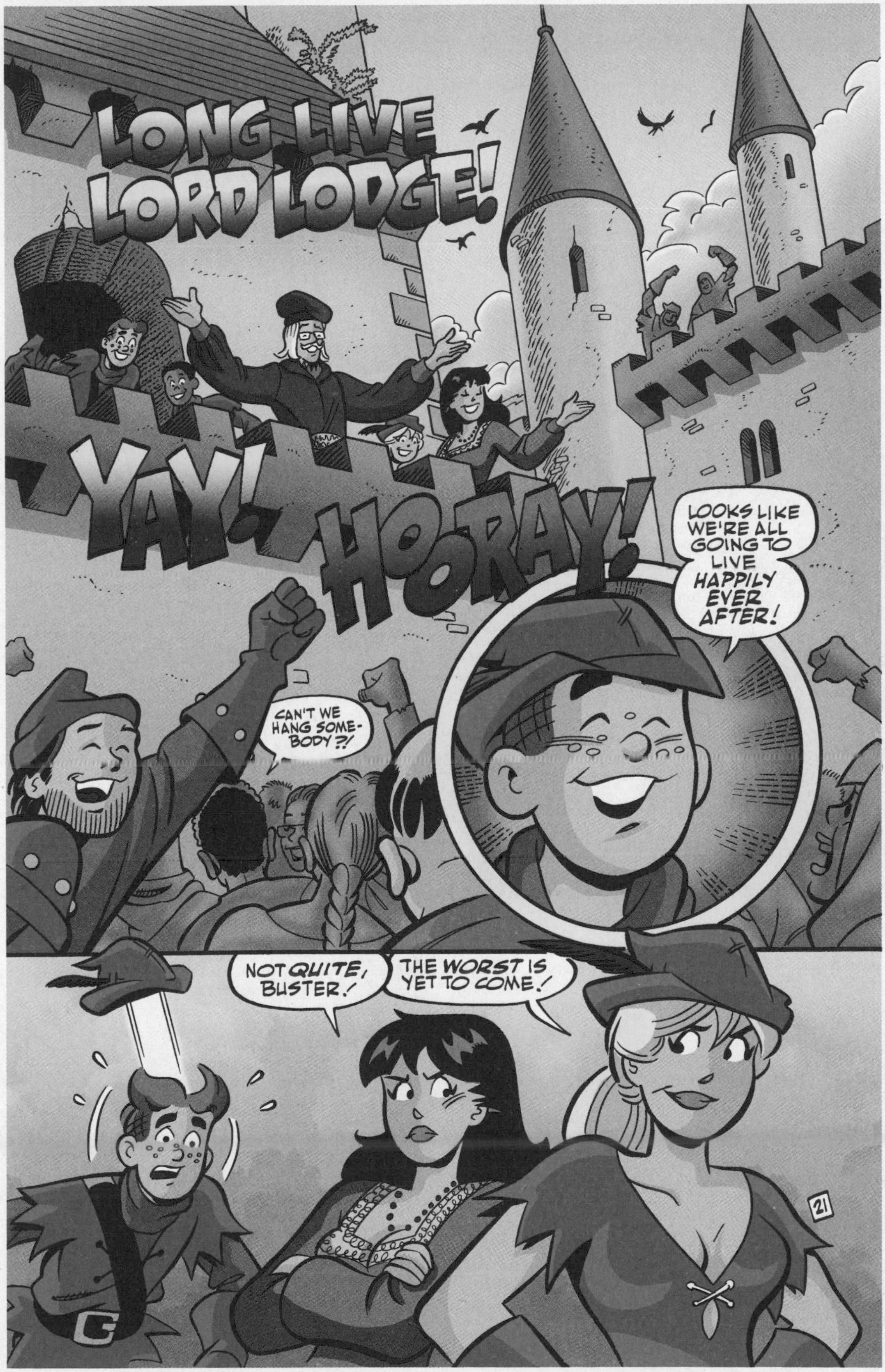
LONG LIVE LORD LODGE!
YAY!
HOORAY!
LOOKS LIKE WE'RE ALL GOING TO LIVE HAPPILY EVER AFTER!
CAN'T WE HANG SOME-BODY?!
NOT QUITE, BUSTER!
THE WORST IS YET TO COME!
21

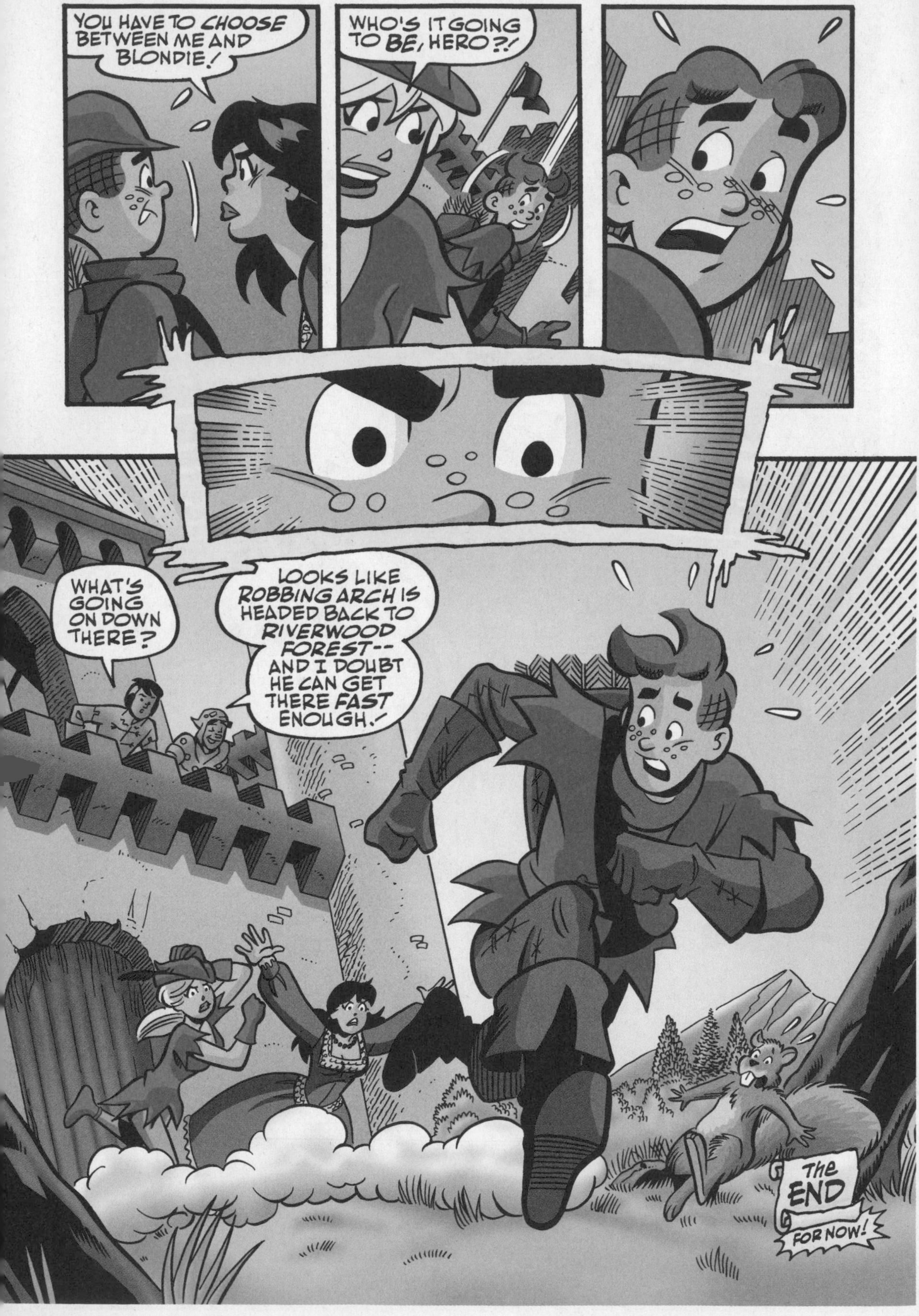
YOU HAVE TO CHOOSE BETWEEN ME AND BLONDIE!
WHO'S IT GOING TO BE, HERO?!
WHAT'S GOING ON DOWN THERE?
LOOKS LIKE ROBBING ARCH IS HEADED BACK TO RIVERWOOD FOREST-- AND I DOUBT HE CAN GET THERE FAST ENOUGH!
The END
FOR NOW!

CHAPTER SEVEN

Game of Phones

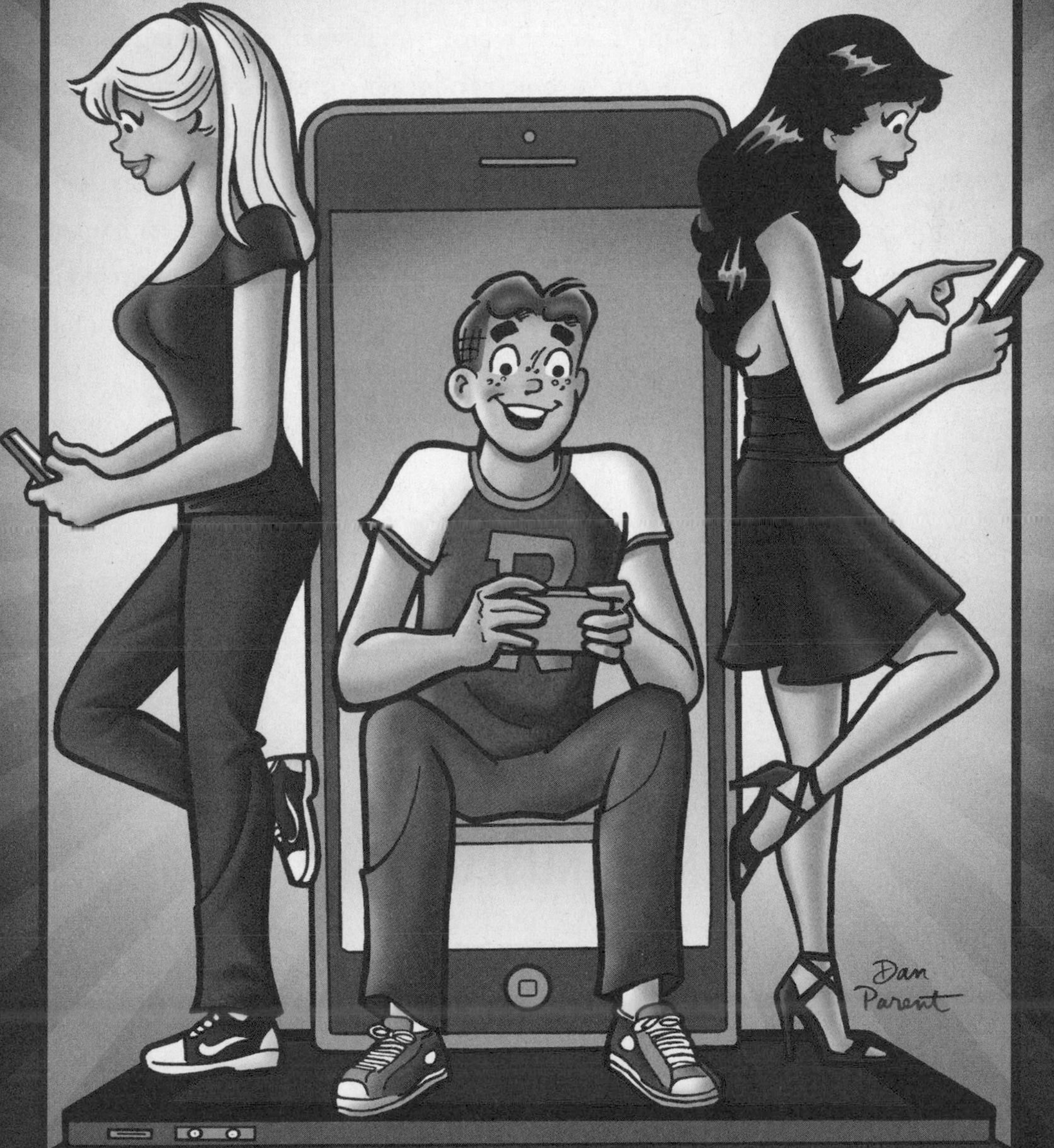
Dan Parent

INTRODUCING GAME OF PHONES

Originally printed in *Archie #664*

Archie stars in "Game of Phones!" Winter is coming... a ten-year long winter—which means ten years of school WITHOUT summer vacation! In a world of many kingdoms, the noble Archie Starch lives with his family and his pal Snowhead in the Kingdom of Riveros. Meanwhile, in the Kingdom of Lodgister, the wealthy princess Veronica Lodgister's greatest desire is to be this year's Prom Queen. Her main rival for the throne is a new girl in school, Princess Betty Cooparian. In yet another kingdom dwell the Braggians, with the pompous, sneaky Prince Reggie who is determined to do whatever it takes to become Prom King—even if that means faking his way to the top. Archie is ready to call his bluff and challenges him to a battle of the kingdoms on the Riveros High Football field. Which Kingdom will preside over all?

WRITER
ANGELO DECESARE

PENCILS
FERNANDO RUIZ

INKS
RICH KOSLOWSKI

LETTERS
JACK MORELLI

COLORS
GLENN WHITMORE

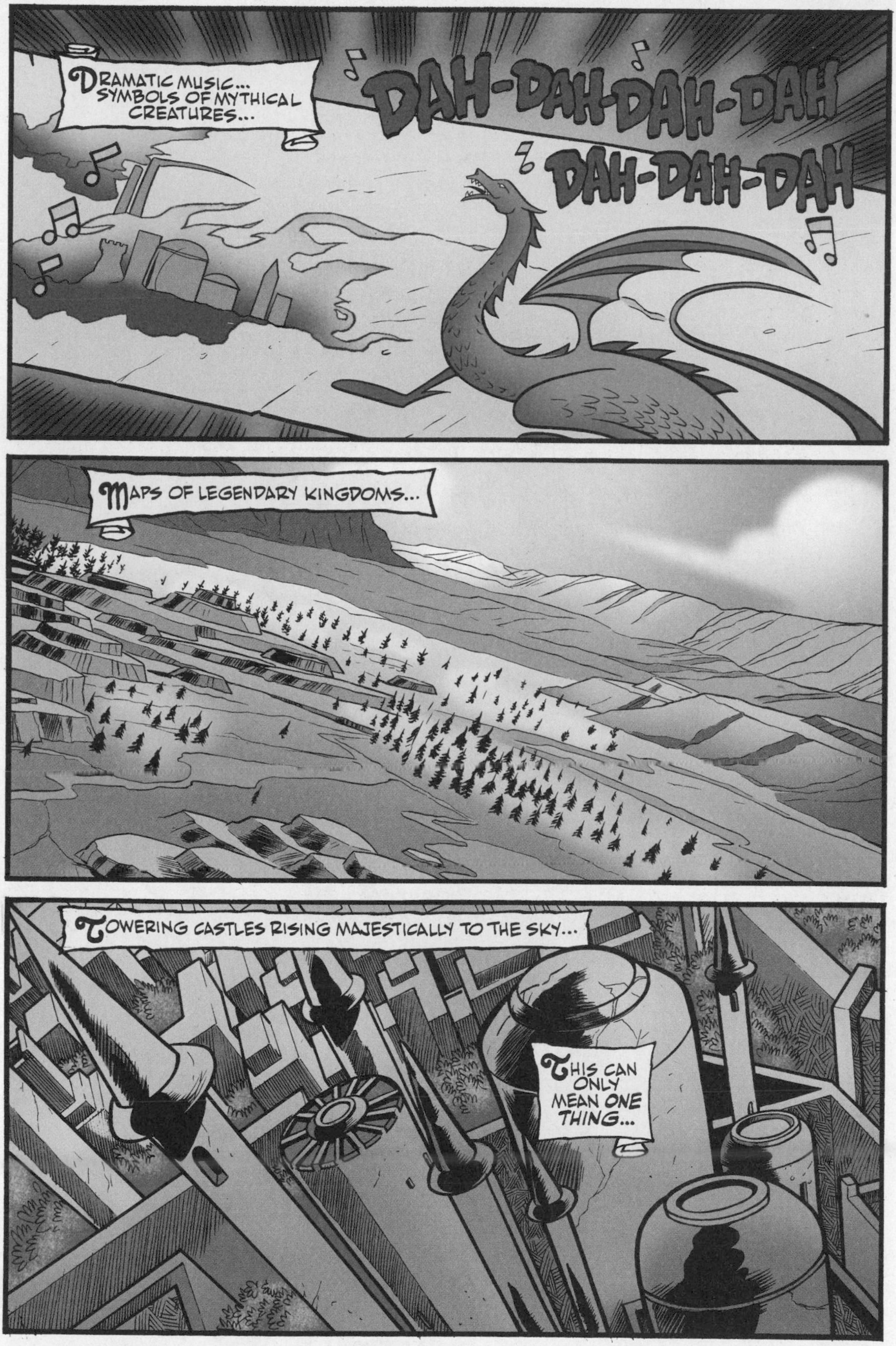

DRAMATIC MUSIC... SYMBOLS OF MYTHICAL CREATURES...
DAH-DAH-DAH-DAH
DAH-DAH-DAH
MAPS OF LEGENDARY KINGDOMS...
TOWERING CASTLES RISING MAJESTICALLY TO THE SKY...
THIS CAN ONLY MEAN ONE THING...

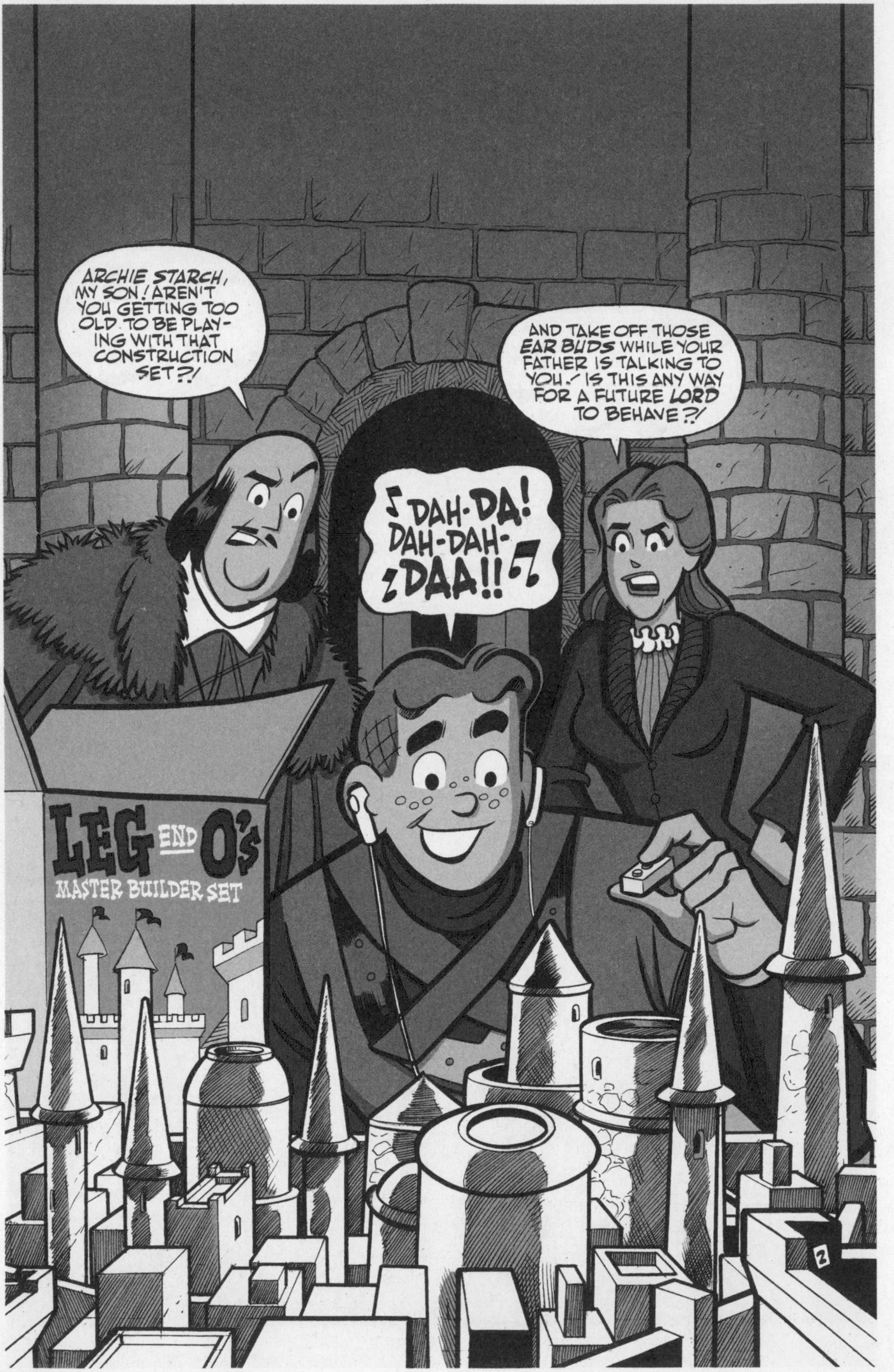
ARCHIE STARCH, MY SON! AREN'T YOU GETTING TOO OLD TO BE PLAYING WITH THAT CONSTRUCTION SET?!
AND TAKE OFF THOSE EAR BUDS WHILE YOUR FATHER IS TALKING TO YOU! IS THIS ANY WAY FOR A FUTURE LORD TO BEHAVE?!
DAH-DA! DAH-DAH-DAA!!
LEG END O's
MASTER BUILDER SET
2

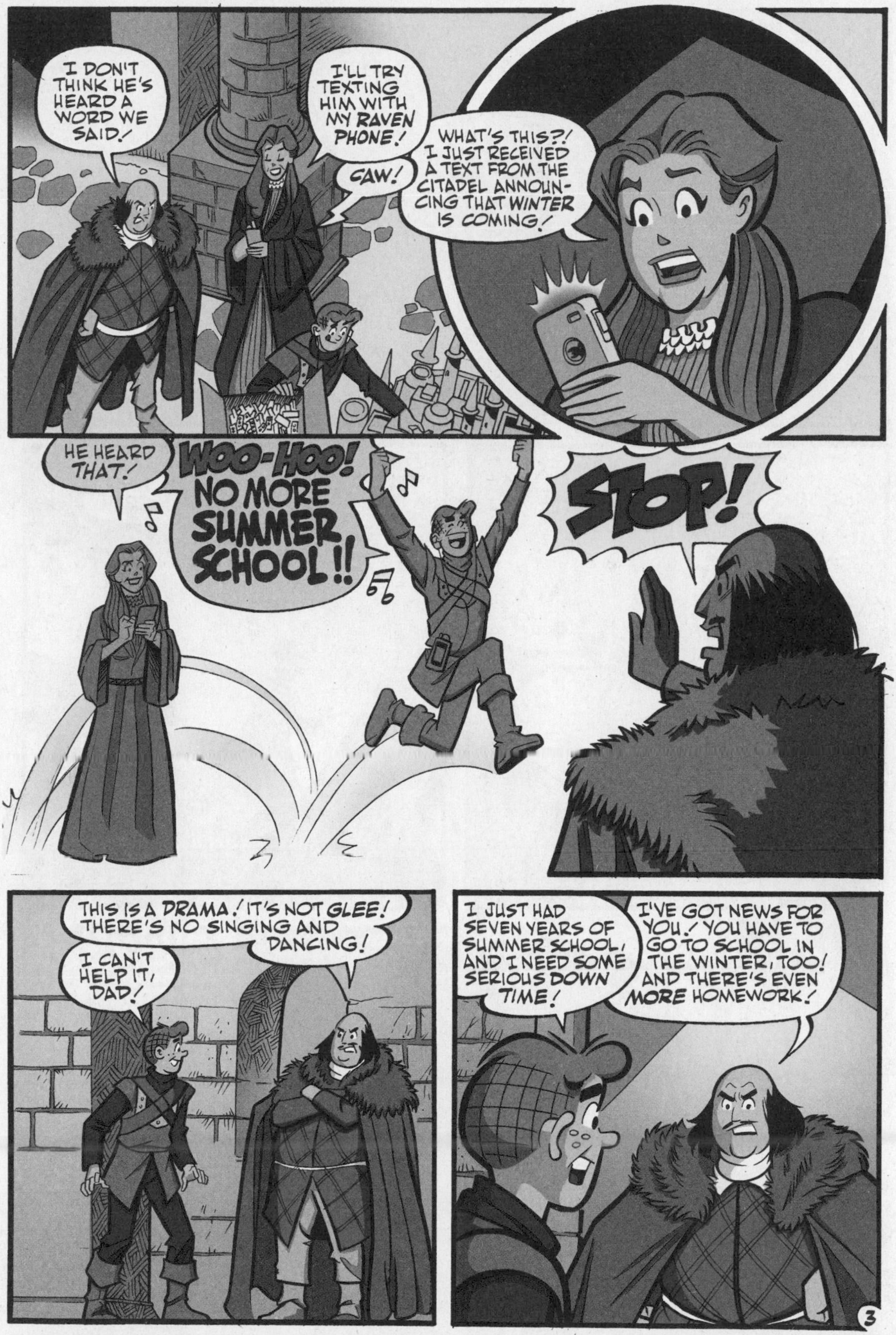
I DON'T THINK HE'S HEARD A WORD WE SAID!
I'LL TRY TEXTING HIM WITH MY RAVEN PHONE!
CAW!
WHAT'S THIS?! I JUST RECEIVED A TEXT FROM THE CITADEL ANNOUNCING THAT WINTER IS COMING!
HE HEARD THAT!
WOO-HOO! NO MORE SUMMER SCHOOL!!
STOP!
THIS IS A DRAMA! IT'S NOT GLEE! THERE'S NO SINGING AND DANCING!
I CAN'T HELP IT, DAD!
I JUST HAD SEVEN YEARS OF SUMMER SCHOOL, AND I NEED SOME SERIOUS DOWN TIME!
I'VE GOT NEWS FOR YOU! YOU HAVE TO GO TO SCHOOL IN THE WINTER, TOO! AND THERE'S EVEN MORE HOMEWORK!
3

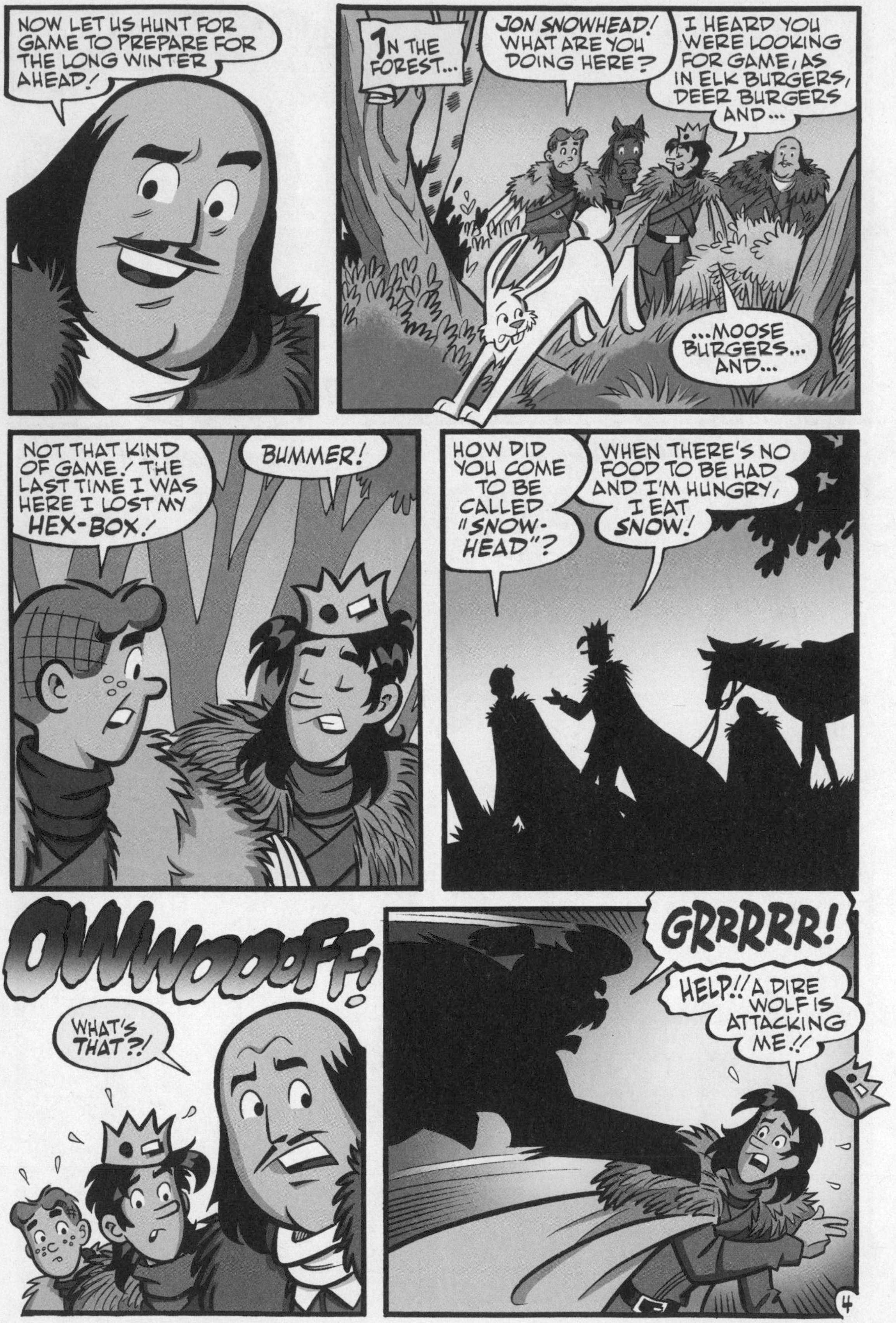
NOW LET US HUNT FOR GAME TO PREPARE FOR THE LONG WINTER AHEAD!
IN THE FOREST...
JON SNOWHEAD! WHAT ARE YOU DOING HERE?
I HEARD YOU WERE LOOKING FOR GAME, AS IN ELK BURGERS, DEER BURGERS AND...
...MOOSE BURGERS... AND...
NOT THAT KIND OF GAME! THE LAST TIME I WAS HERE I LOST MY HEX-BOX!
BUMMER!
HOW DID YOU COME TO BE CALLED "SNOW-HEAD"?
WHEN THERE'S NO FOOD TO BE HAD AND I'M HUNGRY, I EAT SNOW!
OWWOOOFF!
WHAT'S THAT?!
GRRRRR!
HELP!! A DIRE WOLF IS ATTACKING ME!!
4

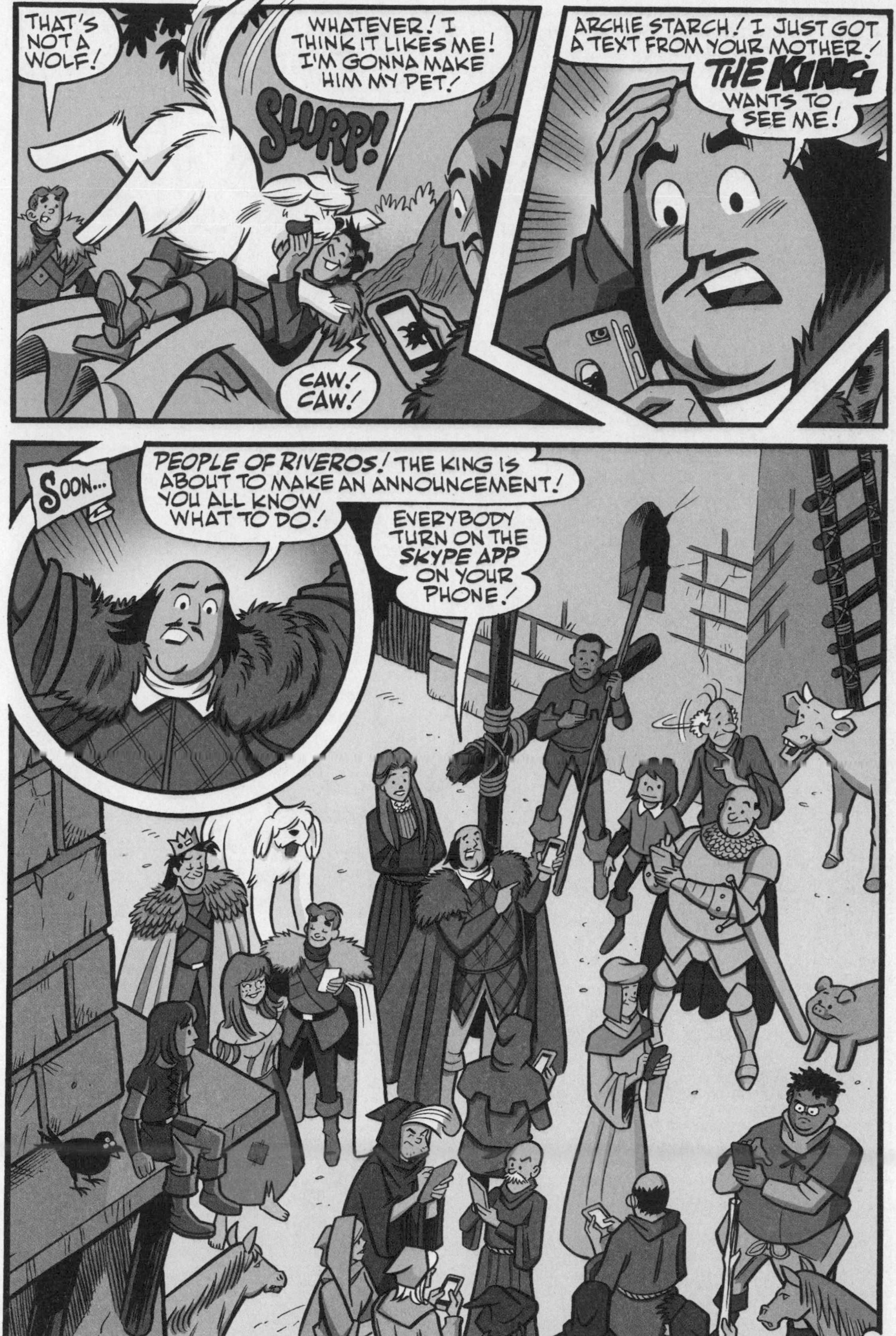
THAT'S NOT A WOLF!
WHATEVER! I THINK IT LIKES ME! I'M GONNA MAKE HIM MY PET!
SLURP!
CAW! CAW!
ARCHIE STARCH! I JUST GOT A TEXT FROM YOUR MOTHER! THE KING WANTS TO SEE ME!
SOON...
PEOPLE OF RIVEROS! THE KING IS ABOUT TO MAKE AN ANNOUNCEMENT! YOU ALL KNOW WHAT TO DO!
EVERYBODY TURN ON THE SKYPE APP ON YOUR PHONE!
5

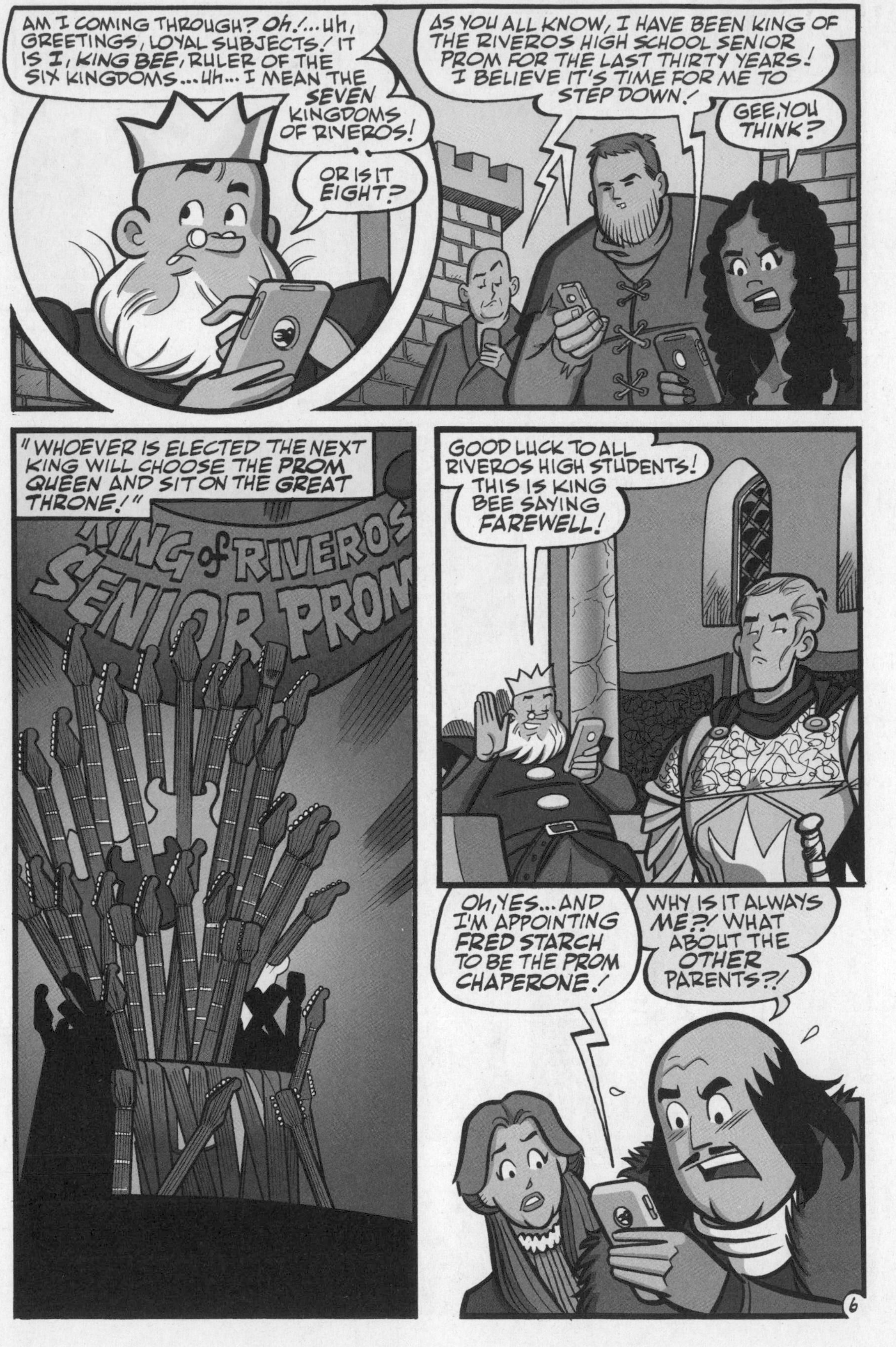
AM I COMING THROUGH? OH!...UH, GREETINGS, LOYAL SUBJECTS! IT IS I, KING BEE, RULER OF THE SIX KINGDOMS...UH... I MEAN THE SEVEN KINGDOMS OF RIVEROS!
OR IS IT EIGHT?
AS YOU ALL KNOW, I HAVE BEEN KING OF THE RIVEROS HIGH SCHOOL SENIOR PROM FOR THE LAST THIRTY YEARS! I BELIEVE IT'S TIME FOR ME TO STEP DOWN!
GEE, YOU THINK?
"WHOEVER IS ELECTED THE NEXT KING WILL CHOOSE THE PROM QUEEN AND SIT ON THE GREAT THRONE!"
KING of RIVEROS SENIOR PROM
GOOD LUCK TO ALL RIVEROS HIGH STUDENTS! THIS IS KING BEE SAYING FAREWELL!
OH, YES...AND I'M APPOINTING FRED STARCH TO BE THE PROM CHAPERONE!
WHY IS IT ALWAYS ME?! WHAT ABOUT THE OTHER PARENTS?!
6

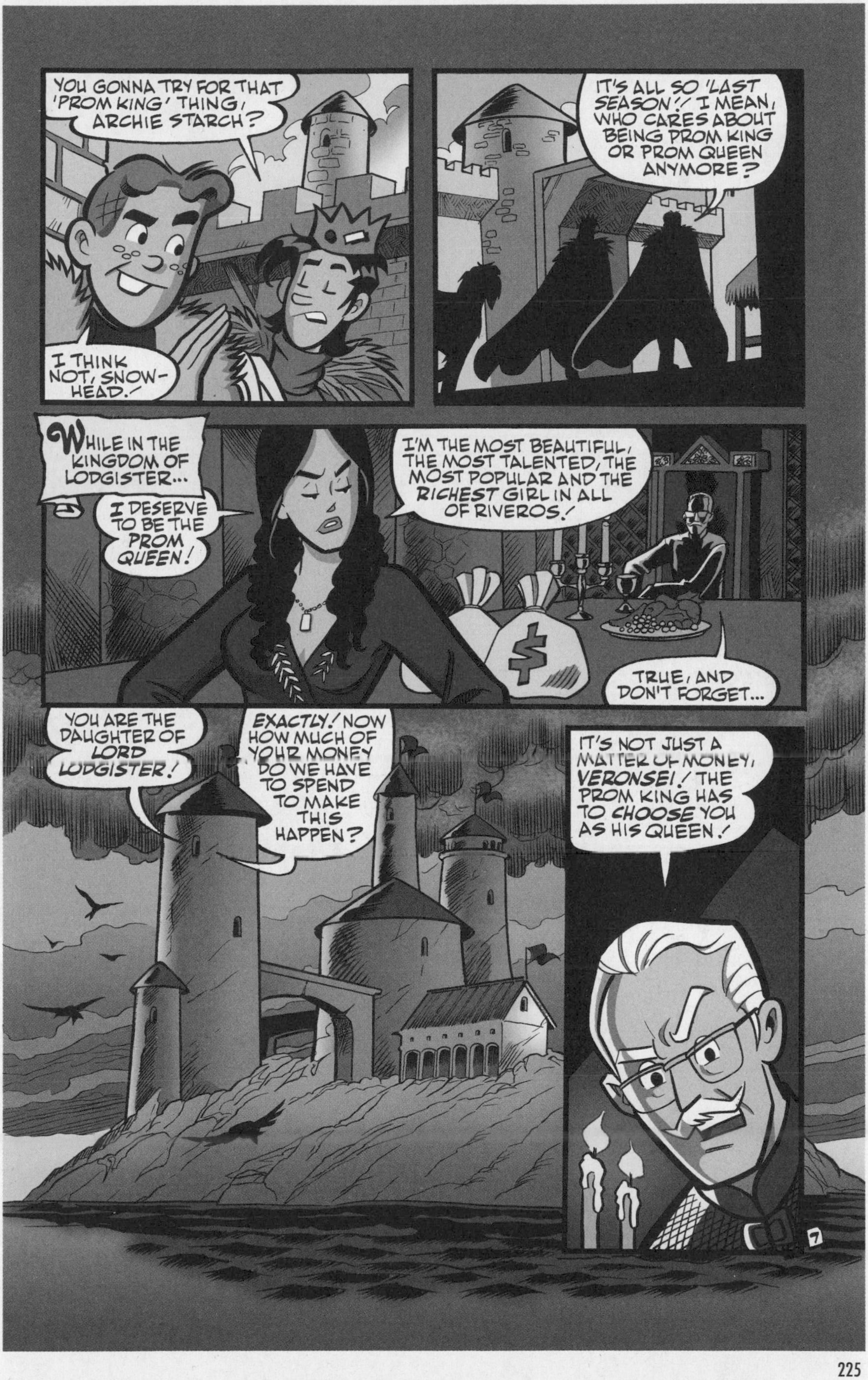
YOU GONNA TRY FOR THAT 'PROM KING' THING, ARCHIE STARCH?
I THINK NOT, SNOW-HEAD!
IT'S ALL SO 'LAST SEASON'! I MEAN, WHO CARES ABOUT BEING PROM KING OR PROM QUEEN ANYMORE?
WHILE IN THE KINGDOM OF LODGISTER...
I DESERVE TO BE THE PROM QUEEN!
I'M THE MOST BEAUTIFUL, THE MOST TALENTED, THE MOST POPULAR AND THE RICHEST GIRL IN ALL OF RIVEROS!
TRUE, AND DON'T FORGET...
YOU ARE THE DAUGHTER OF LORD LODGISTER!
EXACTLY! NOW HOW MUCH OF YOUR MONEY DO WE HAVE TO SPEND TO MAKE THIS HAPPEN?
IT'S NOT JUST A MATTER OF MONEY, VERONSEI! THE PROM KING HAS TO CHOOSE YOU AS HIS QUEEN!
7

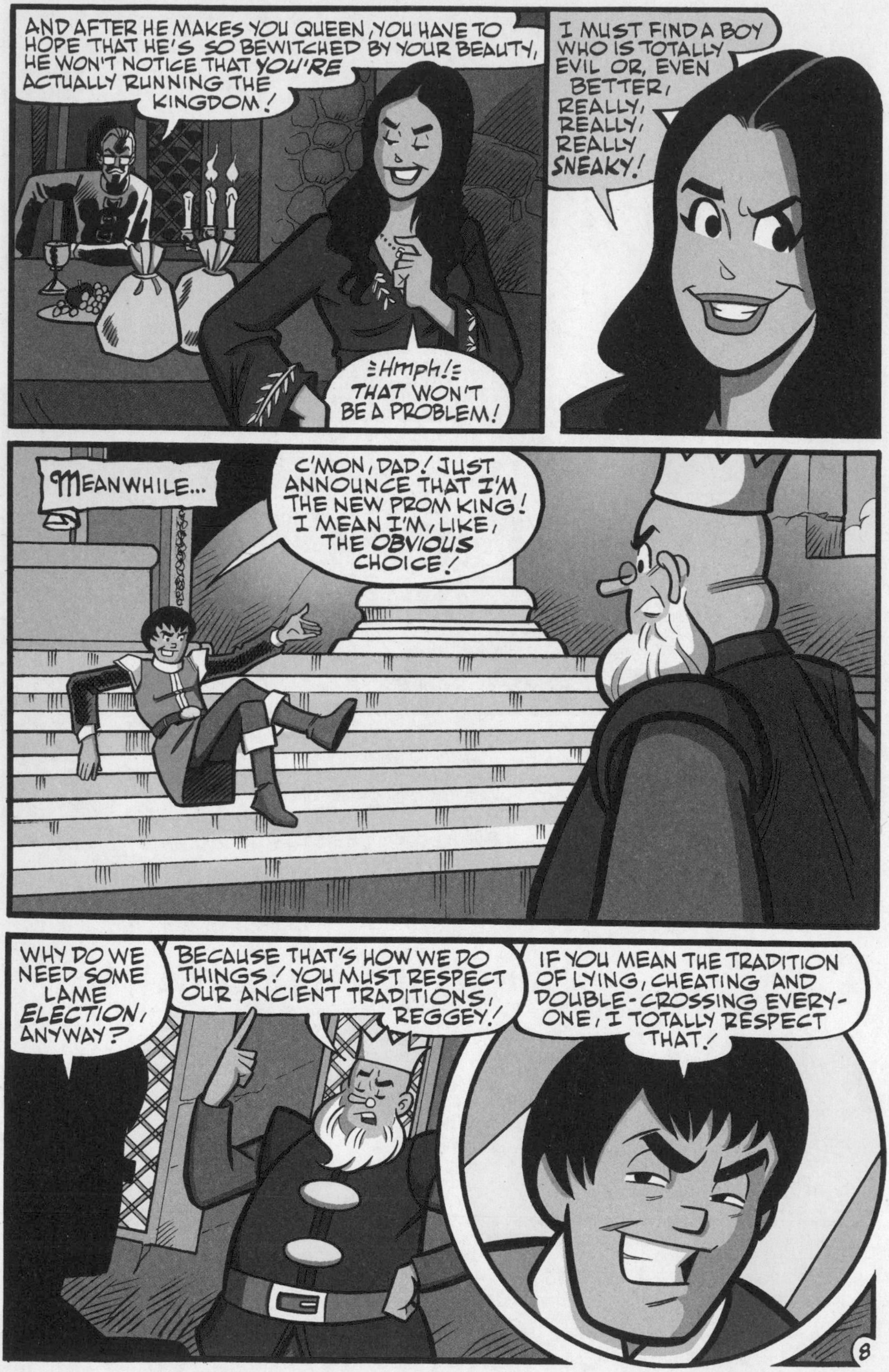
AND AFTER HE MAKES YOU QUEEN, YOU HAVE TO HOPE THAT HE'S SO BEWITCHED BY YOUR BEAUTY, HE WON'T NOTICE THAT YOU'RE ACTUALLY RUNNING THE KINGDOM!
Hmph! THAT WON'T BE A PROBLEM!
I MUST FIND A BOY WHO IS TOTALLY EVIL OR, EVEN BETTER, REALLY, REALLY, REALLY SNEAKY!
MEANWHILE...
C'MON, DAD! JUST ANNOUNCE THAT I'M THE NEW PROM KING! I MEAN I'M, LIKE, THE OBVIOUS CHOICE!
WHY DO WE NEED SOME LAME ELECTION, ANYWAY?
BECAUSE THAT'S HOW WE DO THINGS! YOU MUST RESPECT OUR ANCIENT TRADITIONS, REGGEY!
IF YOU MEAN THE TRADITION OF LYING, CHEATING AND DOUBLE-CROSSING EVERY-ONE, I TOTALLY RESPECT THAT!
8

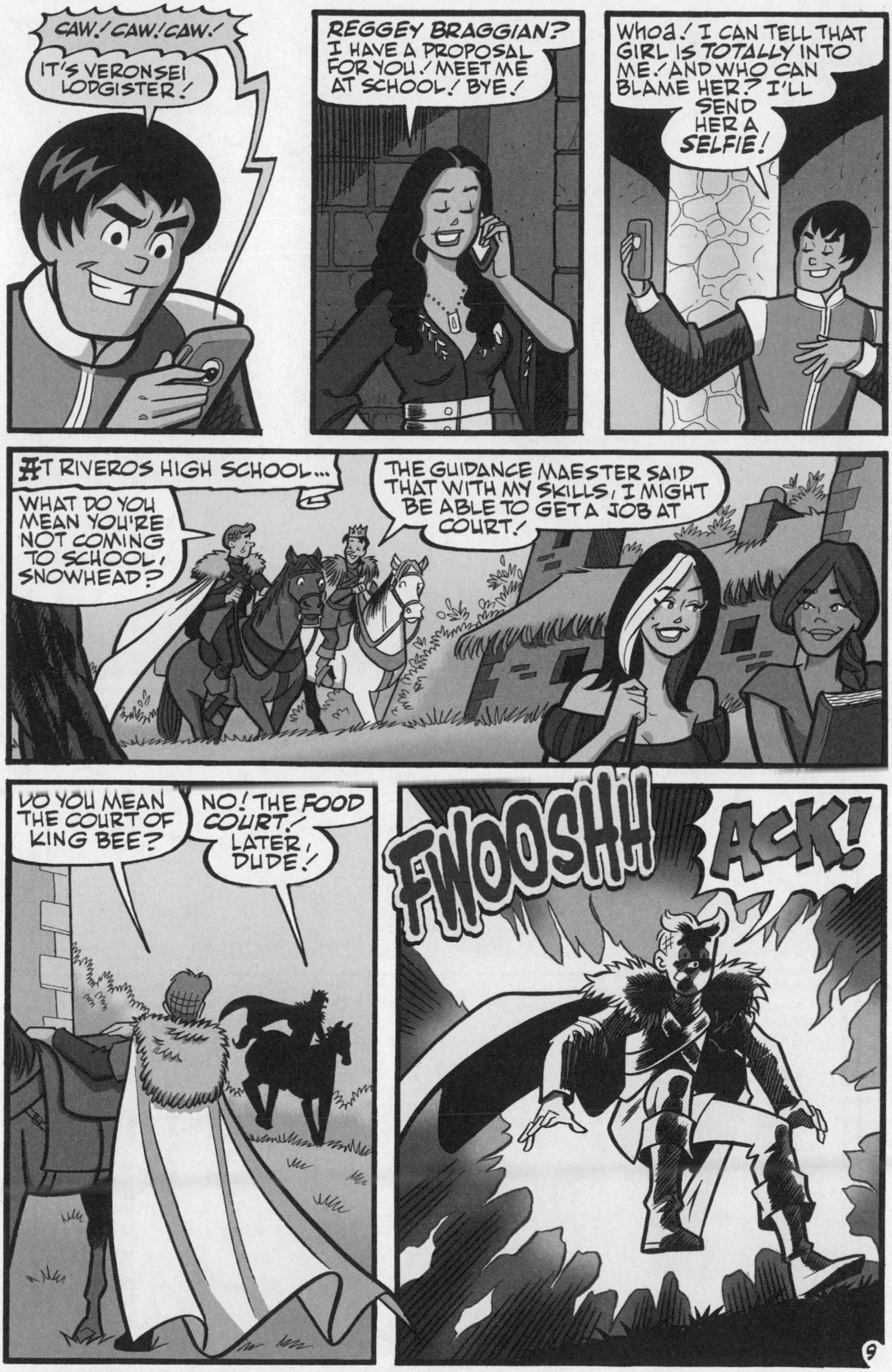
CAW! CAW! CAW!
IT'S VERONSEI LODGISTER!
REGGEY BRAGGIAN? I HAVE A PROPOSAL FOR YOU! MEET ME AT SCHOOL! BYE!
Whoa! I CAN TELL THAT GIRL IS TOTALLY INTO ME! AND WHO CAN BLAME HER? I'LL
SEND HER A SELFIE!
AT RIVEROS HIGH SCHOOL...
WHAT DO YOU MEAN YOU'RE NOT COMING TO SCHOOL, SNOWHEAD?
THE GUIDANCE MAESTER SAID THAT WITH MY SKILLS, I MIGHT BE ABLE TO GET A JOB AT COURT!
DO YOU MEAN THE COURT OF KING BEE?
NO! THE FOOD COURT!
LATER, DUDE!
FWOOSHH
ACK!
9

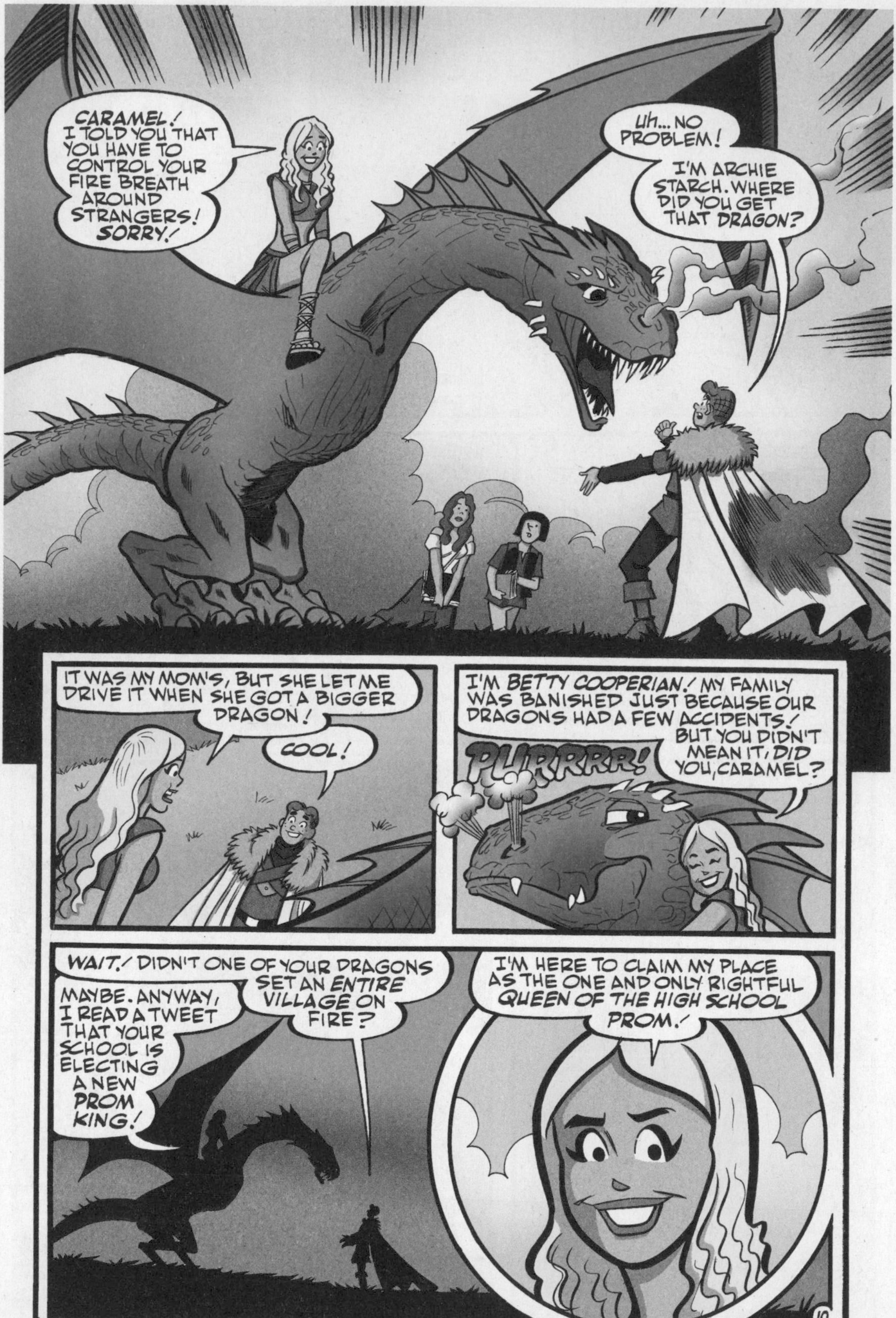
CARAMEL! I TOLD YOU THAT YOU HAVE TO CONTROL YOUR FIRE BREATH AROUND STRANGERS! SORRY!
UH... NO PROBLEM!
I'M ARCHIE STARCH. WHERE DID YOU GET THAT DRAGON?
IT WAS MY MOM'S, BUT SHE LET ME DRIVE IT WHEN SHE GOT A BIGGER DRAGON!
COOL!
I'M BETTY COOPERIAN! MY FAMILY WAS BANISHED JUST BECAUSE OUR DRAGONS HAD A FEW ACCIDENTS!
BUT YOU DIDN'T MEAN IT, DID YOU, CARAMEL?
PURRRR!
WAIT! DIDN'T ONE OF YOUR DRAGONS SET AN ENTIRE VILLAGE ON FIRE?
MAYBE. ANYWAY, I READ A TWEET THAT YOUR SCHOOL IS ELECTING A NEW PROM KING!
I'M HERE TO CLAIM MY PLACE AS THE ONE AND ONLY RIGHTFUL QUEEN OF THE HIGH SCHOOL PROM!
10

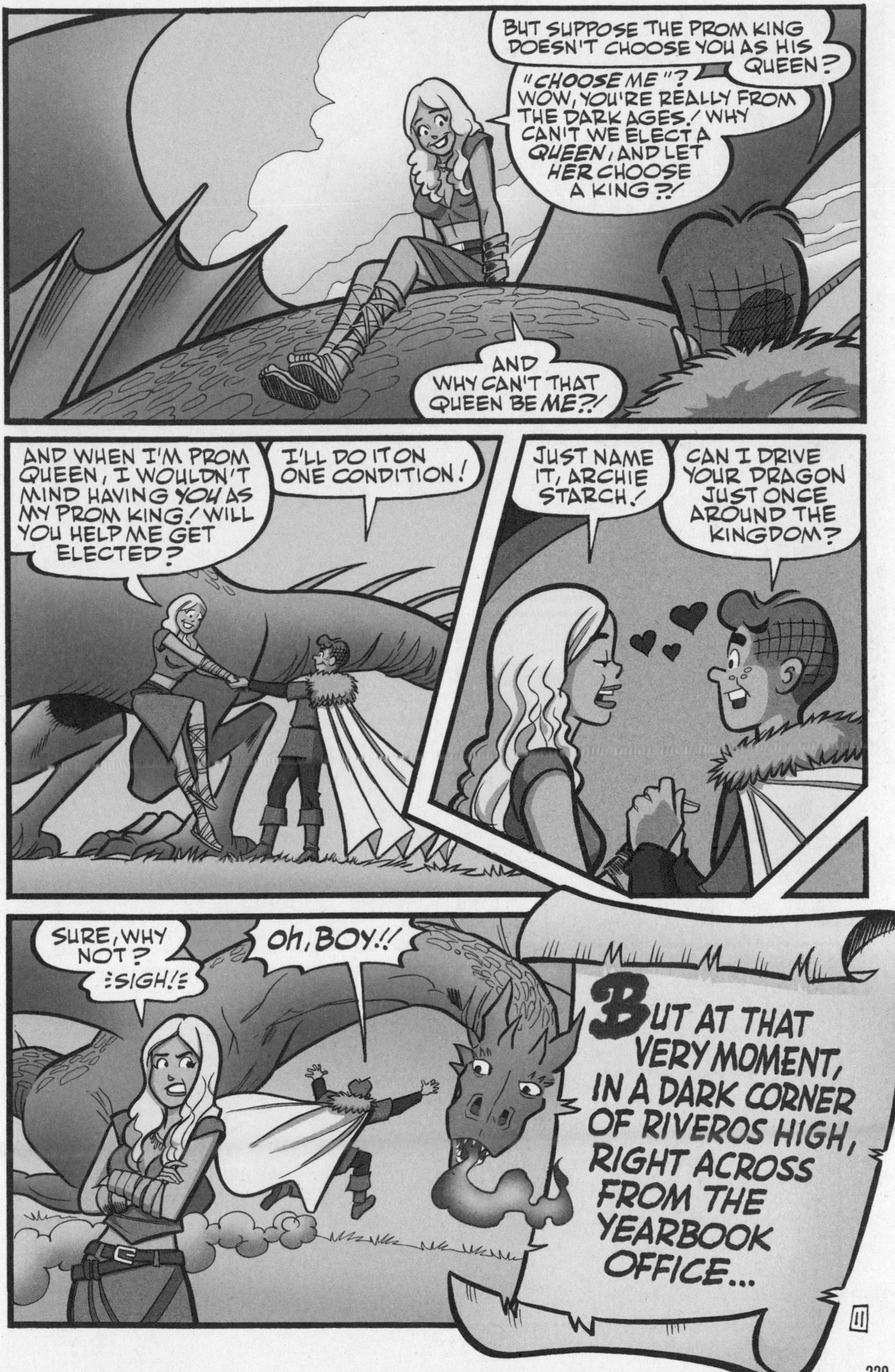
BUT SUPPOSE THE PROM KING DOESN'T CHOOSE YOU AS HIS QUEEN?
"CHOOSE ME"? WOW, YOU'RE REALLY FROM THE DARK AGES! WHY CAN'T WE ELECT A QUEEN, AND LET HER CHOOSE A KING?!
AND WHY CAN'T THAT QUEEN BE ME?!
AND WHEN I'M PROM QUEEN, I WOULDN'T MIND HAVING YOU AS MY PROM KING! WILL YOU HELP ME GET ELECTED?
I'LL DO IT ON ONE CONDITION!
JUST NAME IT, ARCHIE STARCH!
CAN I DRIVE YOUR DRAGON JUST ONCE AROUND THE KINGDOM?
SURE, WHY NOT? SIGH!
Oh, BOY!!
BUT AT THAT VERY MOMENT, IN A DARK CORNER OF RIVEROS HIGH, RIGHT ACROSS FROM THE YEARBOOK OFFICE...
11

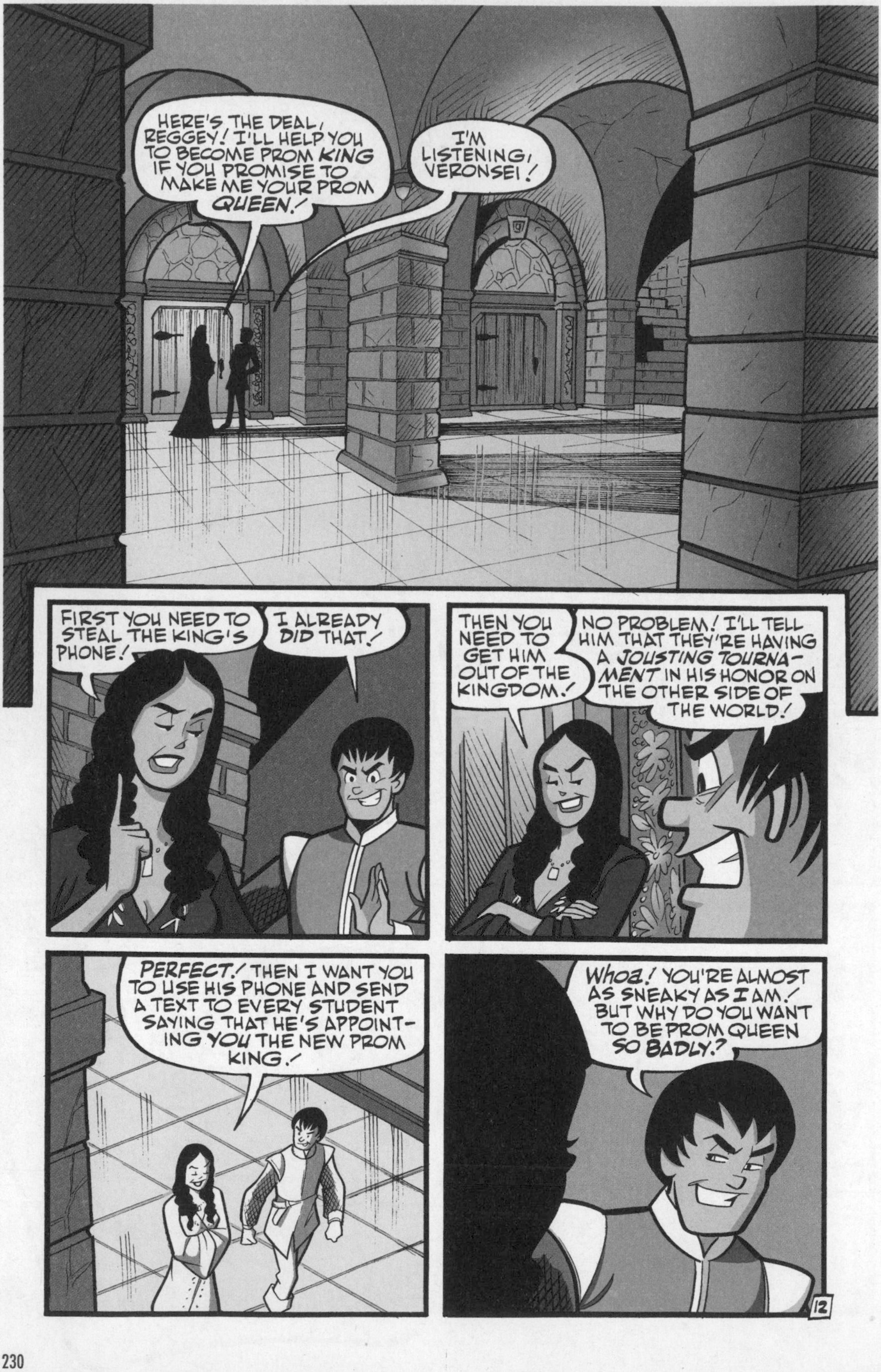
HERE'S THE DEAL, REGGEY! I'LL HELP YOU TO BECOME PROM KING IF YOU PROMISE TO MAKE ME YOUR PROM QUEEN!
I'M LISTENING, VERONSEI!
FIRST YOU NEED TO STEAL THE KING'S PHONE!
I ALREADY DID THAT!
THEN YOU NEED TO GET HIM OUT OF THE KINGDOM!
NO PROBLEM! I'LL TELL HIM THAT THEY'RE HAVING A JOUSTING TOURNAMENT IN HIS HONOR ON THE OTHER SIDE OF THE WORLD!
PERFECT! THEN I WANT YOU TO USE HIS PHONE AND SEND A TEXT TO EVERY STUDENT SAYING THAT HE'S APPOINTING YOU THE NEW PROM KING!
Whoa! YOU'RE ALMOST AS SNEAKY AS I AM! BUT WHY DO YOU WANT TO BE PROM QUEEN SO BADLY?
12

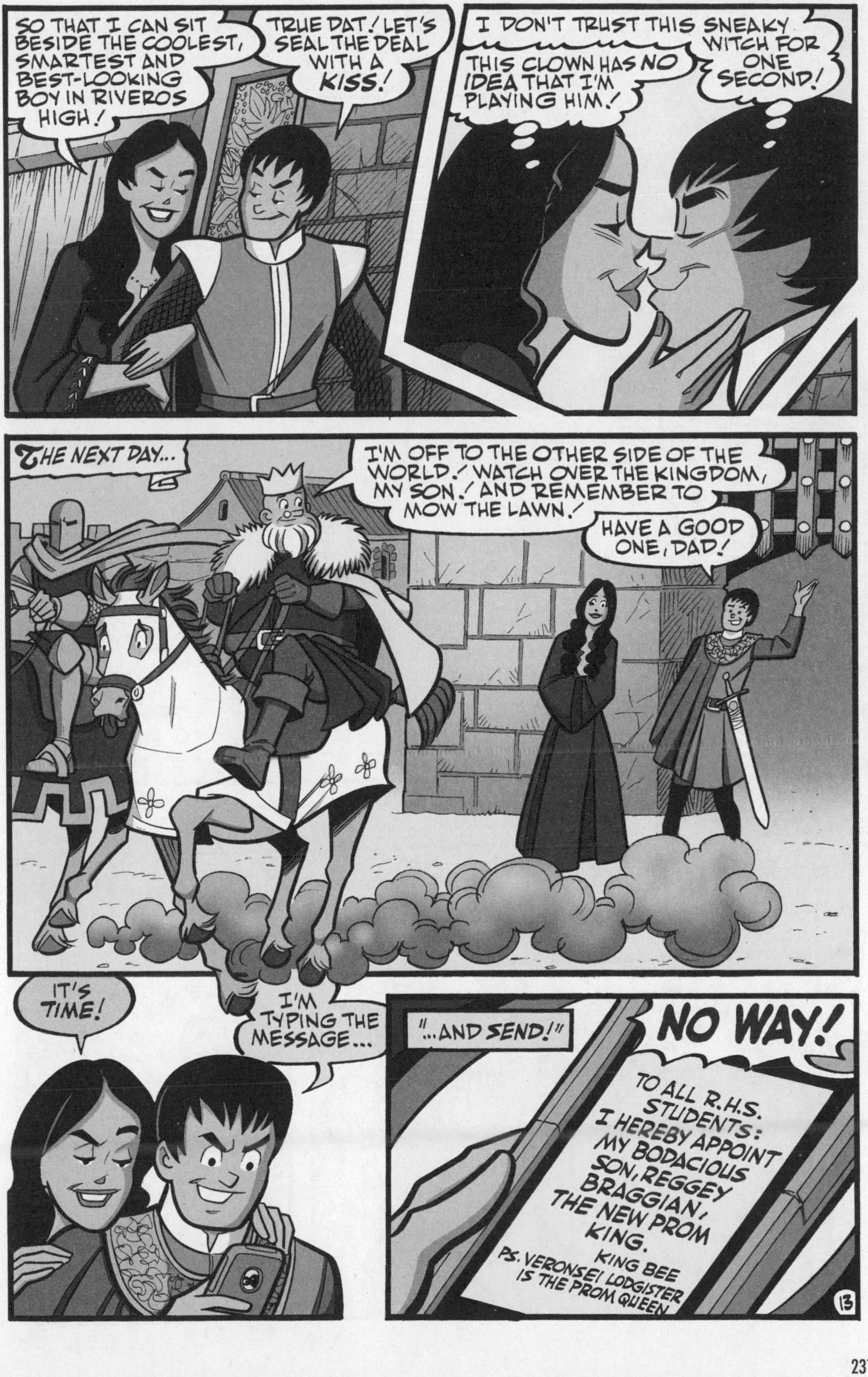
SO THAT I CAN SIT BESIDE THE COOLEST, SMARTEST AND BEST-LOOKING BOY IN RIVEROS HIGH!
TRUE DAT! LET'S SEAL THE DEAL WITH A KISS!
I DON'T TRUST THIS SNEAKY WITCH FOR ONE SECOND!
THIS CLOWN HAS NO IDEA THAT I'M PLAYING HIM!
THE NEXT DAY...
I'M OFF TO THE OTHER SIDE OF THE WORLD! WATCH OVER THE KINGDOM, MY SON! AND REMEMBER TO MOW THE LAWN!
HAVE A GOOD ONE, DAD!
IT'S TIME!
I'M TYPING THE MESSAGE...
"...AND SEND!"
NO WAY!
TO ALL R.H.S. STUDENTS: I HEREBY APPOINT MY BODACIOUS SON, REGGEY BRAGGIAN, THE NEW PROM KING.
KING BEE
P.S. VERONSEI LODGISTER IS THE PROM QUEEN
13

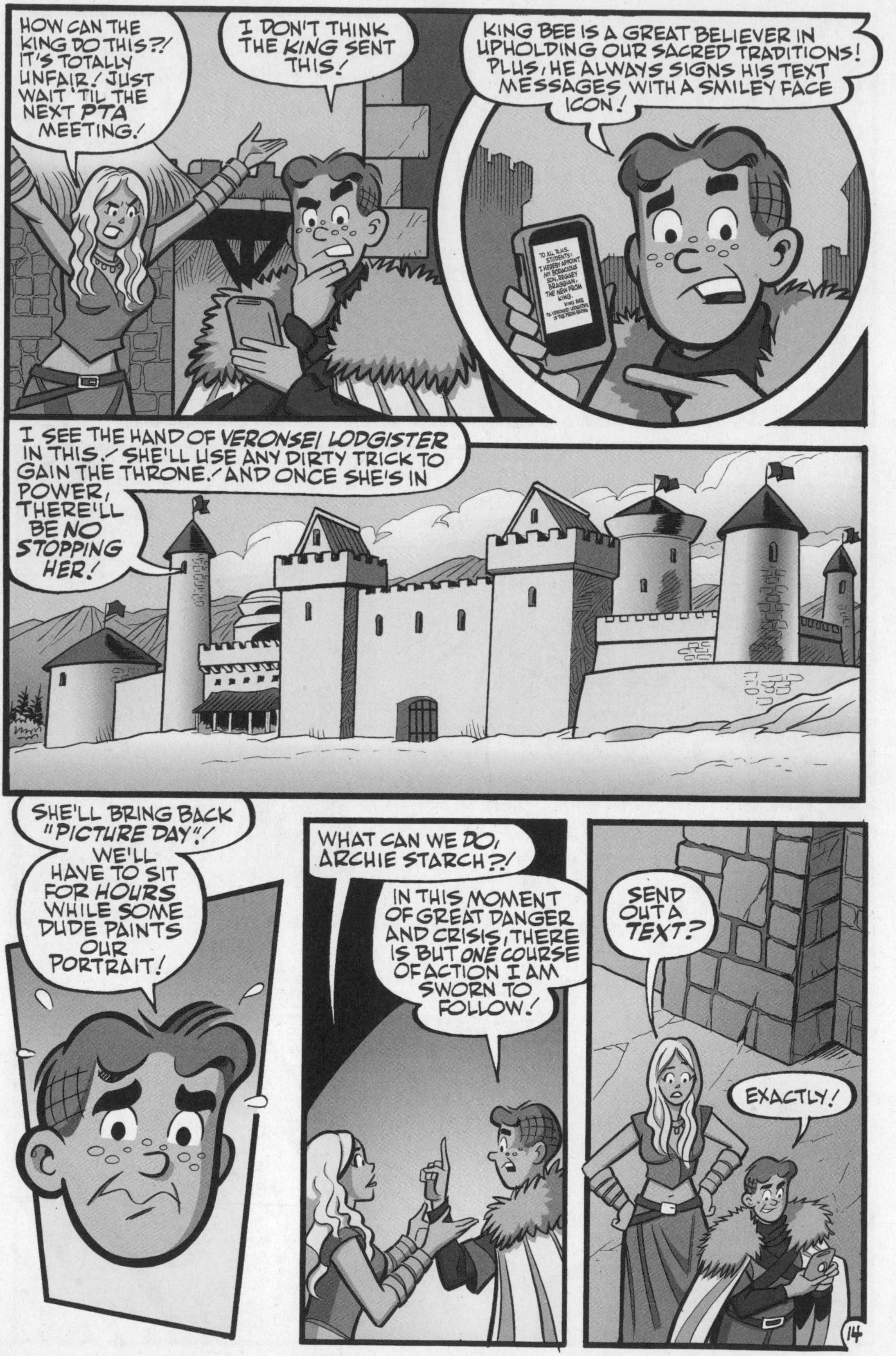
HOW CAN THE KING DO THIS?! IT'S TOTALLY UNFAIR! JUST WAIT 'TIL THE NEXT PTA MEETING!
I DON'T THINK THE KING SENT THIS!
KING BEE IS A GREAT BELIEVER IN UPHOLDING OUR SACRED TRADITIONS! PLUS, HE ALWAYS SIGNS HIS TEXT MESSAGES WITH A SMILEY FACE ICON!
TO ALL R.H.S. STUDENTS: I HEREBY APPOINT MY BODACIOUS SON, REGGEY BRAGGIAN, THE NEW PROM KING.
KING BEE
I SEE THE HAND OF VERONSEI LODGISTER IN THIS! SHE'LL USE ANY DIRTY TRICK TO GAIN THE THRONE! AND ONCE SHE'S IN POWER, THERE'LL BE NO STOPPING HER!
SHE'LL BRING BACK "PICTURE DAY"! WE'LL HAVE TO SIT FOR HOURS WHILE SOME DUDE PAINTS OUR PORTRAIT!
WHAT CAN WE DO, ARCHIE STARCH?!
IN THIS MOMENT OF GREAT DANGER AND CRISIS, THERE IS BUT ONE COURSE OF ACTION I AM SWORN TO FOLLOW!
SEND OUT A TEXT?
EXACTLY!
14

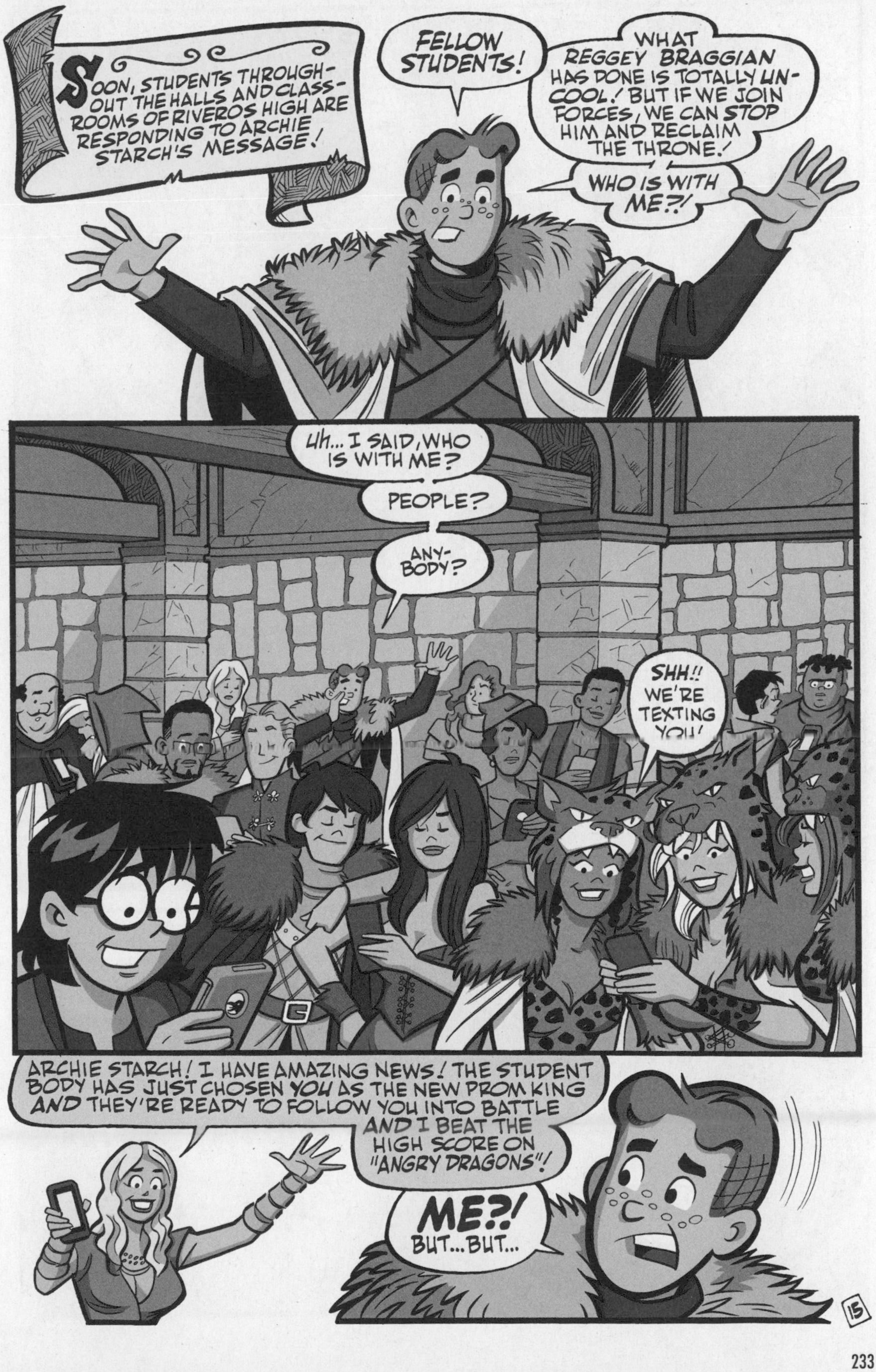
SOON, STUDENTS THROUGH-OUT THE HALLS AND CLASS-ROOMS OF RIVEROS HIGH ARE RESPONDING TO ARCHIE STARCH'S MESSAGE!
FELLOW STUDENTS!
WHAT REGGEY BRAGGIAN HAS DONE IS TOTALLY UN-COOL! BUT IF WE JOIN FORCES, WE CAN STOP HIM AND RECLAIM THE THRONE!
WHO IS WITH ME?!
UH... I SAID, WHO IS WITH ME?
PEOPLE?
ANY-BODY?
SHH!! WE'RE TEXTING YOU!
ARCHIE STARCH! I HAVE AMAZING NEWS! THE STUDENT BODY HAS JUST CHOSEN YOU AS THE NEW PROM KING AND THEY'RE READY TO FOLLOW YOU INTO BATTLE AND I BEAT THE HIGH SCORE ON "ANGRY DRAGONS"!
ME?! BUT... BUT...
15

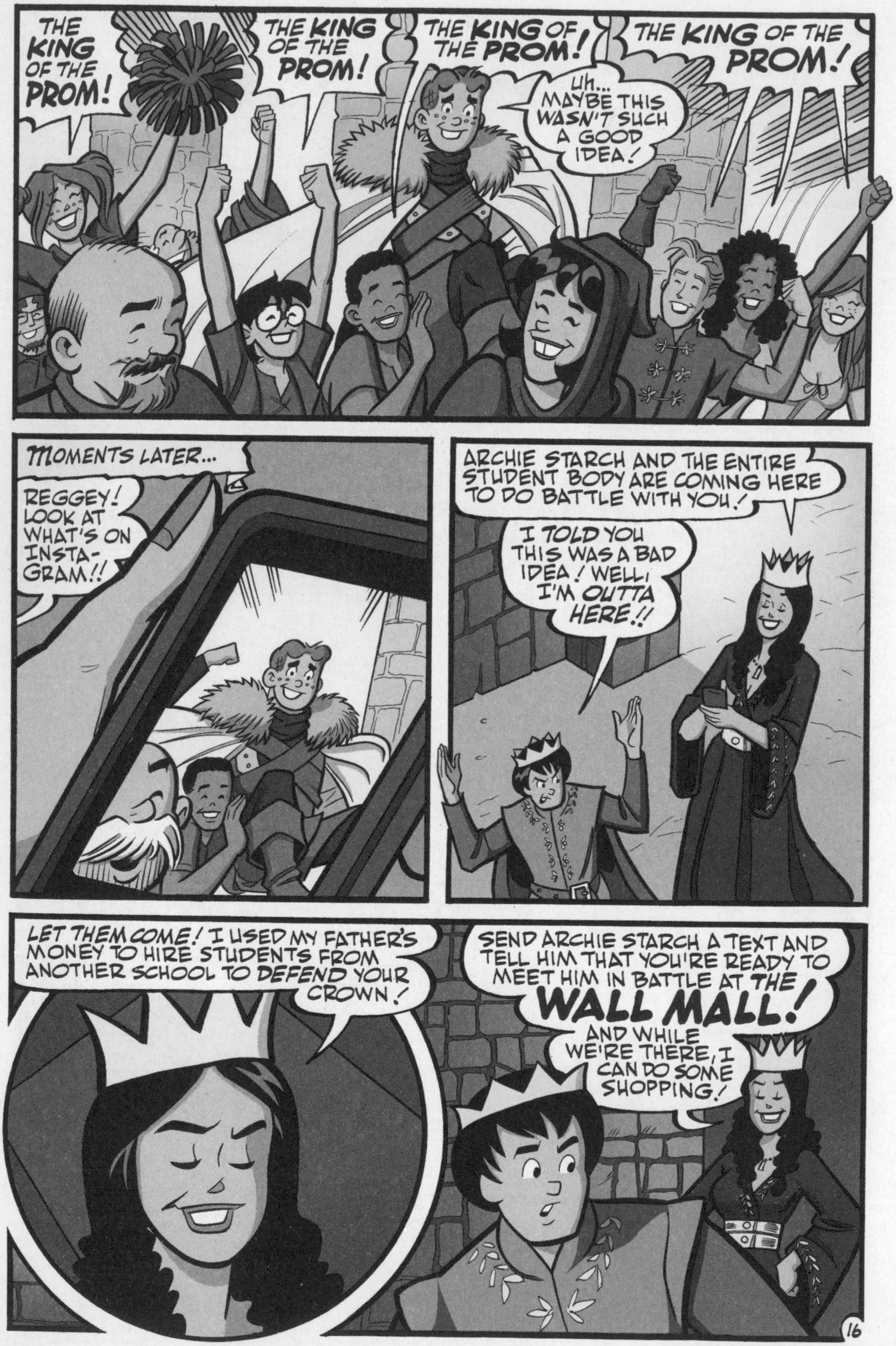
THE KING OF THE PROM!
THE KING OF THE PROM!
THE KING OF THE PROM!
THE KING OF THE PROM!
UH... MAYBE THIS WASN'T SUCH A GOOD IDEA!
MOMENTS LATER...
REGGEY! LOOK AT WHAT'S ON INSTA-GRAM!!
ARCHIE STARCH AND THE ENTIRE STUDENT BODY ARE COMING HERE TO DO BATTLE WITH YOU!
I TOLD YOU THIS WAS A BAD IDEA! WELL, I'M OUTTA HERE!!
LET THEM COME! I USED MY FATHER'S MONEY TO HIRE STUDENTS FROM ANOTHER SCHOOL TO DEFEND YOUR CROWN!
SEND ARCHIE STARCH A TEXT AND TELL HIM THAT YOU'RE READY TO MEET HIM IN BATTLE AT THE WALL MALL!
AND WHILE WE'RE THERE, I CAN DO SOME SHOPPING!
16

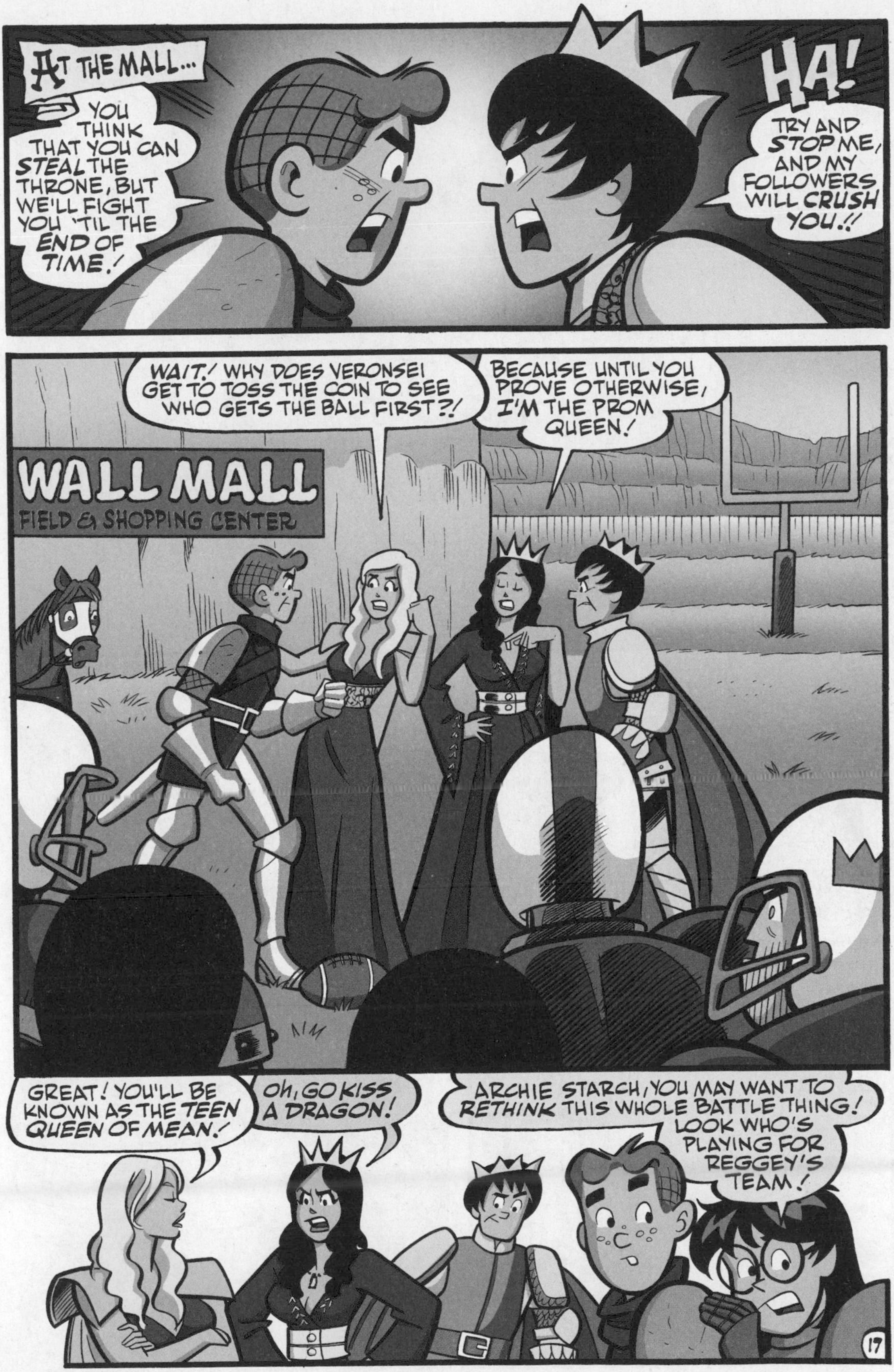
AT THE MALL...
YOU THINK THAT YOU CAN STEAL THE THRONE, BUT WE'LL FIGHT YOU 'TIL THE END OF TIME!
HA!
TRY AND STOP ME, AND MY FOLLOWERS WILL CRUSH YOU!!
WAIT! WHY DOES VERONSEI GET TO TOSS THE COIN TO SEE WHO GETS THE BALL FIRST?!
BECAUSE UNTIL YOU PROVE OTHERWISE, I'M THE PROM QUEEN!
WALL MALL
FIELD & SHOPPING CENTER
GREAT! YOU'LL BE KNOWN AS THE TEEN QUEEN OF MEAN!
OH, GO KISS A DRAGON!
ARCHIE STARCH, YOU MAY WANT TO RETHINK THIS WHOLE BATTLE THING!
LOOK WHO'S PLAYING FOR REGGEY'S TEAM!
17

The MOOSE!!

WE'RE IN TROUBLE! HE'S THE BIGGEST AND STRONGEST PLAYER AROUND! LAST YEAR HE WAS VOTED ALL-KINGDOM!

BRAGGIAN

NICE MOVE! HOW'D WE GET *HIM?*

WE MADE A DEAL! YOU HAVE TO DO HIS MATH HOMEWORK FOR THE *NEXT FIVE YEARS!*

THEN LET THE **BATTLE BEGIN!**

TIME OUT, YOU GUYS!

IT'S MY BEST BUD *JON SNOWHEAD!* HAVE YOU COME TO JOIN US IN BATTLE?

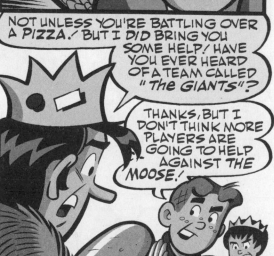

NOT UNLESS YOU'RE BATTLING OVER A *PIZZA!* BUT I *DID* BRING YOU SOME HELP! HAVE YOU EVER HEARD OF A TEAM CALLED *"THE GIANTS"?*

THANKS, BUT I DON'T THINK MORE PLAYERS ARE GOING TO HELP AGAINST *THE MOOSE!*

18

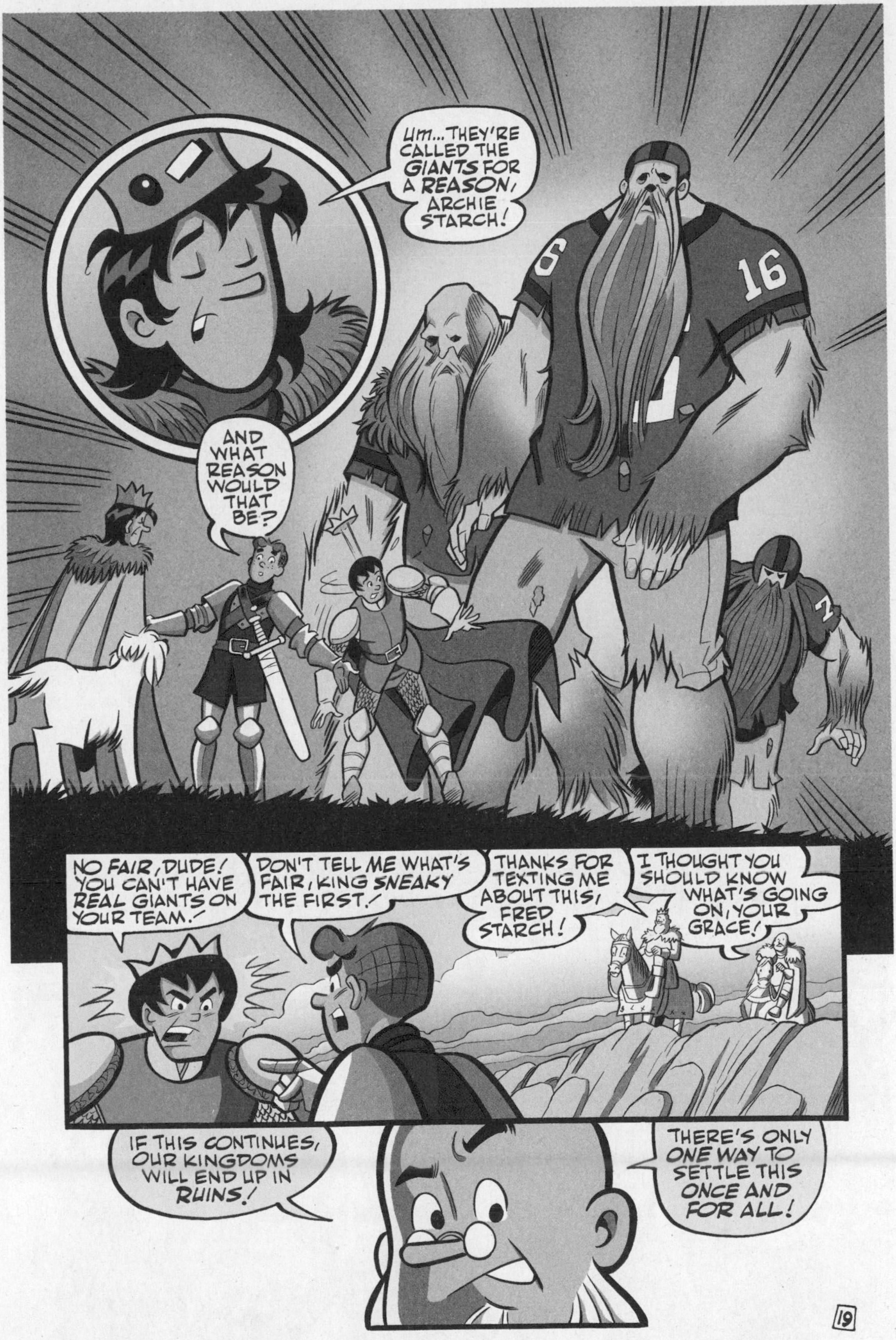
UM... THEY'RE CALLED THE GIANTS FOR A REASON, ARCHIE STARCH!
AND WHAT REASON WOULD THAT BE?
16
NO FAIR, DUDE! YOU CAN'T HAVE REAL GIANTS ON YOUR TEAM!
DON'T TELL ME WHAT'S FAIR, KING SNEAKY THE FIRST!
THANKS FOR TEXTING ME ABOUT THIS, FRED STARCH!
I THOUGHT YOU SHOULD KNOW WHAT'S GOING ON, YOUR GRACE!
IF THIS CONTINUES, OUR KINGDOMS WILL END UP IN RUINS!
THERE'S ONLY ONE WAY TO SETTLE THIS ONCE AND FOR ALL!
19

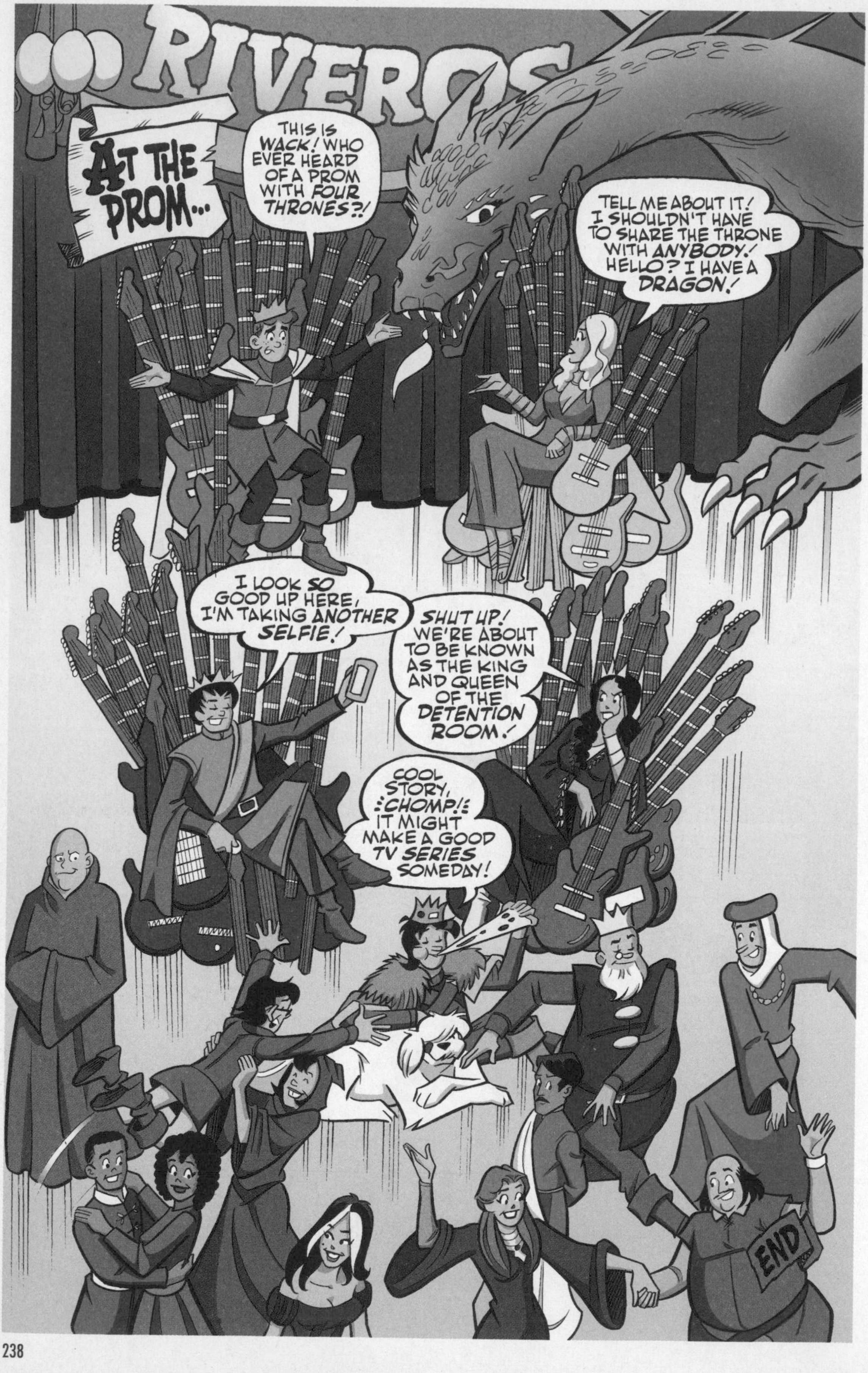
RIVEROS
AT THE PROM...
THIS IS WACK! WHO EVER HEARD OF A PROM WITH FOUR THRONES?!
TELL ME ABOUT IT! I SHOULDN'T HAVE TO SHARE THE THRONE WITH ANYBODY! HELLO? I HAVE A DRAGON!
I LOOK SO GOOD UP HERE, I'M TAKING ANOTHER SELFIE!
SHUT UP! WE'RE ABOUT TO BE KNOWN AS THE KING AND QUEEN OF THE DETENTION ROOM!
COOL STORY, CHOMP! IT MIGHT MAKE A GOOD TV SERIES SOMEDAY!
END

CHAPTER EIGHT

MIRRORDALE

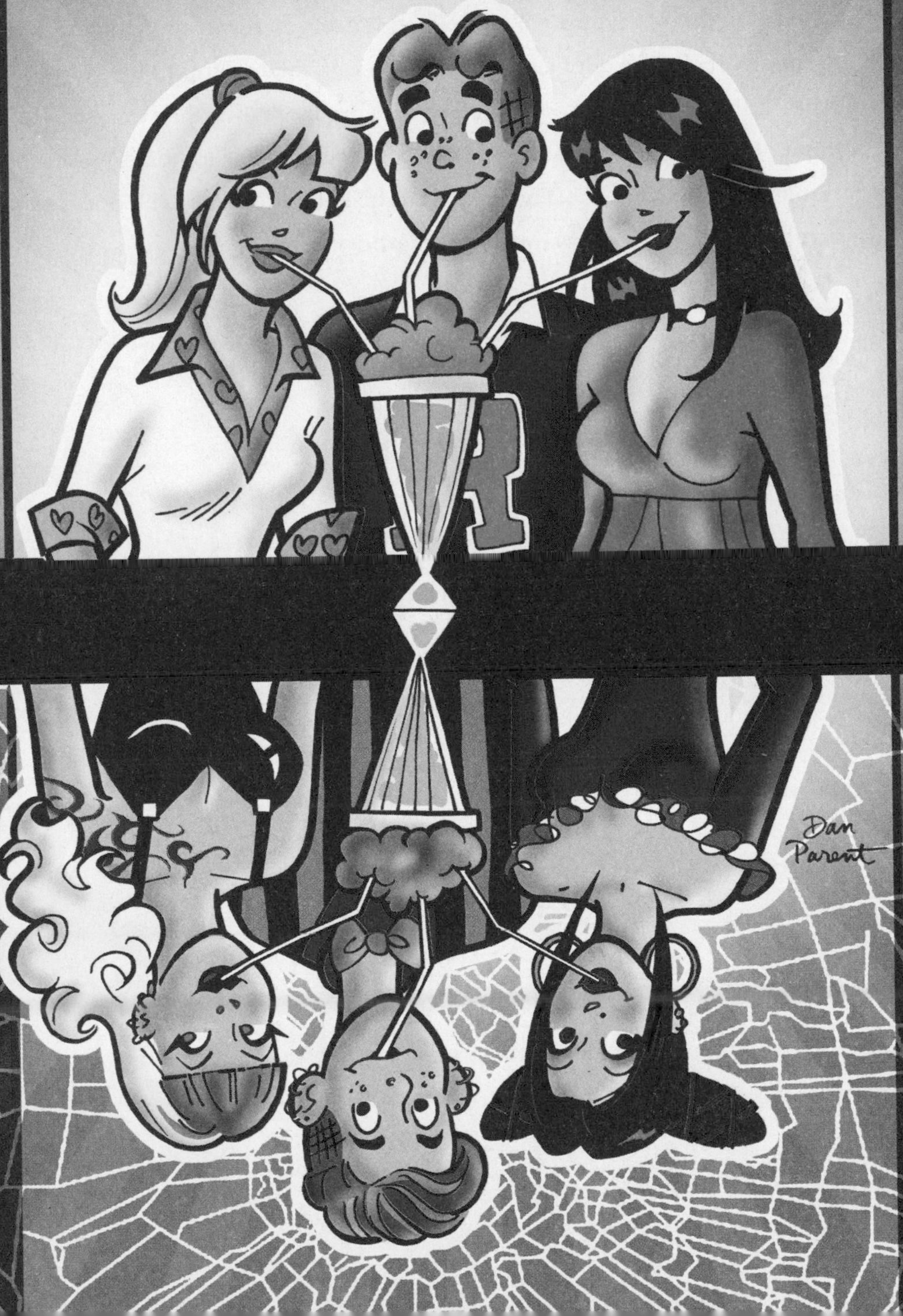
Dan Parent

INTRODUCING MIRRORDALE

Originally printed in *Archie #647*

"Welcome to Mirrordale" tells the story of how a date night with Betty turns into an inter-universe collision when the Madhouse Carnival comes to Riverdale! Archie has a lot to reflect on when he takes a trip to the House of Mirrors, but little does he know those mirrors are more than they appear! He's catapulted into a world where everything seems familiar to home—just a bit different! Can Archie make it back to his date in Riverdale, or is he doomed to switch places with his mirror-world counterpart forever?

WRITER
STEVEN DUVALL

PENCILS
DAN PARENT

INKS
RICH KOSLOWSKI

LETTERS
JACK MORELLI

COLORS
DIGIKORE STUDIOS

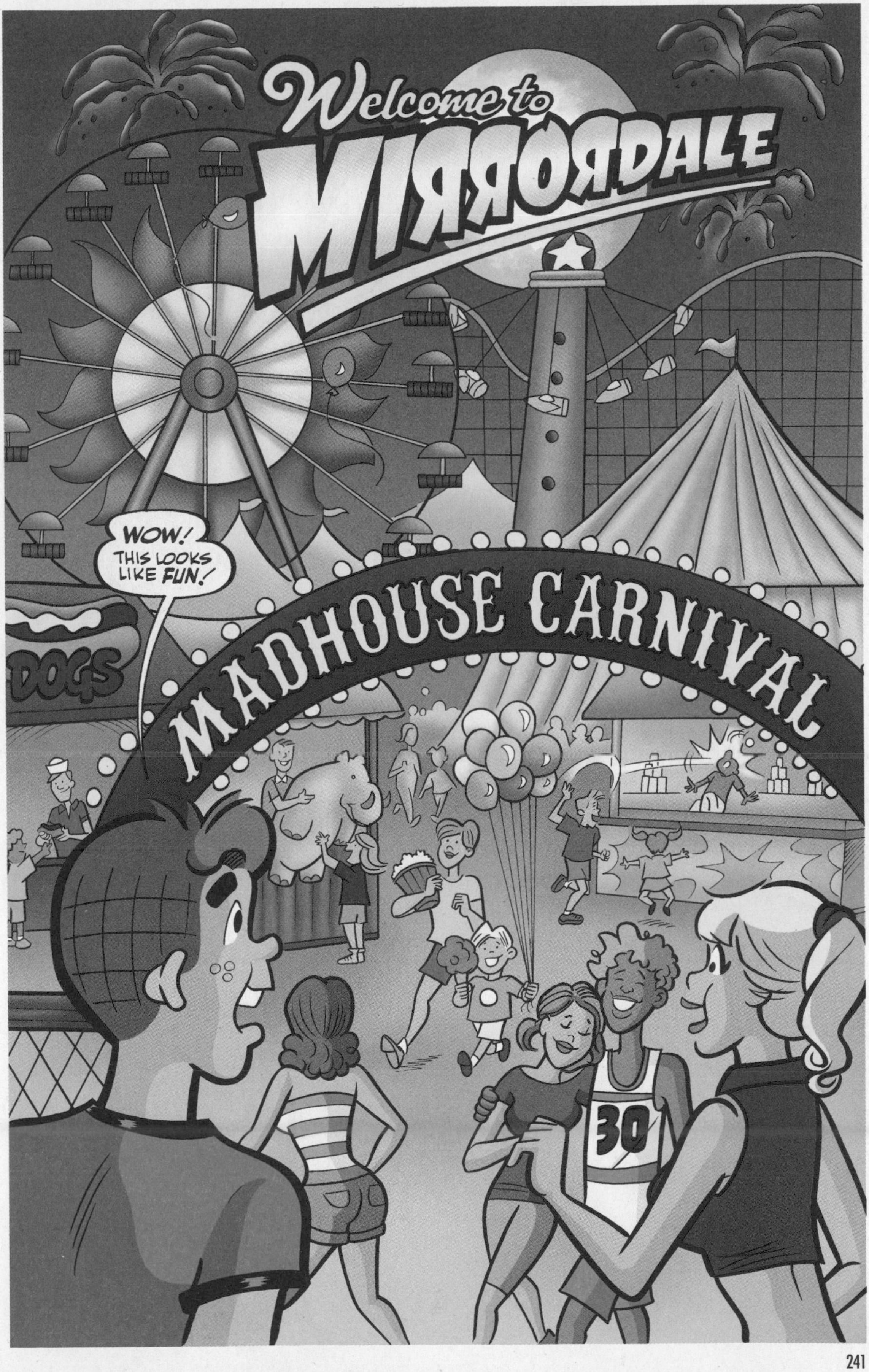
Welcome to
MIRRORDALE
WOW! THIS LOOKS LIKE FUN!
DOGS
MADHOUSE CARNIVAL
30

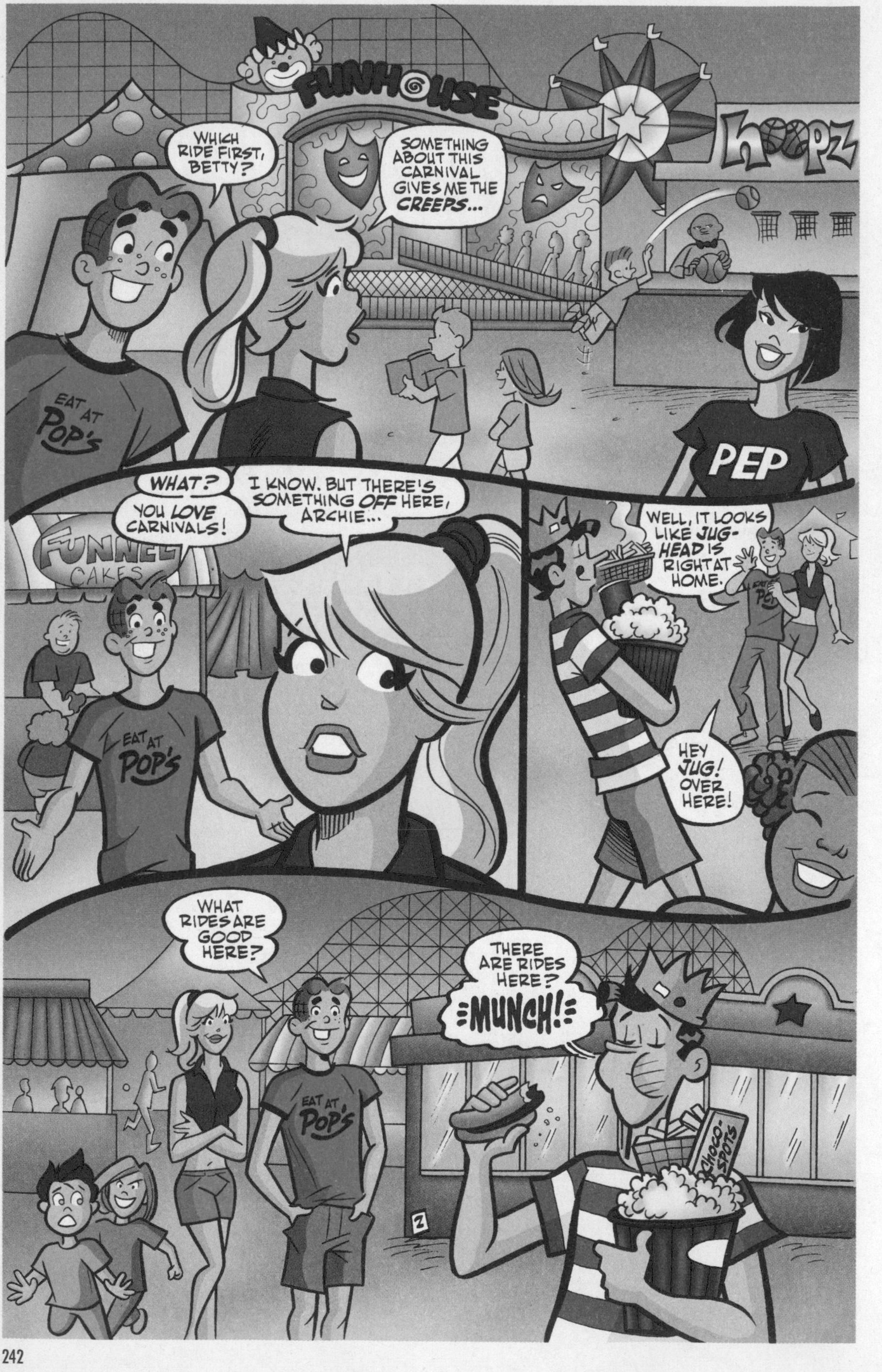
FUNHOUSE
hoopz
WHICH RIDE FIRST, BETTY?
SOMETHING ABOUT THIS CARNIVAL GIVES ME THE CREEPS...
EAT AT POP'S
PEP
WHAT? YOU LOVE CARNIVALS!
I KNOW. BUT THERE'S SOMETHING OFF HERE, ARCHIE...
FUNNEL CAKES
WELL, IT LOOKS LIKE JUGHEAD IS RIGHT AT HOME.
HEY JUG! OVER HERE!
WHAT RIDES ARE GOOD HERE?
THERE ARE RIDES HERE?
MUNCH!
CHOCO-SPOTS

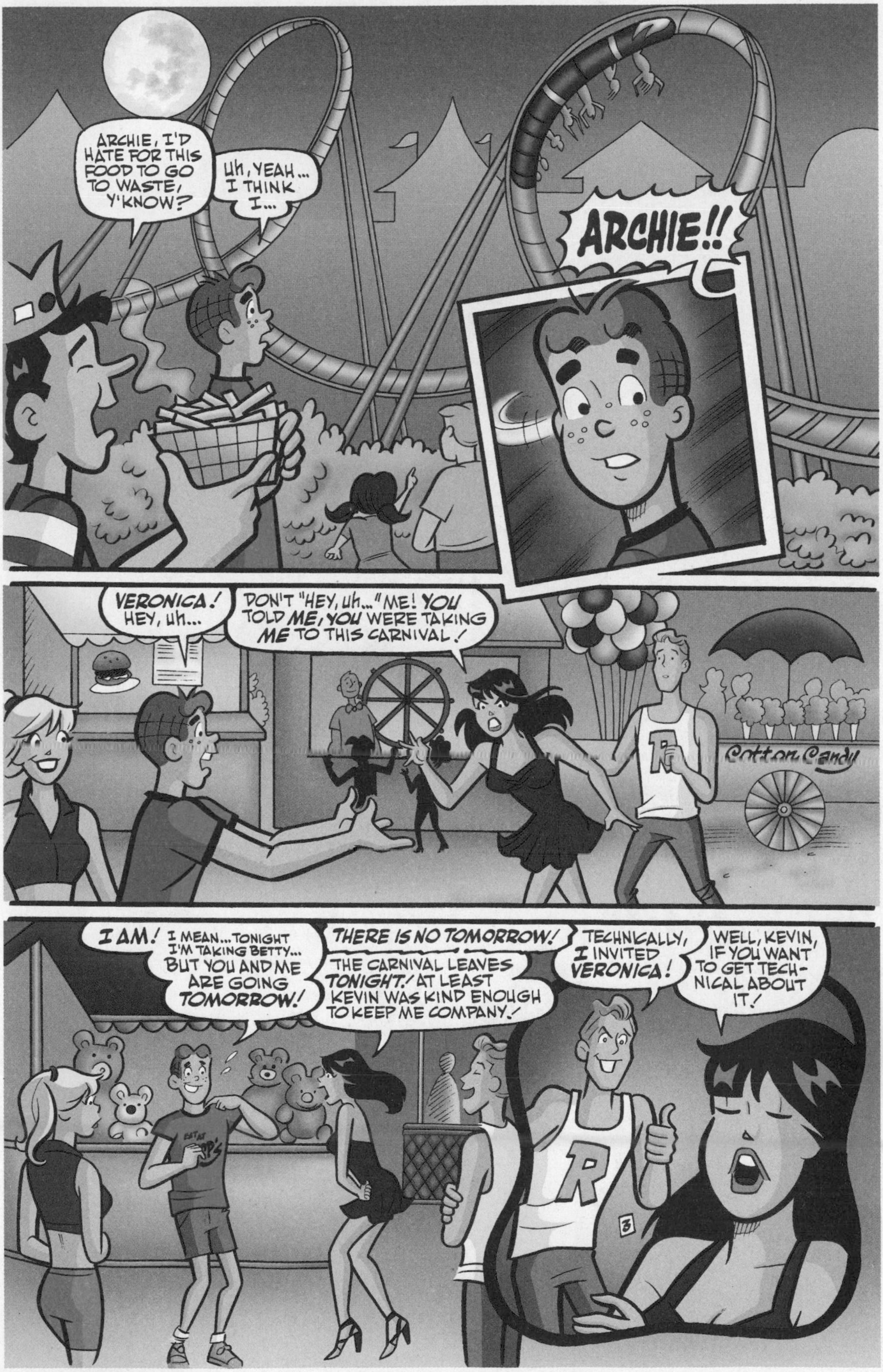
ARCHIE, I'D HATE FOR THIS FOOD TO GO TO WASTE, Y'KNOW?
UH, YEAH... I THINK I...
ARCHIE!!
VERONICA! HEY, UH...
DON'T "HEY, UH..." ME! YOU TOLD ME, YOU WERE TAKING ME TO THIS CARNIVAL!
Cotton Candy
I AM! I MEAN... TONIGHT I'M TAKING BETTY... BUT YOU AND ME ARE GOING TOMORROW!
THERE IS NO TOMORROW! THE CARNIVAL LEAVES TONIGHT! AT LEAST KEVIN WAS KIND ENOUGH TO KEEP ME COMPANY!
TECHNICALLY, I INVITED VERONICA!
WELL, KEVIN, IF YOU WANT TO GET TECHNICAL ABOUT IT!

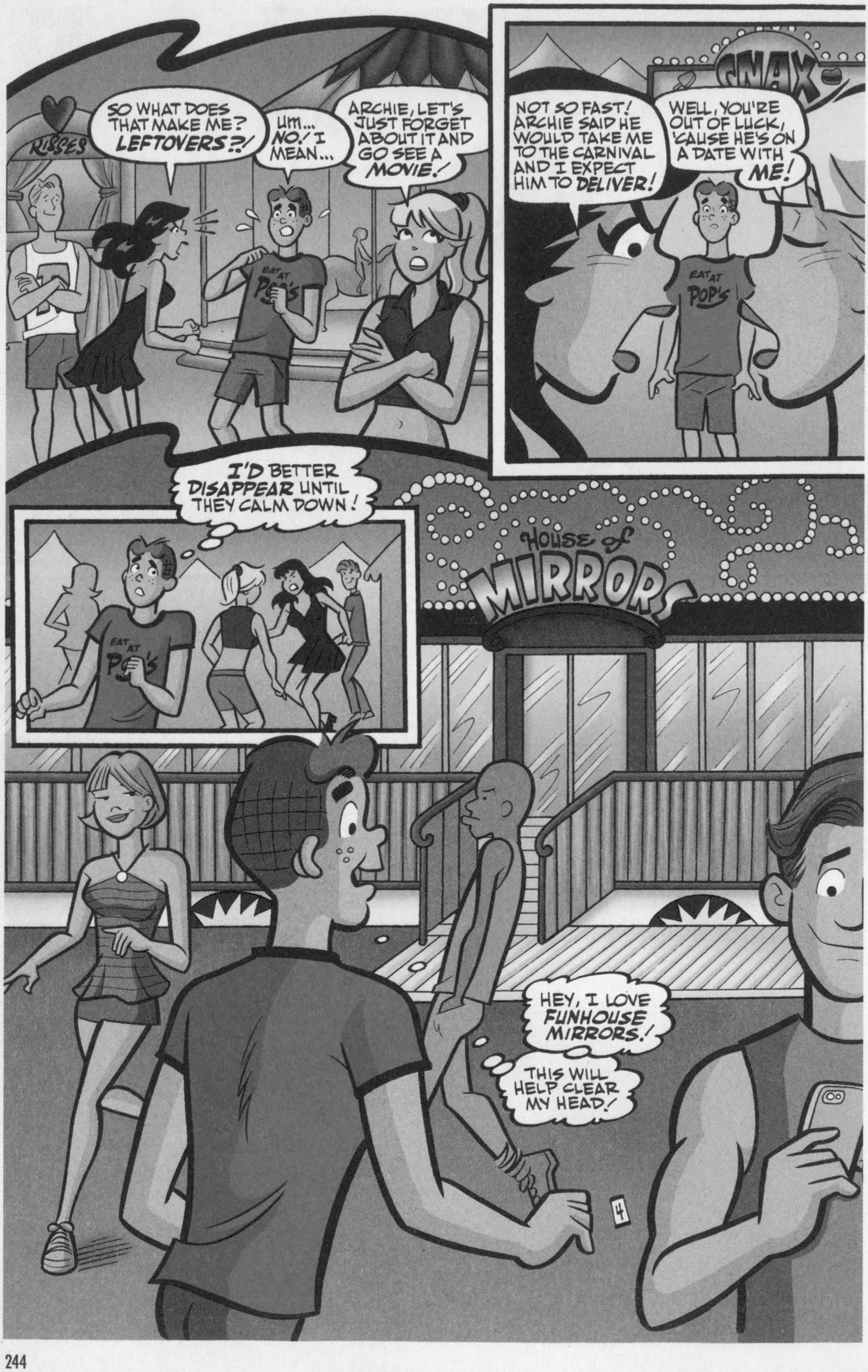
KISSES
SO WHAT DOES THAT MAKE ME? LEFTOVERS?!
UM... NO! I MEAN...
ARCHIE, LET'S JUST FORGET ABOUT IT AND GO SEE A MOVIE!
EAT AT POP'S
SNAX
NOT SO FAST! ARCHIE SAID HE WOULD TAKE ME TO THE CARNIVAL AND I EXPECT HIM TO DELIVER!
WELL, YOU'RE OUT OF LUCK, 'CAUSE HE'S ON A DATE WITH ME!
I'D BETTER DISAPPEAR UNTIL THEY CALM DOWN!
HOUSE of MIRRORS
HEY, I LOVE FUNHOUSE MIRRORS!
THIS WILL HELP CLEAR MY HEAD!
4

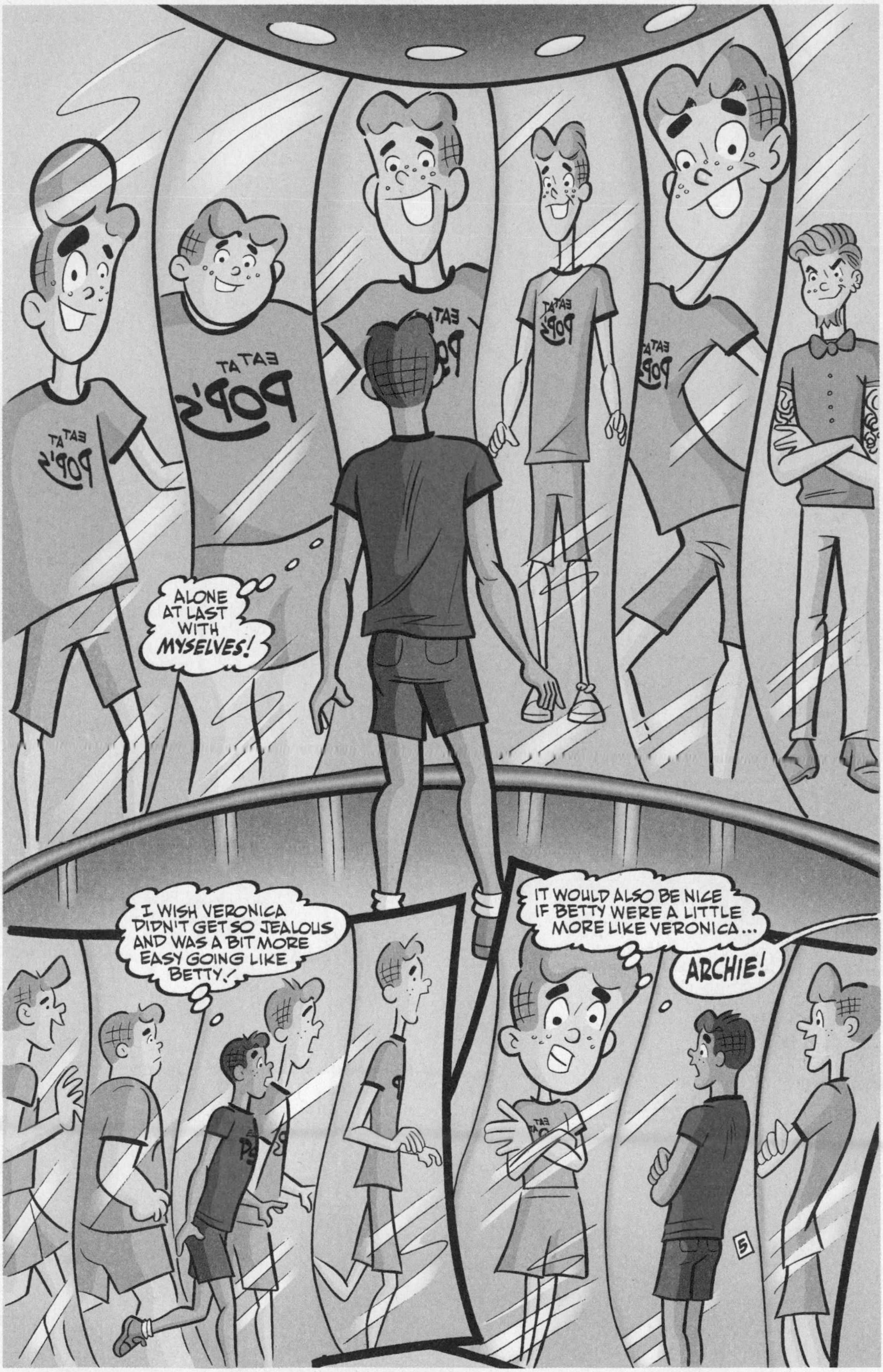
EAT AT POP'S
ALONE AT LAST WITH MYSELVES!
I WISH VERONICA DIDN'T GET SO JEALOUS AND WAS A BIT MORE EASY GOING LIKE BETTY!
IT WOULD ALSO BE NICE IF BETTY WERE A LITTLE MORE LIKE VERONICA...
ARCHIE!
5

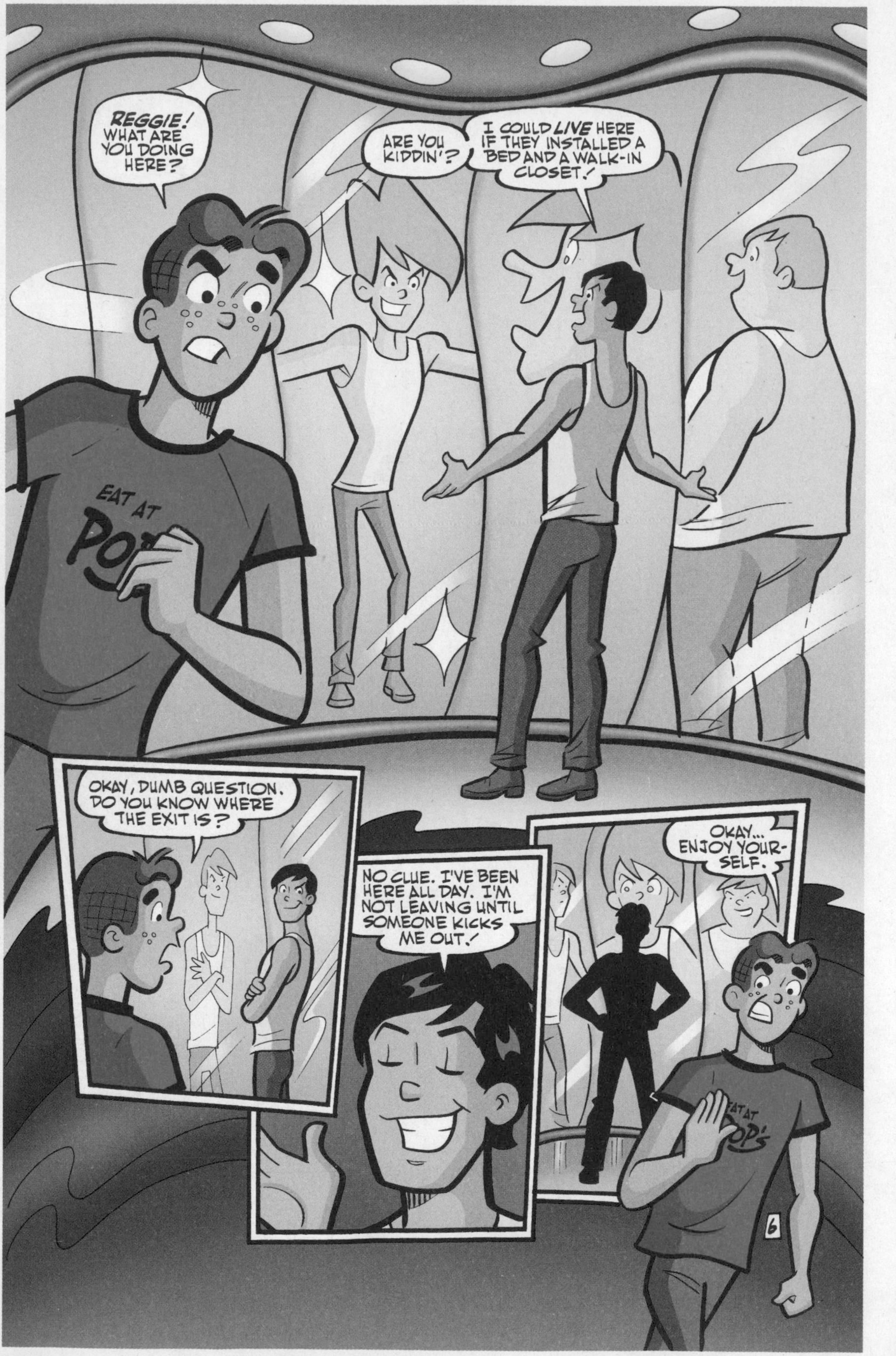
REGGIE! WHAT ARE YOU DOING HERE?
ARE YOU KIDDIN'?
I COULD LIVE HERE IF THEY INSTALLED A BED AND A WALK-IN CLOSET!
EAT AT POP'S
OKAY, DUMB QUESTION. DO YOU KNOW WHERE THE EXIT IS?
NO CLUE. I'VE BEEN HERE ALL DAY. I'M NOT LEAVING UNTIL SOMEONE KICKS ME OUT!
OKAY... ENJOY YOURSELF.
EAT AT POP'S
6

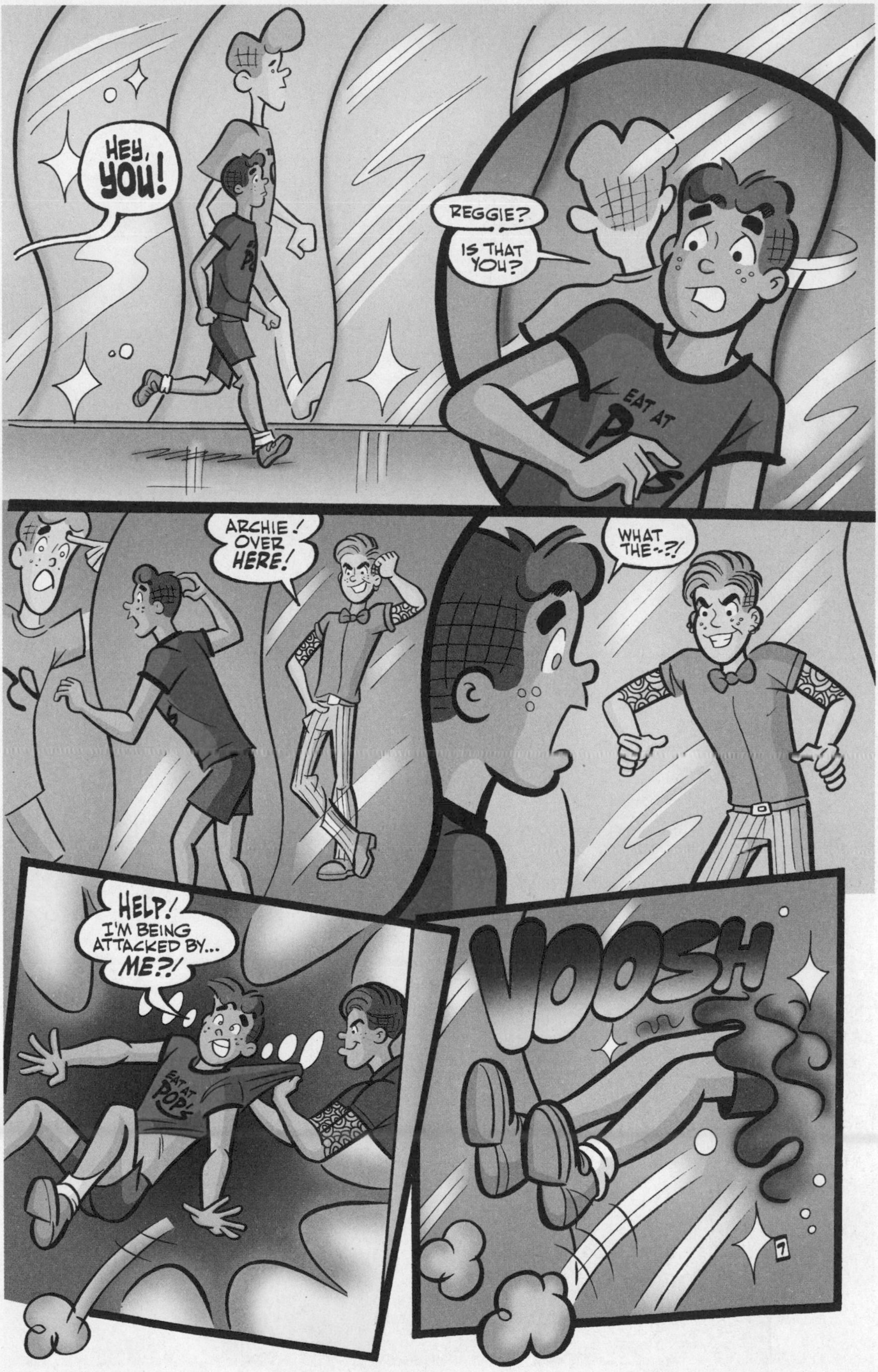
HEY, YOU!
REGGIE?
IS THAT YOU?
EAT AT POP'S
ARCHIE! OVER HERE!
WHAT THE--?!
HELP! I'M BEING ATTACKED BY... ME?!
EAT AT POP'S
VOOSH
7

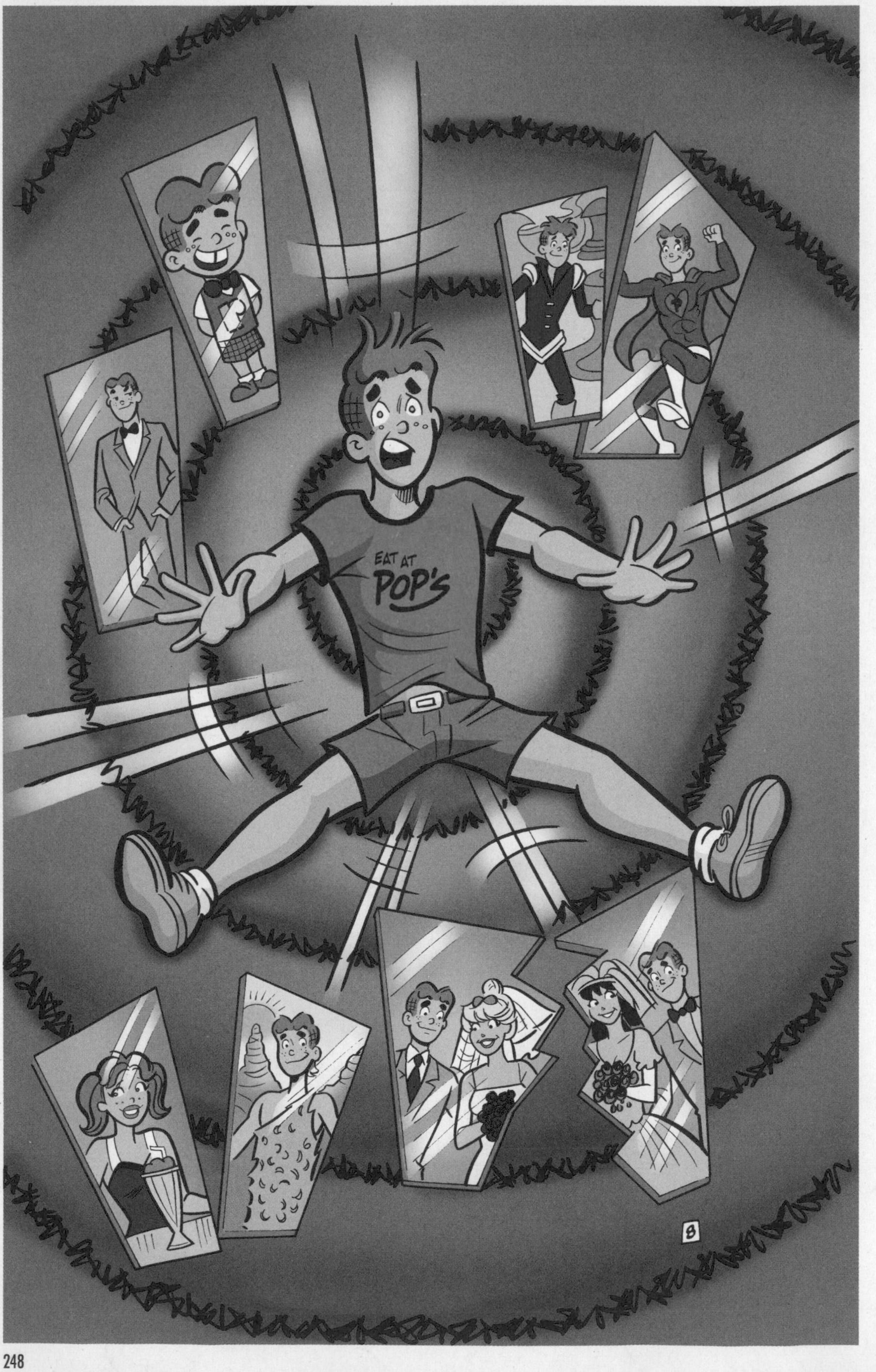
EAT AT
POP'S

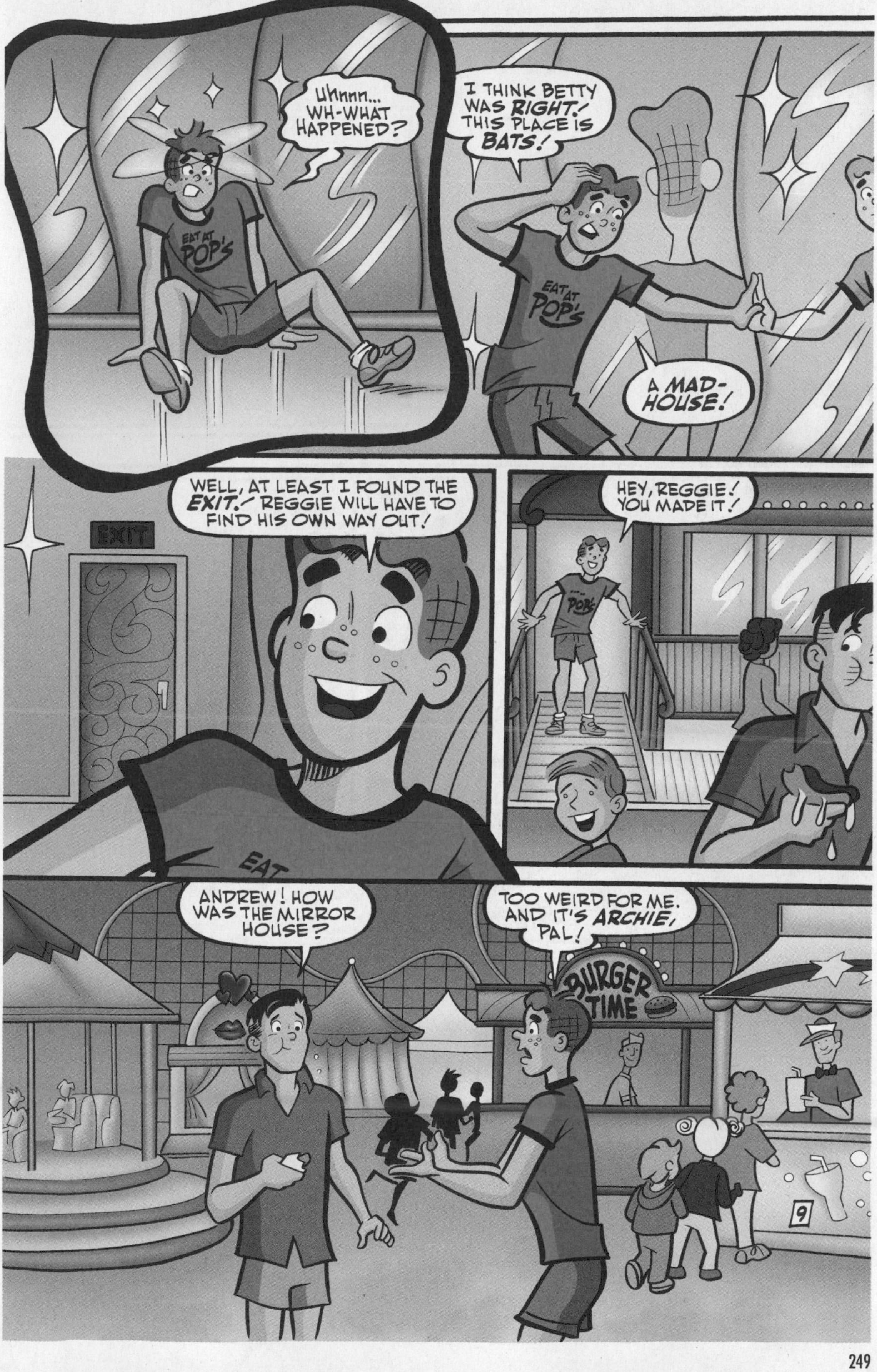
Uhnnn... WH-WHAT HAPPENED?
I THINK BETTY WAS RIGHT! THIS PLACE IS BATS!
A MAD-HOUSE!
EAT AT POP'S
EXIT
WELL, AT LEAST I FOUND THE EXIT! REGGIE WILL HAVE TO FIND HIS OWN WAY OUT!
HEY, REGGIE! YOU MADE IT!
ANDREW! HOW WAS THE MIRROR HOUSE?
TOO WEIRD FOR ME. AND IT'S ARCHIE, PAL!
BURGER TIME
9

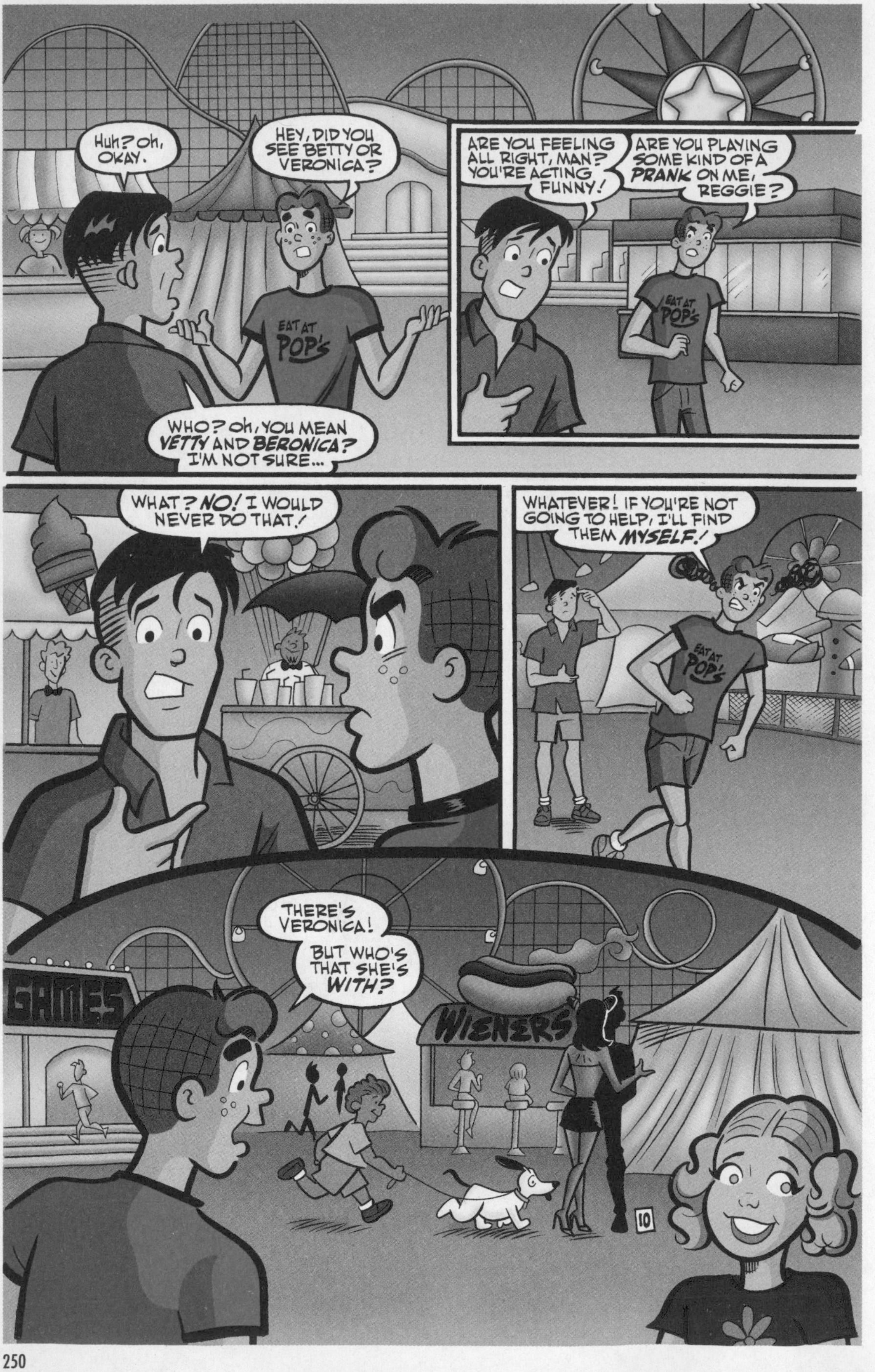
HEY, DID YOU SEE BETTY OR VERONICA?
HUH? OH, OKAY.
WHO? OH, YOU MEAN VETTY AND BERONICA? I'M NOT SURE...
ARE YOU FEELING ALL RIGHT, MAN? YOU'RE ACTING FUNNY!
ARE YOU PLAYING SOME KIND OF A PRANK ON ME, REGGIE?
EAT AT POP'S
WHAT? NO! I WOULD NEVER DO THAT!
WHATEVER! IF YOU'RE NOT GOING TO HELP, I'LL FIND THEM MYSELF!
THERE'S VERONICA!
BUT WHO'S THAT SHE'S WITH?
GAMES
WIENERS
10

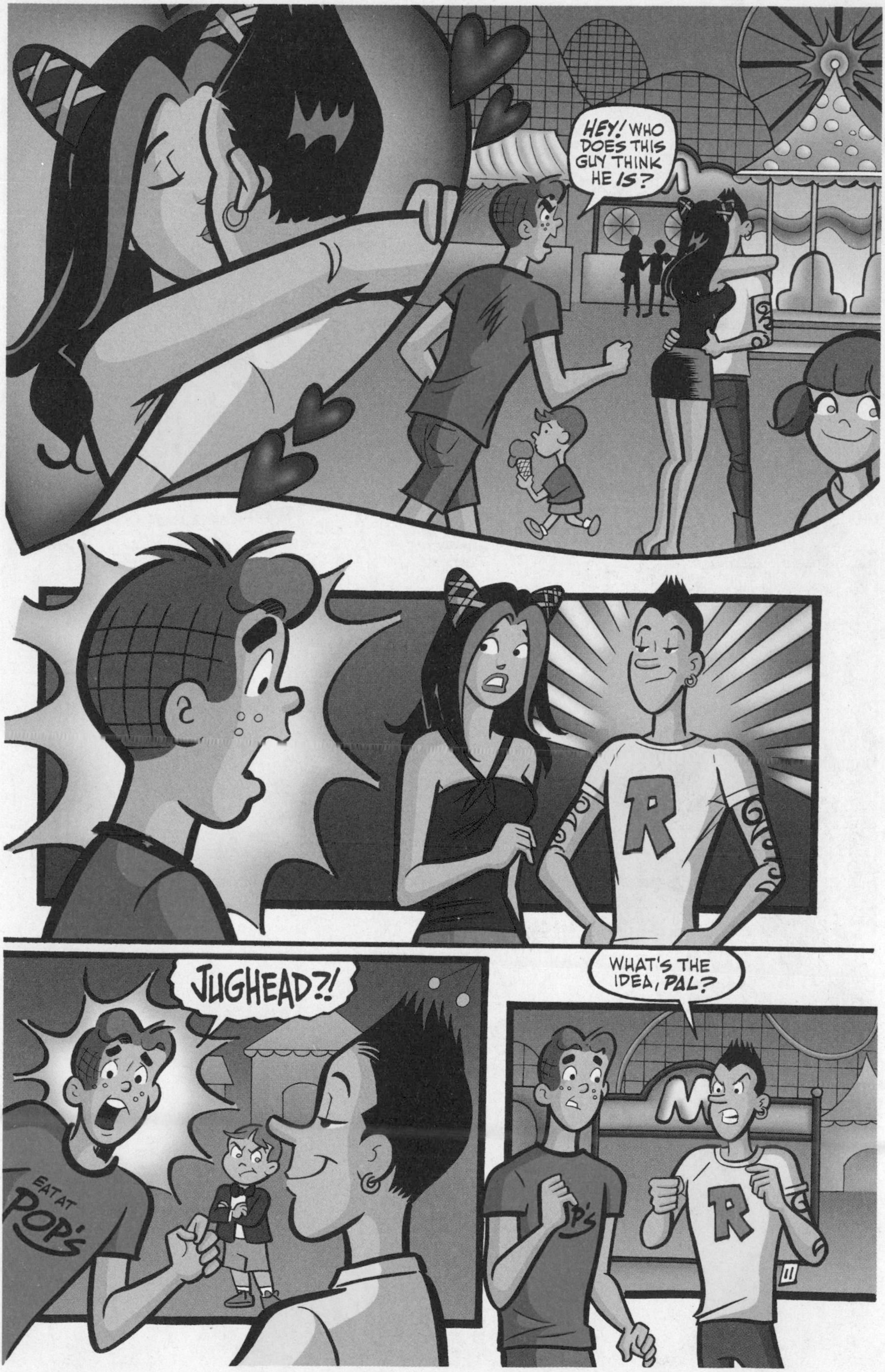
HEY! WHO DOES THIS GUY THINK HE IS?
JUGHEAD?!
EAT AT POP's
WHAT'S THE IDEA, PAL?

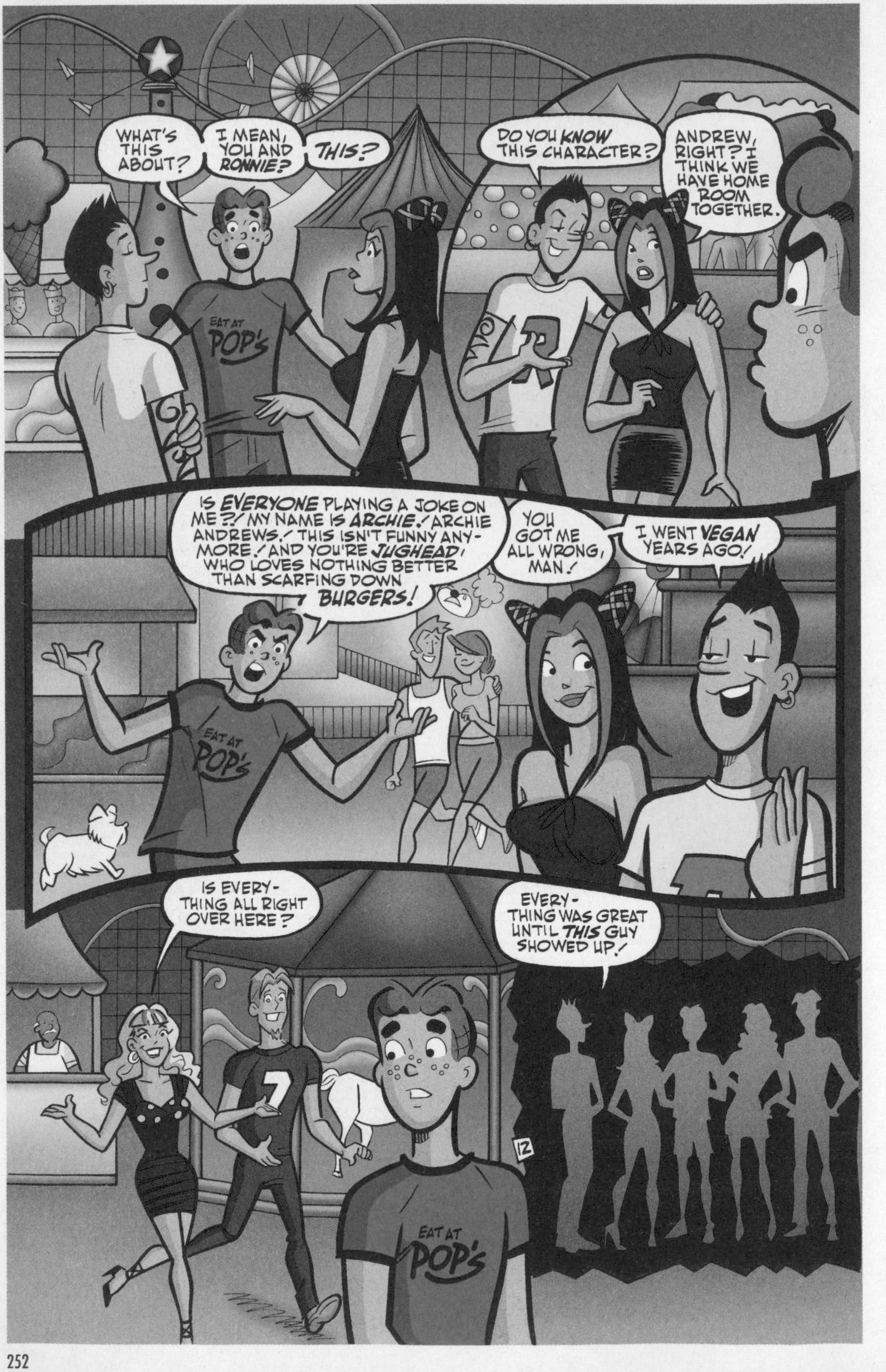
WHAT'S THIS ABOUT?
I MEAN, YOU AND RONNIE?
THIS?
DO YOU KNOW THIS CHARACTER?
ANDREW, RIGHT? I THINK WE HAVE HOME ROOM TOGETHER.
IS EVERYONE PLAYING A JOKE ON ME?! MY NAME IS ARCHIE! ARCHIE ANDREWS! THIS ISN'T FUNNY ANYMORE! AND YOU'RE JUGHEAD! WHO LOVES NOTHING BETTER THAN SCARFING DOWN BURGERS!
YOU GOT ME ALL WRONG, MAN!
I WENT VEGAN YEARS AGO!
IS EVERYTHING ALL RIGHT OVER HERE?
EVERYTHING WAS GREAT UNTIL THIS GUY SHOWED UP!
12

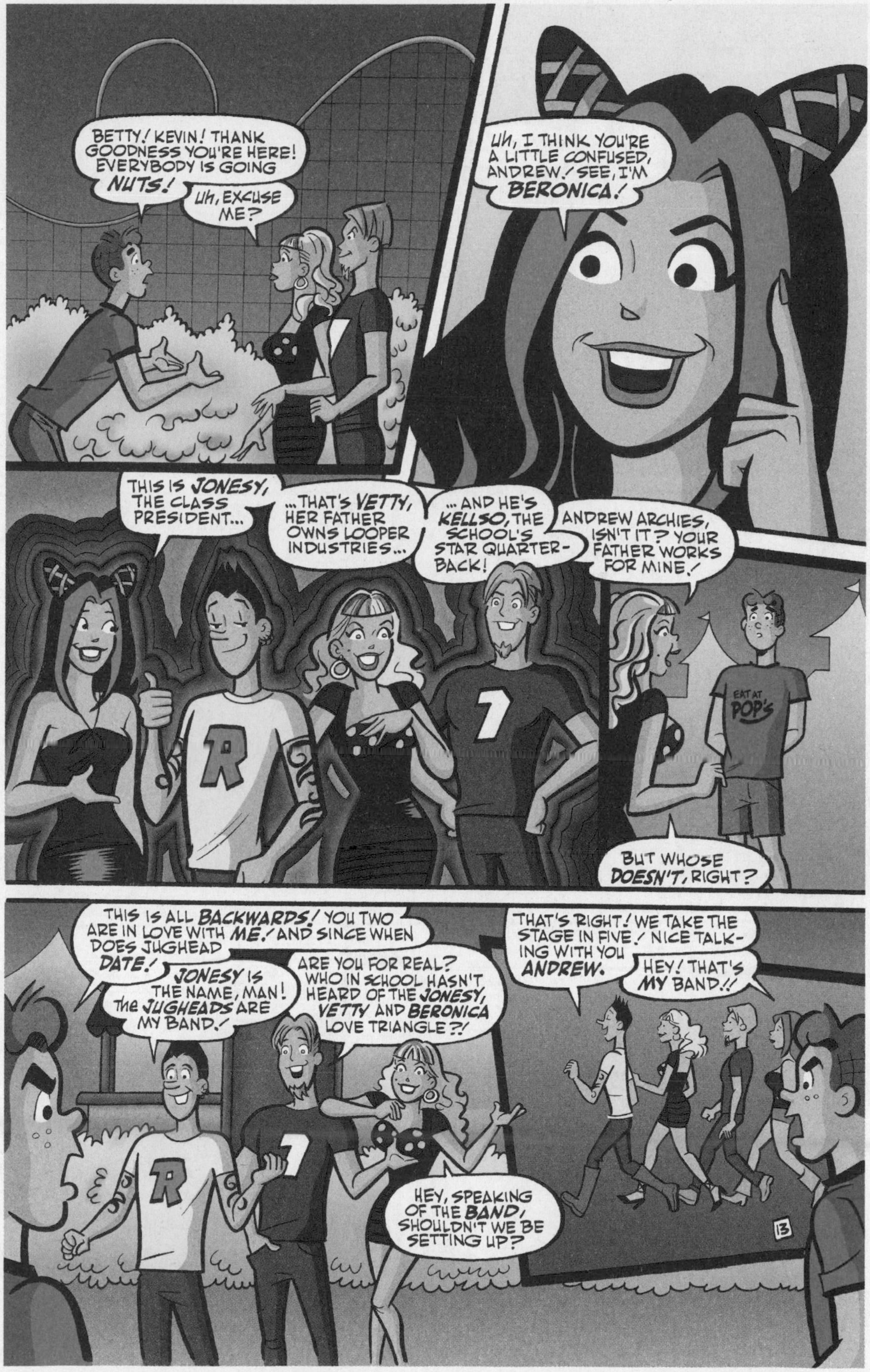
BETTY! KEVIN! THANK GOODNESS YOU'RE HERE! EVERYBODY IS GOING NUTS!
UH, EXCUSE ME?
UH, I THINK YOU'RE A LITTLE CONFUSED, ANDREW! SEE, I'M BERONICA!
THIS IS JONESY, THE CLASS PRESIDENT...
...THAT'S VETTY, HER FATHER OWNS LOOPER INDUSTRIES...
...AND HE'S KELLSO, THE SCHOOL'S STAR QUARTER-BACK!
ANDREW ARCHIES, ISN'T IT? YOUR FATHER WORKS FOR MINE!
EAT AT POP'S
BUT WHOSE DOESN'T, RIGHT?
THIS IS ALL BACKWARDS! YOU TWO ARE IN LOVE WITH ME! AND SINCE WHEN DOES JUGHEAD DATE!
JONESY IS THE NAME, MAN! THE JUGHEADS ARE MY BAND!
ARE YOU FOR REAL? WHO IN SCHOOL HASN'T HEARD OF THE JONESY, VETTY AND BERONICA LOVE TRIANGLE?!
HEY, SPEAKING OF THE BAND, SHOULDN'T WE BE SETTING UP?
THAT'S RIGHT! WE TAKE THE STAGE IN FIVE! NICE TALKING WITH YOU ANDREW.
HEY! THAT'S MY BAND!!
13

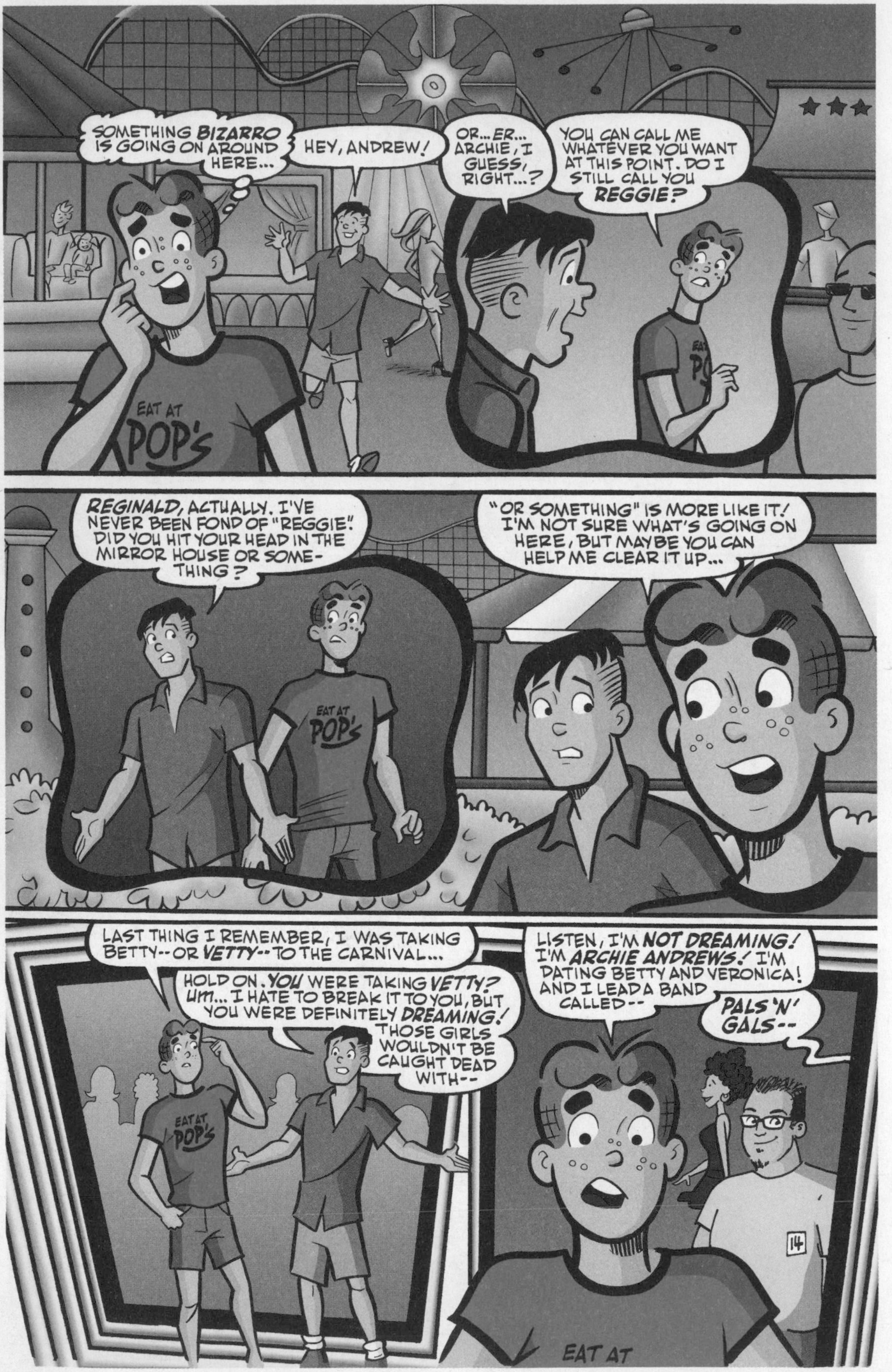
SOMETHING BIZARRO IS GOING ON AROUND HERE...
HEY, ANDREW!
OR... ER... ARCHIE, I GUESS, RIGHT...?
YOU CAN CALL ME WHATEVER YOU WANT AT THIS POINT. DO I STILL CALL YOU REGGIE?
EAT AT POP'S
REGINALD, ACTUALLY. I'VE NEVER BEEN FOND OF "REGGIE". DID YOU HIT YOUR HEAD IN THE MIRROR HOUSE OR SOME-THING?
"OR SOMETHING" IS MORE LIKE IT! I'M NOT SURE WHAT'S GOING ON HERE, BUT MAYBE YOU CAN HELP ME CLEAR IT UP...
LAST THING I REMEMBER, I WAS TAKING BETTY-- OR VETTY-- TO THE CARNIVAL...
HOLD ON. YOU WERE TAKING VETTY? UM... I HATE TO BREAK IT TO YOU, BUT YOU WERE DEFINITELY DREAMING! THOSE GIRLS WOULDN'T BE CAUGHT DEAD WITH--
LISTEN, I'M NOT DREAMING! I'M ARCHIE ANDREWS! I'M DATING BETTY AND VERONICA! AND I LEAD A BAND CALLED--
PALS 'N' GALS--
14
EAT AT

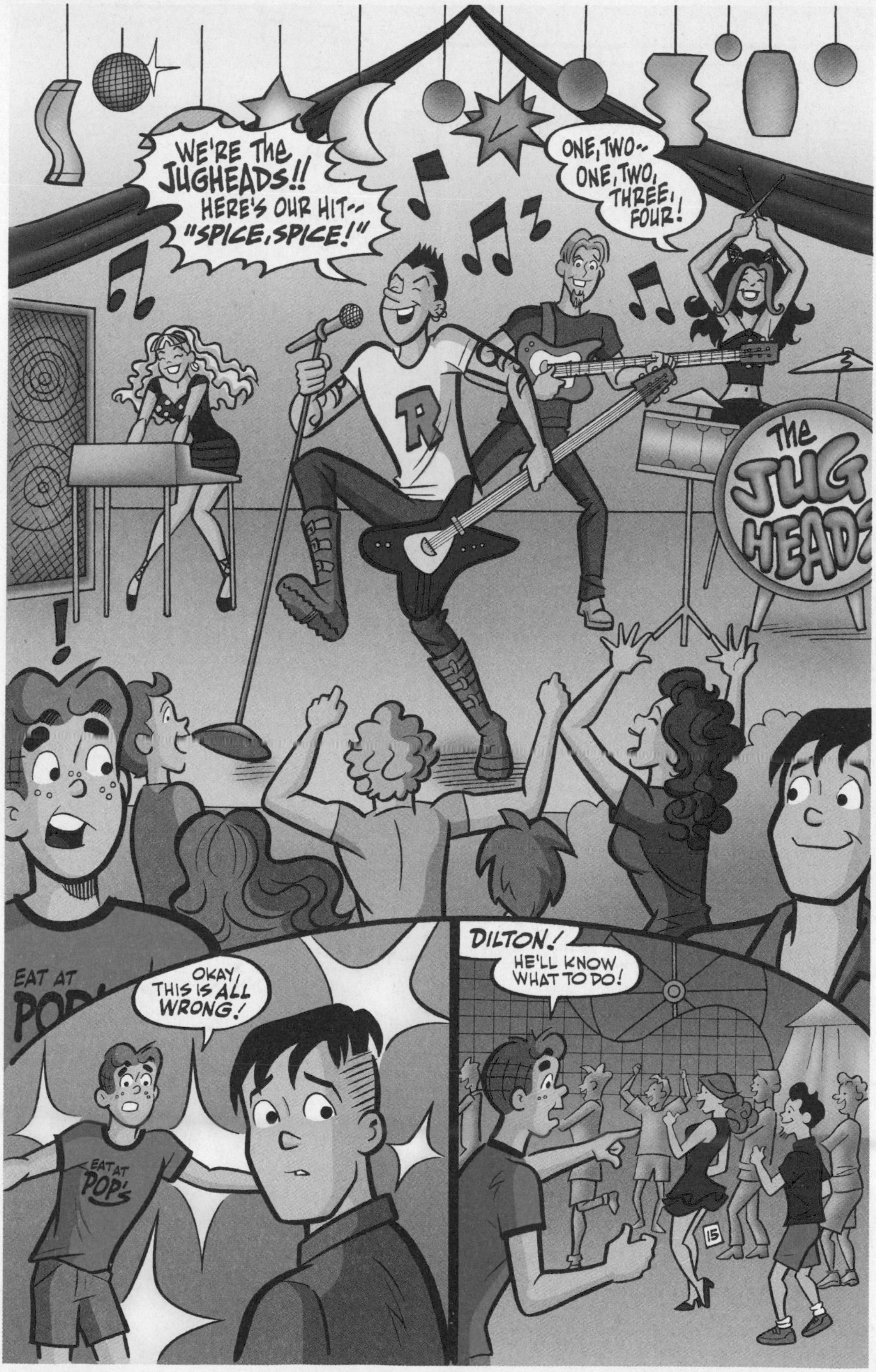
WE'RE THE JUGHEADS!! HERE'S OUR HIT-- "SPICE, SPICE!"
ONE, TWO-- ONE, TWO, THREE! FOUR!
The JUG HEADS
!
EAT AT POP'S
OKAY, THIS IS ALL WRONG!
EAT AT POP'S
DILTON! HE'LL KNOW WHAT TO DO!
15

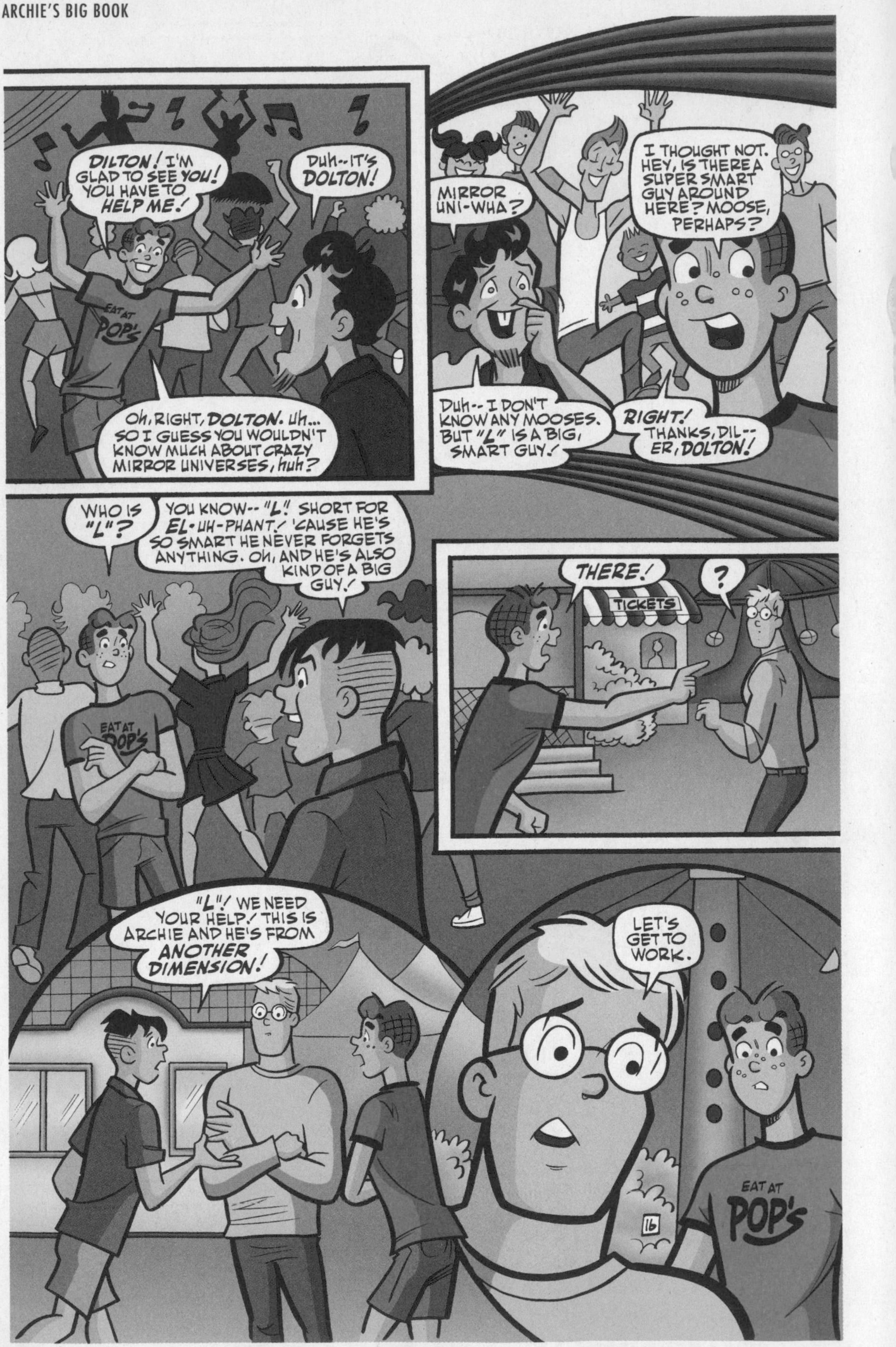
DILTON! I'M GLAD TO SEE YOU! YOU HAVE TO HELP ME!
Duh--IT'S DOLTON!
Oh, RIGHT, DOLTON. uh... SO I GUESS YOU WOULDN'T KNOW MUCH ABOUT CRAZY MIRROR UNIVERSES, huh?
MIRROR UNI-WHA?
I THOUGHT NOT. HEY, IS THERE A SUPER SMART GUY AROUND HERE? MOOSE, PERHAPS?
Duh-- I DON'T KNOW ANY MOOSES. BUT "L" IS A BIG, SMART GUY!
RIGHT! THANKS, DIL-- ER, DOLTON!
WHO IS "L"?
YOU KNOW-- "L"! SHORT FOR EL-uh-PHANT! 'CAUSE HE'S SO SMART HE NEVER FORGETS ANYTHING. Oh, AND HE'S ALSO KIND OF A BIG GUY!
EAT AT POP'S
THERE!
TICKETS
?
"L"! WE NEED YOUR HELP! THIS IS ARCHIE AND HE'S FROM ANOTHER DIMENSION!
LET'S GET TO WORK.
EAT AT POP'S
16

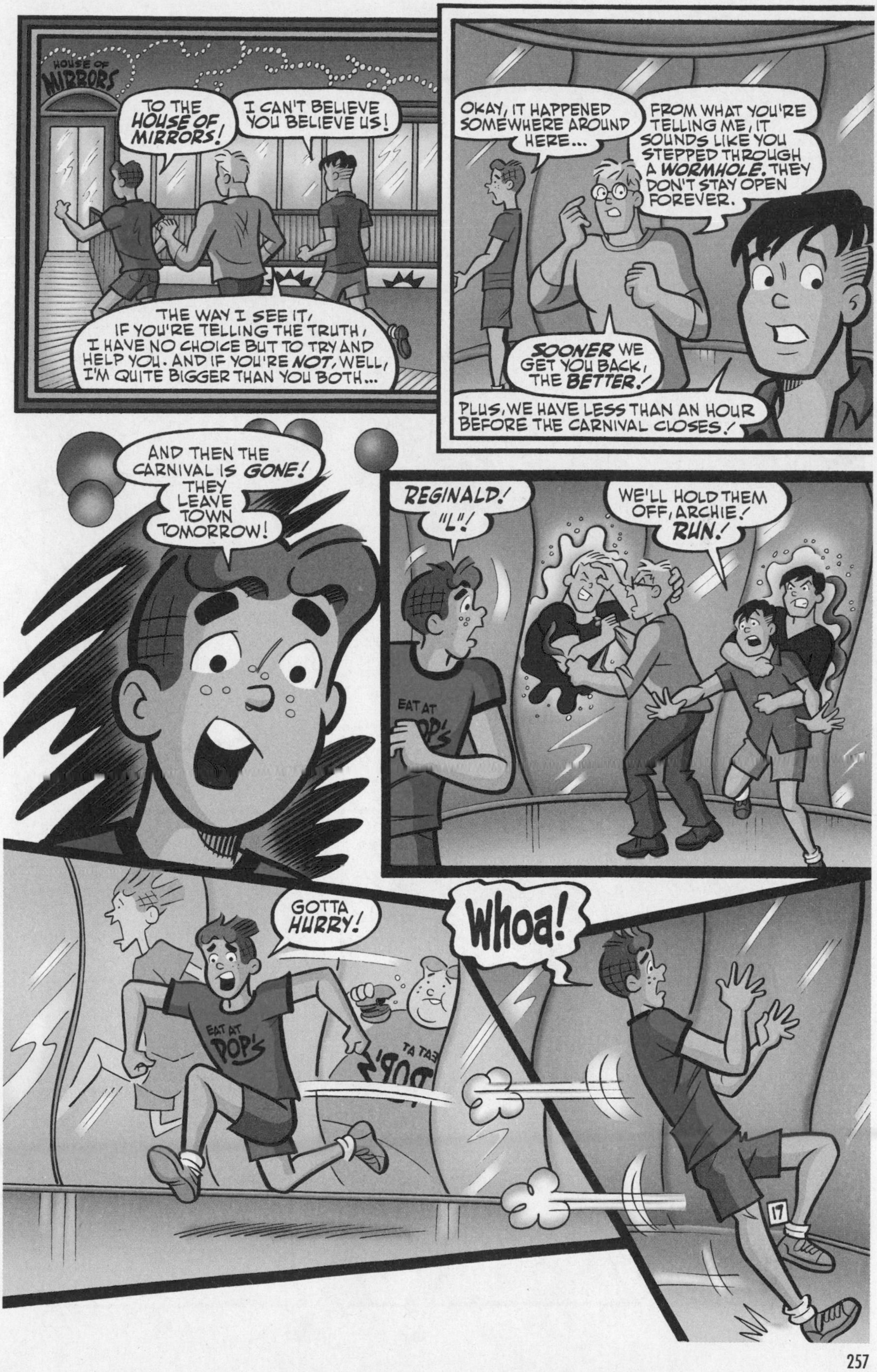
HOUSE OF MIRRORS
TO THE HOUSE OF MIRRORS!
I CAN'T BELIEVE YOU BELIEVE US!
THE WAY I SEE IT, IF YOU'RE TELLING THE TRUTH, I HAVE NO CHOICE BUT TO TRY AND HELP YOU. AND IF YOU'RE NOT, WELL, I'M QUITE BIGGER THAN YOU BOTH...
OKAY, IT HAPPENED SOMEWHERE AROUND HERE...
FROM WHAT YOU'RE TELLING ME, IT SOUNDS LIKE YOU STEPPED THROUGH A WORMHOLE. THEY DON'T STAY OPEN FOREVER.
SOONER WE GET YOU BACK, THE BETTER!
PLUS, WE HAVE LESS THAN AN HOUR BEFORE THE CARNIVAL CLOSES!
AND THEN THE CARNIVAL IS GONE! THEY LEAVE TOWN TOMORROW!
REGINALD! "L"!
WE'LL HOLD THEM OFF, ARCHIE! RUN!
EAT AT POP'S
GOTTA HURRY!
EAT AT POP'S
Whoa!
17

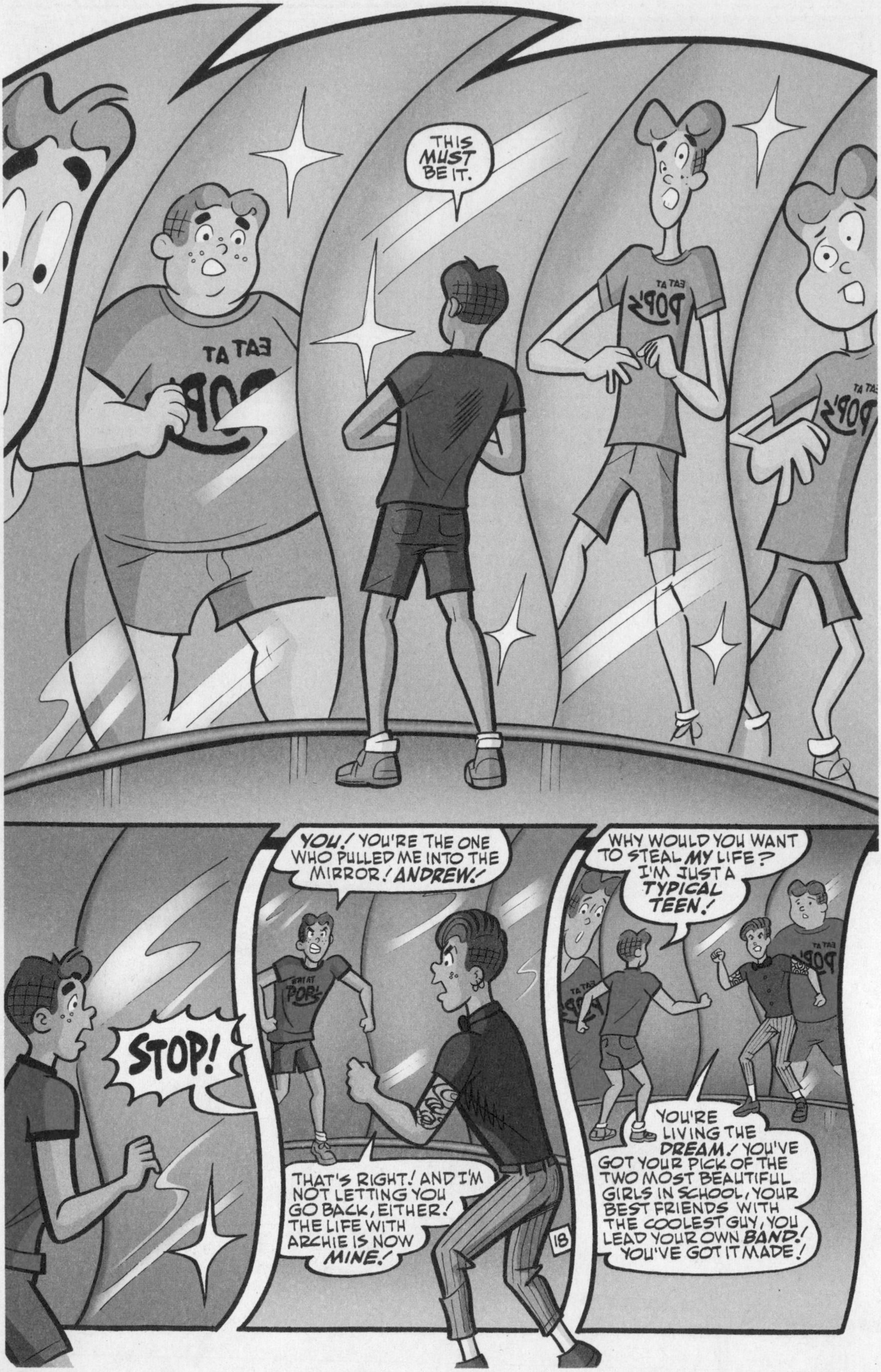
THIS MUST BE IT.
STOP!
YOU! YOU'RE THE ONE WHO PULLED ME INTO THE MIRROR! ANDREW!
THAT'S RIGHT! AND I'M NOT LETTING YOU GO BACK, EITHER! THE LIFE WITH ARCHIE IS NOW MINE!
18
WHY WOULD YOU WANT TO STEAL MY LIFE? I'M JUST A TYPICAL TEEN!
YOU'RE LIVING THE DREAM! YOU'VE GOT YOUR PICK OF THE TWO MOST BEAUTIFUL GIRLS IN SCHOOL, YOUR BEST FRIENDS WITH THE COOLEST GUY, YOU LEAD YOUR OWN BAND! YOU'VE GOT IT MADE!

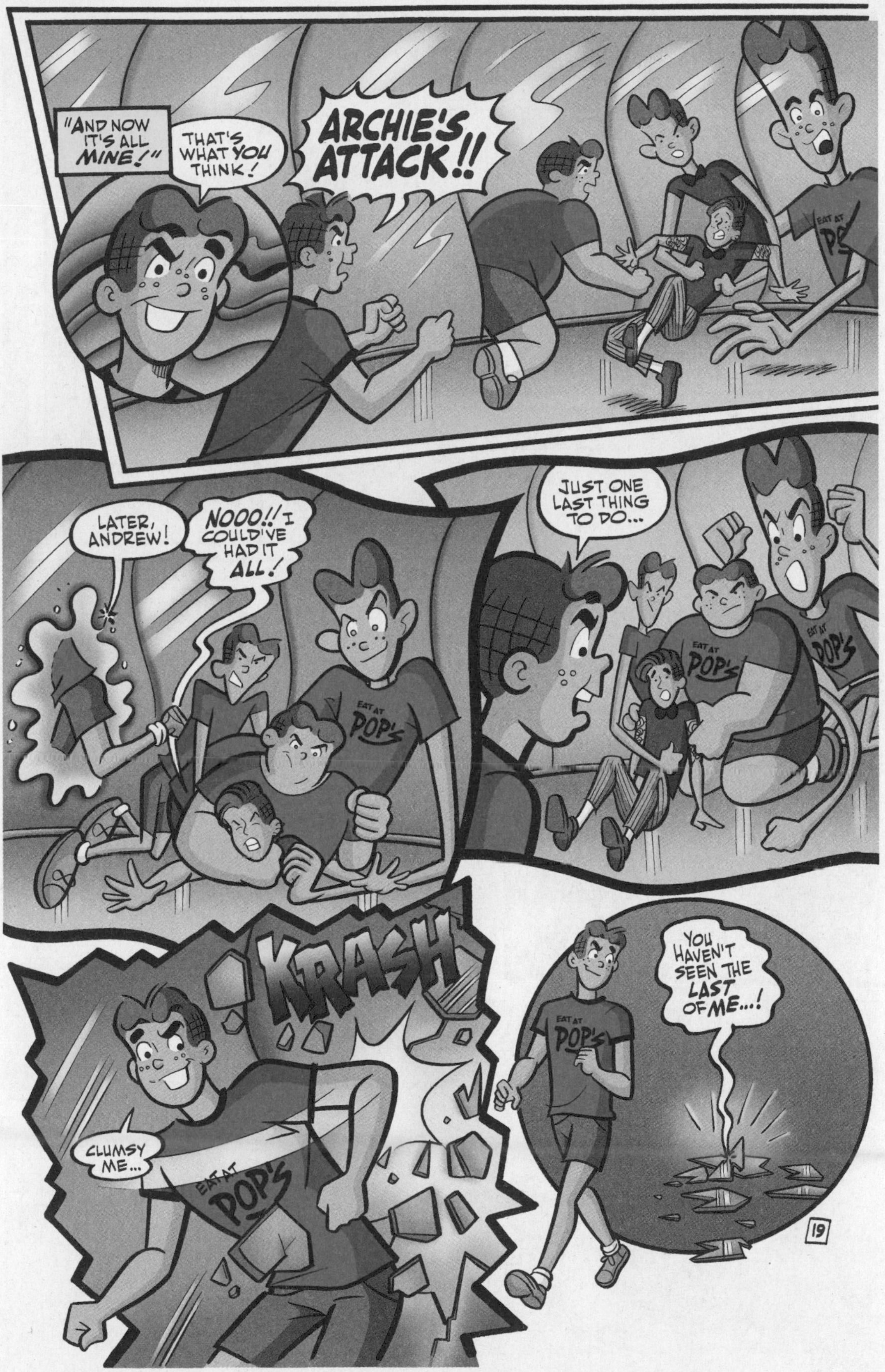
"AND NOW IT'S ALL MINE!"
THAT'S WHAT YOU THINK!
ARCHIE'S ATTACK!!
LATER, ANDREW!
NOOO!! I COULD'VE HAD IT ALL!
JUST ONE LAST THING TO DO...
EAT AT POP'S
KRASH
CLUMSY ME...
YOU HAVEN'T SEEN THE LAST OF ME...!
19

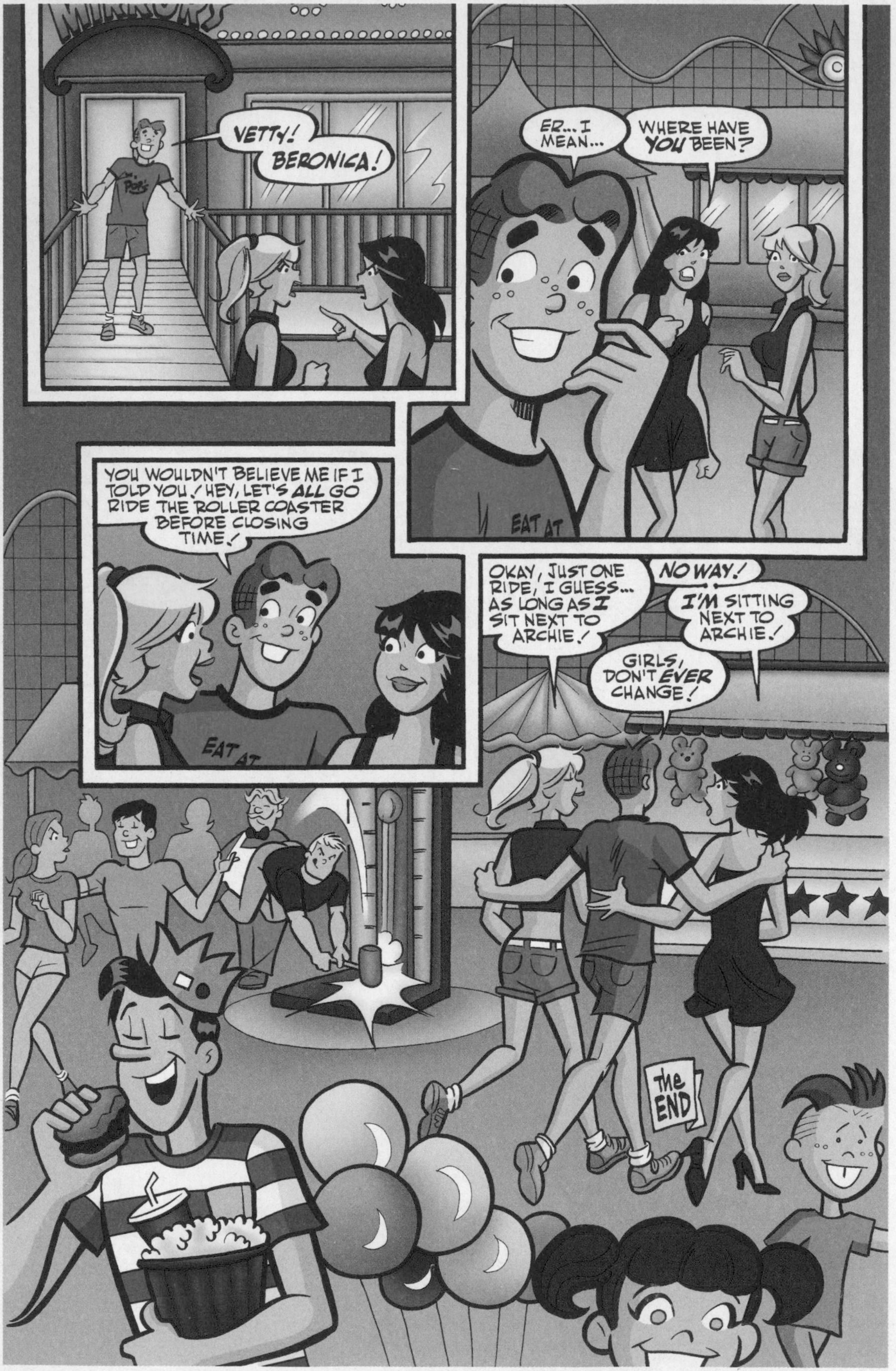
VETTY! BERONICA!
ER... I MEAN...
WHERE HAVE YOU BEEN?
YOU WOULDN'T BELIEVE ME IF I TOLD YOU! HEY, LET'S ALL GO RIDE THE ROLLER COASTER BEFORE CLOSING TIME!
OKAY, JUST ONE RIDE, I GUESS... AS LONG AS I SIT NEXT TO ARCHIE!
NO WAY!
I'M SITTING NEXT TO ARCHIE!
GIRLS, DON'T EVER CHANGE!
THE END

CHAPTER NINE

The Great Switcheroo

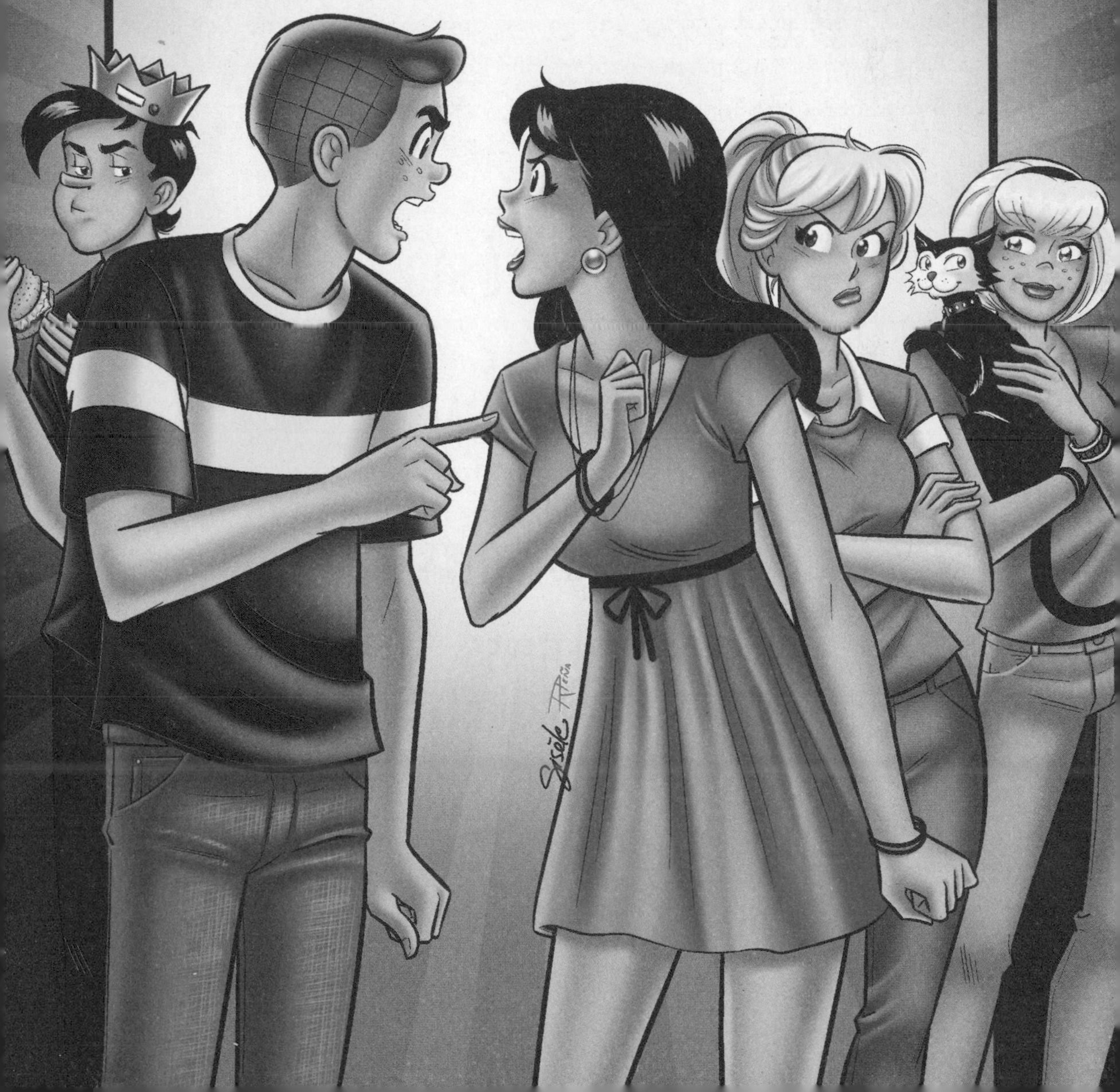

INTRODUCING THE GREAT SWITCHEROO

Originally printed in *Archie #636*

Growing up as a teenage boy can be rough! But not more so than a teen girl, right? Upon overhearing the guys and gals of Riverdale grumbling over how the other half has it easier, Sabrina's mischievous cat Salem turns the town upside down when he dishes out the ultimate gender makeover! Chaos ensues as the teens discover it's not as easy to walk in each other's shoes (or heels!) as they originally thought, so it's up to Sabrina to set things right! Will Salem's spell wear off, thus giving the gang a new appreciation for who they are, or will the switch up become permanent? Find out in this off-the-wall story guest-starring Sabrina the Teenage Witch!

WRITER
TANIA DEL RIO

PENCILS
GISELE LAGACE

INKS
RICH KOSLOWSKI

LETTERS
JACK MORELLI

COLORS
DIGIKORE STUDIOS

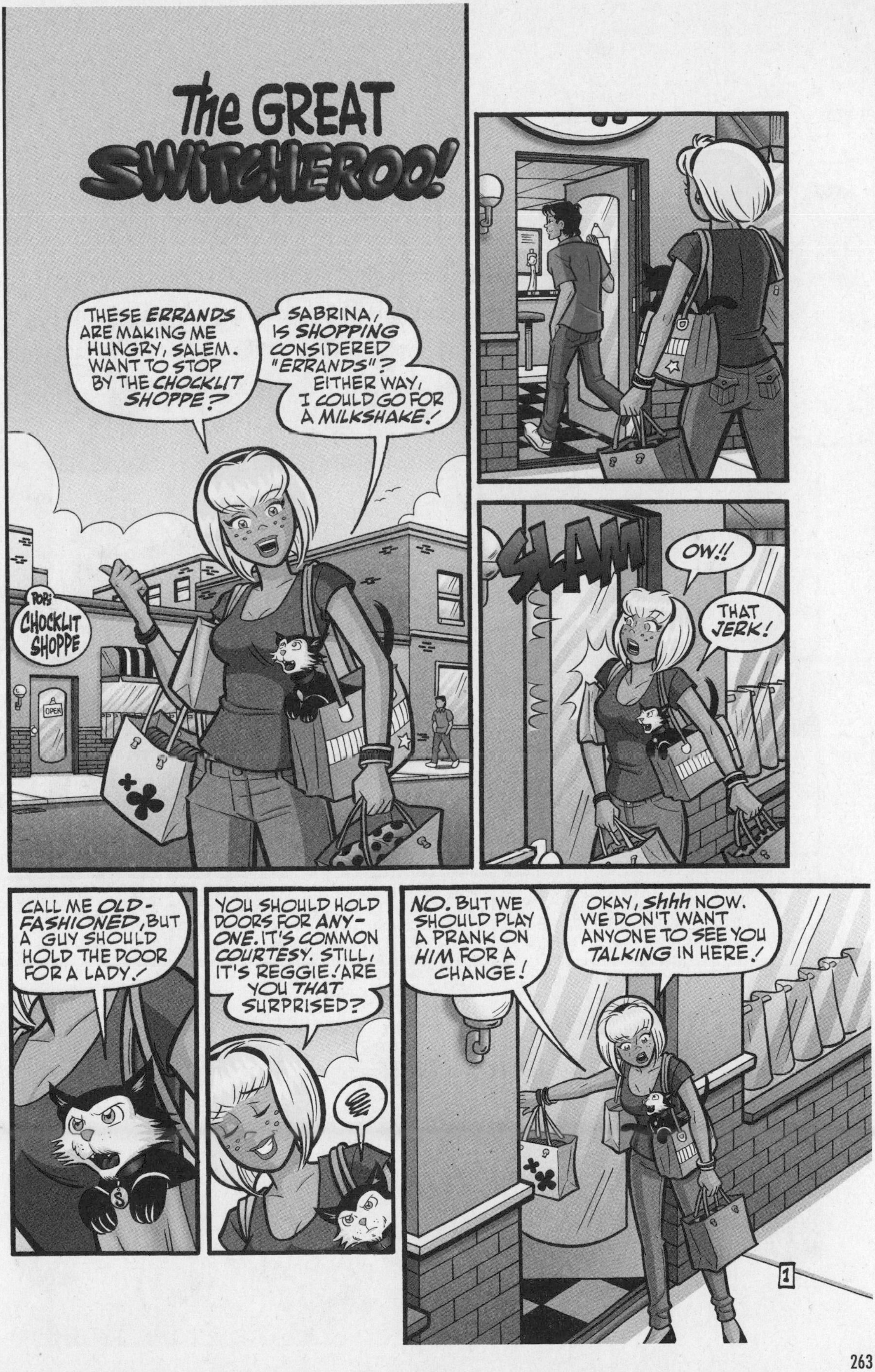
The GREAT SWITCHEROO!
THESE ERRANDS ARE MAKING ME HUNGRY, SALEM. WANT TO STOP BY THE CHOCKLIT SHOPPE?
SABRINA, IS SHOPPING CONSIDERED "ERRANDS"? EITHER WAY, I COULD GO FOR A MILKSHAKE!
POP'S CHOCKLIT SHOPPE
OPEN
SLAM
OW!!
THAT JERK!
CALL ME OLD-FASHIONED, BUT A GUY SHOULD HOLD THE DOOR FOR A LADY!
YOU SHOULD HOLD DOORS FOR ANYONE. IT'S COMMON COURTESY. STILL, IT'S REGGIE! ARE YOU THAT SURPRISED?
NO. BUT WE SHOULD PLAY A PRANK ON HIM FOR A CHANGE!
OKAY, shhh NOW. WE DON'T WANT ANYONE TO SEE YOU TALKING IN HERE!
1

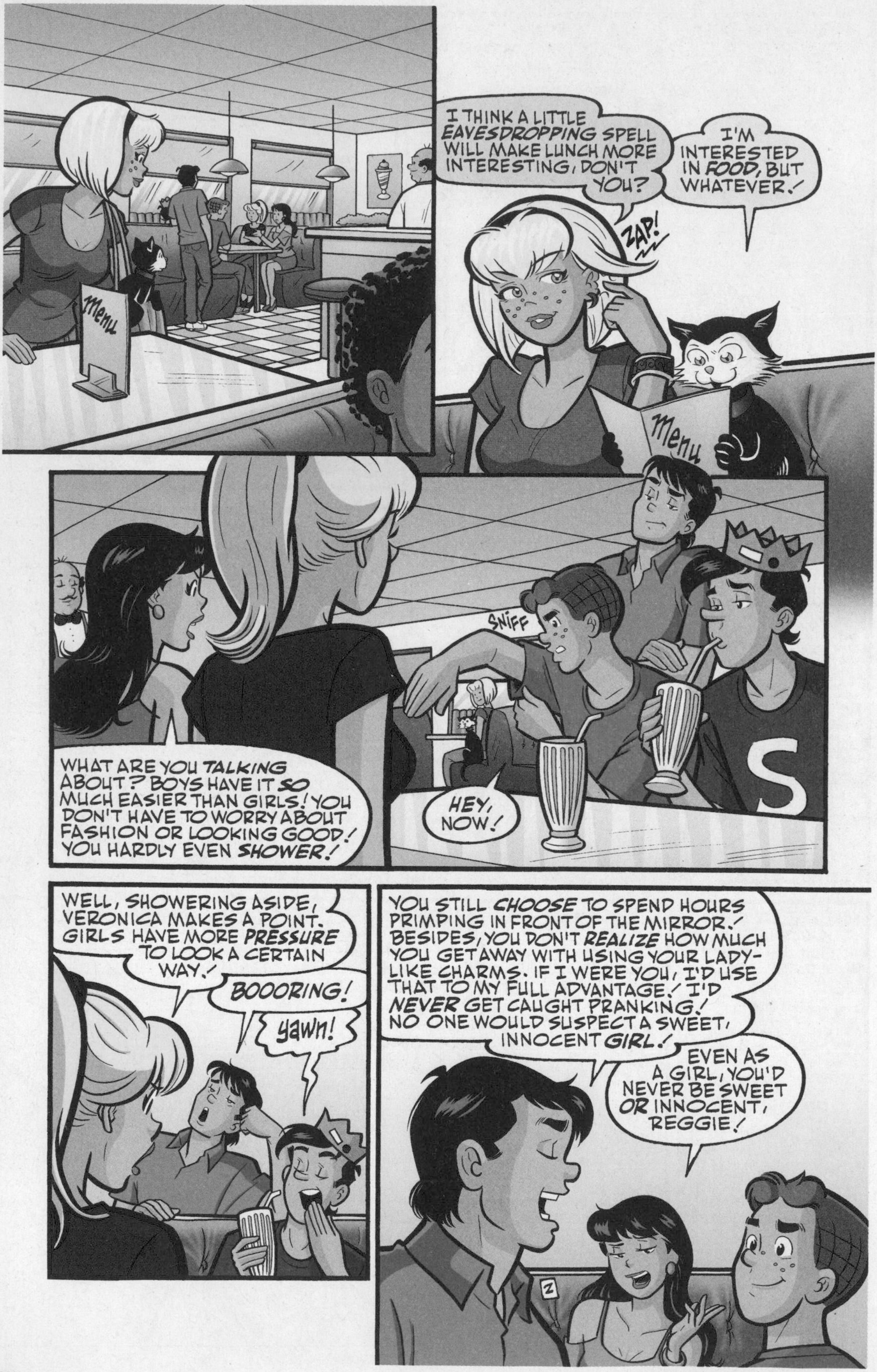

Menu
I THINK A LITTLE EAVESDROPPING SPELL WILL MAKE LUNCH MORE INTERESTING, DON'T YOU?
I'M INTERESTED IN FOOD, BUT WHATEVER.!
ZAP!
Menu
SNIFF
WHAT ARE YOU TALKING ABOUT? BOYS HAVE IT SO MUCH EASIER THAN GIRLS! YOU DON'T HAVE TO WORRY ABOUT FASHION OR LOOKING GOOD! YOU HARDLY EVEN SHOWER!
HEY, NOW!
S
WELL, SHOWERING ASIDE, VERONICA MAKES A POINT. GIRLS HAVE MORE PRESSURE TO LOOK A CERTAIN WAY.!
BOOORING!
yawn!
YOU STILL CHOOSE TO SPEND HOURS PRIMPING IN FRONT OF THE MIRROR.! BESIDES, YOU DON'T REALIZE HOW MUCH YOU GET AWAY WITH USING YOUR LADY-LIKE CHARMS. IF I WERE YOU, I'D USE THAT TO MY FULL ADVANTAGE.! I'D NEVER GET CAUGHT PRANKING! NO ONE WOULD SUSPECT A SWEET, INNOCENT GIRL.!
EVEN AS A GIRL, YOU'D NEVER BE SWEET OR INNOCENT, REGGIE!

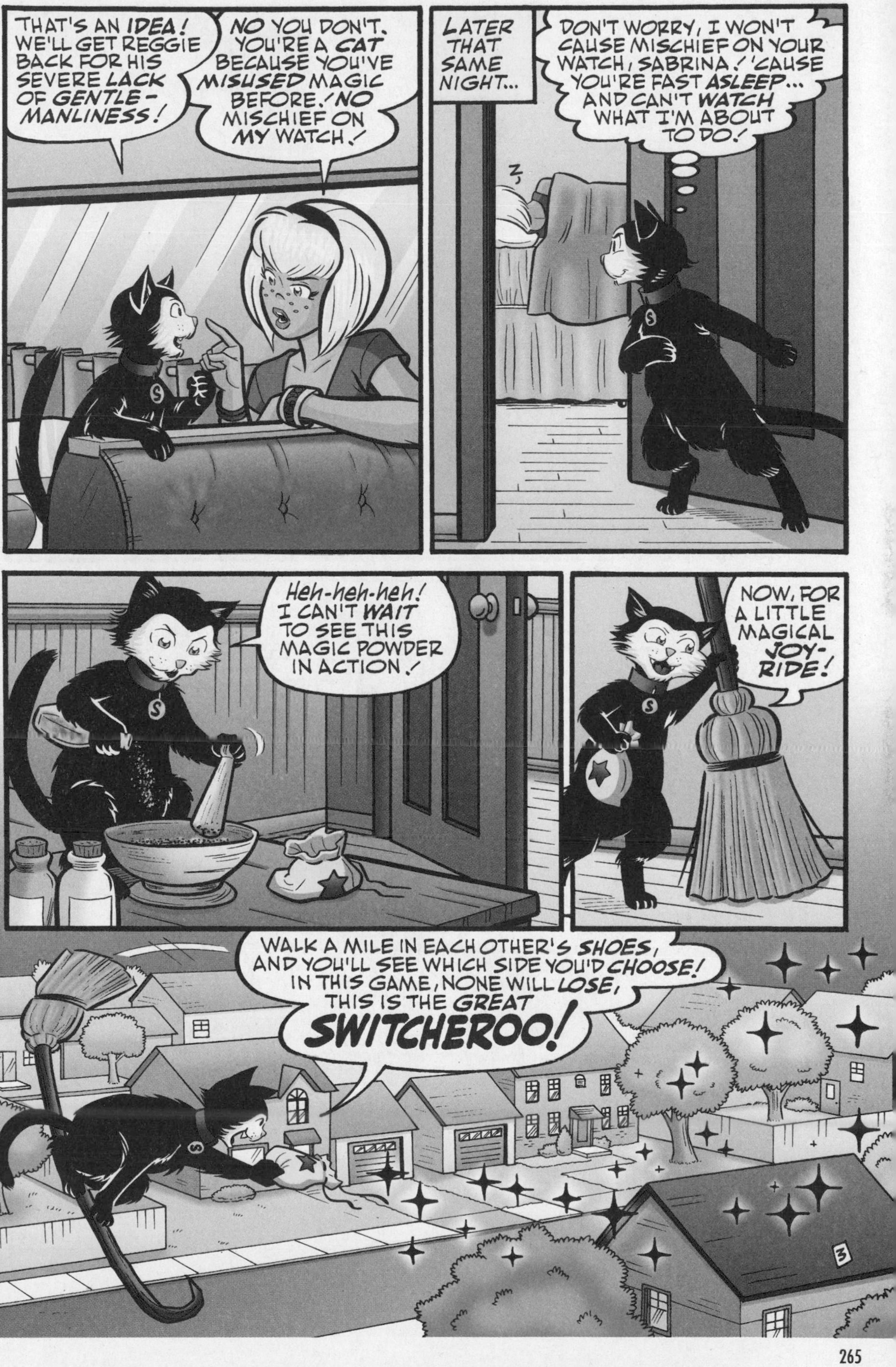
THAT'S AN IDEA! WE'LL GET REGGIE BACK FOR HIS SEVERE LACK OF GENTLE-MANLINESS!
NO YOU DON'T. YOU'RE A CAT BECAUSE YOU'VE MISUSED MAGIC BEFORE.! NO MISCHIEF ON MY WATCH!
LATER THAT SAME NIGHT...
DON'T WORRY, I WON'T CAUSE MISCHIEF ON YOUR WATCH, SABRINA! 'CAUSE YOU'RE FAST ASLEEP... AND CAN'T WATCH WHAT I'M ABOUT TO DO!
Z
Heh-heh-heh! I CAN'T WAIT TO SEE THIS MAGIC POWDER IN ACTION!
NOW, FOR A LITTLE MAGICAL JOY-RIDE!
WALK A MILE IN EACH OTHER'S SHOES, AND YOU'LL SEE WHICH SIDE YOU'D CHOOSE! IN THIS GAME, NONE WILL LOSE, THIS IS THE GREAT SWITCHEROO!
3

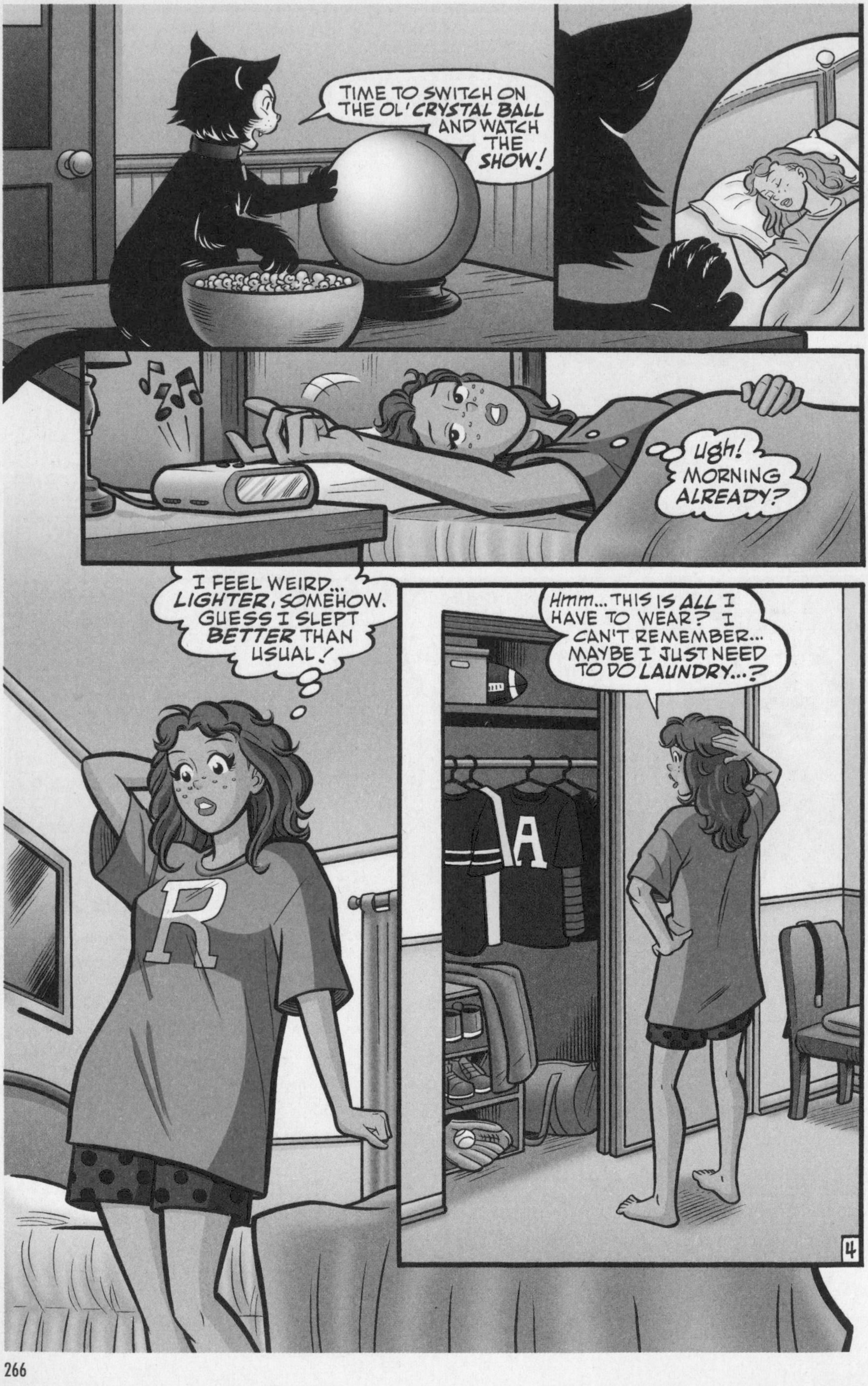
TIME TO SWITCH ON THE OL' CRYSTAL BALL AND WATCH THE SHOW!
Ugh! MORNING ALREADY?
I FEEL WEIRD... LIGHTER, SOMEHOW. GUESS I SLEPT BETTER THAN USUAL!
Hmm... THIS IS ALL I HAVE TO WEAR? I CAN'T REMEMBER... MAYBE I JUST NEED TO DO LAUNDRY...?
A
R
4

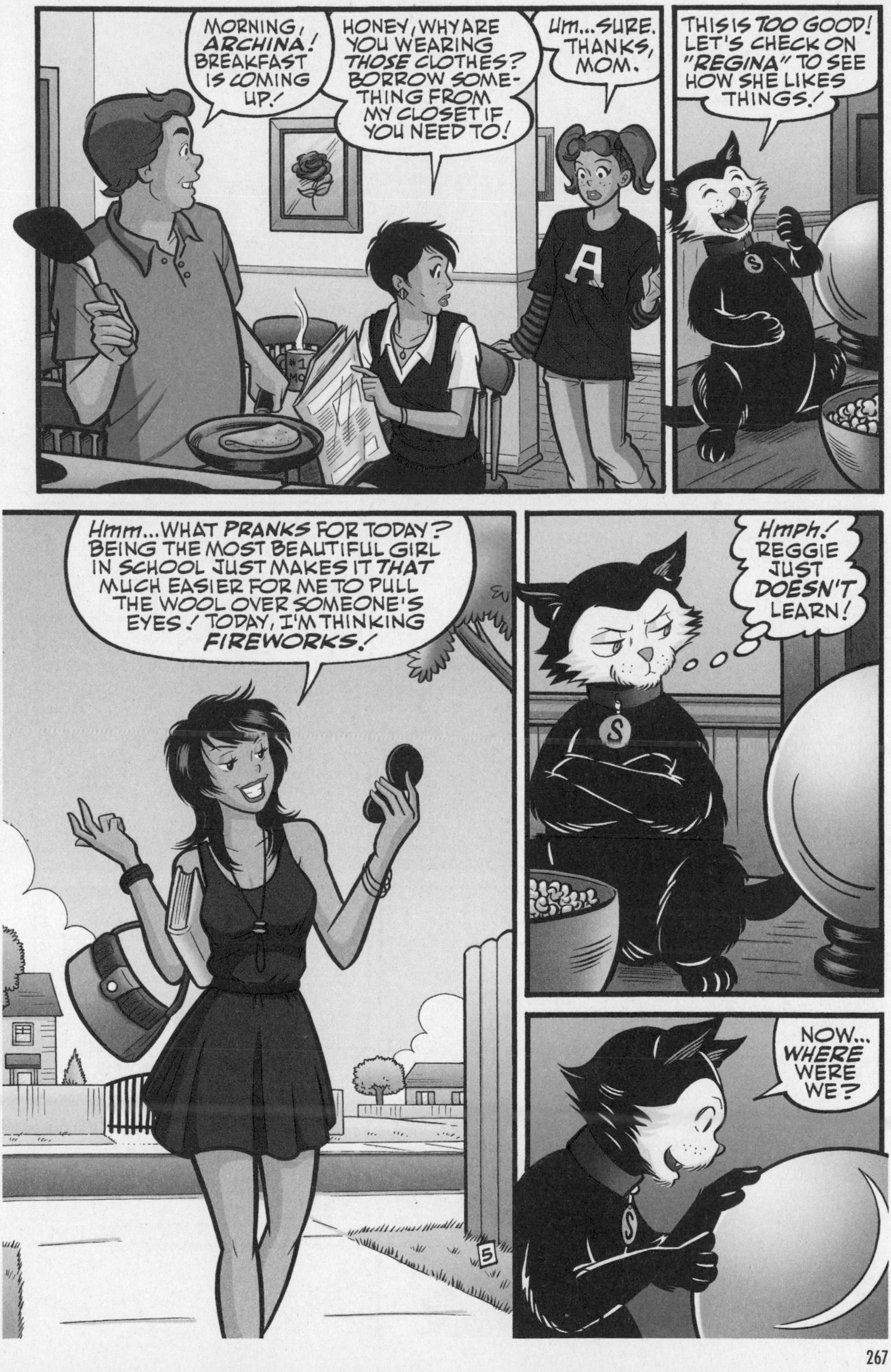
MORNING, ARCHINA! BREAKFAST IS COMING UP!
HONEY, WHY ARE YOU WEARING THOSE CLOTHES? BORROW SOMETHING FROM MY CLOSET IF YOU NEED TO!
Um... SURE. THANKS, MOM.
THIS IS TOO GOOD! LET'S CHECK ON "REGINA" TO SEE HOW SHE LIKES THINGS!
Hmm... WHAT PRANKS FOR TODAY? BEING THE MOST BEAUTIFUL GIRL IN SCHOOL JUST MAKES IT THAT MUCH EASIER FOR ME TO PULL THE WOOL OVER SOMEONE'S EYES! TODAY, I'M THINKING FIREWORKS!
Hmph! REGGIE JUST DOESN'T LEARN!
NOW... WHERE WERE WE?
5

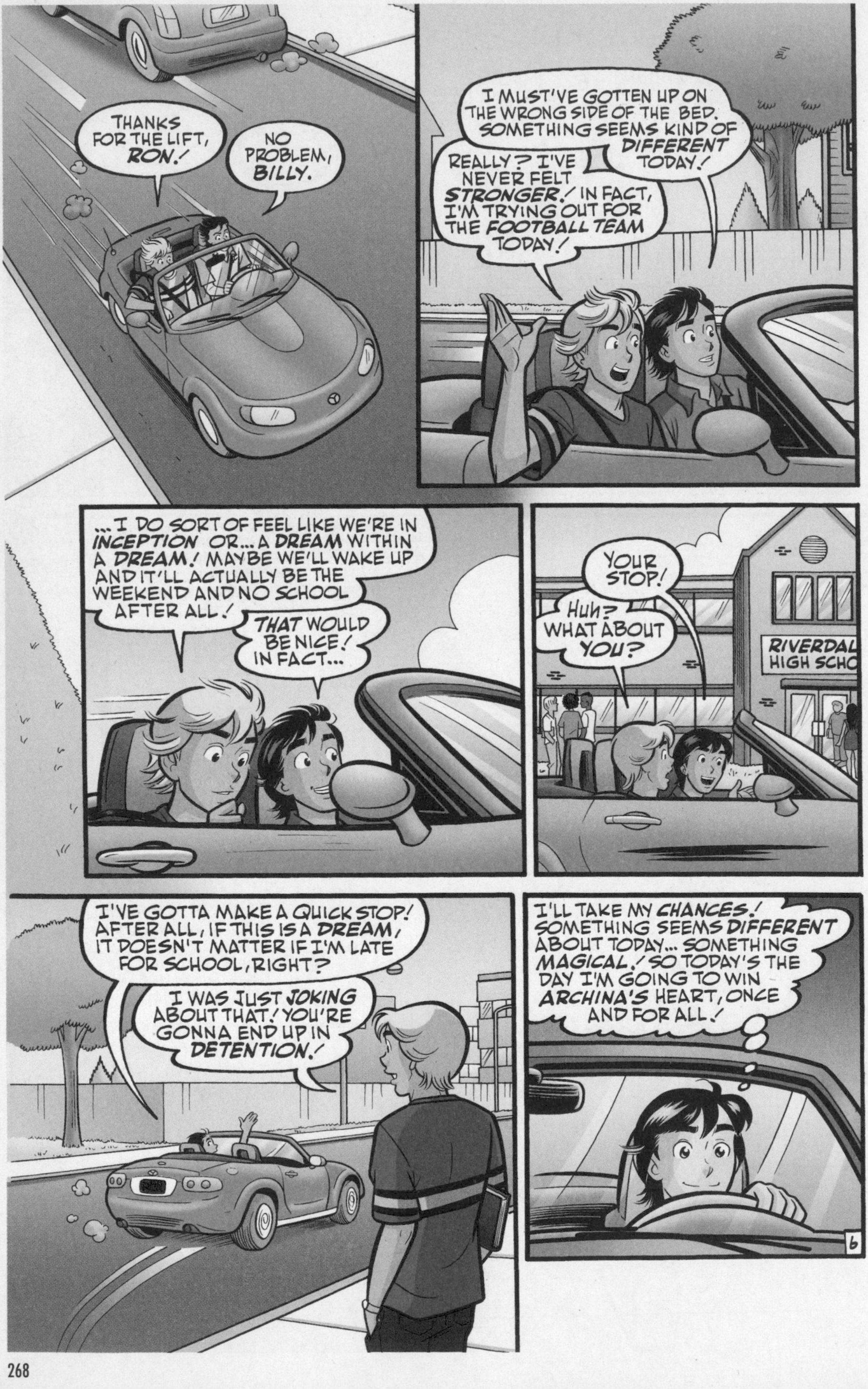
THANKS FOR THE LIFT, RON!
NO PROBLEM, BILLY.
I MUST'VE GOTTEN UP ON THE WRONG SIDE OF THE BED. SOMETHING SEEMS KIND OF DIFFERENT TODAY!
REALLY? I'VE NEVER FELT STRONGER! IN FACT, I'M TRYING OUT FOR THE FOOTBALL TEAM TODAY!
...I DO SORT OF FEEL LIKE WE'RE IN INCEPTION OR... A DREAM WITHIN A DREAM! MAYBE WE'LL WAKE UP AND IT'LL ACTUALLY BE THE WEEKEND AND NO SCHOOL AFTER ALL!
THAT WOULD BE NICE! IN FACT...
YOUR STOP!
HUH? WHAT ABOUT YOU?
RIVERDAL
HIGH SCHO
I'VE GOTTA MAKE A QUICK STOP! AFTER ALL, IF THIS IS A DREAM, IT DOESN'T MATTER IF I'M LATE FOR SCHOOL, RIGHT?
I WAS JUST JOKING ABOUT THAT! YOU'RE GONNA END UP IN DETENTION!
I'LL TAKE MY CHANCES! SOMETHING SEEMS DIFFERENT ABOUT TODAY... SOMETHING MAGICAL! SO TODAY'S THE DAY I'M GOING TO WIN ARCHINA'S HEART, ONCE AND FOR ALL!
6

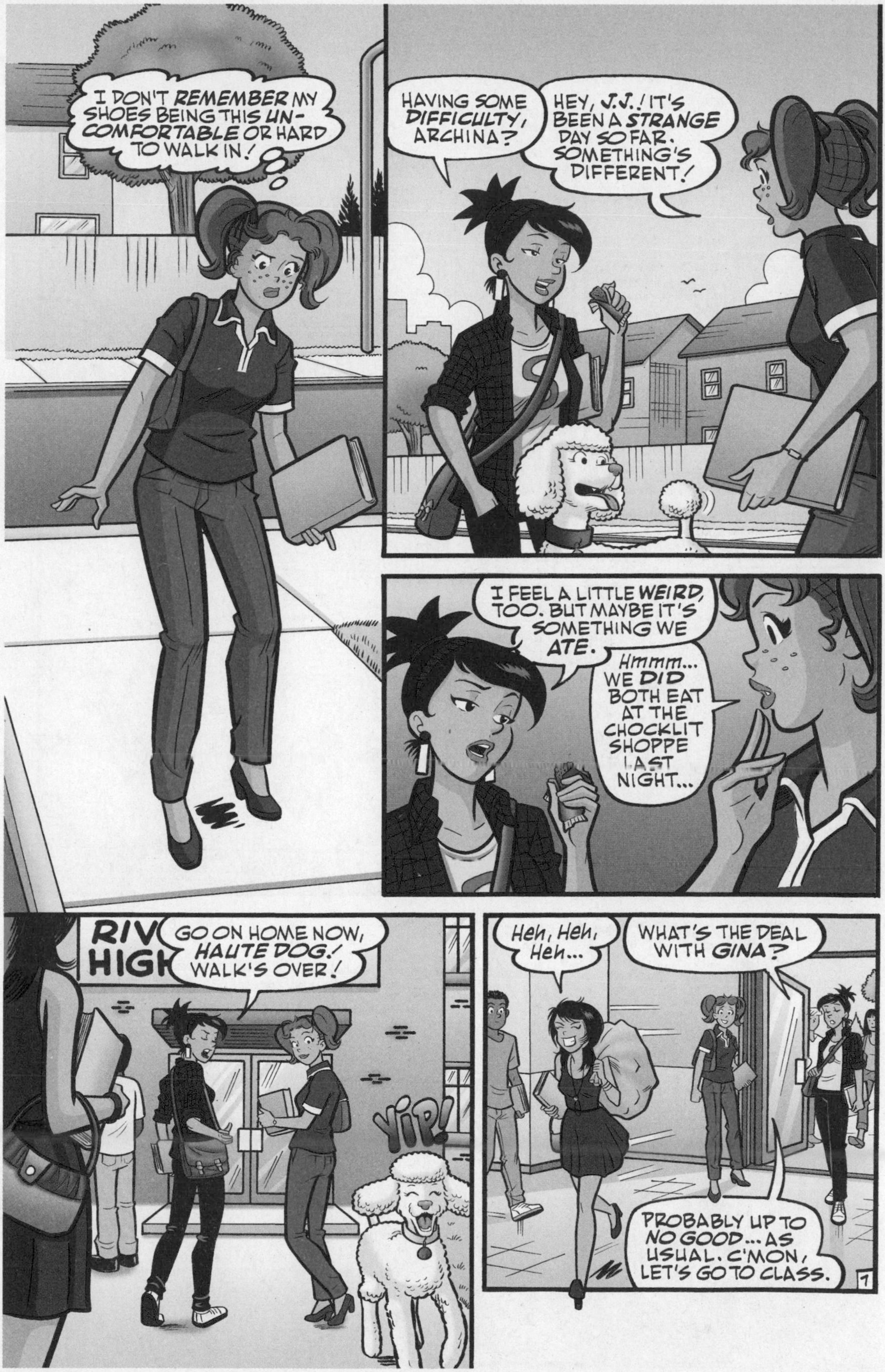
I DON'T REMEMBER MY SHOES BEING THIS UN-COMFORTABLE OR HARD TO WALK IN!
HAVING SOME DIFFICULTY, ARCHINA?
HEY, J.J.! IT'S BEEN A STRANGE DAY SO FAR. SOMETHING'S DIFFERENT!
I FEEL A LITTLE WEIRD, TOO. BUT MAYBE IT'S SOMETHING WE ATE.
Hmmm... WE DID BOTH EAT AT THE CHOCKLIT SHOPPE LAST NIGHT...
RIV
HIGH
GO ON HOME NOW, HAUTE DOG! WALK'S OVER!
YIP!
Heh, Heh, Heh...
WHAT'S THE DEAL WITH GINA?
PROBABLY UP TO NO GOOD... AS USUAL. C'MON, LET'S GO TO CLASS.
7

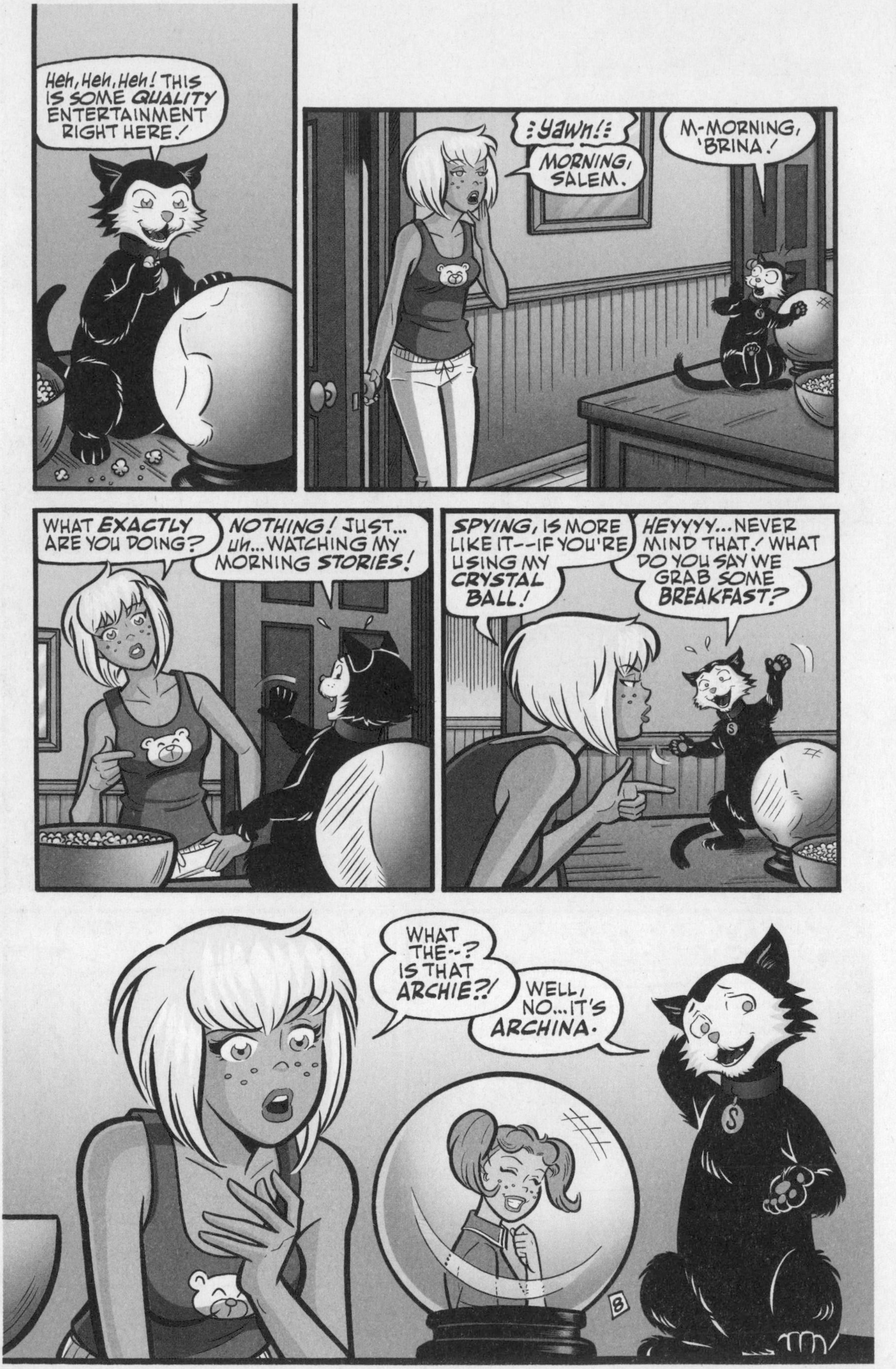
Heh, Heh, Heh! THIS IS SOME QUALITY ENTERTAINMENT RIGHT HERE!
:YAWN!:
MORNING, SALEM.
M-MORNING, 'BRINA!
WHAT EXACTLY ARE YOU DOING?
NOTHING! JUST... uh... WATCHING MY MORNING STORIES!
SPYING, IS MORE LIKE IT--IF YOU'RE USING MY CRYSTAL BALL!
HEYYYY... NEVER MIND THAT! WHAT DO YOU SAY WE GRAB SOME BREAKFAST?
WHAT THE--? IS THAT ARCHIE?!
WELL, NO... IT'S ARCHINA.
8

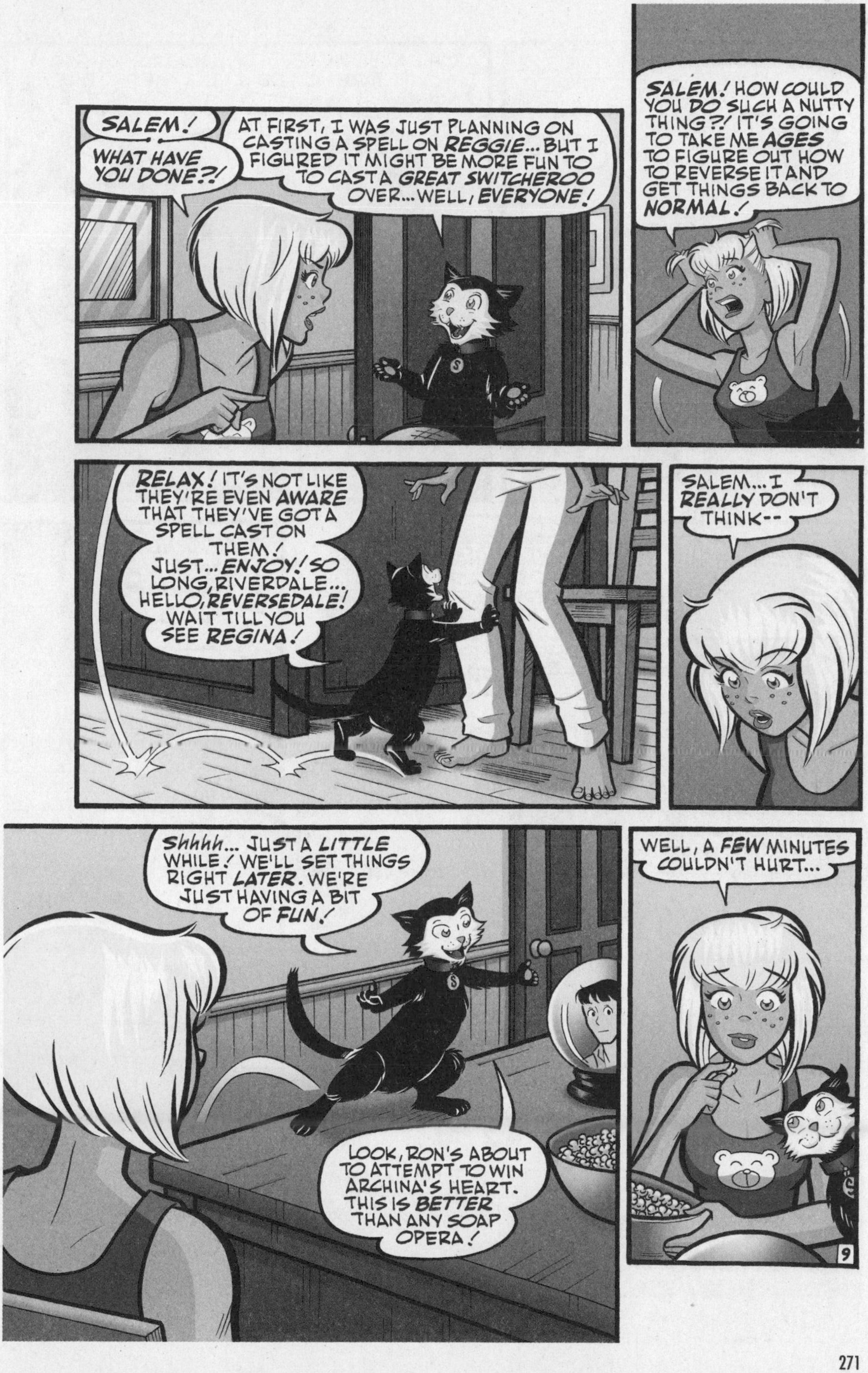
SALEM! WHAT HAVE YOU DONE?!
AT FIRST, I WAS JUST PLANNING ON CASTING A SPELL ON REGGIE... BUT I FIGURED IT MIGHT BE MORE FUN TO TO CAST A GREAT SWITCHEROO OVER... WELL, EVERYONE!
SALEM! HOW COULD YOU DO SUCH A NUTTY THING?! IT'S GOING TO TAKE ME AGES TO FIGURE OUT HOW TO REVERSE IT AND GET THINGS BACK TO NORMAL!
RELAX! IT'S NOT LIKE THEY'RE EVEN AWARE THAT THEY'VE GOT A SPELL CAST ON THEM! JUST... ENJOY! SO LONG, RIVERDALE... HELLO, REVERSEDALE! WAIT TILL YOU SEE REGINA!
SALEM... I REALLY DON'T THINK--
Shhhh... JUST A LITTLE WHILE! WE'LL SET THINGS RIGHT LATER. WE'RE JUST HAVING A BIT OF FUN!
LOOK, RON'S ABOUT TO ATTEMPT TO WIN ARCHINA'S HEART. THIS IS BETTER THAN ANY SOAP OPERA!
WELL, A FEW MINUTES COULDN'T HURT...
9

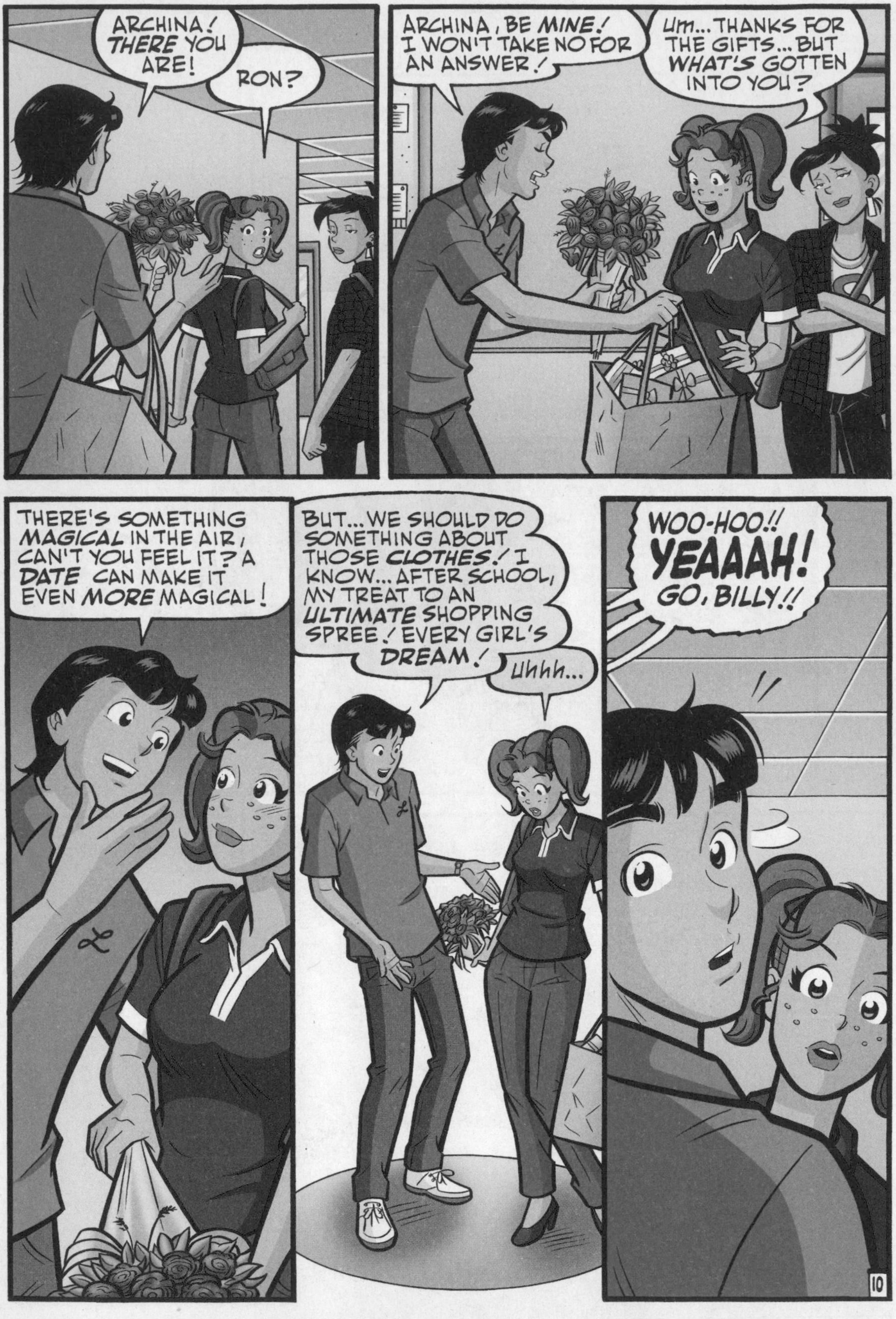
ARCHINA! THERE YOU ARE!
RON?
ARCHINA, BE MINE! I WON'T TAKE NO FOR AN ANSWER!
UM... THANKS FOR THE GIFTS... BUT WHAT'S GOTTEN INTO YOU?
THERE'S SOMETHING MAGICAL IN THE AIR, CAN'T YOU FEEL IT? A DATE CAN MAKE IT EVEN MORE MAGICAL!
BUT... WE SHOULD DO SOMETHING ABOUT THOSE CLOTHES! I KNOW... AFTER SCHOOL, MY TREAT TO AN ULTIMATE SHOPPING SPREE! EVERY GIRL'S DREAM!
UHHH...
WOO-HOO!! YEAAAH! GO, BILLY!!
10

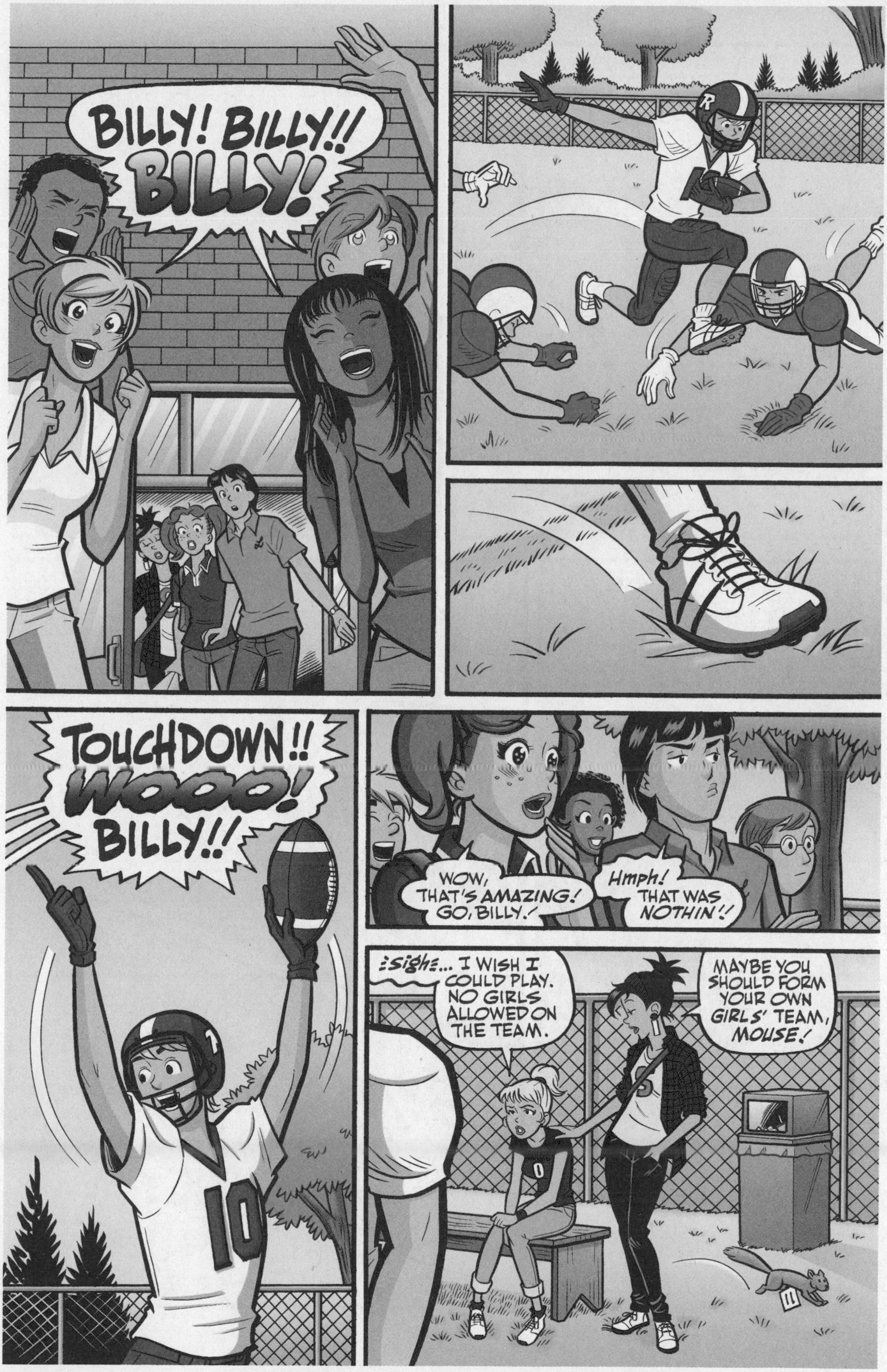
BILLY! BILLY!! BILLY!
TOUCHDOWN!! WOOO! BILLY!!
WOW, THAT'S AMAZING! GO, BILLY!
Hmph! THAT WAS NOTHIN'!
:sigh:... I WISH I COULD PLAY. NO GIRLS ALLOWED ON THE TEAM.
MAYBE YOU SHOULD FORM YOUR OWN GIRLS' TEAM, MOUSE!

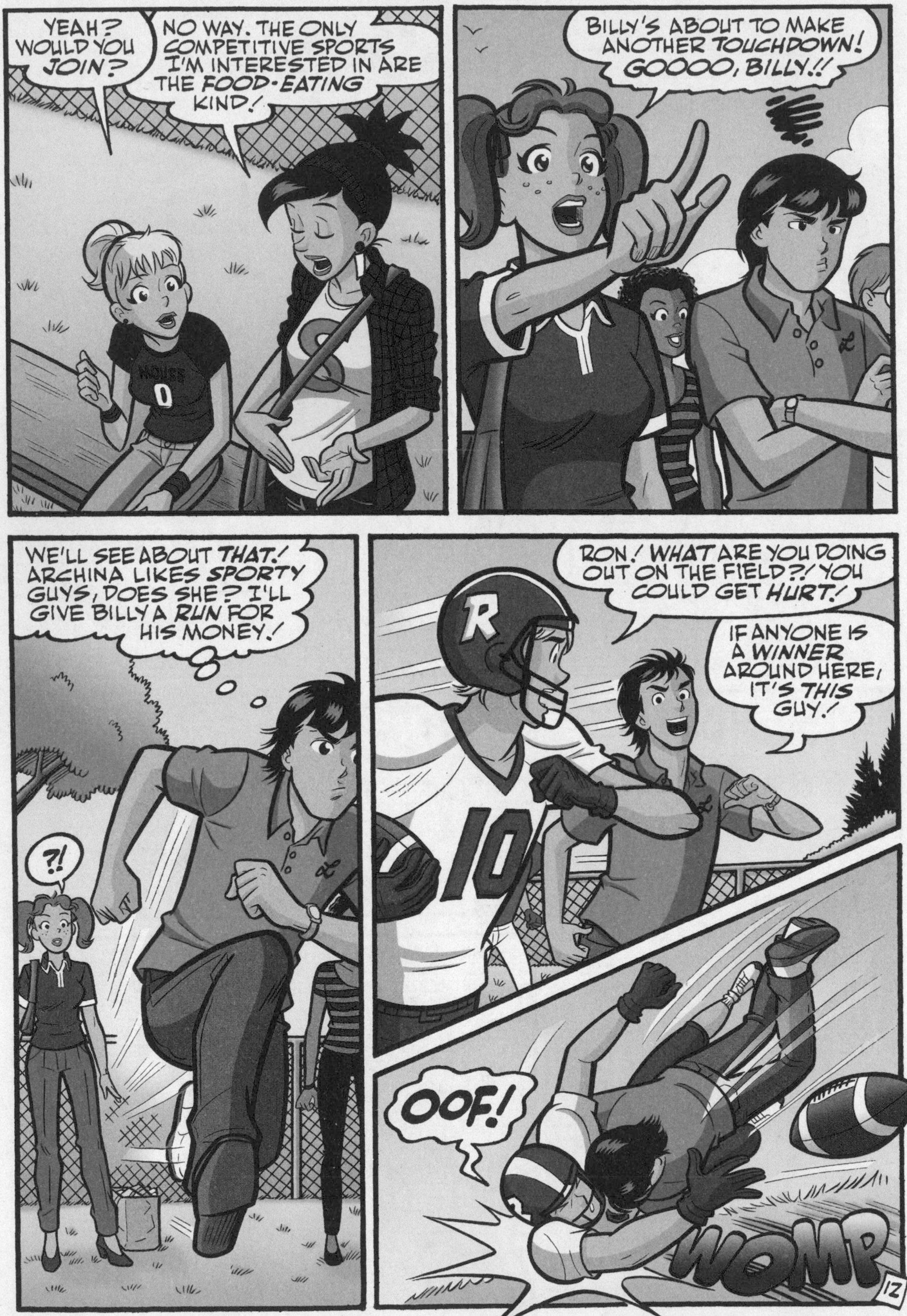
YEAH? WOULD YOU JOIN?
NO WAY. THE ONLY COMPETITIVE SPORTS I'M INTERESTED IN ARE THE FOOD-EATING KIND!
BILLY'S ABOUT TO MAKE ANOTHER TOUCHDOWN! GOOOO, BILLY!!
WE'LL SEE ABOUT THAT! ARCHINA LIKES SPORTY GUYS, DOES SHE? I'LL GIVE BILLY A RUN FOR HIS MONEY!
?!
RON! WHAT ARE YOU DOING OUT ON THE FIELD?! YOU COULD GET HURT!
IF ANYONE IS A WINNER AROUND HERE, IT'S THIS GUY!
OOF!
WOMP
12

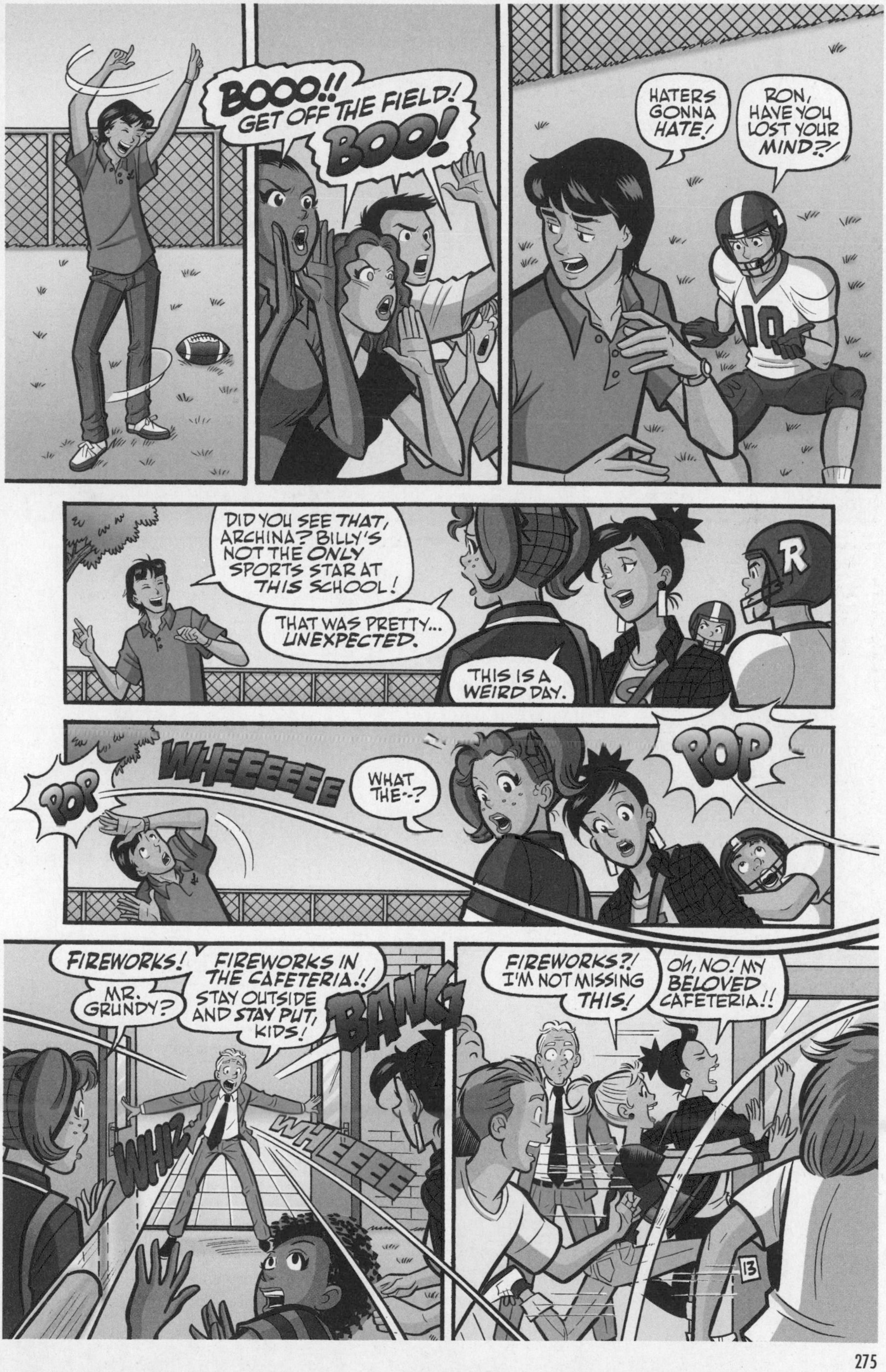
BOOO!! GET OFF THE FIELD! BOO!
HATERS GONNA HATE!
RON, HAVE YOU LOST YOUR MIND?!
DID YOU SEE THAT, ARCHINA? BILLY'S NOT THE ONLY SPORTS STAR AT THIS SCHOOL!
THAT WAS PRETTY... UNEXPECTED.
THIS IS A WEIRD DAY.
POP
WHEEEEEE
WHAT THE--?
POP
FIREWORKS!
MR. GRUNDY?
FIREWORKS IN THE CAFETERIA!! STAY OUTSIDE AND STAY PUT, KIDS!
BANG
WHIZ
WHEEEE
FIREWORKS?! I'M NOT MISSING THIS!
OH, NO! MY BELOVED CAFETERIA!!
13

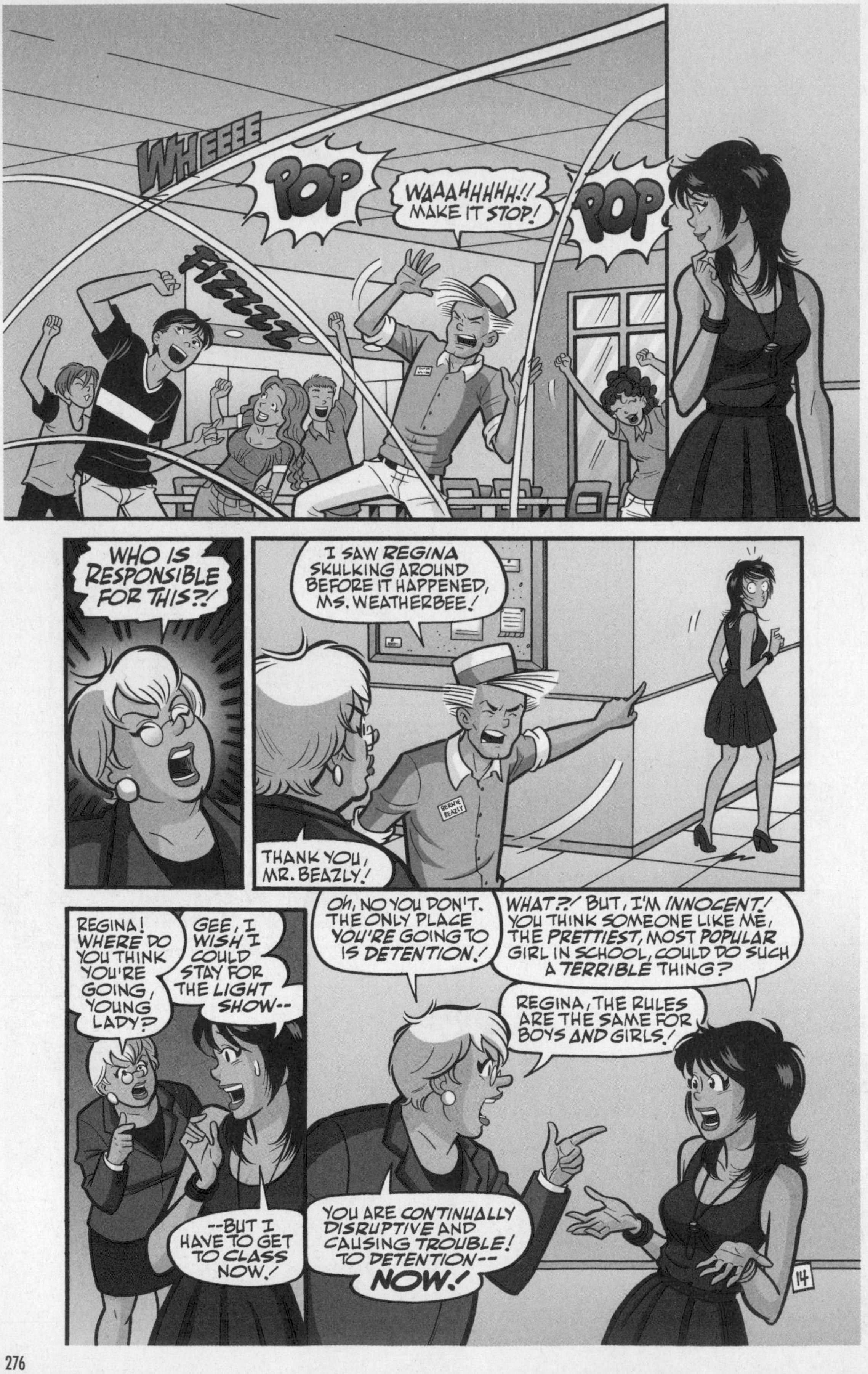
WHEEEE
POP
WAAAHHHHH!! MAKE IT STOP!
POP
FIZZZZZ
WHO IS RESPONSIBLE FOR THIS?!
I SAW REGINA SKULKING AROUND BEFORE IT HAPPENED, MS. WEATHERBEE!
THANK YOU, MR. BEAZLY!
REGINA! WHERE DO YOU THINK YOU'RE GOING, YOUNG LADY?
GEE, I WISH I COULD STAY FOR THE LIGHT SHOW--
--BUT I HAVE TO GET TO CLASS NOW!
OH, NO YOU DON'T. THE ONLY PLACE YOU'RE GOING TO IS DETENTION!
WHAT?! BUT, I'M INNOCENT! YOU THINK SOMEONE LIKE ME, THE PRETTIEST, MOST POPULAR GIRL IN SCHOOL, COULD DO SUCH A TERRIBLE THING?
REGINA, THE RULES ARE THE SAME FOR BOYS AND GIRLS!
YOU ARE CONTINUALLY DISRUPTIVE AND CAUSING TROUBLE! TO DETENTION-- NOW!
14

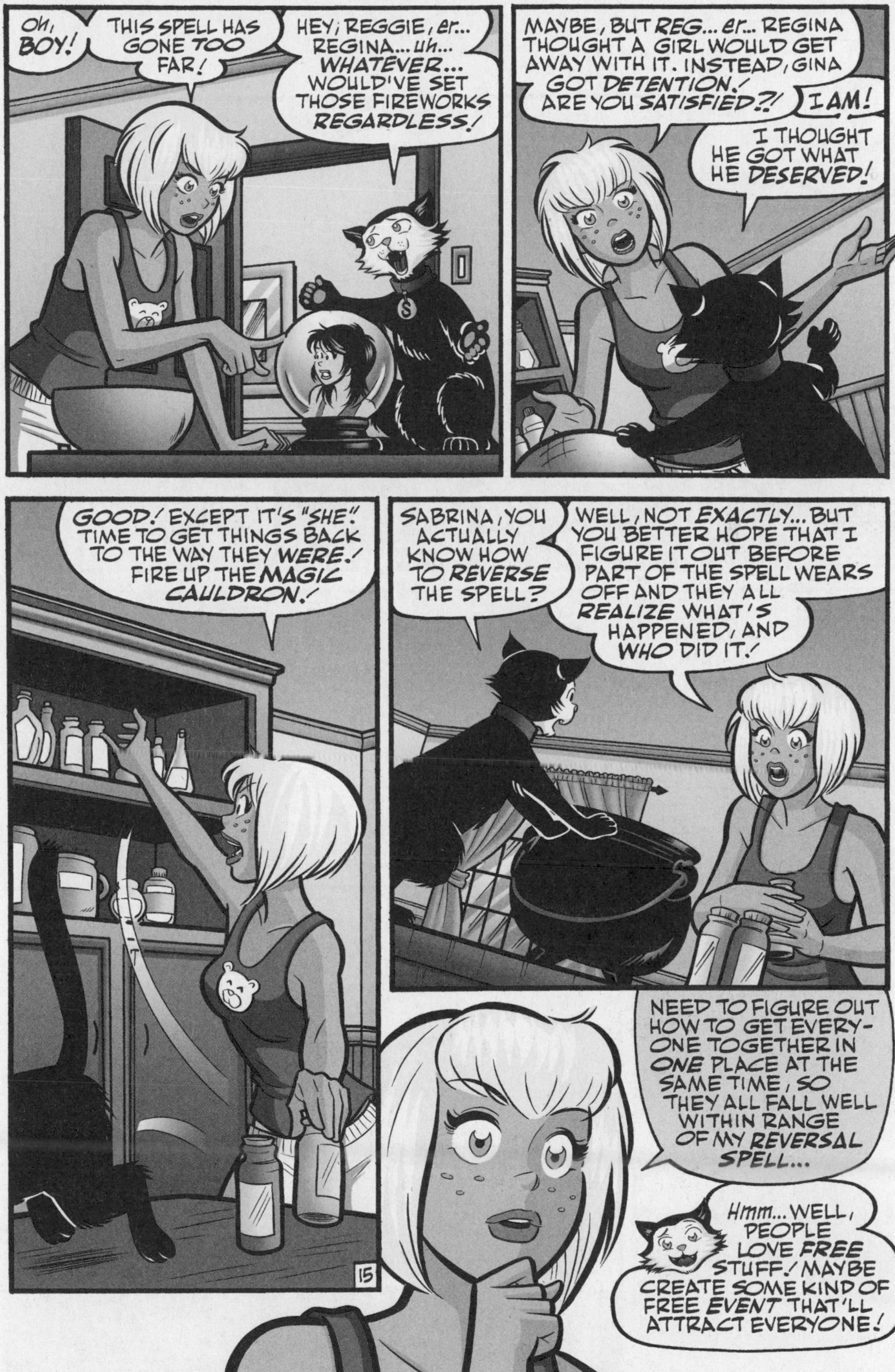
OH, BOY!
THIS SPELL HAS GONE TOO FAR!
HEY, REGGIE, er... REGINA... uh... WHATEVER... WOULD'VE SET THOSE FIREWORKS REGARDLESS!
MAYBE, BUT REG... er... REGINA THOUGHT A GIRL WOULD GET AWAY WITH IT. INSTEAD, GINA GOT DETENTION! ARE YOU SATISFIED?!
I AM!
I THOUGHT HE GOT WHAT HE DESERVED!
GOOD! EXCEPT IT'S "SHE"! TIME TO GET THINGS BACK TO THE WAY THEY WERE! FIRE UP THE MAGIC CAULDRON!
15
SABRINA, YOU ACTUALLY KNOW HOW TO REVERSE THE SPELL?
WELL, NOT EXACTLY... BUT YOU BETTER HOPE THAT I FIGURE IT OUT BEFORE PART OF THE SPELL WEARS OFF AND THEY ALL REALIZE WHAT'S HAPPENED, AND WHO DID IT!
NEED TO FIGURE OUT HOW TO GET EVERY-ONE TOGETHER IN ONE PLACE AT THE SAME TIME, SO THEY ALL FALL WELL WITHIN RANGE OF MY REVERSAL SPELL...
Hmm... WELL, PEOPLE LOVE FREE STUFF! MAYBE CREATE SOME KIND OF FREE EVENT THAT'LL ATTRACT EVERYONE!

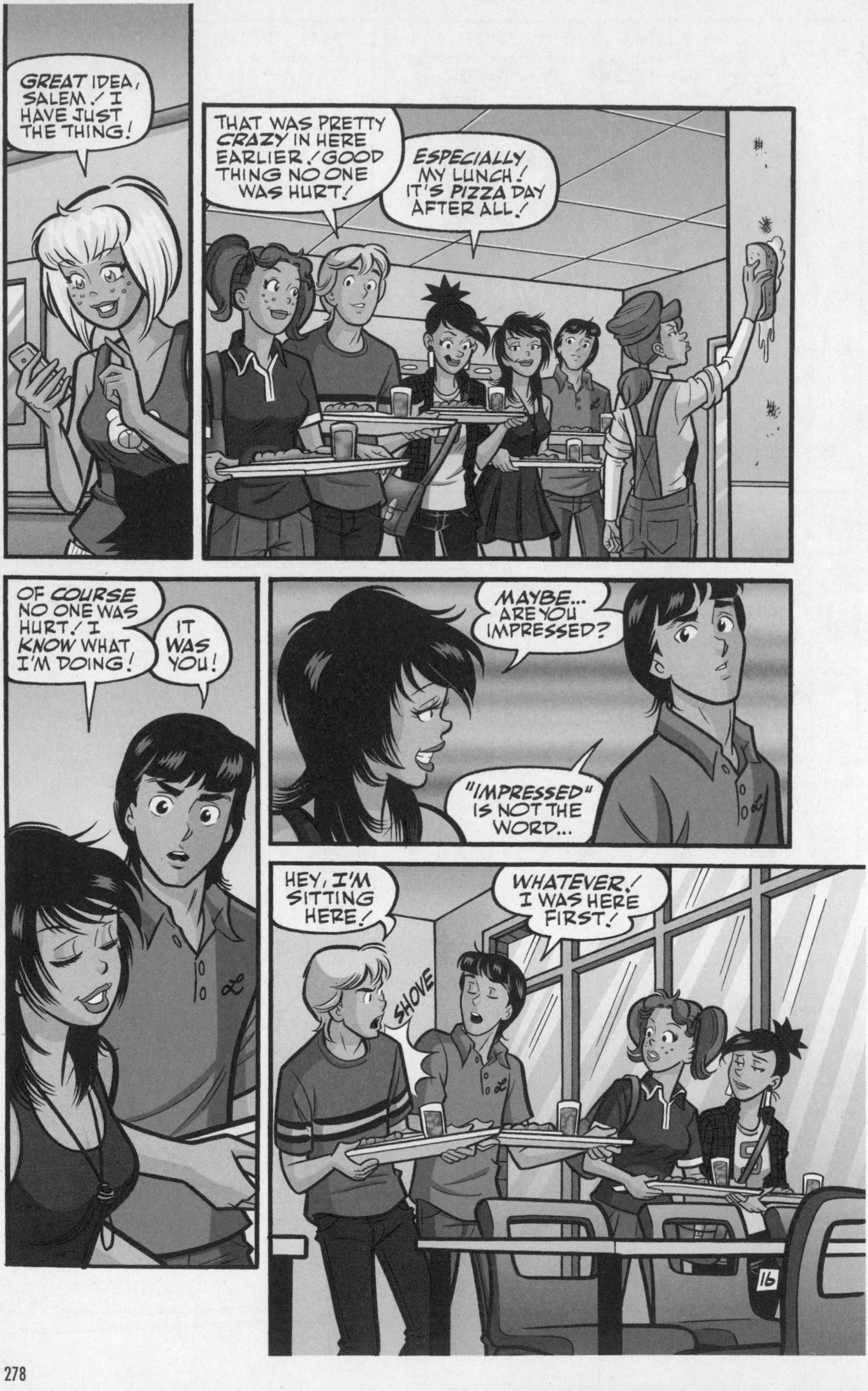
GREAT IDEA, SALEM! I HAVE JUST THE THING!
THAT WAS PRETTY CRAZY IN HERE EARLIER! GOOD THING NO ONE WAS HURT!
ESPECIALLY MY LUNCH! IT'S PIZZA DAY AFTER ALL!
OF COURSE NO ONE WAS HURT! I KNOW WHAT I'M DOING!
IT WAS YOU!
MAYBE... ARE YOU IMPRESSED?
"IMPRESSED" IS NOT THE WORD...
HEY, I'M SITTING HERE!
WHATEVER! I WAS HERE FIRST!
SHOVE
16

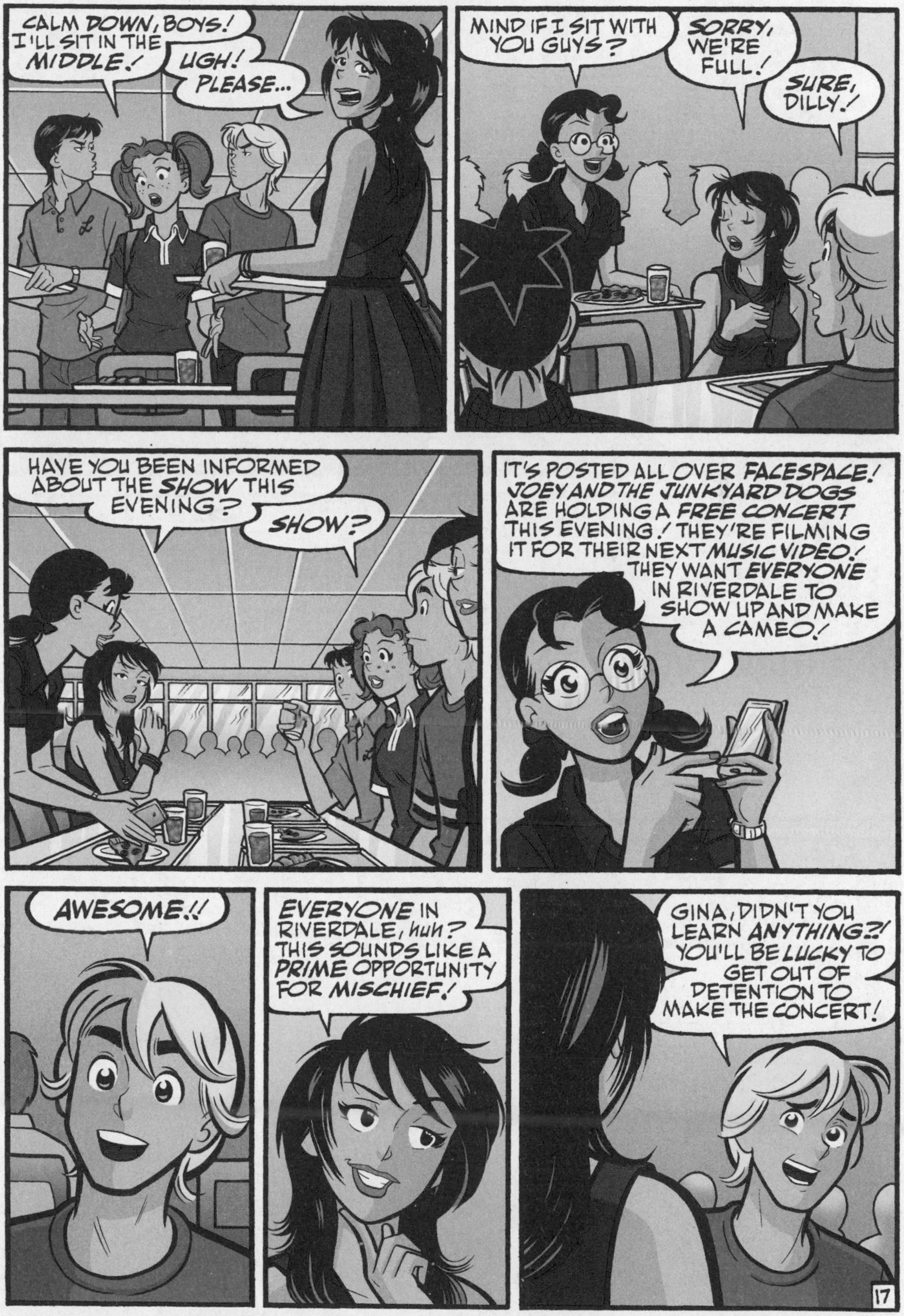
CALM DOWN, BOYS! I'LL SIT IN THE MIDDLE!
UGH! PLEASE...
MIND IF I SIT WITH YOU GUYS?
SORRY, WE'RE FULL!
SURE, DILLY!
HAVE YOU BEEN INFORMED ABOUT THE SHOW THIS EVENING?
SHOW?
IT'S POSTED ALL OVER FACESPACE! JOEY AND THE JUNKYARD DOGS ARE HOLDING A FREE CONCERT THIS EVENING! THEY'RE FILMING IT FOR THEIR NEXT MUSIC VIDEO! THEY WANT EVERYONE IN RIVERDALE TO SHOW UP AND MAKE A CAMEO!
AWESOME!!
EVERYONE IN RIVERDALE, huh? THIS SOUNDS LIKE A PRIME OPPORTUNITY FOR MISCHIEF!
GINA, DIDN'T YOU LEARN ANYTHING?! YOU'LL BE LUCKY TO GET OUT OF DETENTION TO MAKE THE CONCERT!
17

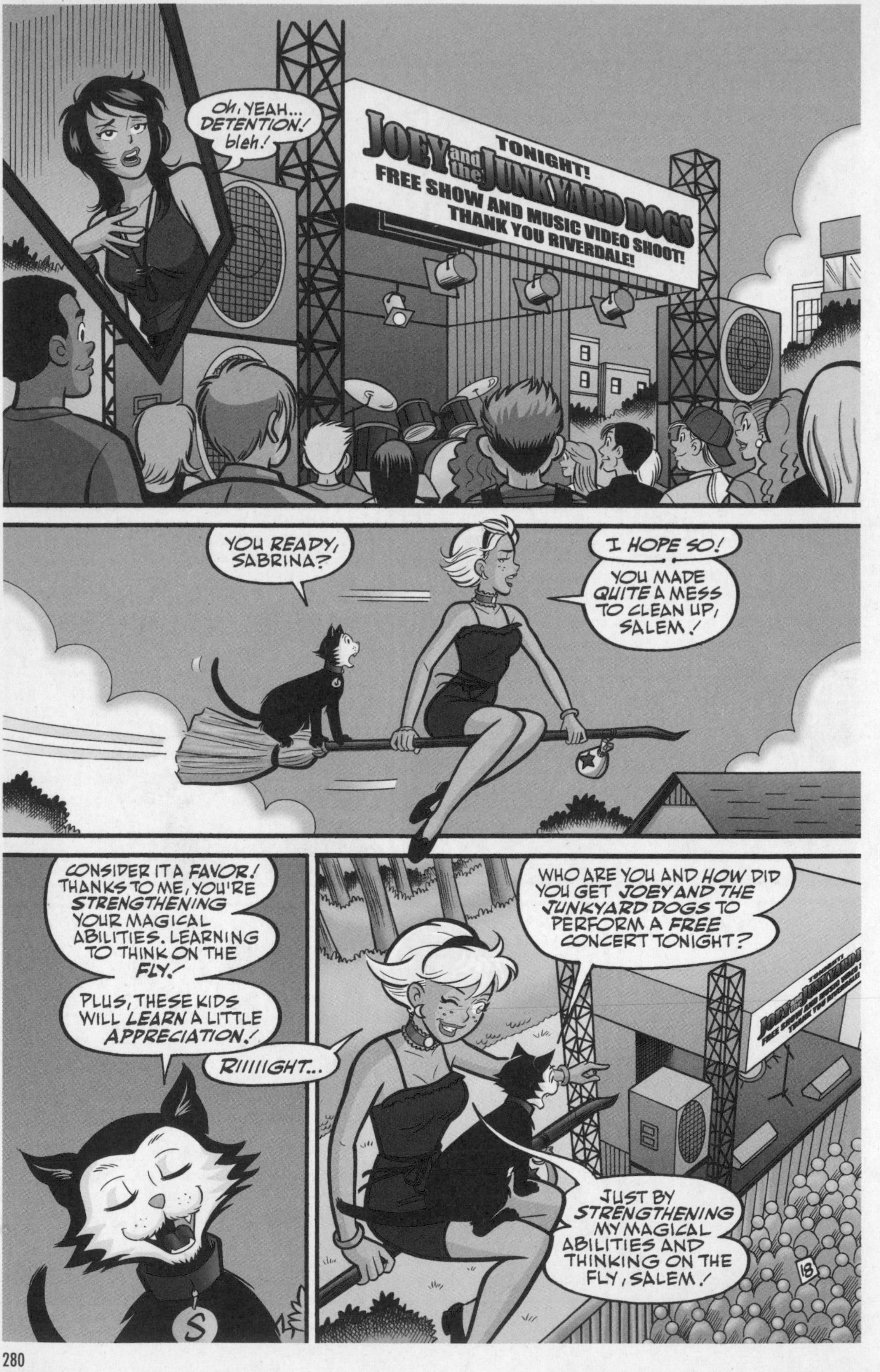

Oh, YEAH... DETENTION! bleh!
TONIGHT! JOEY and the JUNKYARD DOGS FREE SHOW AND MUSIC VIDEO SHOOT! THANK YOU RIVERDALE!
YOU READY, SABRINA?
I HOPE SO!
YOU MADE QUITE A MESS TO CLEAN UP, SALEM!
CONSIDER IT A FAVOR! THANKS TO ME, YOU'RE STRENGTHENING YOUR MAGICAL ABILITIES. LEARNING TO THINK ON THE FLY!
PLUS, THESE KIDS WILL LEARN A LITTLE APPRECIATION!
RIIIIIGHT...
WHO ARE YOU AND HOW DID YOU GET JOEY AND THE JUNKYARD DOGS TO PERFORM A FREE CONCERT TONIGHT?
JUST BY STRENGTHENING MY MAGICAL ABILITIES AND THINKING ON THE FLY, SALEM!
18

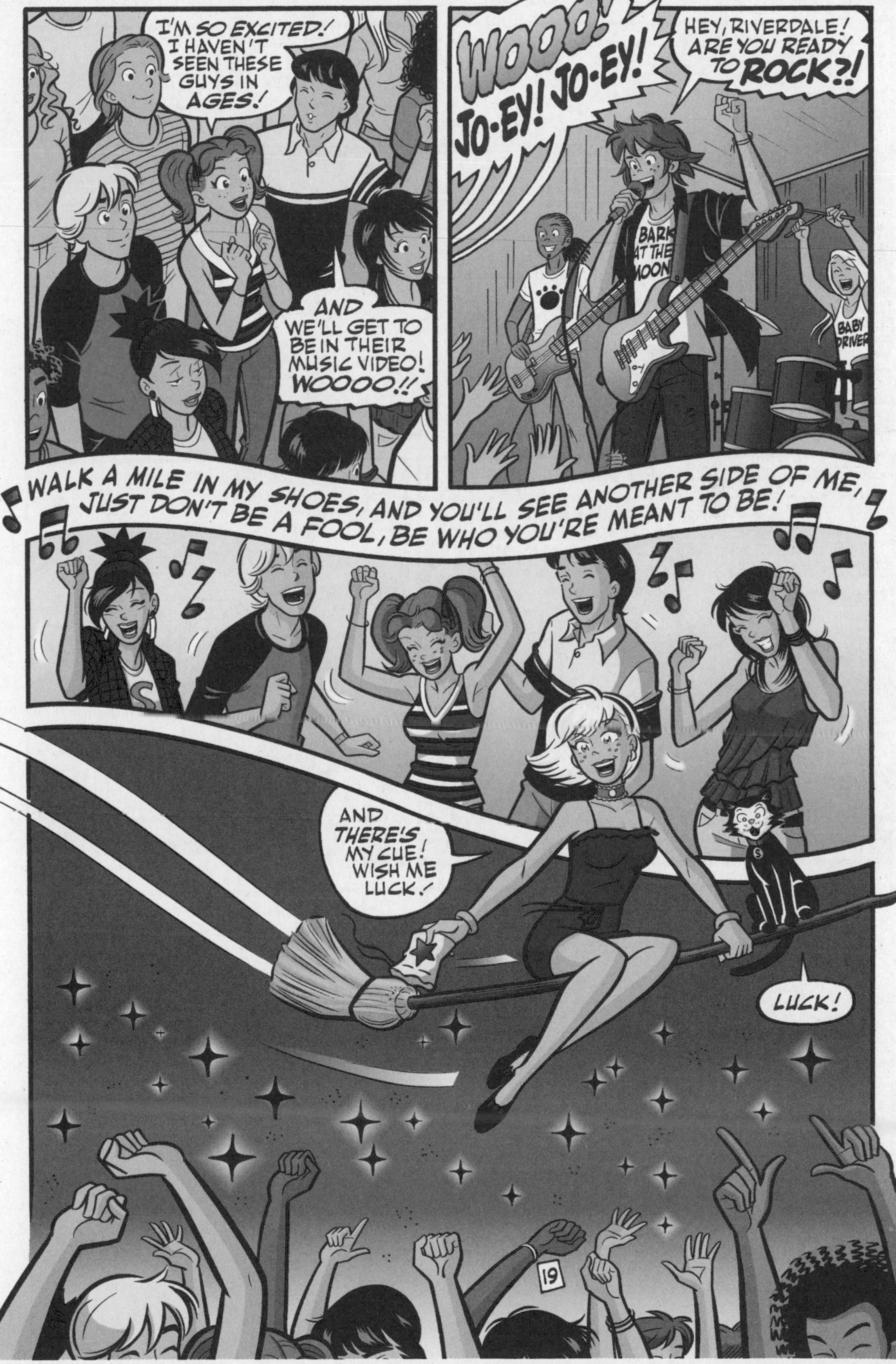
I'M SO EXCITED! I HAVEN'T SEEN THESE GUYS IN AGES!
AND WE'LL GET TO BE IN THEIR MUSIC VIDEO! WOOOO!!
WOOO! JO-EY! JO-EY!
HEY, RIVERDALE! ARE YOU READY TO ROCK?!
BARK AT THE MOON
BABY DRIVER
WALK A MILE IN MY SHOES, AND YOU'LL SEE ANOTHER SIDE OF ME, JUST DON'T BE A FOOL, BE WHO YOU'RE MEANT TO BE!
AND THERE'S MY CUE! WISH ME LUCK!
LUCK!
19

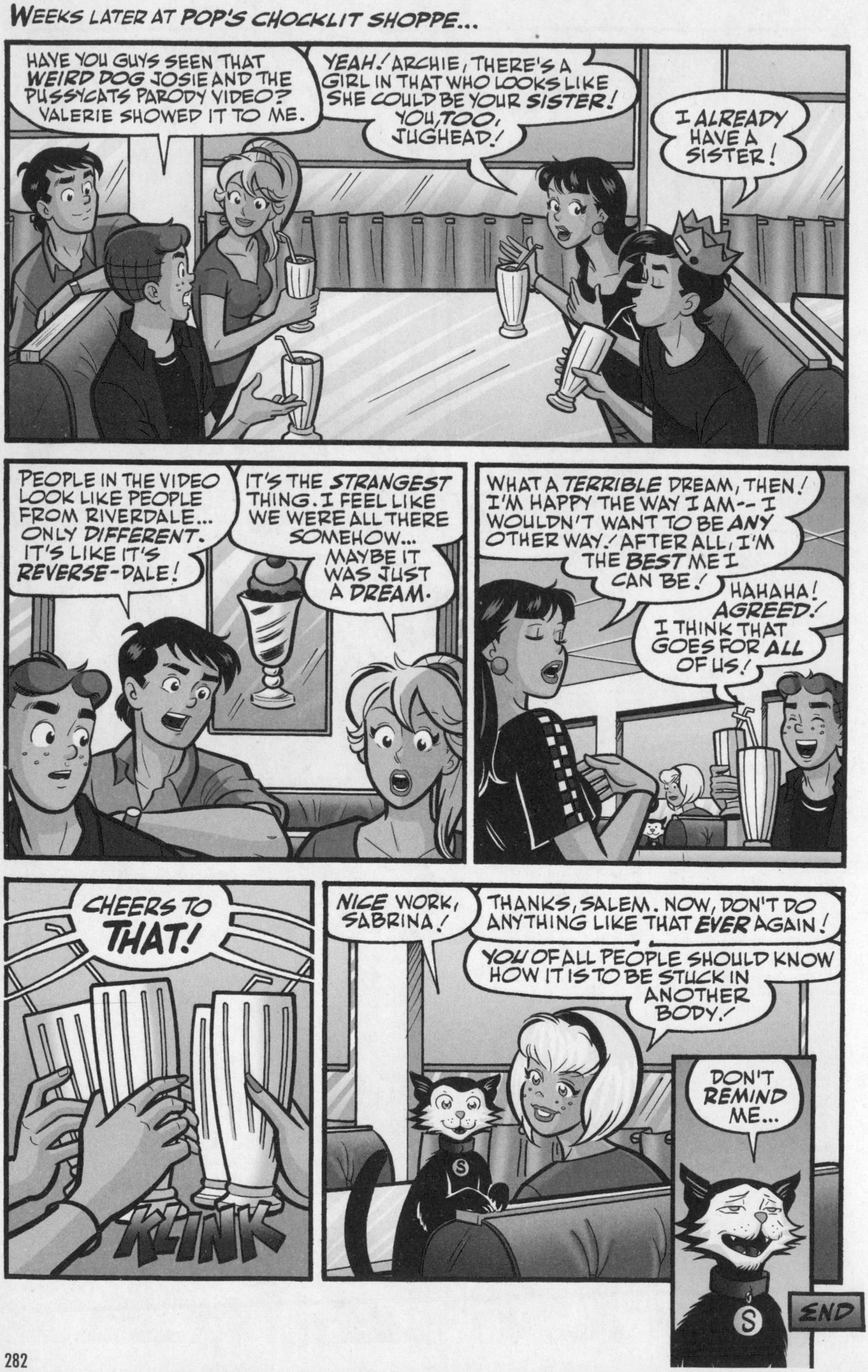
WEEKS LATER AT POP'S CHOCKLIT SHOPPE...
HAVE YOU GUYS SEEN THAT WEIRD DOG JOSIE AND THE PUSSYCATS PARODY VIDEO? VALERIE SHOWED IT TO ME.
YEAH! ARCHIE, THERE'S A GIRL IN THAT WHO LOOKS LIKE SHE COULD BE YOUR SISTER! YOU, TOO, JUGHEAD!
I ALREADY HAVE A SISTER!
PEOPLE IN THE VIDEO LOOK LIKE PEOPLE FROM RIVERDALE... ONLY DIFFERENT. IT'S LIKE IT'S REVERSE-DALE!
IT'S THE STRANGEST THING. I FEEL LIKE WE WERE ALL THERE SOMEHOW... MAYBE IT WAS JUST A DREAM.
WHAT A TERRIBLE DREAM, THEN! I'M HAPPY THE WAY I AM-- I WOULDN'T WANT TO BE ANY OTHER WAY! AFTER ALL, I'M THE BEST ME I CAN BE!
HAHAHA! AGREED! I THINK THAT GOES FOR ALL OF US!
CHEERS TO THAT!
KLINK
NICE WORK, SABRINA!
THANKS, SALEM. NOW, DON'T DO ANYTHING LIKE THAT EVER AGAIN!
YOU OF ALL PEOPLE SHOULD KNOW HOW IT IS TO BE STUCK IN ANOTHER BODY!
DON'T REMIND ME...
END

CHAPTER TEN

Walk on the Wild Side

KENNEDY
SMITH

INTRODUCING WALK ON THE WILD SIDE

Originally printed in *Archie #659*

A Riverdale Zoo field trip goes bonkers in "Walk on the Wild Side!" When Sabrina's magical cat Salem mis-casts a magical spell, Archie and the gang are turned into animals! Not only that, but they're turning everyone they meet into animals as well. Can the gang escape the zoo and reverse the spell before they're stuck in their animal bodies forever?

WRITER
ALEX SEGURA

PENCILS
PAT & TIM KENNEDY

INKS
RICH KOSLOWSKI

LETTERS
JACK MORELLI

COLORS
DIGIKORE STUDIOS

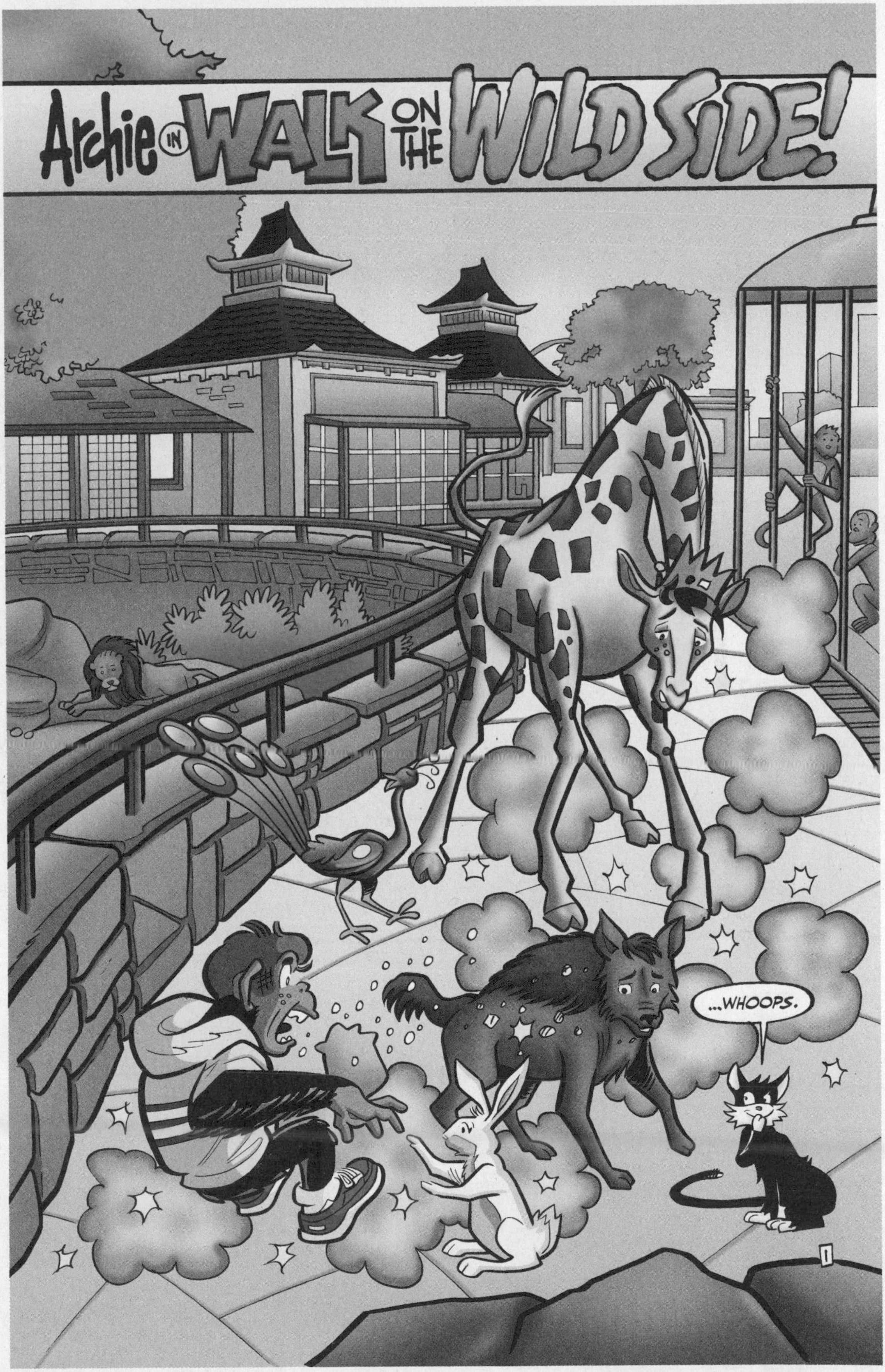
Archie in WALK ON THE WILD SIDE!
...WHOOPS.
1

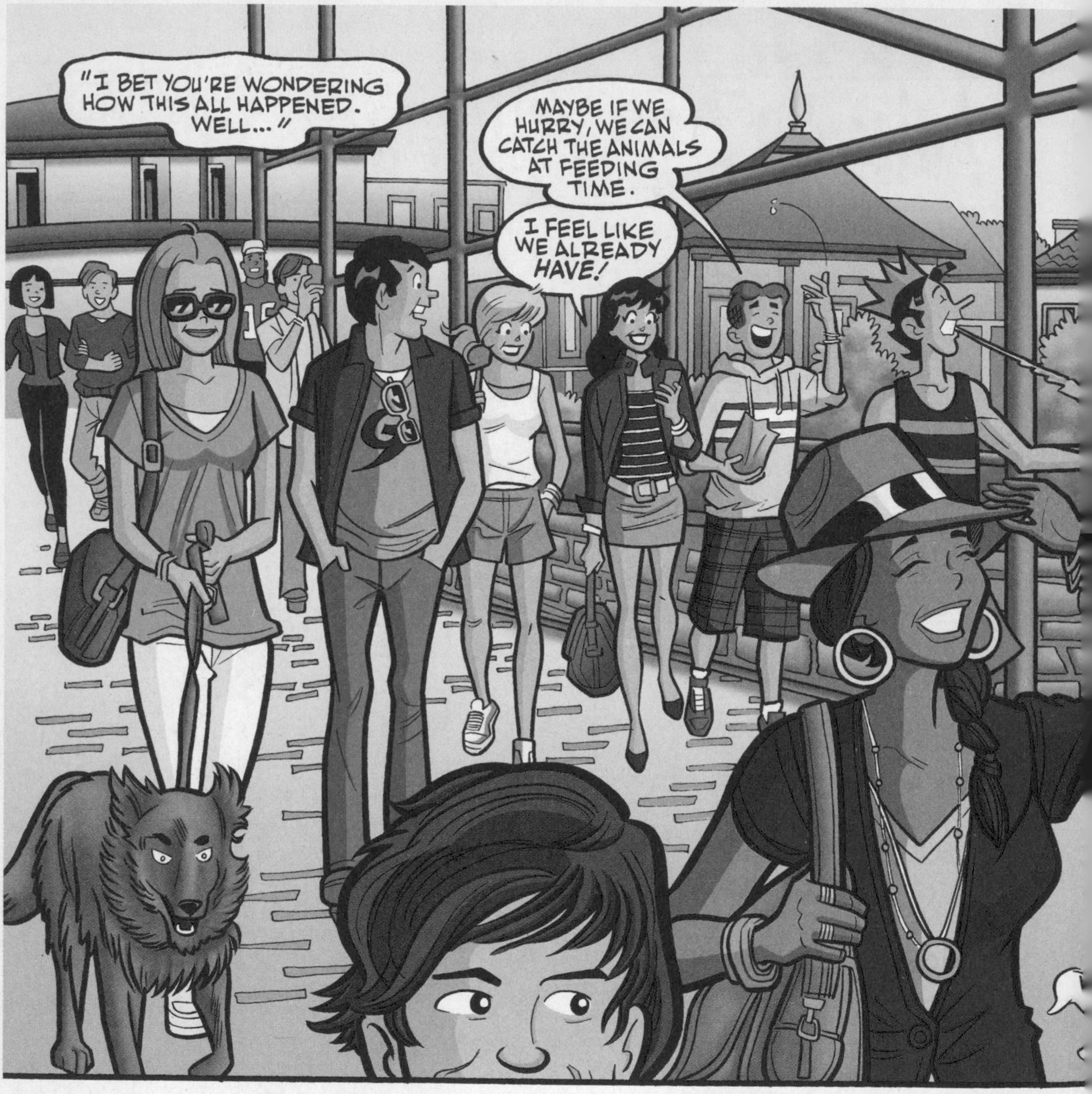
"I BET YOU'RE WONDERING HOW THIS ALL HAPPENED. WELL..."
MAYBE IF WE HURRY, WE CAN CATCH THE ANIMALS AT FEEDING TIME.
I FEEL LIKE WE ALREADY HAVE!

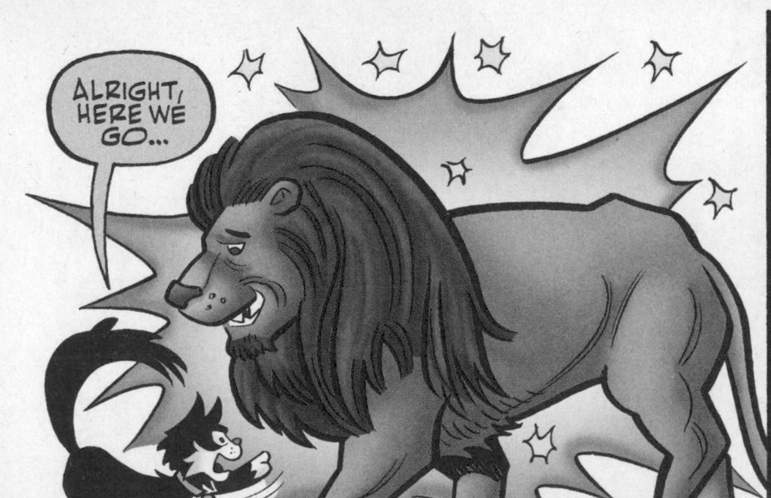
ALRIGHT, HERE WE GO...

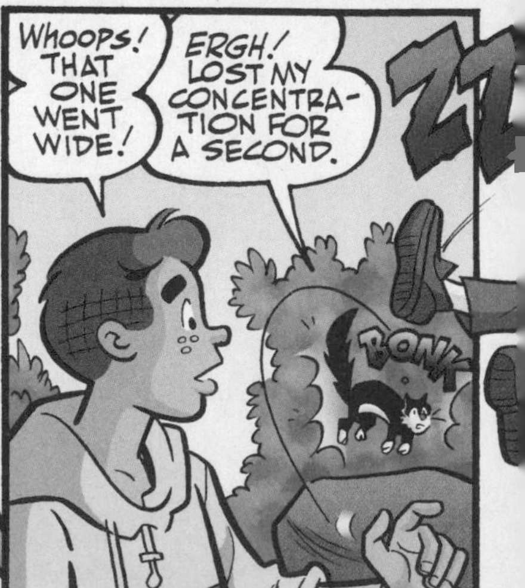
Whoops! THAT ONE WENT WIDE!
ERGH! LOST MY CONCENTRATION FOR A SECOND.
BONK

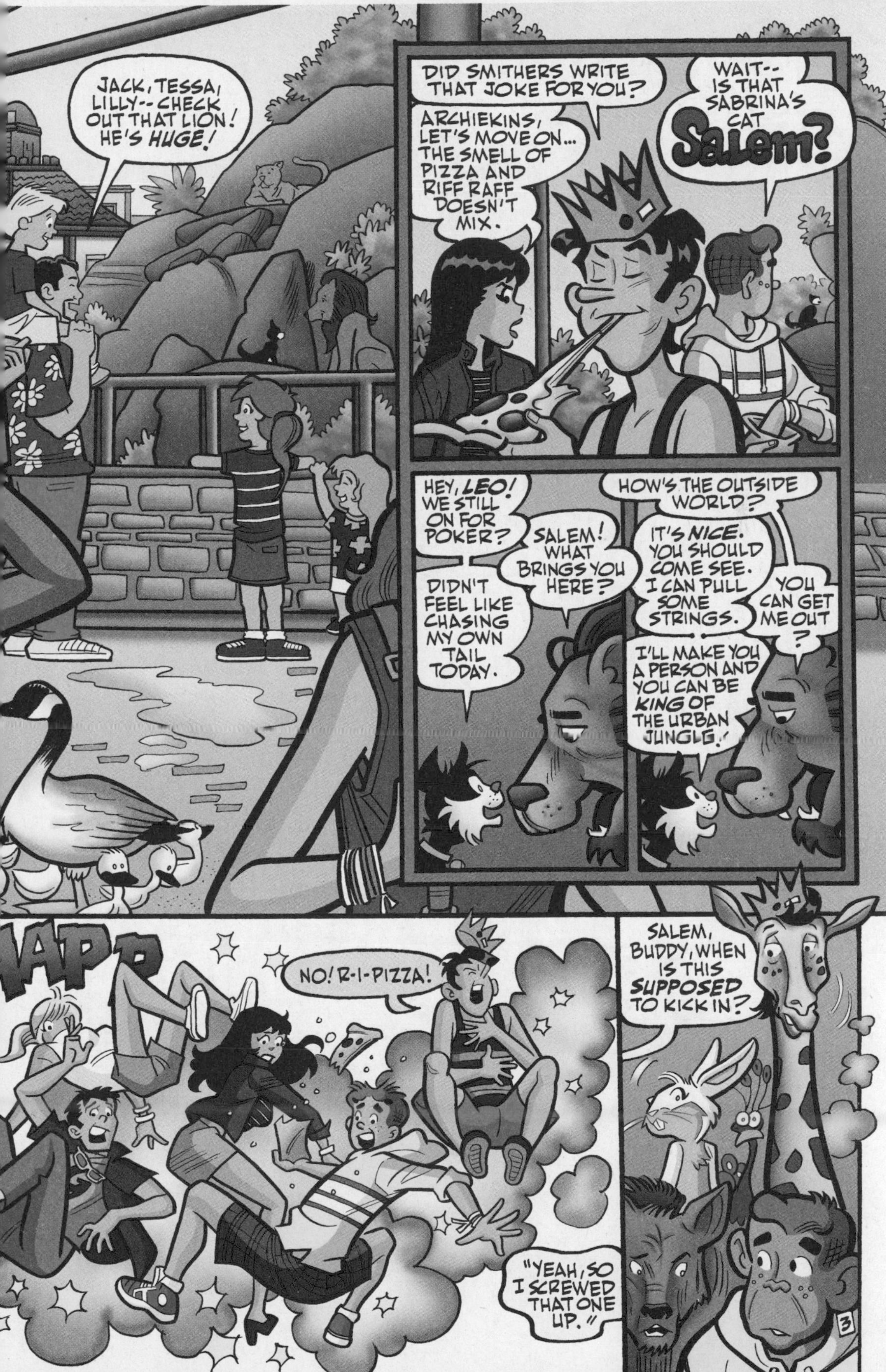
JACK, TESSA, LILLY-- CHECK OUT THAT LION! HE'S HUGE!
DID SMITHERS WRITE THAT JOKE FOR YOU?
ARCHIEKINS, LET'S MOVE ON... THE SMELL OF PIZZA AND RIFF RAFF DOESN'T MIX.
WAIT-- IS THAT SABRINA'S CAT Salem?
HEY, LEO! WE STILL ON FOR POKER?
SALEM! WHAT BRINGS YOU HERE?
DIDN'T FEEL LIKE CHASING MY OWN TAIL TODAY.
HOW'S THE OUTSIDE WORLD?
IT'S NICE. YOU SHOULD COME SEE. I CAN PULL SOME STRINGS.
YOU CAN GET ME OUT?
I'LL MAKE YOU A PERSON AND YOU CAN BE KING OF THE URBAN JUNGLE!
NO! R-I-PIZZA!
SALEM, BUDDY, WHEN IS THIS SUPPOSED TO KICK IN?
"YEAH, SO I SCREWED THAT ONE UP."

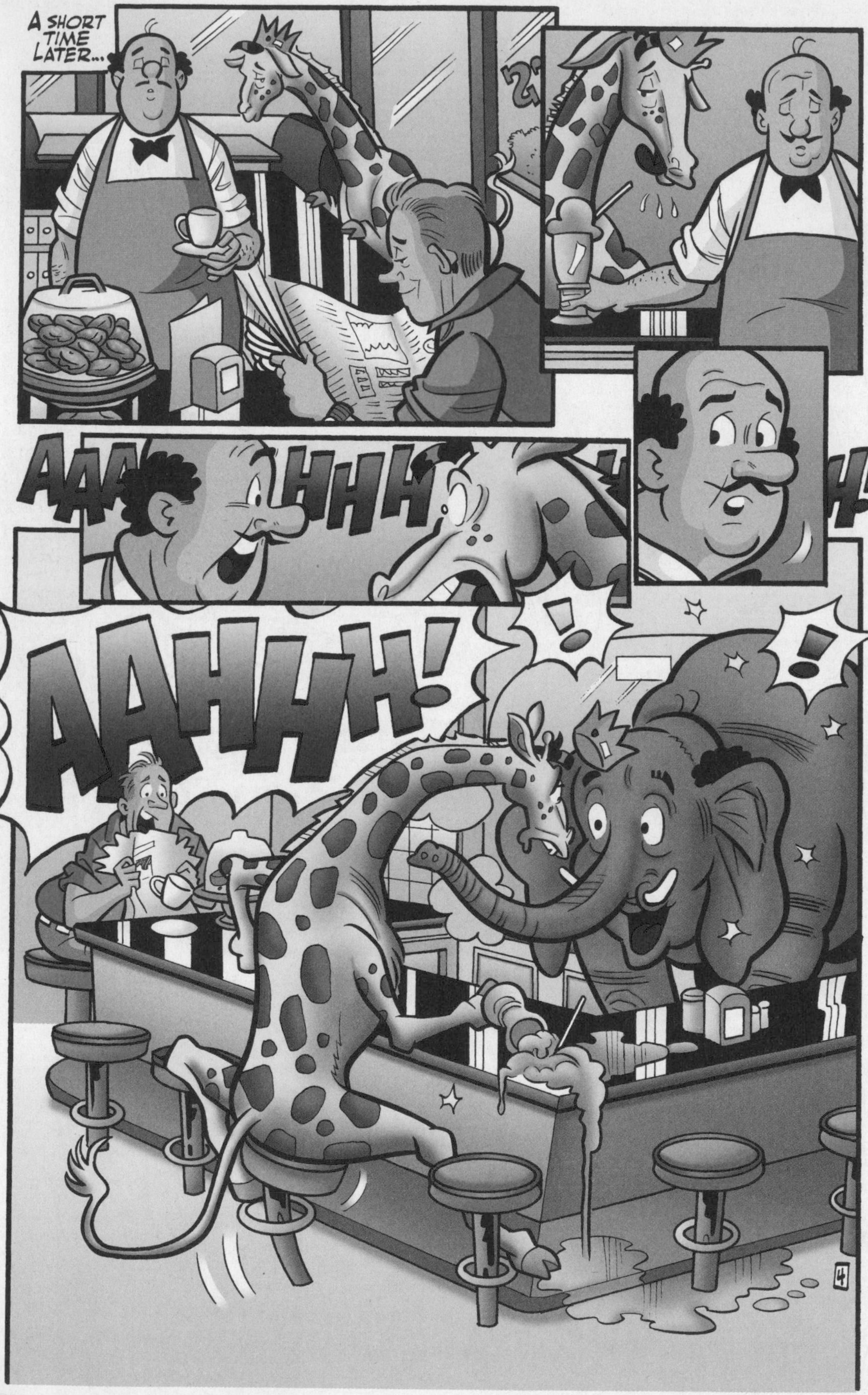
A SHORT TIME LATER...
AAAHHHH!
AAHHH!
!
!
4

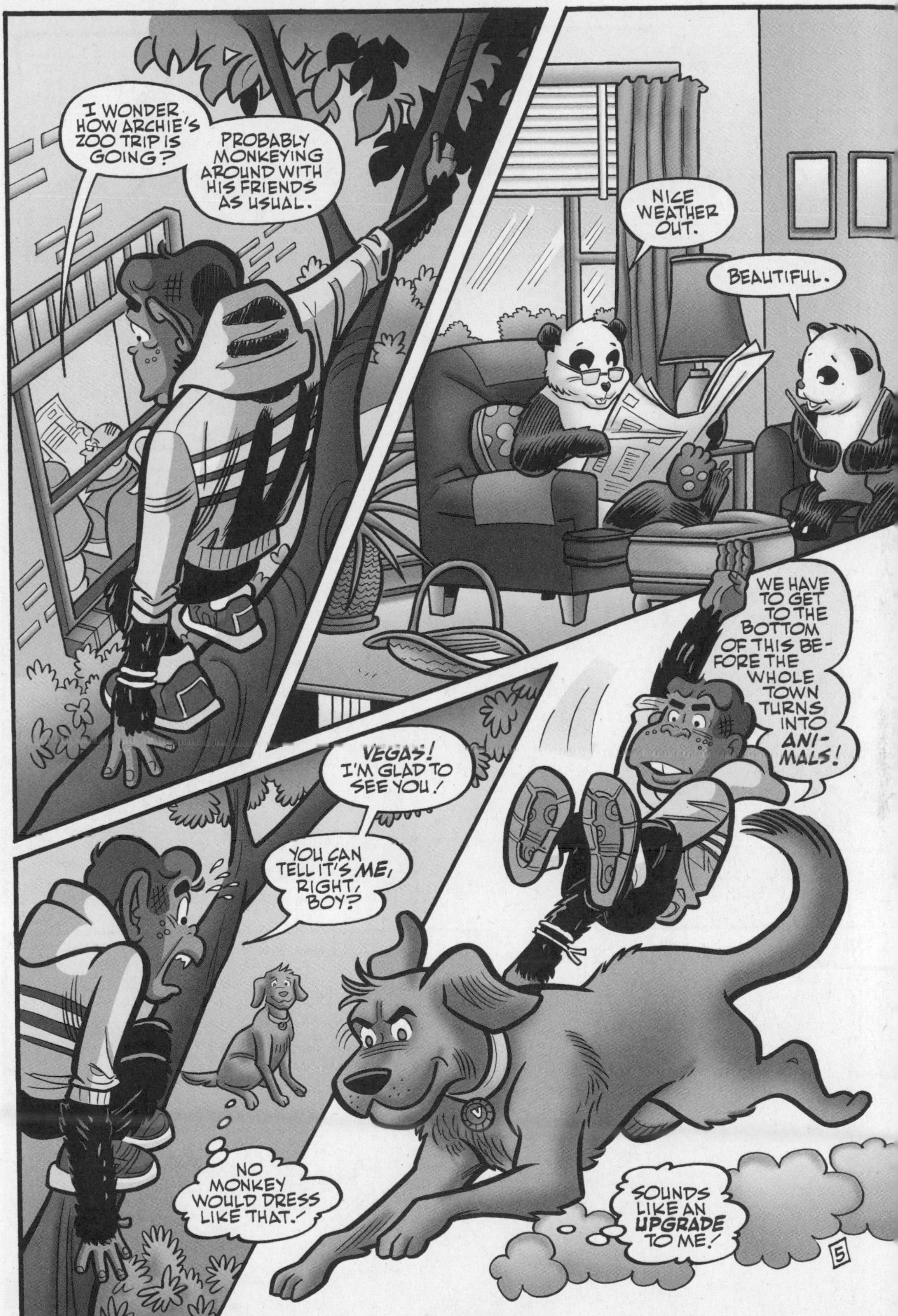

I WONDER HOW ARCHIE'S ZOO TRIP IS GOING?
PROBABLY MONKEYING AROUND WITH HIS FRIENDS AS USUAL.
NICE WEATHER OUT.
BEAUTIFUL.
WE HAVE TO GET TO THE BOTTOM OF THIS BEFORE THE WHOLE TOWN TURNS INTO ANIMALS!
VEGAS! I'M GLAD TO SEE YOU!
YOU CAN TELL IT'S ME, RIGHT, BOY?
NO MONKEY WOULD DRESS LIKE THAT.
SOUNDS LIKE AN UPGRADE TO ME!
5

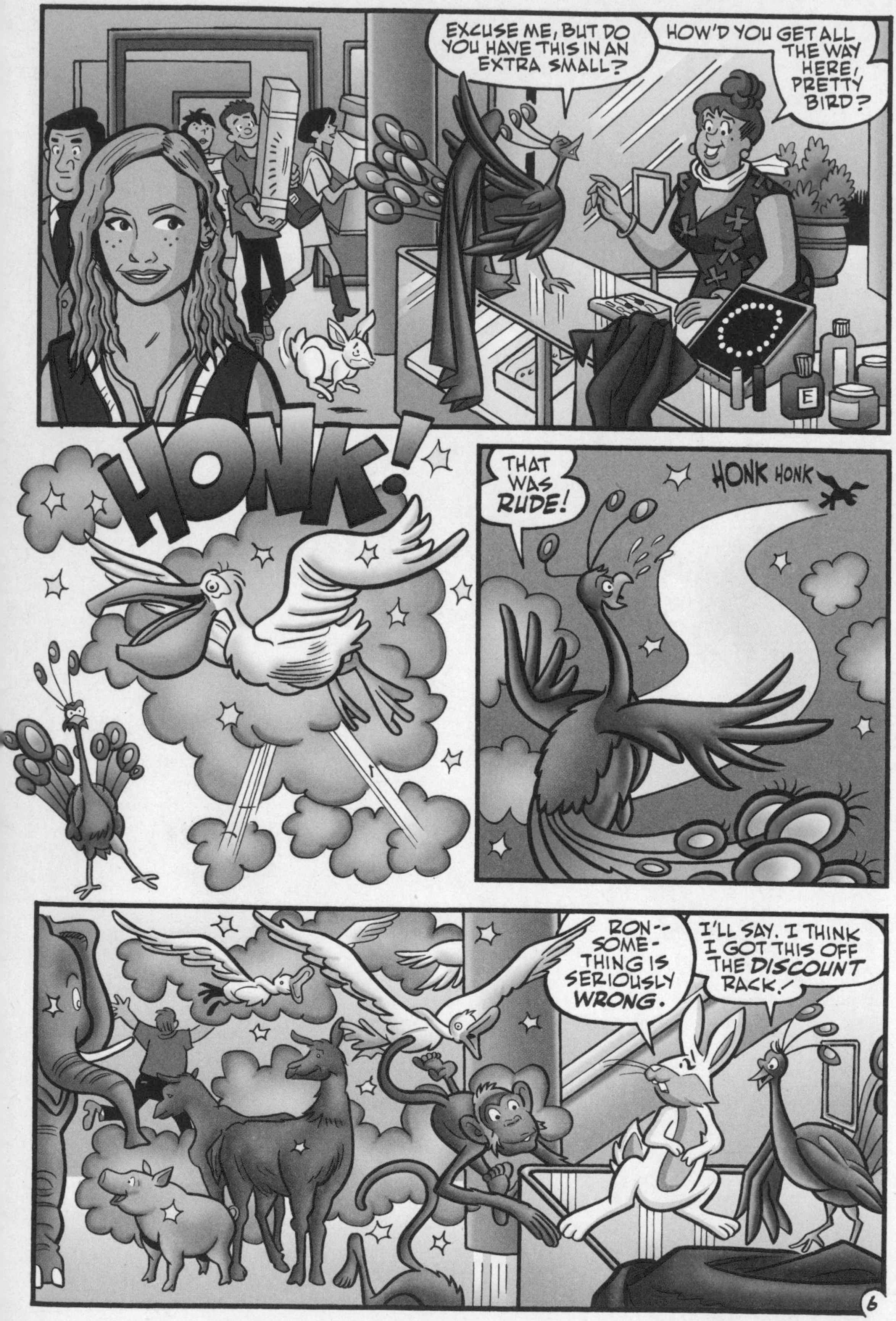
EXCUSE ME, BUT DO YOU HAVE THIS IN AN EXTRA SMALL?
HOW'D YOU GET ALL THE WAY HERE, PRETTY BIRD?
HONK!
THAT WAS RUDE!
HONK HONK
RON-- SOME-THING IS SERIOUSLY WRONG.
I'LL SAY. I THINK I GOT THIS OFF THE DISCOUNT RACK!
6

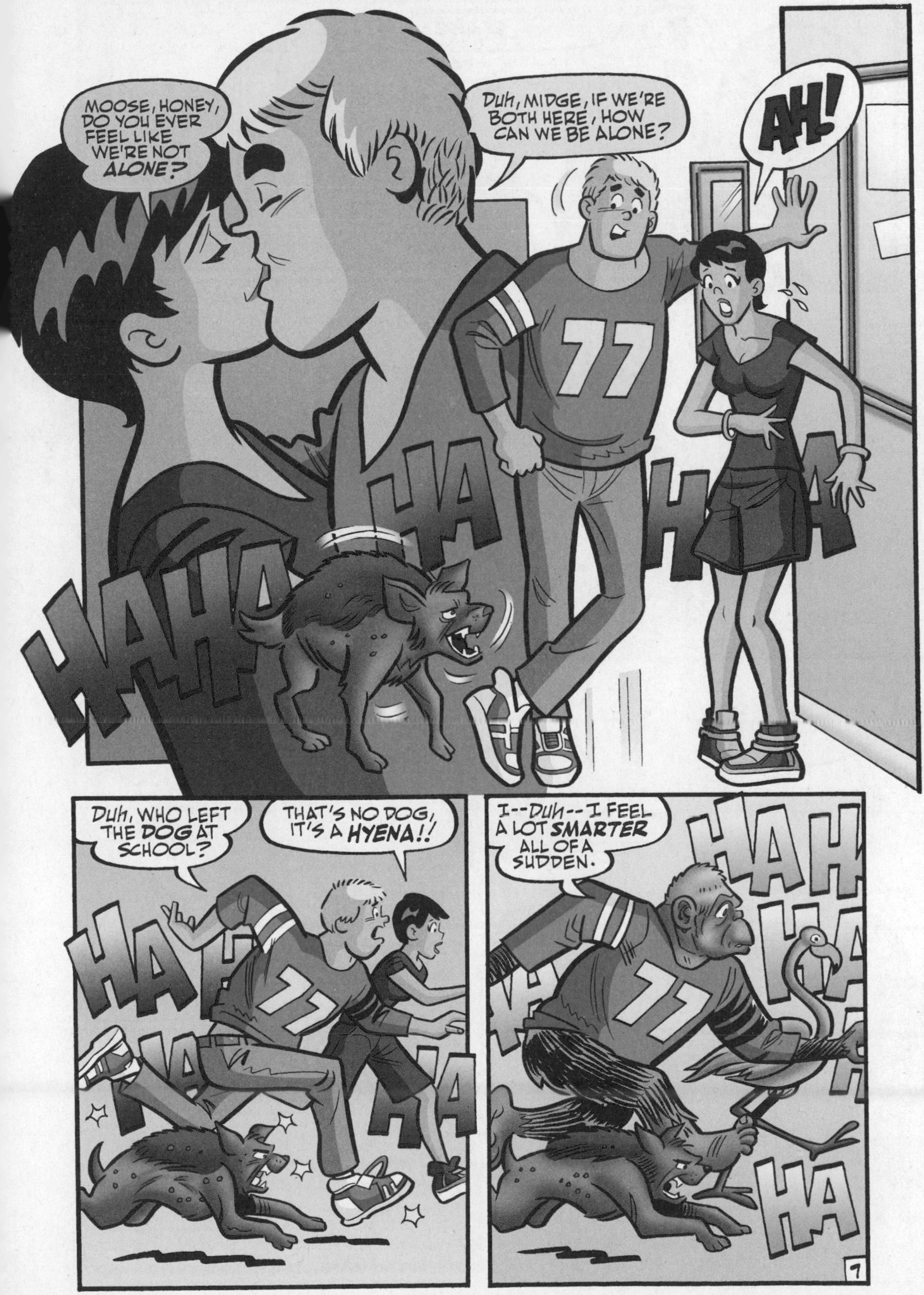
MOOSE, HONEY, DO YOU EVER FEEL LIKE WE'RE NOT ALONE?
DUH, MIDGE, IF WE'RE BOTH HERE, HOW CAN WE BE ALONE?
AH!
HAHA
HA
HA
DUH, WHO LEFT THE DOG AT SCHOOL?
THAT'S NO DOG, IT'S A HYENA!!
I--DUH--I FEEL A LOT SMARTER ALL OF A SUDDEN.
HA
HA
7

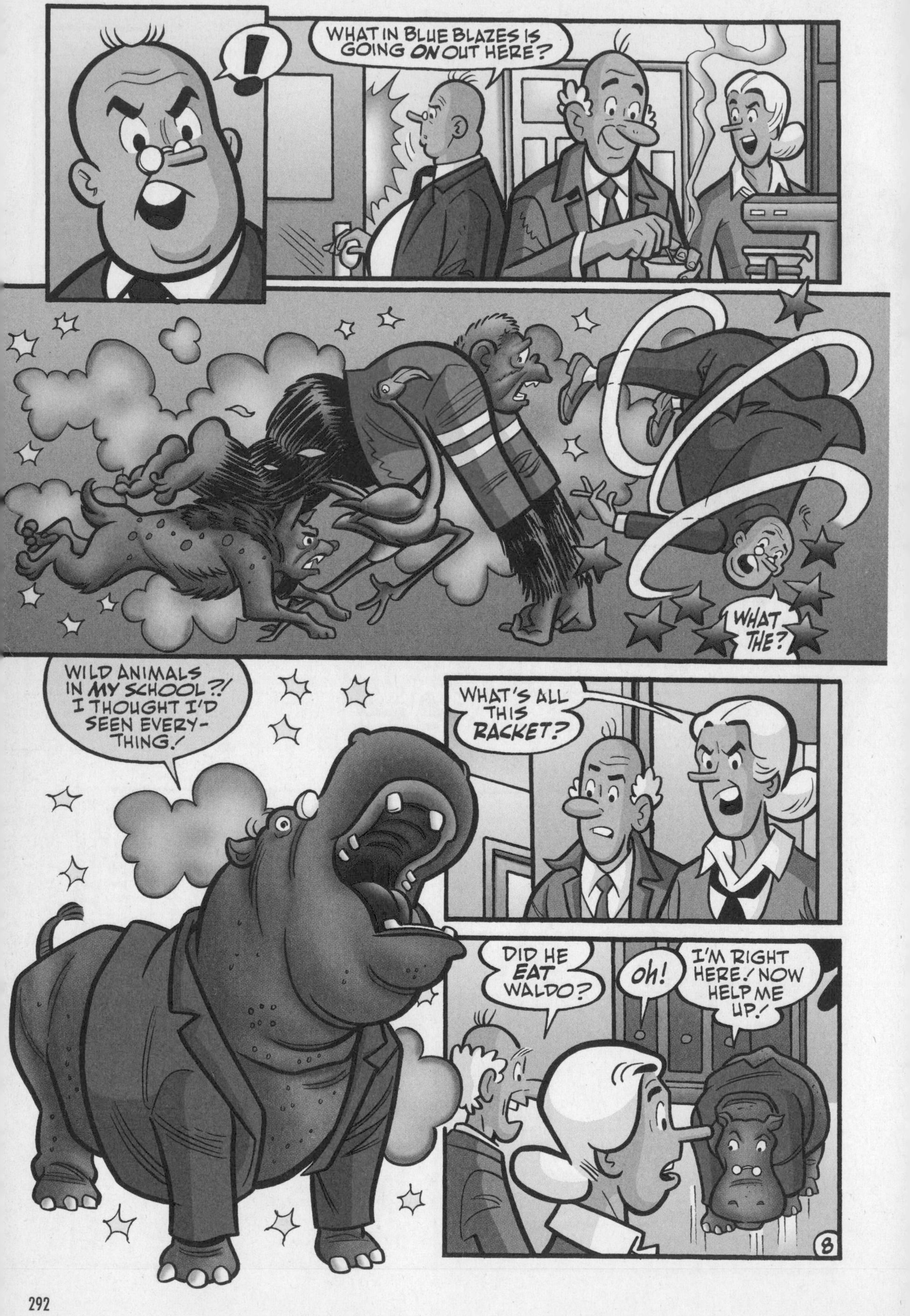

!
WHAT IN BLUE BLAZES IS GOING ON OUT HERE?
WHAT THE?
WILD ANIMALS IN MY SCHOOL?! I THOUGHT I'D SEEN EVERY-THING!
WHAT'S ALL THIS RACKET?
DID HE EAT WALDO?
oh!
I'M RIGHT HERE! NOW HELP ME UP!
8

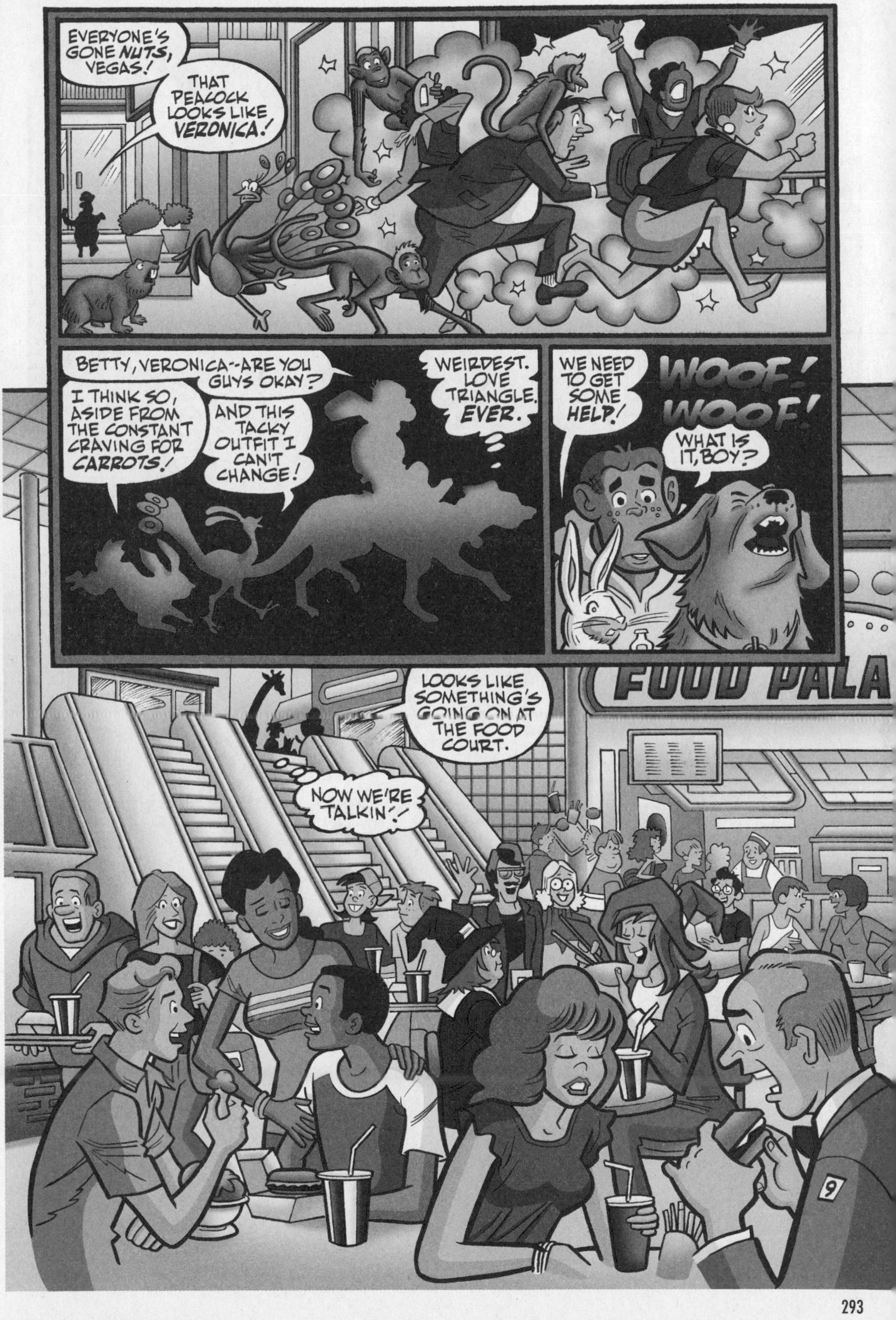
EVERYONE'S GONE NUTS, VEGAS!
THAT PEACOCK LOOKS LIKE VERONICA!
BETTY, VERONICA--ARE YOU GUYS OKAY?
I THINK SO, ASIDE FROM THE CONSTANT CRAVING FOR CARROTS!
AND THIS TACKY OUTFIT I CAN'T CHANGE!
WEIRDEST. LOVE TRIANGLE. EVER.
WE NEED TO GET SOME HELP!
WOOF! WOOF!
WHAT IS IT, BOY?
FOOD PALA
LOOKS LIKE SOMETHING'S GOING ON AT THE FOOD COURT.
NOW WE'RE TALKIN'!
9

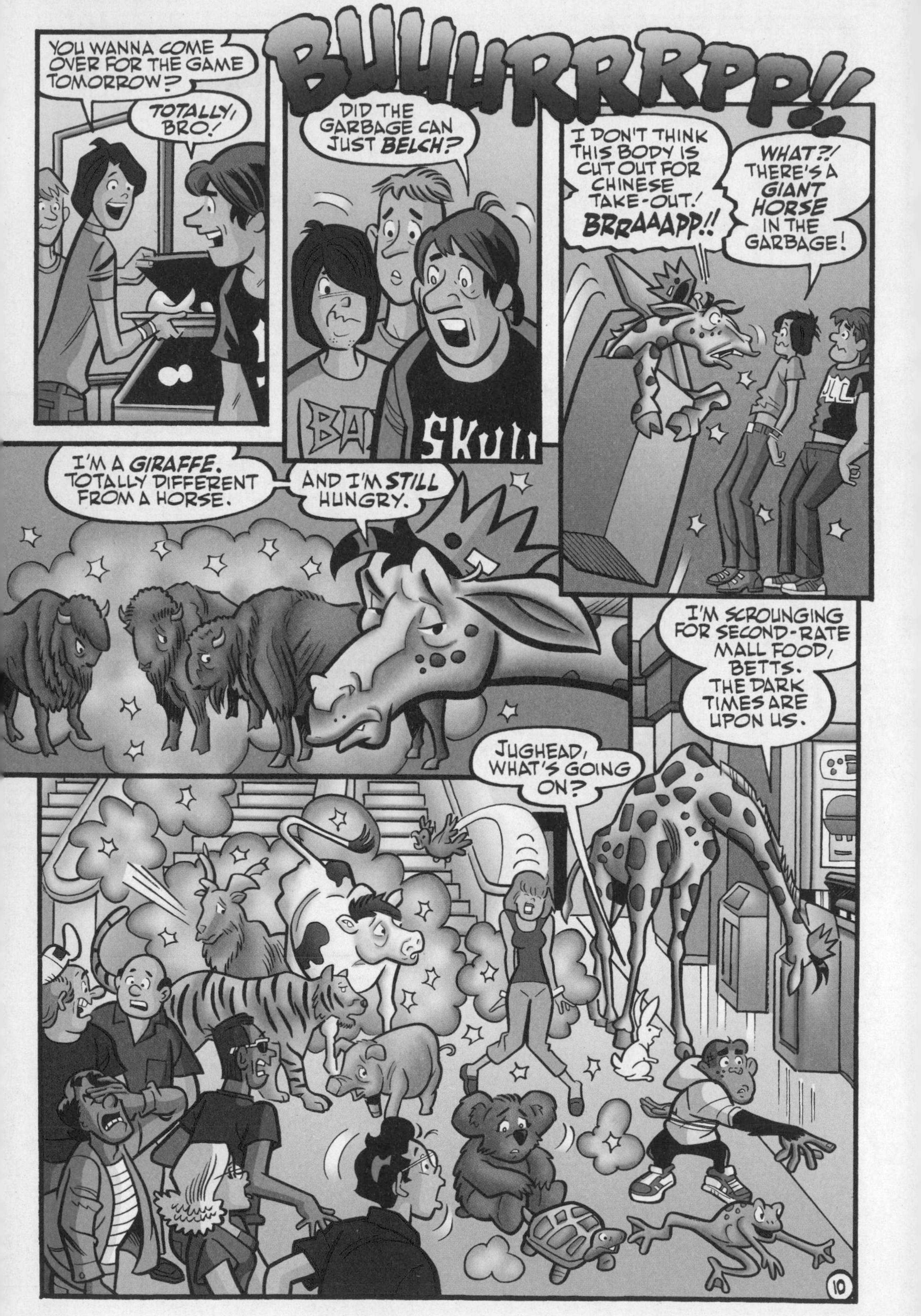
YOU WANNA COME OVER FOR THE GAME TOMORROW?
TOTALLY, BRO!
BUUURRRPP!!
DID THE GARBAGE CAN JUST BELCH?
I DON'T THINK THIS BODY IS CUT OUT FOR CHINESE TAKE-OUT! BRRAAAPP!!
WHAT?! THERE'S A GIANT HORSE IN THE GARBAGE!
I'M A GIRAFFE. TOTALLY DIFFERENT FROM A HORSE.
AND I'M STILL HUNGRY.
I'M SCROUNGING FOR SECOND-RATE MALL FOOD, BETTS. THE DARK TIMES ARE UPON US.
JUGHEAD, WHAT'S GOING ON?
10

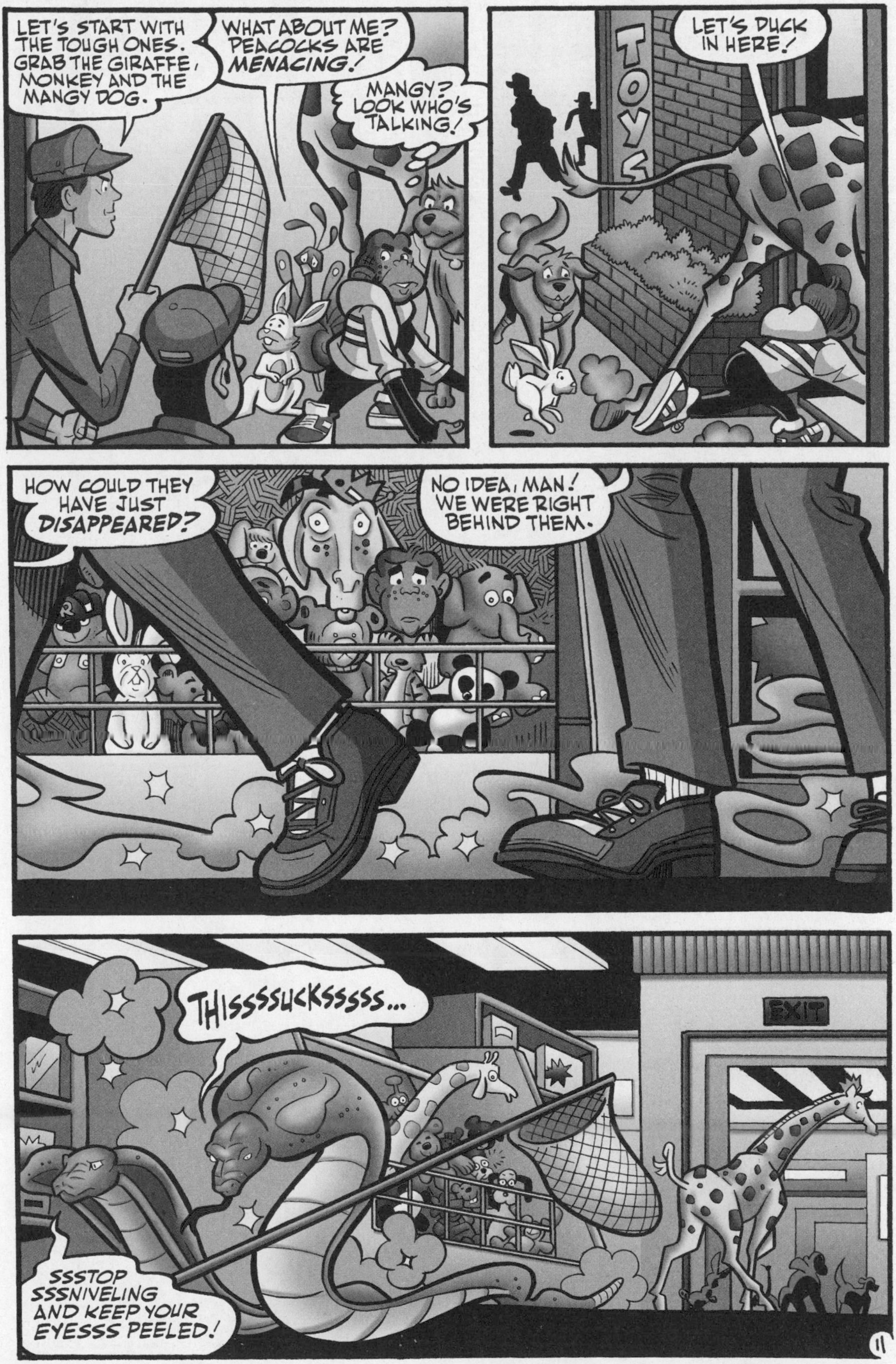
LET'S START WITH THE TOUGH ONES. GRAB THE GIRAFFE, MONKEY AND THE MANGY DOG.
WHAT ABOUT ME? PEACOCKS ARE *MENACING!*
MANGY? LOOK WHO'S TALKING!
TOYS
LET'S DUCK IN HERE!
HOW COULD THEY HAVE JUST **DISAPPEARED?**
NO IDEA, MAN! WE WERE RIGHT BEHIND THEM.
THISSSSUCKSSSSS...
EXIT
SSSTOP SSSNIVELING AND KEEP YOUR EYESSS PEELED!
11

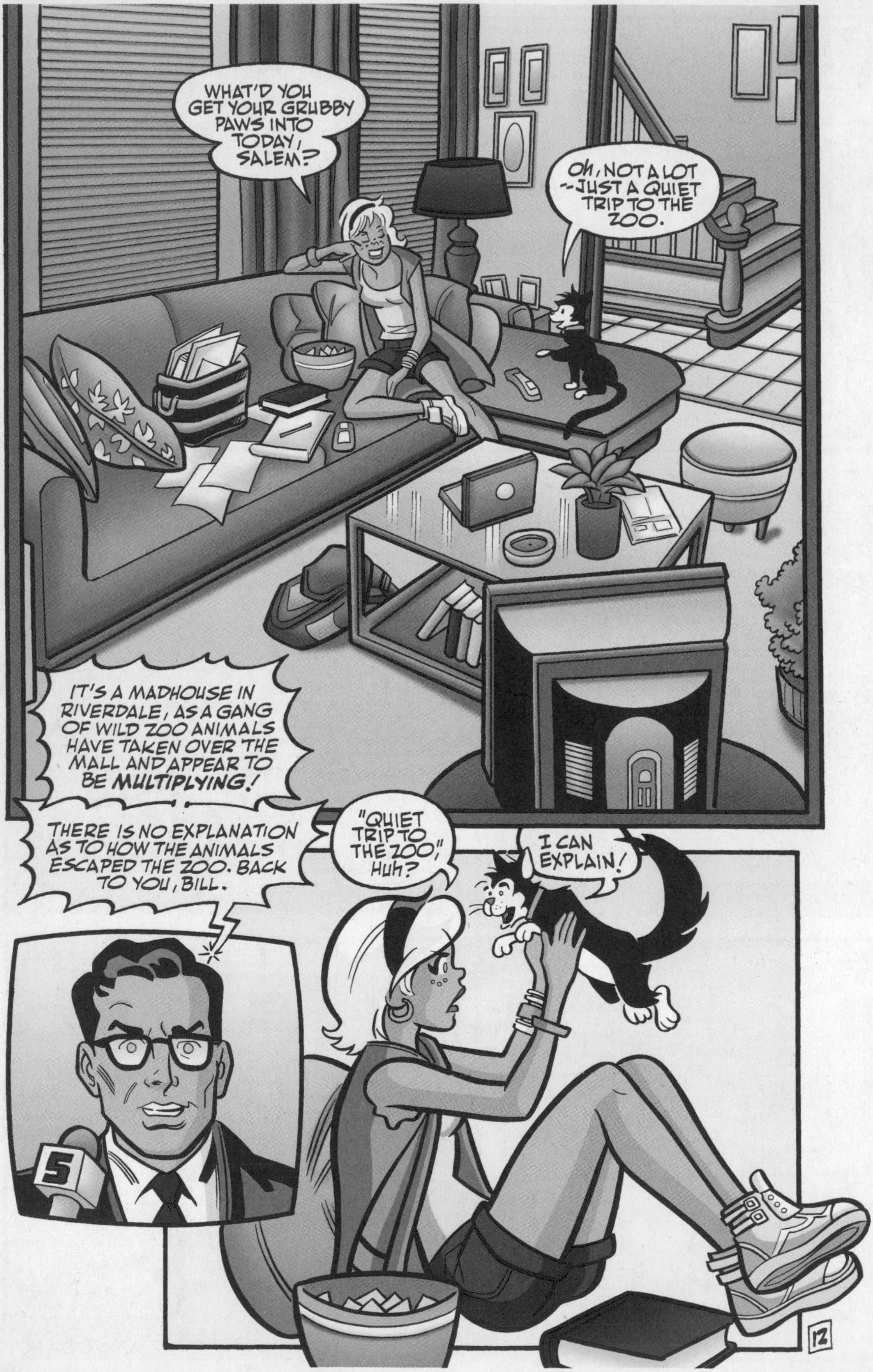
WHAT'D YOU GET YOUR GRUBBY PAWS INTO TODAY, SALEM?
OH, NOT A LOT -- JUST A QUIET TRIP TO THE ZOO.
IT'S A MADHOUSE IN RIVERDALE, AS A GANG OF WILD ZOO ANIMALS HAVE TAKEN OVER THE MALL AND APPEAR TO BE **MULTIPLYING**!
THERE IS NO EXPLANATION AS TO HOW THE ANIMALS ESCAPED THE ZOO. BACK TO YOU, BILL.
"QUIET TRIP TO THE ZOO," HUH?
I CAN EXPLAIN!
5
12

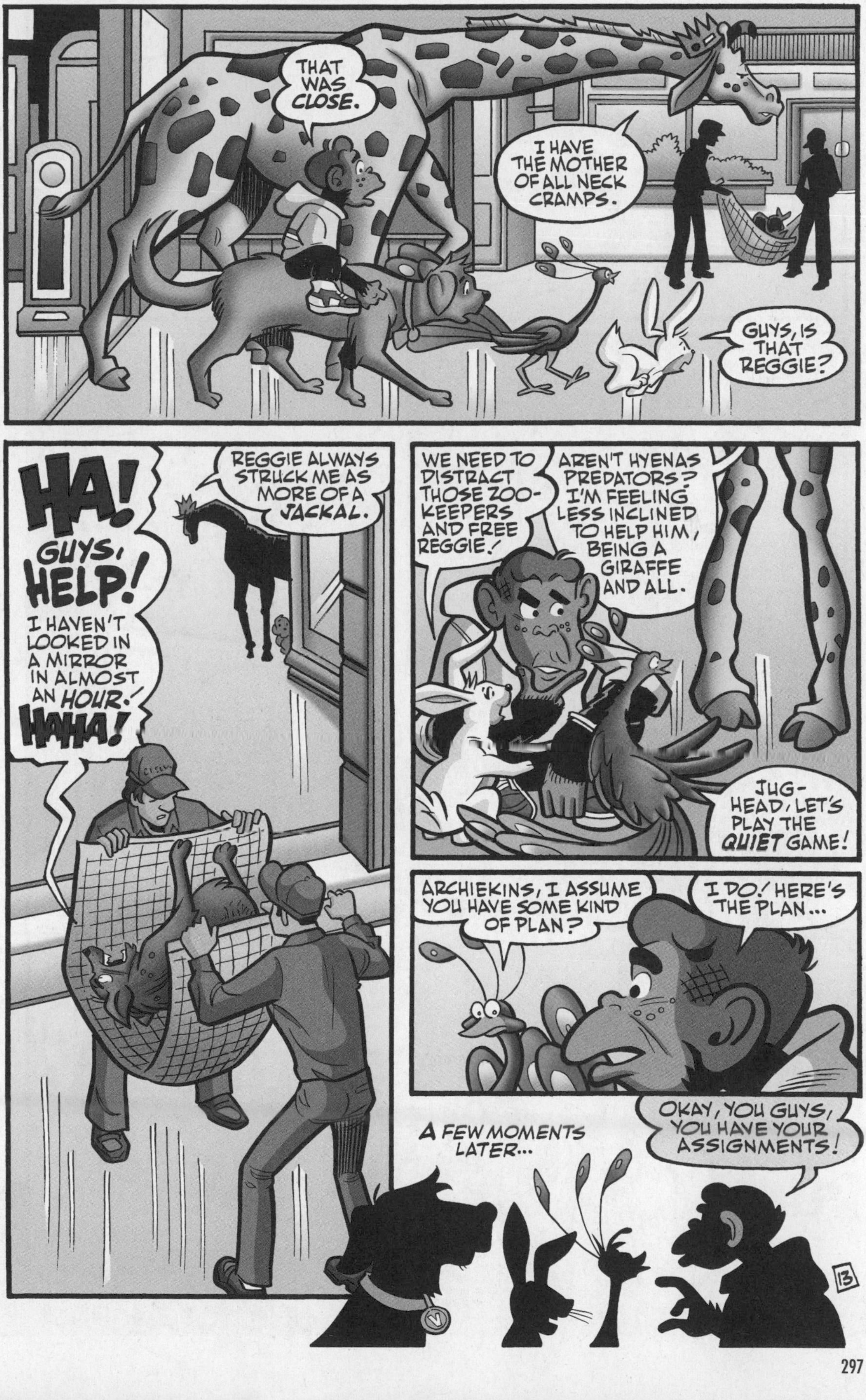
THAT WAS CLOSE.
I HAVE THE MOTHER OF ALL NECK CRAMPS.
GUYS, IS THAT REGGIE?
HA! GUYS, HELP! I HAVEN'T LOOKED IN A MIRROR IN ALMOST AN HOUR! HAHA!
REGGIE ALWAYS STRUCK ME AS MORE OF A JACKAL.
WE NEED TO DISTRACT THOSE ZOO-KEEPERS AND FREE REGGIE!
AREN'T HYENAS PREDATORS? I'M FEELING LESS INCLINED TO HELP HIM, BEING A GIRAFFE AND ALL.
JUG-HEAD, LET'S PLAY THE QUIET GAME!
ARCHIEKINS, I ASSUME YOU HAVE SOME KIND OF PLAN?
I DO! HERE'S THE PLAN...
A FEW MOMENTS LATER...
OKAY, YOU GUYS, YOU HAVE YOUR ASSIGNMENTS!
13

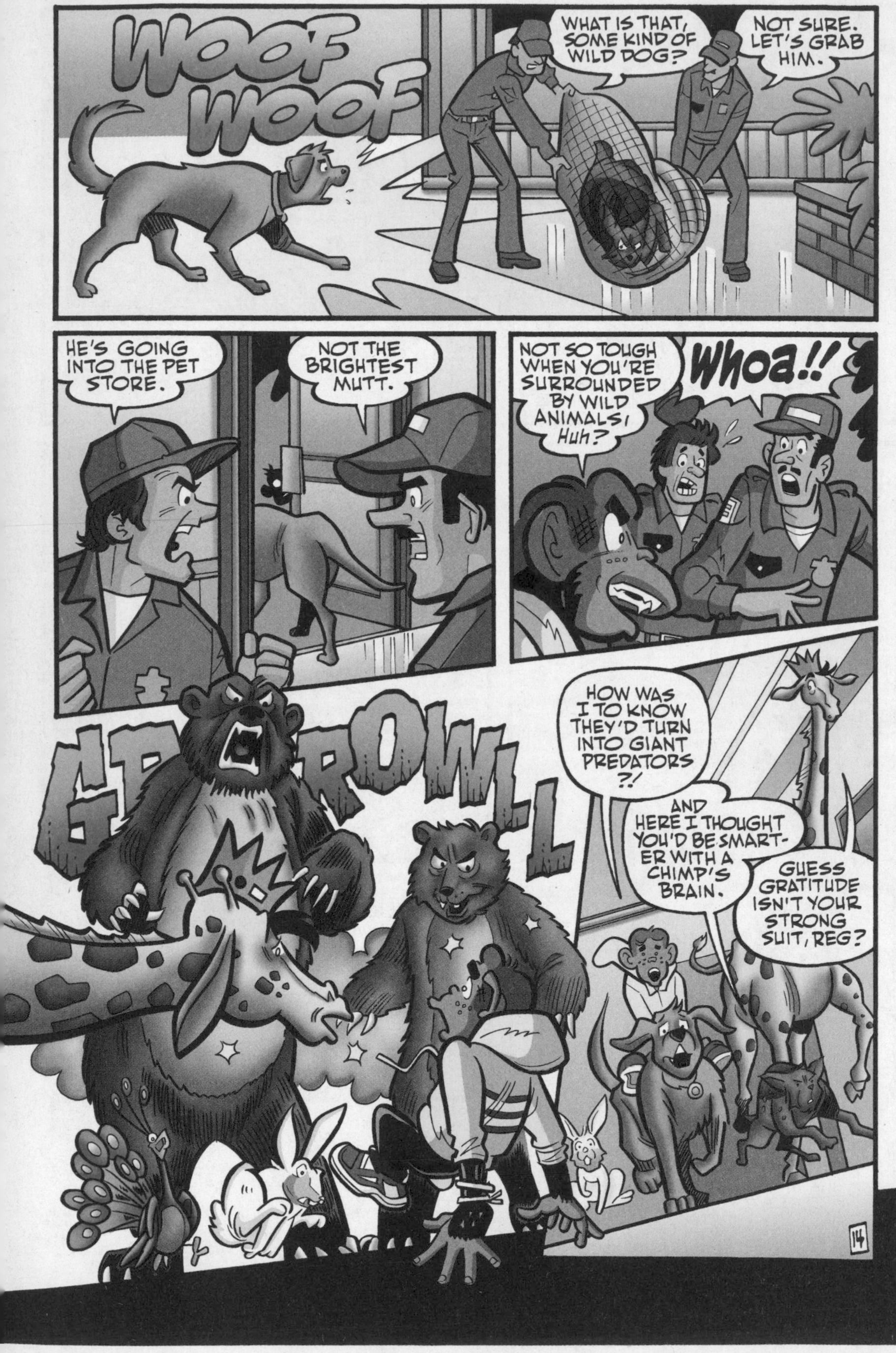
WOOF WOOF
WHAT IS THAT, SOME KIND OF WILD DOG?
NOT SURE. LET'S GRAB HIM.
HE'S GOING INTO THE PET STORE.
NOT THE BRIGHTEST MUTT.
NOT SO TOUGH WHEN YOU'RE SURROUNDED BY WILD ANIMALS, Huh?
Whoa!!
GRROWLL
HOW WAS I TO KNOW THEY'D TURN INTO GIANT PREDATORS?!
AND HERE I THOUGHT YOU'D BE SMART-ER WITH A CHIMP'S BRAIN.
GUESS GRATITUDE ISN'T YOUR STRONG SUIT, REG?
14

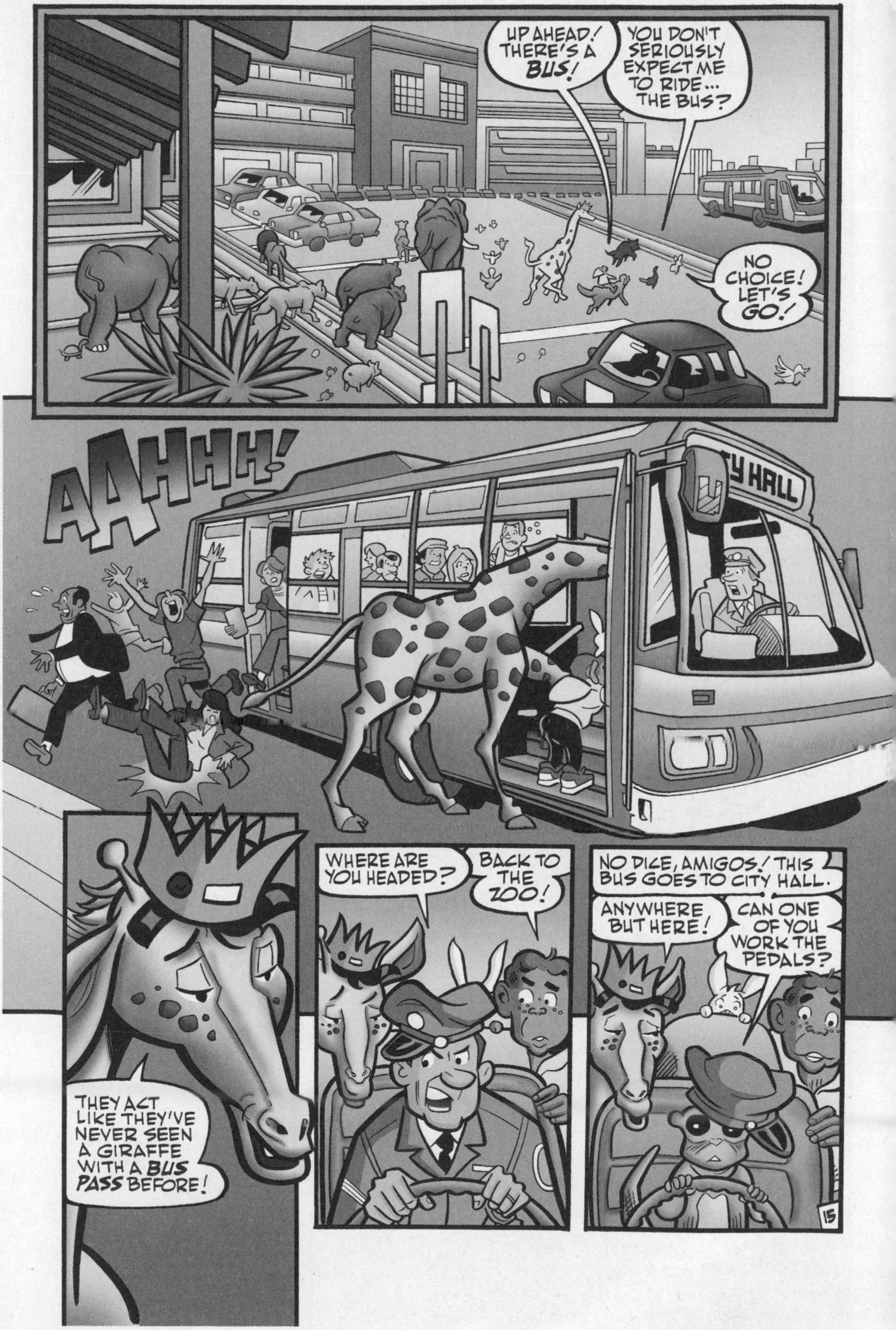
UP AHEAD! THERE'S A BUS!
YOU DON'T SERIOUSLY EXPECT ME TO RIDE... THE BUS?
NO CHOICE! LET'S GO!
AAHHH!
THEY ACT LIKE THEY'VE NEVER SEEN A GIRAFFE WITH A BUS PASS BEFORE!
WHERE ARE YOU HEADED?
BACK TO THE ZOO!
NO DICE, AMIGOS! THIS BUS GOES TO CITY HALL.
ANYWHERE BUT HERE!
CAN ONE OF YOU WORK THE PEDALS?
15

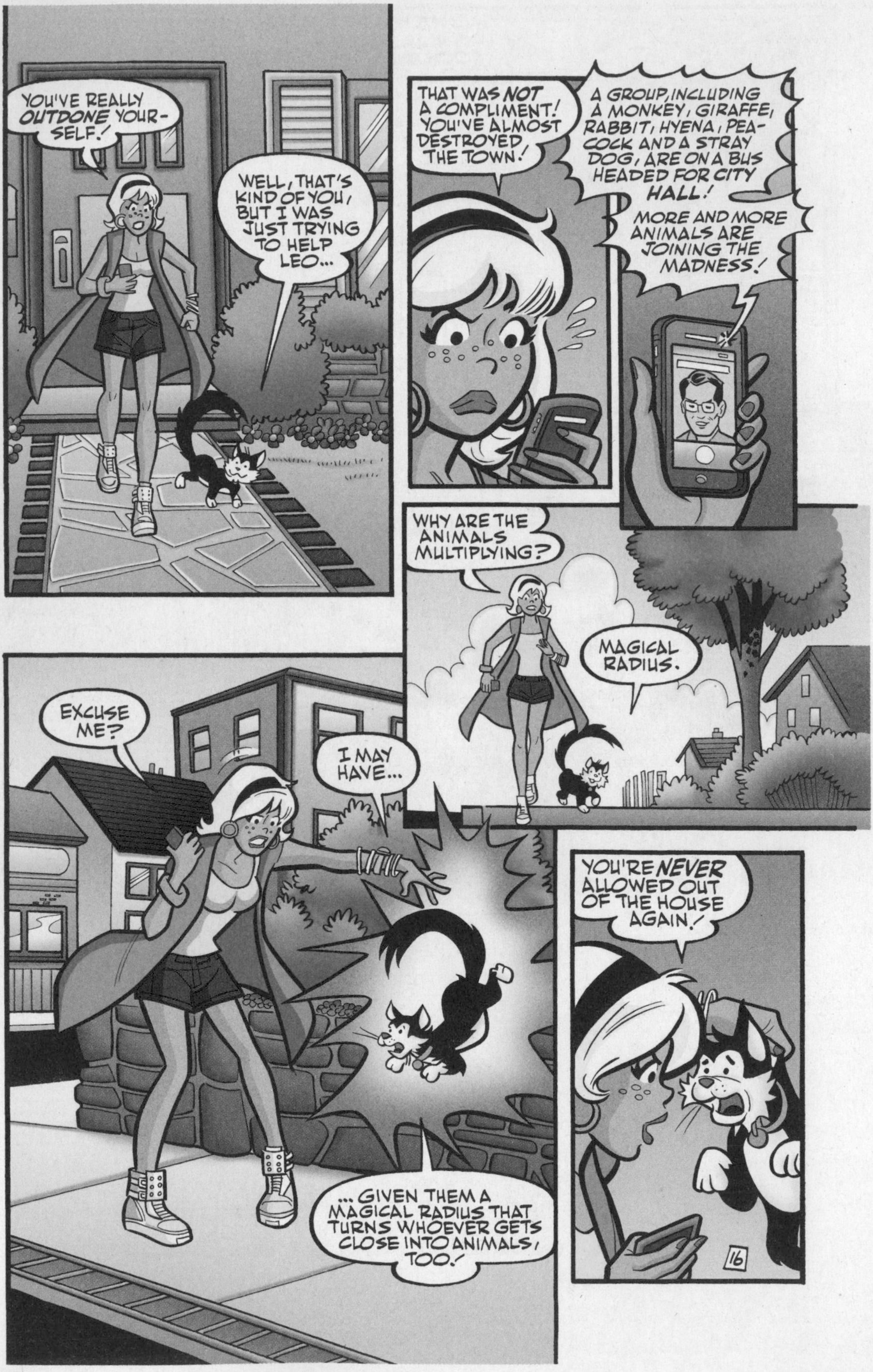
YOU'VE REALLY OUTDONE YOUR-SELF!
WELL, THAT'S KIND OF YOU, BUT I WAS JUST TRYING TO HELP LEO...
THAT WAS NOT A COMPLIMENT! YOU'VE ALMOST DESTROYED THE TOWN!
A GROUP, INCLUDING A MONKEY, GIRAFFE, RABBIT, HYENA, PEA-COCK AND A STRAY DOG, ARE ON A BUS HEADED FOR CITY HALL!
MORE AND MORE ANIMALS ARE JOINING THE MADNESS!
WHY ARE THE ANIMALS MULTIPLYING?
MAGICAL RADIUS.
EXCUSE ME?
I MAY HAVE...
...GIVEN THEM A MAGICAL RADIUS THAT TURNS WHOEVER GETS CLOSE INTO ANIMALS, TOO!
YOU'RE NEVER ALLOWED OUT OF THE HOUSE AGAIN!
16

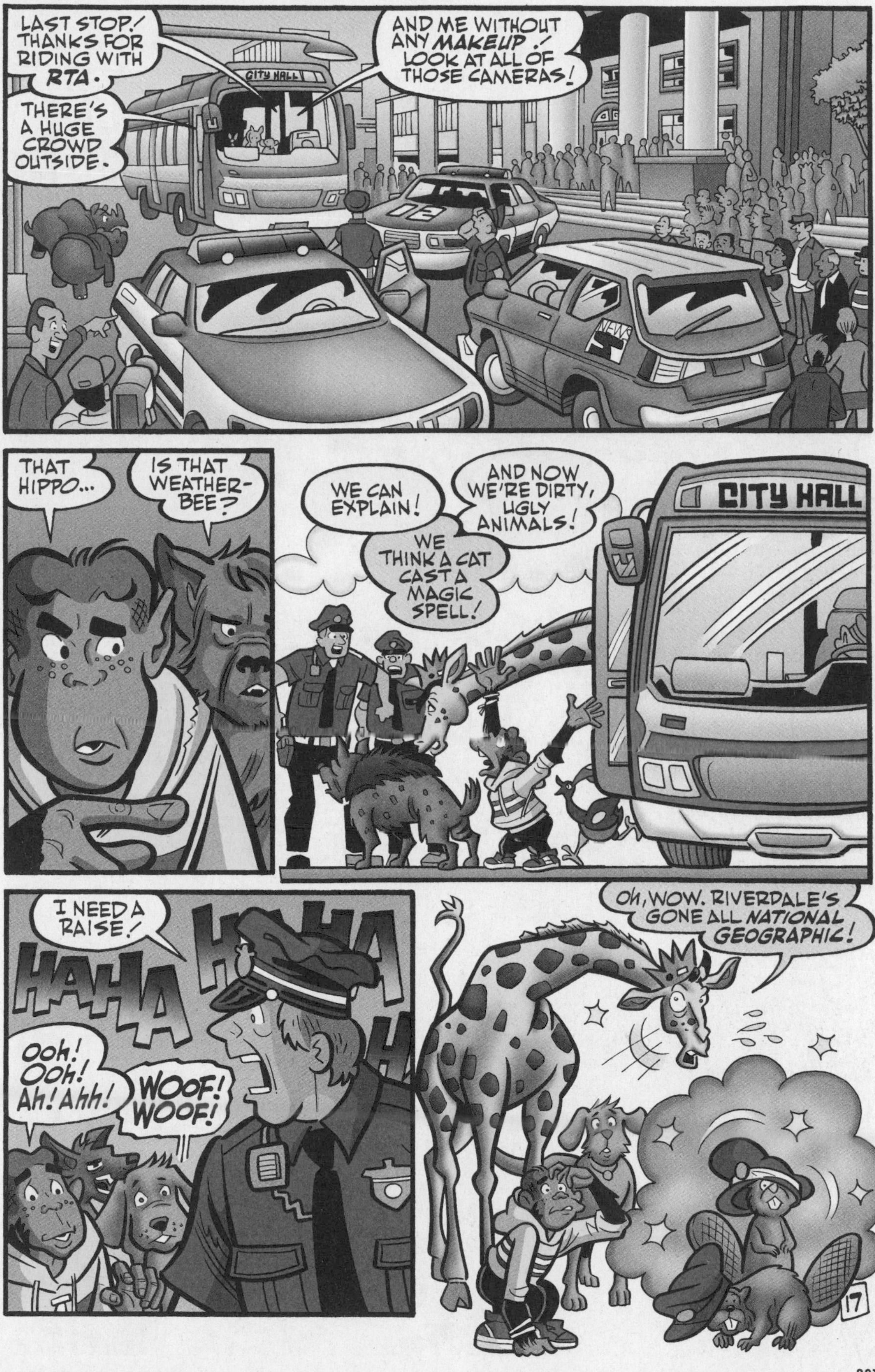
LAST STOP! THANKS FOR RIDING WITH RTA.
AND ME WITHOUT ANY MAKEUP! LOOK AT ALL OF THOSE CAMERAS!
THERE'S A HUGE CROWD OUTSIDE.
CITY HALL
NEWS
THAT HIPPO...
IS THAT WEATHER-BEE?
WE CAN EXPLAIN!
AND NOW WE'RE DIRTY, UGLY ANIMALS!
WE THINK A CAT CAST A MAGIC SPELL!
CITY HALL
I NEED A RAISE!
HAHA HAHA H
Ooh! Ooh! Ah! Ahh!
WOOF! WOOF!
Oh, WOW. RIVERDALE'S GONE ALL NATIONAL GEOGRAPHIC!
17

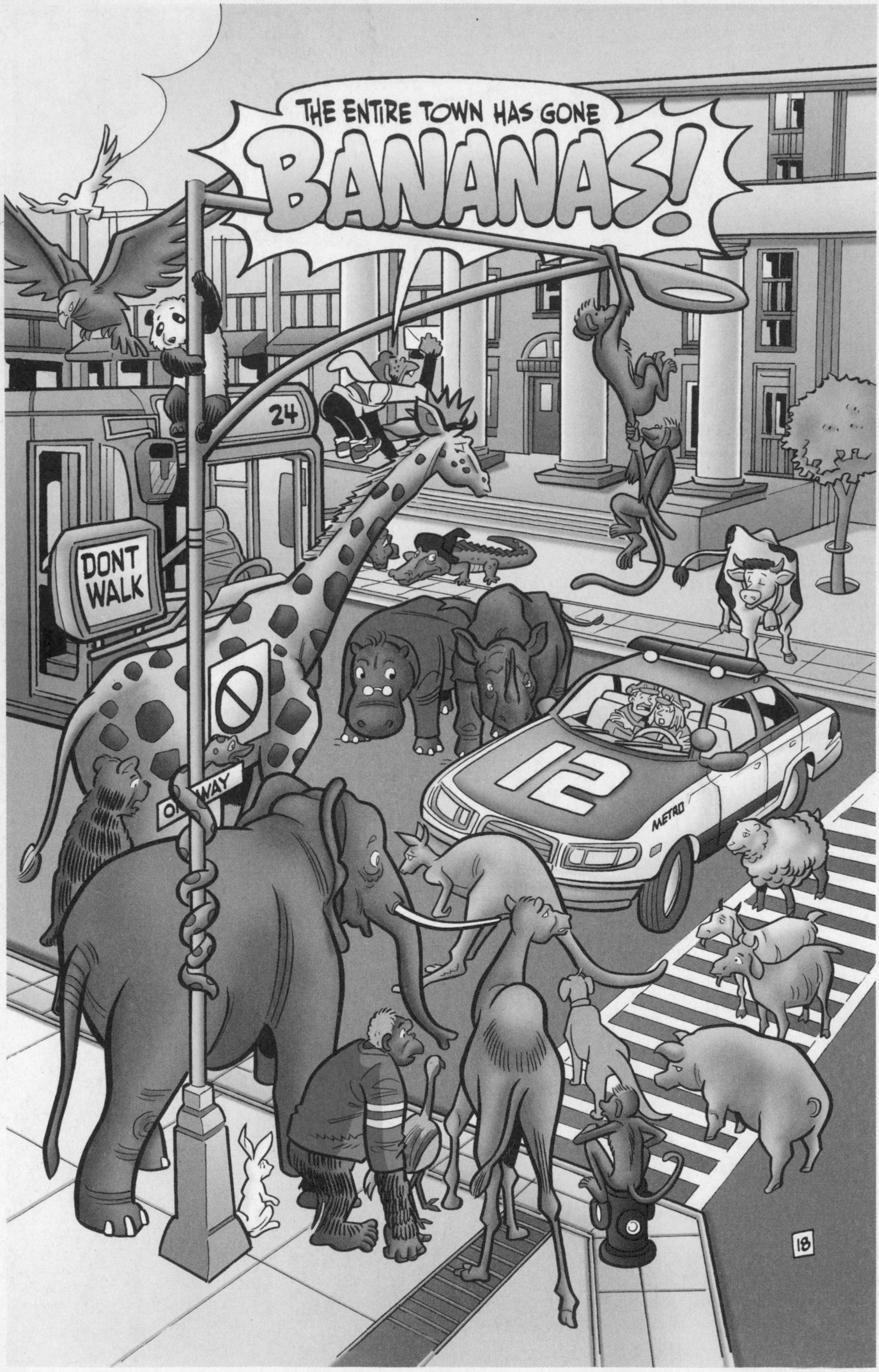
THE ENTIRE TOWN HAS GONE
BANANAS!
24
DONT WALK
12
METRO
18

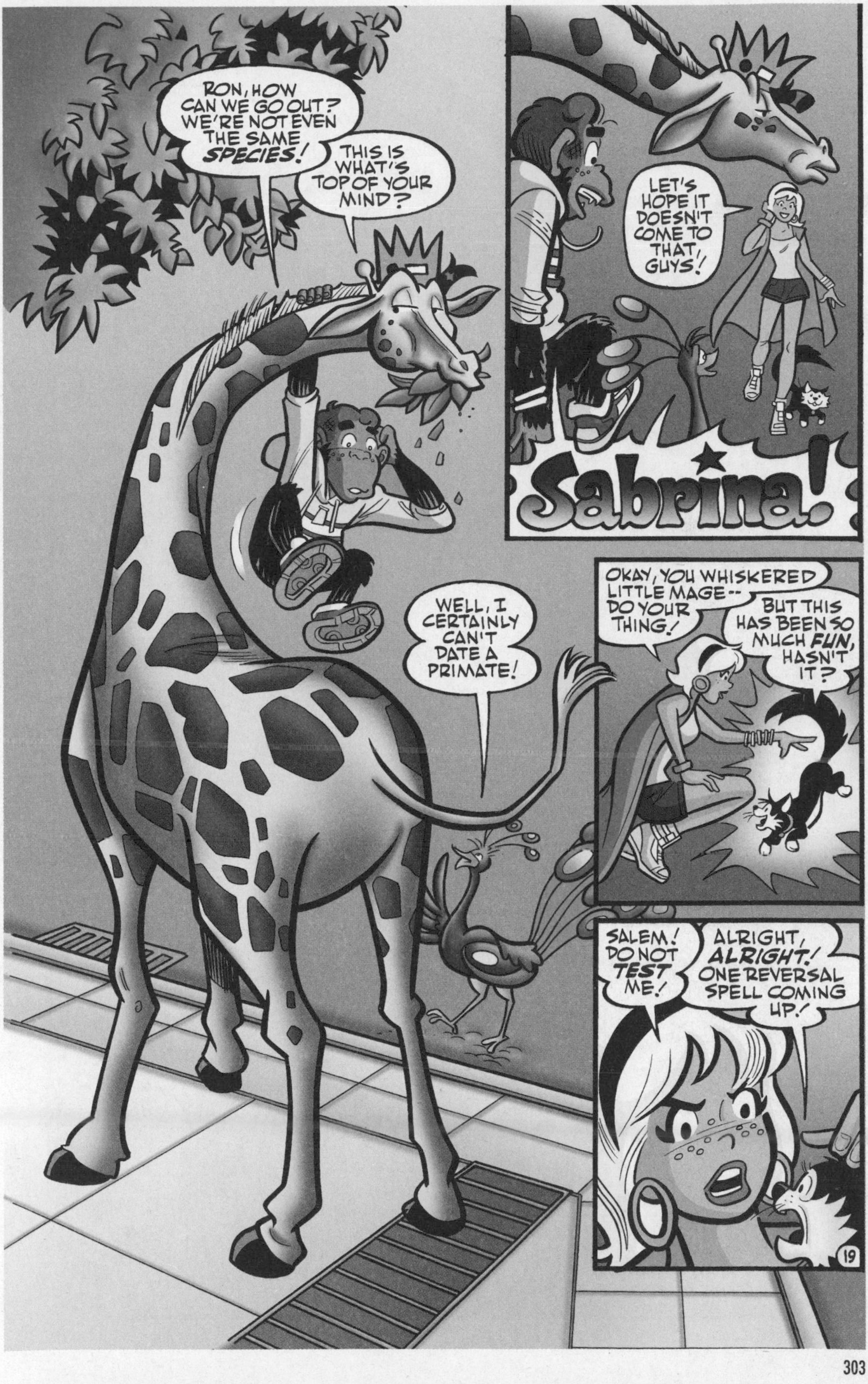
RON, HOW CAN WE GO OUT? WE'RE NOT EVEN THE SAME *SPECIES*!
THIS IS WHAT'S TOP OF YOUR MIND?
WELL, I CERTAINLY CAN'T DATE A PRIMATE!
LET'S HOPE IT DOESN'T COME TO THAT, GUYS!
Sabrina!
OKAY, YOU WHISKERED LITTLE MAGE -- DO YOUR THING!
BUT THIS HAS BEEN SO MUCH *FUN*, HASN'T IT?
SALEM! DO NOT *TEST* ME!
ALRIGHT, *ALRIGHT*! ONE REVERSAL SPELL COMING UP!
19

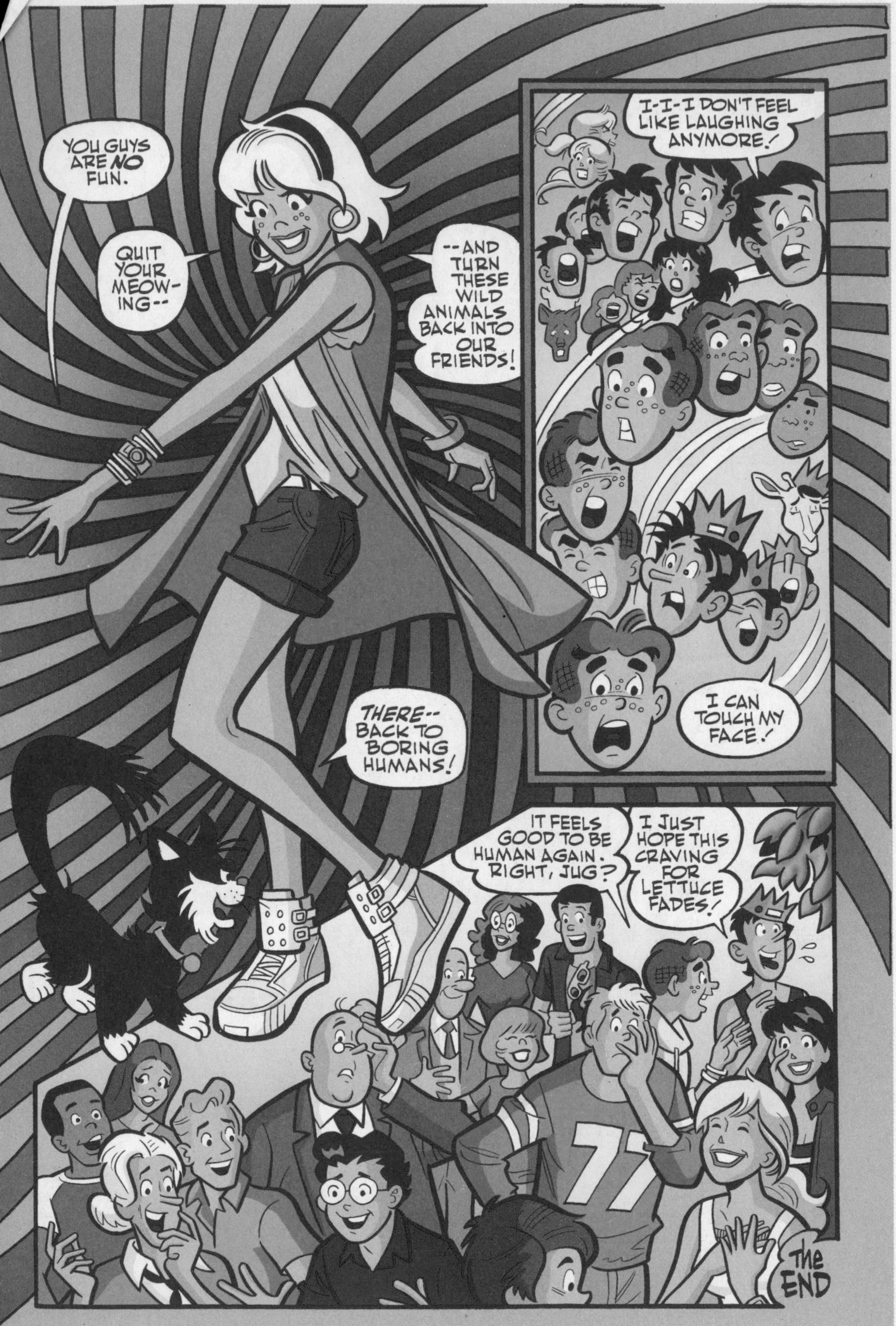
YOU GUYS ARE NO FUN.
QUIT YOUR MEOWING--
--AND TURN THESE WILD ANIMALS BACK INTO OUR FRIENDS!
THERE-- BACK TO BORING HUMANS!
I-I-I DON'T FEEL LIKE LAUGHING ANYMORE!
I CAN TOUCH MY FACE!
IT FEELS GOOD TO BE HUMAN AGAIN. RIGHT, JUG?
I JUST HOPE THIS CRAVING FOR LETTUCE FADES!
THE END